Scandale D'Amour

Erotic Memoirs of Paris in the 1920s

Anne-Marie Villefranche

BLUE MOON BOOKS
NEW YORK

Scandale D'Amour

More Erotic Memoirs
© 1984 by Jane Purcell

Mystere D'Amour
© 1988 by Jane Purcell

Published by
Blue Moon Books
An Imprint of Avalon Publishing Group Incorporated
161 William St., 16th Floor
New York, NY 10038

First Carroll and Graf edition 1995
First Blue Moon Books edition 2003

ISBN 1-56201-323-8

9 8 7 6 5 4 3 2 1

Printed in the United States of America
Distributed by Publishers Group West

MYSTERE
D'AMOUR

Foreword

This is the fourth volume in English of Anne-Marie Ville-franche's improper stories of love affairs in the Paris of her youth, the 1920s. From the first volume on (*Plaisir d'Amour*) her stories have had a wide international appeal, transcending the boundaries of national culture and custom. In her native France her work was selected by Le Grand Livre du Mois, in Germany and England by the book clubs and in the USA by the Literary Guild. Other languages in which her stories have been published are Italian, Dutch, Icelandic, Japanese and Hebrew.

Earlier volumes have told of the pleasures of love, the joys of love and, most entertainingly, the follies of love. This present collection tells of its mysteries – the title is taken from the story of Nicolas and Chantal. The mysteries of love described in this and the other stories in this volume deal with the shadowy and hidden side of human nature. Some readers may question whether love is the appropriate word for the curiously complicated emotions that emerge between the men and women who appear in these stories. That they have love-affairs is one thing, whether they love each other in any ordinary sense of the word may be less clear.

Anne-Marie knew that love can take many forms, some of them mysterious indeed. She found all of them interesting and most of them amusing.

Jane Purcell, London 1987

The Duel

Julien Lambert and Edouard Taine were of almost the same age – one was a month or two short of his twenty-third birthday, the other a month or two past his. They were not friends, but they knew each other slightly – enough to nod and say good day or good evening to each other – for they moved in the same social circles and were invited to the same parties. They did not look anything like each other – Julien was taller and light-complexioned, Edouard was more compact in build and had darker skin that suggested an origin in Provence. Both men had somewhat exaggerated ideas of their own importance and of the absolute need to keep their honour bright and untarnished, whatever that meant to them.

Julien did not take note of it, for there was no reason in the world why he should, but for some months past whenever he had run across Edouard Tainè, he was accompanied by the same pretty girl. Eventually, at some function or other, Julien was introduced to her and learned that her name was Paulette Sorel. She was a chestnut-haired, vivacious girl of perhaps twenty, and she smiled a good deal as she talked. She was not very tall, but she was well-formed and, in Julien's private opinion, she had the roundest and most interesting breasts under her thin white frock that he had been close to for ages. It was a pleasure to talk to her, and he would have continued their conversation indefinitely, except that Edouard spotted them together from the other side of the room. A few steps brought him to Paulette's side, he took her arm and led her away, with only the briefest and least convincing of apologies to Julien.

Julien was displeased by what had happened, not only because he had been deprived of the pleasure of talking to Mademoiselle Sorel and the greater pleasure of observing at close quarters the shape of her thinly-covered breasts, but because he thought Taine had been rude in his manner to him. So what if the wretched fellow was jealous of his girl and rushed round to protect her from anyone who came near her? Many men were jealous in that way, but they controlled their feelings and behaved with the politeness required in good society. No doubt Mademoiselle Sorel was an enthusiast for the intimate pleasures which lovers shared with each other, and Taine was besotted – even so, none of that gave him any right to behave with less than perfect courtesy towards other men, and in particular towards Julien Lambert! If it happened again, he would have to be taught a sharp lesson.

Two or three weeks passed after Julien's introduction to Paulette Sorel and in that time no further occasion for offence arose, in that Julien found himself very suddenly and very profoundly involved with Madame Marie Lacoste and he did not attend any of the parties or other gatherings at which he might have encountered Edouard Taine. Madame Lacoste had started as a casual acquaintance he had seen around the better nightclubs for months; a mutual friend introduced them and an hour later Julien was in her bed, lying on her belly and pumping hard into her, while she wailed and gripped his waist with her knees. Two hours later he knew Marie Lacoste very well indeed, and she knew him perhaps better than he realised. By dawn, when the light crept slowly under the lower edge of the curtains at her bedroom window, he had performed so expertly and thoroughly that they fell asleep at last in each other's arms, their bodies wet with the perspiration of love-making, their tender passions assuaged. The affair began, as it were, like a thunderstorm breaking without warning – and after that it became more and more passionate, until Julien began to wonder whether he had been blessed with the good fortune to make the acquaintance of a true nymphomaniac – a creature he had never before believed to have any existence.

8

Be that as it may, on the evening in question coincidence – or the hand of fate, perhaps – brought together two events, neither of very great importance in themselves, but which led irrevocably to the momentous duel fought between Julien and Edouard – a duel which caused the whole of Paris to gossip for days on end, which scandalised some and angered others, but which was judged, on the whole, to be in keeping with the best traditions of self-respect, good reputation and honour.

Julien's plan that evening was to escort Marie Lacoste to the opera, a form of musical entertainment for which she had a marked liking. Afterwards they would dance and drink a little – though not much, because Marie was opposed to keeping late hours. Not on grounds of health or morality, of course, but because she liked to be in bed, on her back and floating towards her first little crisis of the evening well before midnight. But at about five o'clock she telephoned Julien and said that she had developed a ferocious migraine, which made it impossible for her to go anywhere that evening.

Julien murmured his regrets, promised to enquire the next day to see if she were better, and made a scribbled note on the pad he kept by the telephone to remind himself to have suitable flowers delivered to her the next morning to show how desolate he was at missing a night in her bed. When he put his pencil down and looked at his note, he became thoughtful and stood silent for some time with his speculations.

Yes, Marie might have a migraine, that was true, though not for the reason that women usually have headaches, the calendar assured him of that. All in all she was an extremely healthy woman of a robust disposition. Julien had more than once seen her eat a hearty meal very shortly after she had enjoyed enough climactic releases in a couple of hours to cause the average young woman to slide into a deep sleep to recover. Somehow, in his opinion, this story of the sudden migraine did not ring true. If that were the case, then the only reason he could think of why she would want to cancel their evening together must be that she had met someone new and wanted to be with him.

Well, all might be fair in love and war, but the galling aspect for Julien was that, if his speculation was correct, Marie had met someone she believed could do more to her in bed than he could! The thought was intolerable to his male pride. That he, who by his skill and tenderness had given Marie more crises in a night than she had ever experienced before – or so she had assured him at the time, after her twelfth – that she now cast him casually aside in favour of some unknown person who . . . who what? His train of thought stopped at that point.

He had no intention of going to the opera by himself, of course. On the other hand, he did not intend to stay at home and think miserable thoughts all evening of who was with Marie and what he was doing to her. He dressed and went out to dinner, confident that he would meet people he knew and go on with them afterwards to drink and dance – and perhaps find a companion to console him for his unexpected loss.

To compensate for his disappointment he decided that it would be only fitting to have a very good dinner in a very special restaurant. Consequently, at about eight o'clock he was approaching Maxim's and it was then that there occurred the second event in the chain of circumstance that was to lead to the most improbable venture of his life – and Edouard Taine's. As he was about to enter Maxim's, a girl ran out across the pavement, one hand to her face.

Julien recognised her at once, though her back was to him. It was Paulette Sorel and she was wearing an evening frock of jet black taffeta that rustled as she moved. Her arms were bare and she had a little wrap in one hand, as if she had snatched it up in a hurried departure. Julien forgot about his dinner at Maxim's and went to Paulette, who was standing at the edge of the pavement, looking as if she were lost. He raised his hat and greeted her politely, and when she turned to stare at him in surprise, he saw that her pretty face was stained with tears. At once he took her arm, and led her solicitously towards the taxis parked by the kerb close by.

'You are distressed, Mademoiselle Sorel,' he said gently. 'You must not wander about the streets in this condition – who knows what might happen? Allow me to see you safely home.'

He put her in the first taxi and she told him the address.

'We are almost neighbours,' he told her. 'I live only a few streets away from you, close to the Parc de Monceau. Do you live with your family?'

'I don't want to go home,' said Paulette, beginning to recover her emotional balance. 'My parents will be curious about why I am back so early. Do you mind if we sit somewhere and have a drink, to pass an hour or so?'

'With the greatest of pleasure,' Julien replied. 'Perhaps you would like to come to my apartment – I have an excellent champagne.'

'We hardly know each other,' she said, looking at him somewhat doubtfully. 'A café would be far more suitable, I think, Monsieur Lambert.'

'Or even a restaurant,' he suggested. 'I have not dined and you did not have much time to eat before you left Maxim's.'

'I've lost my appetite completely,' she said, her tone friendly, 'but you must eat – choose somewhere and we can talk while you dine.'

After a little thought Julien directed the taxi to a little restaurant not far from where he lived. He ate there once or twice a week when he was alone, and knew that the food was good and that he would be treated with respect as a regular. While Paulette went to repair her make-up and erase the traces of her tears, he studied the menu and ordered for himself. The lady does not wish to eat, he explained to the waiter, but bring the very best wine you have and she will take a glass with me. The waiter, who in fact was the son of the married couple who owned the restaurant, gave Julien an understanding smile and promised to produce something very special.

When Paulette came back to the table and sat down, her usual cheerful nature had reasserted itself. She looked exceptionally pretty and she was smiling again. Julien noticed that her mouth was a wide and generous one, a small indicator of her nature, perhaps. At least, he hoped that it was so. The neckline of her black frock was cut high

11

and she wore two heavy gold necklaces round her long and slender throat. The manner in which the taffeta draped itself over her breasts was, in Julien's view, enchanting. Her necklaces are of gold, he told himself, and that is because she is still so young – in a few years from now a girl of her prettiness and charm will have diamonds round her neck.

'I suppose you must have guessed why I ran out of the restaurant,' she said. 'I had a quarrel with Edouard.'

Julien nodded sympathetically, poured wine for both of them, and made a start on the thick soup he had ordered.

'Lovers' tiffs,' he said. 'Something of the same sort happened to me, which is why I was dining alone. Though I swear that I did nothing to cause my banishment.'

Far from it, he was thinking – it was probably what someone else had promised to do that persuaded Marie to cancel their visit to the opera. Or what she believed someone else might do for her.

Paulette drank a little wine, smiled as she recognised its excellence, and drank a little more.

'You and Edouard don't really know each other, do you?' she asked. 'The truth is that I like him very much, but there are times when he makes me furious.'

'I thought it extraordinarily uncaring of him to make you cry and run out into the street,' said Julien. 'He did not even follow to look after you.'

'Because I told him I never wanted to see him again,' said Paulette, by way of explanation.

'But even so!'

'And I'm sorry to have to say it, but I was so angry with him that I threw my plate of soup into his face. I think he was too busy wiping it off to see me go.'

'Good god! What did he do to provoke you like that?'

'It doesn't matter,' she answered with a tiny shrug. 'We've had fights before.'

'But the man is impossible, to behave towards you like that! You should not see him again.'

Paulette's generous mouth opened in a broad smile.

'That's all very well for you to say, Julien Lambert – but I wonder how much you are concerned for me and how

12

much you are trying to promote your own interests.'

'My own interests? What do you mean? My concern is for you.'

She emptied her wineglass and smiled at him again.

'Do you remember when we were introduced?' she asked. 'At Odette's party, I think it was. There was no mistaking the way you looked at me. I'm not a child, you know.'

'How did I look at you, Paulette?'

'You were staring at my breasts with an expression on your face that said you wanted to pull my frock off and feel them. Edouard saw it and came rushing over to rescue me. He was annoyed with me all evening because you'd looked at me like that – which is why I haven't forgotten it.'

'But surely,' said Julien softly, 'most men look at you like that, don't they?'

She laughed and he filled her glass again. 'Most men are a little more polite,' she told him. 'They don't make their thoughts as obvious as you do. You were looking at me in the same way a little while ago, when I sat down. Don't you know when you're doing it?'

'An interesting question! You are the first person to have commented on it, so perhaps you are the first to have noticed this expression of mine.'

'Really? I'm the first girl whose breasts bring that look to your face – is that what you expect me to believe?'

The waiter brought the ragout Julien had ordered for himself – a thick and rich stew with an aroma to stir the most jaded appetite.

'You should try some of this,' Julien told Paulette. 'They cook it here to perfection.'

'It certainly smells very good,' she answered, wrinkling her nose prettily, her appetite evidently returning.

Julien asked the waiter to divide the ragout between the two of them and then bring more. They attacked it greedily, with pieces of crusty bread to chew on with it.

'That's better,' said Julien. 'It is a pleasure to see you eat with such zest. It tells me that you've got over the upset of earlier on.'

'I'm not one to mope – life is so enjoyable that there is no time for useless regret. Do I know the girl who left you on your own this evening?'

'I doubt it. She's older than you are – Marie Lacoste.'

'I've heard her name from my brother – he's much older than I am. Doesn't she spend all her time in nightclubs?'

'Not all of it,' Julien said shortly.

'What did you quarrel about?' Paulette persisted.

'We didn't quarrel. I think she's met someone she likes better – it's as simple as that.'

'Poor Julien – there's no way to argue against that, is there?'

They finished the ragout and the wine and inspected the cheeses. Both settled for brie, with another bottle of the excellent wine. After that Julien nibbled a few grapes and Paulette ate a peach. By then they were on very friendly terms and she did not demur when Julien put his hand lightly on hers as it rested on the table.

'The evening started badly for both of us,' he said, 'but see how it has improved! Why don't we go dancing somewhere nice and drink a bottle of champagne?'

If he could get her that far, he was thinking, it was not her little hand he would be touching – he would have his hand on her knee under the table. And when she accepted that caress, he would feel up above her garters to the warm flesh between her stockings and her underwear. Nightclubs were always full of couples in corners, the man's hand hidden by their table as he slid it under his companion's clothes. At least, the men convinced themselves that the table hid what they were doing, though everyone who glanced at them knew what was going on. It was in just such a club that Julien had first touched Marie Lacoste's well-used delight, his hand up her frock and inside her underwear.

'I don't feel like dancing tonight,' said Paulette.

For a moment Julien wondered whether she knew all about men's hands up her frock in dark nightclubs, young as she was. But her smile was so sweet as she declined his invitation that he reproved himself for being cynical.

'I'm content to stay here and talk,' she went on, 'unless you find that too boring for words?'

14

'But of course not! I suggested that we might go dancing because I was afraid that I might be boring you.'

'No girl could possibly be bored while you've got that wicked look on your face,' she said with a giggle, 'and it's back again.'

Julien was well pleased with the evening so far, though sorry that she had refused to accompany him to a club. He enjoyed her conversation, which was a little franker and more suggestive than he had any right to expect, and he saw no reason not to nudge matters forward a little.

'That wicked look, as you call it, seems to happen without my knowledge. Perhaps you can describe it, to make sure that I understand.'

'Oh, you understand very well! While you talk to me, every now and then your eyes drop and there's that look on your face. Your mouth opens a little as if you were going to smile, though you don't, and there is a sort of gleam in your eyes – how can anyone describe a look? But what it says very clearly is that you want to get my clothes off and feel my breasts.'

'And do I have this look on my face now?'

'No, but it was there when you suggested we should go dancing.'

'What can I say?' Julien said with a charming smile, 'You have described the expression very well. I cannot deny the truth of your interpretation of it, because that is exactly what I wish to do – remove your frock and stroke your breasts.'

'You like the look of them?' she asked, giving herself a little shake to make them sway under her black taffeta. 'My sister says that they're too plump for my height.'

'They are beautifully shaped,' Julien assured her, his sincere appreciation very evident in his voice. 'and they are exactly the right size, believe me. If you don't let me see them soon I shall die.'

'A likely story!' she said with a wide grin. 'I'm sure you've noticed that half the population of Paris has a pair of these on their chest. I've never heard of anyone dying because he couldn't look at a particular pair.'

'And I'm sure that you are aware that the other half of

15

the population has an extra limb,' said Julien, grinning back at her. 'There is one particular limb which at this moment is standing up like a flag-pole because its owner is looking at your breasts and wishing that you were not wearing that frock – or any other clothes.'

They chattered and made jokes and soon it was well after ten o'clock. They would have been happy to stay longer, teasing each other over a glass of fine cognac, but by then they were the only ones left in the restaurant and the owners were making it politely apparent that they wished to close and go home.

Paulette insisted that her home was too close for a taxi to be necessary, and that anyway she would prefer to walk. They strolled arm in arm along the Rue de Monceau. It was a pleasant evening, though a little cool, and Paulette drew her wrap about her shoulders and bare arms.

'I had a pair of gloves when I went out this evening,' she said, 'but in the fuss I must have left them at Maxim's. At least I didn't leave my handbag behind.'

'I am glad that I decided to have dinner at Maxim's and equally glad that I got no further than the door,' said Julien. 'The evening has been better than the one I had originally planned.'

He was hoping that she would respond by saying that she felt the same, but in this he was disappointed.

'Is that true?' she asked. 'I'm sure you'd rather be with your lady-friend than walking a stranger home.'

'How can you say that we are strangers to each other now?' he demanded.

'You've told me a little about yourself,' she agreed, 'and I've told you a little about me. But it seems to me that all we have established for certain is that you admire my breasts – and even then you may not be telling the truth.'

'Tomorrow I shall find the office of a notary and swear a statement before him that I admire your breasts more than those of any other woman in the world. And I shall present you with a copy of this sworn statement.'

'But what good will that do you, Julien? You would do better to give a similar statement to your friend – I'm sure that when *she* sees that look on your face she can't wait to pull her clothes off for you to play with *her* breasts.'

'They are not half as beautiful as yours,' he replied.

'How can you be so certain of that? You've played with hers enough times, no doubt, but you've never seen mine. What you think is me might in reality be a pair or two of stockings stuffed down my front.'

'Impossible! I say that with complete conviction because when you move quickly your breasts roll a little under your frock in a way that no padding ever could.'

'Is that so?' she asked. 'Am I so flabby that I roll about in my clothes? Is that what you are telling me?'

Hand on her arm, Julien drew her to a standstill on the pavement and kissed her cheek lightly and quickly. 'You jiggle in a delightful way,' he said. 'Open your wrap and jump up and down a few times.'

'Here, in the street? You wish me to make a spectacle of myself?'

'No one's watching us,' he whispered. 'Jump just once – for me.'

She grinned as she opened her little wrap and jumped up and down on her high heels half a dozen times. Both she and Julien were staring closely at her bosom, she giggling and he sighing amorously, as her plump breasts bounced under her frock.

'There, that's the proof,' said Julien. 'Old stockings don't bounce like that.'

'You are observant,' she said, 'perhaps unnecessarily so. My breasts are prettier than your friend's – is that what you were saying before you made me jump up and down like an idiot?'

'She is no longer my friend,' said Julien, coming to a decision that was to have far-reaching results. 'I shall not see her again.'

'But if she is waiting for you to arrive and play with her breasts – it would be cruel to leave her frustrated and lonely!'

'I suspect that at this moment she is neither alone nor frustrated.'

'Yes, I remember you said before that you think there is someone else. So perhaps they are still dining together, or are dancing somewhere.'

17

'My acquaintance with the lady leads me to the view that by this time of the evening she will be in bed with her new friend.'

'That must be very distressing for you, to believe that.'

'Strangely enough, it doesn't distress me at all. I feel almost as if I had stepped out of a hothouse where orchids are grown. It is only now that I am breathing the cool fresh air that I realise how oppressive it was inside the hothouse. I am grateful to you, Paulette.'

'To me? But why?'

'Being with you this evening was my exit from the hothouse.'

'No more orchids for you?'

'The fact is, dear Paulette, that I would like to become your friend.'

She laughed a little as they walked along.

'You find that amusing?' Julien asked.

'At the beginning of this evening I had a friend. At least, I thought I had, but it became necessary to pour soup over his head. Now you want to be my friend. Yes, I find it amusing.'

They turned off the Rue de Monceau into the street where Paulette said she lived. Julien was reasonably sure that she liked him enough to respond to his further advances, but the evening was fast coming to an end. There was little chance that she would invite him up to her apartment and even if she did, there would be no opportunity whatsoever of making further progress with her parents present. Before they reached her apartment building he saw a dark doorway and, seizing the opportunity, pulled her into it and kissed her lingeringly. She returned his kiss and put her arms round him.

'Did you find that amusing too?' he asked.

'It was very nice. You can do it again if you want to.'

Julien kissed her again, a long, hot kiss that left her in no doubt of his desire – in the improbable circumstance that she entertained any doubt on that score. He put his hand under her wrap to touch her breasts through her frock. They were soft and bouncy to his fingers, but the intervening taffeta maddened him with frustration.

18

'Poor Julien,' Paulette said, when the kiss eventually ended. 'It's too dark to see here but I'm sure you've got that look on your face again. But you'll never get your way while I'm wearing this frock – it fastens up the back, and that's no use to you at all.'

'Come to my apartment,' he suggested quickly. 'I'll get you home by taxi by midnight.'

'No, it's too late for that.'

'When I suggested it hours ago it was apparently too early!'

'I didn't know you then. And to be honest, I hardly know you now. How do I know if I can trust you? If I went to your apartment you might rape and murder me.'

Julien chuckled at her teasing and put his hands round her hips to grasp the cheeks of her bottom and pull her close to him.

'Ah, the celebrated extra limb!' she said at once. 'I can feel it pressing against me.'

Julien pulled her even closer to him, so that his hard stem was squeezed against her soft belly.

'It must be extremely inconvenient sometimes to be a man,' said Paulette. 'I mean, the walk home will surely be very uncomfortable with that baton inside your clothes.'

'Every step of the way will be agony!' he told her.

He wanted to put his hand up her frock and caress her a little between the thighs, but she was standing with her legs together and when he slid a hand over her belly, down towards the join of her legs, she quickly took his wrist and guided his hand back to her soft bottom.

'Yes, agony for you,' she murmured. 'I can imagine it all too well – this swollen thing rubbing against your underwear with each step you take. The rubbing will certainly bring on a crisis before you have taken more than a hundred steps and the passers-by will stare at you and wonder what is wrong with you as you stand there shaking with involuntary ecstasy and doing it in your trousers. Perhaps there'll be a policeman there and he'll arrest you!'

Julien sighed as she slid her hands between them and he kissed her again as she unbuttoned his trousers. A moment later her cool palm enclosed the distended head of his upright stem.

'I feel that I must accept some part of the responsibility for the condition that you are in,' she said. 'Unfortunately for you, dear Julien, there is no possibility whatsoever of reducing your tension by allowing this twitching thing to enter the part of me that you are thinking about.'

'There is no one about,' he whispered, 'The street is entirely empty – pull your frock up and your underwear down a little and we can do it here without the least problem.'

Her hand was stroking him pleasantly. 'Do I hear a note of pleading in your voice, Julien?' she asked.

'I implore you – pull your frock up and let me do it to you!'

'Young ladies don't make love in the streets at night,' she told him, her hand moving very firmly now on his spigot. 'I am astonished that you could even think such a thing, let alone suggest it to me.'

He could hear the rustling of her frock as her wrist moved rhythmically against it. He brought a hand round from her bottom and felt with trembling fingers down her belly for the mound under her frock where her thighs met. This time she didn't try to stop him touching her through her clothes, but with her free hand she reached up and pulled off his handsome black felt evening hat.

'I adore you,' Julien was murmuring, half-delirious with the sensations the caress of her hand was producing in him. 'I adore you, Paulette . . .'

He glanced down in the dark and saw in amazement that she was holding his hat over his exposed spindle while she manipulated it briskly.

'What are you doing?' he gasped.

'If someone comes past we don't want them to see what's going on down here,' she answered, giggling. 'I wonder if anyone's ever done it in his hat before?'

The thought flashed through Julien's mind that it was a very expensive hat and it would surely be ruined if she continued what she was doing to him – and yet it felt so very good that he was not going to argue, whatever she wanted to do.

'Come on, then,' she said. 'We're ready for you, Julien.'

Julien's breath rasped through his open mouth as his belly clenched in the first spasm, and his hands fell to his sides. Paulette stepped very quickly to her left and pulled the hat out of harm's way. The fleshy spout she was grasping thrust itself upwards and forwards and poured out its passionate offering on to the stone doorstep below.

'That *was* quick!' Paulette exclaimed.

Julien was still trembling as he pulled her close to him and kissed her in gratitude and affection.

'Tomorrow,' he said, 'I shall be waiting for you at three o'clock.'

'And what will you do with me?'

'I shall do what the look on my face told you I wanted to do hours ago – I shall take your clothes off and play with your breasts.'

'Only that? No more? It's hardly worth the walk to your apartment.'

'What I do to your breasts will be only the beginning. After that I am going to make love to you as you have never experienced it before.'

'Bragger!' she said, with a little giggle.

Naturally, she did not arrive at his apartment at three the next afternoon, for that is not the way of pretty women with their admirers. Ten minutes went by, and then fifteen, in which time Julien became first impatient and then fearful that she might not come at all. She had given him no firm promise that she would visit him – he was well aware of that. But she had joked about what he might do to her *if* she visited him. And the most reassuring aspect was that she had shown that she was sympathetic towards his desire by the intimate little service she had performed for him in the doorway. And yet, he was compelled to admit, she had turned that into a joke by means of his hat! Perhaps what she had done for him was little more in her estimation that a gesture of gratitude for taking care of her after she had run out of Maxim's. Or worse – it might be that the little episode in the doorway was her way of getting rid of him when she wanted to go home. It was, after all, an easy way of dismissing him without letting herself become involved in his desire. Could it be that it was no more than a way of indicating *goodbye*?

A prey to such dismaying thoughts, Julien was in a condition of great nervousness and doubt when, eventually, the doorbell sounded, twenty minutes after the time he had told her. And there she stood, smiling broadly when she saw the strained expression, and the relief, on his slightly pale face. She laughed aloud at the fervour with which he kissed her hand, and when he tried to put his arms round her and draw her into a close embrace, she laughed again and evaded his grasp.

For Julien it was most disconcerting – not to say disappointing – that she insisted on behaving as if this were an ordinary social visit. She took a chair in his sitting-room, sat with her legs crossed gracefully, and talked of totally unimportant things. Julien sat opposite her, almost in despair, as he forced himself to respond to her mood and keep the trivial conversation going. What made it even more difficult was that she looked extremely attractive that afternoon and the way her legs were crossed gave a little glimpse of the underside of her thigh, but only as far as her garter. She was wearing a long knitted jumper of bright green, with a broad diagonal cream stripe from her left shoulder to her right hip, and a finely pleated skirt in a shade of dark brown. She had a little green felt hat pulled down over her ears, and her chestnut hair curled from under its brim. Julien thought that the jumper was particularly elegant – and more than that, it clung closely to her breasts and displayed their roundness to perfection. His obstinate little friend overcame his disappointment and stood upright inside his trousers.

'Your flowers were not the only ones I received this morning,' Paulette announced suddenly.

He had ordered a dozen pink carnations to be delivered, with just his name on the card and the figure three as a reminder of when he would be waiting anxiously for her. Roses had seemed to him inappropriate for the limited intimacy of the previous evening. He was not pleased by Paulette's words.

'Three dozen yellow roses from Edouard,' she went on, 'with a long message expressing deep regret and a

22

thousand apologies. The handwriting was a little jerky, and the message confused in places, so perhaps he was not completely sober when he wrote it. He was sober when I left him, but who knows where he went or what he did after our quarrel. In his place, where would you have gone, Julien?'

She had asked him an impossible question, of course, and he knew it as well as she did.

'I would have gone at once to the banks of the Seine and thrown myself in if I had been him,' he declared, and Paulette laughed at him.

'How very absurd!' she said. 'He went to a bar somewhere and got drunk and began to feel guilty towards me. Isn't that what men usually do when they have behaved badly towards someone dear to them? Then they send flowers and plead for forgiveness.'

'Then you have forgiven him?' Julien asked.

'Have I? I'm here with you,' she answered, smiling at him.

Julien's emotional little friend had sulked and drooped his head during the talk of yellow roses and their sender. Paulette's more encouraging words about being with Julien instead of Edouard revived his ardour and he shrugged himself and stood at his full height in Julien's underwear. Julien was staring at Paulette's breasts and he was taking no trouble to disguise his admiration.

'That look on your face – it's back again!' she exclaimed, and giggled.

'A look of respectful devotion,' he said, smiling at her.

'Ah that, naturally! Yet I seem to recall something was said about pulling my clothes off and feeling my breasts – or perhaps I was mistaken. Perhaps it wasn't you who said that.'

Julien was out of his chair in an instant and holding out both hands to her. She took them and he pulled her upright and into a warm embrace, the tip of his tongue pressing between her lips to touch her tongue, his hands stroking the round cheeks of her bottom through her linen skirt. In the natural course of things, as men and women have since the beginning of civilisation, they found their way to his bedroom a few minutes later and lay down

23

together. Their kisses became hotter and more passionate, their tongues almost entwined. Paulette's green jumper was up under her armpits and Julien's hand down the front of her loose silk underwear to fondle her breasts.

'Oh, yes, yes,' he was murmuring to himself.

'Does that mean that you like them, now that you've got your hands on them?' she enquired.

'They are superb, Paulette, magnificent! I adore them!'

There was good reason for his enthusiasm. Paulette's breasts were plump and round, the most enticing and sensual playthings Julien had ever handled. He put his lips to one of the dark pink buds that stood firmly upwards and flicked it insistently with his tongue.

'Yes, you *do* like them,' Paulette murmured. 'Let me take off my jumper so that you can play with them properly.'

She sat up on the bed and Julien assisted very gladly in pulling her jumper over her head. She slipped off the narrow shoulder-straps of her camiknickers and pulled the garment down to her waist. Julien stared in silent appreciation at her bare breasts, until Paulette grinned and shook herself to make them sway a little from side to side.

'They're not just for looking at,' she told him.

Julien reached out with both hands to stroke them. 'You like having them touched?' he asked.

'All women like having them touched,' she said, laughing.

'Yes, but what I mean is – you especially like having your breasts touched.'

'How do I know whether I like it more than any other girl? Why don't you stop asking foolish questions and play with them.'

Julien pressed her down on the bed and devoted his attention to her beautiful breasts. He felt them, stroked them, squeezed them, titillated their buds with his fingers, his lips and his tongue, becoming very aroused by what he was doing. As also did Paulette, though Julien had no idea of how frenzied her excitement had become until she jerked her hand up her skirt and, an instant later, her body arched off the bed in a shaking climax. When it ended she fell back limply, looked at Julien and giggled.

24

'That surprised you, didn't it?' she asked.

'It was marvellous to watch! Does playing with your breasts bring you to a climax every time?'

'Not every time, but usually. It depends on who's playing with them. You did it beautifully, Julien – you gave me a fantastic thrill!'

He put his hand up her skirt and she moved hers away to make room for him. Her legs were a little apart and he stroked the soft flesh of her thighs above her stockings.

'Higher,' she said. 'There's something very special waiting for you up there.'

She had pulled aside the strip of silk between her legs during her little crisis and Julien's fingers touched the curls of her fleece and then the warm lips they covered.

'Oh yes, I can tell that's very special indeed,' he said, pressing a finger between those moist lips.

'Very, but you must let me get my breath back before you go any further,' said Paulette, rolling on to her side towards him so that she could use both hands to open his trousers wide and hold his quivering friend.

'What do we have here?' she asked. 'It was far too dark to see what I'd got hold of last night. Apart from which, it was hidden inside your hat, for the sake of modesty.'

'Modesty? I have never put it into a hat before, but that's as good a reason as any,' said Julien, smiling with pleasure as she stroked him slowly.

'I didn't think you had. When you know me better you'll find out that it amuses me to think of unusual places to put *stiff things*. It took me ages to go to sleep last night because I kept laughing at the thought of your *stiff thing* ready to go off pop in your best hat. You thought I was going to let you do it there, didn't you? I nearly did, for a joke, but you might have been annoyed if you'd ruined the lining. So, in the nick of time I aimed your revolver somewhere else. Don't you think that was very kind of me?'

'Unusual places may be amusing, dear Paulette, but believe me, at this moment I am dying to put my *stiff thing* in the usual place.'

Under her skirt his fingers had parted the soft petals between her thighs and were inside, teasing her slippery little bud, and by now she had no objection to his attentions.

'You have got your breath back, I believe,' said Julien.

'Perhaps. But will putting it in the usual place be amusing for me?'

'I promise that it will amuse you greatly. In fact, I'll go further and say that it will delight you.'

'You promise that it will delight me if I let you do what you want to do to me?' she sighed tremulously.

'It will thrill you beyond belief . . .'

They were both far too excited to stop and undress. Paulette rolled on to her back obligingly and pulled her skirt up to her hips, and Julien was lying on her at once. He did not pause to unbutton her camiknickers between the legs, merely held the loose silk aside so that he could present the distended head of his male adjunct to the pink opening under her chestnut curls and slide into her with a gasp of delight.

She had got rid of her hat and shoes when they first entered the bedroom and lay down together, but Julien had managed to shed no more than his jacket. He lay fully clothed between her raised knees and made love to her with long and fast strokes, his blue bow-tie still knotted round his neck and the toes of his beautifully polished shoes digging into the bed to give him a firm base for his rhythmic movements.

'Julien – darling – you were right!' Paulette moaned, 'What you are doing is very entertaining – I like it! Is it entertaining for you?'

'Extraordinarily entertaining!' he gasped. 'You must agree that the usual place is best for *stiff things!*'

'Is that what you think? I wish I had let you do it in your hat last night – that would teach you about the pleasure of unusual places!'

'Nowhere you can think of will ever give me more pleasure than I feel now,' Julien gasped out, hardly able to speak coherently as an ecstatic sensation gripped his sweating belly.

'You promised to thrill me!' Paulette cried out, her loins lifting off the bed to thrust hard against him.

26

'Ah!' he moaned, beyond words, his body convulsing. 'Julien! Harder, harder!'

He rammed hard and fast between her widely-parted legs, his movements automatic and unstoppable now that his crisis of sensation had arrived. An instant later he delivered his warm tribute into Paulette's shaking belly and she uttered little staccato cries of unbearable pleasure. Her wet mouth clung to his in a sudden long kiss, her fingernails scratched at his back as if she would rip his shirt to shreds, and her belly was bucking hard up against his with an enthusiasm that promised well for the future of their friendship.

After that it took a long time before they were both tranquil enough to speak again. Paulette found her voice first.

'My skirt will be terribly creased, up round my waist like this. I must let it hang out properly before I leave, or everyone I pass in the street will guess what I've let you do to me. And what my Mama would say if she guessed, I cannot imagine! She naturally believes that I am a virgin.'

'Naturally,' said Julien. 'All daughters are virgins until they marry – it is a well-known fact. Just as it is a well-known fact among those of our age that their parents abandoned love-making twenty years ago.'

'My parents are fifty,' said Paulette. 'You are not suggesting that they do what you and I have just done – that's absurd!'

'Absolutely absurd,' Julien agreed. 'I am sure that your respected Papa has not had his *stiff thing* between your Mama's legs since the night you were conceived. How old are you – nineteen?'

He watched with interest while she got off the bed to remove her skirt and put it on a hanger she took from his wardrobe. It needed little persuasion to get her to remove her stockings and pale mauve camiknickers. Julien took the opportunity to strip naked and they sat together on the bed, their backs against the headboard and his arm round her waist.

'I shall be twenty in August,' she said. 'And what you said about Papa and Mama is ridiculous. Of course they

27

don't do what we've just done – it's out of the question!'

'Of course,' Julien agreed with a grin.

He was stroking her breasts, unable to take his eyes off their round perfection. He told her that he adored her, which was perfectly true, and of the anxiety he had felt when she didn't arrive at three. She grinned and put a hand into his lap to hold his limp toy.

'After I attended to this little fellow last night – you thought I wouldn't come to see you today? Did you think it was no more than a handshake of a special kind I gave you in the doorway? Do you think I do that for every man I meet? What strange girls you must know, if you have ideas like that about me!'

'I thought that you had taken pity on me and gave me a little consolation, as I would have consoled you, if you had let me. After all, we were both on our own, having lost close friends. But to be honest, I was afraid that you might have forgiven Edouard Taine this morning and gone somewhere with him to make up yesterday's quarrel.'

'No, I haven't forgiven him. And you – have you forgiven your close friend? Were you on the telephone to her this morning, asking to see her?'

'No, I shall not see her again.'

'You sound very determined – but if she telephones you and asks you to go to her apartment because she can't live another day without you and you go rushing round to her – and there she is lying on her bed naked and begging you to make love to her . . . don't tell me that you wouldn't!'

'I wouldn't go there, whatever she said. It's you I want, Paulette. You are the most beautiful and the most desirable girl I have ever known.'

'Your little friend down here doesn't seem to agree with you. He doesn't find me desirable at all – he's fast asleep.'

'When he was between your legs he was in heaven,' said Julien. 'He needs a little time to recover from so overwhelming an experience.'

'Or is it that he's easily satisfied?' Paulette asked, tugging at his limpness. 'Now I think of it, yesterday evening he blurted out his little message before I'd held him for more than a few seconds.'

'You will observe that he is standing to attention again now like a well-trained soldier.'

'At last – I've been trying to wake him up for ages. I'm glad to see that he knows his duty and has presented himself for action, instead of lying about idle.'

Julien's fingers felt gently between her thighs and played with her. 'He knows his duty, I assure you. He will take up his position in the sentry-box appointed for him and remain there until he is relieved.'

'Until *he's* relieved?' Paulette exclaimed, raising her arched eyebrows. 'I am changing his orders – he is to remain in his sentry-box until I tell him that *I* have been relieved. Does he understand that?'

'He will stand to attention in your sentry-box until you dismiss him,' Julien promised.

'Then I shall give him a kiss before he goes on duty,' said Paulette, and slid down the bed until she could trail her wet tongue up the length of Julien's upstanding part.

Less than a week after Paulette's first visit to Julien's apartment and the beginning of their intimate friendship there took place a development that was much less entertaining. Edouard Taine, the rejected lover, sought out Julien in public and deliberately insulted him! This startling event took place in the foyer of the Theatre Danou, as Julien and Paulette were entering, with hundreds of others, for the regular evening performance. Out of nowhere, as it seemed, Edouard marched up to them through the crowd, stood in their way and announced angrily that he had been looking everywhere for Julien.

'Really?' Julien replied coldly. 'I cannot imagine what you want with me, but there is no secret about where I live.'

'Nor about who you sleep with!' Edouard exclaimed, glaring furiously at Paulette.

While he uttered his public insult to her, he slapped Julien across the cheek, not at all hard, but the gesture was enough to draw cries of astonishment and alarm from the onlookers, some of whom may have thought that this was entertainment of a more dramatic and interesting level than they expected to see on the stage of the theatre.

Julien would have struck back at once, but a strong hand seized his arm and held it firmly. For the first time he noticed that Edouard was accompanied by two other young men, and it was one of these who was preventing him from retaliating by smacking Edouard's face.

'Enough, Monsieur Lambert,' said the man holding Julien's arm fast, 'this is no occasion for a vulgar brawl. You have insulted Monsieur Taine and he has taken the appropriate steps to inform you of his intentions. Satisfaction is required, Monsieur. If you will be so kind as to name a friend who will act for you, I shall call upon him in the morning to agree arrangements acceptable to both sides.'

'A duel!' Julien said incredulously. 'That's absurd!'

'Monsieur Taine believes you to be a man of honour.'

During this exchange Paulette had retreated to the side of the foyer, to be in a position of comparable safety in the event of a fist-fight breaking out. Edouard was staring at her with an expression in which anger, disappointment, jealousy and desire were mingled – if anyone present had been sufficiently well versed in the study of the human face to be able to distinguish so fraught a mixture of emotions.

'Come back to me, Paulette!' he blurted out suddenly.

'Oh, Edouard – you are impossible!' she replied.

'Edouard, be silent!' said the man who had been holding Julien's arm. 'That can be arranged between you and the young lady after you have settled accounts with Monsieur Lambert on the field of honour.'

'The man's a lunatic,' said Julien, 'but if he insists that I disgrace him in a duel, then you may call upon my good friend Claude Torcy to make your arrangements. I shall take great pleasure in humbling the excessive conceit of Monsieur Taine.'

Having delivered his words of scorn, Julien took Paulette's arm and walked her quickly out of the theatre. After what had happened he had no wish to sit and watch a play. He found a bar a little way along the boulevard and asked Paulette what she thought of the little drama which Edouard Taine had staged. He was surprised to hear that she thought it very amusing.

'You spoke very well for yourself, Julien,' she said, raising her glass to him in salute. 'It was most impressive.'

'But this is a serious affair! I could be hurt – perhaps killed!'

'There's no chance of that,' she said, laughing at his earnestness. 'Edouard has a quick temper and speaks bravely, but at heart he is not brave at all. He will not fight any kind of duel with you which involves danger. You may forget about swords and pistols – you are quite safe.'

'Oh,' said Julien in relief. 'But what, then?'

'How can I say? Edouard wants to be able to say that he has beaten you at something and it doesn't much matter what it is. He fought a duel once before, with someone he thought had put his hand on my bottom while we were dancing together – that was a car race through Paris by night.'

'What happened?'

'Edouard won, of course. The other man went round a corner too fast and hit a lamp post sideways.'

'But I have no car.'

'Then it will be something else – some activity in which Edouard is convinced that he can beat you.'

'And what then?' Julien demanded. 'If this idiot beats me, what will you do – go back to him?'

Under cover of the little table at which they sat, Julien slid his hand under her clothes, forced her thighs apart and clasped her soft little mound through her underwear, as if to assure himself that he had rights of ownership in it. Paulette smiled and let him hold her, though her smile was non-committal.

In the event, she was proved correct in what she had told Julien about Edouard's intentions, though it took almost another week of negotiations before Claude Torcy and Alexandre Molyneux, acting for Julien, could reach a mutually acceptable form of contest with Edouard's friends. Every practical possibility was discussed, from swimming across the Seine to a game of *boule*, and rejected either because one of the duellists couldn't do it, or it was too risky, or too trivial. But eventually there came the moment when Julien was invited to meet his seconds on

31

the terrace of Fouquet's on the Champs-Elysées to hear what had been decided. They explained to him the difficulties they had faced and what had been ruled out.

'In the end,' said Claude, trying to preserve a suitably serious expression, 'it came down to two activities with which both of you are familiar, to ensure that the duel will be a fair one.'

'And what are these activities?'

'Drinking is one of them. But the more we discussed it with Taine's seconds, the less appealing it became to all of us. We could imagine you and Taine lurching about in the bar selected for the duel, grossly drunk and forcing yourselves to continue until one fell unconscious. An ugly sight, you will agree, and both winner and loser would be incapacitated for days afterwards.'

'The idea is appalling,' said Julien. 'I refuse to engage in a drinking-match.'

'We have already refused on your behalf. That brings us to the final possibility.'

Julien stared across the table at his two friends. He was becoming suspicious of the seriousness of their attitude towards the impending duel. They both had smirks on their faces, which he took as a sign that they found something amusing in the circumstances – something which perhaps he himself would not find so amusing.

'Tell me,' he said briefly.

Claude caught the waiter's eye and ordered more drinks. He waited until they were served before he would continue, in spite of Julien's efforts to prise any fragment of information out of him. Alexandre was even less helpful – he sat staring at two women sitting at a nearby table and pretended not to hear Julien's questions. It seemed an age before the waiter returned and transferred glasses from his tray to the table.

'Now will you tell me!' Julien exclaimed, pink-faced with impatience.

'Drink your drink and I'll explain,' said Claude, and he insisted on waiting until Julien had drained his glass before he would go further.

'The other activity in which we believe you and Taine to

be skilled is, naturally, making love. And since the reason for the quarrel is a woman and the question of who is to enjoy her favours, it seemed reasonable to all the seconds that the duel should take the form of love-making, and the weapons to be used are those with which nature has provided you and Taine.'

Julien stared at Claude as if he had gone mad. But as the explanation continued in detail, his astonishment vanished and the plan began to seem reasonable – and, after a time, amusing. He learned that on a day to be agreed, at a time to be set, he and Taine and their seconds would meet at one of the better establishments where the services of young women were available. The duellists would select a girl each, retire into separate rooms and, at the end of an agreed length of time, the winner would be declared as the one who had made love the most times to his girl.

'How long shall we have?' Julien asked, his imagination caught at last. 'I like a bit of a rest between bouts.'

'We understand that your opponent does too. We've agreed on two hours as the duration of the duel. Does that suit you?'

'How will you make sure that Taine doesn't cheat by bribing his girl to declare more than he actually performs?'

'His seconds asked the same question about you.'

'The devil they did!' Julien exclaimed, outraged that it should be thought that he was capable of any such underhand methods of winning.

'We have discussed the possibility of having an observer present in each of your rooms, but no satisfactory solution seemed possible. If it was another girl, then that would simply mean bribing two girls instead of one – no problem for you or Taine. The alternative is that one of us observes Taine and one of his seconds observes you, but it was not considered acceptable or in keeping with the tone of high honour we are endeavouring to preserve.'

'I should think not! Nothing is more guaranteed to put me off and spoil my chance of winning than having one of Taine's friends watching me from a corner!'

'What it comes to is this,' said Claude. 'His seconds have given us their word that he is a man of honour and will not cheat, and we have given the same assurance on your behalf. Therefore, both sides will play by the rules.'

'I hope that you are right,' said Julien.

Neither his friends nor Taine's friends saw any reason to remain silent about the extraordinary duel that had been arranged – except as to the location, sightseers not being required. In consequence, the story spread like a forest-fire before a strong wind, until it seemed that half of Paris was talking of nothing else. Bets were laid on the outcome, and it did nothing to help Julien's self-assurance to be told that most people were betting on Taine, he being physically the stronger-looking of the two. At least half a dozen pretty women Julien hardly knew accosted him in night-clubs and restaurants and gave him to understand that they were entirely at his disposal – for which he thanked them with all the charm he could convey and noted their names for possible later meetings. Certainly he had no intention of depleting his strength in advance of the duel, not even with Paulette, to her great disappointment, for like the women who had approached Julien, she had become excited by the prospect of what was going to take place.

The duel was arranged for Thursday, at the Maison Junot, an establishment of good repute not far from the Stock Exchange, in the Rue St Fiacre. The seconds were so diligent in their negotiation of the arrangements that they visited the place on two successive days and both visits were long ones. On the appropriate day Julien lunched with Claude and Alexandre, eating sparingly and confining himself to no more than half a bottle of wine. Since he was paying, his seconds took the opportunity of indulging their appetites freely, and by the time they left the restaurant, both were in a mood of exhilaration. They arrived at the field of honour at exactly two-thirty, to find that Edouard Taine and his seconds had entered a moment or two previously.

Maison Junot had only just opened for the day and its usual afternoon clients were still lingering over lunch and business deals in nearby restaurants. This meant that all the girls of the house were available and had been assembled in the large downstairs room. Julien and Edouard did not speak to each other – they stood well apart, studiously ignoring each other and glancing round the room which, with its small tables and chairs, looked much like a bar or restaurant. Except, of course, the only persons sitting at the tables were partly-dressed young women.

The four seconds assembled in a tight little group and talked among themselves in a way which showed that they were on the best of terms – as well they might be, having enjoyed together two separate visits of research to the establishment in the last three days. They all laughed at some remark made by one of them, then stepped back from each other.

One of Edouard Taine's friends spun a coin high into the air and said, 'call!'

'Heads,' said Claude Torcy and the four of them bent over to watch the coin hit the floor, bounce and roll, until it came to a standstill.

'Monsieur Taine has the first choice,' said Claude, not even sounding sorry for this minor stroke of misfortune for Julien.

Edouard Taine grinned contemptuously at Julien and went round the room looking at the girls sitting at the tables. He chose a girl with yellow-bleached hair, wearing a pink chemise and nothing else. He led her across the room to stand by him and his seconds, one of his arms round her waist so that the chemise was hitched up enough to give a half-view of the brown fleece between her thighs. She was half a head taller than Taine himself, but whether he had guessed that when he chose her sitting down, who could say. In any case, Julien thought, when a man and a woman lie down together, they find by some miracle that they are of the same height.

At a gesture from Claude Julien made his choice. The first client of the afternoon had arrived and was asked by the formidable Madame Junot to take a seat and have a little drink on the house until the young gentlemen had completed their business. Julien did not linger over his deliberations. There were seven girls left to choose from and he had already studied them while waiting for the seconds to get on with the arrangements. The seven were all under twenty-five, that being the policy of the house, and although none could be described as pretty, they looked friendly and wholesome. They were in varying stages of undress, though none was wholly naked. The one to whom Julien held out his hand was no more than twenty, a round-faced girl with straight dark-brown hair. She was wearing a negligee of black artificial silk, black stockings and garters. Her cheap negligee was open all the way down the front to display a very plump mound with thick and protruding lips under an untidy patch of hair. But it was not for that Julien chose her – it was for her impudent grin and the sparkle in her eyes, under her fringe.

The seconds drew the duellists and their girls together, face to face, in the centre of the room, as if they were boxers before a match.

'Gentlemen, you both understand the rules,' said one of Taine's friends, speaking in an impressively formal way. 'These ladies will show you to rooms upstairs in a moment. The duel begins promptly at three o'clock, which is fifteen minutes from now, and ends on the stroke of five. During those two hours you may not leave the room, or you will be deemed to have withdrawn from the duel and conceded defeat. A bottle of good champagne has been placed on ice in each room by way of refreshment. You may order anything you want to be delivered to your room – more champagne or other drink, food, cigarettes – but not another girl. The ones you have chosen are the ones you must remain with.'

'Why can't we have two girls each?' Taine asked. 'Why should we be confined to just one?'

'The rules were negotiated freely with your seconds, Monsieur,' said Claude Torcy. 'It is too late now to change them.'

'I am surprised to find myself in agreement with Monsieur Taine on anything whatsoever,' said Julien, 'but in this matter I do. Why should we not have two girls each to stimulate our appetites? Why not three – I would be happy to entertain three.'

The seconds looked at each other doubtfully, until the matter was settled by Edouard Taine, who had only suggested having two girls to impress on Julien that he was a man of above-normal virility.

'There is no time now to rewrite the rules of the engagement,' he said. 'One girl each was agreed and I am prepared to abide by what my friends thought most suitable in this delicate matter. One girl or three girls – I shall acquit myself mightily.'

'Very well then,' said his principal second, 'to continue, gentlemen – at five o'clock precisely the ladies will be collected by Madame Junot herself from your rooms for questioning. If either of you is in close contact with his girl when Madame Junot enters the room, she will allow thirty seconds' grace for the completion of the act, and no more. If it is not completed in that time, she will simply roll you off the girl and take her from the room, and the attempt will not count. Understood?'

Julien and Edouard nodded, astonished by the thought of being pushed off a girl in mid-stroke by the formidable proprietor of the establishment.

'At fifteen minutes past five o'clock you will both present yourselves to us here in this room,' Taine's second continued. 'By then the girls will have been questioned thoroughly by Madame Junot, in our presence, and the winner will be announced. It has been agreed that the loser will pay for everything today – the use of Madame Junot's rooms and girls, whatever is drunk by the seconds during the wait, and any incidental expenses.'

'By god!' Julien exclaimed. 'I wasn't told that!'

'Nor was I,' said Edouard. 'What made you agree to that, Jacques?'

'It is reasonable,' said his second, 'otherwise how is the loser to know that he has lost, if he has passed a couple of hours pleasuring himself with a girl?'

Julien and Edouard looked at each other and both shrugged their shoulders – it was impossible to disagree now with what the seconds had arranged.

'It suits me,' said Edouard, 'as I shall be the winner. I

37

fear that Monsieur Lambert will be required to pay a heavy bill at five o'clock.'

'Ha!' Julien exclaimed scornfully.

'Are there any questions before the duel begins?' the second asked.

'Yes,' said Edouard instantly. 'If I find it impossible to check my ardour in the presence of Mademoiselle Marguérite here and make love to her before three o'clock, I assume that counts towards my total?'

'No, Monsieur,' Claude Torcy replied. 'What you do before three o'clock is for your own amusement and will not be included in the final score.'

'Let it count, for all I care,' said Julien, derision in his voice. 'Whether Monsieur Taine runs out of steam at ten past three or half-past three is of no importance to anyone.'

Now that the moment was here, Julien was enjoying himself – and so evidently was Edouard Taine, whose question had been mere rhetoric to overawe Julien. He retorted with spirit to Julien's taunt.

'It may be that Monsieur Lambert's nature is so insipid that he can wait indefinitely before stirring himself to action with his girl, but I am a hot-blooded man and with my hand on Mademoiselle Marguérite's bare backside I find it almost impossible to prevent myself from paying her the courtesies due to her.'

'Whether your hand is on her backside, her bosom or between her legs,' Julien riposted, 'twice will see you finished – and the second time will take you an hour and the assistance of the young lady's hand to achieve.'

'What?' Edouard roared magnificently. 'Twice? That shows how little experience you have of the world and of human nature. I intend to have the young lady on her back every fifteen minutes for the full two hours! And if Madame Junot attempts to pull me off Mademoiselle Marguérite's belly at five o'clock, she will find herself thrown down on her back and ravaged in her turn!'

'By god – I've yet to meet the man who could ravish me in my own house!' Madame Junot exclaimed, her heavy face flushed purple.

The seconds were listening enthralled to this exchange of opinions between Edouard and Julien and they bowed politely towards Madame Junot in acknowledgment of the truth of her assertion, then their faces turned to Julien again, waiting for his reply to Taine.

'For the full two hours?' he sneered. 'Yes, Mademoiselle Marguérite will be on her back and asleep from boredom for the last hour and a half, for all the action she will get from you.'

Edouard's girl had been standing dumbly, letting him feel her bare bottom under her pink chemise. She ran a hand over the front of his trousers and grinned.

'No, he'll be all right for two or three times,' she announced, 'I can feel something as hard as a flagpole in there.'

'I fear it may prove to be only a green sapling that will bend in the middle and be useless, Mademoiselle,' Julien said politely.

'Is that what you think?' Edouard demanded. 'I see that you have not been informed of my capacities by a certain young lady who has reason to be familiar with their extent.'

'To be truthful, it never occurred to me to ask of such a trivial matter,' said Julien dismissively, 'and after being with me she obviously thought that whatever capacities you possess were not worth mentioning.'

'Gentlemen,' said one of Taine's seconds, his gold pocket-watch in his hand, 'the time is ten minutes to three. I suggest that you accompany the young ladies you have chosen upstairs and prepare to sustain your honour in the trial of strength that lies ahead.'

'Certainly,' Edouard agreed. 'Come along, my dear – I want my first success to be exactly on the stroke of three.'

They went towards the stairs, his arm round her waist pulling up her chemise so that the fat cheeks of her bottom were uncovered and wobbled excitingly as she walked. Julien and the seconds stared in rapture at the sight.

'Mademoiselle Marguérite!' Julien called after her.

'When Monsieur Taine overtaxes himself and collapses in half an hour's time, come to my room – this young lady will need a rest by then.'

'That's what you think!' said Julien's girl, sliding her hand into his trouser pocket to grasp his upright baton. 'I'll take care of this without any help from her, believe me.'

Edouard turned his head to scowl over his shoulder at Julien and Claude reminded him solemnly that if the other girl did come to his room, then under the rules he would have lost.

'Have no fear,' he answered. 'Taine will not let her out of his sight, since he intends to keep up the pretence that he will be still on top of her at five o'clock. And as this young lady says, she will take care of me very adequately.'

'You can be sure of that,' she said, squeezing his stem hard through his pocket.

She waited until Taine was out of sight before leading Julien up the stairs. Her name was Babette, she told him, while she helped him to undress in the pleasantly-furnished bedroom to which she took him.

'Madame Junot told us all about your duel with the other gentleman,' she said, pulling his trousers down. 'We're getting a special bonus, the two of us taking part. It's none of my business, but I don't know why you're doing it – is it for a bet, or are you trying to prove something?'

She had Julien naked and stood close to him, clasping his fleshy handle and stroking it to make it grow as big as it would.

'I'm not trying to prove anything, Babette – it's that idiot Taine. He wants the world to know that he's superior to me at something.'

'But why?' she asked.

Julien slipped her black negligee off her shoulders and let it slide down her body to the crook of her elbows to uncover her breasts. They were a good size and pleasant in his hands, though a little slack, even at her young age, from the amount of handling they had been subjected to.

'It's about a girl,' he said. 'She was his and now she's mine.'

'Now I understand,' said Babette, giving him her

40

enchantingly impudent grin. 'He wants her back – is that it?'

Julien nodded, enjoying what she was doing to his spindle.

'So he's out to prove that he's better at it than you,' said Babette. 'But that won't get her back – girls don't fall for the man with the biggest or who does it the most. They want affection and fun besides love-making.'

Julien slipped her negligee off completely and lay on the double bed with her to play with her breasts and arouse himself further. Babette's words cheered him, since in some way she could be regarded as an expert in one aspect of love-making – or at the very least as a professional. However, he knew enough to be wary of generalisations. 'I used to know a woman who really did go for the biggest and the most often,' he said.

'There's always an exception,' said Babette. 'But is the girl you took from the other gentleman like that? I'm sure she wants more from you. Does she know about this competition?'

'Yes, she thinks it is amusing,' he answered, his hand between Babette's legs to feel her plump mound and its pouting lips. 'She wanted to stay with me all last night and make love because she was excited about today. I had to send her home before she had a chance to exhaust me.'

'She didn't do that,' said Babette, her grip on his stem relaxing. 'You'll never be harder than you are now – do you want to put it in and make a start? It's after three by now.'

She rolled on her back and spread her legs for him. Julien mounted her and her fingers forced the head of his male part into her fleshy vestibule. A long push sank it into her depths, though not with the ease that he was accustomed to.

'But you are not in the least excited, Babette,' he said, lying still on her pale belly.

'What of it? You're the one who's got to win the duel, not me. I'm here to help you score in any way I can, but I don't have to have a climax every time you do.'

'No, I suppose that in your line of work it would be

41

impossible for you to do that,' he said thoughtfully.

'I'd be dead inside a week!' she said, grinning at him. 'How many men do you think I have up me in a day's work? If I had a climax every time I'd be worn to a rag in twenty-four hours, and in hospital after three days. But I know how to help you reach your climax, and that's what matters.'

'This bonus you're being paid for this afternoon, Babette – I'll double it if I win.'

'Then I'll make sure you win. How many times do you want to do it to me?'

'I don't know . . . let's find out.'

He rode her lightly and she encouraged him by spreading her black-stockinged legs as widely as she could and stroking his bare back firmly with her palms.

'Nice and easy this first time,' she said, 'Save your strength as much as you can.'

When his rhythm became a little faster, her hands moved down to his bottom, to grip the cheeks and squeeze them hard and tug them apart and then pinch and scratch them lightly with her nails. Julien gave a long and pleased sigh and discharged his first tribute into her, shaking in a light and ecstatic crisis of sensation.

'Good boy,' said Babette, 'that's the way – no big explosions to wear you out, just a nice, gentle little climax.'

Julien rested beside her, his hands roaming over her body to arouse himself as soon as possible.

'This girl of yours,' said Babette, 'is she pretty?'

'Marvellously so.'

'Is she light or dark?'

'She has chestnut-coloured hair and plump little breasts that are a dream to feel and play with.'

'Would you call mine plump?'

'Yes,' said Julien, handling them with pleasure, his fingers gently busy with their prominent pink tips, 'yours are nice and plump, Babette.'

'Did you make love to her at all yesterday?'

'In the afternoon, twice. Then I made her go home, or she would have drained me dry, she was so excited. I did it to her with my fingers, but she still wanted more.'

42

'It sounds to me as if she wanted you to lose today,' said Babette, massaging his half-limp stem to make it grow big.

'Oh, I hadn't thought of that!' Julien exclaimed in dismay. 'But why should she want Taine to defeat me – she could go back to him at any time she wished.'

'Girls are not always as logical as you men pretend to be. Lie on your back now.'

Julien did as she said and she lay on him, her legs outside his, and spiked herself neatly on his stiff part.

'We'll soon have you doing it again,' she promised, her impudent grin lighting up her face.

Now it was Julien's hands that clasped the cheeks of her bottom and played with them. Babette rode him briskly, jabbing her loins against him in short quick movements to drive him into her. At first Julien thought that the ease with which he was gliding inside her was entirely the result of his own earlier offering, but as Babette's breathing became faster and louder, he understood that she had become aroused and was doing it to him for her own pleasure, apart from her professional reasons. The thought pleased him and he lay comfortably under her and let her attentions carry him up the long slope of arousal to another climactic discharge into her now very slippery entrance. She kept going after he had finished, her jabbing harder and faster, until eventually she gasped loudly and achieved her release.

'That was very nice indeed,' Julien told her, when she opened her eyes and grinned down at him. 'Why did you change your mind and let yourself become aroused?'

'I was thinking – after this afternoon Madame Junot won't be able to argue if Marguérite and I have the rest of the day off. So I might as well let myself go and enjoy it with you – after all, you did promise to double my bonus from Madame.'

'If I win, was what I said.'

'You leave it to me and you won't lose,' she assured him.

During the rest period that followed he asked her what sort of men frequented Maison Junot in the ordinary course of events.

'Businessmen, mostly,' she said. 'Over forty, all of

43

them, and some of them fifty and over. Nice, educated, presentable gentlemen – they're never any trouble. They know what they've come here for and they're always grateful for a little help in getting results, if you know what I mean.'

'I'm not sure that I do, Babette – tell me what you mean.'

'The sad fact is,' she said, 'that a gentleman of fifty-something has lost his youthful strength – too many expensive dinners and lunches, too many bottles of wine and cognac, too many big cigars. They don't worry about how many times they're going to do it – they are happy enough to do it once. Often they're over-weight – or if I'm blunt instead of polite, they've got bellies on them that make it impossible for them to see their things, even when they're standing up stiff. Usually they like to lie on their backs and let the girl do the work – probably because it would never happen if they lay on the girl – they'd run out of breath after half a dozen pushes.'

'I see that I am in very skilled hands,' Julien murmured, as she massaged his chest and belly vigorously, making his skin tingle and his limp part twitch.

'The best,' she agreed, grinning at him. 'What time is it?'

He glanced at his gold wrist-watch and told her that it was a little after three-thirty.

'Twice in half an hour – that's a good start,' she said. 'Turn over and I'll massage your back.'

He lay face-down on the bed while she sat on him and sank her fingers into his shoulders and the muscles of his back. By the time she had worked her way slowly down to his bottom he was beginning to grow hard again. When she squatted over his thighs and smacked his bottom lightly with her open hands for a minute or two, he was fully ready again. He turned over beneath her and pulled her down beside him, his fingers between her legs to open the pouting lips there.

By half-past four he had done it to her four times, though the fourth time was slow and, when he reached the critical moments, exhausting, though very satisfying. He lay on his back recovering, smoking a cigarette that Babette had given him and wondering if he'd done enough to win the duel.

44

'What do you think, Babette?' he asked.

'Four times is not to be despised,' she said, grinning. 'I doubt if most young men could equal that in the time. The only thing is – your opponent is a strong-looking man. He might have done more.'

'So I fear. But it is going to take me more than the time we have left to recover enough to do it again, I fear.'

'Don't give up before you're beaten,' she said. 'Let's see what can be done.'

She spread his legs apart so that she could lie between them and use her mouth on his wilting stem. Her tongue assaulted it vigorously, and the suction she applied was almost strong enough to rip if from his body, Julien feared. Meanwhile her fingers were tugging and rolling his slack dependents. It took some time, but eventually she was rewarded by a twitch that hinted at a revival of his limp morsel. The suction she was applying redoubled and her fingers slid underneath his dependents to probe mercilessly between the cheeks of his bottom. Julien's body woke up and he gasped at the sensations that coursed through it.

Babette was sitting up between his legs, one hand clasping his restored part and massaging it brutally, the fingers of her other hand out of sight and jammed viciously inside him.

'Yes, you're good for one more time,' she exclaimed. 'You can do it!'

Julien shook his head, afraid that his rearing stem would collapse the instant she let go of it.

'Oh yes you can.' Babette insisted. 'I'm the expert and I say you're going to do it again. I will not let you lose!'

'Yes, I can do it if you do that to me!' Julien gasped, suddenly hopeful, staring at her hand tightly grasping his appendage and flicking up and down furiously.

'Ah, but it doesn't count like this,' said Babette. 'That was explained to us by Madame before you made your choice even.'

'What?' Julien exclaimed in dismay.

'That's right – if you do it in my hand it doesn't count. It has to be inside me, that's the rules.'

'Babette – help me!' he implored her.

'As long as you're sure you want to give me the bonus you promised . . .' she said hesitantly, her hand jerking up and down so hard that unimaginable sensations were racking Julien.

'Twice the bonus if you can help me win!' he moaned.

'Give me your word and I'll make sure you don't lose,' she promised.

'Yes!'

Her brutal treatment of the two most tender parts of his body had brought him to so high a pitch of arousal that he was, so to say, *in extremis,* though hardly aware of it, so frantic were his emotions. At the psychological moment Babette changed her position rapidly to sit across his loins and thrust the distended head of his tormented part into the thick lips between her legs. She sat down on him hard, forcing him into her so abruptly that it brought on his crisis at once. Julien screamed shrilly and bucked in frantic spasms as he squirted his last two drops into Babette – at the very moment when the door opened to reveal Madame Junot.

Madame stood in the doorway, a formidable figure in her ankle-length frock of very dark blue, her arms crossed beneath her massive bosom. She stared impassively at the scene on the bed – Julien squealing in an ecstasy so intense that it was almost indistinguishable from pain – and Babette bouncing violently up and down on him. Babette turned her head and grinned at her employer, her movements slowing as the man beneath her started to collapse.

'He's finished,' said Madame Junot. 'Leave him and come with me, Babette.'

Immediately, Babette freed herself from Julien, jumped off the bed and put on her black negligee. Julien was left panting on his back, his demolished stem flopping on his belly. His wits had not yet returned after the cataclysmic sensations he'd experienced and he stared open-mouthed and without comprehension at Madame Junot.

'Dress yourself, Monsieur,' she said. 'Your friends are waiting for you downstairs.'

'Where is Babette?' he asked, his legs and belly still twitching from the experience he had undergone at her hands.

Babette had slipped out of the door and was waiting in the passage for Madame Junot.

'If you wish to spend more time with her company, that can be arranged,' said Madame Junot, always alert for an opportunity to promote business. 'I have no doubt that she will be delighted to entertain a handsome young fellow like you for the rest of the day, if you like. I can see that you're well-made and have the necessary to amuse a girl.'

Julien's *necessary* had collapsed completely and shrunk to the size of his little finger. He sat up and stared at it.

'You can be proud of Babette,' he said. 'She is a credit to your house, Madame.'

'It is the custom for gentlemen to make their gratitude known by giving the girl who has pleased them a little present,' she reminded him.

'I shall most assuredly do that. Do you think that my poor little thing will recover? It looks as if it has been ruined.'

Madame Junot laughed briefly, crossed the room and reached down to flick at his limp affair with an extended forefinger. 'It won't stand up again today – nor tomorrow,' she said judiciously. 'You've had a busy afternoon. Now get dressed and come downstairs.'

Julien felt a little light-headed as he got his clothes on slowly, his fingers fumbling with buttons. In the large room he found his and Edouard Taine's seconds sitting round two tables pushed together. They were chatting and laughing in the friendliest possible way and had very obviously been drinking champagne continuously while the duellists were upstairs with the girls. Madame Junot was with them, a smile on her face and a glass in her hand. Julien's legs seemed a little uncertain under him as he crossed the room and sat down.

Claude handed him a glass of champagne.

'Drink that – you look worn out,' he said with a chuckle.

'Where is Edouard Taine?' Julien asked.

'He'll be here in a moment,' Madame Junot assured him.

'I removed Marguérite from his room at the correct time, have no fear.'

'And was he, as he boasted before we went upstairs, in the very act when you entered his room at five?'

She stared at him for a moment before replying. 'How does that concern you, Monsieur? What goes on in my rooms with my girls is as confidential as the confessional.'

'That would be a sight worth seeing,' said Claude with a grin, 'Julien and one of Madame's girls doing it in the confessional – confidentially.'

'You found me at an interesting moment with Babette,' said Julien. 'I have no objection to that being known – confirm it to the company here, please.'

'That is a matter for you – my lips are sealed. If ever I spoke of what I have seen upstairs, I should be out of business inside a week.'

In another minute or two Edouard Taine came slowly down the stairs and took a seat at the table. Julien scrutinised him carefully and noted that there were dark shadows under his eyes and that his hand shook a little as he raised a glass to his lips.

'We are ready to proceed,' Taine's principal second, Marc Duhamel announced. 'Madame, have you questioned the two young ladies thoroughly?'

'With the greatest rigour,' she answered.

'And we may be certain that the truth has emerged?'

'You may have every confidence. I have had years of experience in these matters and I know when a girl is lying or telling the truth. I have questioned Marguérite and Babette separately and together and I am sure that they have given me an accurate account of what these two gentlemen achieved during their two hours upstairs.'

'Excellent! Then what have you to report to us, Madame?'

She reached down the front of her dark blue frock and extracted a folded paper from between her mountainous breasts. Duhamel took it from her and raised it gallantly to his lips.

'I salute it for the sake of the most interesting place in which it has rested,' he said, a slightly drunken smile on his handsome face.

'If I'd known that I'd have put it down my knickers, said Madame Junot, with a throaty chuckle.

'Are you ready, gentlemen?' he asked, looking first at Edouard and then at Julien. They both nodded, unable to speak for suppressed emotion at this moment of truth, when the matter was to be decided.

He unfolded the paper and read from it. 'Monsieur Julien Lambert – seven times.'

There were gasps of surprise and admiration round the table.

'Ah, she's a good girl, Babette,' said Madame Junot. 'She knows how to get the best out of a man. I was just the same when I was a young girl.'

Adorable Babette Julien was thinking – she had augmented his actual performance to ensure him the victory! She was well worth the bonus he had promised her.

He glared defiantly across at Edouard Taine, who looked away and reached quickly for the champagne bottle to refill his glass.

'Well done, Julien,' said Claude, reaching across the table to shake his hand warmly.

Alexandre added his congratulations, murmuring, 'Seven times in two hours – what a man!'

'If you please, gentlemen,' said Taine's second, 'you have heard only half of what is written here. The winner has not yet been decided.'

'Then continue,' said Claude, 'though I refuse to believe that your man did better than ours. What sort of show did he put up?'

'Monsieur Edouard Taine,' Duhamel read out, 'seven times.'

He put the paper down on the table, so that they could read the words for themselves. There was a moment of stunned silence, then an outburst of laughter and acclamation. Julien stared with open suspicion at Edouard, who returned his gaze with equal doubt. After a moment or two they both realised the absurdity of the situation and broke into laughter.

'The duel has ended in a draw,' Duhamel announced, when he could make himself heard again.

'The best possible result,' Madame Junot declared, rising to her feet. 'I congratulate you both, young gentlemen. You have made good use of my best two girls and you will be welcome here at any time. As will you other gentlemen, of course. Satisfaction is guaranteed here, as you know. Now, if you will excuse me, I have other visitors to look after.'

Indeed, her early evening clients were beginning to drift in, on their way home from a busy day and in need of a little relaxation and amusement before facing their wives and families. As Babette had told Julien, the clients sitting at the little tables with girls, drinking a glass of wine and talking, were all middle-aged and portly – except for one in a black frock-coat, being assisted up the stairs by a girl on either side of him, his arms round their shoulders for support. He was nearing seventy, to judge by his shock of snow-white hair and manner of dress, and would certainly require all the skilled assistance the girls could give him when they got him on to a bed.

Claude Torcy rose to his feet, a filled glass in his hand. 'Gentlemen, honour is satisfied,' he said. 'Both men have acquitted themselves with extraordinary gallantry and courage, not to mention stamina and endurance. Let us salute Julien and Edouard. I propose that they should now shake hands and let the rivalry between them end here.'

In the true spirit of reconciliation, Julien and Edouard rose to shake hands and embrace each other. Both were aware that Madame Junot and her girls had rigged the result and, unless they confided in each other, neither would ever know whether he had beaten the other or not. But the expression on their faces said as they embraced, does it matter? The truth was that both had emerged with enhanced reputations and were well-pleased with themselves. A comfortable conspiracy of silence was very clearly the best policy for them. As for the issue unresolved between them – that of Paulette – as Julien and Edouard released each other and sat down side by side in new-found respect and the beginnings of friendship, they grinned at each other in a way that suggested that all was possible to men of goodwill. She could perhaps be shared between them.

A problem shared
is a problem doubled

For Michel Loubet it was a great inconvenience at the age of twenty-eight to have no profession and a very small income from investments. The traditional way of resolving this problem, for a man of taste and spirit, was, as everyone knows, to marry the daughter of a rich family – pretty if possible, but that was not of prime importance compared with the size of her father's estate. But like many young men before him, Michel learned that the traditional solution presents serious problems of its own. Rich and important parents expect their daughters, pretty or not, to marry the sons of other rich and important parents. Not only do they expect it, they take pains to instil this same expectation into their daughters too.

Naturally, it was not at all difficult for a young man as good-looking and charming as Michel to persuade suitable young ladies to visit his tiny apartment for an hour or two of the pleasures of love. But when, after delighting a young lady with his skill, passion and virility, he presumed to suggest that he was seriously in love with her and contemplated the possibilities of a permanent union – ah well, the mood changed at once! The naked young lady who had writhed in his embrace in ecstasy and had cried out *Je t'adore, Michel!* for the last hour or more, would smile fondly at him and shrug her pretty shoulders. And that was that.

There were older women, it was true – widows for the main part – who might well have been content to listen with more attention and interest to Michel's suggestions, but the prospect was not a pleasing one for him. If he had not secured the prize he sought by the time he reached his

51

thirty-fifth birthday, he told himself, then he might well be compelled to reconsider the availability of well-to-do widows. But that was far away – he was young enough to entertain serious hopes of a better arrangement. And so he continued to circulate in good company, even though he could not really afford to do so, and he was steadily accumulating debts. Eventually they would have to be settled, but that was something he chose not to think about.

These being his circumstances, Michel's heart gave a sudden bound when he was introduced one day to Mademoiselle Vivienne Lesurques at a reception. She was about his own age – certainly under thirty – dark-haired, slender and very pretty. Best of all, she was unmarried and she was wearing expensive clothes. Michel enquired of his men friends whether Mademoiselle Lesurques was perhaps maintained by a rich friend and was assured that she was of independent means. That being so, he set out to turn a casual acquaintance into something more interesting and useful. He succeeded to the point where he was invited to call upon her the next day.

Her apartment was in the Boulevard Haussmann, between the Rue de Courcelles and the Place St Augustin, on the second floor, and very handsomely furnished. Her manner was vivacious to the point of nervousness, which Michel interpreted as an indication that she was hoping that he would make love to her – the slight nervousness of anticipation. He took it that she would not reject his advances, if they were civilised and considerate.

The situation suited him very well and it did not take long for a man of his experience to persuade her to let him sit beside her on the Recamier-style chaise-longue in her salon. He kissed her hands repeatedly and praised her beauty in the most extravagant terms – in short, he availed himself of every device known to eager males since time immemorial. He realised that she had in all probability been subjected many times before to this ardent performance, for she was most attractive and he considered it impossible that she was still a virgin at twenty-nine.

Be that as it may, she gave every sign of being pleasingly flattered by his development of the slight acquaintance between them. Soon he had an arm round her slender waist and was kissing her lips, first tenderly and then with rising ardour. Vivienne responded completely and without reservation and sighed into his open mouth when his hands lightly caressed her breasts through the green silk of her frock.

In due course his persistent praise of her beauty and the increasing tempo of their embraces made it opportune to suggest that she should remove her long-sleeved frock and her slip, so that he could pay his devotions more openly to her breasts. She obliged him at once and, in the nature of things, his admiration did not confine itself to mere words after he had assured her, a little breathlessly by now, that her breasts were of an exquisite shape. This was no more than the simple truth – Vivienne's breasts were small, well-separated and with up-turned russet buds. Michel's admiration for them expressed itself freely through his hands and he fondled her pretty playthings to an extent that was as satisfactory to her as it was to him. He brought his lips to her buds and gave further expression to his devotion by kissing them and rubbing the tip of his wet tongue over them, so that she was left in no doubt whatsoever of his total admiration for her.

Everything was proceeding extraordinarily well. Michel congratulated himself on having found this delightful woman and having reached this advanced state of acquaintance with her in so short a time. It was his intention, after making love to her on her own chaise longue and raising her to the heights of delirious pleasure, to invite her to dinner that evening – and then hopefully to return with her to her apartment and give her a night of further enjoyment. In the morning he would send flowers and a further invitation to dinner. A week or ten days of this intensive courtship, though it would cost far more than he could afford, would make him indispensable to her, he calculated. After seven successive nights of ecstatic love-making with him, she would not be able to bear the thought of sleeping alone on the eighth night. The time would be right for gentle hints at a longer-lasting relationship between them – and if at the time of his declaration of undying love his hand was between her thighs, giving her tiny thrills of delight, he had little doubt but that she would murmur that she loved him too. After that, it was just a question of making arrangements for marriage.

That was in the future that existed only in Michel's head. At the very moment in question, Vivienne was half-reclining on her chaise longue, supported by his arm about her, while he continued to display his deep appreciation of the beauties of her breasts. Because she had removed her frock and slip to permit him to do this, she was wearing only her stockings and loose knickers of eau-de-nil silk. Michel could hardly believe his luck – that a beauty like Vivienne, of independent means, had come into his life and was encouraging him in this way – it was like winning a million francs in the state lottery.

When he judged that the moment had arrived to advance his cause a little further, he let his hand stray from her breasts to stroke her bare and narrow belly. She was a very slender woman, with long thin arms and long thin legs, if plain words were to be used, though there is no good reason why they should be. In Michel's experience she was the very slender type who often display a more than ordinary sensuality when properly aroused. He was convinced that hidden fires burned in her nature and he was eagerly anticipating the moment when she would erupt like a volcano in a lava-flow of passion.

His anticipation was so eager because, apart from any consideration of his future fortunes, he was himself a sensual man and he intended to have Vivienne three times for his own satisfaction before pausing to talk about taking her to dinner. His hand slid down inside the top of her silk knickers and stroked the smooth skin of her narrow belly. A little deeper and he touched thick and springy curls and combed through them with curled fingertips to excite her more. He felt for the warm treasure he hoped shortly to impale – and judge his astonishment when Vivienne seized his wrist to prevent his fingers from investigating further.

'But what is the matter, *chérie*?' he asked, looking at her pink-flushed face. 'I adore you and I want to caress you between your beautiful thighs.'

'It's no good,' she said. 'It was a mistake to ask you here, I'm sorry.'

'But why do you want me to stop now – at this golden moment?'

'I can't help it.'

Michel's male part was clamouring in his trousers for the solace to be found between Vivienne's tightly-closed thighs. But because Michel's designs were more ambitious than immediate gratification, he suppressed his understandable annoyance at being so discourteously frustrated and spoke with sympathy in his voice. 'My dear Vivienne, I see that there is a difficulty,' he said, removing his hand from her knickers until he could again establish a mood in which she would welcome it there. 'Perhaps I have been too enthusiastic or too forward, but the sight of your charming little breasts set me on fire. Forgive me if I have offended you.'

'You haven't offended me at all,' she said, looking away from him awkwardly. 'It was so thrilling when you stroked my breasts that I thought things would be all right. But I should have known better. It's my fault.'

'Let us not speak of faults until we understand each other better. Your little buds stood up firmly under my tongue – you were excited.'

'But not enough,' she said flatly.

'Not enough for what? We were about to reach the next stage of excitement with my hand between your legs to play with the treasure that is hidden there.'

'It's no treasure,' she said unhappily. 'It's a useless thing.'

'That I cannot believe – why do you use such unkind words about something I am sure is delightful?'

'I know you're trying to be kind to me, even though you must be disappointed. Thank you for that, at least.'

'The disappointment is on both sides. If I can help you to overcome whatever problem oppresses you, dear Vivienne, I am at your service.'

'I've heard that before,' she said, with a trace of bitterness. 'Do you think that you're the first to try?'

55

'The number is not important, only the outcome.'

'Oh, you men!' Vivienne exclaimed. 'You never understand. For you it's all so simple.'

'What do you mean?' Michel was beginning to think that perhaps after all she was still a virgin and terrified of making love for the first time. Her hand reached into his lap and took hold of his stiffness through the cloth of his grey trousers.

'What do I mean? I mean that *this* stands up the moment you touch a pair of breasts,' she said. 'You push it into a woman and one minute later it does its business and that's all there is to it for you.'

She was gripping him so tightly that it was deliciously painful.

'How sad that you reduce the immeasurable delights of love – the kisses, the murmurs, the rapture – to a simple question of a quick penetration,' he said. 'Surely you have enjoyed those marvellous emotions and sensations – on happier occasions than this, I mean?'

'You can hide it all you want to with words,' said Vivienne fiercely, 'men are good at that. But the reality is that a few strokes with *this* inside a woman gives you all that you want – and that's the end of the kisses and rapture.'

'I can only guess that you have been unfortunate in your choice of lovers,' said Michel, feeling his spindle jerk in her squeezing fingers. 'Has some brute used you insensitively in the past – abused you, perhaps even forced you? Not all men are like that, I assure you.'

'Yes, you are,' she answered. 'You use pretty words like rapture when all you mean is a quick thrill.'

'You are mistaken. It was my intention to kiss your charming body from nose to toes and caress every part of you until you were on fire, before proceeding to the ultimate intimacy. And then, when you had accepted me eagerly inside you, I would have made love to you with such delicacy and finesse that you would have pleaded with me to carry you up to the very pinnacle of ecstasy.'

Vivienne's hand was moving feverishly on his trousers, rubbing his uprightness through the thin cloth.

'Hypocrite!' she exclaimed, 'Liar! Everything you say is directed towards one selfish purpose – to get *this* inside me, push five times and do your business. Men talk of love and their words are empty. They tell a woman she is beautiful, that she has pretty breasts – it's all flattery.'

'But you *are* beautiful, Vivienne,' Michel gasped, as her frantic grip increased in tightness on his abused stem.

'The truth is that when a man's *thing* stands up, any woman will do for him,' she said, her vehemence over-riding his words. 'Even ugly old women are persuaded to lie on their backs and open their legs if a man has had enough to drink. Half a bottle of cognac and a man will stick it up his own grandmother! And the final truth is this – that the woman is not even necessary, plain or ugly. All that you need to get your quick little thrill is what I'm doing to you, isn't it? Answer me.'

'Ah, ah!' Michel moaned as her savagely-moving hand carried him past the point of control and he squirted his passion up his quaking belly inside his underpants.

'Animal!' Vivienne exclaimed, rubbing even faster. 'You have proved everything I said!'

He seized her thin wrist and pulled her hand away from him as his throes subsided. Vivienne freed herself from his encircling arm and moved to the end of the chaise longue. She sat staring at him in contempt, her arms crossed beneath her bare breasts, pushing them upwards, so that their pink buds were like gun sights aimed at him.

'My god, why did you do that?' Michel asked.

'To prove my point. You're the same as the rest of them, for all your fine words. Well, you've had what you came here for – you can go now.'

'You are mistaken, Vivienne. That wasn't what I came here for,' he answered, looking with curiosity at this extraordinary woman.

'You don't have to lie now – it's all over,' she said in a dismissive tone of voice.

'It is obvious to me that you are a deeply unhappy woman and I ask myself why.'

'What do you care?'

Michel was a man of very considerable charm and

intelligence – and no stranger to the irrational moods of women. He began to talk to her gently, his words well-chosen and his manner easy. Slowly the hard look left Vivienne's face and she became less hostile. Ten minutes later she was apologising to him for the way she had spoken to him, and Michel knew that he was on the road towards gaining her confidence. Whether it would be worth the trouble and time, he was no longer sure, but his instincts suggested that if he could arouse her and then satisfy her, an interesting and rewarding friendship might in time develop between them.

'If you will excuse me for a moment,' he said, with a smile, 'I will make use of your bathroom to remove my underwear. It is becoming a matter of urgency if my suit is not to be stained.'

She smiled briefly and showed him where to go. When he returned she had opened a bottle of wine and poured two glasses. That was an encouraging sign, he judged. Far more encouraging was the fact that she had not put her frock back on – she was still wearing only her stockings and knickers, her breasts bare. Michel interpreted this as a silent plea on her part to do something to her – to make her yield, to take her by force, perhaps, and compel her to endure the ecstasy which eluded her. Perhaps.

Michel thought it prudent to wait and find out what it was that she really wanted him to do to her. Their conversation as they drank the wine, sitting apart on the chaise longue, was friendly. There was none of the hostility she had displayed towards him earlier, when she had been at the height of her frustration. By the time the bottle was empty she was smiling at him, though not in a way that invited him to move any closer or attempt to touch her. Nevertheless, she gave signs of being pleased when he gazed at her breasts.

'There is so much I would like you to tell me,' he said, smiling at her. 'I wonder if you ever will?'

She shrugged her bare shoulders.

'The things of real importance are never told,' she said.

An idea of how he might advance matters came into Michel's head. 'Yes, they are told.' he said. 'One of the wise dispensations of the Church is the confessional. Do you make use of it regularly?'

'I have not spoken to a priest since I was eighteen. Why do you ask?'

'Because, dear Vivienne, you and I are still strangers to each other, in spite of what started to happen between us and then did not.'

'And in spite of what actually did happen for you?' she asked, with a half-grin.

'Let us agree that it never took place,' he said, returning her grin. 'No significance need be given to that little episode. You had no intention of giving me pleasure and I had no expectation of receiving any. You were demonstrating what you believe to be true of men in general.'

'I was angry and unreasonable,' she said softly. 'It was a dreadful thing to do – I am ashamed of myself, Michel.'

'There is no need to be – as you will understand in a moment. The reason why I mentioned the confessional is that I believe that you could disembarrass your soul of what is troubling it by making your confession.'

'Tell a priest!' she exclaimed, aghast.

'No, make your confession to me. Afterwards I will go away and you need never see me again. The act of telling all will bring you calm and understanding.'

'But you're no priest! Ten minutes ago you had your hand inside my knickers!'

'So much the better. I am no celibate candle-snuffer – I have experienced everything that men and women do together. Therefore I am well-placed to understand and sympathise.'

'But I should feel such a fool!'

'It is not easy, but it could free you from your problems.'

'You don't know what you're talking about,' Vivienne protested, but he could see that his suggestion had caught her imagination and that there was something exciting in the idea of telling him her innermost secrets.

'Try,' he urged her. 'If it becomes too difficult to continue, you can stop and tell me to leave. It is in your hands. But consider – this may be the only opportunity you will ever have, unless you go to a real priest.'

She sighed deeply, her naked breasts swaying, and thought for some moments.

'A real priest is no use to me, Michel. How do you propose that we should start this little game?'

The apartment was bright from the afternoon sun streaming in through the windows. Michel drew the long curtains to bring a restful dimness to the room and then persuaded Vivienne to lie full-length on the chaise longue. He placed a chair for himself just behind her shoulder, so that he was close to her but out of her sight.

'Compose yourself,' he said in a soothing tone. 'Make yourself comfortable as if you were going to have a little sleep. Let your arms rest down by your sides. Close your eyes lightly and relax yourself.'

'Do penitent women in the confessional show their breasts to the priest like this?' she asked mockingly.

'I don't know – but if I were a priest I would insist that they did before I listened to them. Tell me about yourself, Vivienne – where were you born and who were your parents?'

She began to recite her life-story to him. He listened to her account of well-to-do parents of good repute, her schooling and growing-up. It all sounded normal and dull, except that both parents had died in the influenza epidemic at the end of the War and left her everything.

'Tell me about your first lover,' Michel suggested, now that she was talking freely about herself. 'How old were you?'

'Nineteen, and madly in love with him. It thrilled me when he kissed me and stroked my breasts. I longed to be married to him – I thought it would make me the happiest girl in France to be with him all day and all night. What a fool I was when I was young!'

'Did he do more than stroke your breasts? Did he touch you between the legs?'

'Yes, when he got bolder he felt me there. I urged him to continue and he pulled out his *thing* and asked me to hold it.'

'Was that enjoyable?'

'It was very interesting, because I'd never felt one

before. After a while he lay on top of me and pushed it in. I was a virgin and I'd been told by friends that the first time with a man was not very agreeable. He bounced up and down on me and turned red in the face and finished his business – and it did nothing for me at all, nothing! And there you have the story of my life – I feel nothing when a man makes love to me.'

'You have tried with others since then?'

'In the ten years since then I have tried with twenty or thirty men – always hoping that the next one would be able to achieve what none of the others had. But you saw what happened twenty minutes ago – I became pleasantly aroused when you touched my breasts, but I can no longer let a man put it in me because I know that it will be a fiasco.'

She had become agitated during the telling of her unhappy tale, as she had every right to. Her arms were in the air, waving and gesticulating meaninglessly, and her body twitched about on the chaise longue in her nervous distress. This caused her pretty breasts to shake and quiver in a way which Michel found very exciting. He leaned forward with an outstretched hand to touch them, thought better of it and stroked Vivienne's forehead lightly instead.

'Be calm, my dear. We shall arrive in due course at the heart of the matter. Have you consulted a good doctor to ascertain if the problem is physical?'

'I don't need a doctor to tell me about myself. There is no physical impediment, I know that for certain.'

'Ah, you mean that there have been occasions when you have achieved a climax?'

'Thousands of times.'

Michel considered this information and its implications.

'With other women?' he asked.

'Certainly not!' she replied in indignation.

'Then how?'

'I've told you enough.'

Michel smoothed her forehead again and found that it was moist with the perspiration of her agitation.

'Gently, gently,' he said. 'We have reached the central point, I perceive. You are telling me that you pleasure yourself – is that it?'

'Yes,' she groaned faintly, her face scarlet.

'You have feelings of shame, I see. You are afraid that I shall think less of you because I know your little secret. But as the saying goes – to understand all is to forgive all. Not that you need my forgiveness – you need to forgive yourself. Tell me your secret boldly and rid yourself of this unnecessary guilt.'

'I can't,' she said forlornly, and covered her face with her hands.

'Here in the confidentiality of friendship you can say anything you like, Vivienne – that you have murdered people, stolen money, committed adultery, robbed banks, debauched priests, offered your bottom for an unnatural act – anything you like.'

She took her hands away from her face and breathed in deeply. 'Since you know the truth already, you might as well hear all the details,' she said. 'When I was a child of twelve or thirteen I fell into the habit of playing with myself. This has persisted all my life.'

'So now you can stop worrying about it,' said Michel. 'You've told me and it's no longer your own little secret. After all, it's not so terrible, is it?'

'It prevents me from experiencing the pleasure I ought to enjoy with men.'

'The act of self-love does not prevent you – it is your misplaced sense of guilt that causes the problem.'

'If only you knew!'

'What should I know? Tell me and let everything be clear between us now that we have made a start. Then we can decide on how best to relieve your unhappiness.'

'How often does a normal woman enjoy love-making with a man?'

'There is no general answer to that. It depends on circumstances and personal inclination.'

'When you are with a woman, do you make love to her more than once?'

'Twice is my usual custom, and three times if she is not in a hurry. Once is for those snatched moments of pleasure in unobserved corners.'

'And if I tell you that I am in the habit of doing it to

62

myself never less than four times a day – then what?'

From his seat behind her right shoulder Michel observed the roll of her bare breasts as she gestured with her arms again. In his trousers his appurtenance was standing firmly again and asking for attention.

'I am impressed,' he answered, his belief that hers was a more than usually sensual nature confirmed, 'but with so much daily pleasure in your life, why do you want a man at all?'

He gazed down the length of her slender body, past her up-tilted little breasts and her flat belly, down to her loose silk knickers, where the faint shadow of dark curls beneath showed through the thin eau-de-nil silk. He thought that it was a great pity that all this was wasted. If only she were not so neurotic he could be lying on that narrow belly of hers with his hard spike sunk into the warm flesh between her long thin thighs.

His question had taken her by surprise. She was silent for a while and he wiped her forehead gently with the silk handkerchief from his breast pocket, then dabbed lightly under her chin. He would have liked to wipe the tiny trickle of perspiration he could see between her breasts, but that was to try to go too fast for her.

'There was a time when I would have agreed with you,' she said at last, 'five or six years ago, when I'd had twenty lovers or more and not one was able to thrill me. I vowed never to let another man touch me – I didn't need them. I had all the enjoyment I wanted from pleasuring myself three or four times a day – and I really enjoyed it, believe me.'

'What changed?'

'After a year or two of that, it became boring,' she said, her voice unhappy and strained. 'It is not a pleasure any more – even while I am doing it to myself I am bored. It has become a compulsion – do you understand that? For those few seconds of relief I must endure agonies of mind.'

'I am glad that you told me this – it has a bearing on what we eventually decide to do to help you.'

'There is nothing to be done,' she said, sounding as if she were on the verge of tears. 'It has gone too far.'

63

'Impossible – you are young and healthy and strong. There is much that can be done.'

'I haven't told you everything yet, Michel. In the last month or two I have become so desperate that I have been doing it to myself more and more often – six, seven times a day. You were my last hope. I found you so attractive that I invited you here in the hope that you would succeed for me. But you failed, as everyone else has failed. That is why I said that things have gone too far.'

'If I had known what was expected of me I would have gone about things a little differently,' he said, keeping his voice cheerful, though he was fast losing confidence that he would be able to do much for her – and there went the golden opportunity he had almost had in his grasp.

'It wouldn't have made any difference,' she said miserably, 'it is four days now since I was able to make my body respond to my fingers. Nothing happens any more! It's finished for me.'

She burst into sobs. Michel left his chair and knelt by the chaise longue to cradle her in his arms and comfort her. She clung to him fiercely, her wet cheek pressed to his.

'You must think me a fool,' she gasped through her sobbing.

'No, no, I think you have been most unfortunate. And you have hugged this sorrow to yourself for too many years, instead of confiding in a trusted friend.'

'How could I?' she asked, her weeping subsiding. 'I am too ashamed. I shall never be able to look you in the face again.'

'What nonsense! We are going to be the best of friends and together find a way out of this impasse.'

'Impasse!' she sighed, her face hidden against his jacket. 'Suppose that our positions were reversed and that your *thing* refused to stand up.'

'That happened to me a year or two ago,' he answered, chuckling, 'but I had been overdoing things – continuous late nights, too little sleep, too much champagne and too many enthusiastic girls. One afternoon it shamed me by hanging limp when I had a particularly beautiful girl naked in my arms. For a while I thought that the end of the world had come.'

'What did you do?'

'I sent the girl home unfulfilled. And I went to bed for three days. I had nourishing meals sent in from a little restaurant near where I live and for most of the time I slept. And one morning I awoke to find my little friend as stiff as a broom-handle in my pyjamas.'

'Ah, if it were only that easy for me,' Vivienne sighed.

She was half-sitting and half-lying in his arms. He stroked her long and narrow back to soothe her.

'Mental anxiety will prevent your body from responding as surely as drunkeness,' he said. 'What happened four days ago?'

'That terrible day!' she answered in a whisper. 'I couldn't stop myself. I woke up with my nightdress round my waist and my fingers between my legs. Between then and falling asleep exhausted about eight that evening it was as if I were demented – wherever I sat in the apartment, whatever I tried to do to distract myself I found that I had my hand in my knickers to play with myself. My maid served me lunch and I even did it to myself sitting at the dining-table, while she was out of the room. Ecstasy between courses! But it wasn't ecstasy – it was agony leading to a second or two of calmness. I went out for a walk after lunch to stop myself doing it – and I became so desperate that I stood behind a tree in the park while I put my hand up my skirt and made myself climax. By the evening I had done it a dozen or more times. I told my maid that I was unwell and went to bed very early. And exhausted as I was, I had to do it to myself again before I could go to sleep. The next day I woke utterly exhausted and stayed in bed all day, asleep most of the time. But towards evening I felt the urge to do it again – and that was when I discovered that my body would no longer respond, whatever I did to arouse myself. Since then I have been almost frantic – I can't sleep properly – I wake up and pace round the apartment. I play with myself in desperation to try and achieve release, so that I can sleep – and nothing happens! Can you help me, Michel – I am at the end of my tether.'

'Things will begin to change for you now you have had

the courage to speak out and confess all,' said Michel, not believing his own words. 'What you need is a glass of wine to revive your spirits.'

She fetched another bottle of red wine and they sat together on the chaise longue, he still fully dressed and she in only her silk stockings and knickers. They talked in an intimate way, as good friends, though of nothing of importance, for Michel wanted her to become more tranquil. He made sure that she drank most of the bottle of wine and by the time it was empty she was slightly drunk, leaning back casually with her long slender legs crossed. Some of her problem, Michel guessed, sprang from the fact that she had no real friends – only men who she took as lovers and who proved to be a disappointment to her.

'Now that you understand that I am a true friend,' he said, 'and not a predatory male seeking a quick thrill at your expense, perhaps you will permit me to examine more intimately what is causing you so much anxiety.'

She looked at him doubtfully, not wholly certain what he meant.

'The unresponsive little thing which is the source of your annoyance,' he explained, reaching over to hook his fingers in the waistband of her fragile knickers.

Vivienne raised her bottom to allow him to pass the garment under her and down her legs to her ankles. The curls between her thighs were thick and very dark, almost black. Michel ran his fingers through them and her legs parted a little.

'Useless thing!' she said with a sigh.

'Let us not be too hasty in our judgment,' Michel advised.

He slid off the chaise longue and removed her knickers completely so that he could separate her legs and sit between them on his haunches.

'Very pretty,' he said. 'Such dramatic colouring against your ivory skin – and such luxuriance of growth. Absolutely charming!'

'You are wasting your time, my friend,' Vivienne whispered. 'I have been trying for days to wring a thrill from it – and who should know better than I how to make it respond?'

Michel brought his head down between her legs until he could kiss the warm lips within the dark curls. He put out his tongue and licked them with delicacy – and after a while he used his fingers to open them to let his tongue enter and moisten her dry interior.

'Yes, that is the spot – but it is as unfeeling as if it were made of wood,' she exclaimed, at the tip of his tongue touched her hidden bud and played over it.

Michel was not discouraged by her words. He continued the treatment and, after a long time, was rewarded by a slight tremor of her thighs. He redoubled his efforts and in due course caused her to utter a little sigh. He raised his head to smile at her.

'Admit it,' he said 'you felt some little sensation of pleasure then.'

'It was nice,' Vivienne answered, 'not enough to arouse me, but you are a good friend to take so much trouble with me.'

'You trust me now?'

'Completely – to the point where you may do anything you wish to this enervated and useless body of mine. If you want to put your *thing* in me for your own pleasure, do so. It means nothing to me any more, but you deserve that at least for your kindness.'

'Such defeatism in one so young and pretty!' said Michel. 'If you could give yourself half a dozen thrills a day, then I am reasonably certain that I can give you one at least.'

'If only you could!' she sighed, stroking his face.

Determined to win her eternal gratitude by succeeding, Michel bent to his task again. His thumbs pulled wide apart the fleshy petals between her slender thighs and he used his tongue vigorously on her exposed bud. Although it seemed to take forever, Vivienne eventually began to sigh and tremble.

'That feels good,' she murmured.

She appeared to have reached a plateau of gentle excitement, neither climbing any higher nor sinking back into indifference. Michel put his fingers where his tongue had been and caressed her now slippery bud in a slow rhythm.

'When you play with yourself, Vivienne, what do you think about?'

'But I can't tell you that!'

'You can tell me anything you choose – I am your intimate confessor.'

After a pause, in a voice that was only a whisper, she described to him a fantasy of walking along the Rue de Rivoli in broad daylight, to be seized brutally from behind by a drunken workman in shabby clothes. In spite of her screams he throws her to the pavement, on her back, and rips off her knickers with a large and grubby hand. The passersby ignore her shrieking for assistance and gather round in a circle to watch – they comment on the thinness of her thighs and the fullness of the black bush between them. Exclamations of admiration greet the appearance of the huge truncheon the workman releases from his baggy trousers. Vivienne screams in terror as he plunges it violently into her body, almost splitting her tender flesh. She claws at his unshaven face as he stabs viciously at her, but to no avail – with a great grunt he squirts a hot flood into her ravished body.

'Ah!' she squealed suddenly, breaking off her narrative, her loins jerking upwards under Michel's caressing fingers.

At once he slid two joined fingers deep into her, his thumb rubbing quickly over her wet bud.

'Yes, the brute is spouting up inside you, Vivienne!' he said urgently. 'He is flooding your belly – ravishing you – you can feel his gushing inside you!'

'Ah, ah!' she shrieked happily, her fingers twining in Michel's hair.

As suddenly as it had arrived, her climax left her. She fell forward against Michel, her head on his shoulder. He lifted her back on to the chaise longue and stretched her legs out comfortably, then sat on the floor beside her, holding one of her hands and stroking her hot and shuddering belly.

'My dear friend,' she murmured, her eyes closed, 'you made me do it! How can I ever express the gratitude I feel towards you or repay your devotion?'

'Between close friends there is no need for words of gratitude,' he assured her.

'I wish that I had met you years ago, Michel. You could have saved me from all this terrible suffering.'

'But now that we have met, the worst is over, my dear. I shall not let you fall back into your old ways and become over-anxious again.'

'How will you stop me, when my body is crying out for me to stroke myself between the legs?'

'Leave that to me. For the moment, be content.'

'How can I be content, Michel?' she whispered. 'My blood is on fire now. I have been without that marvellous pleasure for days – and now you have reminded me of what I have been missing. I must feel those sensations again.'

'And so you shall,' he answered, as anxious to placate the stiff and unruly part making its presence felt inside his trousers as he was to pleasure Vivienne again.

He arranged matters so that he sat on the chaise longue with his legs together and Vivienne, naked but for her stockings, straddled his thighs, her back towards him. He released his vibrating part from his trousers, took Vivienne by her narrow hips and guided her downwards until he pierced her dark-curled flower and entered her fully.

'You are so beautiful,' he murmured, his arms round her so that he could play with her breasts. 'You and I will share immense pleasures together.'

'I hope it will be so,' she whispered, 'but I am afraid, Michel – I know myself better than you do.'

'This is no moment for doubts. Close your eyes and enjoy the sensations of your body. What do you feel?'

'Your hands on my breasts – tender and firm in their touch.'

'What else?'

'Your hard *thing* inside me, strong and demanding. If only I could respond to its demand!'

He gave her breasts a final squeeze before sliding his palms down over her hot belly, until his fingers touched her thick curls and then, between the soft lips he held open, her secret bud. He fondled it slowly and yet insistently.

'Your touch calms my fear and makes me feel so good,' Vivienne sighed. 'If only we could stay like this forever.'

'Then I am making you happy?'

'You are making me very happy, dear Michel. I think that you must be the best lover in the whole world!'

Michel considered that very little recommendation from a woman whose experience of lovers had been so profoundly unsatisfactory, but it pleased him to know that he was able to awake her enthusiasm, and he thought that promised well for the future. Of her own accord she was swaying backwards and forwards slowly on his embedded stem, to make it move inside her.

'Let your body decide for itself how fast or slow it wishes to move,' he said, kissing the back of her neck. 'There is nothing to be gained by forcing yourself to reach the critical moment sooner than necessary. We can stay like this for a very long time, enjoying the sensations together.'

'Oh, yes, yes – you're right,' she murmured.

But in the event they did not have as much time as Michel thought. Now that he had awakened Vivienne's nature from its coma of insensibility, her sensuality reasserted itself. While Michel's fingertips teased her exposed bud, her narrow belly began to contract rhythmically, so that it felt as if a slippery hand was massaging his upright part. And she was rocking faster – deliberately so – and he could hear her breath gasping out through her open mouth.

'Oh, Vivienne!' he whispered, showering kisses on her bare shoulders and back as his own excitement grew.

'Oh, Michel!' she moaned, her hands squeezing her own breasts.

A moment or two later she shrieked loudly, bouncing up and down furiously on his lap to drive him deeper into her, and Michel fountained his passion into her.

'Oh god, god!' she screamed in her ecstasy.

As Michel's pleasurable throes faded slowly and his breathing became more normal, he had reason to congratulate himself silently on what he had achieved that afternoon. When he arrived two hours ago she was unable to wring even the feeblest response from her body by her own efforts – and now she had attained a climax through normal love-making! His male pride was greatly flattered – though as he was to find later, his achievement was not all that he thought it was.

But for the present all was rapture, gratification, gratitude, loving affection and intimacy. When they went out to dinner that evening Vivienne put on an elegant frock of apricot silk, with a deep-cut wrap-over bodice that made no secret of the fact that her little breasts were bare and free under the clinging silk. The strained expression was gone from her pretty face, as well it should after the ecstatic peaks she had climbed with Michel's careful assistance on the chaise longue.

She proved to be an entertaining companion now that her anxieties had been relieved for the time being. She liked the little restaurant which Michel chose, she ate well and talked in a vivacious manner – in short, she enjoyed herself. Throughout the meal Michel basked in inner content and pride of accomplishment. The contrast between the hostility she had shown him in her frustration, when she had almost twisted his spindle off inside his trousers and her delightful attentiveness to him now gave him very great joy – the way she put a hand briefly on his arm to emphasise a point in her conversation, the little smiles she directed towards him, the way her foot touched his foot under the table . . . Michel felt that things could not have been better. He was also impressed by the diamond necklace Vivienne wore round her long and slender neck.

They left the restaurant some time after ten, replete with excellent food and wine. In other circumstances the size of the bill would have made Michel wince, but he paid with a smile and added a generous tip. He regarded the expense as an investment in his own future and even suggested that Vivienne might like to go to Les Acacias to dance and drink a bottle of champagne.

'I would rather that you took me home,' she answered, squeezing his arm.

'Certainly – are you a little tired, perhaps? You have not

slept well for the last few nights, you said.'

'That is true, but I am wide awake and feel more truly alive than I have for a long time – a very long time.'

That boded well, Michel considered. In the taxi they held hands, quite decorously, at first. But before long Vivienne was stroking the inside of his thigh, and so he put his hand under her evening wrap of pale fur and into the loose front of her frock to clasp a soft breast. It was obvious that Vivienne intended to make up for lost time now that her confidence in herself had returned – and why not? At the same time, Michel flattered himself that there was more to it than that – in his estimation, now that she had at last experienced the climax of passion with a man inside her she wished to repeat the experience many times to convince herself that she was as normal as any other woman.

At the apartment door Vivienne's maid hurried into the entrance hall at the sound of a key in the lock. Vivienne removed her wrap and gloves and told the maid to bring a bottle of cognac to the salon and then go to bed. Almost as an afterthought she added that she was not to be disturbed in the morning until she rang.

'Where was she this afternoon?' Michel asked, when they were alone. 'Out, I hope.'

'No, I don't think so.'

'Then she must surely have heard those delicious little screams of yours.'

'What of it? This is my home and I do what I choose in it.'

They were sitting side by side on the chaise longue, which seemed to be Vivienne's favourite place, though the salon had enough chairs and sofas for a dozen people. She looked extremely attractive, sipping her little glass of cognac, her brown eyes glowing and her expression one of enjoyment and exhilaration. Michel put his glass down and took her in his arms. Vivienne got rid of her glass and pressed her body against him, her red-rouged mouth open a little to show her white teeth and the tip of her pink tongue. Michel's hand found its way into the wrap-over bodice of her frock and fondled her breasts under the apricot silk.

'That's very nice,' she said, pulling his hand away gently, 'but there is something I wish to know.'

'Something about me?'

'Naturally.'

'Whatever you wish – you have only to ask.'

Her fingers were at his trouser buttons, undoing them somewhat awkwardly, until she had them open and was able to pull out his stiff affair.

'You will think me innocent, perhaps, but I want to understand why *this* was able to achieve what none of the others could.'

'The question is one I cannot answer. Perhaps we were destined for each other.'

She was stroking it fondly, making it grow even harder.

'Perhaps,' she agreed, 'but I would prefer a more logical explanation.'

To his surprise she slid off the chaise longue and knelt between his spread thighs to inspect closely what she was holding.

'The size is satisfactory,' she said, 'and the shape is elegant.'

'You are an expert?' Michel asked, amused by her verdict.

'I have seen twenty or thirty in this condition of hardness,' she reminded him, 'some larger, some smaller, some thicker and some thinner. I am not so ignorant of male anatomy as you suppose.'

'And you have had all of them inside you?' he asked, tremors of pleasure running through him as she handled his hard spike.

'Of course – that's what they're for, isn't it?'

'Most certainly that is what they are for.'

'And yet,' she sighed, as if puzzled, 'this is the only one that has given me pleasure. I do not understand why.'

'Reasons are not important,' Michel murmured. 'Leave such questions to philosophers. For us what matters is that we enjoy what we have.'

'Ah, easy for you to say – but you have not endured the agonies of mind that I have suffered for years,' Vivienne pointed out. 'You do not know how desperate I was before

73

you arrived here today and did things to me which I have always believed impossible. This morning I thought that everything was at an end. But this blessed *thing* of yours has saved my life and given me new hope.'

She lowered her head and pressed kisses of fervent gratitude on the tip of his fleshy sprig.

'You do it great honour,' Michel exclaimed. 'If you continue like that it will become so bold that it will present you with its little gift.'

'Will it?' she breathed, her pretty face flushed a delicate pink. 'That is something I have never seen.'

'Not once? Not with any of the men you have known?'

'Never,' she replied, her eyes fixed on the quivering stem that she was stroking.

'But when you were angry this afternoon, you gripped me through my trousers and you knew well enough what to do.'

'I've done that plenty of times when I've been angry,' she murmured, 'to show men that I despised them for their inability to please me. But always in their trousers.'

'But you caress me so cleverly that this cannot be the first time you have excited a man with your hand, apart from punishing him by making him throw his little present away.'

'Oh, enough men have showed me how to make them excited by playing with them. But every man I have ever known has put me on my back and pushed it into me – a most discouraging experience for me until today! I have never played with a man as lovingly as I play with myself.'

'Then play all you wish and see all you want,' Michel sighed.

'I intend to.'

Michel stopped trying to understand this complicated woman and let himself be engulfed in pleasurable sensation.

'It's grown very big and hard,' Vivienne whispered. 'The head is purple and its little eye is opening . . . oh!'

Her exclamation of surprise was occasioned by Michel's sudden gush of passion in gouts that spattered his shirt-front.

'Oh,' she said again, 'how remarkable! What a fascinating *thing* you have, Michel!'

She continued to play with him until she had seen the

entire process. 'Was what you saw interesting?' he enquired.

'Very enlightening. Now I know what it did inside me this afternoon. Though that does not explain why it made me feel so much pleasure.'

Michel helped her up from the floor to sit beside him on the chaise longue. His arm was round her waist, holding her close, and she still clasped his now diminished affair, as if afraid to let go.

'You have enjoyed today?' he asked.

'Today has been the most marvellous day of my life, Michel. First you restored me to life when my body had become numb – and then you went on to give me my first climax with a man's *thing* in me. I could throw open the windows and shout my joy to all Paris!'

'You can inform the whole of Paris later,' said Michel, smiling at her enthusiasm, 'First I intend to make you enjoy another climax or two.'

'Yes!' she exclaimed, 'Come with me.'

She led him by his limp handle to her bedroom. Michel was pleased by this initiative of hers – it confirmed his view that she now regarded him as her source of sexual delight. At the right time he would be able to take full advantage of her dependence on him. She turned on no lights in the bedroom, but there was light enough from the windows to show him that it was a spacious and well-furnished room. Long before he had shed his clothes Vivienne was naked and on her back on the bed. He lay beside her and took her in his arms to kiss her.

'Later,' she said, turning her head away. 'First thrill me.'

He ran his hand down her belly to her thick tuft of curls. Her legs were splayed wide in expectation and his fingertips touched the warm and moist lips between them.

'Do it the way you did it to me the first time,' she said, her voice jerky, 'When you saved my life. I want to savour that divine moment again.'

He knew what she meant, of course, and slid down the satin bedcover until he was face-down between her long legs. His thumbs parted her fleshy petals and his tongue touched her secret button.

75

'Oh my god!' she cried out, writhing in joy, 'that's it, Michel – make me do it!'

After the interlude in the salon, when she had satisfied her curiosity about the performance of his peg, Michel was glad to have time for it to regain its strength before being called on again. He used his tongue diligently and listened to Vivienne's rising crescendo of moans and sobs of pleasure, marking her steady progress towards her goal.

'Michel – I adore you!' she sobbed in delight, her legs jerking up and down on the bed and, though he could not see them, her hands were tugging at her own breasts.

When he judged that she was far enough gone, he inserted his fingers into the slippery alcove below her button and slid them quickly in and out. In moments her bottom jerked upwards off the bed and she uttered a long squeal of ecstasy.

Michel kept her spasms going for as long as he could, determined to make sure that she enjoyed full measure with him. Only when she lay still did he crawl back up the bed to gather her in his arms. She lay limply against him, her breasts pressed to his chest and her perspiring belly close to his.

'And how was the *divine moment*?' he asked. 'As good as the first time?'

'Better,' she whispered, so softly that he could only just hear her words, 'better because this time I knew for sure that it was going to happen to me.'

'And the first time you were not sure?'

'I was sure that it wouldn't happen – right up to the very moment when it did.'

Michel's stem was hard again, aroused by her ecstatic cries. He reached down to lift her long thin thigh over his hip and arranged matters so that the tip of his trembling little friend was touching Vivienne's wet entrance.

'Oh, no,' she sighed, as he pushed slowly into her, 'not again so soon, dear Michel – I am exhausted.'

'Lie still and rest, chérie – my *thing*, as you call him, feels the need of a soft and cosy hiding place, that's all. He will behave himself and give you no cause for complaint, I promise.'

'Then he can stay,' she murmured.

Michel caressed the smooth skin of her narrow back to soothe her.

'Rest, rest,' he said softly. 'A day of discoveries like today is fatiguing.'

'More than you realise, perhaps,' she whispered. 'The pleasure you have given me today has been so intense that I am utterly satisfied – and I never thought I would say that in my life.'

'But you have satisfied yourself many times in the past.'

'Never once. Even when I played with myself six or seven times a day I was never satisfied like this, only exhausted. You are wonderful, Michel, and I love you.'

These were very gratifying words to hear! In the course of an afternoon and an evening he had pleasured her three times, twice with his tongue and once with his spindle – and she was in love with him! Michel was hardly able to believe his good fortune. He reckoned that by the time he had pleasured her three times a day for a week, she would be begging him to marry her.

He lay still, his stiff part inside her as she lay facing him. It felt very good and he knew that he had only to thrust a dozen or so times to jettison his passion. But that might be to risk undoing all the good work he had accomplished. Vivienne trusted him because she was convinced that his first thought was for her and her pleasure, not the pursuit of what she had called a quick thrill. He kept his feelings under firm control, though it was not easy.

Very soon Vivienne's quiet breathing and the slow movement of her soft little breasts on his chest told him that she was asleep. For Michel, sleep was impossible – his warmly embedded baton was sullenly hard and demanding. He decided to ease it out of her, in the hope that the loss of contact with her soft flesh would allow him to become tranquil, but Vivienne had her leg and an arm over him and to pull away would disturb her.

He lay awake for what seemed like hours, though it was probably no more than thirty minutes. His excitement had built itself up stealthily to the point where he was no longer capable of denying his raging little friend what he desired – and so he began to make slow little thrusts into Vivienne's warm pocket. After a while he heard her give a long sigh, but she did not wake from her sleep – the deep sleep of contentment and fulfilment. He continued his furtive love-making until he was balanced on the brink of sensation – two more movements would hurl him over the edge into delirium.

At this delicate moment Vivienne stirred and mumbled in her sleep and at once Michel was still, fearful of waking her. But he was not taking proper account of the pent-up force of his own nature, which refused to accept this final insult. Though Michel's body was as immobile as a figure carved from wood, his spindle jerked mightily of its own volition and spat its outrage into Vivienne's belly.

She groaned and mumbled in her sleep, as if dreaming, then fell silent again. Michel was gritting his teeth and using all his willpower to prevent himself from thrashing about in his climactic moments, his anxiety overriding his pleasure, so that it was the least satisfactory climax he had ever experienced.

When it was all over he congratulated himself on his narrow escape, for he was certain that Vivienne would have been angry with him if she had woken to find her body being used for his pleasure without her consent. But at least he had rid himself of his tension. Remembering her little outcry and the change in the rhythm of her breathing at the instant of his discharge, he wondered whether he had by chance pleasured her again in her sleep. His softening part soon slid out of her and he too fell asleep.

From that day on Michel and Vivienne became inseparable, as he had predicted to himself. Whether she loved him or not he found impossible to determine, though she often said that she did – and she was constant in her desire for him to make love to her. It did not take her many days to ascertain the facts of his unfortunate financial position and she insisted, with only a token protest from him, in arranging a monthly payment into his bank account. Nor was that all – her gratitude, as Michel thought of it, extended to shopping expeditions to equip him with silk shirts, ties, shoes, suits, hats, gloves, socks and whatever else she considered he had need of. They went to restaurants, theatres, nightclubs and other places of entertainment and the money with which Michel paid was always hers, handed to him in her apartment before they went out for the evening.

As for entertainment in bed, on which her loving goodwill depended, that was more satisfactory to Vivienne than it was to Michel. No doubt it was the result of her years of solitary amusements, but what she preferred above all else was to be made to reach her little crisis two or three times a day by the use of Michel's tongue or fingers. When she had been gratified a time or two she would invite him to slip his *thing* into her wet pouch and take his own pleasure. He understood perfectly well that she did this by way of recompense for what he had done for her, not because she wanted him inside her. It was true that he could always now make her attain another climax with his plunger, as long as he used a fingertip on her hidden button at the same time, but these little crises of hers were never as profound as those she experienced when he lay with his head between her thighs and held her fleshy petals open for his tongue to pierce her.

Nor did she ever again show any interest in treating herself to a demonstration of how his spigot functioned when she stroked it until it released its torrent. On that first occasion together she had been naturally curious about his stiff part, having just experienced something surprising with it in her. But as Michel came to realise, she wasn't really interested in it at all.

Indeed, Michel came to understand over the course of a month or two much about Vivienne's character, and not all of it was agreeable. She was generous with her money to him, for example, but to no one else – she often displayed traits of meanness which Michel found embarrassing. She believed, or at least she frequently told him – that he was the most marvellous person in the world. Again, he was an exception, for she made her dislike of other men apparent enough. This Michel put down to her disappointing experiences at the hands of men – though it did occur to him to wonder sometimes whether her disappointment perhaps sprang from her dislike of men. She was possessive and jealous – he did not realise how jealous she could be until an evening when they formed a party with friends to dance at a nightclub.

There were three other couples with them and Vivienne gave every sign of enjoying herself until Michel asked one of the other women to dance with him. He brought his partner back to the table after a sensuous tango and saw with alarm that Vivienne's face was flushed with rage and she was glaring at him as if she wished him dead.

'Do you feel unwell?' he asked solicitously, amazed that she could think that he might be lured away from her by a pretty face and a good figure.

Vivienne's emotions were so intense that she was unable to speak. She made ugly little gurgling noises, the colour of her face and neck becoming redder. Under the table her high-heeled shoe stamped down viciously on his foot, sending a wave of agony up his leg.

'It is very hot in here,' Michel told their friends. 'Vivienne needs a little fresh air. I shall take her outside for five minutes.'

Her bare arm was rigid as steel as he took it, pulled her to her feet and led her out of the club. Outside in the street she tried to pull away from him, but he held her tightly and walked her along the pavement until they came to a doorway. Michel glanced round quickly. It was after one in the morning and there was no one about. He pushed Vivienne into the doorway, until her back was against the locked door, and held her there. She was still making the same furious little gurgling noises and her clenched fists beat at his chest.

He could think of only one way to calm her. Swiftly he put his hand under her frock and into her loose silk knickers until he had hold of her thick tuft of curls in his palm. He was too close to her then for her to be able to punch his chest. Her arms fell to her sides and she stared over his shoulder into nothingness, her mouth open and moving wordlessly. By then Michel had his fingers inside the fleshy lips between her slender thighs and was caressing her lightly.

80

'Gently, gently,' he murmured in a soothing tone, 'move your feet a little apart, dear Vivienne.'

Whether she understood his words was doubtful, but at the touch of his fingers on her most treasured possession her body reacted and her shoes made a little scraping sound on the doorstep as they moved away from each other.

Michel knew that his position was very grave indeed. Unless he could regain her trust and affection quickly, it would be the end of their friendship – and for him a sudden descent from relative affluence into genteel poverty once more. He needed to persuade her that she was the most important woman in the world to him – and he had to do it quickly.

'You are so beautiful and so desirable that I could not wait another moment,' he said, his fingers moving with great delicacy at their task. 'My feelings for you overcame me so completely that I had to touch your beautiful, beautiful body!'

'Ah, ah!' she exclaimed, her legs parting a little wider, giving Michel a little hope that he might succeed.

'Forgive me for being so impetuous, my darling,' he murmured, 'but can you understand the effect which the sight of you has on me? My hands tremble to feel your pretty breasts and this exquisite delight between your legs.'

'Michel!' she gasped – the first intelligible word she had uttered since she saw him dancing with another woman, his hand stroking her bottom through her evening frock – a sight which had thrown Vivienne into a paroxysm of jealous rage.

'Yes, I know what you must think of me for dragging you away from our friends to gratify my mad desire to touch you – but I could not wait any longer! Forgive me, I implore you, dear Vivienne.'

'You don't love me,' she gasped, 'all you want from me is my body to stick *this* into!'

She was gripping *this* through the thin material of his trousers so tightly that he feared that she might crush it flat. Her accusation was so bizarrely unjust that Michel might have laughed, except for the acute discomfort between his thighs.

'But of course I love you,' he groaned. 'How can you doubt me? Remember the night last week when we lay in each other's arms naked all night long – and I made you die of ecstasy eight times between midnight and dawn?'

It was a night Michel had reason enough to remember. She had wanted to enjoy the touch of his wet tongue on her secret bud every time. His jaws and tongue ached so badly the next day that he was hardly able to speak or eat. By way of thankyou Vivienne had bought him a gold cigarette case with his initials engraved on it.

'You didn't do it for me,' she moaned, her back hard to the door behind her as his fingers teased her bud more insistently, 'After you'd exhausted me you insisted on sticking your *thing* into me for your own selfish pleasure!'

Her grip on his *thing* had slackened to a point where it was bearable, but she was jolting it up and down now, her intention to shame him by bringing on his crisis. But Michel had already taken her too far for that to succeed. He brought on her climax, and her intense anger was transformed into another emotion, equally intense, though far more delightful. Her head went back so fast that it thudded against the wooden door behind her, her eyes rolled up to show the whites, and she screamed loudly and shrilly as her loins convulsed fiercely against his busy fingers.

'Yes, yes, yes,' said Michel, drawing out her ecstasy to the very limit of possibility, 'you are adorable!'

She was, he knew, an extremely selfish person. Not just in the ways that everyone he knew was selfish – but selfish beyond all reason. She had no regard for anyone in the world but herself. She despised and disliked people and didn't care whether they knew it or not. She treated Michel well, but only because he had made himself indispensable to her in the one way she had discovered that she could not be satisfactorily self-sufficient.

He had relieved her of her insane jealousy in an unexpectedly delightful way and she responded well. She let go of his tormented part and put her arms round his neck and kissed him lovingly. Michel breathed a little sigh of relief – all was well again, though it had been a close thing. In future he would never dance with another woman while Vivienne was present, or be seen even speaking to another woman under the age of sixty!

'Dear Michel,' she whispered against his cheek, 'that was incredible! I love you.'

'And I love you, Vivienne,' he answered.

'Of course you do,' she murmured, 'you love me because I give you everything, including my body. Without me you would have nothing, my dear. Do it to me again, Michel, before we go back to the club and dance together till dawn.'

The Barras sisters

They were sitting at a small round table on the terrace of a restaurant halfway along the Avenue des Champs-Elysées, two elegantly dressed women in their twenties. Their modish handbags and gloves lay on the table with the aperitifs they had ordered, while the women talked in a friendly and unhurried way to each other, glancing from time to time at newcomers to the terrace and at the people walking past on the pavement.

Though both women had been married for some time, everyone who knew them still referred to them, in their absence, as the Barras sisters, instead of Madame Duroc and Madame Tourneur. Perhaps this was because they were always to be seen together, as on this fine spring morning, when the sun promised warmer days to come before long. Certainly no one ever invited either of the sisters to a dinner or a party without also inviting the other one.

All of which may sound most agreeable for two sisters who were good friends, but in effect it concealed a certain unhappiness. The sisters had been married off by their parents at the earliest possible age to young men of suitable family and prospects. Each had performed her marital duty excellently well by bearing her husband two children within five years of being married – two boys for Fleurette, the older sister, and a boy and and a girl for Félice. The Duroc family, the Tourneur family and the Barras family were highly satisfied that a benign providence had arranged matters so completely to their satisfaction.

Naturally, no one thought to ask Fleurette and Félice whether they were pleased or not, because it was obvious

84

that they doted on their children. Apart from that, it was well-known that the sisters were not very intelligent – in fact, it had been known for the malicious to describe them both as slow-witted. That was one reason why they were always invited out together – so that they could talk to each other and not burden the quicker-witted and sharper-tongued with the effort of sustaining a conversation with either of them.

It took the Barras sisters longer than most to reach an understanding of their position, but they were not stupid. By the time that Fleurette was twenty-eight and Félice twenty-six they had, in years of conversation together, come to a reasonably accurate assessment of the situation in which they found themselves. Their principal function in life, they now realised, had been to produce heirs for their respective husbands – and that duty was now discharged. The attentions lavished upon them by those husbands in the first few years of marriage – the intimate attentions which had caused their bellies to swell – all this was now a thing of the past. It was only occasionally now that either Duroc or Tourneur had his wife's nightgown up under her armpits and his hand between her legs to prepare the way for his stiff part, from which unsatisfactory state of affairs the sisters concluded, after much hesitation, that their husbands had established interests with other women.

What was left to Fleurette and Félice was the upbringing of their children and the accompanying of their husbands on social occasions – of which, in the nature of things, they attended a great many. It required courage for the sisters to question the validity of the tenets by which they had themselves been brought up, but eventually they reached the point of asking themselves whether this was what they had expected of life. It took even more courage for them to agree that, while they loved their children and respected their husbands, they had hoped for rather more from life.

'There is only one answer,' Fleurette declared with unaccustomed boldness. 'We must fall in love – that will change everything.'

'But who shall we fall in love *with*?' Félice demanded.

'The men we know are all married. And if gossip is to be believed, nearly all of them have very young girlfriends hidden away somewhere in little apartments. Who is interested in you and me? Everyone says that we are dull.'

Before Fleurette could reply, if she had any reply to her sister's question, a man's cheerful voice wished them good day. They looked up to see Charles Brissard, in a beautifully-made suit of dove-grey, raising his hat to them. The sisters greeted him with pleasure and pressed him to sit down and join them for a moment. Evidently he was in no hurry and accepted their invitation.

They asked after his wife, whom they had last seen only five days ago, and his children. He asked after their husbands and children, though he had seen Duroc the day before. But as he knew from some years' acquaintance with the Barras sisters, this was safe ground – an exchange of trivialities. If the conversation moved to anything more complicated than that, the difficulties would begin and the speaker would find two pretty faces staring at him somewhat blankly.

He wondered, while he sipped a glass of white vermouth, why the sisters were looking at him with more interest and animation than he could recall their displaying in the past. Naturally, he prided himself on being the type of handsome and well-dressed man any woman was pleased to be seen with in public. But that in itself hardly seemed enough to account for the gleam he discerned in two pairs of velvety-brown eyes.

'We were talking about love,' Félice blurted out, very unexpectedly, and she blushed pink at her own forwardness.

'Ah, love!' said Charles, giving her his most charming smile, 'what else is there to talk about except that strange, fugitive, inescapable and incomprehensible emotion which raises us to the heights of joy and plunges us into the depths of despair? Whatever one says about love is totally false and totally true and has been said millions of times before.'

Fleurette and Félice looked at each other in surprise and delight at his words, meaningless though they were. No one had ever addressed words like those to them before, not even their husbands in the tenderest moments before they were married. To them Charles seemed marvellously clever, touched with glamour and a delicious danger they had never been aware of in the past.

'You are an expert in love!' Fleurette exclaimed. 'How fortunate that you arrived at the exact moment when we needed someone who could inform us about things we don't know.'

'An expert – me? I assure you I am not,' said Charles, smiling at her across the little round table. 'Believe me, there *are* no experts – neither those who have enjoyed the ecstasy and endured the torment of love, nor those who pass through life serenely untouched and unscathed by love.'

'But surely,' said Félice, wrinkling her pretty forehead as she tried to understand what he meant, 'those who have experienced love must understand something about it?'

'No more than the soldier understands of the battle in which he is wounded and left lying on the field of action.'

'But is it always so tragic?'

'Not always. Sometimes love thrives and prospers and blossoms. A few fortunate lovers are nourished and blessed. It is as if they were walking hand in hand through soft green meadows with spring flowers at their feet.'

While he was talking nonsense to keep them entertained, Charles studied the sisters more carefully than he ever had in the past. They were not twins, but there was a strong family resemblance in their oval-shaped faces, their slightly-dimpled chins and the ripeness of their bodies. They both dressed well, as was to be expected. Fleurette was in a long-sleeved frock of dusky tangerine, with a little cloche hat of the same colour. Félice wore a jacket and skirt of ivory silk, with a primrose blouse. Her white hat had a wide brim, but it was less at that than at her perfectly rounded and crossed knees that Charles glanced.

It seemed to him that perhaps the reason why people considered the sisters dull was because their lives *were* dull. Their husbands were engrossed in business affairs, their children and households were cared for by servants. They met the same hundred or so people in differing permutations on social occasions through the year – the truth was that Fleurette and Félice must be permanently and insufferably bored.

This flash of insight on the part of Charles Brissard was caused in some measure by his own circumstances – he was not very happy at that time in his life. Matters between him and his wife had somehow drifted into a state bordering on indifference – not unlike that between the Barras sisters and their husbands. For Charles there was an obvious response to this boredom – his own or another's – and that was to launch into an immediate love-affair, to make the blood surge again and to elate the flagging spirit. As with all the Brissards, to decide was to act – and Charles had made his decision before he even sat down on the terrace with Fleurette and Félice.

'We shall have lunch together, ladies,' he announced, 'inside, where they can serve us properly and the dust of the street will not settle on our food. I am delighted to have you as my guests.'

He could have added to the reasons for going inside the restaurant that they would then be away from the sight of casual passersby who might recognise them, but that would be to run ahead of himself. The gentle glow in the eyes of the sisters and the tinge of pink that came to their cheeks informed him better than any words that he was on the right track and needed only to proceed with tact and delicacy. The Barras sisters were restive and in urgent need of a man to be kind to them and make them feel that they were desirable women.

Over an excellent lunch and a couple of bottles of very good wine Charles entertained them with a discourse on love. They listened in rapture, having heard nothing like it before. Though he tried to involve them in the talk, they were both so impressed that they hardly dared to interrupt, and did no more than interject an occasional word of agreement – and at some points, surprise. The early stages of Charles' discourse touched lightly and perhaps too poetically upon his chosen subject, but by the time the plates had been cleared away and the second bottle was empty, he was speaking quietly of the intimacies between lovers – the intimate acts which brought the greatest delight this world has to offer.

Fleurette and Félice were enthralled, staring adoringly at Charles' handsome face across the table and from time to time glancing at each other in wonder. He was speaking openly of matters they had never discussed with Monsieur Duroc or Monsieur Tourneur! Indeed, these were matters they had talked of to each other only in hints and half-sentences. By the end of the meal Fleurette and Félice were looking at Charles as if he were a popular matinee-idol and they his most devoted admirers.

Charles smiled at them with affection and asked what their plans were for the afternoon.

'Oh!' Félice exclaimed in dismay, glancing at her tiny wrist-watch, 'I have to meet my mother-in-law in less than ten minutes! I shall be late!'

Charles told the waiter to get her a taxi at once. 'You will be no more than five or six minutes late,' he assured her, his hand on hers in a gesture of friendship and support. 'What a pity you must leave so soon! And you, Fleurette – do you have to meet your mother-in-law?'

'No,' she said, smiling at him. 'I have nothing arranged for this afternoon.'

'Then you have time to drink a little glass of cognac with me before we leave.'

The taxi arrived, Charles kissed Félice's hand charmingly and said he hoped they would meet again soon – a hope in which she joined most fervently before she rushed away. Charles returned to the table, moved to a chair next to Fleurette and ordered cognac. Under the table his hand found her silk-stockinged knee and rested on it. The touch startled her and her immediate reaction was to push his hand away – but his smile promised such revelations of happiness she could only dimly guess at that she restrained her first impulse and let his hand stay where it was. And soon its gentle stroking became very pleasant – so much so that when his hand slid further under her clothes and touched the bare flesh above her garter, her response was to blush but not to clamp her thighs together.

The sisters met at Fleurette's apartment the next day, in mid-morning. Félice could hardly wait for the maid to leave the room before demanding to know what had happened the day before after she had gone.

'We stayed in the restaurant and talked for a while,' Fleurette answered with a little smile.

'You can't deceive me like that!' Félice exclaimed, 'I know you too well. You look five years younger this morning – what happened?'

'I don't know where to begin!'

'Where did you go from the restaurant?'

'Charles took me to a sort of hotel – well, it was something like a hotel, but very discreet – the sort of place where the guests stay only an hour or two and have no luggage.'

'Oh, Fleurette – suppose you had been seen going into a place like that. Think of the scandal!'

'Whoever owns the establishment has already thought of such problems,' said Fleurette, not in the least nervous. 'No one sees you go in or come out.'

'How is that possible?'

'It is just off the Boulevard Haussmann. There is a plain entrance door, without even a number, between two shops. The door was opened the instant that Charles rang the bell and we went up to the first floor and a maid showed us to a room without a moment's wait. When you leave it is by another door into another street – all very discreet, I assure you.'

'What sort of room?' Félice demanded, not at all interested in the exit arrangements, only in what had taken place.

'A large room, furnished in the style of fifty or sixty years ago. There was a four-poster bed with curtains of dark red velvet and gold cords with big tassels. It was very romantic, I thought.'

'A bed! Oh, Fleurette – you didn't!'

'But I did! And so would you if you had been there with Charles instead of me. Admit it.'

'Perhaps you're right,' Félice sighed. 'After the marvellous way he talked of love at lunch, and the looks he gave

90

us, I would have let him make love to me on the restaurant table, if he had wanted to.'

'Félice!' Fleurette exclaimed, a little shocked by her sister's words at first, until the incongruity of the thought struck her and she gave a little laugh. 'Well, at least the bed was more comfortable than that!'

'I want to know everything! What did he do when you were in this room?'

'He took me in his arms and kissed me – what else would you expect him to do?'

'You know very well what I mean – did you let him touch you?'

'He took all of my clothes off – everything – and made me lie naked on the bed while he touched me everywhere. That's what you want to hear, isn't it? And that's exactly what happened.'

'You let him touch you everywhere?' Félice sighed.

'And not just once or twice – he caressed my body until I was on fire and could hardly breathe.'

'My god!'

'Then he kissed me all over, especially my breasts and between my thighs.'

'He kissed you between the thighs – oh my god!' Félice gasped, her face burning red. 'And you let him – how could you?'

'He had aroused me so much that I wanted him to. He pushed my legs as wide apart as they would go and I felt his tongue touching my *belle chose*, as he called it. Did you know that you have a *belle chose* between your legs, Félice? Has Roger ever called it that and kissed it?'

'Don't change the subject – get back to Charles. Did he take his own clothes off?'

'He was as naked as I was. He is very well-proportioned – broad shoulders and a narrow waist and strong thighs!'

'Yes, yes – but did you see *his*?'

Fleurette nodded and smiled, her face a faint pink at the recollection.

'Must I drag it out of you word by word?' Félice complained.

'He has a long, thick and very agile one,' said Fleurette.

91

'He was not in the least shy about letting me see it – he let me hold it and stroke it for as long as I wanted. I was so excited by then that I even kissed it!'

'Oh, Fleurette – I can't believe what you're telling me! Things like this don't happen to people like us – to go to secret hotels in the middle of the day and strip naked for a man to kiss you between the legs!'

'I have told you the simple truth. Yesterday I would have agreed with you – people like us don't do things like that. But I know now that they do.'

'You let him make love to you properly?'

'Of course – though he was in no hurry to do so. We must have played with each other for an hour before he pressed me on to my back. And what an hour – he did so much to me that I felt more pleasure than I normally do in the act of love itself.'

'And he claimed that he was no expert on love! From what you say it seems to me that he is very experienced in love.'

'Very expert,' Fleurette agreed. 'All the time he was lying on me and pushing inside me he was kissing me and saying pretty things and stroking my breasts – believe me, he really knows how to make love to a woman.'

'And he took you all the way – that's obvious.'

'All the way and beyond! It was no affair of two or three minutes – he did the most exciting things to me for ages while he was on top of me and I was out of my mind with pleasure. And then he made me explode like a bomb! I've never known it to be so stupendous before.'

'It's too much,' Félice murmured, her voice wistful, 'I am madly jealous of you, my dear.'

'You will envy me even more in a minute. He didn't lose interest and roll away afterwards – he held me in his arms and we lay entwined, side by side, while he said the nicest things to me.'

'What sort of things?' Félice asked, her curiosity aroused.

'He praised my breasts and my complexion and my warm nature – which I'd never realised I had until he told me. And he made me laugh with his compliments to my *belle chose*.'

'He paid compliments to your . . . now I'm really jealous!'

'There's more,' said Fleurette, smiling contentedly at her sister.

'How could there be, after what you've told me? By then you'd done it all.'

'Charles wanted to do more. And not more than a quarter of an hour after my colossal explosion, he did it to me again.'

'I don't envy you that. Roger used to do it to me two and sometimes three times when we were first married, but I never enjoyed it after the first time. It was a question of lying with my legs apart and waiting for him to finish.'

'I know what you mean,' said Fleurette, 'but it wasn't like that with Charles. He took care to arouse me slowly, so that I was ready for him. At first I didn't notice what he was doing – we were talking and laughing, and I talked to him more than I ever have to any man before. His hands were caressing me gently – casually, you might say – but in fact he was arousing me skilfully. I became excited all over again without realising what he was doing to me, until his fingers were inside me and I wanted him to love me again.'

'And the second time was as good as the first – is that what you're telling me?'

'Better!' Fleurette declared. 'The first time was absolutely amazing, but the second time round the sensations were so enormous that I think I must have fainted for a second or two. I never dreamed that my body could feel so much.'

'Ah, lucky Fleurette! Will you go with him again?'

'Any time he wants me.'

'Life is unjust,' said Félice. 'If it had been you who had to rush off yesterday, then I would have been the one to enjoy this marvellous afternoon! We were talking about the necessity of falling in love, you and I, and the very same day you find a superb lover, but I do not.'

'Don't speak too hastily,' said her sister. 'I don't know how to explain this to you, but Charles wants to be your lover as well as mine.'

'What are you saying?' Félice demanded in stupefaction.

'I know that it must sound very strange to you. It sounded strange to me at the time. I too was outraged by the suggestion. But Charles explained it so clearly to me that I understood the rightness of what he proposed.'

'Then perhaps you will explain it to me.'

'You know I'm not very good with words – neither of us is. You must let Charles explain it to you himself. It's all perfectly sensible and logical, I promise you.'

'So why can't you tell me?'

'Because I've forgotten what he said,' Fleurette confessed.

'But he persuaded you at the time?'

'Completely! I have no reservations at all about having him as my lover if he is also yours.'

'Listen to us,' Félice said with laugh, 'we are talking about whether we can share a lover between us! Not long ago we would have been talking about dinner-parties and children. What has happened to us?'

'I don't know, my dear. You and I talked about love yesterday – and Charles Brissard, whom we have known for years, pops up and offers us love! It is as if the good God Himself heard us and answered our prayer.'

'Hush! The good God is not likely to condone adultery.'

'Call it what you like, Félice – I don't care. My eyes were opened yesterday to the possibilities of life that have always been hidden from me. I love Charles and I intend to hold on to him.'

'You love him! Then there is no hope for me.'

'On the contrary – you can share him with me or you can be virtuous and have nothing to do with him. I am happy to share him with you. You must make your choice, little sister.'

'But can one man love two women, Fleurette?'

'I don't know, but if it is possible, then Charles is the man.'

To Félice it was a matter of some importance to ascertain for herself the truth or otherwise of her sister's assertions about Charles Brissard. It was not a question that could be left indefinitely – in fact the very next day, in consequence of her intense curiosity, she found herself with Charles in the room with the red and gold draped bed. She stared at the old-fashioned furniture and was surprised that such a room could have survived the change in taste.

'Is the whole hotel like this, or only this room?' she asked.

'All of it that I have seen is in the same style as this,' Charles replied. 'The rooms are exactly as they were when they were first furnished – in the days when our grandfathers brought their little friends here.'

'A strange idea – to make time stand still.'

'I find the idea very sympathetic – the room reminds us of the great days of the last century and makes us feel for a moment or two that we are part of the pleasure-loving and full-blooded society of that epoch.'

'Were they so different then?' Félice asked. 'Apart from clothes and furniture, has anything changed very much? I mean, people are still the same, surely?'

'Perhaps,' said Charles. 'You and I know only our own times and so we are not able to make comparisons with the past. But by all accounts people have changed greatly since the War and I think we are aware of that, though not very clearly. We are living in the Jazz Age, I regret to say, when foreign styles and foreign manners are eroding our French traditions. Everyone is in a hurry now and women try to look like boys.'

He had at last said something which she could relate to her personal interests and of which she could make sense.

'Do I look like a boy to you, Charles?'

She had taken extraordinary care that afternoon to look very feminine, very chic and very attractive. She was wearing a belted frock of olive-green shantung and a little turban of the same colour, with a diamond brooch pinned to it above one ear. Charles took her by the waist and kissed her gently.

'You look very beautiful,' he told her, 'and I am delighted that you are here with me.'

'As to that,' she said, her gloved hands resting on his forearms to prevent any further familiarities, if he should have any in mind, as she suspected he did, 'I hope that there is no misunderstanding on your part, Charles. I did not agree to come here with you so that you could make love to me – I would like that very clearly understood between us.'

'Of course!' said Charles, 'There is no misunderstanding, dear Félice. You are here because your sister told you certain things which you found a little surprising. You believe that she perhaps misrepresented certain things I said to her – at all events, you think it important to clear these questions up.'

'That's right,' she said, very pleased by the way in which he had made it easier for her to begin a discussion of the important issues that were in her mind, 'there are confidential matters we must talk about and we are in this place only because Fleurette gave me to understand that it is a suitably private place to talk in. It is most regrettable that there is a bed in the room, but we shall ignore its presence.'

'By all means let us ignore it,' Charles agreed.

He led her politely to a large sofa in heavy crimson velvet that stood beneath a window obscured by criss-crossing lace curtains. They sat a little way apart, turning slightly towards each other.

'If I may be permitted . . .' said Charles, as Félice started to remove her gloves.

Without waiting for a reply, he took her nearest hand in both of his own. Her gloves were of the finest and softest white kid, with lines of hand-stitching to decorate the backs. Charles removed her glove slowly and skilfully – and in some way which Félice found inexplicable, he made the simple process shockingly intimate as if he had stripped off her silk knickers. She blushed furiously as he kissed her bare fingertips one after the other, and then the soft palm of her hand, remembering what Fleurette had told her about Charles kissing her between her legs. If kissing her hand did this to her, what would that do, she asked herself tremulously. She stared fascinated while he drew off her other glove and she knew that she was becoming sexually aroused, though she found it impossible to say why.

'There,' said Charles, and as he kissed the palm of her hand she felt the tip of his tongue touch it for a moment, 'now we must talk, you and I, about very confidential concerns. How would you like to begin – is there any question you would like to ask me, dear Félice?'

There were many questions Félice would have liked to ask him, questions mainly to do with what he did to women to produce the stupendous effects which her sister had mentioned – and whether he would like to do those marvellous things right now to Félice herself – but naturally she was incapable of asking such questions. Instead she made an oblique approach.

'Have I been correctly informed that you and my sister have become close friends?' she asked cautiously.

'Yes, we are very close friends,' Charles answered, amused by the circumspection of her question.

'Would it be true then to say that you have become intimate friends?' Félice persisted, not at all sure where this was leading her – if anywhere.

'Very intimate,' said Charles, 'To be frank with you, Fleurette and I are lovers.'

'Lovers! In the fullest sense of the word?'

'Most surely! Fleurette and I lay naked together on the bed over there which we have agreed to ignore today. I kissed her from head to foot and she caressed me. She lay on her back for me to mount her and penetrate her – and together we experienced the most exquisite sensations of pleasure. Does that answer your question as fully as you would like?'

Félice's cheeks were red. She had not expected so detailed an answer. Besides which, to hear of what had taken place from her sister was one thing, but to hear it from the man concerned was quite another! It was almost as if he had done all those things to Félice herself, to hear him speak of them. Yet she was unable to look away from his face, in spite of her confusion, and she was wholly unaware that he held both her hands between his own and was stroking them rhythmically.

'What can I say?' Félice murmured confusedly. 'I hope that you and she will make each other happy.'

'I hope so too – but that depends on you.'

'On me? Surely not! How can your friendship with

97

Fleurette involve me in any way?' she gasped, knowing that the moment she had been waiting for had arrived.

'You sound surprised,' said Charles, who sounded very reasonable himself, 'and I suppose that you have a right to be. Let me assure you, my dear Félice, that I was surprised too when I first came to realise how unusual a situation had developed. Fleurette was greatly surprised at first, but she has a practical nature and she soon came to understand how matters stood between the three of us. Has she said nothing of this to you?'

'We have talked about it a little.'

'Then you know her mind.'

'I know *her* mind, but I don't know my own,' she answered.

In some way which she found impossible to understand, the distance between her and Charles on the sofa had dwindled to nothing, though she had no recollection of either of them moving. She was now sitting very close to him – closer than she had ever been to any man except her husband, and that seemed very strange and unsettling to her. Charles had an arm round her shoulders in a friendly attitude that seemed not in the least familiar or distasteful, and his other hand was stroking her face in a manner that she found comforting and, at the same time, thrilling. Her own hands were not folded modestly in her lap, as she had thought they were, but were pressed flat against Charles' chest inside his unbuttoned jacket. On reflection, she was not trying to push him away, but to touch him! She could feel the warmth of his body through his shirt and she found that very pleasant.

'Tell me frankly what it is that troubles you,' Charles said in a sympathetic tone.

Félice summoned up all her courage and asked the impossible question.

'Why do you want to be my lover as well as Fleurette's? Isn't one of us enough for you?'

'Straight to the point! I admire that in you, Félice.'

That was not all that he found to admire. He slipped off her little green turban so that he could stroke her dark brown hair.

'You ask a simple and direct question,' he went on, 'and I shall give you an equally direct answer – the same answer I gave to your sister when she asked the same question.'

'In this room?' Félice murmured, losing her grasp of the conversation as Charles pressed little kisses to her forehead, her cheeks and her full red lips.

'In this room,' he murmured back between kisses, 'on that bed – both of us naked.'

'Oh, oh,' she sighed, her face turned up and her eyes half-closed as the kisses continued down her neck.

As if in a dream she felt Charles' fingers unbutton the bodice of her frock. She felt for a moment that she ought to stop him before the situation got completely out of hand – after all, she was here only to discuss certain complicated matters with him. But by then his hand was inside her frock, down the top of her silk chemise and he was fondling her bare breasts.

'Listen to me carefully, dearest Félice,' he said. 'Do not be offended by what I say – hear me out and consider my words before you make up your mind.'

She nodded, her body trembling against him. This was what she had come here for – to listen to what he had to say. If he touched her breasts a little while he was talking, it was of no great importance, she told herself. It would not change her decision . . . and in the meantime, as she had to admit to herself, the way he was teasing the tender buds of her breasts was very thrilling.

'First, we must consider and analyse what precisely took place two days ago,' said Charles. 'Was it blind chance, do you believe, that you and your sister were sitting on the restaurant terrace at the same time that I walked past? You and she could have been in any one of five thousand restaurants and I could have been walking along any one of five thousand streets. Was it more chance that I was walking on the same side of the Avenue as you were sitting on? Was it no more than chance that made me see you sitting there?'

His hand undid the belt of her frock and explored the fastenings at the waist while he was talking. He unbuttoned the long tight cuffs of her sleeves and, with a little assistance from Félice, eased the frock from under her bottom and up over her head. Her silk chemise followed it and he fondled her exposed breasts with every sign of appreciation.

'Tell me – is life ruled by chance?' he asked her.

'No,' she sighed, 'by fate.'

Charles' head was lowered to kiss the firm and russet tips of her breasts and he did not reply for a little while. Félice was trying so hard to concentrate on what he had said about blind chance and their meeting that she let him slip a hand down the front of her embroidered silk knickers, though she had never consciously intended to allow him such incredible familiarities. She was here, after all, only to clarify certain questions which she found puzzling!

Somehow matters seemed to have become even more puzzling in the past quarter of an hour, she reflected – it was puzzling why Charles thought he had permission to put his hand between her thighs, as he was doing, to stroke her curls. On the other hand, she had to admit that there was nothing puzzling about the extremely pleasant feelings his fingers were making her enjoy.

'Fate!' Charles repeated, raising his head from her breasts to kiss her mouth softly. 'You are absolutely right, Félice – it is fate that has guided the three of us and brought us together.'

Presumably it was fate which at that moment guided his fingers to the tender aperture between Félice's legs and then guided them inside. At that instant, as she shook helplessly with pleasurable sensations, Félice was prepared to agree that fate was responsible – a fate she readily embraced.

'I knew that you would understand,' Charles continued, 'just as dear Fleurette did. The three of us are at a strange turning-point in our lives. Two days ago we were unsure of ourselves, of our intentions, of our future. Then fate intervened! In an instant we were brought together and instructed what we must do.'

'What do you mean, instructed?' Félice sighed, her head resting on Charles' shoulder and her body throbbing from what he was doing to her secret bud.

'But it is so obvious! The three of us are destined to be lovers, that's why we met as we did. Fate determined that you were not able to stay after lunch, and so Fleurette and I opened the ball by waltzing together, so to speak – but it could as easily have been you.'

'That's what I told her,' Félice murmured, 'but since it was her, then it seems to me that fate has decided that you and she are to be lovers and I am excluded.'

'By no means! Fate removed one of you so that I and the other could proceed without any embarrassment. But now you are here with me and Fleurette is not.'

'But this is impossible,' Félice gasped, 'one man with two women! And sisters at that!'

'Believe me, I have more experience of love-affairs than you, darling Félice,' he said smoothly, his fingers fluttering inside her slippery little alcove. 'With three of us our friendship will survive the lassitude and satiety which overtakes most lovers when familiarity has removed the excitement of newness. With either of you alone, a love-affair might last for six months at most. With both of you, it will endure for many years – perhaps all our lives.'

'Charles!' she exclaimed sharply.

His dexterous fingers inside her knickers had stirred her little pot so well that it boiled over. Her hands gripped him by his neck and pulled his mouth hard to hers, her body shuddering and her breasts bouncing in paroxysms of pleasure.

He waited until she was calm enough to hear him and understand him before he resumed his discourse on destiny.

'You see, dear Félice, fate has decreed this for the three of us and we can do no other than obey. It is out of our hands.'

'Charles,' she said, slightly reproving him, 'I did not understand what you were doing to me until it was too late to stop it.'

'But why would you want to stop it?'

'I came here to settle certain important questions – not for you to play with as if I were a doll.'

'And we have discussed the really important question

101

and we understand how enormous the stakes are. And while we were discussing it, it seemed to me that there was no harm in caressing you a little as evidence of my respect and devotion.'

'Be truthful,' she said, a little puzzled by his apparently serious answer. 'You want to make love to me. But that's not how people make love. Why didn't you lie on me and do it the right way – I would have let you.'

'Dear sweet Félice,' said Charles, stroking her belly inside her knickers, 'There is no right way. Lovers do what pleases them best, not what other people think is right.'

For Félice, as it had been for her sister, this was an unfamiliar state of affairs that Charles was suggesting. The purpose of love-making with her husband had always been to satisfy his desire, and while he made sure that she was suitably aroused for him to enter her, her own satisfaction was of secondary importance. If she attained a climax by the time that he did, then good – if she did not, then that was a pity. The idea of two people deliberately attempting to give each other the maximum pleasure was one she found strange.

'What you say sounds immoral,' she said, cuddling close to Charles and enjoying the feel of his arms round her. 'You are suggesting a sort of anarchy, where everyone consults their own wishes.'

'What I said was that lovers do what pleases them best. I wanted to please you by caressing you – and so I did. It's as simple as that.'

'You pleased me enormously,' she said, abandoning the pretence that she was only with him to talk, 'but you must be frustrated yourself. Because of what you did to me you denied yourself the pleasure that should have been yours.'

'I sit here with a beautiful woman in my arms,' he replied, easing her knickers down her legs and out of the way, 'a beautiful naked woman, who has permitted me to caress her in the most intimate way. I am excited, dear Félice, but I am not frustrated.'

Are you *very* excited?' she asked solemnly.

He smiled at her, stood up and undressed quickly, dropping his clothes on the carpet. Félice was a little startled by his response to her question but, that notwithstanding, she stared pink-cheeked at his well-made body, the mat of dark hair on his chest – and most of all at his long and stiff handle.

'There,' he said, sitting down close to her and slipping an arm about her bare waist, 'now we have no secrets from each other.'

'Do lovers never have secrets from each other?' she asked.

'As I told you in the restaurant, there are no rules in love.'

'At least *this* is no longer a secret from me,' she said tremulously, touching his upright spindle with her finger-tips, though her touch was a little nervous.

'There is no reason to be afraid,' said Charles with a grin. 'On the contrary – this little gentleman of mine will give you the greatest pleasure you will ever know. Therefore you should cherish him.'

So encouraged, Félice took his projection somewhat timidly in her hand. Its rigidity and strength caused her to give a little gasp of surprise, but then she began to understand and appreciate these virtues. Meanwhile, Charles was caressing her with affection and finesse. He ran his fingers underneath her breasts, between her shoulder-blades, around her deep-set belly-button and along the insides of her thighs.

'I know what you are trying to do,' she said, smiling at him.

'And what is that?'

'You want to arouse me again so that you can put *this* in me. But it's all right, Charles my dear, you don't have to worry about me. Lie on me and do what you want – I don't mind.'

'Well, well,' said Charles, his eyebrows raised, 'What sort of words are these between lovers? *Have me if you want to – I don't mind!* Wives say that to husbands, perhaps, but lovers never say it to each other. They say things like *Take me – I want you!* and *I am dying for you – open your legs for me!* Never mind, we shall make love together, you and I, but not in the off-hand way you suggest.'

103

His words made her blush with shame, the colour spreading from her cheeks down her throat and across her chest until it almost reached her well-shaped breasts. Charles grinned and kissed her tenderly and murmured to her, his hands fondling her breasts gently, until she could look him in the face again. He arranged her along the red velvet sofa on her back, her knees up and apart. Félice thought it odd to be lying naked on a sofa instead of a bed, and this was most certainly the first time she had been in so unlikely a position – unlikely to her, that is. There was something almost indecent about it, she felt, and yet at the same time she had to admit that it was thrilling. And it was comfortable on the deep cushions, with the feel of the velvet under her. It occurred to her that in all probability the sofa had been designed and made for exactly this use. And from that she went on to wonder for a breathtaking moment how many women in the past half-century or so had lain on their backs on this comfortable piece of furniture, their clothes off, to put their charms at the disposal of their lovers. She almost blushed again, then grinned, pleased with herself for having the idea at all.

Charles was on his knees between her stockinged feet, looking down at her body with a look of intense pleasure on his face. His fingers ran through the dark brown curls between her open thighs and she gave him a little smile of encouragement. In spite of what he had said, she supposed, he was going to penetrate her with his quivering projection.

'I am ready for you Charles – put it in me and take your pleasure.'

'Perhaps I am not ready for you,' he suggested, a chuckle in his voice.

'You look ready enough to me,' she said, a tiny frown on her face as she tried to understand what was in his mind.

'When a man's peg stands up, he is in the first stage of readiness, that is true,' he agreed, 'but there are other stages.'

With extreme gentleness he opened the brown-fleeced lips between her parted legs, and then the tender inner lips, until her secret bud stood exposed and vulnerable.

'That's very pretty,' he said, his voice almost a sigh.

Félice stared at him, not wishing to miss the moment when he brought his baton down to her opening and pushed it in. But he crouched down, his bare feet against the sofa-arm and his chest on his bent knees, to bring his face down between her raised thighs. Félice gave a little cry of surprise when she felt the warm tip of his tongue touch her bud.

Fleurette had told her that Charles had *kissed* her all over, between her legs as well as elsewhere. But the words had not produced any very clear image in Félice's mind. If she thought about it at all, what her imagination suggested was that Charles had touched his lips briefly to Fleurette's tuft of curls as a gesture, to impress her with his adoration and desire. What he was doing to Félice now was very far from any such token gesture. There were throbs of unimaginable pleasure in her belly as, with great subtlety, the tip of Charles' tongue stimulated her little button. Before long she was more aroused than she had ever been in her life before.

Her head was thrown back and rolled from side to side on the cushions, her eyes were closed and her hands were rubbing her own tender breasts quickly. Then there was a moment when Charles' tongue went away from her and, a moment later, was replaced by something hard and long that slid into her belly. She opened her eyes and stared, half-stupefied with pleasure. Charles was kneeling close to her bottom, his thighs splayed, and he had her ankles in his hands to hold her legs up out of the way. She looked down the length of her naked body and saw his fleshy baton sliding horizontally in and out of her soft groove.

Even though savage sensations were overwhelming her body and threatening to overwhelm her mind in another instant, the sheer strangeness of Charles' position caught at her imagination, undeveloped though it was. He was not lying flat on her belly, their sexual parts joined in secrecy, as she was used to – he was perched so that he could observe himself making love to her, stroke by stroke. The thought was highly indecent to Félice, but it was wildly exciting.

105

'Oh my god!' she gasped, staring in indescribable delight at the long hard shaft sliding in and out of her like the piston of a steam engine.

Her belly fluttered in and out to the hot spasms of her sudden climax, her sensations so intense that she did not even know when Charles slammed hard against her and fountained his desire into her. She knew only that huge waves of ecstasy were crashing through her body like breakers on a shore, and she could hear their roar and thunder in her head.

The experience was of a different order of magnitude to the brief and nervous twitching of sexual release to which she was accustomed at home. This was a delicious agony that permeated every fibre of her being, as if she had been dipped in liquid fire!

When at last the sensations receded, she was left panting for breath. Her eyes opened slowly and she smiled at Charles between her legs, his thick stem lodged comfortably inside her and at rest, while his hands stroked her still trembling belly. She gazed at him and was unable to speak, but he smiled as if he understood. He freed himself from her and took her by the wrists to raise her off her back and pull her towards him. She was as limp as a rag doll from the effects of her extraordinary climax and let him arrange her as he thought best.

He sat propped up by the sofa-arm, one knee up and one leg stretched out along the cushions, with Félice between his thighs, half-sitting and half-lying against him, her head pillowed on his chest and his arms round her to hold her close.

'You are adorable,' he said, kissing the top of her head.

'Now we are truly lovers,' she whispered, her fingers entwined in the hair on his chest.

It was a statement of the obvious, but Charles smiled and agreed with her.

'As fate decreed,' he said.

'You are right. I didn't entirely understand what you were saying to me before, but I am sure now that you were right. You are destined to be my lover – and Fleurette's too. There is no other way.'

'Are you happy now that you have accepted the situation?'

'I am so happy that I find it hard to believe,' she said, pressing herself against his chest and belly with great affection. 'Two days ago I would have been offended beyond words if anyone had suggested that I could ever find myself naked with a lover – and here I am! And on a red sofa, of all places to be naked!'

'You must remember that when we first arrived here you told me that the bed had no part to play in our meeting and that it was to be ignored. Very well, we have ignored it.'

'You make my words mean something different from what I intended them to mean,' she said with a little sigh. 'The truth is that I am not very clever, as you will quickly find out. I am afraid that you will eventually despise me for that.'

'You do yourself an injustice,' Charles assured her, 'after all, I have known you and your sister for years.'

'I'm sure you think we're as dull as most people do.'

'A good heart is worth more than a glib tongue, Félice.'

'And is that enough for you?'

'The solid foundation of the friendship between us is the enormous pleasure we can give each other – on the sofa, on the bed, anywhere. For that no clever conversation and no elaborate feats of intellect are required. Be content to be with me and let your beautiful body respond to me as it already has, and we shall be happy.'

They talked for a long time of nothing much, as is the way with lovers. Held close to Charles' body in a warm embrace Félice spoke with an ease and openness that she had never before been able to command with any human being, let alone a man. She asked questions and his answers either made her laugh or enlightened her – sometimes both together. A little slow Félice may have been, and Fleurette too, but in the setting of the secret meeting-place she found the self-confidence she had never really had. She became light-hearted and mildly vivacious – she even ventured to express an opinion or two. Most unusual of all, she talked to Charles about her deepest feelings, and he listened with sympathy and encouraged her to open her heart to him.

Half an hour or three-quarters went by in this agreeable way before Félice became aware of something pressing into her side, just above her hip. She moved her position a little between Charles' thighs to see what was causing the slight discomfort and was astonished to see that his appendage had grown long and stiff again.

'Oh, I did not expect that to happen,' she said in some dismay.

'We have so much to learn about each other,' said Charles, catching the startled tone in her voice.

'You want to make love to me again – and so you shall,' she said, with sudden decision. 'for you I will do anything and everything.'

'Dear little martyr,' he said, grinning at her, 'I am your lover, not your husband. You owe me no duty of lying down and parting your legs when I demand. Lovers do only what pleases them – I told you that before.'

'And it would please you to put this in me.'

'But if it does not please you, then I shall not do it.'

'You are very aroused,' Félice observed, touching his upright staff in fascination, so that it quivered and nodded its head eagerly.

'So much the better,' he said. 'Take it in your hand and stroke it – that will relieve my excitement without inconveniencing you.'

She took hold of his heavy spindle and did as he suggested. At first she performed this intimate service with a degree of clumsiness that demonstrated her lack of familiarity with what she was doing. A word of direction from Charles and a little practice soon improved her technique. She stared down at her busy hand, a look of concentration on her pretty face.

'Charles – it has grown so huge! Am I pleasing you?'

'In a few moments you will have the answer to your question expressed more convincingly than mere words could,' he sighed.

His hands were caressing her firmly, one stroking down her back and the other fondling her breasts.

'But this is wrong, what we are doing,' she said suddenly, her hand slowing its massage of his engorged shaft.

'What do you mean?' Charles gasped.

'This is a waste of your strength, for me to do this to you.'

'You had no objection when I did it to you.'

'That was different – you put your fingers inside me instead of this. But it is not the same for a man – I cannot let you waste your strength in this way.'

'Félice . . . I am dying!' he moaned.

'I shall not let you die of unrequited passion,' she told him.

To his amazement, Félice got up on her knees, straddled his thighs and used both hands to pull open the delicate lips between her legs.

'Put it in me,' she said.

Charles was so aroused that he seized his shaking stem and held it to her pretty pink entrance at once, his other hand on her hip, urging her downwards. She settled on him slowly, embedding his throbbing part inside her.

'Now I've got you!' she exclaimed. 'You're my prisoner and I have you safe where you can't waste your strength.'

'For you, Félice – all for you!' he murmured gratefully.

She rode up and down on him, a little jerkily, but this was the first time she had attempted so bold an initiative. Charles' hands were at her breasts, rolling her buds under his fingers and plucking at them softly. Félice looked down to see what his hands were doing to her and liked it. She looked lower, to where his slippery column was sliding in and out of her as she jolted up and down.

'It looks so indecent!' she gasped, 'I love it!'

So did Charles, needless to say – he loved what she was doing to his spike so much that he expressed his appreciation in the most appropriate way. His loins bucked upwards and he gave a long wailing moan as he gushed his passion into her. Félice stared round-eyed at his flushed face and gaping mouth, then down to where their bodies were joined, and her slow imagination caught fire for a moment and she knew what his engorged baton was doing inside her belly at that moment.

'Oh my dear god!' she exclaimed, jerking up and down on him fast and furiously. She felt her belly clench on the gushing spout inside it and, an instant later, ecstasy took her and wiped out her consciousness. She thumped up and down on Charles' lap, her fingernails digging into his bare shoulders, and she shrieked in uncontrollable joy.

Needless to say, Charles did not believe a single word of his so-called explanation of how fate had brought him together with Fleuretta and Félice. The truth was that he had met them on a day when he was gravely dissatisfied with certain aspects of his own life and in a mood to take action to change things. He was a gambler at heart, and he decided to bring luck – or chance – into his plan. He strolled the length of the Champs-Elysées on one side, from the Place de la Concorde to the Arc de Triomphe, and was returning down the other side of the Avenue when he spotted the Barras sisters. The reason for his walk was that he was certain that in the course of it he would meet someone he knew. In fact, he had already met three men he knew before he saw Fleurette and Félice and sat down with them. His intention on setting out that morning was to seduce the first woman he met whom he knew, regardless of the consequences. And they were the first.

When chance – or luck, whichever way one chooses to look at it – put not one but two women he knew in his path, Charles knew that this was a most important moment for him. The consequences of seducing the Barras sisters were incalculable – he would be making a big bet with unknown odds. The idea appealed to him. He considered that he had been right to take his stroll. He had gone looking for a woman to bring back zest to his life, and he had been given two! Could it be fate after all, rather than mere chance?

With each of the sisters he enjoyed a marvellous afternoon – on the bed with one and on the sofa with the other. Both of them good bodies, well-fed and well cared for. Each responded magnificently to his love-making and both were eager to meet him again soon. He did not intend to keep them waiting for long. As soon as the weekend and family duties were out of the way, he had arranged to meet Fleurette on Monday and Félice on Wednesday to introduce them, very tenderly, to more aspects of love-making than they imagined possible.

It was the next step after that which would be the hardest, the one which would call for all of his charm, persuasion and tact. Since the moment he had sat down at their table on the restaurant terrace, his intention had been not merely to have them both, separately, but to make love to them together. It had been the truth when he told Félice that an affair with either of them would last six months at most. She had taken his meaning to be that alternate meetings with her and her sister would prolong the affair far beyond that – and Fleurette had interpreted his words in the same way. Neither guessed – for how could respectable young married women of good family imagine such a thing – that what Charles had in mind for them was a love-affair *à trois* – the three of them in a bed together.

When the time came to explain this to each of them in turn, they would surely blush most enticingly, he guessed. He would set it out in slow and careful words, his revelation of what *fate* had really decreed for them. Naturally, they would immediately declare that such a suggestion was monstrous, that it was impossible and indecent – perhaps even perverse and obscene. That was the natural reaction and Charles would not be abashed by it, however vehemently expressed. The sisters would meet to discuss his proposal, and they would think about it in secret alone. They would recall the boredom of their daily life before he took each of them in turn to the room with the red and gold draped bed. They were warm-natured and affectionate women and they would not want to lose his attentions to them. Perhaps it would take a few days, but Charles was sure that eventually Fleurette and Félice would persuade themselves – and each other – that there was nothing blameworthy about acceding to his wishes. His desires were unusual, perhaps, but they both knew him to be an unusual person – a man who had introduced them to sharper thrills than anyone had ever bothered to show them before.

And then! Ah, what orgies of delight Charles promised

111

himself! He pictured the sisters naked and on the crimson-curtained bed together, their sleek bodies and plump breasts naked and at his disposal. He imagined how it would feel to be entwined with them on that bed, to be almost smothered in their warm flesh, their little hands smoothing his skin and tugging at his baton, a soft and curly-haired mound squeezed against his bare thigh and another, equally delicious, beneath his caressing fingers, while his tongue flicked at the pink tips of breasts presented for his attentions. For the first few times he enjoyed the sisters together he would be gentle and extremly reassuring, covering each of them with love and caresses and little kisses. He would ensure that Fleurette and Félice each enjoyed no less than two climaxes of delight under his hands and tongue before he slid into each of their well-prepared portals in turn and discharged his fiery passion into their hot bellies!

Thus reassured that there was nothing wrong about what they were doing – that it was the most normal thing in the world for the two of them to be rolling about naked with the same man – they would become accustomed to his desires and moods. Slowly he would extend the frontiers of their love-making, little by little, being very careful not to startle them or make them reluctant. Dear Fleurette and darling Félice had been protected all their lives by domesticity – they knew of only one warm entrance that could be used for making love. Under Charles' guidance they were going to learn in the months ahead that they had others which could be brought into service, with surprisingly pleasing results.

The prospect before Charles was so incredibly lascivious that his piston stood up stiffly in his trousers, though it was less than an hour since he had left Félice. He was sitting in a bar on the Boulevard Haussmann, enjoying a restoring drink and assembling his thoughts before returning home to change for dinner. Under cover of the table-top he stroked the bulge in his trousers comfortingly and promised his eager little friend that great days lay ahead.

He would have to find and rent a little apartment where

112

he could take his two friends to play their games. Somewhere discreet and convenient – it needed little more than space for a large bed and somewhere to cool a few bottles of champagne. In his imagination he was already sitting on the side of that bed, his feet on the floor and Fleurette, naked of course, straddled across his lap and spiked on his upright part. Her arms were round his neck and her plump breasts squashed against his chest. Félice stood close behind her sister, so that Charles could fondle her breasts – and then, as Fleurette bumped up and down faster on him, his hand was between Félice's thighs and his fingers teasing inside her. Both women were gasping in the last stages of desire – as was Charles himself! One more second and all three would cry out together in ecstasy.

Yes, great days are ahead, dear friend, Charles silently promised his throbbing part. Imagine the first time that we play at making a daisy-chain! Dear Fleurette on her back, her legs wide apart and my head between them so that I can tickle her button with my tongue – while darling Félice has you in her mouth – her very hot and wet mouth – and is caressing you with her tongue! And to complete the circle, Fleurette's fingers are inside her sister's soft purse, for she is so aroused by what I am doing to her that she will obey my every suggestion. The three of us lie there, shaking and sobbing with spasms of delight! The only question is which of us reaches the critical moment first and triggers off the climactic delight of all of us.

Thus addressed, Charles' sturdy friend jerked so fiercely in his trousers that he wished he had stayed another hour with Félice and satisfied himself – and her – one more time. But she had said that she was expected home for some domestic arrangement or other. There was nothing he could do but kiss her affectionately on the belly just before she slipped on her silk underwear, and find a taxi for her when she was dressed. That last kiss was vivid in his memory, for as his mouth pressed against the satin-smooth skin of her rounded belly, his fingers touched briefly the soft and moist lips below which he had so recently pierced. Félice shivered at his touch and almost

113

changed her mind and stayed for another half-hour to let him make her enjoy those unforgettable and ravishing sensations once more – but then she remembered her wifely commitments, and pulled away from him with regret and reached for her embroidered knickers to indicate that there was time for no more.

Images of delight crowded into Charles' mind as he sat in the bar, staring at his half-empty glass. Two pairs of plump breasts together, soft bellies for his hands to stroke, round bottoms for his teeth to nibble – he felt a little dizzy from the contemplation of such riches, even in his imagination. He reviewed the similarities between the sisters – the shape of their faces, the roundness of their bottoms, the colour of the curls between their thighs – and the differences. Fleurette's breasts were a little fuller than Félice's, but Félice's buds were larger. Félice had a mole on her belly, to the side of her navel, while Fleurette's belly was unmarked, but she had a mole on the inside of her right thigh.

By the time that Charles had taught the Barras sisters all that he knew of the infinitely varied and labyrinthine ways of love, they would be very experienced young women. Outwardly they would remain the same dull and reliable young wives everyone knew them to be – but inwardly – what a transformation! An exciting part of the affair would be Charles' secret knowledge of the transformation – of the differences between the outward and the inward. There would be long afternoons of making love to them, doing everything he could imagine to them – and evenings when he would meet them with their husbands on social occasions. He alone would have the power to stare, in his imagination, right through the elegant frocks the sisters wore, to see the breasts he had fondled and kissed that very afternoon. If the others present could guess what was in his mind! If Duroc or Tourneur had the least suspicion that, while he talked to their wives of indifferent matters, he was in his mind's eye seeing the curly little fleeces under their clothes and the warm alcoves into which he had plunged that afternoon!

The truth was, of course, that Charles was a hopeless

romantic, easily made happy and just as easily made sad. At that moment he was very happy and elated – he had made love to Félice all afternoon and he still wanted more. *There, there,* he sighed to himself, *Lie down and be good, dear friend, your reward will come later,* yet he could not help stroking himself a little under cover of the bar table. Happiness was his – it lay in making love to Félice and Fleurette, singly at the moment, but together in another ten days or two weeks.

If one pretty woman in bed was good, two together was not merely twice as good, he thought – it was at least ten times better. It did not occur to Charles that the qualities that Fleurette and Félice brought to his bed might eventually become disadvantages. They were not volatile by nature, as he was himself, they were almost stolid. They might call him their lover when they spoke of him to each other, but the only relationship they understood between man and woman was that of husband and wife. However much and however often Charles thrilled them with ecstatic sensation, the traits of character which had made them dull and reliable young wives would begin to assert themselves. By degrees they would begin to manage Charles. He might believe as he lay between them and held a naked breast in each hand that he was a sultan in his harem and these were two of his adoring odalisques, eager to offer him their bodies for his pleasure – but in truth it would be as if Charles had a wife on either side of him – not as undemanding as the two of them were with their legal husbands, for he had made them aware of pleasures that should be theirs by right. For Charles the enjoyment would not be diminished, for he would not know what subtle changes had taken place between the three of them and the bounties of their bodies would be his for the taking – yet in effect, the Barras sisters would have taken him over and made him their slave.

Sunbathing with Madame Gaumont

Before the War, as everyone knows, women of style took the utmost pride in the creamy whiteness of their complexions. When they ventured out of doors in the summer, little lace-trimmed parasols and hats with wide brims kept the sun off their faces and necks and, however low-cut at bosom and back their grand evening gowns were, the skin displayed was of a most delicately pale tint, with just the merest touch of face-powder to give it a hint of colour. The fortunate lover of such a lady, removing her long and elaborate clothes in the privacy of his apartment, could be sure of uncovering milky white breasts and a rounded belly and smooth thighs of the same creamy texture for his delight.

With the progress of time there came a change in custom. In the decade after the end of the War it became the height of fashion to visit the Côte d'Azur during the hot summer months and to lie in the sun in a skin-tight bathing-costume for hours on end. Women of style competed with each other over who had the deepest and most golden suntan, this being seen as a measure of their social status, almost. When they slipped out of their flimsy modern clothes and into the embrace of a lover, they presented to him a strangely striped body for his amorous attention – brown of face and shoulders, white across breasts and belly, and brown again down thighs and legs. Whatever pleasure it gave the women to show themselves with skin tanned by the sun, the sight was not altogether pleasing from the aesthetic point of view when they were naked.

Anyone who was anyone at all passed the entire month

of August by the sea and returned to Paris to display golden skin in short and revealing evening frocks at parties and dances. With the advance of autumn, the tan faded, even with the most skilful application of coloured face-powder to arms and backs, until everyone had reverted to their natural colour. There were those of ample means who stayed for two months, or even three months, by the Mediterranean and achieved so mahogany a shade that it lasted almost to the end of the year, outdoing their friends and thereby winning for themselves a certain prestige. But by January it was all gone and forgotten and, through the first half of the year, the ladies of Paris presented themselves to their lovers the same colour all over – the fine and delicate hue which providence intended.

Every rule has its exceptions, and Madame Gaumont could be seen in April, May and June with a pale gold tan, long before anyone thought of going south for the sun. How she achieved it was her secret and was not shared with even her closest friends. Her husband preserved a discreet silence on the subject, as indeed he did on all matters relating to his wife. It was generally believed by all who knew the Gaumonts that they lived together amicably enough but that they each pursued their own interests separately, and after nearly twenty years of marriage, this surprised no one at all. Charles Gaumont was approaching sixty, an age at which the interest of many men in his position leans towards very young girls. His wife Marcelle was not yet forty, though not far from it – a tall and good-looking woman. Her nose was perhaps a little too long and her jaw a little too square for her to be considered a real beauty, even when she was young, but for all that she was attractive and not lacking in admirers. Her discretion was well-known, but it was widely believed in her circle that some of her admirers had been permitted to remove Marcelle's elegant clothes and delight themselves with her charms.

The Gaumonts had only one child, a son of sixteen. A friend of his was Jean-Louis Normand, also sixteen, a handsome and well-built boy. It was he who discovered the secret of Madame Gaumont's unseasonal suntan – and

117

much else besides – by chance, or so he thought. It was on a day in the school vacation when he called at the Gaumont home for Henri, at about eleven in the morning, to be told that he had gone out. Marcelle Gaumont heard him talking at the door with her servant and asked him in to apologise for her son's forgetfulness. Jean-Louis found himself sitting in the salon, a glass of lemonade in his hand, talking to Madame Gaumont. Eventually they got on to the subject of suntans and Jean-Louis complimented Madame Gaumont on hers, which he considered very beautiful. For reasons best known to herself, but at which one can guess, Marcelle took an unexpected decision – she swore Jean-Louis to silence and offered to show him how she achieved her pale golden colour so early in the year, for it was only the first week of May.

So it came about that the young Jean-Louis was led up to the very top of the house, into a small room under the mansard roof. The windows were shuttered and the room stuffy, but Marcelle threw back the shutters to disclose a view southwards over the Bois de Boulogne. The walls and ceiling of the room were painted white, with no decoration of any sort, and the only furniture was a white-painted cupboard in one corner.

'By this time of the morning the sun is up above the trees,' she said. 'This is my solarium.'

The sun was streaming in through the open windows, throwing a long bright streak of light across the wooden floor.

'How simple when you know the secret!' said Jean-Louis.

'I had it made like this when I found out how health-giving it is to sunbathe,' she said. 'Even in winter, if the sun breaks through the clouds for an hour, I can use this room in comfort – it becomes surprisingly warm. Sometimes in summer it becomes too hot to bear.'

'I can understand why people envy you and wonder how you stay so golden brown,' said Jean-Louis, 'My mother sounds quite furious sometimes when she mentions you.'

'You gave me your word of honour not to breathe a

word of this to anyone,' Marcelle reminded him.

'Of course, Madame. A promise is a promise.'

'It's not just a matter of sunbathing for the sake of health,' she told him. 'In this room I can be alone for an hour or so and compose myself spiritually. The servants are forbidden to disturb me here. I live a busy life and I need a little retreat of my own. You are the first person to have entered this room, apart from my husband. Even Henri has never been here.'

'I am honoured, Madame,' said Jean-Louis, wondering why he was being singled out for this special treatment, 'but there is something I do not understand – there is no furniture here, not even a chair. How do you sunbathe?'

Marcelle stared at him for some moments, as if turning over in her mind some decision of particular importance. She looked long and hard at his pleasant snub-nosed face and his tranquil expression, then smiled.

'You shall see,' she said, as if her mind were made up, 'and you can join me for an hour of relaxation in the sun. It is excellent for your skin, of course, and it has a tonic effect on the nervous system. Did you know that?'

'No, I thought it was just an excuse to doze in the daytime.'

'I have been assured by medical experts that to sunbathe regularly promotes health and vitality,' Marcelle said firmly, 'and I have proved it myself – I never suffer from colds in the winter or exhaustion after late nights, or poor digestion, or any of the ailments which afflict those who live in cities.'

'Then everyone should do it,' said Jean-Louis, impressed by this catalogue of benefit.

'You must understand,' said Marcelle carefully and with emphasis, 'that when I suggested that you should join me in the sun for an hour, it was entirely on account of my regard for your health. It would be embarrassing if you made the mistake of thinking that there is any question of any other motive.'

'I don't understand, Madame – what other motive could there be?'

'None,' she said, very firmly.

Her tone puzzled the boy – it was almost as if he had offended her in some way. That was very distant from his mind – he considered Madame Gaumont to be an attractive woman, even though she was as old as his own mother.

'Open the cupboard and you will find the things I use,' she said, smiling at him.

He did as she said and found that there was a shelf at the top of the cupboard on which stood bottles of sun-oil, while the lower two-thirds was almost entirely filled by a thin and rolled-up mattress standing on end. At her instructions he took it out and unrolled it on the floor where the sunlight fell. He glanced up from his task to see that Marcelle had taken off her grey silk blouse and pleated skirt and was hanging them in the cupboard. She was wearing camiknickers in pale blue and Jean-Louis stared open-mouthed at the round cheeks of her bottom, revealed to him when she bent over to roll down her stockings. She glanced over her bare shoulder at him, still crouched on the floor by the bright yellow mattress.

'It is necessary to remove one's clothes to sunbathe,' she said.

'Why, yes,' he answered slowly, not at all sure where this was leading.

'Come along then,' she said briskly, and he slowly took off his jacket.

It was all very well for Madame Gaumont to talk about this being a project to improve the health, but Jean-Louis was troubled by the thought that the ever-eager little fellow inside his trousers might well shame him by standing upright – as it did on the least provocation. To ward off so inconvenient an event, he turned his eyes away from Marcelle as she took off her silk underwear and forced himself to recite the multiplication tables in his head while he undressed down to his underpants and threw his clothes into the bottom of the cupboard. By then Marcelle was lying face-down on the yellow mattress, her face turned away from him. Her smooth round bottom brought a suppressed sigh to his lips and he looked away quickly while he took his place at her side, also face-down.

Through the wide open windows the sun beat down on his back in a very pleasant way. The room seemed to him hot, but he was not sure whether to attribute that entirely to the sun or to his own dangerous state of mind at finding himself so close to a naked woman for the first time in his life. He clenched his fists and recited Latin irregular verbs in his head, but soon he heard the movements of Marcelle turning over and sitting up.

'But you still have your underwear on!' she said in a shocked tone.

'It seemed more respectful,' Jean-Louis muttered.

'What nonsense! Turn over and look at me.'

He turned only his head. She was not only completely naked, as he knew already – she was sun-tanned all over, from her forehead to her scarlet-painted toenails – breasts, belly and thighs all the same golden shade as her arms and shoulders.

'On beaches people have to wear bathing-costumes,' she said, 'and the result is appalling – when they undress they look like zebras. What is worse, they do not profit as much as they should from the sun because so much of their bodies are hidden from it. You must remove those ridiculous underpants and give yourself freely to the sun.'

'But . . .' he stammered, and blushed crimson as she took hold of his cotton underpants and dragged them forcibly down his legs and threw them across the room.

'That's much better,' she said, giving his upturned rump a playful little smack, 'Nothing looks more foolish on a man than a white bottom above brown legs. Mine looks very good, don't you think?'

Over his shoulder he saw that she had resumed her face-down position on the mattress. The golden-skinned cheeks of her bottom were like the two halves of a succulently-rounded melon and Jean-Louis found that he wanted more than anything in the world to touch them. He suppressed the thought hastily and lay with his arms folded under his head, very conscious that his male part, squeezed between his belly and the mattress, was defiantly hard. That posed a problem that seemed to him insoluble, for he knew from experience how very persistent his stiffness was.

Marcelle chatted inconsequentially for perhaps five minutes, Jean-Louis muttering a vague word of agreement now and then, though his attention was concentrated elsewhere. He was startled when she announced that their backs had enjoyed the sun for long enough and it was time to turn over. He watched her do so, his eyes drawn to her prominent breasts and his disobedient spike twitching underneath him.

'Turn over,' Marcelle said. 'Have you fallen asleep?'

'No, I'm awake.'

'Then turn over.'

'I don't think I ought to, Madame . . . the fact is that there is a sort of problem . . . if I turn over I shall offend your sense of decency . . .'

'I can't imagine why you think the sight of a naked boy might offend me. Do you suppose that I am ignorant of how the male body is shaped?'

'No . . . but the sun seems to have had an effect on me – if you see what I mean.'

'Heavens, is that all that's bothering you!' she said with a chuckle. 'I know exactly what you mean, Jean-Louis. There's no reason to be embarrassed about it – I have seen it happen often enough on the beach. Good manners require that one takes no notice of these little accidents.'

'But on the beach men wear bathing-costumes,' he pointed out. 'I am wearing nothing at all.'

'It is of no consequence. If you had not mentioned it yourself, I would not have taken the slightest notice. Turn over and expose the front of your body to the sun.'

He was reassured by her matter-of-fact manner and it never entered his head that a grown-up like Madame Gaumont could have the slightest interest in him. He turned over slowly to lie on his back, his stiff limb standing well clear of his belly. Marcelle paid no attention at all – she was spread comfortably, her feet a little apart and her hands under her head. It was more than Jean-Louis could do not to squint down at her bare breasts and their soft pink tips. Seeing that her eyes were closed and her head well back to let the sunlight reach up under her chin, he thought it safe to stare at her breasts more openly.

'Do you feel the sun on your body doing you good?' she asked casually.

'Oh yes,' he replied, half-proud and half-ashamed of the way in which his stiff stem was quivering as he stared at her breasts and imagined what it would be like to feel them.

'This is in confidence,' she said. 'An important aspect of sunbathing is to let the rays reach those parts of the body which we take most care to keep covered. Do you understand me?'

'Really?' he said, wondering that she mentioned those parts of the body to him and intrigued to hear that it was good for him to let the sun shine on his secret pride. 'Why is that?'

'But it is obvious! Consider for a moment – as we know, men on the beach often experience a stimulation of the male organ and they believe that this is caused by the heat of the sun. Agreed?'

'Well, yes,' Jean-Louis answered, though privately he considered that the reason was more likely to be the nearness of pretty young women in close-fitting bathing-costumes that showed off the shape of their breasts. That had been in his own experience the summer before when his parents took him with them for the first time to Cannes – the sight of so many half-dressed women on the beach had kept him stiff from morning to night, almost.

'To some extent this is correct,' Marcelle continued, 'the warmth of the sun is a pleasant sensation that stimulates men. But what they do not realise is that the health-giving rays which penetrate the material of their bathing-costumes have a direct effect on the nerve-endings of their sexual organ. I was given this information by a friend who is a doctor.'

'But how could he be sure?'

'By experiment, of course – he is a very eminent doctor. By experimenting on himself he proved that this natural stimulation by the sun's rays is extremely beneficial. It strengthens the male sexual capacity – though that is of no importance to you at present, since you are too young to know about such things.'

'But I often think about such things,' said Jean-Louis at once, unwilling to be thought a child.

He had, after all, persuaded two girls of his own age to let him feel their little breasts and he was in the lengthy process of trying to persuade Madeleine Leroy to let him put his hand in her knickers and feel her there.

'I suppose you have the fantasies of boyhood,' said Marcelle, 'but you will not appreciate the truth of what I mean until you are a few years older.'

Jean-Louis said nothing, though he was surprised that she knew about his fantasies.

She continued, 'So far I have spoken only of men, but the same is true of women. Exposure to sunlight on a regular basis is beneficial to the female sexual parts – you may have noticed that I am lying with my legs apart so that the sun can penetrate between my thighs.'

'I hadn't noticed,' the boy lied. 'But isn't this dangerous, exposing everything to the sun? Sometimes you see people with fiery red shoulders – if this happened between your legs the result would be agony.'

'Thank heavens you reminded me!' Marcelle exclaimed. 'I'd forgotten you're not used to the sun – I should have rubbed you with sun-oil before we started.'

She rose from beside him and went to the cupboard. Jean-Louis stared in desperate admiration at her long back and swaying bottom and then, when she came back to the mattress, at her jiggling breasts and down at the patch of brown curls between her thighs. She knelt beside him, poured scented oil on to his chest and shoulders and smoothed it into his skin with her palm. When her hand moved down to his belly, he almost sighed with pleasure, but thought it better to force himself to be silent in case he upset her. After all, she was so much older than he and it was impossible that she had any interest in his body – certainly not the intense interest he had in hers! She rubbed oil down his thighs and between them and his naughty part gave a sudden jump. Marcelle made no comment – in fact she seemed not to have noticed, though it was in plain view.

'This is an excellent preparation,' she informed him. 'I

get it from an expert in skin-care. It forms an invisible barrier to ward off the rays which cause burning, but it lets the healthy rays through.'

Jean-Louis looked up at her. She was sitting on her heels, her face tranquil as she poured more of the oil into the palm of her hand.

'Nearly finished,' she said. 'Then you will be fully protected.'

He gasped loudly, unable to stop himself, as she clasped his trembling stalk in her slippery hand and rubbed the oil in firmly.

'But Madame Gaumont . . .' he said, blushing furiously.

'Lie still and don't be silly. This is precisely where you are most likely to burn unless proper precautions are taken. And, as you said yourself, that would be agony for you.'

Her hand slid up and down his stiff pole, massaging oil into the skin very thoroughly. Jean-Louis stared, his mind in a turmoil, as she poured oil from the bottle on to the blunt tip of his upright stem and let it trickle down inside her loosely clasping hand.

'As you see, there is nothing to be embàrrassed about, Jean Louis, even though I am touching you. The physical contact is without significance – it is no more than if I were rubbing oil on your back.'

'Of course,' he murmured, his legs shaking from the tremendous sensations that her hand was sending through him. 'It means no more than if you asked me to rub oil on your back.'

'Right,' she agreed, her hand sliding up and down in slow rhythm. 'When I have finished oiling you, I shall want you to do the same to me – to rub all over me, back or breasts – it's all the same, you understand.'

'It's all the same thing,' he gasped, his upstart companion jerking violently in her restricting hand at the thought of rubbing sun-oil into the soft breasts dangling so close to him.

'Back, bosom, legs,' said Marcelle, her voice trembling a little as her hand moved busily at its task, 'especially between the legs, where the skin is most sensitive . . . you must pay particular attention to the skin between my legs . . .'

'I shall!' Jean-Louis exclaimed explosively as his bottom heaved upwards off the yellow mattress and he squirted his boyish passion high into the air.

'Oh!' Marcelle gasped, her scarlet-nailed hand moving faster than ever. 'This is very unexpected!'

'Ah, ah!' Jean-Louis moaned in delirium as she drained him expertly of his outburst.

'I didn't imagine that you would lose control of yourself quite so easily,' she said, almost a hint of reproach in her voice. 'You must be a very sensual boy to react so strongly to a meaningless stimulus like spreading sun-oil on your skin.'

Jean-Louis sat up, his thoughts whirling, and began to apologise for what had happened.

'There is no need for apologies,' she said, with a little laugh. 'These accidents happen to men sometimes. It is of no importance. You will find a towel in the cupboard – wipe yourself and then attend to me – my skin feels hot and sensitive.'

When he came back from the cupboard he found Marcelle lying face-down ready for him. He squatted beside her, poured a generous measure of the oil on to her flawless back and used both palms to spread it and rub it in to her golden skin.

'That's right,' she said, 'make sure you don't leave any patches dry.'

He worked his way slowly from her shoulders down to the small of her back and then, with more oil in his cupped hands, addressed himself to her perfect bottom. The skin was like satin under his hands and his limp sprig, dangling between his thighs, twitched threateningly. He lingered over her bottom for as long as he dared without giving her reason to suspect that he was doing more than follow her instructions. He was astonished when she reminded him that he had missed the delicate skin between the cheeks.

His hands were shaking as he poured a little oil into the cleavage between her cheeks of her bottom and used his fingertips to massage it gently in. He touched a little knot of muscle deep between the cheeks and saw her bottom quiver.

'Yes, use plenty of oil,' she said over her shoulder. 'There's more in the cupboard.'

Jean-Louis separated the round cheeks with one hand and caressed between them with the fingers of his other hand, sliding deeper and deeper, until he touched soft hair and the beginning of fleshy lips. He had been trying for over a week to talk Madeleine Leroy into letting him touch her little slit – and here was Madame Gaumont letting him finger hers freely! Madeleine would get a surprise when they met next – he would tell her that he had felt a better slit than hers and she could either take her knickers down and let him feel her or she wouldn't see him again.

'My legs now,' said Marcelle, evidently of the opinion that he had paid enough attention to the delicate folds between her thighs and that it was time he moved on further.

Her legs were a joy between Jean-Louis' hands – long slender thighs and shapely calves. Her feet were small for so tall a woman and he touched the soles very carefully. He had just started on the second foot when she rolled over to lie on her back.

'The shins are vulnerable,' she told him. 'They can become over-tanned and sensitive and that makes it uncomfortable to wear stockings.'

Jean-Louis pretended to keep his eyes fixed on her shins, though her naked body was spread out before him. He was trying to convince himself that she was speaking the truth when she claimed that it was of no significance when she rubbed oil on him and now that he was doing it for her. Perhaps it was of no significance to her, but Jean-Louis' spigot was giving him a different message by standing up stiffly again.

He worked his way slowly from her slim ankles to her rounded knees, making her skin gleam with the scented oil, and then paused, uncertain of how she wanted him to proceed. Her arms lay loosely at her sides and her eyes

127

were closed – he took the opportunity to stare openly at her sleek belly and at the neatly-trimmed fleece where her legs met. The only result was that his rebellious part grew to full-stretch and he tried to conceal it by pressing it between his thighs.

'What is it?' Marcelle asked, without opening her eyes. 'Have you used all the oil?'

'No, there's still half a bottle,' he answered softly.

'Then do my thighs before they turn red and ugly.'

He used both hands to smooth up her nearest thigh, to within a finger's breadth of her curls. Then the other thigh, starting at the knee – and as his hands approached her curls again, her legs slid apart on the yellow mattress, and Jean-Louis uttered the longest sigh of his life as he caught sight of the long pink-brown lips between them. He did not believe for one moment that Madeleine's could be half so exciting as Madame Gaumont's, even if she took her knickers down and let him examine it.

'Use plenty of oil between the legs,' Marcelle murmured. 'It is a mistake to think that the hair protects the tender skin beneath it.'

Jean-Louis was breathing heavily as he poured oil into his hand and applied it to the plump mound between Marcelle's thighs. At first he smoothed it into the curls with his whole hand, but his natural instincts were too powerful to be held in check for long – as he thought she would expect them to be – and soon he was using his fingertips on the delicate folds of flesh between the curls.

'That's the way,' she said, seeming to be unaffected by this intimate proceeding, 'massage it in softly.'

The boy's up-rearing baton was throbbing hard. He up-ended the bottle over Marcelle's fleece and watched a cascade of thin oil stream down her groin and between the fleshy lips his fingers had opened by their gentle rubbing. A moment later his fingers were inside her, rubbing slowly and softly. Marcelle made no comment, but there was no possibility that she was unaware of what he was doing to her. The resolution of extreme arousal had Jean-Louis in its holds and with his other hand he was stroking Marcelle's belly, no longer even pretending to be oiling her skin. Her dark head rolled slowly from side to side and her mouth was open. Jean-Louis stared at her breasts and saw that their pink tips were larger and firmer than when she had first turned on to her back.

'Yes, you must rub the oil in softly,' Marcelle sighed.

She took his wrist and pulled his hand upwards a fraction until he felt a little button under his fingertips.

'That is the most important place of all,' she whispered. 'Rub the oil on it very slowly and very gently.'

Jean-Louis had become aware in the last few minutes that it was no longer a question of rubbing sun-oil into her skin to protect it. Her face was a delicate pink and her belly was quivering a little – though she was still pretending to herself that what was happening to her was of no significance, the truth was that she was sighing with pleasure, and Jean-Louis was giving her that pleasure! His delight was so immense that he felt dizzy. If Madeleine would cooperate properly when he next met her, he could give her this same pleasure by stroking her!

Marcelle's loins jerked upwards briefly and her heels drummed on the mattress, then she was still again.

'That's enough there,' she said weakly. 'Now do the rest of me.'

'Are you sure?' he asked in a quavering voice, reluctant to take his fingers away from the warm nest he had explored.

'Quite sure,' she said briefly.

There was nothing for it but to take his hand from between her legs and massage oil into her rounded belly. But soon he came to her breasts and the projection he gripped between his thighs to hold it it still shook with frustration as he caressed them. They felt so firm and yet so tender – so much bigger than those of the two girls he had felt. His fingers ranged over their red-brown buds and from being soft they began to feel firm again.

'Your hands are shaking,' said Marcelle, looking up at him through half-closed eyes. 'Why is that?'

'Because you are so beautiful,' he answered boldly.

She shrugged her shoulders a little. 'It is a very great privilege for you to have seen me naked,' she said, 'I rely

129

on you to be totally discreet and keep it a secret.'

'I would bite off my tongue before breathing a word to anyone!' he assured her.

He was kneeling beside her while he fondled her breasts under the pretence of putting oil on them. His desire was sticking out stiffly, unconcealed in his agitation.

'My poor Jean-Louis – I have been very thoughtless,' said Marcelle. 'I lie here in the sun naked so often it means nothing to me. I ought to have remembered what the effect of seeing me would be on a young man. Your accidental emission when I rubbed oil on you ought to have warned me.'

'But it is marvellous to see you naked!' he protested. 'It is I who must apologise for being unable to control myself.'

'No, you are not to blame. I am desolated to have brought you by sheer carelessness to this condition.' And she reached out casually and her hand closed round his quivering pride.

'Oh yes!' he murmured, hoping that she would offer to rub more sun-oil on it.

'I have been irresponsible,' Marcelle told him, 'I must never let you see me naked again.'

'Please don't say that!'

She sat up and, without considering what he was doing, Jean-Louis scrambled over her leg and knelt between her parted thighs, his body close to hers. She still held his outstanding part in her hand – in fact she was holding it in both hands.

'Do you really think I am beautiful? I must seem old to you.'

'You are the most beautiful woman I have ever seen!' he gasped.

'I imagine that I am the only woman you have ever seen. Which part of me do you consider to be the most beautiful?'

'All of you!'

'The enthusiasm of youth! But you must learn to discriminate, my dear. Do you think my breasts are pretty, for instance?'

'They are marvellous!'

130

'You seem to enjoy fondling them. Do it again and make sure.'

Jean-Louis needed no second invitation. His hands played over her soft breasts eagerly.

'Well?' she asked.

'They are beautiful to the touch – and to look at.'

Marcelle lay back on the yellow mattress, her breasts sliding away from his hands. 'What about my belly – does that please you?'

Jean-Louis summoned up all his shattered presence of mind in order to respond in what he hoped was a grown-up way.

'The skin's like silk to touch,' he said, 'and the shape is exquisite.'

'Very good!' Marcelle murmured. 'You are learning. Lie on my belly and stroke my breasts again.'

Jean-Louis thought he would die at that very moment. He was dizzy with pleasure and anticipation as he lay forward on her warm and soft body, his hands under him to feel for her breasts. Marcelle tugged at his straining handle and he felt it touch slippery flesh, and knew himself to be at the very threshold.

'Push forward slowly,' she whispered, her mouth close to his ear.

To slide into that soft and enclosing flesh was for Jean-Louis like entering into paradise, with angels blowing golden trumpets to welcome him.

'Lie still now until I tell you,' Marcelle whispered. 'You are a strong and well-developed young man, Jean-Louis – you will give women a great deal of pleasure when you grow up. Do you like what you feel?'

He was beyond words. His whole body shook continuously and he was panting, so intense were his emotions. Inside Marcelle's body his trapped staff was fluttering like a wild bird in a small cage.

'Greedy little fellow,' said Marcelle with a chuckle, 'he can't wait to enjoy his pleasure slowly – he snatches at it as if it might be taken away from him. You will learn in time. But since this is your first time and you are so very agitated – do it!'

131

Her words sounded only faintly in his ears through the roaring of his blood and the heavy thumping of his heart in his chest – but even so he understood that she had told him he could do what he wanted to do. He was gasping continuously as he lunged in and out of Marcelle's well-oiled enclosure, treating it so roughly that she moaned in pleasure and her knees lifted off the mattress as she opened herself to the full. Moments later a paroxysm of passion shook Jean-Louis and he gushed his sap into her, his belly thumping on hers. He did not hear her little climactic wail, so lost was he to all but his own sensations.

They lay side by side afterwards, the sun beating through the open windows on to their bodies.

'What do you think of your first experience of love-making, Jean-Louis?' Marcelle asked curiously. 'Was it what you expected, or disappointing?'

'It was superb! I shall remember it forever.'

His words made her laugh. 'You are very young. Men's gratitude to women disappears very quickly, I can tell you. I have known men who have enjoyed the most exquisite pleasures with a woman for months and then one day – pfft! – he's off with another woman, a younger one, without a single word of tenderness to the one who gave him so much.'

'I'd never behave like that,' Jean-Louis exclaimed, shocked by what he had been told.

'Ah, come and see me ten years from now and tell me that,' she said, chuckling at his outrage.

'Will you tell me something?' he asked, seizing the opportunity.

'What?'

'Does it feel as incredible for a woman as for a man when they make love?'

'Yes, as long as she wants the man to do it to her. Otherwise no – some married women find that it becomes a boring duty.'

'You mean they just lie there while their husband does it?'

'Exactly – he is no more than a heavy weight on her belly until his emission ends the business.'

132

'Did you enjoy it just now when I did it to you?'

'The question every lover asks!' she said, laughing aloud. 'Yes, I enjoyed it.'

'What about the prostitutes you see on the boulevards – do they enjoy it?'

'I doubt it – they do it for money and their clients may be ugly and brutal. Now it's your turn to answer a question for me.'

'Whatever you like.'

'We can be very frank with each other after what we have done together,' she said. 'There is no reason for you to be embarrassed, any more than there was when I rubbed oil on you and you surprised me with your sudden reaction.'

'I *was* embarrassed,' Jean-Louis confided, 'but you took it so calmly that I saw that it was natural and nothing to be ashamed of at all. If you did it to me again I should not be embarrassed at all.'

'Good, then you will not be embarrassed by my question. Everyone knows that boys relieve their sexual tensions by using their hands. You are a strong and healthy young man of sixteen – you must have played a tune on your violin many times, Am I right?'

'Well . . . yes,' he admitted, 'but if everyone knows that already, why ask?'

'That wasn't my question. What I want to ask you is how often a young man of your age relieves his tensions.'

'We talk about it at school sometimes,' he replied, 'but there's so much boasting that you never find out what the truth is.'

'I see that in these matters men learn to lie very early in life! It is a habit they keep all through their lives. There is a person I know who claims that he regularly makes love to three women a day.'

'No!' Jean-Louis gasped in astonishment. 'Three different women?'

'On occasions when I have been able to put his stamina to the test, his limit proved to be twice. After that he made excuses about overdoing things the night before – in short, his claim was a lie.'

It did not occur to Jean-Louis that Marcelle might have

133

an unspoken reason for enquiring into the sexual capacity of boys of his age – he assumed that she was asking out of pure curiosity.

'There's a friend at school who says he's done it to himself eight times in one day, but I don't believe him,' he offered.

'And how about you, my young friend?' she asked, turning on her side to face him, so close to him that her breasts touched his upper arm. 'How often are you forced to relieve your tensions?'

'It depends,' he answered vaguely.

Marcelle's hand ran lightly up his bare thigh. 'Your tension has been dealt with twice this morning,' she reminded him, 'Do you find that excessive?'

Her fingers touched his limp stem and fondled it. The power of recovery of youth caused it to lengthen and harden at once, and he turned on his side towards her so that he could feel her breasts.

'Well,' said Marcelle, pretending surprise, 'how quickly you have regained your ability – this is most impressive. Do you like my breasts?'

'They are marvellous!'

'You should kiss them.'

Her suggestion opened up new and hitherto undreamed-of vistas of pleasure for Jean-Louis. He put his head down to nuzzle her breasts, while her fingers played with his stiff pride, and it did not take him long to discover the delights of tickling her soft buds with his tongue.

'That's very good,' Marcelle whispered, 'you learn quickly. Put your hand between my legs.'

His fingers touched the crinkly dark-brown fleece and, a moment later, found their way between the half-open fleshy lips there.

'Do you like that?' she asked.

'Oh yes – you are so warm and wet inside,' he murmured. 'If I push my finger right into you like this it's as if a hand in a soft glove was gripping it.'

His spindle was twitching in her hand.

'Like the way my hand feels clasped around you?' she asked.

'Something like that – only softer and warmer.

'It is time for you to remove your finger and put *this* in its place,' she told him, giving his baton an affectionate little tug. 'Lie on top of me again, Jean-Louis.'

She rolled on her back and spread her knees wide as he scrambled on to her hot belly and pushed into her without any assistance from her this time.

'Now how does that feel?' she asked, her brown eyes staring at his pink-flushed young face.

'Marvellous – like a soft hand holding me!'

'Lie still!' she said, gripping him by the hips to immobilise him as he began to jerk inexpertly into her. 'Listen and learn, Jean-Louis! The first time you made love to me you treated me roughly, because you were over-excited – simply because for you it *was* the first time. But a woman's body is not to be battered and beaten with your own body – it is a thing of great beauty and sensitivity to be enjoyed. There is no hurry – do you understand me?'

He demonstrated his understanding by riding her to the rhythm she set with her hands on his hips – firm and steady strokes that after a while had her murmuring *Yes, yes, yes!* Jean-Louis forced himself to take note of what he was feeling, not to let it all merge into an amorphous feeling of excitement that would make his sap leap. He identified the distinct pleasures of her warm belly under his, of her soft breasts squashed beneath his chest, of the gentle grip of her interior on his baton as it slid to and fro. The sun was hot on his bare back and he had never before in his life experienced so complex and sensual a combination of feelings, physical and mental, as he did at that moment. This time it was Marcelle whose critical moments arrived first. She moaned and squirmed under him until he was carried away by her passion and stabbed into her slippery warmth and squirted his ecstasy into her.

He would have stayed on top of her after that, for the position of dominance pleased him tremendously, but after a time Marcelle pushed him gently away. He nestled close to her side, she still on her back, and put his head on her shoulder.

'You did that very well, my dear,' she said contentedly.

135

'You are a good student and I must be a good teacher.'

'What is it like when you reach your climax?' he asked. 'I mean, how does it feel?'

'Ah, the lesson is not yet over, I see. But there is no way I can describe to you the sensations that rush through my body in those moments. It is like being swept away by a great tidal wave and drowning – that's all I can tell you.'

'A very nice tidal wave,' he suggested. 'That's three times you've drowned this morning.'

'Three – why do you say that? You've made love to me twice.'

'I know, but you did it before, when I was rubbing oil between your legs. I didn't understand then, but I do now. Why did you pretend nothing had happened to you?'

'So as not to embarrass you, perhaps. After all, I am a grown woman and you are many years younger. I did not wish to discomfort you with something you had never seen before – a woman's passionate release.'

'But you weren't embarrassed when I squirted in your hand before that,' Jean-Louis pointed out.

'I am more experienced than you, my little student. I know what to expect when a man reaches his climax.'

'It seems to me that if I made you feel ecstasy by rubbing between your legs with my fingers, then girls can play the violin just like boys,' said Jean-Louis, pursuing a train of thought of his own.

'Naturally,' she answered, amused by his interest. 'Didn't you know?'

It had never come into Jean-Louis' head that Madeleine Leroy, whose little breasts he had felt and into whose knickers he was trying to talk his way – though only to feel her a little – that this quiet little sixteen-year-old perhaps put her own hand into her knickers and rubbed herself until she experienced a climax! But perhaps young girls didn't amuse themselves like that – perhaps only grown up ladies like Marcelle did it when they had no lover.

His hand lay on Marcelle's belly. She felt it move down across her oiled and sun-hot skin to touch her between the thighs.

'Let me play a little tune on your violin,' he whispered

136

urgently, 'I want to watch you properly this time and see what happens.'

'What a little monster you are!' she said, still amused.

Her legs opened wider and his finger slid into her easily.

'A little higher,' she murmured. 'Find the bud I showed you before and caress it gently – that's how to arouse a woman. Yes, now you've got it – touch it with delicacy and love, never roughly.'

'Like this?'

'That's it – kiss my breasts while you play with it.'

Jean-Louis needed no instruction to move his head down from her shoulder and take the red-brown tip between his lips and use his tongue on it. During the next five or six minutes he learned in the most thorough and practical way how to excite a woman to the very limit. Marcelle's explosion of passion, when it came, was spectacular and made a lasting impression on the boy. Her belly and loins rose upwards and for long moments she was balanced rigidly on her shoulder-blades and heels, shuddering violently and gasping.

He by then had abandoned her breasts so that he could observe the progress and extent of her climactic release, his mouth open in wonder at it. He would have liked it to last for hours, so entrancing was the sight, but in the natural course of things Marcelle collapsed after only a few moments. She lay trembling while her throes faded, her eyes closed and her arms loose at her sides. Without a moment's hesitation Jean-Louis rolled on to her belly and pierced her deeply, his stalk at full-stretch again from what he had observed.

'Ah no!' Marcelle exclaimed weakly. 'No more – I can't.'

But he was too aroused by her ecstatic explosion to pay any attention to her words. She pushed at his shoulders to indicate that he must withdraw from her body and leave her alone, but Jean-Louis was broaching her with a boldness and vigour beyond his years. His previous pleasure with her slowed him down this time and, as he swung in a firm rhythm in and out of her, her own body began to respond to what he was doing. Her eyes remained tight shut, but her arms and legs were twined over him to hold him close.

137

'No, it's too much . . .' she murmured in broken little words, 'I can't . . . This is impossible . . .'

Jean-Louis was not deceived this time – her slippery passage was gripping his distended baton and was massaging it and squeezing it.

'You're enjoying it!' he gasped, stabbing more quickly. This time she squealed when he fountained his rapture into her very wet aperture.

'You've killed me!' she cried out, her body convulsing so furiously in her release that but for her arms and legs around him he might well have been thrown off her, like an inexpert rider from a bucking horse. But she gripped him tight, her body seeming to suck his stem deeper into her, until they both collapsed.

Jean-Louis slid out of her and lay by her side, gasping and panting, his body wet with perspiration and sun-oil.

'We both drowned at the same time,' he murmured in satisfaction.

'We're drowned and lying at the bottom of the sea,' she agreed, speaking so faintly that he could only just discern the words.

'You really like to be drowned, don't you?' he said, making a statement rather than asking a question.

'Every woman does,' she whispered, 'but some refuse to admit it.'

'Why do they do that?'

'No more questions!' she said, her voice stronger as she recovered from the impact of her climactic sensations. 'You are a strong young man – stronger than I imagined! Though perhaps I should have guessed when you squirted so easily into my hand. Ah, if men could only retain this virility of youth throughout their lives!'

'What do you mean?' Jean-Louis asked in alarm. 'That I won't be able to make love when I'm grown up?'

'*If youth only knew, if age only could,*' Marcelle sighed, quoting the well-known words that meant nothing much to Jean-Louis.

'If youth knew what?' he demanded.

'If young men only knew how wonderful it is to be young!' she replied. 'But you need have no fear – ten years from now *you* will be the one who can make love to three women in a day, not the boastful idiot I told you about.'

'Do you think so?' he asked in pride.

'I'm sure of it.' She rolled over to lie face-down, her long gleaming back exposed to the sun.

Jean-Louis lay propped on an elbow beside her, his hand stroking her shoulder.

'You never did answer my question, did you?' she said lazily.

'What question?'

How often you pleasure yourself – judging from what you've done to me it must be often – you have a very sensual nature. Every day, I suppose.'

'Most days,' he said. 'Shall I put more oil on your back – the sun's very hot now.'

'That's a good idea,' she answered drowsily. 'I see that I shall get no answer to my question – does it make you shy to talk about pleasuring yourself?'

Jean-Louis began to rub sun-oil into the skin of her back. His touch had a confidence that was not present the first time he had done this for her – now that he had been admitted to every intimacy there was perhaps a touch of the proprietorial in his massage. Young as he was, he was not immune to the general male pride of possession after he has enjoyed a woman's body.

'I'm not shy to talk to you about it,' he said, his palms gliding slowly over her satin skin. 'Some days once, some days more – it depends.'

If Marcelle had any inkling of his changed attitude towards her, she made no comment. She was in fact almost asleep and the slow passage of his hands from her shoulders down to the small of her back served to lull her into further contentment and a light doze.

With the enviable resilience and curiosity of youth, Jean-Louis' interest in Marcelle's naked body was undiminished. He felt that he had come of age this day and he was still avid to feel the breasts and belly on which he had lain during his ecstatic passage from childhood to adult experience. Her sleepy acquiescence pleased him – it gave him full scope to enjoy the touch of her warm skin under his

139

palms. By the time that her back gleamed with oil from the nape of her neck to her bottom, his dangler was stiffening itself again in a most satisfactory manner. His attention became fixed on Marcelle's upturned bottom and he fondled the fleshy cheeks as if they were the big sisters of her breasts. Though he had no previous experience and was therefore in no position to make useful comparisons, the truth was that for a woman of her age Marcelle's rump was still well-shaped and pleasing, soft to the touch but not over-large or flabby.

Eventually the boy's well-oiled fingers slid down the long valley between Marcelle's cheeks and explored everything they encountered, until the tip of his middle finger touched the moist entrance into which he had earlier been welcomed. It could have been no more than a reflex action that sent Marcelle's legs sliding slowly apart at his touch, for she was dozing peacefully and not truly aware of anything but a feeling of gentle well-being.

Jean-Louis was trying to picture what it would be like if he had Madeleine Leroy with him, face-down with her knickers off and his fingers between her thighs. She was only just sixteen – would she have this exciting fleece of dark curls to play with? Were the lips of her little purse as plump and pouting as Marcelle's – or was there just a plain little slit between her legs? When at last he was able to persuade her to let him put his hand in her knickers and feel her, would she let him play a little tune on her violin? It would be fascinating to see cool and self-assured little Madeleine gasping and squirming in a climax brought on by his fingers – but he was fairly sure that she would not let him do that to her. Would she lie on her back and let him slide into her little slit and squirt up her? He was certain that the answer to that was absolutely no! But what did any of that matter when he had this marvellous grown-up lady naked and ready to let him do anything he liked to her! Poor Madeleine – in comparison she had nothing to offer at all.

His probing fingers were well inside Marcelle and tickling her button very lightly. He was rewarded in a while by the sight of her legs sliding even further apart, so that he could kneel between her thighs and use his whole hand to rifle her secrets.

Marcelle woke from her doze with a little gasp and raised her head to look at him over her shoulder.

'Oh!' she exclaimed, seeing his upright stalk. 'What are you doing?'

'Spreading oil on your back,' he answered readily.

'My back? With your hand between my legs and your fingers inside me! The sun does not penetrate that far.'

'Better take no chances,' he said. 'You wouldn't want to get sun-burned there, would you?'

Marcelle put her head down on her arms and relaxed again.

'My poor Jean-Louis,' she said, a chuckle in her voice, 'I know very well what you are trying to do – you want to make me aroused so that I will lie on my back for you again. But you are wasting your time – you have exhausted me completely.'

'But we've only done it once or twice,' he said, puzzled by her words.

'My god – what sort of insatiable beast have I released from its cage,' she murmured. 'Four times in quick succession and he expects more! No, it is impossible, I tell you. You must learn, my active little friend, that there is a limit for everyone.'

'I thought you would want to do it more times than me because you're grown up.'

'Sadly, no. My god – what are you doing?'

'It's all right,' he said, 'I won't disturb you.'

In effect, he had stretched himself along Marcelle's back, his belly on her rump and his legs down between hers. The idea had come to him that if he could reach her entrance from behind and below with his fingers, then it ought to be possible to reach the same desirable aperture with his stiff equipment.

'Ah, you little devil,' Marcelle exclaimed when she felt its warm tip press between the lips he had been caressing a moment earlier. 'It will do you no good!'

Jean-Louis was gratified to find that his idea had been correct. He pushed into Marcelle as far as the constrained position allowed him.

141

'If you lie still I can do it without making you any more exhausted,' he told her.

'I don't know whether to laugh or to cry!' Marcelle exclaimed as she felt him moving to and fro inside her. 'An hour ago you knew nothing about making love and I had to teach you – now you are forcing me against my will!'

She could, if she had wanted to, have rolled him off her back and put a stop to the exercise, for she was bigger and heavier than he was. But she did no such thing. For reasons of her own, of which curiosity may have been one, she chose to lie still and play the martyr, while he thrust busily into her slippery vestibule.

'*Some days once*!' she said, repeating his earlier words. 'And what about the other days, Jean-Louis – how many times do you pleasure yourself then?'

'Three or four, perhaps,' he gasped, his belly pounding at her bare bottom.

'Ah . . . and on special days?'

'On my birthday . . . six times!'

'Six times!' Marcelle shrieked.

It had been on his birthday that Françine had let him feel her little breasts, as a sort of special present. Her cool skin and delicate flesh had aroused him so enormously that, after she had gone, he had no choice but to relieve his own sexual tension in the only way he could – not merely once but, during the rest of the day, a record number of times.

'Ah, no,' Marcelle moaned suddenly, as she felt him convulse on her back and deposit his warm tribute just inside her entrance, so that it flooded over her hidden bud.

'No, no!' she moaned again, as the familiar but totally unexpected sensations of climactic release blossomed in her belly. 'It's not possible!'

But it was possible, and her bottom heaved upwards to drive Jean-Louis deeper into her as she sobbed in delirious pleasure. In her whirling mind was the astonishing thought that, of all the lovers she had known, not one of them had ever given her so many climaxes in so short a time as this sixteen-year-old boy. Indeed, until this moment she had no idea that she was capable of so many so quickly. For a woman approaching forty that was an

142

unusual and interesting discovery to make.

When her tranquility returned, she rolled Jean-Louis off her back and raised herself on an elbow to stare at him.

'If only you were six or seven years older,' she said fondly, 'you could be my acknowledged lover and I would visit you in the afternoons to be loved like this. Such pretty presents I would bring you; silk shirts and ties and a gold wrist-watch and a hundred other things. But those few years make all the difference in the world – if it became known that I had let you make love to me, everyone would laugh at me. And in six or seven years' time, when you are old enough, you will have a string of pretty young women and will scarcely remember me, except for your first, perhaps.'

Jean-Louis said nothing. He lay on his back, an arm across his face to shade his closed eyes from the glare of the midday sun. His male affair had lost its hardness and lay limply between his thighs. Marcelle gazed at it with respect – in its present condition it gave the impression of being small and harmless. But as she had found out, it was capable of a more sustained performance than that of any grown man with whom she was acquainted.

'Are you tired?' she asked.

'Just a bit. How about you?'

'I am beyond the point of total exhaustion – thanks to you,' she replied with affection. 'I am crushed and it will take a week before I think of making love again with anyone. I suppose you know that you made me reach another climax when I least wanted to?'

'But you enjoyed it,' he pointed out, grinning at her.

'Yes – and this evening I shall be good for nothing at the dinner party I am attending.'

'Will you tell me something?'

'What is it this time?'

'When Monsieur Gaumont makes love to you, how many times does he do it?'

'Your question is impertinent!'

'I'm sorry – I didn't mean to be. I was worried about you.'

'In what way?'

143

'When Monsieur Gaumont makes love to you tonight, you may be too tired to enjoy it.'

'You need have no worries on that score. Monsieur Gaumont will not want to make love to me tonight.'

'Why not? If I were married I'd do it every night at bedtime.'

'One day, when you are married, you will come to understand that things are not as you imagine them.'

She touched his shoulder and the skin was very hot from the sun.

'You will burn in another minute or two,' she said, and knelt up to pour sun-oil on his chest and belly and rub it in with a light touch.

'In fact, it would be better for you to be out of the sun altogether now,' she added. 'You are not used to it, as I am. I think you must shower and put your clothes on.'

'I don't want to go yet – I'll be all right.'

To Marcelle's utter amazement, while her slippery hand smeared oil into the fine skin of his belly, his limp part quivered. And by the time that she had finished with his belly and was rubbing the oil on the insides of his thighs, his affair was not soft at all, but pointed boldly upwards.

'This is incredible,' she murmured.

Jean-Louis stared at her bare and heavy breasts with greedy eyes.

'I want to do it again,' he said, the merest trace of male insolence in his voice.

'So I observe,' Marcelle answered drily.

'You needn't do anything – just lie still and let me,' he assured her.

She poured oil into her palm, clasped his stiff baton and massaged it quickly.

'I shall find a girlfriend who likes to do it as much as I do,' he murmured, his eyes closing and his legs trembling as he let her excite him more and more.

'I wish you good luck in your search, Jean-Louis. It will not be a simple matter to find a girl who can match your remarkable stamina.'

'It will be easy enough it I try girls of my own age,' he told her. 'You said yourself that older people can't do it as

144

often as when they were young . . . I bet I can find a girl who wants to do it ten times in a row.'

'Ah, my boastful little man!' Marcelle exclaimed, her oiled hand pulling him up the long slope towards release. 'Do you have any particular young lady in mind?'

'Yes,' he sighed, his legs wide apart in his excitement and his belly quivering. 'A friend of mine – her name is Madeleine and she is very pretty. She lets me feel her breasts!'

'Does she have nice breasts?'

'They're smaller than yours – she's only sixteen – but they're nice to play with.'

'And does she play with you as I am doing now?' Marcelle asked.

'She won't touch me – I don't know why. I tried to push her hand down the front of my trousers while I was feeling her breasts, but she pulled it away. Why do you think she did that?'

'Because she was not aroused and so her fear or her modesty prevented her from taking hold of you. But like all girls of that age, she must be dying of curiosity to see what you have hidden in your trousers. You must play with her breasts with more delicacy until you arouse her, and then she will let you touch her between the legs – and she will want to play with you.'

Jean-Louis was trying to imagine what it would be like if Madeleine played with his stem, as Marcelle was doing. He tried to picture her with her blouse wide open and her soft little breasts on show to him, her hand massaging him – and perhaps her skirt up and her knickers down to let him see the slit between her thighs . . .

'Oh, oh, oh,' he moaned, and two pearly drops leaped from his throbbing part and fell on Marcelle's hand – the last of his youthful endeavour.

'There!' she said, grinning in triumph now that she was sure that she had exhausted his capabilities for that day. 'You must rest for a few minutes before you leave, Jean-Louis.'

The meagreness of his output had no relation to the intensity of the sensations he had experienced. He lay limply on his back, his face pale and his chest heaving. In Marcelle's hand his pride shrank rapidly until it slipped out of her oiled palm. She was satisfied at last that she had brought his interest in her body to a natural conclusion and that he would not approach her again – but to be safe, she lay face-down and with her legs close together. Her pleasant fatigue soon carried her into a light sleep.

A quarter of an hour passed before Jean-Louis sat up slowly and looked at her. He wasn't sure how many times he had done it with her, but he knew that it was enough. Not any amount of fondling the cheeks of her bottom or, if she had been on her back, no amount of playing with her breasts would stiffen him again that day. He got up from the mattress quietly so as not to disturb her sleep and went to the cupboard. There was a towel with which he wiped the oil from his body before putting on his clothes and leaving, without a word of farewell.

Marcelle drifted into a deeper sleep, contented beyond measure by the boy's unexpected virility. She had been wrung out sexually to the limit that morning and was totally satisfied, mentally and physically. No one came to disturb her in her solarium and, when she awoke three hours later, the afternoon sun had moved far enough to the west for her to be lying in the shade. But, alas, the overlong exposure to its rays during her sleep had turned the backs of her legs to a painful scarlet and her tender bottom was so red and sore that she was unable to sit comfortably for a week – and what was worse, unable to lie on her back.

Chantal's new lover
teaches her to love

Chantal Lamartine was blonde and beautiful – not the bleached blonde of young women trying to improve on what the good God gave them, nor the light brown which is claimed as blonde by women born with that colour of hair – but a delicate golden shade which made her admirers think that the sun itself had touched her hair – that she was in some way a true daughter of Apollo. Those who observed more closely noted that on her forearms there was the faintest trace of blonde fluff, a detail so endearing that more than one young man, kissing her hand politely when she was wearing a sleeveless evening frock, had so far forgot himself as to attempt to extend his kiss from the back of her hand up her forearm. Naturally, they were laughingly rebuked for so exuberant a breach of polite manners, though in a way that made them feel pleased with themselves – for Chantal knew how to please men.

It is possible that the same providence that tinted her hair blonde and adorned her arms also intended that her legs should be touched with blonde. If so, that was a secret between Chantal and her maid, for her legs were always as smooth and fine as satin. Of course, there were those admirers who let their minds range over other intriguing possibilities – for with so great a beauty it was almost impossible not to speculate about her charms – and these admirers were given to wonder from time to time what was the colour of the little fleece where Chantal's smooth legs joined under her clothes.

There was no way in which they could satisfy their curiosity, these admirers who would have liked to undress

Chantal and kiss her little fleece. She was the particular friend of André Belfort, and had been for almost three years. Those others who were attracted to her for her vivacious personality and great charm – and by the desire to unveil her slender body and possess it in a day-long acts of love-making – these people tormented themselves in vain. They were not above making her certain offers in secret, as one would expect, offers which would have seemed almost irresistible to another woman. But Chantal remained infuriatingly faithful to André.

One of her most devoted admirers was André's good friend Nicolas Darcy. He made no secret of his feelings – whenever he and Chantal met he kissed her hand with excessive delicacy and paid her extravagant compliments. He more than once proposed that she should detach herself from André and put herself under his protection, for he adored her, and so on. He even said these things when André was present, and seemed serious about what he was saying. Nevertheless, there was never anything between Nicolas and Chantal – the most she ever bestowed upon him was a warm smile and a pat on the cheek. She had good reason for her loyalty to André – he kept her in style, and it would have been foolish of her to risk that. Nicolas and others like him had no choice but to lavish on lesser women the desire they felt for Chantal and quench their passionate longings between other thighs than hers.

The situation changed completely and without warning when André, having remained a bachelor until he was twenty-nine, decided to marry a girl his family thought very suitable. He confided this information to Nicolas one evening when they were having dinner together in a restaurant. Nicolas was so surprised that he put down his fork with a tender morsel of best veal on his plate instead of in his mouth.

'But what of Chantal?' he asked, not even congratulating André on his forthcoming nuptials.

'We shall part as friends,' said André, shrugging his shoulders. 'There will be an arrangement to relieve her of any immediate financial problems. As for the future – she

148

is young and beautiful – she will be able to look after herself.'

'You sound so callous!' Nicolas exclaimed, 'You and she have been lovers for so long – to the envy of many. You adore her!'

'That may be, but there are times when it is necessary to be realistic in one's assessment. As you say, Chantal is adorable – she makes love better than any woman I have ever known – a thousand times better than my little goose of a wife will, I should think! My wedding-night will be like a school-room, I imagine, with me teaching her which bit goes where and what for. She is only eighteen, you know, and my guess is that she is a virgin. According to my Mama, her Mama insists that dear little Ambrosine is untouched by human hand! Nevertheless, the advantages of this marriage are very considerable, believe me. There was sadness in my heart when I made the choice, but there was never any doubt as to what the choice would be.'

Nicolas thought about the possible developments that might ensue and drank a little wine to give himself a moment. Was it possible, for instance, that when André left her, Chantal might accept himself as her lover? She knew of his feelings towards her, but whether she took him seriously was another matter. All the same, a bold man steps forward and puts his fortune to the test – and this Nicolas intended to do. After a little interval, naturally – it would be insensitive to rush in on Chantal while she was perhaps still shedding a tear for André. On the other hand, it would be far from safe to leave matters for long – Nicolas knew half a dozen men who would present themselves at Chantal's door when they heard of André's intention to marry.

With such thoughts in his head already, imagine Nicolas' pleasure – and surprise – when André suggested, in plain words, that he should take over Chantal.

'You've always had warm feelings for her,' said André with a knowing grin. 'You'd have had your hand up her clothes a long time ago if she'd let you. Now's your chance – I'm vacating the premises, so to speak, and you can be the next occupier if you wish.'

'She might not want me.'

'Yes, she does. I asked her.'

'What?' Nicolas exclaimed in amazement.

'Look here, my friend – when I made my decision the first thing I did was to have a frank talk with Chantal. She is a very intelligent woman and we've always been straight-forward with each other. She was hurt and disappointed, as you'd expect, but she understood my position.'

'What has this to do with me?'

'We talked about her future. I told her what I was prepared to do by way of a goodbye present and suggested that she started looking around for someone else. Your name came up in the list of possibles.'

'This is extraordinary, to be discussed in such a way! What did she say?'

'She thought about it for a while and said that you'd do very well – if you are seriously interested and not just flirting about. Are you seriously interested in her? She's fairly expensive, but well worth it.'

'I don't know what to say! I've never heard anything like this.'

'Don't let your surprise divert you too long. There is a serious rival on the scene – or at least there will be when he hears the news.'

'Who?'

'Jean-Jacques Laugier. At present the advantage lies with you – you're under thirty and he's over forty – you're not bad-looking, and he has a face like a frog. But don't rejoice too soon – he has a formidable reputation with beautiful women – he can charm their clothes off, they say. He's got more money than you and he's interested in Chantal.'

'How do you know that?'

'Because she always tells me when another man makes an approach – flowers delivered to her apartment, little notes, invitations to grand occasions.'

'He does all this, this Laugier, the evil beast? How dare he even think of laying a finger on her!'

'He'll lay far more than a finger on her if he gets the

chance. You remember the evening when we were dining with Michel Brissard and his wife – there were about twenty of us altogether. You were there with that simpering little Carpillon girl you picked up somewhere – god knows what you wanted with her! I'm sure she bursts into tears every time she has it up her.'

'Mademoiselle Marie-Claire Carpillon,' said Nicolas formally, letting it be seen that he was offended by André's coarseness. 'A very worthy and presentable young lady. Her father is . . .'

'I know what her fat and boring father is!' André interrupted. 'Anyway, at that dinner Laugier somehow managed to get himself seated next to Chantal. And would you believe it – he had his hand in her lap before the first course was on the table!'

'She told you that?'

'She said his grip was so strong that she had little red marks from his fingernails right through her clothes. But she imagined that bit – I couldn't see any marks on her thighs when I took her to bed afterwards.'

Into Nicolas' mind there came a picture of beautiful Chantal sitting on a bed, her frock up round her waist and her elegant underwear on show, while André had his head down between her slender thighs, pretending to look for fingernail marks and in reality kissing the insides of her thighs to arouse her. Now he, Nicolas, could be the man with his lips pressed to the satin skin of Chantal's thighs . . . the prospect was so very exciting that Nicolas' stalk stood hard and upright in his trousers. And then a less pleasing thought entered his mind.

'Chantal tells you everything about other men?' he asked.

'Always,' André replied, smiling at him. 'Even about your little attempt to interest her. Forgive me, but I had to laugh.'

'André, it was all a mistake!' said Nicolas quickly. 'I didn't know that Chantal was in the room – it was an accident.'

'At least it gave her an opportunity to observe what you have to offer. That may have been pointless at the time, but it is of some interest now.'

151

André was referring to an occasion when, at a New Year's Eve party when most of the guests were drunk, Nicolas had gone so far as to allow his trousers to become *accidentally* undone and his spigot – in a condition of furious erection – to protrude nakedly, in a corner where only Chantal could observe it. Reminded of the incident now, Nicolas could only blush.

'I hope that Chantal has forgiven me for that little incident,' he said, 'It was entirely accidental, I assure you.'

'Of course, *accidental*! She didn't think any worse of you for it – she was amused at the time. You must remember that with someone as desirable as her men are always trying to make an impression on her – and sometimes they go to astonishing lengths! Not that your length is astonishing, from what she told me.'

'André!'

'Sorry – I couldn't resist the joke. At least she knows what you've got, which is more than she knows about Jean-Jacques Laugier.'

'You are laughing at me!' Nicolas said indignantly.

'What you did was comical, my friend. I remember showing mine to a girl I wanted – but neither of us was more than twelve at the time. But that's beside the point. Do you want Chantal or not?'

'Naturally, I want her!'

'Then present yourself at her apartment in the Rue Bayen and take her to bed. You will enjoy yourself more than you have in your life before. Afterwards you and she can discuss your arrangements at leisure.'

'You're not serious! Knock at her door and take her to bed – it can't be that simple!'

'The important things in life are usually very simple, in my experience. It is only idiots that make them complicated. As soon as you've had her, she will be yours.'

'When do you suggest that I call upon her to . . . commence proceedings?'

André stared at him across the table as if he had taken leave of his senses.

'As soon as we've finished dinner, of course. She's waiting for you.'

'You mean that you've said your last goodbyes already?'

'Why do you think I asked you to dinner this evening, Nicolas? It's all arranged for you.'

Throughout the rest of the meal Nicolas found it impossible to think seriously of anything but Chantal. Even the excellent crêpe Suzette hardly gained his attention – he prodded it indifferently with his fork. The last time he had seen Chantal was the previous week. On that occasion she had worn a frock of some fine white material that clung deliciously to her well-shaped breasts. Her blonde hair was cut short and brushed back over her ears, her dark blue eyes aglow with *joie de vivre*. Since then she had received bad news from André, of course, and no doubt needed to be comforted with kisses and little caresses – and eventually by that intimate embrace which is the true solace of pretty ladies left abandoned.

At the end of the meal Nicolas drank a little glass of cognac with André and thanked him cordially for all he had done. They shook hands and left the restaurant in separate taxis – André heading for who knows where, and Nicolas en route for the adventure with Chantal which he had many times dreamed of but never truly expected to embark upon.

And yet . . . as he sat in the back of a taxi rattling along the Avenue des Ternes, his mood was undergoing a change – a disconcerting and most unwelcome change. His male part drooped limply inside his underwear, in spite of the fact that there was every prospect of it being between Chantal's beautiful legs within the hour.

The fact was, Nicolas realised at last, that his friend André had unburdened himself of an inconvenient mistress by handing her over as if she were a suit of unfashionable cut he couldn't wear again. Or to look at it another way, Mademoiselle Chantal was planning to exchange lovers as casually as she might change her silk underwear – André off, Nicolas on, with no more ado than that! Seen in this light, the situation was profoundly unsatisfactory to any man of pride.

'Rue Bayen,' the taxi driver announced. 'What number do you want?'

153

'I'm not sure now that I want to get out here,' Nicolas told him. 'Turn round and take me back to the Place de la Concorde, and then back here again. That will give me time to think.'

'You're paying,' the driver said indifferently, turning eastwards again.

In his silent and uncomfortable deliberations Nicolas reached a stage at which the proposed love-affair between himself and Chantal strongly resembled a business arrangement. The consideration did not please him in the least – it made him a little angry to think of her in the same terms as the young women in a certain private establishment he sometimes visited – an agreed price for specified services. His feelings towards Chantal, he realised, were too sincere for it to be comfortable for him to see her in this way, even if the offer through André was in some ways remarkably similar to that which big-breasted and wide-hipped Judith offered for a few francs in the Maison Suzy.

By the time the taxi arrived for the second time in the Rue Bayen, Nicolas had still reached no firm conclusion. It was useless to go on another tour, for the unpalatable truth was that even if he drove about Paris all night long he would still not succeed in resolving his emotional conflict. In essence it was simple enough – he desired Chantal madly, as he always had, and he welcomed this unforeseen opportunity to secure her intimate friendship and enjoy her charms to the full. On the other hand he detested her for having conveyed, through André, that she was available to him and that his desire could be satisfied, on the appropriate terms. To desire and detest a woman at the same time is an awkward and painful predicament in which to find oneself.

What made it worse was that Nicolas knew his position was without reason or logic to support it. Chantal made no pretence of being a woman who gave all for love. Her lack of guile added to Nicolas' irritation – he was angry with her and angry with himself. He paid off the taxi and climbed the stairs to Chantal's apartment.

It was not at all late – only about half-past ten. Even so,

the maid said that she thought that Mademoiselle Lamartine might have retired for the night, but if he would wait a moment, she would go and enquire. That annoyed Nicolas too. After being told by André that Chantal was waiting for him to arrive and make love to her, this little pretence by the maid was ridiculous. He could hardly stand still for impatience until she returned to inform him that Mademoiselle Lamartine was in the very act of retiring for the night, but that she would receive him.

She ushered him into the salon, where Chantal was waiting for him – looking so absolutely radiant that she almost took Nicolas' breath away. She was reclining gracefully on her side on a long sofa, and she wore an ankle-length negligée of ivory silk. With her pale gold hair brushed back and very little make-up on her face, she looked almost like a nineteen-year-old bride tremulously waiting for her husband on the first night of her honeymoon. She stretched out an arm for Nicolas to kiss her hand, and her broad-cuffed sleeve slid back almost to her elbow, revealing a slender forearm with a little bracelet of diamonds about the wrist. Soon I shall kiss the tender inside of that beautiful arm, Nicolas thought in wonder, as he swallowed her bait like a hungry carp snapping at a barbed hook.

'Dear Nicolas,' she said softly, staring up at him with eyes that brimmed with affection and trust, 'I was on my way to bed when Sophie announced you. It is very late for a social call, but I am always delighted to see *you*.'

She sounded so utterly sincere that Nicolas' heart melted. He looked up from the little hand he had been kissing, into her dark blue eyes, and he was ready to swear eternal devotion. He gazed briefly at the rounded little breasts outlined by the silk of her negligée and was ready to assert that he adored her beyond his own life. And so he would swear devotion and assert adoration, he told himself, when he reached the stage of opening her negligée and pressing kisses on those charming breasts of hers.

In the middle of this traditional and banal romanticising, he remembered the true situation and his misgivings about it in the taxi. His annoyance returned doubled – he stood up straight and looked at her with less respect.

'Chantal – I am not here to play a game of pretence. You've been expecting me for the last hour – that's why you're half-undressed. We both know why I am here.'

She stared at him thoughtfully. In the past he had always spoken to her with a certain warm charm – that of a man who is trying to persuade a woman that there was much to be gained by allowing him into her bed. This was the first instance she had experienced of Nicolas speaking bluntly.

'You are angry about something,' she said. 'Why *are* you here, then?'

'I am your new lover,' he informed her categorically. 'You want it, André wants it, I want it. So everyone is satisfied and there is no more to be said.'

'That settles it, does it?' she asked in annoyance. 'You think that all you need do is march into my home and drag me into the bedroom?'

'That's exactly what I think,' he retorted.

'Get out of my sight!' she exclaimed sharply.

She swung her legs off the sofa to sit upright and point dramatically towards the door with a shaking finger.

'Be silent and listen to me,' Nicolas replied with contempt. 'I will not be treated as a complete fool by you and André. I'm not the rich country cousin with a pocketful of money and his handle standing up stiff at the first girl who winks at him!'

'Is that so?' Chantal demanded with great scorn. 'My impression is that your handle not merely stands up but sticks out as well – and in public – even before a girl winks at you! Or have you conveniently forgotten New Year's Eve?'

'I haven't forgotten,' he said, angry that she had brought up that silly episode against him, 'but I've learned a thing or two since then.'

'That girls are not impressed by men who wag their middle fingers at them?'

'What I have learned since then is that I can have you for the asking!'

'You are grossly insulting,' Chantal exclaimed, her

156

cheeks suddenly red, 'and I want you to leave now! Get out!'

She stood up, her elegant negligée gathered closely about her, and would have left the room, but Nicolas seized her by the shoulders and held her still.

'I haven't finished yet,' he said. 'You are going to hear me out, whether you want to or not.'

'There is nothing you can say that I wish to hear – let go of me or I shall call for my maid!'

'You are a hypocrite,' Nicolas told her. 'You don't want me to let go of you at all – you want me to hold you even closer! You want me between your legs so that you can grapple me to you and make me your property!'

'This is monstrous! You must be drunk!'

'I am not in the least drunk. It seems to me that a few moments of total frankness at the beginning of our friendship would help us avoid misunderstandings later on.'

'Friendship – with you? I never want to see you again!'

'So you say – but consider this: if we strip away the pretence and the politeness that screens harsh fact from our eyes . . .' and suiting the action to the words, he let go of her shoulders to hook his hands into the closed top of her negligée and rip it open with one savage pull.

'No!' Chantal gasped, her hands flying up to cover her exposed breasts.

He seized her slender wrists and pulled her hands away, to feast his eyes on the enchanting breasts he had longed to touch for the past three years. They were well worth his sustained admiration, being round and firm, with prominent buds of a pretty dark pink shade.

'. . . in this way we lay bare the truth,' he continued. 'The facts are these – you are the fortunate owner of a commodity for which there is a certain demand. As a consequence, this commodity has a price that is established by the economic laws of supply and demand, as is the price of other commodities offered for sale – coffee, cognac, champagne, for example.'

Chantal was glaring at him with such fury that, if looks could have killed, he would have been struck dead on the

157

spot and fallen to the floor. But instead, he continued to stare at her breasts and continued his diatribe.

'I understand that there is a Monsieur Laugier in the bidding against me, Chantal. His drawbacks are obvious to all – he is ugly, middle-aged, and has a wife and family concealed in some remote suburb. Let us eliminate him from our considerations. That leaves me – and I am able and ready to pay the market price for the commodity I wish to enjoy.'

'Brute! Turk! Cannibal!' Chantal snarled at him.

She struggled to free her wrists and perhaps to smack his face, but her struggles were not fierce enough to achieve that end, only to make her pretty breasts bounce in a tantalising manner.

'I do not wish to buy your commodity outright, as in marriage,' Nicolas went on. 'I propose that I should rent it, like an apartment. Let us agree on a year's lease to start with, and the option of renewing the lease for a further agreed period after that, if that is satisfactory to both parties.'

'I hate you! I detest you!'

Her once-elegant negligée hung down from her waist, held there by a knotted belt. Her golden hair had become a little ruffled in her struggling – in all, she was no longer the gracious lady reposing in tranquillity on a sofa to await her lover.

'Hate me or love me,' said Nicolas, 'what does it matter to either of us? Do you accept my terms?'

'Never! You are a monster!'

'And I am also your new lover – agreed?'

'Why must you make everything sound so brutal and loathsome?'

'Because I choose to. For the last time – do you accept my terms?'

'Yes,' she whispered, her eyes cast down.

'On your knees when you say that!' Nicolas insisted, and forced her downwards by his grasp on her wrists.

'This is too much!' she protested bitterly.

'A few minutes ago you amused yourself by being scornful about an unfortunate incident on New Year's Eve,' he said.

He let go of her wrists, undid his trousers and pulled out the part in question. It was no longer limp – his aggression when he ripped open her negligée had stiffened it most forcefully, and it pointed up boldly at the ceiling.

'Observe it closely,' he told her. 'On New Year's Eve you hardly glanced at it – you can have little idea of its size and strength. Now is your opportunity to familiarise yourself with it – and for the best of reasons! It was an object of derision to you not long ago, but it has now become an object of supreme importance to you, in your changed circumstances.'

'I despise you!' Chantal exclaimed, refusing to look at his protruding handle.

'That is your privilege. But I tell you openly and with all due warning that I intend to gratify this part of me you despise in an amazing variety of ways, using all parts of your body for the purpose. Not only the obvious one which André came here to make use of, but parts of you which perhaps you never imagined could be used by a man to gratify himself. That is my privilege.'

'You are a beast!' she cried out. 'A pervert!'

'Call me what you like – our bargain is made. Prove to me that you have accepted me fully as your lover by kissing the part you despise.'

Chantal stared up into his face, saw the determination there, and shuffled closer to him on her knees. She took hold of his upright stem and kissed its flushed head.

'I am the master here,' said Nicolas. 'Do you understand that?'

She nodded.

'Good,' he said. 'You know what I want.'

Indeed, Chantal had understood well enough that when he told her to *kiss* his swollen stalk he intended more than a chaste and gentle touch of her lips. She opened her mouth and let his long spout slide inside.

'Ah, yes,' said Nicolas softly, 'you amused yourself by deriding it – now you may amuse me by licking it.'

This was certainly not the first time in her life that Chantal had gratified a lover by taking his stem into her mouth. But to be engaged in this now and in these circumstances, her negligée round her hips and probably ruined

159

from the way Nicolas had wrenched it open, was very far from what she had expected of her first time with him. She had anticipated a tender and loving approach from Nicolas, that was why she had undressed and put on the expensive ivory silk, to give a touch of first-night glamour to the occasion – perhaps even a slight ambience of innocent young love! If anyone were to kneel, it ought to be Nicolas, she felt, as he kissed the insides of her thighs while she lay gracefully back on the sofa. That was how it should have been – not this assault on her dignity.

But as she knew, men are moody creatures at the best of times. Something – she had no idea of what it could be – had upset Nicolas and made him angry. He was determined to make use of their first encounter to assert his masculinity in the most brutal and ridiculous ways he could think of. Well, if that's how he wanted it . . . who-ever paid the pianist's wages was entitled to arrange the programme of music. For the present, at least.

She used her wet tongue more skilfully than any of the young women at the Maison Suzy who had performed this little service for him. His knees began to shake and he moaned lightly, his hands reaching for her bare shoulders to steady himself.

'Now you know who is master here,' he gasped, hardly able to speak rationally. 'We shall get on well together if you remember that.'

Chantal made no reply. Her mouth was fully occupied, it was true, but apart from that, there was no sense in replying to what he said – it was male vanity speaking, the blind pride of his standing part, urged on by the feelings racing through him from what her tongue was doing to him. Another second or two would see his pride deflated.

'Ah!' he wailed, as his passion was released in a sudden surge.

Ready for this moment, Chantal pulled her head back quickly and worked his pump-handle by hand, so that he squirted his ecstasy over her bare breasts. He shook and swayed, so violent were his sensations and clung to her. Chantal gave him no respite, but used his handle with great vigour to drain him of emotion.

When the shaking in his legs subsided to a mere tremble, Nicolas shuffled backwards until he found an arm-chair and collapsed into it. He was still breathing heavily, his wet pink column standing up out of his open trousers. He stared at Chantal with eyes that were slightly unfocused – she was on her knees where he had left her, the traces of his passion trickling down between her breasts. She looked back at him curiously, waiting to see if his mood had changed now that she had short-circuited his electricity supply.

'You are my slave,' he said at last. 'You will be obedient when I desire to make use of your body.'

Chantal said nothing. She stood up and undid the tie-belt round her waist, so that her hanging negligée fell to the carpet. She was not completely naked under it, as Nicolas had assumed. Whether her intention was to appear a trifle virginal, a touch coquettish – or a hint of both together – she was wearing loose-legged knickers that were a confection of white ninon and Alençon lace.

'You're entitled to see the rest,' she said, her voice calm.

She slipped the knickers off and sat down in a chair opposite Nicolas, her knees and silver-slippered feet apart, to afford him a perfect view of the blonde-curled delight between her thighs.

'Enchanting!' Nicolas sighed. 'As beautiful as I always imagined!'

Who but a monster could have been angry with a beautiful woman who so freely bared to his gaze that most private and tender part of her body in which he could take his delight whenever he chose? And yet, even while he stared at her enticing blonde treasure, Nicolas began to wonder how many times André had split that golden peach for his delight. A thousand times? Two thousand times? More? Not that there was any sign that it had been abused or even over-used – or, for that matter, that it had ever been used at all! Chantal's tender entrance was as delicate and pretty as that of a girl of fifteen. Yet knowing André and his appetites, Nicolas was certain that he had pierced that innocent-looking morsel at least twice a day on most days of the week – and perhaps much more often than that!

Nicolas' face flushed with anger again. He leaped to his feet, determined to assert himself again, to try to free himself from the painful emotions that rose unbidden and unwanted in his breast. He took hold of Chantal, not in the least tenderly, and made her get down on her hands and knees on the carpet. Her pretty breasts hung forlornly beneath her, uncaressed and unkissed, her round and soft bottom exposed to Nicolas. He knelt close behind her and thrust his reinvigorated stalk into her blonde-haired alcove, with no more care or consideration than if he had been putting a brass key into a door-lock. Chantal did not complain at this rough usage – but she turned her head to stare at him over her shoulder, a look of piteous distress on her beautiful face that would have softened a less obdurate heart than Nicolas' and brought tears of compassion to eyes less blinded by anger than his. He held her very tightly by the hips while he lunged in and out, glorying in the position of domination he had over her.

'You have the pleasure of entertaining me in your belly for the first time,' he sighed loudly.

'Be gentle!' Chantal moaned, her body shaken by his heavy lunging.

'Gentle? What a strange thing to say at a time like this! Gentleness is for the very young discovering the mysteries of love in each other – it is not for people like you and me, my dear Chantal – we have both known many lovers and we know that love has no mysteries at all.'

'Not for you, perhaps!' she exclaimed.

'Love is a question of skin sliding on skin, of hardness piercing softness, of nerves stimulated until involuntary spasms intervene,' he gasped. 'There is no mystery for us.'

'Love is more than that!' Chantal insisted. 'Much more!'

The irony of the situation was perceived by neither of them. Chantal, whose way of life depended on making her charming body available to a chosen man was convinced in her heart that love was a tender emotion which bound men and women together in bonds that were almost indissoluble. And Nicolas, a romantic in love with her, was denying that love was any more than the gratification of the senses. And while they debated this question, he was mounted on her back and suffering the agonies of the damned in his heart because he was ill-treating Chantal – while she, protesting that love was supreme, was already responding to his tyranny – for all her complaints, the fact was that hardness *had* pierced softness, and little thrills were running through her belly.

As Nicolas approached his crisis he slammed harder against her rump. His fingers sank cruelly into the soft flesh of her hips, his pitiless ram-rod sank ever deeper into her tender burrow – and with a loud cry of triumph he delivered himself of a torrent of passion. His furious strokes made Chantal cry out too – though it was more of a wail than a cry – as waves of ecstatic sensation rolled through her.

As soon as he had finished, he pulled away from her body, as if he were extracting a cork from a bottle of wine. He buttoned his trousers, staring all the time at her blonde-curled aperture, loose-lipped and wet from his violence towards it. In another mood he might have been impelled to touch it gently and with affection, for it had served his purpose well – but not all emotion had been drained from him into the misused and vulnerable alcove he was contemplating. There was still anger in his heart – anger that his love for Chantal had been in some way betrayed by the offer to him of her body. There was an expression of gloating on his face, unseen by her, for her head was hanging and she was sighing a little as she recovered from what Nicolas had done to her – he was gloating over the fact that he had prised open her soft petals of flesh and discharged his passion into her without a thought for her pleasure – or even comfort! He was, of course, blindly unaware that he had pleasured her by accident.

'I shall take my leave now,' he said, getting to his feet. 'Be ready tomorrow morning about ten-thirty and I will call for you. Your negligée is torn, I imagine, from my usage of it – it will give me pleasure to replace it and to buy you a few other items of lingerie.'

Without another word – not even bidding her goodnight – he was gone, leaving Chantal still on her hands and knees on the floor of her salon, her bare bottom in the air, asking herself whether Nicolas was entirely sane.

So began, in this atrocious manner, the love-affair between the two of them. In public Nicolas behaved towards her with such tender devotion that all her friends envied her so attentive lover. She appeared in elegant new day clothes and evening frocks from the most expensive couturiers in Paris, she wore diamonds at her throat and wrists. Never had she looked more beautiful – her delicate skin bloomed with health and her pale gold hair had a sheen that reduced men to wondering silence and women to sharp jealousy.

They were to be seen everywhere together – at balls and parties, at the theatre and the opera, in restaurants and nightclubs, at fashion shows and at the races. Their private entertainments were utterly different from what their friends imagined – Nicolas did not demonstrate his regard for her in the traditional ways – he did not caress her and kiss her breasts as a prelude to lying lightly on her enchanting body to slide delicately into her. On the contrary – after long and enjoyable outings together, no sooner had Chantal's bedroom door closed behind them than Nicolas was likely to seize her by the nape of the neck and throw her roughly on to the bed, on her face with her legs kicking in the air. In an instant he would flick up the back of whatever elegant frock she was wearing and tear her flimsy knickers from her body with a brutal hand. *No, no!* Chantal would sob as she heard the tearing sound of her silk underwear snatched from her body – but to no avail – Nicolas' thick and heavy peg would already be ramming itself into the soft folds of flesh between her exposed thighs, as if it would split them apart!

Helpless and humiliated, poor Chantal lay face-down, pinned to the bed by Nicolas' crushing weight. She jerked like a rag doll to the rhythm of his cruel thumping into her belly, until a sudden hot gush signalled the arrival of his crisis. And, though Nicolas was always too preoccupied with his own triumphant ravishing of her body to notice anything else – Chantal's jerking movements under him would reach a climax as she too sobbed in ecstasy. That this should happen in such improbable circumstances was a source of surprise to her every time. However, it was most enjoyable and she disguised it as much as possible from Nicolas, thinking that if he once realised that he was giving her pleasure, he would become angrier and not avail himself of her body again.

And so, as soon as his weight was lifted from her back Chantal got up at once and pulled her frock down to cover her bare bottom, as if ashamed! Nicolas would laugh at what he thought to be her confusion and sit in a chair to rest, the instrument with which he had just ravaged her lolling out of his open trousers as it lost its stiffness.

'Take your clothes off, Chantal – I want to see you naked,' he invariably commanded at this point.

To plead with him, she had learned, merely incited his harsh desires further. At any show of reluctance he would raise his voice and insist, until she gave way and removed all her clothes and stood beautiful and naked in front of him. She had come to know well the gloating expression that disfigured his otherwise handsome face as he stared at her body.

'Bring your knickers here,' he ordered.

'Not again, Nicolas – I beg you!'

'At once!' he said fiercely.

She picked up the scrap of torn crêpe de chine from where he had dropped it on the bed and brought it to him. She knew what he wanted her to do – this was a routine he had forced her into many times. His eyes glared at her, daring her to defy him, until she was compelled to drop her own eyes, unable to bear the intensity of his stare.

She knelt humbly between his spread knees and wrapped the thin folds of her ruined knickers round his by now deflated affair, so that she could massage it slowly through the fine material. While she was doing this Nicolas amused himself by fondling her breasts, having stripped her of her frock – and he handled them as roughly as if they were the worn-out and flabby breasts of a fifty-year-old whore instead of the delicate little playthings they were.

In due course his baton became upright again and

165

Chantal massaged it more quickly through the flimsy crêpe de chine to end her ordeal by bringing on his emission. Once or twice she had succeeded – he had become so aroused that he had let matters go too far and, even as he tried to halt her moving hand, he had squirted into the torn knickers in which his spike was enfolded. But far more usually his hand gripped her wrist in time and stopped her. Chantal's eyes pleaded silently with him to spare her this, but he only smiled a thin and cruel smile in return. She freed him from the crêpe de chine, bent her long and slender neck, and took his engorged baton into her wet mouth.

'Do it to me, my little slave!' he commanded.

With the gleam of unshed tears in her dark blue eyes, Chantal used her tongue on the exposed head of his projection, until he was gasping and twitching in his chair. Her long fingers extracted his dependents from his open trousers, to tug at them gently, slowing their retreat into his groin as his critical moments approached. Eventually, with a cry of *Faster*! his whole body quaked furiously and he spurted into her mouth – for he insisted on using that and not spilling his passion on to her breasts, as he had on their first encounter.

Usually that concluded his interest in her for the time being. If it was the afternoon, he would then sleep for an hour to refresh himself before taking Chantal to some marvellous function for the evening. And if they had returned from an evening's entertainment, then after his emission they would settle down to sleep for the night. His custom in this too was unkind – he fell asleep with his hand clasped between her legs, gripping her blonde-curled mound. The first time he did this Chantal mistook it for a mark of affection, but she came to doubt that very soon and asked him the reason. Nicolas laughed and said that he was protecting his interests in case any intruder tried to enter while he slept.

It was only on the couple of nights a week that he stayed with her all night that she ever saw him naked. For his brief and violent bouts of love-making he never undressed – he merely unbuttoned his trousers and pulled out his

166

baton to impale her on – or to force into her mouth. Yet each time he was with her he would, at some point, not necessarily while he was enjoying her body, make her strip naked and look at her. Very often this took place in the salon instead of the bedroom – to make her feel uncomfortable. There was an afternoon when he made her feel very uncomfortable indeed – attracted either by her cries or by sheer curiosity, her maid entered the salon at the crucial moment! Chantal was on her hands and knees on the oriental carpet, her skirt up over her back and her bare bottom on show, while Nicolas, fully-clothed, was perched above her, slamming into her. They were sideways on to the maid, who stood with a hand to her mouth as she saw Nicolas' thick and heavy instrument stabbing into the blonde-curled lips between Chantal's spread thighs. Nicolas did not hear the maid's gasp as he emptied his ecstatic emotions into Chantal's belly, but Chantal glanced round at the sound of the door and blushed scarlet to know that her maid was watching what her lover was doing to her.

The thought occurred to her one day that Nicolas might treat her with more tenderness if he woke up in the night and found himself aroused – he would be a little confused and disorientated from sleep and his true nature would perhaps be allowed to show itself. She waited for the right opportunity, when he was sleeping in her bed after enjoying her twice between midnight and one in the morning. When the relaxation of his grip between her thighs told her that he was asleep, she turned towards him and took hold of his limp sprig. She tickled it with the lightest of touches and succeeded admirably in what she intended – Nicolas was at full-stretch and throbbing in her hand, as if about to discharge his energy. And in this condition he awoke. Chantal's hope was that he would roll her on to her back and lie on her, his mouth seeking hers, while he pushed into her warm entrance and made love to her in the way she had not enjoyed for so long.

Perversely, he did nothing of the kind. He woke gasping and close to his climax. He put his hands on her shoulders and pushed her swiftly down the bed until her breasts were opposite his belly – and used both hands to squeeze those beautiful breasts round his engorged affair! He thrust fiercely between them and, in only an instant or two, Chantal felt his hot wetness squirt up her chest to her throat, and she groaned in frustration and dismay.

There were days when his desire endured longer – when it survived the face-down ravishment of Chantal on the bed and the excitement of her hot mouth in the chair. On days like these, when his stem grew hard again, he submitted Chantal to the greatest indignity of all. He varied the position – sometimes he would make her lie on her side with her knees drawn up until they almost touched her breasts, sometimes he made her bend forward over the padded back of an arm-chair, so that she was bent almost double – but the purpose was the same. He approached her from behind, ignoring her pitiful little pleas for mercy, his fingers grasped and pulled apart the cheeks of her bottom. For long seconds, while Chantal almost wept in fearful anticipation, he stared with unholy joy at the tiny aperture he had exposed between her cheeks, then he forced his hard and pitiless stalk into it and penetrated her body not by the natural portal but by the back door! Chantal shrieked and shrieked – in vain – as he drove into her and took his savage pleasure. Once she had caught sight of his face reflected in her dressing-table mirror as he did this to her – he had made her get on the bed on her hands and knees on that occasion. She scarcely recognised him – his face was crimson, his eyes bulged out and his mouth hung open – it was as if a demon was riding her back and stabbing into her.

It was Nicolas' own words that set Chantal thinking of revenging herself on so unfeeling and ferocious a lover. With his hand clasped tightly between her legs, he had spoken of keeping intruders away. Naturally, the idea grew in Chantal's mind that someone else should be offered an opportunity to enjoy her beautiful body – someone who would appreciate her and treat her tenderly. She had no lack of admirers to choose from, even now that her affections, as one might say, had been transferred to Nicolas for some months. Jean-Jacques Laugier was still interested in her and sent her little messages from time to time, accompanying huge bouquets of flowers, indicating that he was anxious to take her into his protection the moment she said that she was ready. But with Laugier it would be a more serious matter, she knew, implying the beginning of another long-standing relationship. For the present she thought it sensible to leave Jean-Jacques sighing in unrequited passion and in hope, since her immediate purpose was simply to avenge herself on Nicolas.

After some consideration, she chose Robert Nevers, a handsome man of thirty she had known for a long time. To get him to invite her to his apartment without seeming to was the easiest thing in the world for so intelligent a young woman as Chantal. Robert was unable to believe his good luck in persuading the beautiful and charming Chantal Lamartine to put herself at his disposal! The result was that he excelled himself for an entire afternoon. He undressed Chantal with the tender care she had once known from André, even going down on one knee to roll down her silk stockings for her. He touched her flimsy black knickers with gentle fingers and slipped them off – pressed his lips reverently to her little blonde fleece and murmured a hundred pretty and flattering things. He kissed the tips of her breasts until they were as hard as cherry-stones, he caressed every part of her, his touch on the secret bud between her thighs was as delicate as the fluttering of a butterfly's wing. His male equipment was not thick and heavy like Nicolas', but slim and elegant of appearance – it fitted snugly into Chantal's hand when she stroked it and it slid very comfortably into her entrance when she was ready for it. Between two o'clock and six o'clock that day Robert made love to her three times on her back and once with her sitting over his loins. Each time he guided her skilfully to an enchanting climax, making her sigh with the delight of being a woman loved and not an object with a slit to be used.

When she kissed Robert goodbye and promised to telephone him, it was with real affection and gratitude. The contrast between what he had made her feel and the brutality with which Nicolas took her for his own satisfaction was so enormous that Chantal could hardly believe that, in essence, both of them had been engaged in the same activity – gratifying themselves on her. Robert did it so gracefully – and with as much regard for her pleasure as for his own – while Nicolas simply stuck his vicious thing into her and satisfied himself. On reflection she came to the conclusion that, generous though he was towards her in every way except that of love-making, her friendship with Nicolas was not what she wanted, expected, or could tolerate. A change of lover seemed indicated. Robert Nevers was not in the running, sadly – excellent lover though he was, he had no money. The time had come to explore the possibilities of Jean-Jacques Laugier, she believed. Older and married he might be, but that could well mean that he would be so pleased to have so beautiful a young woman as Chantal at his disposal that he would treat her with very tender care, shower gifts and money on her, and cosset her in bed.

She was not meeting Nicolas that evening, her intention being to have a quiet evening at home – the first for some time – to recover a little from her delightful afternoon with Robert. This would also give her time to think seriously about Laugier. Could he be persuaded, perhaps, to write down some sort of agreement – a *dowry*, one might almost call it – before she let him touch her? If she wore the appropriate frock, with a low-cut neckline, she was reasonably certain he would be panting to get his hands on her breasts in no time at all – and that would make him more susceptible to suggestions about financial arrangements.

With these thoughts revolving in her blonde head, Chantal was very surprised when, about eight o'clock, her maid announced Nicolas. Since the afternoon when she had caught a glimpse of Nicolas ravishing her employer on the salon floor, the maid always blushed when she mentioned his name. Perhaps she was embarrassed by what she had seen, or perhaps her emotions were stirred by it and she could picture herself down on her hands and knees with no knickers, and Nicolas' long and heavy implement sliding into her burrow!

'Nicolas!' said Chantal, her curved eyebrows rising in

surprise as he entered the salon, and she held out her hand for him to kiss.

Evidently he had been dining alone – and dining well! His handsome face was slightly flushed and his gentures a little too emphatic as a result of the wine he had drunk.

'I couldn't stay away from you,' he explained, kissing her hand. 'You may not believe me, Chantal, but I am in love with you – always have been, even when you were with André.'

She looked at him in even greater surprise at that. For months he had been at some pains to make it clear to her theirs was a convenient arrangement – financial favours for sexual favours.

'You love me, Nicolas?' she asked, not believing him.

'To desperation!'

He still held the hand he had kissed. His fingers closed round it tightly and he hauled her unceremoniously out of her armchair and flung her across the room. She fell against the sofa, landing on her side on its cushions. At once Nicolas was at her, as if they were engaged in hand-to-hand combat to the death! He gripped her thighs up under her skirt and wrenched her over so that she was face-down. She wailed as he dragged her skirt up over her bottom and tore her silk knickers away.

'This is love?' she cried.

He was on the sofa behind her, between her thighs, forcing them as far apart as they would go to expose her blonde-curled mound. She felt him slide his bent knees under her belly, raising her loins to make it easier for him to penetrate her – and she wailed again as his great spike stabbed at the tender lips between her legs, parting them roughly and forcing its way deep into her.

'Nicolas – not like this!' she moaned.

His hands were under her and wrenching at the front of her pink silk blouse – she felt the buttons go and heard the silk rip – then he had dragged her breasts out of the top of her chemise, snapping one of her shoulder-straps – and he was handling her with the utmost callousness. His assault on her yellow-haired mound was not of long duration, for he had already been very aroused when he arrived at her

171

apartment – the result of nursing his grievance against her during dinner and the two bottles of wine he had drunk with it. The pace of his barbarous thrusting into her rose to a frenzy and she squealed as his brutal passion flooded her abused belly.

'Chantal – I love you, I love you!' he cried out.

She shook under him, not in protest or in discomfort but in a paroxysm of ecstasy. Forgotten were the little climaxes which Robert had given her that afternoon – in retrospect all that he had done to her seemed more appropriate to a girl of fifteen or sixteen, when set against what Chantal was experiencing now from Nicolas' atrocious desire – the delirium of release that is like dying!

When she could speak again she murmured over her shoulder to him. 'Stay in me, Nicolas – there is something I want to say to you.'

Usually he pulled out of her and pushed her away from him the moment he had satisfied himself. This time he did as she asked, his knees tucked under her belly and his softening limb shrinking gradually inside her.

'Do you truly love me?' she asked.

'It was foolish to tell you that,' he answered. 'You will use it against me.'

'How can you believe such a thing? I'm sorry you didn't tell me long ago – it would have made a difference to us.'

'You mean the first time I made love to you – that evening I dined with André – I had you here on this same sofa.'

'Before then,' she said. 'Remember the party on New Year's Eve – when you showed me your handle sticking out? If only you had said then that you loved me, I would have stroked it for you and kissed you, instead of laughing at you.'

'Chantal! Would you really?'

In all the time that she had been André's friend, André had never once told Chantal that he loved her. He had murmured a thousand times that he adored her, usually when he was lying on her belly and on the verge of delivering his little gift to her. But *love* – that never! Nor, for that matter, had Robert said he loved her that afternoon, even after so much delight. No man had told Chantal that he loved her since she was sixteen, and the boy who had said it was merely trying to get her to open her legs so that he could feel her. And here was Nicolas, who appeared to believe that he was a descendant of the Marquis de Sade, confessing his love! Men were strange creatures.

'How much do you love me?' she asked, snuggling her bare bottom into his lap now that his sprig had wilted and slipped out of her.

He was very willing to tell her, now that the words had slipped out unintentionally, and so he told her at great length and in detail how much he loved her, how long he had loved her, and all the things that men in love feel obliged to say. He did not seem to notice when Chantal's hands felt round her hips and into his lap, to hold his limp affair and stroke it. Or if he did notice, which seems far more probable, he did not object.

'But can *you* ever love me?' he asked eventually.

'And if I did – what then?'

'Chantal, my dearest – you must believe me when I say that I am absolutely serious about this – if I thought that you truly loved me I would ask you to marry me at once.'

'What?' she exclaimed, amazed by his words.

'It is true,' he assured her, 'I swear it!'

'Perhaps,' she said, feeling his spindle growing fatter and harder between her fingers.

'I know what you are thinking,' he said. 'There are those who would laugh at me if I married you – but what of that? If you truly loved me I would be the happiest man in the world and people could say what they liked – it would make no difference.'

Over the years Chantal had been very fond of several men – one at a time, of course – but whether she had actually loved any of them she was not sure. She had missed one or two of them, but she had not been desolated when any of them ceased to be her intimate friend. Nevertheless, she was convinced that love was the supreme emotion of which men and women were capable and she was equally convinced that she would herself experience it one day. Had the day come, she asked herself? She had certainly not loved Nicolas yesterday – she was his dear friend and he maintained her in 'style, but his sadistic treatment of her made it impossible to entertain any kind of tender emotion towards him. That, when all was said, was why she had betrayed him so very pleasantly and so very thoroughly with Robert that very day.

And yet – five minutes ago Nicolas' ravaging of her had given her a climactic release so profound that she had been shaken to the foundations of her being. Nor was this the first time – his brutality spoke wordlessly to a primitive urge hidden deep in her soul – an urge she would have been ashamed to have admitted to, for it responded only to the outrageous and uncivilised. But when it did respond – when Nicolas' cruel and unfeeling abuse of her summoned up that urge from its sub-human hiding-place – it racked her with sensations that made the little crisis induced in her by Robert feel like little more than sneezing! So if Nicolas could make her feel as profoundly as that, perhaps she loved him, or so she reasoned.

'Are you telling me the truth, Nicolas – would you really marry me?'

'Without a moment's hesitation – if you loved me half as much as I love you.'

His male affair was long and stiff in her manipulating hands. She released it to grip the cheeks of her round bottom and pull them apart to show Nicolas the little knot of muscle between them.

'Put it in me – if you want to,' she whispered.

He gave a long sigh of pleasure and, a moment later, his thick piston forced its way into Chantal's forbidden aperture with barbarous strength and insistence. His hands replaced hers on her bottom, wrenching the cheeks apart as he stabbed into her hard and fast. For a moment or two Chantal squealed in pain, but fell silent as a huge wave of ecstasy gathered in her belly and began to roll towards the shore, where it would break in a crash of white spray.

'Nicolas, Nicolas!' she moaned, hardly able to speak for the sensations that were about to destroy her. 'I love you!'

174

She meant it, too. At that moment she was utterly sure that this is what she wanted – this atrocious misuse of her beautiful body that brought her such profound and perverse ecstasy.

'Chantal – I love you!' Nicolas sobbed, lunging furiously.

The well-matched couple

'Bonjour, Madame,' the concierge greeted Diane Guichard warmly as she entered the apartment building in the middle of the afternoon.

Madame Guichard was her favourite tenant, a fine-looking woman in her middle thirties whose comings and goings lent a certain distinction to the building. It was generally understood that she was a widow, for no Monsieur Guichard had ever been in evidence, but this was no more than surmise, since Madame Guichard herself was silent on the subject. Whatever the truth of it, her income was evidently more than adequate, as could be seen from the fact that she occupied the best apartment in the building, one floor up from the street, and the equally impressive fact that she wore beautiful clothes from expensive couturiers. On this particular windy autumn afternoon she looked magnificent in a close-fitting coat of black vicuña, with deep trims of astrakhan on the cuffs and hem.

She returned the concierge's greeting with a nod and a little smile of acknowledgment. She found the goodwill of Madame Blanc the concierge most useful on occasions and tipped her regularly and generously in order to ensure that any little favours she required would be forthcoming at once.

There trotted across the pavement behind her Madame Guichard's current gentleman friend. He had been paying off the taxi and he was encumbered with a dozen neatly-tied packages. Obviously he had accompanied Diane Guichard on a shopping expedition, the concierge told herself – after all, that was what gentlemen friends were for. She

176

greeted Monsieur Marquand politely and wondered, for the hundredth time, what were the attractions which Madame Guichard held for him.

She was good-looking, naturally, but in a slightly forbidding way that would not have been to the taste of many men. She was perfectly-groomed, that went without saying, visiting her hairdresser and manicurist never less than three times a week. There could be little doubt that she was amply experienced in those intimate activities in which men fully expected to indulge themselves at various hours of the day and night. Yet none of that seemed to explain the friendship between her and Yves Marquand, at least to the concierge's mind.

He was an extremely handsome young man – and one with plenty of money to spend, if he accompanied Madame Guichard on her shopping trips. With a good face and a full purse he could have had his pick of ten thousand beautiful young Parisians – and for some reason he had chosen Diane Guichard. To the concierge's experienced eye she was ten years older than he was, and she was by no means always good-natured. There were times when her temper got the better of her and she spoke very sharply to whoever had incurred her disfavour – and also to anyone else who happened by chance to be in the vicinity.

Love is a great mystery, the concierge thought, shrugging her plump shoulders as the lovers went up the stairs towards the first-floor apartment. From past experience she knew that they would probably stay up there for the next few hours, until it was time for him to take her out to dinner. In the six months or thereabouts that he had been Diane's regular visitor, he had never once stayed the night with her, that the concierge knew for certain, for she paid particular attention to her tenants' night-time visitors. Information of that sort was sometimes most valuable, she had found. More than once in her years as a concierge she had been encouraged by generous gifts of money to forget that a certain man or a certain woman had ever set foot inside her building. On one memorable occasion the inducement to forget had been very large, when serious matters had been involved and it was a question of being

177

unable to identify a particular man for the police. Her savings had benefited considerably from that little episode of forgetfulness and, when the time came for her to retire from the cares and duties of being a concierge, she would be able to live comfortably. Apart from being a great mystery, love was also very profitable, she had found.

If young Monsieur Marquand never stayed overnight with Madame Guichard, then evidently he and she made love during the daytime. As, for instance, now, Madame Blanc said to herself as she returned to her own little room just inside the street-door of the building. By now the young man had put down the expensive packages he was carrying and Madame would have taken off her beautiful coat. What frock she was wearing under it, who could say – but whatever it was, the young man would surely be helping her out of it. She would be wearing silk underwear, of course – the concierge was utterly certain that a lady like Madame Guichard wore only the finest and most delicate silk next to her skin. That too would be removed and she and the young man would be in bed, doing what men and women do in bed together.

Madame Blanc, who had been widowed by the War, had pleasant enough memories of what she and her late husband had done together in bed. When they were first married, Henri worked in a furniture factory not very far from where they had set up home. Not content, it seemed, with his nightly enjoyment of his young wife's charms, Henri Blanc had the habit of dashing home at midday. The workers were given a break of only half an hour and so his daytime performances were of necessity hurried, though no less pleasing for that. There was no time to undress and go to bed – Henri bent her over the dining-table, flicked her skirts up and her long drawers down and did his business rapidly from the rear. Then with a loud and smacking kiss on her bare rump, he was off again and struggling to fasten his trousers as he went speedily down the stairs from their top-floor apartment to the street.

Madame Blanc had found it enjoyable and comforting to be wanted so frequently by her husband and she encouraged him in every way she could think of. On Sundays she went to early Mass at St Médard down the road, while Henri, who was a disbeliever, stayed in bed. By the time she returned she always found him up, though still in his night-shirt, making coffee for them both. They drank it at the table and ate the fresh bread-rolls she had bought on her way back from church – at that solid table which supported her through their weekday episodes, the table at which another appetite was slaked besides that for food. After a while Henri would begin his nonsense.

'Have you been thoroughly blessed by the priest?' he asked with a grin.

'You know that I have.'

'Was this hairy little thing included in the blessing?' he demanded, his hand up her skirts to grasp her between the legs.

'The good father does not do things by halves,' she said, opening her legs wide. 'His blessing is inclusive, I am sure.'

'Then this bit of warm rabbit-skin I'm holding is holy – is that what you're telling me?'

'Whether it's holy I can't say,' and she grinned back at him. 'At least it has been blessed along with the rest of me.'

By then his baton was standing up stiffly under his loose night-shirt, holding it up above his lap.

'Then as your husband it is only right that I have a share in this blessing. Come to bed and let me take my share.'

She went with him very willingly and by a deep insertion and vigorous movement he enjoyed as much as he could of the blessing that had been bestowed on her – though perhaps if the priest had got to know of this unorthodox way of passing on his benediction, he would have objected strongly.

All that was a long time ago. The son produced by Henri's frequent attentions to his wife's rabbit-fur was grown up and married himself. Madame Blanc's daughter was still with her, though she had a job and a boyfriend. It's different for the rich, Madame Blanc thought, looking up at the ceiling above which was the apartment where her favourite tenant and her friend were together – Madame Guichard invites her men friends to provide her with a little diversion when she feels like it, and she takes good care not to be made pregnant – that would ruin her elegant life.

If the concierge could by some miraculous means have seen through her ceiling and the parquet floor of Diane Guichard's apartment, she would have been astounded by what was going on. She would have had good reason to repeat that *love is a great mystery*, but this time she would have spoken the words with shock and incredulity.

The lovers had paused on the landing while Diane searched through her white glacée leather handbag for the key. Her maid was in, she knew, but it pleased her to assert her self-sufficiency by unlocking the door herself and not ringing to be admitted. Inside, in the small entrance hall, she waited in silence for Yves to put down the packages he was carrying and remove his grey homburg hat. She was a tall woman, elegant of figure for all that she was as tall as Yves himself, and she stood motionless, her arms a little out from her sides and her handbag in one gloved hand. Yves stood near to her and opened the concealed buttons down the front of her beautiful black coat, took her handbag and then, as she turned slowly until her back was to him, he slipped the coat off her shoulders and down until her arms were free of it.

'Leave it there,' she said indifferently. 'Thérèse can put it away later.'

Yves shrugged himself out of his own overcoat, draped it over the hall-table with the vicuña coat and picked up the packages. Diane had gone into her drawing-room and sat upright on an armchair of dark red leather, the skirt of her turquoise frock hitched up a little to show her silk-clad knees. She was still wearing her hat and black suede gloves.

'Put those things down somewhere,' she said, frowning slightly at the packages as if they were of no interest to her.

Without being sent for, the maid, a plain woman of no more than thirty, entered the room.

'Is there anything I can get for you, Madame?' she asked. 'There have been no messages while you were out.'

'Nothing, thank you,' Diane answered, taking off her

gloves. 'If anyone telephones or calls I am out and you do not know when I shall be back. If I want anything I shall ring for you. Otherwise, I am not to be disturbed.'

'Very good – I understand,' said the maid, and indeed she understood Diane Guichard's ways very well, having been in her service for over two years.

The position at the moment was clear enough to her. Madame's new friend had taken her shopping and bought her some expensive gifts – she was now going to take him into her bedroom for the next hour or so to show him that she was suitably grateful. Not that Monsieur Marquand was all that new – he had been visiting Madame for about six months. That he was still as eager as ever to take her shopping signified that the little episodes they enjoyed together in the bedroom were much to his taste.

Unlike the concierge below, Thérèse had no misconceptions about what went on in Diane Guichard's bedroom. She was in a better position to know the truth, being inside the apartment, where she could hardly fail to overhear things. Nor was she above listening with an ear to the bedroom door if she was in the appropriate mood. But more than that, Madame talked to her quite frankly about her men-friends.

'You seem very silent and a little out of humour, my dear,' said Diane to Yves. 'Why is that?'

He was standing by the window, his face blank of expression. He crossed the room quickly to her and, at her gesture, fell to his knees in front of her.

'How could I be out of humour when I am with you?' he murmured.

'That's better.'

She took his chin in her hand and stared into his eyes.

'You are so very handsome,' she told him. 'When we are out together I can literally feel the waves of envy directed at me by other women. I love that feeling!'

'Oh, Diane – you flatter me!'

'You are too modest,' she said, squeezing his cheeks in her long fingers. 'You are the best-looking man I have ever seen in my life. And yet, I like this modesty in you – it makes it possible for us to create a special bond between us.'

'Yes,' he breathed earnestly, 'a very special bond.'

She laughed, pulled off her close-fitting hat and shook out her brown hair.

'I am going to my bedroom for an hour or so,' she said, stretching her arms above her head as if she were tired, but to make her breasts more prominent under the thin turquoise frock. 'Do you want to come with me or would you prefer to stay here?'

'Let me come with you!' he begged at once.

In the bedroom Diane sat on a chair, crossed her knees and held out her upper foot towards Yves. He was trembling with excitement as he went down on his knees and removed her black glacée leather shoe.

'Your feet are so beautiful,' he murmured, his hand under her heel to support her leg. 'The finely curved arch, the exquisite little toes!'

She ignored his raptures and crossed her knees the other way to offer him her other shoe.

'My feet are a little cold,' she complained. 'Make them warm for me.'

He removed her other shoe, clasped her foot between his palms and massaged it.

'Yes,' he sighed, 'they are chilled by the weather outside. But they will soon be warm and comfortable again.'

He rubbed both of her feet until she told him to stop. He stared at her with a downcast expression, as if he had been deprived of a special treat. Diane gave him a brief smile and asked him to take her stockings off.

If she had done it herself it would have taken five seconds at the most. But Yves made of this simple act an almost religious experience that lasted for over five minutes. He began by reaching delicately under the hem of her short frock with both hands until his fingertips touched her garter. He slid it down to her knee very slowly, and all this time he was looking up into her face, devotion in his eyes and his cheeks faintly pink with suppressed excitement.

The garter was over her knee and he brought it down her well-shaped leg, only his fingertips in contact with it. Then, the garter gone, he felt under her frock again to find her stocking-top and roll it down. This time, by accident, he touched the warm flesh of her thigh for a fleeting moment and blushed a fiery red at the thought of what he had done.

'Be careful!' said Diane sharply, her deep brown eyes holding his gaze while he rolled her silk stocking down to her slim ankles and drew it over her foot.

'Forgive me,' he sighed, 'it was an accident, I swear!'

She rested her bare foot against his thigh and held out the other leg towards him. Still staring into her eyes, Yves put his hand under her frock once more and, perhaps because he was shaking, he felt a little too high and touched smooth skin well above her stocking-top.

'Oh, excuse me!' he gasped, and Diane took hold of his ears and pulled them painfully.

'I told you to be careful! Instead of which you are remarkably clumsy. What am I to think – that your usual delicacy of touch has deserted you or that you are deliberately taking liberties by trying to feel me?'

'Oh no, Diane,' he exclaimed. 'I would never do anything to offend you!'

'Then pay attention to what you are doing,' she said, releasing her hold on his ears.

By concentrating very hard, Yves succeeded in removing her other garter and stocking without incurring her further displeasure. She stretched out her leg, flexed her toes, and kicked him lightly twice where his thighs joined.

'Diane!' he gasped, his face bright red, though he made no attempt to protect himself with his hands as her foot swung forwards and backwards ominously.

'Beware!' she said. 'Do not let that idiotic thing in your trousers mislead you into thinking that you can sully my body whenever you feel the itch to do so. You must control your selfish lust if you are to be anywhere near me. Only I decide when and how I am to be touched – understand?'

'Yes, yes,' he murmured and she gave him one more playful little kick and laughed at the grimace that distorted his handsome face.

'You deserved that,' she said, 'and more! You have exhausted me, dragging me into all those shops.'

183

'I am so sorry! It was thoughtless of me.'

'If you expect me to go out to dinner and then dance with you this evening I must have a little rest first. Or would you deny me that and make me stay awake to listen to your nonsense?'

'You must rest, my darling. Then you will be at your best this evening and so beautiful that I shall die of love for you.'

He was still on his knees before her. She stood up and stroked his hair, much as if he had been her pet poodle.

'Ring the bell for Thérèse,' she said. 'She can undress me so that I can lie down for an hour.'

'Please – let me do it for you! I can do it just as well as Thérèse.'

'Is that so?' Diane asked in doubtful voice. 'The trouble with you, my dear Yves, is that your hands go wandering about where they have no right – as a moment ago you were pretending to take my stockings off and in reality you were attempting to feel inside my underwear and touch me between the legs. How can I trust you after that?'

'You can – I swear it!'

'Perhaps I am a fool, but I shall give you one more chance.'

He was on his feet at once, his face beaming. With the lightest touch in the world he undid the side-fastening of her frock, so skilfully that it was only by looking that she knew he had done it. She raised her arms and he lifted the turquoise frock over her shoulders and head so expertly that not a hair of her perfectly coiffeured head was displaced.

'You are improving,' she said, the faintest touch of approval in her tone to incite him. 'Perhaps you are capable of playing the part of a lady's maid without remembering that you are a male and grabbing for my breasts or trying to force your hand inside my knickers.'

'Yes, Diane,' he babbled, his face shiny and pink with delight and anticipation of what was yet to come.

'Put that frock in the wardrobe,' said Diane, the touch of approval gone as quickly as it came, 'and hang it with care – I do not want to see creases in it.'

That done, he turned from the wardrobe to look at her fully. She was at the dressing-table, standing and bending over to look closely at her face in the big mirror. Yves caught his breath as he contemplated her, she had so intense an effect on him. She was wearing a silk chemise and matching loose silk knickers in an eau-de-nil shade and the fineness of the material left little of her tall and well-kept body to the imagination. She turned from the mirror and gave him one of her rare smiles when she saw the look on his face.

'Am I beautiful, Yves?' she asked, her tone slightly mocking, for she had no illusions about her appearance.

'You are the most beautiful woman in the world,' he replied, without a moment's hesitation, and he meant it.

'I seem to remember that you offered to undress me as well as my maid could – and here I am, standing like a fool in my underwear, though I am dropping with fatigue.'

He was at her side at once, murmuring his apologies. Diane watched him critically as he took hold of the lace hem of her chemise and lifted it above her hips and up towards her breasts. He kept his eyes on her face for as long as she could see him, but when she raised her arms high for him to lift the chemise away and her face was hidden for a moment or two by the upward passage of the thin garment, he could not stop himself from staring at the breasts he had bared. To him they were the most exciting breasts there had ever been on a woman, though the truth was that they had always been flattish and very widely-spaced. The tip of Yves' tongue peeped out between his lips as he stared at the small reddish-brown buds of Diane's breasts. Then the chemise was off and he held it loosely in one hand and Diane was glaring at him with suspicion.

'You are becoming insolent again,' she accused him. 'I warned you!'

'But Diane – I did not touch you! You know that!'

'You were staring at my breasts as if you intended to grab hold of them and feel them,' she said, and put her hands under them and pushed them upwards to make them fuller and more pointed.

185

'How could anyone resist snatching a quick glance?' Yves sighed heavily. 'They attract the eyes as a beautiful flower attracts the bees in summer. But I would never dare put my hands on them, Diane.'

'Do not let your imagination get out of control,' she said. 'Bees in summer on flowers! What you mean is that you'd like to put your mouth to my breasts and suck at them – isn't that it?'

At the suggestion he trembled from head to foot and she laughed softly to herself.

'You still have work to do,' she told him.

His handsome face was scarlet with emotion as he sank to his knees at her feet.

'I warn you for the last time,' she said, 'be very careful indeed now or you will regret it bitterly.'

With the extreme tips of his fingers and thumbs he gripped the waist-band of her eau-de-nil silk knickers and undid the two small white buttons that closed it round her. If he had been in a church at Mass, on his knees before the altar, his mouth open to receive the sacrament from a priest, he could not have been more hushed and reverent than he was at this moment. Diane stood perfectly still, letting him have his few moments of rapture as he began to slide her knickers down over her rounded hips. She saw how intense and fixed was his gaze at her belly as he uncovered it and then, as the silk moved down her thighs, and he saw her fleece of dark-brown curls, he gave a long gentle sigh that contained so much emotion that Diane could hardly prevent herself from snorting in derision.

This was a game she understood very well, this game of pull and push, of discouragements and little encouragements, so that the man in question was kept suspended in a state of frenzy and frustration for as long as he could stand it. After the earlier discouragements, a moment or two of encouragement was in order just now, by her calculation, though it must not be allowed to last too long. So she stood upright and naked, her knickers round her ankles, a cynical little smile on her lips as she let Yves stare at her fleece and endure the agonies of thwarted desire for a little longer.

But when he swayed forward, as if to close the distance between them and kiss her belly, she smacked his face at once, just hard enough to make him aware of her deep displeasure.

'Watch what you are doing!' she said sharply. 'You are dreaming again and trying to take liberties with me.'

'I adore you, Diane, I adore you!' he moaned.

'I know what your adoration amounts to – you thought you would press your mouth against the most tender part of my body and force your slavering tongue inside me,' she said, deliberately fuelling his fervid imagination by her choice of words. 'Is that adoration? I call it selfish lust on your part.'

'Not selfish,' he murmured, his imagination so soaring that he was carried away and spoke too boldly. 'If you let me put my tongue just a little inside you I would give you such pleasure as you cannot believe.'

'How dare you!' she said at once.

She kicked the knickers off her ankles to liberate her feet and then kicked Yves with the sole of her foot where his thighs joined – not hard enough to cause him any real pain, for that was not her way, but enough to make him acutely aware of that part of his body and what it wanted of him.

'Diane – I shall die of love for you,' he moaned.

'And while you are dying of love on my bedroom carpet, I am left standing naked to get chilled – I suppose it doesn't matter what happens to me while you grovel there indulging your sordid fantasies of doing unspeakable things to me with your tongue? Get my lounging pyjamas for me from the wardrobe at once,' and she gave him another little kick in the same place to urge him into action.

The pyjamas were a creation of high fashion, a tunic and wide-bottomed trousers of lilac satin with broad orange cuffs to the sleeves and trouser-legs. To Yves' intense disappointment Diane did not give him another opportunity to savour the blissful moments of staring at her round belly and curls – and her way of denying it to him was cruel. She made him kneel and hold the trousers out for her to step into, but she had one hand twined in his

187

brown hair and the other under his chin, so that she was able to force his head painfully upwards and back. Unable to observe what he was doing, he fumbled a little as he pulled the trousers up her legs and thighs and over her hips. The side of his hand grazed gently over her belly as he pulled the trousers right up and groped for the shiny buttons that held them at her waist. His touch on her flesh was met with an angry hiss from Diane and a painful wrench of his hair.

'You do not trust me,' he gasped, as she forced his chin relentlessly upwards.

'Why should I take chances?' she retorted. 'First you ogle me when you pull my knickers down and then you try to assault me between the legs with your tongue in the most vulgar manner imaginable! I cannot think where you get ideas like that from – you must have associated with some vile people before I met you.'

All the same, however painful it was to have his head almost torn off, he had a very good view of her breasts from below. And again when he held up the lilac tunic for her to slip into.

'I hope that I am at last safe from your unwanted attentions,' she said, turning away from him.

She arranged herself on the bed in an alluring pose – on her side and propped up on one elbow, her ankles crossed and her little bare feet peeping out of the wide bottoms of the trousers. The thin satin of the tunic lay close to her breasts and outlined them nicely. Yves stood staring at her with desperate devotion.

'You may take your clothes off,' Diane informed him.

She watched with complete indifference while he removed his suit and tie, his shirt and underpants, his shoes and socks. When he was naked she pointed to a comfortable chair upholstered in grey velvet that stood facing the bed and not at all close to it. Yves sat down, shaking with excitement. He was completely naked and the woman he adored was staring at him – the sight of him so exposed must surely move her to take pity on him . . .

'As I thought,' said Diane, glancing casually at the pink

188

column rearing up from between his thighs, 'your condition is one I would prefer not to know about. Why do you allow yourself to become aroused so easily?'

'How could it be otherwise, Diane? To be so close to you and to help you undress! To glimpse, even if only for a moment, the beauties of your body!'

'That's a miserable explanation,' she retorted. 'I am looking at your naked body and I am not in the least aroused.'

'What can I say?' he pleaded. 'This is what the sight of your beautiful naked body does to me.'

'That's not the truth,' she said. 'You were aroused before you helped me out of my underwear, long before you saw me naked. You were in that state when you took my stockings off.'

'How do you know that?' he asked in naive surprise.

'Because I kicked you – or have you forgotten? And my toes encountered something hard. You might as well tell the truth – you have been in this condition of arousal from the moment you set foot inside this bedroom, before I allowed you to do anything at all.'

'I beg you not to be angry with me, Diane. I love you so much that it tears my heart in two when you lose your temper with me.'

'Then tell me the truth.'

'The truth is that I have been in this condition ever since we arrived at your apartment and you let me help you take your coat off.'

'What? This monstrous thing of yours has been standing up in your trousers since then – before I allowed you into my bedroom?'

Yves nodded, unable to guess how she would respond, so uncertain was he of her moods and games. Deep down, though he hardly dare admit it to himself, he guessed that she was pleased when he became aroused because it demonstrated her hold over him. But pleased or not, she was quite capable of saying cruel things about his upright part.

'Well,' she said after a pause, 'I suppose that I shall never understand your depraved nature. But there is no

189

point in being angry with you. At the same time, there is no reason why I should be compelled to look at this offensive object which you insist on making stiff for hours on end. Cover it up at once – put my underwear on.'

'Oh my god, I shall die!' Yves moaned, his baton leaping so furiously that he was terrified that he was about to disgrace himself in front of Diane by suffering an involuntary emission, so strongly had her suggestion aroused him.

'Stand up straight and breathe deeply!' she ordered him loudly and fiercely. 'Pull your belly in and put your shoulders back!'

He was so accustomed to obeying her orders that he was off the chair at once. The impending overflow subsided, though it left him shiny with perspiration on his face and chest.

'Put my underwear on,' Diane repeated. 'and control yourself!'

Yves was a thin young man, with practically no hips or backside, and a narrow chest. He was no taller than Diane and not much more than she was around the waist and chest. He was able to get into her discarded knickers and chemise without any great difficulty, though on her they were loose and on him they were a close fit. He resumed his place on the chair, facing the bed, his mind awash with sensations from the silk she had worn.

'That's better,' said Diane, smiling at the incongruous sight. 'Now the wretched thing is concealed, as it should be.'

She settled her head on the pillows and closed her eyes. 'I am tired,' she murmured. 'Sit there without a sound while I sleep for an hour. If you disturb me I shall be annoyed.'

Yves stared at her with devotion and desire. She lay on her side, facing towards him. The way her breasts hung forward to fill out the lilac satin of her tunic made him breathe faster as he caressed her with his eyes. And lower down, the little triangle where her thighs met and where, behind the flimsy material of her trousers, her curly fleece lay hidden! She had let him see it for a few moments when he had taken her knickers off for her and the memory burned within him. Fire raged in his blood and his long spike was twitching inside the knickers that held his loins in a silken grip. His whole body was clamouring and there was a roaring in his brain that he knew he could not ignore forever.

Diane was breathing regularly and lightly, evidently in a gentle sleep. After a while she sighed and turned on to her back, her breasts rolling under her flimsy tunic in a way that made Yves gasp loudly and shiver. It was this scene which, if Madame Blanc down in her concierge's lodge could have seen through the ceiling, would have made her doubt whether she knew anything at all about the intimate relations between men and women. There lay Diane asleep on her bed in her chic pyjamas, not in the least interested in her young lover. And there sat the lover himself, wearing Diane's silk underwear, two metres from the bed. His face was flushed a dark red and he was breathing heavily through his open mouth – the very picture of a man so excited that his critical moment is not far away. Yet he had not touched Diane, except fleetingly and by accident. She had spoken to him with contempt and by flaunting her body and denying it to him she had deliberately humiliated his manhood.

He adored it, of course. This is what excited him, the humiliation and the refusal to let him do more than catch a glimpse of her body. He had been with a dozen or more pretty girls of his own age who were very willing to let him undress them and feel them all over – and lie on their back for him with their legs apart. Not one of them had made him experience the sheer intensity of sensation which Diane could arouse in him without letting him do anything at all. Which goes to prove, if it were ever in doubt, that love is not merely a combination of affection and friction, as cynics claim, but a supremely mysterious affair.

By the time Diane had been sleeping for a quarter of an hour Yves' state of mind – and of body – was critical. His heart thumped almost painfully in his chest and the stiff projection trapped against his belly by Diane's tight-fitting knickers was throbbing in a steady rhythm of its own that announced its forthcoming intentions. In short, Yves was a human bomb with the fuse almost burned away, only moments before the explosion. He got to his feet, shaking from head to toe, and took half a dozen unsteady steps to bring him to the side of the bed. He stared down at Diane, sleeping so calmly, his mind a raging volcano of desire.

Her short tunic had ridden up a little when she turned on to her back. Yves could see a narrow strip of bare flesh between the waistband of her trousers and the lower edge of her tunic. His breath rasped loudly as he contemplated that small glimpse of her and, whether the noise of his breathing penetrated her sleep or not, she mumbled a little and slid one arm slowly up to pillow her head. The movement raised her tunic a little further, so that Yves saw her round belly-button.

His knees buckled beneath him and he fell to the floor, his hands clutching at his middle as outraged nature took its revenge and his upright messenger spluttered out its torrent of words into the silk of the knickers he was wearing. He moaned and cried, racked by long wet throbs that seemed never to end. How long he was down there on the floor gasping for breath there was no way of knowing – it appeared to him to be a very long time – and he felt as if he had been struck by a thunderbolt. So violent had the discharge been that he was not even sure that he would survive the experience and it was almost as if he were sinking slowly into unconsciousness and then into extinction.

But in due course his heart-beat returned to normal and his breathing slowed, the last little thrill of pleasure faded from his belly and his fully satisfied stem lost its hardness and began to sag downwards. Yves recovered sufficiently to crawl across the carpet to the grey armchair and drag himself up into it.

Diane had turned on to her side, away from him, as if even in her sleep she was somehow aware that his crisis was over and she need pay no attention whatsoever to him. He stared in adoration at the round cheeks of her bottom outlined by her pyjamas and even permitted himself the impertinence of thinking for a moment of pressing his spindle into the warm crease between those cheeks. No woman had ever made him as happy as Diane did, he was clear about that – he loved her to distraction and would never part from her. He closed his eyes in contentment and, in spite of the wet and sticky patch of silk against his belly, he fell asleep.

How had it come about, one might enquire, that a good-looking and well-educated young man of independent means had entered into so strange a liaison with Diane Guichard? The truth was that he had not consciously chosen to do so – it was she who had chosen him. They had been introduced by mutual friends at a nightclub and Diane, who was always on the look-out for agreeable young men, made herself extremely charming to him. They danced together, a tango which he performed with style and verve, and Diane made a slow and careful assessment of his suitability.

There was something in the way he held her as they danced – as if she were an *objet-d'art* of enormous value – and a yielding look in his eyes – that suggested to Diane that she had here a likely candidate for the sort of friendship in which she was most comfortable. This is to say, a friendship in which the man adored her, body and soul, lavished his attention and money on her, and made no distastefully intimate demands on her in return.

Not that she was any stranger to love-making as it is generally understood – her experience with men went back to her seventeenth year – but she was a woman who understood her own nature. It was necessary to form friendships with men of means, partly for economic reasons and partly for reasons of prestige and self-esteem. But that said, she took no great pleasure in men's embraces. In consequence, she had, over the years, developed ways in which she could enjoy the benefits of close friendships without submitting herself to what she perceived as the disadvantages.

To succeed in her ambitions it was vital to meet a certain type of man – a rare type who was without the normal assumptions of male superiority and could therefore be brought into subjection. Why there should have been men at all with so unusual a temperament, she did not trouble to ask. She assumed that it was to do with their childhood and upbringing, but beyond that she had no interest. For her, life was a matter of practical arrangements, not of theories.

The man who had enjoyed for a long time the privilege of her friendship before she met Yves was a good example of the type she sought. His name was Gaston Ladèle and he was in his late forties, a stocky and vigorous man who provided himself with a large income from dealings on the stock exchange. Yet when he was alone with Diane in her bedroom, his vigour and decisiveness deserted him. He would sit on the grey-upholstered armchair, his mouth open in rapture while she, at a safe distance from him, removed her clothes slowly, garment by beautiful garment, letting him see her naked breasts, until she retained only her silk knickers. By that time Gaston would be breathing heavily, his face dark red and his hands shaking as if he had palsy. Very graciously, keeping out of arm's reach, Diane would give him permission to undo his trousers and let his short and thick spout protrude without hindrance.

'I have never thought it in the least flattering to have *that* effect on a man,' she would tell him coldly, her hands stroking her breasts sensually to arouse him further. 'I regard it as proof that you want to hold me down on the bed and force it into my helpless body for your own degenerate pleasure.'

'No, Diane,' Gaston replied at once,' I would not dare think so monstrous a thought!'

He was telling a little less than the truth. When he was with her and when he was elsewhere going about his affairs, the thought of holding Diane down on the bed was uppermost in his mind. Most often he saw himself with one brutal hand on the nape of her neck, pressing her face down into the pillows and, while she struggled and screamed, reaching with his other hand under her clothes and ripping away her silk underwear, to bare the dark-curled mound he had been allowed to glimpse from time to time, but never touch. But how he would touch it then —

he would ravish it with his fingers, making her cry out with fear, until it was open and wet – and then – ah, that supreme moment in his fantasy when, still holding her down by the nape of her neck, he jammed his hard spigot into her and profaned her helpless body with his torrent!

But this was all fantasy. This otherwise forceful man was so confused in his attitudes towards women, and in particular towards Diane, that he was no more capable of pushing her on to the bed and taking his pleasure between her legs than he was of flying to the moon. And in the innermost recesses of his being, he had what he really wanted and knew it – to be abused and taunted by a beautiful woman who flaunted her naked body before him while he sat powerless. The excitement of the contrived situation was so enormous that he was usually reduced to a wordless babble at the moment when Diane removed her final silk garment and allowed him to see the dark curls between her smooth and pale thighs.

The disadvantage she found in her otherwise near-perfect friendship with Gaston was that no matter to what heights she aroused him by the display of her body and her cruel and inflammatory comments, in order to bring the scene to its destined conclusion it was necessary for her to approach him, go down on her knees between his parted legs and, with her own hand administer the *coup de grâce* by giving his quivering handle the final half-dozen tugs it needed. Mercifully, from Diane's point of view, it never took more than half a dozen tugs, and sometimes fewer, to release his passionate flood into the fine linen handkerchief she took from his breast-pocket for the purpose.

With Yves Marquand there was no such inconvenience. She guessed that he was an ideal subject for her the first time they met and danced together. She made sure that he had numerous opportunities to glance down the front of her low-cut evening frock and see her bare breasts – and the look in his eyes was like that of a poodle when it sits with raised paws to beg for a chocolate. Diane recognised the look and told herself that here was a man who could be trained satisfactorily. And he was so much younger and better-looking than Gaston, though that in itself counted for little if events did not prove conclusively that he was suitable in all other ways.

Diane arranged matters skilfully after that first meeting, so that Yves believed that he was pursuing her. She kept him in suspense for four days and through long telephone conversations during which Yves thought that he was struggling to overcome her resistance to his invitation to dine with him. For the most part he talked, and Diane only now and then interjected a seemingly innocent comment that inflamed his imagination. She was as sure as anyone could be that while he was talking to her he was sitting with his trousers unbuttoned and his male part sticking stiffly out so that he could fondle it a little.

On the fourth day of this improbable courtship Diane's experienced ear detected a change in his voice – even though the shortcomings of the telephone system made his voice a little shrill and crackly, as it did everyone's. There was something different this time, and she knew at once what it was. Yves was daring to go beyond the mere exposure of his projection while he talked to her – he was actively pleasuring himself and he intended to make himself discharge at a suitable moment when he was listening to her voice, preferably speaking his name.

She cut the conversation short at once, saying that a visitor had arrived and ringing off. It was not only the conversation she cut off so sharply, it was the tremulous pleasure Yves thought he was going to enjoy. Her imaginary visitor blocked the arrival of *his* visitor in his hand! She waited for an hour and telephoned him back. The delight in his voice at hearing from her was very apparent and, before he had time to reach for his trouser-buttons, she told him that if he called for her that evening she would dine with him. He gasped in surprise, she said *au revoir* and rang off quickly.

It could be said that the game was won and lost on that first evening, except that these words have no significance in so complicated a situation. In reality, two people were negotiating the unusual terms on which their friendship would be based, to the satisfaction of both. And this negotiation was necessarily carried through without either of them ever putting into words what the terms were to be. After they had dined well they went to dance and Diane took care that Yves should become aroused. She let her thighs and belly brush with great delicacy past his loins while they were dancing and, when they were sitting and sipping champagne, she let one narrow shoulder-strap of her frock slip accidentally down so that, for a moment or two, her left breast was almost completely uncovered – but not quite. In the taxi on the way home she sat close to him so that her thigh touched his thigh and, when the taxi took a corner much too fast as is the custom of taxis in Paris, she fell against him and, in her confusion, gripped the inside of his thigh to stop herself from sprawling right across his lap. In her apartment he helped her off with the evening cloak she was wearing – and by some curious chance, as she turned, his hand touched her breasts. In short, by the time they were sitting in her drawing-room sometime after midnight, Yves was in a condition bordering on controlled frenzy.

For the first, the last, and the only time in their friendship she sat beside him on the red leather sofa instead of in a separate armchair. She permitted herself to lounge – something she never normally did, one arm along the sofa-back, so that her knee-length frock was pulled up her thighs by her position, revealing the tops of her silk stockings and her pretty garters.

Yves was pink-faced and embarrassed by his own excitement – and also embarrassed that he was enjoying being excited. He tried to keep his eyes on Diane's face as they talked, but he was unable to prevent himself from casting, every few seconds, a quick glance downwards at her legs. She stretched her legs out a little further and pulled her belly in sharply, so making the hem of her frock ride up higher still. She heard Yves' sigh as he gave up struggling with himself and stared fully at her thighs.

'I hope you will not be offended,' she said in a casual tone, 'but my maid is in bed by now and there is a small service I require.'

Offended? There was no possible way in this world she

could have offended him at such a moment, even if she had told him to strip naked and run up the Champs-Elysées. When she mentioned what the small service was, it was as if a cherished dream had come true.

'Your garters?' he gasped, not believing his ears.

'If you don't mind – they're new and they feel uncomfortably tight. I'm sure they're making ugly red marks on my legs.'

In Yves' state of mind it did not occur to him that no maid was needed to slip off a pair of garters. He understood the request as a tremendous privilege granted to him and he was off the sofa and on his knees in an instant. He knelt to the side of her legs, of course, not opposite them, since that might suggest to so fastidious a woman as Diane that he had some dark and secret expectation of slipping between her knees. That would have been an unpardonable liberty, even as a thought, let alone as a deed! Diane smiled at his timidity in this and stretched out one well-shaped leg. Yves was trembling so much that he had a little difficulty in getting hold of the exposed garter, but after a few fumbles he got it down her leg to her ankle.

'And the shoe,' she told him.

He was almost delirious with joy as he put his palm under the sole of her high-heeled shoe and eased it slowly off, and then removed the garter. She stretched out her other leg and he repeated the process, his fingers shaking.

'That's better,' said Diane. 'Have I got red marks?'

The invitation to scrutinise her long and smooth thighs was almost beyond Yves' comprehension at that moment. He stared into her face, his mouth foolishly agape, until she laughed and patted his cheeks to bring him to himself. *Perfect*, she was saying to herself, *a perfect plump pigeon for plucking*.

'Slip my stockings down and see if the garters have marked my thighs.' she prompted him, making it sound extremely off-hand.

He bent his head to look and Diane shifted her position on the sofa so that she had a leg on either side of him and her knees well apart. Yves' fingers touched the gossamer silk of her stockings and eased them down a little to examine the pale and satin skin for imaginary marks.

'Can you see?' she asked, using both hands to hoist her frock higher still, until the black-laced edge of her knickers was revealed to him.

'There's no mark, thank god!' he sighed, 'What beautiful legs you have!'

'Are you sure? Have a good look.' And she pulled her frock up higher.

The hem was at her groin and Yves had a perfect view of her silk underwear. His shaking fingers pulled her stocking-tops down further, right down to her knees, and he examined her thighs at close range for as long as he dared. He would have given her everything he had in the world for the privilege of kissing the insides of those warm thighs, but he was incapable of doing any such thing without her express instruction.

Diane was not enjoying the feverish touch of his fingers on her bare thighs as he sought for marks that were not there. But it was sometimes necessary to suffer a little in the larger cause. She promised herself that as soon as she had Yves properly submissive, he would never again have an opportunity to touch her so close her tenderest part.

'My legs ache,' she said. 'That's because you made me dance too much in high-heeled shoes.'

'Oh, I didn't realise . . . forgive me, Diane.'

'You caused the ache, so you can cure it,' she said. 'Massage my calves.'

To Yves utter amazement she raised her legs and put a silk-stockinged foot on each of his shoulders.

As if in a dream, he raised his hands to clasp her calves and his body shook at the contact as if he had touched an electric wire. While his fingers squeezed and rubbed, he stared fixedly between her thighs – for he could do no other. Her position, sprawled back on the sofa with her feet up on his shoulders, revealed to Yves, as it was intended to, more than he had ever expected to see of her. Her knickers were thin to the point of transparency and loose-fitting round the thighs. Because her legs were raised, the ivory coloured material had slipped back and the narrow strip of silk between her legs could not conceal the treasure between her parted thighs. Yves stared at the dark-brown curls and plump pink lips so openly exposed to him as if he were being vouchsafed a vision of the Holy Grail.

This was the vital moment that would decide the future course of their friendship, Diane knew. She was putting everything to the test by giving him this view of paradise – a paradise into which he would never be allowed to enter. If he reached out to fondle it with his hot hand, or ducked his head between her thighs to kiss her warm alcove, then that would indicate that weeks of patient training would be necessary to teach him his place and to disabuse him of any notion he might have that her body was for him to touch.

When she put Gaston Ladèle through this same test, eighteen months earlier, he had turned pale at the sight of her treasure, and stammered something, before letting go of her calves to rip open his trousers. As his swollen spike emerged Diane thought for a moment that he intended to hook her legs over his shoulders and penetrate her! Not that he would have succeeded – her fingernails would have been in his eyes before he had time to guide his ugly thing to the pouting lips between her legs. But in the event she had not been mistaken about him – he was incapable of dominating her or even trying to. The worst that happened was that he grabbed his engorged part and flicked it a few times, staring at the fleece revealed by her immodest position on the sofa and her inadequate underwear – and discharged his emotions in quick jets against the front of her red leather sofa. After that it had not taken her many meetings to secure control over him and make sure that he had his messy little spasms on a regular basis.

When Yves was subjected to this test of his initiative and inclinations, the outcome was most satisfactory – to Diane, that is. With her feet on his shoulders he stared intently at her half-revealed treasure and gasped so long and loud that Diane thought he would wake the sleeping maid at the other end of the apartment. She watched him closely as the blood rushed to his face, turning it a darker and darker red, his body shaking so furiously that it was only his grip on her legs that kept him from collapsing on the floor.

'You're a very lucky man, do you know that?' she asked. 'I'm letting you see something which men are never allowed to see. Do you think it's pretty?'

He gurgled, as if trying to speak, and his eyes rolled up in his head until only the whites were showing. Diane watched in absolute fascination as his head rolled backwards, his body twitched fiercely and he gave a low moaning cry that went on and on and finally faded away in a soft whimper.

She waited for some time, until his breathing was normal again and the hectic flush had left his cheeks, then removed her feet from his shoulders and tucked them underneath her on the sofa. She pulled her frock down modestly to hide her underwear.

'If you will excuse me for a moment . . .' said Yves.

'No, stay where you are,' she said, a little edge in her voice. 'I haven't finished with you. I asked you to massage my aching legs – was that your idea of massage?'

'I am so sorry,' he answered with humility, 'I don't know what happened . . . I lost control of myself for a moment or two.'

'There is no point in pretending not to know what happened,' she told him, sounding offended. 'I know very well what happened – you ejaculated in your clothes. If that's what you call losing control . . . well, I personally would use harsher words than that. Does this happen very often?'

'No, no,' he said, shame-faced. 'I must have had too much to drink this evening.'

'What nonsense! The reason that you lost control of yourself, as you put it, was because you had the impertinence to stare at my underwear – and at god knows what else!'

His eyes were downcast and he said nothing.

'Open you trousers,' she ordered him. 'I want to see for myself the unfortunate results of this lack of self-control.'

'No – please don't ask me to do that! It would be too embarrassing!'

'I'm not asking you to open your trousers,' she replied, 'I am ordering you to do so. Open your trousers – now!'

This too was a key point in her exploration that evening of the degree of Yves' submissiveness. To her secret delight he obeyed her without further protest. He undid the buttons of his black evening trousers and held them open to let her see the stain seeping through his shirt.

'Really,' she rebuked him, 'what messy creatures you men are! Pull your shirt up and open your underwear.'

Without a word he did as she said. His softening spindle flopped out and drooped its head towards the carpet. Diane stretched out a leg and lifted his deflated balloon on her toes.

'I'm sure that the good god created woman first and that men were an afterthought,' she told him, 'and not a very bright afterthought at that. It is extremely untidy to have this awkward thing sticking out between your legs. I'm sure it was a mistake on god's part.'

She dropped her foot and his pointer sagged downwards.

'Oh!' she exclaimed in simulated disgust, 'Look at that – you've wet my stocking – it's sure to stain! This is a new pair of stockings and I must throw them away because of your messiness! Well, tomorrow you can buy me a dozen pairs – that will teach you.'

'Yes, Diane,' he said at once, 'two dozen if you like! Anything!'

'You'd better go to the bathroom and clean yourself up. I'm tired and I want you out of this apartment before I go to bed. Now that I've seen what you're capable of when you see my garters I would not dare to sleep with you anywhere near me.'

'But I would stay awake all night and guard you, watch over you and protect you, Diane!'

'From what? It would be against you that I would need protection! I should fear every second that you were lurking in the dark, ready to hurl yourself on top of me and force my legs apart so that you could ram that fat evil thing into me and sully my body!'

The picture she was planting in his mind made his *evil thing* twitch and she smiled a little smile of satisfaction. The first training session with him had gone very well.

202

From now on he would be her special friend in place of Gaston. Not that she intended to lose touch completely with Gaston, of course – he was too useful and too generous to dismiss like that. But in future he would have to be content with meeting her once a week.

So it began with Yves, and thereafter Diane took control of him more and more. She made him enjoy the way she dealt with him, however outrageous it could be when she was in a bad mood. By the time of the afternoon when he fell asleep in her grey chair he was a very happy and fulfilled man. Three or four times a week Diane summoned him peremptorily by telephone to take her shopping, or to lunch, or to dinner, or the theatre, or whatever else she wanted to do. No matter what the occasion, she always looked marvellously chic and svelte – as she could afford to at his expense – and very exciting. By the time that they had enjoyed their outing and were back in her apartment she would have Yves in an advanced state of arousal. Events after that depended on her whim that day – she might treat him with indifference and coldness, sometimes with contempt and even cruelty – all of which he adored. Eventually, under some pretext or other, he would be permitted to see her naked, or near-naked. The long process of over-stimulating his nerves, which she understood well, would at last culminate in a climactic release which left him weak and shaken.

He was enjoying a sweet dream of Diane. She was wearing a nun's black habit and she was holding him face-down over a chair-back. She had pulled his trousers down and was spanking his bottom with her bare hand and he was pleading with her to stop. A hand gripped his shoulder and he awoke with a start and looked round to get his bearings. He was curled up in the armchair in Diane's bedroom and it was the maid who was shaking his shoulder. He glanced at the bed and saw that Diane was no longer there.

'Wake up, M'sieu Yves. It is almost six o'clock.'

As he could see, it was dark outside the windows and there was a light patter of rain on the glass. Thérèse had switched on the electric lights.

'Where is Madame Guichard?' he asked.

The maid stood back, folded her arms and looked at him thoughtfully. Plain of face she might have been, but she had a sturdy body under her black frock and starched apron and was not averse to the pleasures of love, when opportunity served. If this Monsieur Marquand had been up to it in her estimation she might well have given him to understand that she would not object in the least if he decided that he wanted to roll her on the bed while Madame was elsewhere. But there seemed little point – there he was, handsome enough, if a bit thin, dolled up in Madame's underwear. With a splash-mark on the front that demonstrated clearly that his pleasure had not been taken between Madame's legs.

What an idiot, the maid thought to herself. He could be on top of pretty girls three times a day if he wanted to. Then she remembered that this idiot represented an important part of Madame's income at present, and therefore a part of her own wages. She gave him a friendly smile.

'There was a telephone call,' she told him. 'An old friend. Madame has been called away very urgently. She told me to give you her regrets about this evening.'

'But I have a table booked! When will she be back?'

'She will be back very late – if it becomes too late she will stay with her friend overnight and return in the morning.'

Yves slowly realised that he was wearing, before a stranger's critical eyes, a silk chemise and knickers. He blushed pink and crossed his legs to hide what drooped between his thighs. The maid's smile broadened.

'There is a further message for you,' she said.

'What is that?'

'It concerns Madame's underwear,' said Thérèse, trying not to burst out laughing as Yves' face turned pinker still.

'Well?' he demanded, his eyes turned away from her.

'Madame said that as you have soiled her underwear, you are to take it home with you and sleep in it tonight and tomorrow night.'

Yves was thunderstruck. He gaped foolishly at Thérèse.

'Tonight and tomorrow night,' she repeated firmly.

The thought of wearing Diane's silk underwear in bed was so exciting that Yves' peg immediately began to grow in length and girth. Though he had his legs crossed, he was not used to the fit of women's knickers and he blushed scarlet as he saw the head of his eager member thrusting itself out from under the lace edging on his thigh.

'Madame's instructions please you, I see,' said the maid, gesturing down with her chin at his shame.

'Thérèse, do not laugh at me,' he said earnestly, 'I can't help what affects me.'

'That I understand. Is there any way in which I can be of service to you?'

'What do you mean?'

She reached down to touch his bare thigh and then the engorged head that peeped out from under the lace. He gasped, not used to being touched by a woman just there – Diane never did.

'By the look of this you are in need of the assistance a woman can provide,' she suggested.

In Thérèse's mind there had formed a desire to score secretly over her employer by making this idiotic young man of hers perform properly for once. If he was able to, that is.

'Stand up,' she said.

He had been made so thoroughly subservient to a woman's instructions by Diane that he stood up and let the maid pull the eau-de-nil knickers over his hips and down his legs. His stiff part, freed from its close confinement, stuck out boldly. Thérèse grasped it as if it were a handle and dragged him towards the bed.

'Thérèse – no!' he exclaimed, aware at last of what she had in mind.

'Why not?' she demanded, turning him and pushing him down until he was sitting on the bed. 'You do it with Madame – why not with me?'

'But I love her,' he informed her, 'and besides, we do not do it in the way you are suggesting. That would be out of the question.'

'Yes, she's very mean about opening her legs for a man. Lie back.'

He was still wearing the silk chemise, which came to just below his waist. When he lay back on the bed, his feet still on the floor, his lower half was totally exposed and his stanchion pointed stiffly upwards. Thérèse had made her mind up. Madame's boyfriend was a pathetic creature and a natural victim – and if for Madame, then why not a victim for herself? She had learned a good deal from Diane Guichard during her service with her – mostly about how to deal with men so that they volunteered to pay bills and buy presents, without becoming a nuisance. A little application of what she had learned could well reward Thérèse with a small part of the largesse this miserable idiot on the bed had to offer. At least his handle was still hard – the important thing was to keep it that way.

'Madame thought you were a little tired,' she said in a soothing voice, 'That's why she did not disturb you when she had to go out. And she was right – you slept until I woke you a moment ago. Did you sleep well in the armchair?'

'Yes, very well,' said Yves, who had just lost his nervousness of the maid as a result of her approach, 'I had a marvellous dream.'

'Ah – what was it about?'

'I can't tell you that!' he exclaimed.

'So it was a naughty dream, was it? About Madame, I'm sure – what were you doing to her?'

'It's too private,' he said, blushing pink at the memory of what he had dreamed that Diane was doing to him.

'You must rest for a little while so that I can explain what Madame said to me before she left – there is more for you to hear concerning her underwear.'

Yves was a comical sight, lying on the bed in the chemise, his spout aimed at the ceiling. The maid leaned over to take hold of it and stroke it.

'Madame was wearing her lilac lounging pyjamas,' she said slyly. 'What a fortunate man you are to be allowed to see her dressed like that – she looks very exciting.'

'You cannot imagine how very exciting she is,' Yves replied, his eyes tightly shut to that he could pretend that it was not his stem that was being handled and stimulated

– that what the maid was doing had nothing to do with him.

'The way the thin material clings round her thighs and bottom – have you noticed that?' Thérèse asked, 'Sometimes I think that she shows more of herself when she wears those pyjamas than when she is naked.'

'Oh, oh,' Yves sighed, his imagination caught by her words, as she had intended it should be, 'she was sleeping on her back, and the tunic was pulled up a little – I saw the soft skin of her belly and it was smooth and very beautiful in colour.'

'Her skin is exceptionally beautiful,' said Thérèse. 'When she asks me to bath her I smooth creamy lather over her entire body with my hands – everywhere – under her soft armpits, over her breasts, across her belly and between her legs. What do you think of that?'

Yves, manipulated physically and mentally in this way, was breathing hard and shuddering with spasms of pleasure. To him Thérèse was not a person, as Diane was a person and as he himself was a person. She was no more than a handy presence who attended to things that needed doing – such as stroking his eager part – and a voice that suggested exciting possibilities about Diane. To bath her and have the freedom to run one's hands over every part of her body and cover it with scented lather! His hands would not descend below the level of her breasts before an involuntary crisis brought him to his knees by the side of the bath and wet his underpants – but to dream about proceeding further and slipping a hand between Diane's legs was entrancing.

'You've never had your hand between her legs, have you?' said the maid, guessing at the truth from his squirming and moaning. 'But you'd like to, wouldn't you? Shall I tell you what she feels like there?'

She let go of him to reach under her black frock and pull her plain cotton underwear down round her thighs. In another second she was on the bed, squatting over Yves' loins, gripping his projection again and guiding it to where she wanted it. Yves twitched and gasped, his eyes closed very tightly, as she sat down on him and he was forced deeply into her portal. In some way he had separated his consciousness from his bodily sensations, to protect himself from feelings of guilt about this act of unfaithfulness towards his beloved Diane. What was going on below his waist had no connection with him, he was convinced.

'You understand about Madame's underwear, don't you?' the maid asked a little jerkily as she rode up and down quickly on his embedded part.

'She wants me to sleep in it tonight,' he murmured.

'Yes, and tomorrow night. She wants you back here on Saturday evening to take her to dinner, and you are not to call or phone in the meantime. Have you got that?'

'Two nights of torment – I shall not sleep for even a moment!' he moaned.

'Yes, you will,' the maid contradicted him. 'Madame said that you would squirt off soon enough in her knickers and fall asleep, both nights. And if you wake up in the night, the same thing will happen. She said that you'd probably squirt off three or four times a night and give her underwear a tremendous soaking.'

'Ah!' Yves exclaimed shrilly at the image evoked in his mind by her words. 'You must stop this at once!'

An instant later he squealed again as Thérèse's pumping loins drained him of his passion. He flopped about on the bed like a fish hooked and pulled on to a river-bank, while Thérèse panted and jolted hard as she gratified herself on his fountaining insertion. It was good that he had remained hard through her administrations – at the outset she had not been at all sure that he would not wilt at the touch of the real thing, after the way Madame Guichard had trained him for the past few months.

When it was all over Yves opened his eyes and stared at the maid's black-stockinged knees protruding towards him as she squatted on his belly, at the white cotton knickers dragged down and bunched round her thighs. He considered the weight of her bare bottom on his belly and the warm clasp round his stem, and he was forced at last to acknowledge what had been done to him. He looked up at Thérèse's face with an expression not far short of terror.

'Thérèse – you must promise me that Madame will never hear about this!'

'Why? Do you think she would object to a little fooling about between you and me on her bed?' and she grinned at him with mockery in her eyes.

'She would send me away and never let me see her again!' he exclaimed in panic. 'I implore you, get off me at once.'

'But it's very comfortable sitting like this with your big strong thing inside me,' she countered, adding to his perturbation of mind. 'Surely it feels good to you too?'

'No!' he said at once, frantic to deny that he had in any way consented to his act of infidelity or had taken the least pleasure from it.

'That's not very flattering,' said Thérèse. 'I know half a dozen men who would be only to pleased to have their things where yours is now. But I suppose you might be right – Madame might be annoyed and show you the door if she found out that your worm's been between my legs. And you didn't even take her chemise off while you did it to me! Yes, I can see that she might be offended by what you've done.'

'But I didn't!' he protested weakly. 'It was you who did it to me! I never wanted anything like that to happen – you violated me!'

'Fine words for a man to use!' she retorted, grinning at the incongruity of the situation. 'Very well then – you have my permission to tell Madame that I held you down against your will and violated you. Do you imagine that she'll believe that? Especially after I tell her that you deceived me into letting you make love to me by saying that you had her permission to do so. No, it will be good-bye and good-riddance to you.'

Eventually Thérèse allowed herself to be persuaded – for a large cash sum – to make sure that Madame Guichard did not find out that Yves had committed an act of disloyalty to her on her own bed. As soon as the sum had been agreed, the maid climbed off Yves and treated him to a look at her dark-haired portal before she pulled up her underwear. Yves looked away, terrified of what she might do next, though all she did was to bring him his jacket so that he could give her the money. She tucked the bank-notes into the pocket of her short white apron and smiled contentedly. It had been a satisfactory half-hour and she was not certain which was the best part of it – the cash or the pleasure of putting one over on her employer.

'Now, M'sieu Yves,' she said briskly, 'it is time for you to dress and go. Put Madame's underwear into your pocket and take it with you. Do not forget her instructions.'

'As if I could forget!'

'There is one final instruction for you. When you return here on Saturday evening, you are to bring the underwear with you – washed, clean, pressed, immaculate and scented with Madame's favourite perfume – the Chanel. The set is to be immaculate – that is the word she used.'

Needless to say, there had been no telephone message to call Diane away urgently while Yves slept in the grey armchair facing the bed. After an hour's doze she had woken feeling refreshed and glanced across the room towards Yves. She expected to see him bolt-upright in the chair, half-mad with thwarted desire. In fact, he was asleep and the dark stain that had seeped through the front of the eau-de-nil knickers he was wearing confirmed that he had experienced his little crisis and required no further attention.

Diane thought about the plans for the evening, and frowned slightly. At another time she would have been pleased enough by the entertainment proposed, but in the mood in which she had woken up it seemed boring. And there was the prospect of bringing Yves back to her apartment at one in the morning so that she could precipitate another little spasm for him – the idea was too tedious to contemplate.

She got off the bed and, bare-foot and silent, went to the wardrobe by the wall. From it she took a well-cut little jacket and skirt in midnight blue wool, a plain white blouse and shoes. Her stockings and underwear were kept in the drawers of the dressing-table that stood by the window, close to Yves' chair and she did not want to wake him and become involved in explanations. Consequently she simply left the bed-room, on tiptoes, carrying the clothes she had chosen. Safe in the drawing-room she rang for her maid while she dressed.

'I may be back late tonight or I may be back tomorrow, Thérèse.'

'Very good, Madame. What about M'sieu Yves?'

'He is asleep. Leave him for another hour and then send him home with these instructions.'

Thérèse listened carefully to the orders for Yves, grinning at the enormities Diane got away with in her dealings with her men-friends.

'Leave it to me – I'll make sure he understands what you want him to do. But Madame – you cannot go out into the street bare-legged like that!'

'Bare legs and a bare behind,' said Diane. 'It doesn't matter – I'll get a taxi at the end of the street.'

'Yes, Madame. Are you going far?'

The maid got no answer to her question, nor did she really expect one. Two or three times a week, when Yves was not expected, Diane Guichard disappeared on her own for the whole evening. She wore day clothes for these mysterious outings, dark clothes which would not draw attention to her. Sometimes she was back about midnight, sometimes she returned the next morning. Naturally, her visits had to be to a secret lover – there was no other possible explanation. But her maid was unable to think of any reason why the lover must be so secret and why the meetings always took place away from Diane's apartment. Of course, it was possible to speculate that the lover was so important that no risks could be taken – the President of the Republic, perhaps – but Thérèse did not think that her employer aspired to such heights.

Apart from her regular expeditions to wherever she went, there was almost nothing else about which Diane was not prepared to talk openly to her maid: the little degeneracies of Yves Marquand, for instance, and the inconveniences of Gaston Ladèle, before him. In fact Ladèle still came to the apartment from time to time, when Madame let him – two or three times a month – for his gratification. Diane had no fear that her maid would reveal that little arrangement to Yves. But on the subject of where she vanished to so frequently, there was not a single word said.

Thérèse tried to think of ways of finding out where Madame went, but it was not easy. To creep out of the apartment after her and follow her by taxi was an uncertain business, with the obvious danger of being recognised and dismissed. If there had been anyone the maid trusted enough, she would have had him loitering down by the taxi-rank ready to follow Madame. Unfortunately, Thérèse's present boyfriend, though handy enough at what men were useful for when they were undressed, was not to be entrusted with so delicate a mission. There was some danger that he would keep the information to himself and try to make use of it, instead of passing it on. So, for the time being, the matter rested.

Diane's secret destination was not, as her maid suspected, the house of some vastly important person in the best part of Paris, but a run-down apartment building in the Rue Mouffetard, a long, straggly, seedy street on the Left Bank. By coincidence it was not far from the church of St Médard, where Madame Blanc the concierge had gone on Sunday mornings twenty-five years ago, to have her bit of rabbit-skin blessed after Mass.

From the street Diane climbed four flights of dirty stairs to the apartment she was visiting and knocked gently with an expensively gloved knuckle at a door from which the paint had long ago peeled. After a pause the door opened and there stood Lucille Devrais. The two women embraced and kissed each other on both cheeks and Lucille drew her visitor into the room. It was a large, all-purpose room, with a low bed by the far wall, chairs and an old sofa in the middle, and a cold-water sink and gas cooker in a corner. It was not as dingy as the outside of the building might have suggested, but it was very cheap and ordinary in appearance. A young man sat on one of the chairs, drinking red wine. He was poorly dressed and not polite enough to rise to his feet at Diane's entrance.

'You know my brother Emile,' Lucille said almost

apologetically, 'He's out of work again and he came round for a chat.'

'Good evening, Emile,' said Diane, a little coldly, and he grinned and nodded his head at her.

'Sit down,' Lucille urged, clearing a stack of washed but not yet ironed clothes from the sofa. 'Would you like a glass of wine?'

Diane smiled and took the glass poured for her. The wine was drinkable, though it fell a long way below the quality she normally drank.

'So you've lost your job, Emile?' she said, staring at him. 'What will you do now?'

He mumbled inarticulately, not being used to being challenged so directly by a woman. Diane harassed him relentlessly, enquiring what skills, if any, he could offer an employer, how many different jobs he'd had since he left school, and what was the longest he'd ever kept a job. She deliberately made him feel uncomfortable and inadequate, because she wanted him to leave. In this she succeeded – within a quarter of an hour he got to his feet, red-faced and irritated, and told his sister that he must go. He put on an ugly black proletarian cap and took his leave without a word of farewell to Diane.

'What a horror he is!' she said, 'I suppose he came here to ask you for money.'

'Poor Emile,' Lucille defended him. 'He always seems to have bad luck.'

'Luck has nothing to do with it – he's shiftless and idle. I expect he'll go to prison one day.'

'Oh, Diane, don't say that!'

'Come and sit here with me.'

Lucille Devrais was twenty-four, a good ten years younger than Diane. The most remarkable thing about her was her size – her pretty face was round and chubby, her shoulders meaty, her belly prominent and her backside as big as a regimental drum. But it was her breasts that dominated everything – they had grown to a gigantic size. She was wearing a brown skirt and white blouse – the largest size it is possible to buy – and it was strained tight over that stupendous bosom.

'I've missed you,' said Diane, stroking her friend's plump cheek.

She undid the buttons down the front of Lucille's blouse and opened it wide to reveal a chemise of artificial silk stretched tight over the rotundities it covered. At once Diane's hand was down the top of the chemise to fondle Lucille's fleshy masses.

'You'll break my shoulder-strap like that,' said Lucille, as Diane's hand delved deeper. 'Wait a minute and I'll take my blouse off.'

Diane helped her off with it and pulled the chemise down to her waist, exposing her swollen breasts to the tender assaults of her hands and mouth. Their sheer weight made them droop down to the level of her waist and, because of their unnaturally distended size, their pink buds were stretched almost flat.

'That's enough!' Lucille said five minutes later. 'You'll make me do it before I want to if you keep on feeling me like that. I want to see you with your clothes off, you know.'

Diane raised her face from her friend's breasts and kissed her tenderly on the mouth.

'Let's lie on the bed,' she suggested.

They crossed the room hand-in-hand to the bed, Lucille's melon-sized playthings rolling and bouncing as she walked, and Diane gave a little laugh of sheer pleasure at the sight. They stood beside the bed, facing each other, embracing and kissing, the bulk of Lucille's breasts holding Diane away from her. As their mouths and tongues pressed together and aroused them both, Diane's hand forced itself down the waistband of her friend's skirt and tried to reach the join of her thighs.

'We'll see about that!' said Lucille, starting to undress Diane. Off came the well-cut little jacket and skirt – and she stood in only her shoes and blouse.

'No underwear!' Lucille exclaimed, with a knowing grin. 'What were you up to this afternoon? Had a man's length up you, I suppose,' and her hand clasped Diane's dark-curled mound.

'No such thing!' Diane answered, wriggling her hips to

rub herself against Lucille's palm. 'But I had a visitor and I didn't want to wake him up, so I crept out half-dressed.'

Lucille's hand clenched more tightly on Diane's warm mound and her other hand was behind her, fondling the bare cheeks of her bottom and then probing down between them, so that Diane was held in a double grip.

'Your visitor was asleep, was he? That means he'd had all he wanted from you. Where did he squirt it up you – front or back?'

This was the game they played together to excite themselves – accusing each other of intimacies with men that neither of them would dream of allowing. Lucille was a girl of the people and her suggestions were often down-to-earth – which aroused Diane. In turn, Diane's more restrained language had its effect on her friend, though when it came to deeds instead of words there was nothing to choose between the two of them for earthy sensuality. But that stage was still to come.

'Front or back – what a thing to say!' Diane gasped, feeling herself pierced front and back by Lucille's agile fingers. 'What self-respecting woman would lie face-down and let a man do it to her rump!'

'Thousands of them do,' said Lucille sagaciously, 'so if it wasn't that, then he stuck it in the front door.'

'He never touched me! I refuse to let him.'

'I'm sure you let him have a quick feel.'

'Never!'

'So if he didn't feel you, then you must have used your hand on him to make him do it.'

'Ridiculous . . .' Diane sighed, her belly surging with delightful little sensations from the action of her friend's fingers, 'I've never touched his long, ugly thing.'

'But you've had a good look at it if you know it's a long one!' She ceased her pleasurable attentions to Diane's lower half and pushed her on to the bed. Diane quickly removed her expensive blouse before it became creased, and Lucille took off her brown skirt and capacious underwear. Then she had one knee on the bed and, before Diane could move or protect herself, she flung herself on top of her, squashing her down into the mattress by her bulk and weight.

'Oh my god,' Diane gasped, 'I can't breathe!'

Lucille had her arms and legs locked tightly round her. She rocked backwards and forwards, making her massive breasts roll between them like half-inflated balloons, and her fat hot belly crushed Diane's belly flat.

'You spend the afternoon with a man,' she exclaimed, grinding Diane beneath her, 'you let him feel you and stick his thing in you – and then you come to me and say you've missed me! The only reason you're here is because you hope I'll let you play with my lovely big breasts! Do you take me for a fool? I know you let men do dirty things to you to pay the rent of your fancy apartment.'

'I'm dying . . .' Diane whimpered, 'smother me to death, Lucille . . .'

A moment before Diane fainted from lack of breath, Lucille rolled off her and used both hands to raise and lower her chest, as if she were reviving a half-drowned woman pulled from the Seine.

'Don't you dare to pass out on me!' she said. 'I haven't even started on you yet.'

Diane was breathing normally again. Lucille stroked her belly in a comforting way and chuckled.

'I nearly smothered you that time,' she said. 'Your face was purple.'

Diane put her hands on the enormous breasts that hung down over her like impossibly ripe fruit.

'You are unjust to accuse me of letting a man touch me,' she said. 'It is fifteen years since the last time I lay on my back for a man. I was young then and knew no better.'

'You were twenty-one – that's not so young! At twenty-one I knew better,' Lucille replied scornfully. 'I still don't believe you about this afternoon.'

So saying, she reached down to put a hand between Diane's legs and, an instant later, her fingers were inside her.

'Yes, I thought so when I felt you before – you're wet inside. That's because you let your boyfriend do his business there. There's no point in denying it.'

'Oh, Lucille,' Diane murmured, as her friend's fingers busied themselves expertly with her secret bud, 'it's

216

because you had your hand there, not because of a man.'

'I know you're lying to me,' Lucille insisted, shifting her position on the bed slightly so that her gross danglers were over Diane's face.

Diane seized them with both hands and nibbled at their flattened tips to make them more prominent.

'No, its the truth!' she gasped. 'Yves didn't touch me once, nor I him. I made him put my knickers on and he had his little emission inside them.'

'So you did let him look at you, when you took your knickers off! Now we're getting at the truth at last. What was he doing while you were standing about with a bare behind – playing with himself?'

'No, no, no! I'd never let him do anything as coarse as that in front of me.'

'Why not?' Lucille demanded, her fingers fluttering deftly between Diane's soft folds of flesh. 'You used to let the last one do it to himself – you told me so. In fact, you did it for him often enough.'

'But he's been gone for ages,' Diane sighed, though not with complete truth. 'Yves is easier to manage – I can bring on his climax by saying the right things to him.'

'So you claim, but I'm not fool enough to believe that. Listen well, rich Madame, this part of Paris is rougher than where you live. Things go on round here that would make your hair stand on end. I've heard it all – from fathers with their ten-year-old daughters to men whose pleasure is to stick their tongues up a woman's backside – but I've never heard of a man who can be *talked* into squirting off.'

Diane's loins lifted jerkily off the bed and she screamed at the top of her voice as her climax hit her. She burrowed her face into the ample flesh of Lucille's breasts and her legs kicked and thrashed about convulsively.

'Well!' Lucille exclaimed in mock surprise, her fingers still busy to prolong the throes for as long as he could. 'I'm trying to talk to you seriously and you're not even listening to me.'

'Darling,' Diane sighed, her breathing slowing down at last, 'that was fabulous!'

They lay cuddled in each other's arms, whispering and

kissing, enjoying the warm feel of each other's bodies so close. After a while Lucille's fingers stroked Diane's flat little breasts with more than affection, and Diane understood. She sat up and glared down angrily at Lucille.

'You did that to me to throw me off the track,' she said, 'but I'm not that easily deceived, Mademoiselle Devrais – you're not the only one with some experience of the world, though your experience seems to me to have been mainly in the gutter.'

'What do you mean?' Lucille asked, turning on to her broad back.

Her loose breasts rolled off her chest like bowling-balls and hung against her upper arms. Diane sank her fingers into the soft flesh of her friend's belly and gripped two handfuls of it.

'You are so enormously sensual to look at that everyone wants to have you,' she said, 'but what you did was wrong – you know that! All that marvellous soft and warm flesh of yours makes men's hands itch to grab hold and feel you – they can't stop themselves getting hold of your fantastic breasts and rolling their faces in them. You are a walking temptation and a danger to men – but there are times when you go too far.'

'I don't understand you,' Lucille sighed, stretching her plump legs wide apart so that Diane could stroke the soft flesh of her thighs. 'What have I done? No man has ever laid as much as a finger on my breasts! There's many that would like to – and round here they tell you outright what they want, they don't drop polite hints. But they never get anywhere with me.'

'I know what happens, though,' said Diane, her hands caressing the insides of Lucille's thighs and finding the wispy hair that adorned the lips between them.

'What?'

'They go home disappointed, but then they pleasure themselves by hand while they enjoy their little fantasies about your breasts – they pretend that they are squirting over them.'

'You're only guessing,' Lucille sighed, shivering a little in delight as Diane's fingers touched her secret place delicately.

218

'How do you know what men get up to on their own?'

'I made Gaston confess his fantasy to me once, that's how I know.'

'How did you make him?'

Diane's thumbs parted the somewhat underdeveloped lips between Lucille's thighs and slowly uncovered her very small bud.

'We were sitting opposite each other and his trousers were unbuttoned and his ugly pink thing sticking out. He was very excited and desperate to be relieved – I had been tormenting him one way and another for the best part of an hour. I ordered him to tell me what he thought about when he was alone, but he refused – he was too embarrassed, so I knew that it involved me in some way. That made me determined to find out – whatever it took to drag his furtive little secret from him.'

'Diane, what are you doing to me?' Lucille moaned, well aware of what her friend was doing. 'You're splitting me apart!'

Diane's fingertip was teasing gently round her exposed bud, never touching it directly.

'Has any man's thing ever been inside this pink tunnel?' she demanded.

'Never – I swear to you, Diane! Plenty have tried, but I've never let one even touch me there with his hand, let alone anything else!'

'But they do it to you in their thoughts,' said Diane, 'just like Gaston Ladèle.'

'What does he do in his thoughts – tell me!' Lucille sighed, her fat belly shaking with pleasure as Diane's fingers caressed her slowly. 'How did you make him tell you?'

'Ah yes – how I made him suffer until he confessed to me. I pulled up my skirt above my stocking-tops, so that he caught a glimpse of my thighs. At once he reached for his twitching thing, to relieve himself – but I commanded him to put his hands behind his back.'

'Surely he was too far gone to listen to you . . .' Lucille breathed.

'He was far gone, believe me, but after I have trained a

219

man he never dares let himself go too far and disobey me. He put his hands behind his back at once and sat there groaning softly. I pulled my skirt even higher, until he could see my underwear.'

'Diane . . . I'm going to explode in a minute!'

'Not till I let you! Be quiet and listen to my story and you will learn something – how to twist a man's will so that he will do whatever you tell him.'

'I don't care about that – *I'll* do anything you tell me!' Lucille murmured.

'At this moment there is only one thing you want to do, Diane told her, 'but you will have to wait until I let you – what do you think I visit you for – a back-alley stand-up thirty-second job? I am trying to teach you better and more pleasurable ways, dear Lucille.'

'Yes, yes, yes . . . go on with your story, then!' Lucille gasped.

'I let Gaston see my underwear – and then I put my hand inside and touched my *little sister*. That made his eyes stand out of his head, believe me! I pulled my knickers aside and let him see my fingers stroking myself. I thought he would die, his face was so flushed!'

'I'm the one who's going to die!' Lucille moaned, her body shaking.

'So I told Gaston to confess. He shook his head and babbled, and I slipped two fingers inside and caressed myself. When he saw what I was doing, his will was broken. He blurted out in shame that when he was alone, between visits to me, he pleasured himself by imagining me lying naked on his bed and letting him squirt over my naked breasts. Can you believe the insolence of the man, to use me that way, even in his thoughts?'

'Oh, oh, oh,' Lucille was gasping, 'over your breasts! Oh my god!'

'And now you know how the men around here treat you in their fantasies!'

'Never! It isn't true!'

'Perhaps you know less about men than I do, my dear, in spite of living in what you call a rougher district. They get their ugly hard things out and imagine your huge

220

voluptuous breasts in front of them as a sort of target.'

Lucille shrieked loudly as she reached her moment of crisis. Her dome of a belly inflated and deflated rhythmically to the waves of her ecstasy.

'Yes, you may well squeal!' said Diane. 'This is the real delight of love, this great climactic burst – not the feeble twitchings in your belly you experienced before you met me.'

'Look who's talking!' Lucille retorted, a little breathlessly, her body still shaken with tremors that sent her melons of breasts jerking and rolling. 'You were so busy training men to pay your rent that you never had time to find out what love was all about until you met me and felt my breasts for the first time. Your own hand in your knickers was the most you ever enjoyed in those days.'

Diane settled herself comfortably between Lucille's parted thighs and applied the tip of her tongue to the little bud she had made defenceless. Lucille shrieked softly at the warm touch and stopped talking. As Diane well knew, once she had been aroused it required more than a single climax to calm her nature. Her fingers replaced her tongue and she resumed her mental stimulation as well as her physical stimulation of her friend.

'I know very well why Emile was here,' she said. 'It wasn't just to borrow money. He came here to have you. He knows about you and me, doesn't he?'

'Everybody knows about us,' Lucille answered. 'People aren't stupid – they see you coming here two or three times a week – it didn't take them long to guess what you came for.'

'He's jealous of me, your brother,' said Diane. 'He had you this afternoon to spite me.'

'But he's my brother,' Lucille protested.

'As if that made any difference in a district like this! He had you on this bed before I arrived – you might as well admit it. His fingers were between your legs, where mine are now, doing the same thing to you.'

'Oh no, oh no,' Lucille moaned.

She gripped the tiny tips of her huge breasts between thumb and forefinger and stretched them cruelly.

'But your precious Emile wasn't satisfied with that,' Diane said. 'What does he understand of the gentle pleasures of touching and caressing? His long sticker was out of his trousers in no time, I'm sure of that, and up *here*,' and she slid two joined fingers into Lucille's tender depths.

'I'd never let him do that to me!' Lucille gasped.

'Little liar! Today wasn't the first time – Emile's been having you for years, ever since he could make his thing stand up straight and spit.'

Diane put her head down and used her tongue to lap gently at the pink interior she was exposing by holding Lucille's fleshy folds apart. Lucille moaned, as if *in extremis*, Diane's tongue became more imperious in its attentions and Lucille lifted the weight of her melons by the tender tips she was gripping, and held them up as high as they would go above her heaving chest – a sight to amaze anyone other than Diane, who had witnessed this before: Lucille's breasts lifted upwards like two gigantic hot-air balloons lifting away from the ground at the beginning of a soaring flight into the sky.

'I'm exploding!' Lucille cried out.

Her second crisis was more profound and lasted longer than her first. Throughout it her heavy body rolled from side to side on the creaking bed, while Diane held her plump thighs wide apart by force and used her tongue mercilessly. At long last, ravaged by the strenuous emotions of her release, Lucille let go of her cruelly stretched buds and her breasts collapsed back on to her chest, their flight into the empyrean completed. They lay slackly on her, earth-bound and heavy.

Diane sat up and smiled. 'Now you know how it feels to be made love to properly, my dear,' she said, a trifle smugly. 'I think you will agree that it is infinitely superior to anything you may have experienced when your useless brother was pumping in and out of you.'

Lucille burst into laughter, her breasts jumping, and Diane joined in. They lay down in each other's arms, well pleased with the progress of their little game so far.

'How long will you stay?' Lucille asked, stroking Diane's hair.

'All night. It is my opinion that you are falling into unsocial habits living here on your own. I propose to exercise you thoroughly between now and tomorrow morning.'

'What bad habits?'

'If your brother's not here having you, then you're lying on this bed all evening with your knickers off, playing with yourself.'

'Yes, but I always think about you while I'm doing it, Diane.'

'That's sweet! We'll go for dinner to the restaurant in the Rue Monge in a while – the one we've been to before. We'll have as good a dinner as they can provide and then come back to bed so that I can exercise you properly. Unless you collapse and go to sleep!'

Lucille reached over Diane to sink her fingers into the warm flesh of her bottom and pinched her hard.

'Asleep – me? You seem to have forgotten what happened the last time you stayed all night!'

'How can I remember every trivial event?' Diane teased her.

'It is a trivial event for you, is it, when I let you have the pleasure of doing it to me half a dozen times?'

'Half a dozen – is that what it came to? I know that you are a little glutton when you begin, but that seems excessive.'

'And I suppose it wasn't excessive when I made you do it half a dozen times?'

'Not in the least! I waste so much of my time arousing the sordid passions of my so-called lover Yves – which I may say I find utterly boring – that my own poor need for love and affection is ignored and forgotten.'

'Half a dozen times isn't being ignored!' Lucille exclaimed. 'It was all right for you – I left you asleep here in my own bed when I got up and went to work – and you'd done so much to me in the night that I was late and the boss told me off!'

'Tomorrow morning I shall get up with you and we will have coffee and croissants together in the café down the road before you go to work,' Diane assured her.

'So you say! More likely the alarm clock will wake us and before I can get out of bed you'll have your fingers up me and I'll be late for work again!'

'It is only just that when I visit you and let you caress my beautiful body you should devote yourself to giving me a little pleasure,' said Diane. 'And if I want it half a dozen times, what of it? And then friendship demands that I return the compliment and do it to you a few times. I have a very loving nature, a fact which most people do not understand.'

'Ah, you!' said Lucille. 'You think you can come here with your grand manners and impress me because I'm only a poor girl! You come here because you're crazy about my balloons – you can't keep your hands off them! It's nothing to do with having a loving nature – it's just pleasure you're after. You think you can come here whenever you want to and practically rape me! I'll make you pay for that – I'm going to roll on you until I've squashed you and your skinny little breasts flat!'

'Oh, yes, Lucille!' said Diane happily. 'Roll on me – lie on my belly and flatten me – I love you!'

The colour of
Claudette's hair

It was on a fine warm night in early autumn that, as the hour approached midnight, Pierre Fauvel strolled leisurely along the Boulevard des Italiens. He was on his way home after dining very well with his fiancée and her parents – the food had been excellent and the wines superb, the conversation interesting and far-ranging. Nathalie's father approved of Pierre as a future son-in-law and made his approval known in every possible way. More important, perhaps, her mother liked Pierre and displayed none of the signs of a possessive and interfering mother-in-law to be. It was understood that Pierre would join his father-in-law's practice after the marriage, with the unspoken promise that he would take it over when Monsieur Binet decided to retire in ten or twelve years time. As for Nathalie herself, twenty years old and pretty, she was well-educated, docile and had all the qualities which would enable her to become a devoted wife and mother. What more could any young man ask?

There had been no opportunity for Pierre to make love to Nathalie this evening – nothing more than a kiss on parting and a quick caress of her breasts through her frock, with one eye cocked anxiously towards the door in case Monsieur Binet came to see why his daughter was taking so long to see her fiancé off. But she had been at his bachelor apartment the previous afternoon, as on a good many occasions before, and had denied him nothing. As ever, she had been a little constrained in her love-making, but that was to be expected of a young woman of her upbringing and background. She let him undress her completely and lay on his bed while he gratified his sense

225

of touch by caressing her soft body and kissing her breasts. She became aroused quite easily, he had discovered early on in their relationship, but her arousal had a mildness about it that kept it within bounds. She lay passively on her back to let him mount her and introduce his male part into the soft aperture between her thighs – she even exclaimed *Oh, Pierre!* as if she were pleased when he jetted his passion into her warm belly. As far as she knew, this was the whole of love-making – it was the woman's role to lie on her back and let her partner have his way. All that would change, Pierre promised himself, when they were married and he could stop worrying about whether she knew enough not to become pregnant before it was convenient. He intended that under his tuition she would blossom into a sensual wife.

Normally he would have taken a taxi back to his apartment, but the night was so pleasant that he decided to walk, even though it was a considerable distance. He was about halfway when he paused for a drink and a brief rest in a bar in the Boulevard des Italiens. It was not a bar he remembered being in before, but it looked decent enough, and inviting. Events were to prove the truth of this impression – though the invitation extended to Pierre was not one that he had expected.

He stood at the zinc-topped bar, drinking a little glass of cognac, thinking of nothing very much, when he noticed a young woman at the other end of the bar. He made the obvious assumption that, alone in a bar at midnight, she could only be a professional looking for clients – or perhaps refreshing herself with a drink between clients. His assumption became a certainty when she smiled broadly at him and moved along the bar towards him.

It was only on rare occasions that Pierre availed himself of the facilities offered by professionals and he had no thought of doing so then, for he was hoping to get Nathalie into his bed the next afternoon. But he was in a good humour and well-disposed towards all the world.

'Good evening, Mademoiselle,' he said, touching the brim of his hat politely.

She was twenty-two or three, he guessed, and better-looking and more elegantly dressed than women he had seen looking for clients in bars before. She wore a very striking frock of black and white chevron stripes, with a white leather belt, and a white felt cloche hat. She was slender of body and her pale-complexioned face was heavily made-up, her mouth a scarlet gash and her eyelashes thick with some black cosmetic. She sounded a little drunk when she returned his greeting, but she immediately accepted his offer of a drink.

'I'm Claudette,' she told him, 'What's your name?'

'It is of no consequence,' said Pierre, putting money on the zinc for the drinks. 'I must be on my way.'

'Don't be in such a hurry – we've only just met. Have another drink – I'll pay.'

He had never heard of a girl of the town buying a drink for a prospect before. The idea ran counter to all the established laws of nature and economics, as Pierre understood them. He was sufficiently amazed to accept and even more amazed when she opened her handbag and paid the bartender from a thick bundle of bank-notes.

'You have had a successful day,' Pierre commented.

'Is that what you think?' she exclaimed, staring hard at him. 'Successful! This has been the worst day of my life and I feel like jumping into the Seine and drowning myself.'

'My apologies. Mademoiselle – I meant nothing disrespectful.'

'Disrespectful – what sort of stupid word is that?' she said angrily. Pierre was wishing that he had not allowed himself to become involved with her. To extricate himself from what might become an awkward scene he gave her his most charming smile.

'Your face becomes a very pretty pink when you lose your temper,' he said, 'and that suits you, for your complexion is naturally a delicate pale shade. You should be angry more often.'

'Do you think so?' she asked, appeased by his words. 'I've always been pale-skinned. I was born like that and it has never changed.'

'You have the complexion which all women wanted when your grandmother was a young girl,' he said, 'a delicate creamy shade.'

227

'Who told you that?'

'My own grandmother, of course. She told me of the days when the dream of every woman was to have a figure like an hour-glass – full above and full below, with a tiny waist. Today every pretty woman wants to be slender, as you are.'

'But not too slender,' she replied. 'A woman needs a bit up top and a bit behind, or men don't look at her. I don't know which would be worse – being flat-chested or having a pair like a dairy cow.'

The bartender looked at Pierre and then at the empty glasses and Pierre indicated that they should be refilled.

'To you, Mademoiselle Claudette,' he said, raising his glass. 'A last drink and I must go.'

'Why the rush?' she asked. 'Don't you want me?'

'Thank you for the offer, but I really must go home.'

She sidled very close to him and he felt the gentle pressure of a pointed little breast against his arm.

'You said I was pretty,' she said. 'I'm even prettier when I take my clothes off.'

'Of that I have no doubt, but you must understand that I have a fiancée to whom I am devoted. It would be an act of bad faith on my part, I regret to say, if I made love to you – or any other woman, however pretty.'

'Bad faith – that means nothing!' she said, in a dismissive tone of voice. 'There's no such thing as good faith, everyone knows that. It won't cost you anything to see me naked, if that's what is bothering you.'

'What do you mean?'

'I'm not asking you for money – I want you to make love to me, that's all. It's not much to ask – most men would leap at the chance.'

Pierre stared uncertainly at her pretty face and tried to imagine it without the thick layer of make-up.

'But why?' he asked.

'Stupid question! I want to make love and you're young and good-looking. Forget about your fiancée for one night – she'll still be there waiting for you tomorrow.'

'But I love her,' Pierre protested, though his resolve was weakening as the little breast against his arm continued its soft pressure.

'So what if you do? You'll have the entire honeymoon to make love to her. With me you've got only tonight.'

'This is madness!' Pierre exclaimed.

So great was his confusion that, without wholly realising what he was doing, he touched her hip and his hand slid round to her bottom. Claudette gave him a dazzling smile when she felt him touch her and he was lost.

'One night of madness in a lifetime of sanity will do you good,' she informed him. 'When did you make love to her last?'

'Yesterday,' he answered, his fingers squeezing the soft cheeks of her bottom through her frock.

'Not today? Then you must be feeling frustrated and ready for a woman,' said Claudette, turning slowly so that his fingers trailed from her bottom round to her belly.

For one dizzy moment Pierre's fingertips were brushing across a plump little mound, with only two layers of very thin material between. Claudette linked arms with him and led him out of the bar and towards a destiny he could not begin to imagine. Her apartment was within walking distance, east along the boulevard for a little way and then off to the left. She lived on the third floor and, in her slightly drunken condition, it took her some time to rummage about in her handbag for the keys. Once inside the apartment she took him straight to a bedroom. It was furnished with more style than Pierre had expected, though the bed was unmade and rumpled, as if it had been used recently for some energetic activity or other. A bedside lamp had been left on.

Claudette pulled off her hat and shook her head to make her hair spring free. Pierre gave a little gasp of appreciation at the sight – her hair was thick and curly and as black as a raven's wing. She pressed herself close to him and reached up to put her arms round his neck, for he was taller than her by a head.

'Did you tell me your name?' she asked, her greenish eyes staring up at his face. 'Not that it matters. If you wish to be my nameless lover, that's all right by me.'

'My name is Pierre,' he murmured, becoming excited by the touch of her body against his belly and loins.

'Pierre – that's a good name,' and she raised her face to bring her red-painted lips towards his.

Pierre kissed her and tasted cognac on her lips and on her breath, and smelled the heady perfume she had dashed a little too liberally behind her ears and under her chin. His arms were round her, his hands caressing her back, from her slightly prominent shoulder-blades all the way down to the round little cheeks of her rump. His emotions were hopelessly confused and his thoughts – or what served him for thoughts at such a moment – were no less confused. On the occasions he had made use of the services of a professional in the past it had never been like this. Normally it was down to business at once and a speedy goodbye.

'Claudette,' he murmured when the kiss ended, 'I ought not to be here. I am not the sort of man who looks for a girl to make love casually.'

'Nonsense,' she said. 'All men do it all the time. A few francs change hands and the girl is on her back immediately.'

'That may be, but we are not in that situation.'

'What difference does it make? Do you want me to pay you?'

'There is no need to insult me!' said Pierre.

'Do you want me?' she asked, and slipped a hand down the front of his trousers to grasp the long upright bulge under his shirt. 'Yes, you do. Take your clothes off and you can have me.'

While he was undressing she turned her back to him and removed her own clothes – a gesture of modesty, perhaps, but if so, one which surprised him. Her chevron-striped frock came off to reveal a rose-pink slip which she pulled over her head to show her matching knickers. Pierre stared at her slender back and thought that her slightly prominent shoulder-blades were charming – and her little round rump delicious! Without taking the trouble to remove her black silk stockings, Claudette got into bed, keeping her back towards him, and pulled a single sheet up over her to her chin.

'What's taking you so long?' she asked.

'The graceful line of your back,' he replied. 'I could do no other than stand and admire it.'

'My front is even nicer than my back,' she said.

Pierre discarded his final item of clothing and joined her under the sheet. He tried to throw it aside so that he could look at the front she had spoken of so well, but at once she had an arm round his neck to pull him towards her, while her other hand secured a tight hold on his stem. He touched the breasts he had not yet seen and found them cool and small and pointed – he would have played with them for a long time, but Claudette was impatient. Her hand massaged his stiff part so vigorously that he was left in no doubt of her urgent need.

'Put it in me,' she whispered.

Her legs opened like a pair of scissors as he rolled on to her belly and her hand tugged his projection towards its appointed goal. When he sank deep into her he found that, though her breasts had been cool to his touch, the alcove in which he was now ensconced was very warm and very wet. The sensation made him sigh with pleasure and he started to see-saw back and forth.

'Oh, yes, that's what I want!' Claudette moaned. 'Do it to me!'

At that moment Pierre required no encouragement to continue what he was doing. He was aroused and all thoughts of Nathalie were forgotten. Claudette's exhortation to do it to her was strange, it being his understanding that girls of the streets did not become excited, as ten or a dozen times a day would be far too exhausting for them. But in view of the fact that she was making herself available to him for nothing, and therefore for her own pleasure, he obliged her by accelerating his rhythmic movements. Almost at once she shrieked loudly and unmelodiously – and she writhed beneath him in what was an unmistakable climax of passion, though it was brief.

'Stop,' she whispered, as her shuddering subsided. 'Stop for a moment.'

Pierre lay still, at a loss what to make of this strange woman, but pleased to be in the intimate position he was in – and able to defer his own pleasure for a while in the expectation of a greater pleasure later.

'You were very quick, my dear,' he said. 'Quicker than you wished to be, I'm sure. I shall be gentler with you now.'

Claudette drew a deep breath. 'Again,' she said. 'Hard and fast!'

So urged, Pierre resumed his energetic exercise. Soon he groaned in delight as his belly clenched in ecstatic spasms and fountained its little burden in Claudette's shaking body. This time she screamed shrilly, almost as if she were being murdered, her back arching off the bed so strongly that Pierre was lifted by her. But intense as it was, her climax was again brief, and she collapsed under him.

'You are very good, Pierre,' she murmured. 'You make me do it so easily! But I'm worn out now, and I must sleep.'

Pierre uncoupled himself from her. 'Then I will take my leave,' he said, somewhat disappointed.

'Don't go! I shall wake up in an hour or so and want you again. Rest a little until I am ready and you can have me again – as many times as you like.'

While he watched her, her eyes closed – those eyes of so unlikely a shade of green – and she fell asleep. Pierre began to consider his situation. Claudette had behaved oddly since the moment they had met in the bar – but no doubt she had drunk a great deal and that might account for her words and actions. He guessed that it was probable that she would be less welcoming towards him after she had slept off the effects of the cognac, and to continue the involvement with her was to run the risk of unnecessary difficulties. She had let him satisfy the desire she had aroused and the prudent course was to slip quietly away before she awoke.

He eased himself out of the bed and put his clothes on, moving very quietly. When he was ready to go, even to the hat on his head, he took a last look at her and thought that, without the exaggerated make-up, she had a very pretty face. Presumably the rest of her was pretty too, though her back was the only part he had seen naked. He would never meet her again, so it was a pity to leave without one glance at the delights he had enjoyed, but which she had kept concealed under the sheet.

He stood at the side of the bed and raised the thin sheet – a simple and human act, an act which no man in Pierre's position could have resisted – but the consequences of it were to prove catastrophic. He gazed at Claudette's sleeping body and, like Lot's wife who paused in her escape from the cities of the plain to cast a last glance behind her, he was turned to a pillar of salt. That is to say, he stood open-mouthed and unable to move.

She lay exactly as she had when he had made love to her – on her back, with her arms down by her sides and her slender legs well apart – almost as if she were waiting for him to remount and repeat his performance. Her pointed little breasts rose and fell to the slow rhythm of her breathing, their buds a delicate blush-pink. Lower down the dimple of her flat and narrow belly was enchanting, being more oval than round. In effect, she had a charming body, though perhaps not more so than other women to whom Pierre had made love. It was what he glimpsed between her parted thighs that affected him so strongly.

The plump little mound he was staring at was covered in thick curls of a bright ginger colour! Pierre's eyes swivelled to look at the raven-black hair of her head on the pillow, then back to the vivid ginger between her legs, his whirling thoughts unable to grapple with the contrast. She is a girl of astonishing contradictions, this Claudette, he told himself – a girl of the night who takes a man to bed without payment, a black-haired woman who is ginger between the thighs – what could it mean?

Though he had known several women intimately and was engaged to be married, Pierre understood as little about women as other men, or the answers to his puzzles would have been obvious. As it was, his own ignorance allowed him to become bewitched by Claudette as she lay sleeping. He lowered the sheet gently over her and, instead of going home like a prudent man, he undressed again and got back into bed with her. He told himself that he owed it to himself to solve this mystery before he went home – though in this he was being less than honest with himself. He wanted to enjoy Claudette's ginger mystery, not solve it! The hour was late and he was more tired than he thought, and before long he fell asleep.

When he awoke he found himself alone in the bed. He had no idea what time of day or night it was and his watch was somewhere in his discarded clothes. He stumbled to the window and drew the heavy curtain aside a little, and saw that it was still dark. He pulled on his shirt and trousers and went in search of Claudette.

She was in the kitchen, wrapped in a flowered dressing-gown, and she was sitting at a table, slumped over it, head on her folded arms, as if she had been weeping. Pierre put a chair beside her and an arm round her shoulders to comfort her.

'Leave me alone,' she said miserably. 'There's nothing to be done.'

'No man of feeling could abandon you to your grief – what is it that troubles you?'

'Why should I tell you? You can't help me.'

'An hour or two ago you were anxious enough to have my help – in bed!'

'It wasn't you I wanted,' she said unkindly. 'Just your few centimetres of gristle.'

'I'm glad that it at least was of some service to you!' Pierre exclaimed, at first insulted and then amused by her words.

'It sent me to sleep for a couple of hours,' she replied. 'That was more than the others did.'

'The others?' he said, aghast. 'Were there many?'

'Five or six. I forget.'

'There is only one calamity in life which can cause so total an abandonment of all sense and reason and bring on this urge to self-destruction,' said Pierre, in a moment of insight, 'a tragic love-affair! Am I right?'

Claudette nodded, her face still hidden.

'Perhaps if you tell me the circumstances?' he suggested.

'What is there to tell? I loved him. I thought he loved me. For two years we were ecstatically happy together. And when I came home yesterday he was gone and there was only a note.'

'A dreadful shock! Were you married?'

'Of course not. Who gets married these days?'

'Some do, I assure you. But leaving that aside, were you dependent on him financially in any way – or was he dependent on you, in the circumstances?'

Claudette sat up and wiped her face. She was glad to have someone to talk to at three in the morning. Pierre learned, to his secret embarrassment, that she was not a woman of the town but an actress. The shock of her lover's desertion had so unhinged her that she had prowled the bars of the Boulevard des Italiens picking up men at random and taking them to her apartment to make love to her in some frantic effort to wipe out the memory of the one man she wanted and no longer had. She mentioned some of the plays in which she had appeared and Pierre realised that he had taken Nathalie to one of them and must therefore have seen Claudette on the stage, not that he recalled her.

'And your friend – is he also in the theatrical profession?' he enquired, wondering what sort of idiot deserted a charming young woman who had ginger curls between her legs.

'Denis? Yes, of course.'

'And you and he lived here together?'

'Until yesterday. Now he has gone off with that little whore Josette Ligny!'

'A friend of yours?'

'Not any more!'

'I think that you should wash your face with cold water,' Pierre suggested. 'You have been weeping and that has made it red and swollen.'

'My god, I must look a sight!' and she jumped up from the table and ran to the bathroom. She was gone for some time, and Pierre guessed that feminine vanity was reasserting itself – a very good indication that the worst emotional storm was over. When she came back to the kitchen Claudette's face was smooth and pale and she had brushed out her jet-black hair.

'Now you have heard my story,' she said, lighting a cigarette, 'banal and boring as it is, you will be leaving, I suppose?'

'I am in no hurry, Claudette – not at three in the morning. I like you.'

'You don't have to say that just because you've had me.'

'No, seriously, I like you very much.'

He wasn't telling the whole truth, which was that he was so enormously and desperately attracted to her that nothing, short of calling the police, would have got him out of her apartment at that moment. But the occasion did not seem convenient for so open a declaration just then. Claudette sat down at the table again and they talked. He learned that she was currently rehearsing for a play that was to open in three weeks.

'Then your evenings are free at present,' he said with a smile. 'Good – we can have dinner together this evening.'

'Because I called upon your services in an emergency it does not necessarily follow that I wish to become acquainted with you socially,' said Claudette. 'I know nothing about you. Who are you?'

Pierre gave an account of himself. 'Compared with your life, mine is drab and dull,' he concluded, 'but even so, we could have dinner together this evening.'

'Yes, we could,' she agreed, a little thoughtful now that she was able to form an assessment of Pierre's social and financial background. 'Indeed we can – we will! But let it be somewhere grand – I have had enough of the cheap bistros frequented by theatricals who never know from one week to the next whether they have a job or not.'

By grand she did not mean one of the handful of restaurants where the art of preparing fine food has been elevated to such heights that to dine there is an experience almost religious in its intensity. Pierre's guess at what Claudette understood by grand was the sort of fashionable place where she could be seen and admired by persons of importance. He took her to Le Boeuf sur le Toit, where a fair portion of the café society of Paris could be observed drinking and chattering incessantly. Claudette adored it. She ate, she drank, she talked and she danced – and she was a different person from the drunken depressive of the evening before.

She was wearing a simple and short black evening frock,

well-cut and evidently from a good house. Pierre guessed that it was probably the best that her wardrobe could offer and he was enchanted by the way in which it set off her figure. It had a narrow halter and dipped low in front, so that her pointed little breasts were only just covered – and at the back there was nothing at all above the waist. When they danced Pierre found his hand in delightful contact with the bare skin of her back, and he seized the opportunity to caress – just lightly – her slightly prominent shoulder-blades.

The touch of his hand brought a smile to Claudette's face – a slow smile that hinted at her greater understanding of his attachment to her.

'Darling Pierre – why are you so fond of me when you hardly know me?'

'I feel that I know you very well,' he protested.

'What nonsense! You've made love to me once. We've talked for an hour in the middle of the night. The truth is that I am a stranger to you, as you are to me.'

'I know all that I want to know about you, Claudette,' he insisted.

'Do you? We shall see.'

It was after two in the morning when they returned to Claudette's apartment off the Boulevard des Italiens. They were both in a very good mood from the champagne they had consumed and Pierre's heart was singing joyfully in his chest at the prospect of what was to come. The moment he had Claudette in her bedroom he took her in his arms and kissed her furiously, his hands stroking down her bare back until he could grasp, through the thin georgette of her frock, the little round cheeks of her bottom.

As on the previous evening, her hand slid down inside the front of his trousers, to take hold of his stiff shaft through his shirt.

'You still want me, I see,' she observed.

'More than you can imagine!' he gasped.

Her frock came off very easily, as did her underwear and silk stockings. Pierre shed his evening jacket and bow tie and bore her backwards onto the bed, his mouth locked on hers in a long and passionate kiss. He fondled her pretty breasts and kissed their pink tips and then – whatever Claudette might have expected to happen next – he slid down the bed until he was lying with his chest and shoulders between her legs. His hands caressed the pale skin of her thighs and his mouth pressed in a long kiss to her bright ginger mound.

'So spectacular a colour!' he murmured at last. 'How is this possible when you are so dark-haired?'

'But that is my natural colour,' Claudette answered in some surprise. 'My hair is dyed black – there are few opportunities for an actress with ginger hair, believe me. It may be popular at the Folies Bergères, where the audience only go to look at naked girls, but for a serious actress it is impossible.'

'Then this is the real you,' Pierre exclaimed in delight, his fingers slowly parting the warm folds of flesh beneath the ginger curls.

'It certainly is,' said Claudette with a giggle. 'The real me!'

Her giggle turned to a gasp as Pierre's wet tongue thrust itself between the ginger-curled lips and sought out her hidden bud. Soon her gasp became long sighs of pleasure, for Pierre's tongue was arousing her to heights of passion that she had not thought to experience with him that night. He was, in her estimation, an amiable young man who could well afford to look after her, but she had no strong feelings about him. She expected that he would make love to her agreeably a time or two before they fell asleep – she was unprepared for the typhoon of passion he was stirring up.

What she did not know about at this stage was Pierre's obsession with her brightly-coloured plaything. From the moment he had caught sight of it the night before, when she was asleep, he had been gripped by so powerful a monomania that he had been able to think of little else. Whether his eyes were open or closed, in his mind there glowed that vivid ginger jewel, to the exclusion of every-thing else. And here he was – Claudette naked and open to him on her bed – her plaything at his complete disposal! He was like a famished man led to a banquet.

Claudette writhed on her back in pleasure and wondered dimly what kind of insatiable lover she had gained, being brought to no less than three dramatic crises of passion in the next twenty minutes by Pierre's tireless tongue. After the third time she lay panting weakly, while Pierre ripped off his clothes and hurled them away from him. Before Claudette could get her breath back, he was on top of her, his belly on hers and his hard spout deep inside her very wet treasure. Without a moment's pause, he rode her firmly towards yet another outburst.

'It's too much . . .' she whimpered, as his belly pounded hers and his hands clenched on the soft flesh of her rump.

But it was too late to complain about what he was doing to her. She moaned loudly when she felt his fleshy probe leap and spurt inside her and, an instant later, she clawed his back with her fingernails in the convulsions of her own release.

After that she fell asleep as if drugged, as in a sense she was – by the emotional fatigue of so much love-making. However much poor Pierre kissed her and stroked her breasts and belly, she lay in a stupor and he was unable to wake her. Her ginger curls lay exposed to his feverish gaze – his ram-rod was hard again and shaking in anticipation – it was utterly impossible that he could sleep until he had enjoyed her at least once more. He turned her gently on to her side, facing away from him, folded at the waist, so that her bare little bottom was thrust towards him. It was easy enough then to grip her just below the smooth cheeks and hold her thighs open enough for his pump-handle to slide into her slippery burrow from the rear. He rocked himself to and fro in a pleasant rhythm, until at last his passion discharged itself into her belly and he was able to turn off the lights and go to sleep.

He had a most marvellous dream of making love to her again – a dream which defied logic and anatomy, as dreams often do. He seemed to be enjoying her ginger alcove with his tongue and his stiff part at the same time! It was so exciting that he woke up – woke slowly to the knowledge that his stem was jutting straight up above his belly, thrills of delight flickering through it just as if he were really making love to Claudette. The thrills became steadily stronger and Pierre knew that he was only instants away from his crisis – he could hear himself giving little moans of pleasure. He opened his eyes slowly, afraid that the wonderful sensations of the dream would disappear if he woke up completely.

There was a good reason for his dream and for the sensations that he was enjoying. He was lying on his back, the bed-sheet thrown aside, and Claudette was lying naked beside him. Her pretty little breasts bounced up and down to the movement of her arm – her long-fingered hand was clasped round his upright staff and she was massaging it firmly.

'Oh,' Pierre sighed, as he grasped what she was doing to him.

Seeing that he was awake at last, Claudette smiled at him, her hand moving more quickly.

'Bonjour, Chéri,' she murmured and, three seconds later, Pierre fountained his desire over his chest and belly.

'I'm glad you woke up in time,' she said. 'I thought you were going to sleep right through it and never know what I'd done to you.'

When he was tranquil again, Claudette released him and slid off the bed. It was with some surprise that he saw that she was pulling on a pair of stockings.

'What are you doing?' he asked lazily.

'Getting dressed.'

'But I want you here in bed with me! There are things I want to do to you, Claudette – lovely things!'

'I thought you might wake up in that state of mind,' she replied, pulling up her skirt and fastening it at the waist, 'so I took the precaution of softening your resolve. It is soft now, I see.'

'But where are you going?'

'I am due at the theatre in half an hour for my rehearsal. There is no time for what you want. Besides you don't really want to make love to me now after what I've done to you.'

'Give me a chance and I'll show you!'

'Later,' she said, sliding a pullover over her head.

'When?'

'You may call for me at eight this evening and take me to dinner.'

She combed out her full black hair and stood up, fully dressed and ready. At the bedroom door she halted to blow a kiss towards Pierre.

'Au revoir, Pierre,' and she was gone.

Pierre lay thinking for a while, content in body and mind after his surprising early-morning call, as one might say. That evening he had an arrangement to meet Nathalie and take her out to dinner. To cancel the arrangement would require explanations – not only to Nathalie but to her father and mother, both of whom took the closest interest in their daughter's happiness and well-being. What Pierre had intended was a quiet dinner followed by an hour at his apartment, when dear Nathalie would let him strip her naked and play with her as he pleased. There was a time – and only a short time ago – when that would have seemed an agreeable evening. But not now that he knew Claudette.

He thought of Nathalie's breasts – soft, round and a joy to feel. They had been handled by no one but himself, he was fairly sure of that. He compared them in his imagination with Claudette's breasts – small and pointed and with an air of nervous agitation about them that hinted at paroxysms of delight, past and future. He thought of the soft brown fleece between Nathalie's thighs and then the bright ginger curls that covered Claudette's mound. He thought of Nathalie's gentle passivity when she lay on her back, leaving it to him to do what he pleased. And he thought of Claudette's participation – her boldness to the point of waking him up with her hand on him to make him squirt.

Only to think about Claudette excited him – her little breasts and her ginger tuft of curls – so much so that his pointer had reared up towards the bedroom ceiling again, though it was no more than twenty minutes since she had humbled its pride with her busy fingers. Pierre's hand curled round it affectionately.

241

It was obvious to him that he was going to spend the evening – and the night – with Claudette. And not only this evening – the next and the next and the one after that. The problem was what excuses to make to Nathalie. The damnable truth is, Pierre said to himself, that I have fallen madly in love with Claudette and I must have her. It is not a question of I would *like* to have her, or that I would *enjoy* having her – I *must* have her. In comparison with that, nothing else is of the least importance! Dear little Nathalie, of whom I was so extremely fond until two days ago, has become a nuisance and a hindrance and I must get rid of her.

It was simple enough for Pierre, lying at his ease in Claudette's bed, fondling his stiff stalk a little and promising it an orgy of delight that evening, to tell himself that he must rid himself of his Nathalie. But as all the world knows, for a man of any station of importance in life to disencumber himself of a fiancée of good family and reputation is a wearisome and bad-tempered business. Nathalie's own reaction was bad enough – she burst into tears and accused Pierre of betraying her love, her trust and her honour. Her mother was more aggressive and wounding – she told Pierre that his conduct had been disgraceful, unspeakable and unpardonable – this presumably being a veiled reference to the pleasure he had enjoyed with Nathalie in bed, she having confided in her mother in her hour of need. Nathalie's father said that he intended to see to it that Pierre was never again welcome among decent people – so perhaps Madame Binet had informed her husband that their daughter's innocence had been grossly abused and that she was no longer *intacta*! Unfortunately, Binet had the influence and standing to ensure that many doors formerly open to Pierre were now closed and bolted against him.

Unpleasant though it was, at last it was done and Pierre was free of obligations towards Nathalie. He was sustained through the experience by the intensity of his emotions towards Claudette and the comfort of her friendship. When she was not working he spent all his time with her – in fact, he had more or less moved into her

242

apartment and returned to his own only when he wanted clothes, or to pick up his mail. After the rehearsals concluded and the play opened at the Theatre Danou, he collected Claudette at the stage door after each performance and took her to supper at any one of the half-dozen fashionable places she liked. Then they had the night together – and the next day – until Claudette departed for the theatre again.

She was an intelligent woman and so it did not take her long to discover the object of Pierre's obsession – and this knowledge she put to good use. Left to his own devices, Pierre would have submitted her ginger jewel to such continuous attention in his impossible attempt to possess it utterly that poor Claudette would have been worn away to skin and bone. But with the glove on the other hand, as one might say, it was now Claudette who decided what games of desire and imagination were played out in her bed. She arranged matters so that Pierre's reserves of virility were fully used and exhausted, to his great satisfaction – and applied also to her own gratification.

None of this was in the least difficult for her to accomplish, as a single hour of experimentation showed her. She woke him one morning about eleven with a cup of café au lait and a croissant and sat on the bed watching him. They had enjoyed a late night, but Pierre looked refreshed and full of energy. When he had finished his breakfast, Claudette slipped off her dressing-gown, under which she wore nothing at all, and ran her fingers over the pink tips of her little breasts.

'You are so beautiful,' Pierre murmured at once, his gaze moving down her slim body to the ginger tuft visible above her crossed thighs. 'Lie down and I will make love to you all morning.'

Without answering, she threw aside the sheet that covered him, pulled the pillow from under his head and, on her knees, straddled his face, her feet against the bedhead. She smiled to herself and nodded when she heard Pierre's long and incredulous gasp, and she lowered herself on him slowly until her ginger-haired plaything was pressed to his face.

'There, my darling Pierre,' she said. 'You like to contemplate the real me – now you have a close-up view and I hope that it pleases you.'

She did not need his muffled gasping to confirm that he was enjoying the experience – he had, as always, slept naked, and his appurtenance was standing at full-stretch and jerking about convulsively.

'The big hand of the clock is now almost at twelve,' she said with a laugh. 'The hour will strike very soon!'

She could feel his wet tongue against the soft lips between her thighs, seeking to enter, and she rubbed herself against it.

'There are days when a man can be easily satisfied,' she said. 'As you were the morning I woke you up by stroking you until your desire made your belly wet. And there are days when a man is hard to satisfy – as on the evening when you forced me to experience four or five climaxes without a pause.'

The tip of his tongue had penetrated her and was inducing little tremors of pleasure in her bud.

'What will happen today, I wonder?' Claudette sighed. 'Will you be quickly satisfied, or will you be insatiable? If I ask you that question, your pride will compel you to say that you will make love to me all day and kill me with ecstasy. So I shall not ask you.'

In fact, she was sure that she already knew the answer, but it was prudent to flatter Pierre by letting him think that his virility was tireless and overwhelming, even though she fully intended to satisfy him within half an hour and have him take her out to lunch before an hour had passed. She lifted herself from his flushed face, slid away from his grasping hands that wanted to play with her ginger toy, and reversed her position above him so that she was straddling his loins, facing him.

'This certainly knows where he wants to go,' she said, taking hold of his twitching device.

Pierre stared open-mouthed as she steered the purple head of his stem into her, between the warm lips he had made wet with his tongue. He gave a long sigh of exaltation as she sank slowly down on him, embedding his hard shaft in her, centimetre by centimetre – making it disappear into her ginger-curled haven. His hands gripped her thighs and his belly fluttered in uncontrollable spasms.

'There – now you possess me,' said Claudette, smiling down at him, 'The real me, the true Claudette, hot as ginger – look for yourself – you possess me completely.'

'Oh my god,' Pierre moaned, his face crimson and his eyes bulging as he stared at the joining of their tenderest parts.

'Does that mean that you are enjoying possessing me?' she asked, riding slowly up and down his trapped stalk. 'If so, then you should tell me so, my dear. I have given you my wet little plaything to do as you please with – but you offer me no word of love in return!'

It was more than Pierre could bear. A long moaning cry escaped him and his long probe delivered his tribute to her desirability.

'Ah – a compliment at last!' Claudette exclaimed, feeling his passion flooding into her.

With such evidence of her power over him now that she understood the true nature of his interest, it was easy for Claudette to arrange matters to her own liking. Pierre's crisis had arrived far too quickly for her to achieve release and so she stayed where she was, sitting over his loins, long after he was calm again and his stem was softening inside her.

'The roles are reversed today,' she told him softly. 'Remember the night when you wore me out completely? I was too tired to respond again, yet you insisted on making love to me again. Now you must satisfy mé, whether you want to or not.'

'But that's impossible – let me rest a little and then I will make love to you.'

'You didn't let me rest – why should I let you? You excited me with your tongue when I sat on your face – and you have excited me even more with your spike – I cannot wait while you rest!'

She made use of her well-developed internal muscles to grip him tight and prevent him from slipping away from her. Her fingernails raked the soft skin of his belly and the inside of his thighs.

'But I can't do anything,' said Pierre.

'What! I let you open my jewel-box and rummage about inside until you present me with a string of pearls – though you had more pleasure in giving than I had in receiving your little gift. Now it is my turn to possess you.'

His fallen soldier twitched a little inside her and she used her nails cruelly on his flat nipples.

'Do you like my ginger muff, Pierre? I think it's very pretty – the way it surrounds your stem, don't you?'

It did not take Claudette very long to manipulate him mentally and physically into the renewed stiffness she wanted.

'Now you can rest,' she said, sliding happily up and down the baton on which she was impaled. 'Rest all you want to, dear Pierre, while I wrap my ginger furcoat round you to keep you warm.'

'Claudette – I love you,' he moaned.

'You love my ginger curls,' she answered, grinning, jolting up and down faster as her arousal grew keener.

'Claudette – I want you to marry me!'

'What a marvellous compliment,' she sighed, her breathing fast and ragged, 'but this is no time for talk of marriage, when you are making me feel so happy!'

'I will make you happy!' he said, misunderstanding her.

'You'll never make me happier than you are doing now!' she exclaimed.

'Marry me!' he gasped.

'This is much more important,' she murmured, riding him very fast.

Before Pierre could pursue his matrimonial proposals, she squealed happily as massive sensations of pleasure gripped her and shook her like a puppet. As for Pierre, the effect of her internal convulsions on his embedded part were such that he had no choice but to deliver his second climactic tribute into her quaking belly.

She lay in his arms afterwards, well pleased with the progress she had made that morning. As she had decided earlier on, it was not a day on which Pierre was difficult to satisfy – for after the experience of being forced to make love to her – or perhaps, one might even say, of being raped by her in a perfectly friendly way – he wanted no more just then. Over lunch in a fashionable restaurant he took up the subject of marriage again. Claudette said that she never accepted proposals of marriage from men on the point of squirting into her purse, mainly because their wits had left them in the emotion of the moment and they did not know what they were saying. Pierre pointed out that he did not have his device in her at that moment and he was totally aware of what he was saying. She replied that she never listened to proposals of marriage from men whose pegs were standing up, even in restaurants, because they were so anxious to get her on her back that they would say anything. Pierre denied that his peg was stiff and insisted that she put her hand in his lap under the table to check for herself. She accused him of trying to get her to play with him in a restaurant.

'How far do you expect me to go?' she demanded. 'All the way? You want me to make you squirt in your trousers – is that it?'

'It's perfectly limp,' Pierre insisted. 'There is no fear of that.'

'Ah, this is one of the days when you are difficult to satisfy!' Claudette sighed. 'Twice between waking up and lunch isn't enough for you! My god, if we were married you'd be doing it to me day and night until I died of total exhaustion – I doubt if I'd survive the honeymoon!'

'It is because I love you so much that I desire you so much,' said Pierre.

'The real me – that's who you love and desire,' she replied, grinning.

'Oh yes, the real you,' he said softly, picturing to himself the bright ginger fleece inside her thin silk knickers.

Naturally, the thought caused his spindle to stand up boldly – just as Claudette belatedly accepted his suggestion to check for herself that it was soft.

'I knew it!' she exclaimed. 'Stiff as a flagpole! All this talk of marriage is only to get me back into bed with you.'

However he tried to get her to take the suggestion seriously, she turned it into a joke. *We hardly know each other* was her principal objection, and when he claimed that they did, she countered that making love to someone twenty or thirty times was neither here nor there – and that she could see no advantage to either of them in an official union. Pierre decided to let the matter drop for the time being, content to be her lover for now and sate himself on her ginger treasure, but determined to come back to the subject when the time seemed right. It was important to him to establish, as soon as he could, some kind of permanent right to what obsessed him between her legs.

It goes without saying that to enjoy the regular attentions of Claudette and intimate access to her ginger jewel was a privilege which cost Pierre a certain amount of money, apart from the cost of dinners and nightclubs. She was a prudent young woman in a risky profession – there could be long unpaid intervals between appearances on the stage. In due course Pierre found himself paying, without protest, a year's rent in advance on her apartment. Often he found himself in expensive shops with her and it was with pleasure that he added to the little black frock she had worn on her first evening with him.

He could well afford all this, and, as he found, the rewards of his generosity were extremely gratifying. As for instance on an afternoon when they returned to her apartment after a shopping expedition and lunch. He had been pacified by her ginger muff once that morning, to put him in the right mood for visiting shops, and now Claudette was intent on reinforcing the lesson that a little expenditure on her led to a very pleasant interlude for him.

She took her purchases into the bedroom to try on, leaving Pierre lounging in an armchair in the sitting-room, waiting for the fashion parade she had promised to put on for him. First she appeared in a frock she had chosen – with his encouragement, despite the price. It was a wispy little creation for the evening, in crimson chiffon, that clung to her pointed little breasts, so cleverly designed that it seemed to reveal more of her than any man had the right to expect in public.

'Tonight we will dine and dance somewhere very special to show off your new frock,' Pierre promised, as she twirled before him, making her skirt flare out to show her knees.

'Somewhere special,' she murmured, and planted a delicate kiss on his forehead before disappearing into the bedroom.

When she came out again, Pierre sighed loudly – and well he might! She had taken off the new frock and was wearing some of the underwear he had bought for her that day. He stared in wordless delight at her slender and pale body, hardly covered at all by flimsy camiknickers of peach-coloured georgette, scalloped at breast and leg with bands of lace.

'What do you think – does it suit me?' she asked, posing for him.

Her jet-black hair and ivory skin ensured that it suited her very well. Pierre reached out both arms towards her, to pull her down on to his lap and play with her. She smiled at him and skipped away.

'You don't think it looks a little indecent?' she asked.

'It looks superb!'

'Then why are you trying to grab me and tear it off?'

'Because I adore you!'

'I suppose I ought to be flattered that you are still interested in me after having me on the sofa before we went out,' she said with a grin, 'but are you sure that it is I who excite you – or is it my silk underwear?'

'Only you!' he murmured. 'You know I can never get enough of you.'

'There is certainly a big bulge in your trousers – I can see it from here,' Claudette observed. 'But on the other hand, it wasn't there when I had my new frock on – only now that you see me in my underwear. Can it be that you are a secret fetishist, darling Pierre?'

'Dressed or undressed, I adore you,' he said fulsomely.

'Perhaps,' she said thoughtfully, standing just out of his reach, her head a little on one side.

Pierre stared at her slender thighs and the lace where they vanished into her camiknickers. Only the thinnest of peach-coloured georgette concealed her ginger tuft from him. He was highly aroused, his staff bulging furiously through the material of his trousers – and Claudette was disposed to make him wait a little before she satisfied his desire, so that by waiting he learned to appreciate the value of what she had to offer him.

'I knew someone once who was a secret fetishist,' she said, her fingers stroking the flimsy material that half hid her pointed little breasts. 'His name was Marcel – do you know him? Marcel Chalon. He was madly in love with someone and when she wasn't there he used to make love to her underwear.'

'How do you know?'

'He told me so himself,' said Claudette noncommittally.

'What did he do?'

'He'd lie on her bed when she was out and open his trousers wide and rub himself with a handful of her knickers and stockings and slips. He'd sprinkle them first with her perfume and close his eyes and caress himself until he squirted into her underwear!'

'Is this true?' Pierre asked softly, his imagination caught by the thought of a lover lying on his back with his trousers undone and a double handful of coloured silk underwear wrapped round his hard shaft, gasping and sighing, his body committed to a convulsion of ecstasy that would soak the flimsy silk with his hot passion.

'Oh,' said Claudette, observing the flush in his cheeks, 'I believe that you must be like Marcel – you'd do it in my underwear with as much pleasure as if you were in me!'

'Never – how can you say that?' Pierre exclaimed hoarsely, his aching stalk twitching furiously inside his trousers.

'There is an easy way to settle the matter,' said Claudette.

She reached between her legs to unfasten the buttons of her camiknickers and turned away from Pierre while she lifted the flimsy garment and tucked it up round her waist, exposing the little round cheeks of her bottom to him.

'Does that make your bulge any bigger?' she asked.

'Judge for yourself,' he answered, wanting her to turn

round and let him see her ginger curls.

'No, you tell me,' she said, keeping her back to him, her hands stroking the cheeks of her bottom to excite him more.

'It is huge,' he said.

'Then it must be very uncomfortable in your trousers,' she suggested, glancing at him over her shoulder, 'Why not let it out into the light of day?'

Pink-faced with emotion, Pierre tugged open his trouser buttons and pulled out his upright and trembling pike-staff, long, thick and eager for action. He had no idea what Claudette intended to do, but he was enjoying her little game. He was hoping that she would come to him and sit on his lap with her camiknickers round her waist, so that he could play with her ginger toy.

Instead, she went to the bookcase by the wall, put her hands on one of the shelves and sank down slowly to her kneed, her back still towards him. Her knees were very wide apart on the parquet floor and he saw, below the enchanting crease of her bottom, her soft plaything – looking for all the world like a split peach with bright ginger fuzz on it.

'Now we shall get at the truth,' Claudette said over her shoulder. 'Which is it that excites you – my underwear or me?'

Pierre babbled nonsense as he slid off his armchair and knelt down close behind her. The soft georgette had slipped down from her slender waist to cover her bottom.

'Well?' Claudette asked. 'Can't you make your mind up? Are you going to do it to me or wrap my underwear round your spike and do it to that?'

An instant later his long handle split her peach open and forced itself inside.

'Claudette – I love you!' he gasped. 'One glimpse of the little treasure between your legs and I am lost!'

'Or is it one glimpse of my underwear that makes you stiff?' she teased him.

He put his hands up the front of her camiknickers to fondle her breasts while he pressed his belly close to her bottom and rocked gently in and out of her warm alcove.

251

'This is all very well,' Claudette announced. 'I only let you look between my legs to settle this question of whether you find me attractive or whether you are a fetishist.'

'You know the answer!' he sighed, his strokes a little faster and deeper now.

'Do I, indeed? It seems to me that while I am trying to resolve a point of some importance,' she continued, her arms stretched up and her fingers clenched on the bookcase shelf as she struggled to keep her voice calm in her mounting excitement, 'a point of considerable importance – the question of whether I should let you touch me again or whether I should send you away with a pair of knickers to satisfy yourself – while I'm trying to settle this, you take advantage of my position and force that unruly thing of yours into me! Is this the way to behave towards me?'

'Yes!' Pierre answered at once. 'This is exactly the way for me to behave towards you, Claudette – day and night!'

The buds of her breasts were hard under his fingers and there were little tremors of pleasure in her belly.

'I must admit that there have been moments when you have made me feel happy,' she murmured.

'Moments! Do not mock me – I have made you scream in ecstasy dozens of times – scores of times!'

He was plunging fast and hard, his hands down on her belly to hold her firmly while he gave full rein to his desire.

'Make me scream now, Pierre!' she gasped.

It did not take him long to do as she requested. Her face was pressed against a row of books, her eyes wide open but seeing nothing, unaware that it was against the collected works of those great dramatists Corneille and Racine that she was being so forcefully made love to.

When the storm of passion abated and they were calm again, Pierre brushed her black hair upwards with his hand so that he could kiss the nape of her neck.

'I love fashion shows,' he told her. 'Is there more to come?'

'Oh yes – three more sets of underwear, if you are not too tired to view them.'

'I think that we should go into the bedroom and examine this new underwear to make sure that it fits properly,' Pierre suggested. 'I seem to remember that you bought a pair of thin white satin knickers – I'm almost sure that the colour of your hair will show through.'

'You'd like that, I'm sure! Come on, then – I'l put them on and you can tell me if you can see through them from the other side of the bedroom.'

'I may have to come closer than that to make sure,' he said, grinning.

However interesting and satisfactory their liaison was to both of them, the truth was that Pierre was obsessed by Claudette, but not she by him. And as is well known, imbalances are unstable, in politics, in finance, in love. There came an evening, three or four months after they first met, when Claudette was not at the stage door when Pierre called for her after the performance. None of her friends and others backstage seemed to know where she could be – or so they insisted. Pierre ran about like a man demented and eventually, by means of a large bribe to a stagehand, he extracted the information that she had left with another man seconds after the final curtain came down – still with her stage make-up and costume on.

Pierre was thunder-struck by what he had been told. *What man*? he demanded, but if anyone knew the answer to that, they did not tell him. For want of any better idea, he made his way back to Claudette's apartment, to wait for her there. By one in the morning he had finished a bottle of cognac and was still waiting. He woke up with a fearful headache in an armchair, fully dressed, the next morning. His wrist-watch indicated that it was after eleven o'clock.

What had woken him was the sound of someone moving about in the kitchen. He dragged himself off the armchair, his back and neck aching, fought down the pangs of nausea brought on by his headache, and stumbled into the kitchen. He found Claudette making coffee. Evidently she had been in the apartment for some time – her black hair was fluffed out as if she had washed and dried it, and she was wearing her flowered dressing-gown.

253

'You look dreadful – sit down!' she said sympathetically.

Pierre collapsed into one of the hard wooden chairs by the kitchen table and stared accusingly at her. She put a large cup of strong black coffee in front of him and sat at the other end of the table.

'How long have you been back?' he demanded.

'An hour or so. I thought it best not to disturb you when I saw the empty bottle on the floor. So I had a bath and washed my hair. Drink your coffee – it will help a little.'

He sipped it in silent misery, hardly able to bring himself to ask the question that had tormented him all night.

'Where were you?' he asked finally, dreading the answer.

'With Denis,' she said at once. 'He came to see me backstage during the intermission.'

'But you hate him – he left you to go with another girl!'

'That's right – I threw a vase of flowers and a pair of shoes at his head. And after that we talked. When the performance ended I went with him. I am sorry it was not possible to leave a note for you explaining things – but I didn't know myself how things stood just then.'

'You had to go to bed with him to find out – is that what you're telling me?'

'We had to talk to each other for a long time for us to understand why we parted.'

'You parted because this Denis person went off with your friend Josette.'

'Ah yes – but why did he go with her when I am better-looking and much more intelligent – and a far better actress, of course? That is what we had to talk about.'

'If you found an answer, I don't want to hear it,' said Pierre morosely, a sickening feeling in his stomach telling him that he was the loser. 'Just tell me what you intend doing.'

'I love Denis,' said Claudette. 'I always have. And he loves me – he has been unhappy without me and he's leaving Josette.'

'I love you too – does that count for nothing?'

'I know you do, dearest Pierre, and I am very fond of you. But I don't love you, and you have no reason to think that I ever did.'

254

Pierre finished his black coffee. It did not make him feel any better.

'You want me out of your apartment so that this treacherous actor can move in,' he said sullenly. 'But why should I make things easy for you?'

'You do not own me, Pierre.'

'That may be, but I cannot live without you.'

'Of course you can. You may feel as if the world has come to an end today, as I did on the night we met. But I survived with your help —and so will you, perhaps with someone else's help.'

'There is no one else. I broke off my engagement for you!'

'Not for me, Pierre. I didn't ask you to do that. Whatever you did, you did it for yourself.'

'Because I wanted you so much! And I still do! More than ever!'

'You never really wanted *me*,' she said. 'You don't even know me. The truth is that I have nothing you want. So let us part as friends.'

'But you do!' he said, with great vehemence, striking the wooden table with his clenched fist.

'You are mistaken, my friend,' Claudette said, softly but firmly.

She got up from her chair, untied her sash-belt and held her dressing-gown wide open. Pierre glanced at her pretty breasts and his teeth clenched at the thought that they had been handled and kissed all night by another man. He summoned up his courage to look at the join of her thighs, where another stalk had probed and pushed and slid and gushed its sap for someone else's pleasure. Where he expected to see the bright ginger fleece that aroused him so fiercely, all that was to be seen was a tuft of jet-black curls clipped short.

'But, but, but . . .' he stammered, not believing his eyes.

'I became bored with being different colours – like a pet cat,' Claudette told him, 'so on the way home this morning I stopped at my hairdresser's and persuaded him to put the same colour on as he uses on my head. Heavens –

he was incredibly embarrassed at so simple a job! You'd have thought he'd never seen a woman with her knickers off before!'

'No, no, no!' Pierre gasped. 'Impossible!'

'Very possible, as you can see,' said Claudette, smiling at him. 'The effect is gorgeous, don't you think? I clipped it short in the bath to get that effect against my skin.'

'Oh, my god, you've spoiled everything!' he moaned, staring in horror and outrage at her raven-black little curls. 'There's nothing in the least exciting about that!'

'I'm getting dressed now to go out,' she said, wrapping the dressing-gown tightly about her, the show over. 'When I come back this afternoon I shall not be alone do you understand? Please be gone by then.'

'But why, why . . .' he was murmuring.

'Goodbye, Pierre.' She walked out of the kitchen.

Pierre covered his face with his hands and, overcome by grief for his loss, wept quietly.

An evening at the Opera

Victor Darridan was a dozen years older than his cousin Marc and probably a dozen times richer. The acquaintance between them was cordial enough, but their meetings were infrequent and always at family gatherings, the grandest of which was undoubtedly Victor's marriage. That his cousin should marry at all caused Marc to raise his eyebrows. Victor was approaching forty and he lived very quietly with his widowed mother, his main interest being music. Marc had assumed – when he had troubled himself to think about the matter at all, which was rarely – that Victor contented himself with regular visits to one of the better private establishments when he felt a desire for the intimate company of a young woman for an hour, and then returned home to his music and his mother.

Even more surprising than that Victor should marry at all was his choice of bride – an outstandingly beautiful girl of whose family no one had ever heard. She was not merely younger than Victor, but younger even than Marc! But why not, thought Marc at the wedding ceremony, it seems that poor Victor has discovered the delights of love at last, rather than the easy pleasures of the girls at Maison Junot or elsewhere. And he has found someone admirably suited to the exploration of those joys which form the basis of a satisfactory and enduring relationship between a man and a woman. No doubt Victor's mother was displeased by this show of independence by her son, but the money is Victor's not hers, Marc reflected, observing the pursed lips of old Madame Darridan as she watched the priest bless the union of Victor and Alice – but in time she will adapt herself to the presence of a second Madame Darridan in the household.

Half a year passed before Marc saw his cousin again. He was invited to dine with the Darridans, along with seven or eight other cousins, aunts and uncles. Victor's mother proved to be as formidable as ever, but his wife Alice was even more beautiful than Marc recalled from the wedding celebrations, if that were possible. The food and wine were magnificent – Victor could always be relied upon for that, but otherwise it was an undistinguished party and Marc hoped that at least a year would pass before he was invited again.

But not so. Only a month – less than a month – elapsed before he received another invitation from Victor – this time to attend a performance at the opera with him and Alice. There was a new production of *Samson and Delilah* – an event which held little attraction for Marc, who much preferred the sort of music to be heard at the Folies Bergères and other places of entertainment where pretty girls appeared on stage very lightly clothed. But Victor's invitation was an opportunity for Marc to be seen with people of importance and therefore not to be declined.

At the appointed time he presented himself at the Darridan apartment and drank a glass or two of excellent champagne. On learning that Victor's mother was also to be of the party, Marc's heart sank a little and he held out his glass to the servant to be refilled. Aunt Berthe had always been his least favourite aunt, even as a child. Her permanent expression was one of disapproval – she seemed to disapprove of everyone she knew, with the single exception of her own son, and she disapproved of everything anyone ever did. Marc was puzzled by the thought that she had, though many years ago, opened her legs for Victor's father to make her conceive – presumably she had found the entire process most distasteful and had nagged her husband to get it over with quickly.

Naturally, Victor had one of the best boxes at the opera, being a constant attender there, as well as at symphonic concerts, piano recitals and other forms of musical endeavour. In the foyer Marc bowed to two married women he knew well and they smiled back, both a little surprised to see him there. On the way to the box he said good evening to a deputy he knew slightly, and was pleased to have his greeting returned. Victor introduced him to one or two of his friends and their wives, but the men were professors of music and of no interest to Marc. One of them had a plump and pretty young wife with a certain gleam in her eye, and to her Marc was particularly charming.

Victor and his mother took the two front seats in their box, Marc and Alice the two rear seats. All consulted their programmes and talked of nothing much until the lights were dimmed and the orchestra began to play. Marc attempted to interest himself in the performance, but his attention soon wandered away from the stage, and he occupied himself by gazing surreptitiously at Alice.

If I were a painter, thought Marc, I would paint her portrait and it would be a masterpiece – *Madame Alice Darridan at the opera* – what a subject for an artist of talent!

Indeed, Alice was worthy of any man's attention that evening, painter or not. She was wearing a jet black evening frock, from the hand of a master couturier, made of watered silk, sleeveless and with the bodice cut in so deep and acute a triangle that its point ended deep between her breasts. It fitted her as closely as a second skin and therefore, Marc concluded, it was impossible that she should be wearing anything under it except her silk stockings and the tiniest of knickers, for no line showed through the frock at hip or thigh.

She was in profile to him and he was watching her out of the corner of one eye, not wanting to draw her attention to his study of her beauty. Her face was of classical proportions, with a straight nose and a graceful jawline. Her dark brown hair was arranged in what was thought to be a Spanish style – parted centrally and swept back, with a long ringlet just in front of each enchanting little ear Her long and slender neck was encircled by three strands of matched pearls, and her bare shoulders were deliciously rounded.

Under the dramatic black of her frock her breasts were very well shaped. If a man dared reach out towards them, Marc thought, he would find no more than a thin layer of silk between his hand and those superb adornments! How on earth Victor had managed to find for himself so desirable a wife was a mystery. But there it was – Victor was an exceptionally fortunate man.

Or so Marc thought at the moment. It was during the second act of the opera that he first had reason to ask himself whether relations between Victor and the beautiful Alice were as loving as they might be. She too had lost interest in the work being performed and was fidgeting a little. Victor, sitting in front, was so rapt in the singing that he would not have noticed if Alice had got up and walked out of the box. As for Aunt Berthe, she was a little deaf and was leaning forward, a hand cupped behind one ear, in total concentration.

In due course Marc's watchfulness was rewarded in a way he could never have imagined. From the corner of his eye he saw Alice raise one slender arm and slip her hand into the deep décolletage of her frock. For a moment or two Marc thought she was relieving some minor discomfort – not that one could associate anything as vulgar as an itch with Alice – but, when her hand remained inside her frock, he was forced to the conclusion that she was caressing herself! He almost gasped aloud at the thought, but controlled himself and smiled in the dark. There was not a man present in the opera house that evening who would not have gone down on his knees to beg for the privilege of caressing Alice's breasts – and here she was, performing this little act of love for herself! It seemed to Marc that Victor must be neglecting to pay his regards to Alice's breasts frequently enough to content her – and they had been married for only seven or eight months.

He heard her utter a guarded little cough, as if to reach his ears alone, and he turned his head to look at her fully. Her hand was still in her frock and she was smiling openly at Marc! He smiled back and glimpsed the tip of her tongue briefly between her red lips. Having captured his attention, she took her hand from her décolletage and slipped her frock off one shoulder for an instant or two, so that he saw one delicious pale breast. He reached out cautiously towards her thigh, to stroke it, but she shook her head vigorously at him and hid her breast again. Marc clasped his hands in his lap, where something was growing hard and long, and waited to see what Alice would do next to amuse herself.

When she was satisfied that he would keep his hands to himself, she uncrossed her long legs and took hold of the hem of her frock. She was staring at Marc's face while she raised her frock slowly above her knees, and on up her thighs. Marc could not suppress the sigh that escaped him when she uncovered her stocking-tops and then the bare skin above them. At this point she paused and waited for him to look up from her thighs to her face, and gave him a mocking little smile. Marc nodded his head several times willing her to continue her little game. She pointed a finger towards Victor's back and cocked her head to one side, as if asking Marc whether he minded if Victor looked round and saw what was going on. Marc shrugged his shoulders, indicating his indifference to Victor, and Alice eased her hem up higher still, though very slowly, as if to torture him with anticipation.

What had grown long and hard under Marc's clasped hands in his lap was quivering as the hem crawled higher, centimetre by centimetre, showing him long and pale-skinned thighs. He was waiting for the moment when her underwear came into view, but he waited in vain. What he glimpsed, instead of the silk and lace morsel he expected, was a tuft of dark curls. This time he could not prevent himself from gasping loudly, but by good fortune the singers on the stage were just then performing a fortissimo passage, and he was not heard by Victor.

Alice was smiling broadly at his reaction to the discovery that she had nothing on under her black frock but her stockings. And even as Marc stared, enthralled by the graceful lines of her thighs and the darkness of her curls, she put her fingers to those very curls and started to caress herself. Marc's blood pounded in his head and he could feel his eyes bulging out like a frog's! As for the stiff prisoner in his trousers, that was jerking about furiously in its desperation to be released from its dark confinement.

'Alice!' Marc whispered under cover of the music,

directing his plea to her ears alone.

Her hand left her curls for a moment to point at his lap, and she nodded and smiled at him. Her long fingers resumed their loving task between her legs and Marc understood what she was suggesting – and the thought both excited and terrified him. He looked at the back of Victor's head, and then at Aunt Berthe, both absorbed in the spectacle on the stage, then back at Alice. He unbuttoned his trousers, his fingers shaking so much that he fumbled at them. Alice's smile took on a languorous look and Marc thought that her beautiful eyes narrowed as she caught sight of his released prisoner, standing up stiff and pale from his open trousers. Her fingers continued their work of pleasuring herself and she nodded gently towards Marc's lap, to indicate to him what she expected him to do.

Naturally, Marc was appalled by the risk he was taking. If either Victor or Aunt Berthe glanced round for a moment and saw what he was displaying, there would be a quarrel of catastrophic proportions. Yet he was so aroused that any risk seemed as nothing at that moment. It was the sight of Alice's naked thighs that had brought him to this fever-pitch, of course, and the colossal impact on him of seeing her caress herself between those thighs – and perhaps even more than that, it was the expression on her face – a look he had not seen before on any woman's face – an expression of calm voluptuousness that would have stiffened even a eunuch's appendage.

Marc had arranged his programme, opened like a book, in front of his upright part, to screen it from any casual glance by Victor or his mother. He was trapped in a complicated maze of strong emotions – afraid to take hold of his stalk and do what his body was demanding, but even more afraid to hide it back in his trousers in case Alice took it badly and dropped her skirt in retaliation. He stared at her face, not at her thighs or the moving hand between them, and he saw her eyes close and her mouth pout as she neared her goal. Her breasts were rising and falling in the most exciting manner to her rapid breathing – and Marc lost all control of himself at the sweet sight. He reached quickly between her legs, forced her hand aside

262

and pressed his fingers between the warm lips concealed by her dark little tuft of curls. At once her body went rigid on her chair and her head went back until she was staring blindly up at the ceiling as she struggled to remain silent through a long climax of delight. Marc's fingers were deep inside her wet warmth, forcing her by expert caresses to experience her sensations to the fullest extent to which she was capable. She had hold of his wrist and was trying to pull his hand away from between her thighs, but he was far stronger and he allowed her not the least remission from her long ecstasy.

It was only when she was completely finished and the last tremor had gone from her belly that Marc took his hand away, hearing her sigh faintly as if regretting that the pleasure had ended. He quickly reimprisoned his furiously disappointed part and looked at Alice again. Her frock was modestly down over her knees, and her knees were crossed, effectively barring the way to any exploring hand. Marc smiled at her in a way that was meant to convey that he thought she was adorable, that he was enchanted by what had happened between them, and that he was on fire with impatience to meet her in private so that even more interesting things could happen – all this in one smile was asking a great deal, of course. He was rewarded with a glare so icy that he could feel the marrow in his bones freezing solid – and his prisoner wilted instantly in his trousers. After that Alice turned her face towards the stage and studiously ignored him.

During the intermission she continued to ignore him, not even replying to the most polite of questions on how she was enjoying the performance. Clearly she was deeply offended with Marc, though the reason was beyond him to guess. Was it that she had wanted her pleasure to last longer and was annoyed with him for terminating it by touching her hidden bud so decisively? But that could not be it – she had been about to do it anyway when he touched her. Marc was at a complete loss to account for the sudden and dramatic change in her attitude towards him.

Before the final act of the opera began, Alice asked her husband to change places with her, claiming that she particularly enjoyed this part and would like to see the stage more clearly. Victor changed seats with her and for the whole of the last act Marc saw only the back of her head and her pretty shoulders above the back of her chair. Whether the last act was any better than what had gone before, he never discovered, for he heard not one single note of it. He was far too preoccupied with the vexatious question of what he had done to offend the beautiful Alice. He had gone along with her dangerous little game at her invitation – not all the way, perhaps, if she wanted to see him reach his crisis under cover of the programme – but he had shown his goodwill towards her. He had assisted her to reach her soaring peak of pleasure – perhaps she wanted to do that for herself. But there was no cause that Marc could think of that could possibly justify her coldness to him.

When the opera ended Alice announced that she had developed a headache. In consequence, they did not go on anywhere for a drink or something to eat. Victor put his wife and mother into a taxi, wished Marc goodnight and left him on the pavement outside the opera house. Baffled beyond measure, Marc went home and to bed, puzzled by the ways of women – not for the first time in his life. He dreamed of Alice that night – what man would not, after such an encounter. In his dream they were in the opera box again and her black frock had vanished, as clothes often do in dreams. She was so beautiful naked that he knelt beside her chair to kiss her belly with reverence, and he felt tears running down his face, so strong were his emotions. He knelt between her parted thighs and slid his long stem into the soft slips beneath her dark tuft. She called over his shoulder to her husband – *Victor, look what Marc is doing to me!* And as Marc slid in and out of Alice's warm little aperture, he heard Victor say, *Not now, Alice – wait till the intermission.* And Aunt Berthe's voice said disapprovingly, *Be quiet, the two of you – Victor wants to hear the singing*.

Marc fountained his passion into Alice's graceful little belly, gasping out that he loved her to distraction. As he did so, he woke in his own bed, alone, and found that the prisoner who had been briefly released in the darkness of the opera box and then hurried back to his cell had taken his revenge on his cruel jailer and was blurting his outrage into Marc's silk pyjamas.

When he was finally appeased and losing his rigidity, Marc lay thinking about his dream. It was a poor way to enjoy the delights which Alice had let him glimpse so tantalisingly, but it was useless to reproach nature for insisting on having its own way. In a sense, what had occurred was to be preferred to what had been in his mind when the Darridan family had abandoned him on the pavement outside the opera. His immediate thought then, bearing in mind his arousal and frustration, was to go to the apartment of a woman friend he had known for almost a year and stay the night with her. Though he was tempted, he had decided against it, his reasoning being that he would be thinking of Alice while he made love to Léa, and that would have been unsatisfactory to him and to her. At least he had enjoyed the illusion of making love to Alice – and it seemed so real that he wondered whether, in the unlikely event that the opportunity would present itself to make love to her, the reality could be as marvellous as the dream.

Beyond that, as the dream faded from his mind, there came the thought that the truth often reveals itself in dreams, if the dreamer can interpret them correctly. Not that Marc in any way believed in the mystifications of fortune-tellers who pretended that the future could be foretold from omens, signs and dreams – that would be absurd – but he did believe that in sleep the mind analyses events, causes and reasons and presents its findings in vivid and apparently unrelated images which, like a story in a foreign language, need to be translated properly to be understood. It therefore seemed to him beyond argument that Victor was neglecting his young wife, for there was no other way to account for her behaviour. And it seemed also beyond doubt that she misbehaved in order to spite Victor. The conclusion from that was that Alice might well be eager for a lover. With this thought in mind, Marc fell asleep again and did not wake until after nine.

He was still in his dressing-gown when the door bell rang sharply. That surprised him – as a man of leisure who often brought a woman friend home for the night, he discouraged visits from friends before midday, at which time he usually went out to lunch. He wondered, with a sudden feeling of guilty trepidation, if his unexpected visitor could be Victor, given a false version of events at the opera by Alice and here to seek revenge. But on reflection, that made no sense – Alice was not likely to tell her husband that she had exposed her charms to his cousin.

He was right, of course – it was not Victor ringing the door bell so persistently. It was Alice herself, and her expression was one of furious anger. She pushed past Marc rudely and strode into his sitting-room, her voice shrill as she denounced him for his abominable behaviour the evening before. Marc closed the apartment door and followed her into the sitting-room, amazed by her attitude, and even more amazed by her presence.

They stood facing each other – there being no point in inviting her to sit down in the mood she was in – and Marc kept silent in the face of her noisy rage. While he was trying to make sense of her grievance against him he could not fail to notice how very alluring she was that morning. She was wearing a white silk blouse, which draped itself over her breasts in a most enchanting manner, and a close-fitting black skirt which shaped her slender hips perfectly. Her little black hat was as flat and no larger than a saucer, and had one tall black feather which pointed upwards at an angle. There was nothing much Marc could do but wait for her anger to subside, so that they could converse more normally and he could ascertain the reason for her state of mind. But instead of subsiding, her rage increased, as if his very silence and immobility contributed to it, and she stepped closer to him and thumped at his chest with black-gloved fists.

It was when she threatened to tell Victor that she had been unspeakably molested at the opera and very nearly violated against her will, that Marc saw that the situation was a comic one. Without attempting by word or expression to halt her tirade, he slowly undid the buttons of her silk blouse and unclipped the half-cup brassiere beneath it. Alice did nothing to prevent this baring of her provocative little breasts and, as Marc fondled them, her torrent of abuse slowed to a trickle and then stopped altogether. Her fists rested against his chest, but she was no longer beating him.

'I am so pleased that you came here this morning,' said Marc, trying very hard not to grin, 'it gives me the opportunity to offer my sincere apologies for the misunderstanding between us yesterday evening.'

'I want no apology!' Alice exclaimed, with a final spark of her original fire. 'Some things are unforgivable!'

'Oh, I entirely agree,' said Marc, 'but I respect you very greatly, Alice, and I would be desolated to think that I had offended you beyond the possibility of understanding and forgiveness.'

He spoke this nonsense with all due solemnity while he was unfastening her skirt – and a moment later it slid down her long legs to the floor. He gazed into her dark brown eyes to assure her of his sincerity, while passing a hand down her smooth belly. His sense of touch informed him that she had no underwear on when his fingers reached her tuft of curls.

'This is the strangest apology I have ever heard of,' she said, her voice indignant.

'Words are cheap,' he answered, his hand stroking between her legs 'I feel that something more than words is called for to efface my offence.'

'I've had enough apologies at home to know how little words mean!' she exclaimed, 'But this – you go too far.'

However ridiculous the situation was, Marc was determined to enjoy it to the full. Alice might never be in his apartment again. The stiff part under his dressing-gown was even more determined to take advantage of events, to judge by its trembling.

'You are so very beautiful that I was completely carried away by my emotions,' said Marc, by way of explanation rather than excuse. 'Surely you can understand that?'

'You molested me!' she insisted primly. 'And in the presence of my husband and mother-in-law! You subjected me to a crude and gross act of depravity!'

The undeniable fact that he was at that moment molesting her in exactly the same crude way did not appear to have registered on Alice's mind. Or such was the hypocritical game she was playing.

'I confess it,' said Marc, finding it almost impossible not to grin, 'I molested you shamefully! I ask your pardon on my knees!'

He suited the action to the word by going down on both knees and kissing her bare belly.

'If you are truly sincere . . .' she said hesitantly, trembling a little as the tip of his warm tongue touched for a moment the soft lips between her legs.

'I am,' he assured her, 'completely and utterly sincere, Alice.'

'Then you are forgiven,' she said in a soft voice.

Marc stood up, took her hand and kissed it, pressing his lips to the soft and thin leather of her glove.

'Thank you, Alice,' he said, his tone very sincere indeed as he played out the comedy with her. 'And now that we have cleared up our little misunderstanding, we can be friends. I have wanted to be your friend since I first met you – at your wedding, that was – but until now that has been impossible. Come and sit down and have coffee while we talk – I'd just made it when you arrived.'

She let him lead her to the sofa and they sat together as if this were an ordinary social visit. Each gave the impression of not noticing that Alice was naked except for her shoes and stockings, her white gloves and the little hat with the long feather.

'I can't stay long,' she said in a conversational tone, 'I have so much to do this morning.'

'Naturally,' said Marc, equally casually, his hand stroking her round little breasts and making their pink buds stand firm, 'but I must ask you – what was Victor's opinion of the performance last evening?'

'He rated it highly,' she answered, 'though he had a slight criticism of the orchestra, which he said was at times a little too loud for the singers.'

'He is right,' said Marc, who had no opinion at all on the matter. 'But what of the staging – was that to his liking?'

Alice related Victor's expert opinions, which had been conveyed to her over breakfast, and Marc caressed her thighs above her garters, where her skin was like satin to his touch. He progressed slowly to the curls where her thighs joined, and Alice's voice quavered slightly. Nevertheless, she continued to talk while he parted the fleshy petals under her curls and stroked her where she had stroked herself the previous evening.

'I didn't know that you were so interested in music,' she said at the end of her recital of Victor's opinions, though she was by then flustered by her rising emotions.

'Of all the arts, it is music that interests me the most,' Marc answered – which was in a way true, for his interest in any of the arts was small, unless half-naked girls dancing on the stage at the Folies Bergères could be counted among the arts.

He eased Alice down full-length on the cushions, on her side and supported by the sofa-back. He lay facing her and quickly opened his dressing-gown and pyjamas. Alice's gloved hand took charge of his freed prisoner.

'Which do you prefer,' she asked breathlessly, 'opera or orchestral music?'

'That is not a question to be answered without careful consideration,' he said, his hand raising her left knee to part her thighs widely.

Alice guided her warm handful towards the entrance of her curls and Marc sank it into her with a long, slow push. She gave a little sigh of content.

'It's so nice to be friends,' she said. 'I hate quarrels.'

'Quarrels are only for enemies,' said Marc, establishing an easy rhythm in the velvety alcove he had penetrated.

'And friends help each other with all the difficulties of life,' she murmured. 'They comfort each other and help with problems.'

'You may rely on me to help you with any problem you ever have,' said Marc, his voice becoming very uneven under the pressure of his sensations.

Alice's dark eyes were almost closed and she was breathing quickly as he slid to and fro. On her face was the expression of voluptuous tranquillity he had seen the evening before when she was exciting herself.

'Oh, Alice!' Marc murmured, hardly knowing what he was saying, so fantastic were the waves of pleasure coursing through him. 'I never imagined . . .'

'Don't say anything,' she whispered.

Not that there was time left for him to say anything, even if he had been capable of rational speech. His dream of the night before had come true and he could only gasp while his busy stalk leaped furiously and bestowed in her belly its tribute to Alice's beauty. Alice whimpered in ecstasy and writhed against him.

When at last their throes subsided, Marc tried to kiss her. She presented her cheek to him, not her mouth, and it was all that he could do to keep himself from laughing at so ludicrous a response after the intimacy they had just shared.

'You offered me coffee,' she said. 'Black with no sugar, please.'

Marc disengaged himself from her and went to the kitchen. When he returned with the two porcelain cups, she was sitting up again, her back straight and her legs crossed elegantly, though all that she had on were her shoes, silk stockings and gloves – and her chic little hat! Its long feather had been ruffled badly during her climactic little episode and was bent over at a sharp angle, the tip pointing towards her left ear.

While they drank their coffee they conversed in so normal a manner that Alice might as well have been fully dressed, though Marc was pleased that she was not, for the beauty of her slender body was a joy to see. The gentle sway of her naked breasts as she moved her arms was nothing less than poetry expressed in movement. She asked how long he had lived in this apartment and congratulated him on furnishing it in so modern and pleasing a style. She was enthusiastic about the colour scheme, so that Marc after a while thought it not unreasonable to suggest that she might give him her expert opinion on the bedroom, where the colours were totally different. Alice expressed herself perfectly willing to give him the benefit of her advice and accompanied him to the room in question.

She found the colour-scheme there much to her liking, declaring that while it gave a strongly masculine impression, it was one of harmony and comfort. As if to demonstrate what she meant, she took off her tiny hat with the ruined feather and lay on her back on the bed. She glanced briefly at her little gold wrist-watch set with diamonds and reminded Marc that she must leave quite soon. It would have been impolite to make her late for her appointment, whatever it might be, and so Marc stripped off his dressing-gown and pyjamas and lay beside her to kiss her breasts.

'I am delighted that we have cleared up the misunderstanding which threatened our friendship,' he murmured, his fingers between her thighs.

'And so am I', she replied. 'I have wanted a good friend to confide in for a long time.'

Marc ran the tip of his tongue down her belly towards her curls and assured her that she could confide in him with complete confidence.

'Then that will make four people happy,' she said.

'Four?'

'I shall be happy because I have you to confide in, you will be happy because you enjoy giving me your assistance – that was very clear to me out there on your sofa! Victor will be happy because I shall be better disposed towards him now that my urgent problem is solved, and his mother will be happy because she thinks of nothing but the tranquillity of her son.'

'It is extremely rare that so many people can achieve happiness in so simple a manner,' said Marc, noticing that Alice was still wearing her black suede gloves, 'Does Victor not appreciate you properly?'

'He thinks of nothing but his music,' Alice sighed, as Marc positioned himself between her parted legs.

'I should say that I am sorry to hear that,' said Marc, easing himself forward to embed his stiff device in her furry aperture, 'but on the other hand, to be honest, I can see advantages in the present arrangement.'

'The present arrangement is very much to my liking,' Alice whispered, her hips rising rhythmically to meet his thrusts.

Her arms were round him and he felt the unfamiliar

sensation of the soft suede of her gloves tracing down his back. He murmured her name and continued with what he was doing, enthusiastically assisted by Alice, until their game reached its natural conclusion in convulsions of delight. After that Alice uttered a long sigh of satisfaction and said that she really must go now.

'I was hoping that you would stay for lunch,' said Marc, stretching out beside her in great content, 'Nothing elaborate – but I entertain here so seldom that it would please me very much to have you as a guest.'

'You've had me twice already – wasn't that as a guest?'

'As a friend, dear Alice.'

'It's not even half-past eleven,' she informed him, consulting her tiny watch. 'It's far too early for lunch.'

'But we have so much to talk about,' Marc replied at once, 'it will be time for lunch before we have finished.'

'Is there any more to be said between us?' Alice asked, smiling at him lazily. 'I thought it had all been said for the present – or am I wrong?'

'You underestimate me. Or perhaps you are judging me by Victor. My conversation is of less intellectual weight than his, I grant you – but it is of great interest to a beautiful woman like you.'

'It has been so far,' she admitted.

'Good – I can sustain this conversation for longer than you might guess.'

'Then I was right to choose you as the person in whom to confide!'

'I am ready for your confidences at any time, Alice. It is right that we should confide in each other – you and I are of the same age, almost. We have much to say to each other that older people cannot follow.'

'I was twenty last April,' said Alice, taking her gloves off at last, an act which Marc interpreted to mean that she would stay for lunch.

'Victor is twenty years older than you,' he said. 'He can't possibly enjoy the sort of conversation that we younger people do – or if he did once, he has forgotten.'

'I don't believe that he ever did.' said Alice, pouting a little. 'His mother brought him up to be middle-aged while

272

he was still young.'

'Why did you marry him?'

'Victor is a charming man. He is also a rich man. My parents are neither charming nor rich. I had to make the best choice I could, at an age when girls should be enjoying themselves at dances and parties. I was lucky to meet Victor and even luckier to attract him enough to marry me. There's the whole story!'

'Victor is the lucky one, to meet a girl as beautiful as you! Do you love him?'

'I respect him. He was the answer to many problems in my life.'

'Yet one problem remains – until today.'

'Until today,' she agreed, smiling at him.

Marc turned her over so that she lay face-down on his bed. He massaged her long and slender back with extreme sensuousness, eliciting little sighs of pleasure from her. When he reached her pert little bottom he paid special attention to it, kneading the warm flesh lovingly – and taking the utmost care not to mark her perfect satin skin.

'I've never had that done to me before,' she murmured, her face pressed into the pillow. 'I like it – don't stop.'

'But surely you had a lover before you married Victor?'

'You may laugh if you will, but I was a virgin when I married,' Alice answered with a happy giggle. 'The most I'd let any boy do was kiss me and touch my breasts under my clothes.'

'And that was all you knew?' Marc asked in surprise.

'Well . . . there was one boy I liked so much that I let him put his hand up my skirt and play with me a little. But that was all. Victor was my first lover, on our wedding night.'

'What? He didn't make love to you until then, even though you were engaged?'

'At a concert of Debussy music once he put his hand on my thigh and stroked it a little in the dark. I thought he would make love to me after the concert, but nothing happened.'

'My poor, beautiful Alice!' Marc exclaimed, astonished by what he was hearing about his cousin Victor – he had evidently been wrong to assume, as he had before the

273

wedding, that Victor had been in the habit of visiting private establishments to pacify his desires.

He rolled Alice over gently and massaged her soft belly and the insides of her thighs until she was trembling hard, then slipped two fingers into her wet little entrance to caress her hidden button.

'When I did this to you at the opera, it made you angry,' he said, 'though now you are enjoying it.'

'You are the first man ever to bring on my crisis by stroking me there,' she whispered.

'Surely not! What about the special boyfriend who put his hand up your skirt to play with you?'

'All he touched was my knickers,' she said virtuously.

'Then it is a great honour for me to be allowed to pleasure you in this way,' said Marc, his rearing stem quivering boldly.

He studied the calm and voluptuous expression of her face and thought that she was the most adorable woman he had ever seen – let alone caressed in this most intimate of ways.

'Why was I invited to the opera?' he asked. 'Victor knows I'm not interested in that sort of music.'

'It was my suggestion that he should invite you,' she murmured.

'Ah – you wanted to see me again!'

'I thought that you might be the right person for my confidences,' she sighed, her hips squirming on the bed as he brought her closer to her critical moments. And then closer still, till she was only a hair's-breadth away from ecstasy.

'I'm going to do it!' she gasped, and her bottom lifted off the bed as her sensations reached a climax of delight.

Marc watched in rapture the shaking of her breasts and the trembling of her belly. He continued to caress her until she slid gently down from her peak of pleasure.

'Why were you angry with me at the opera?' he asked. 'After all, it was you who raised your frock and showed yourself to me.'

'I don't know why I did it,' she answered, looking away from him as if embarrassed. 'I was bored – and I was very

274

angry with Victor. It is two weeks since he came to my bedroom.'

'Your bedroom? You have separate rooms?'

'From the day we married, it was his idea, not mine. At first he came to my room three or four times a week, but now his visits are rare.'

'So you wanted a little revenge on him?' Marc asked, smiling at her.

'I wasn't thinking clearly, or I would never have dared pull my frock up like that. Perhaps I hoped that Victor would turn round and see you looking at what he never wants to see now – does that make sense?'

'Yes, you wanted to revenge yourself – I understand that perfectly. And you wanted me to get mine out and stroke it to prove to yourself that you had the power to excite a man – a normal man, at least, if not Victor. But when I put the finishing touch to what you were doing to yourself, you became angry with me. Why was that?'

'The moment my crisis started I was terrified that he would turn round and see your hand between my legs. That would be the end of everything between Victor and me. It was fear, not anger, that made me act the way I did.'

'And today there is no cause for either fear or anger because he is not here to see what you have been doing. You have revenged yourself on him completely.'

'Yes,' said Alice, with a happy smile, 'though it is more a question of what has been done to me, rather than what I have been doing. These two hours with you have been the most exciting of my life, Marc. You have changed my outlook dramatically. I know that I need never be unhappy again, however cold Victor may be.'

'You have only to come here and I will make you happy at any time of the day,' Marc murmured, his hand smoothing over her belly and up to her breasts.

'But it is my turn to make *you* happy,' she replied. 'I see you are ready for it.'

She took hold of his stiff projection and pulled him gently towards her. He put his belly on hers and slid into her like a hand into a soft glove made to fit it.

'I know so little about men,' Alice sighed, though she

275

knew enough to pull her pretty knees up and part them widely to accommodate Marc. 'My only experience has been with Victor, and that has been disappointing.'

'You are made for love, my beautiful Alice,' Marc murmured, plunging firmly.

'In one morning you have been inside me more times than Victor does in a month! Is that how it should be, Marc? If you and I were married, would you make love to me three times every day?'

'At least!' he gasped, his thrusting becoming quicker as his desire mounted sharply towards its zenith.

Alice was not sharing his ecstasy this time. She lay comfortably on her back, watching his flushed face and stroking his cheeks, until he gushed his passion into her belly and lay trembling on her.

'Oh!' he exclaimed in dismay. 'What is it, Alice?'

'Nothing,' she replied. 'It felt nice, but you have exhausted me for the present with your love-making, that's all. I am not used to it on this scale, you must remember.'

Marc pulled away from her and took her in his arms.

'It was inconsiderate of me to continue when you were not enjoying it.'

'But I did enjoy it! Not in the same way as you did, but I had the satisfaction of knowing that you desired me and were demonstrating your desire in the best way possible. Perhaps it is difficult for you to understand how important that is to me.'

Though Marc had told her that he would make love to her a dozen times a day if they were married, he was overstating his capabilities, as all men do. His third effort, delightful though it had been, had fatigued him. He was secretly glad that Alice had come to a standstill. After a little while, she fell asleep in his arms, very content with her morning, and, not long afterwards, Marc sank into a light doze, his hand resting on Alice's warm belly – and he too was very pleased with the way the day had turned out after so inauspicious a beginning.

When he woke up, he craned his neck to look at the little gold watch on Alice's wrist, and saw that it was well after one o'clock. He kissed her face until her eyes opened.

'Marc!' she murmured. 'I was having a lovely dream about you!'

She smiled and stretched and looked at her watch and said that she was hungry.

'So am I,' Marc agreed, 'and you promised to stay for lunch.'

When they got off the bed Alice decided not to put her clothes on, saying that she had so few opportunities to be seen and admired naked that she did not intend to miss this one. Marc put on a pair of trousers as a precaution against minor injuries while he was cooking, and together they went into the kitchen. It was not often that Marc ate at home, but the woman who cleaned for him made sure that light provisions were available in case of emergencies. Marc inspected his supplies and announced that lunch would consist of an omelette aux fines herbes and a bottle of white wine. In due course they sat facing each other across the table and he had the engaging spectacle before him of Alice's round little breasts bobbing and swaying as she ate and drank.

'I understand very well why Victor wanted to marry you,' he told her, 'but not why he sleeps alone at night.'

'You don't understand at all – he didn't marry me because he loved me, not even because he desired me. His mother has been nagging him for years to marry and produce children to continue the family – above all a son. He chose me because I·was young and innocent and because he thought my children would be beautiful. At least, he thought he chose me – but in fact it was I who chose him as a means of escaping my own home.'

'You believe that the initiative was Aunt Berthe's and not Victor's?'

'I am sure of it. Victor did what his mother told him to do. But when I was not pregnant after three months of marriage, he gave up, for he had never really been interested in making love. I know that his occasional visits to my room now are prompted by his mother insisting that he has a duty to give her a grandson.'

'But how dreadful! How can you tolerate it?'

Alice shrugged her bare shoulders delicately, making her little breasts rise and sway, and Marc gave a little sigh of appreciation at the sight.

'What alternative do I have?' she asked. 'Life with Victor is extremely comfortable – in every possible way but one.'

After the omelette had been eaten, followed by a bunch of grapes shared between them, and the wine had been drunk, Marc took her back to bed. The little sleep and the simple meal had refreshed her and renewed his energies, so that she responded vivaciously to his love-making, and they enjoyed another gratifying interlude together on his bed.

She was dressing to leave, about three in the afternoon, when Marc remembered the question he wanted to ask her. He was lying on the bed, smoking a cigarette, his tail limp between his legs, and he was watching Alice smooth her silk stockings up her long legs and then adjust her lacy little brassiere about her breasts. She put on her blouse and buttoned it up carefully, and stepped into her skirt, leaning forward in a way that made her round little bottom stick out, when he remembered.

'Alice – do you ever wear knickers?'

'But of course! I only leave them off when I am angry with Victor.'

'A sort of protest?'

'I don't know why I do it,' she said, wrinkling her nose deliciously at him. 'All my life I've worn them, but after three months of marriage – off!'

'When was the first time – do you remember?'

'Naturally I remember! Victor had stayed away from me for over a week. I was in my room dressing to go out for the evening, and he came in to ask me to help him with his bow-tie. I put my hand down the front of his trousers and took hold of his dangler and tried to get him to lie on the bed with me. But he insisted that there wasn't time and that we'd be late at the Bergsons for dinner – though it wouldn't have taken more than ten minutes to make love if he'd wanted to. He was very gentle with me – he pulled my hand out of his trousers and kissed my cheek and told me to hurry up and finish getting ready. And off he went! I was so furious that I deliberately left my knickers off and went out to dinner with him bare-bottomed. Isn't that odd?'

'In a way you were hoping perhaps that someone more appreciative of your charms might find occasion to view what Victor is indifferent to. As I did, at the opera.'

'You deliberately molested a married woman in public,' she said, grinning at him. 'That was disgraceful!'

'It will forever be one of the most cherished memories of my life,' said Marc, grinning back at her. 'And so presumably you were still angry with Victor this morning when you arrived here bare-bottomed?'

'I was furious with him.'

'Why was that?'

'For one thing there was what you did to me – he drove me to it! And when we got home from the opera I tried to persuade him to sleep with me – I was very excited still. The little climax you gave me hadn't calmed me at all – quite the reverse! But Victor said that he wouldn't dream of sharing my bed when I had a headache and he wouldn't listen when I said the headache had gone! Not that I'd ever had one in the first place – it was only an excuse to get away from you.'

She sat down on the side of the bed and pulled on her black suede gloves.

'Well, Victor has paid for his lack of interest, even if he doesn't know it,' said Marc. 'Did you sleep at all after a rebuff like that?'

'Since my husband refused to come to bed with me and make love to me, my fingers were my husband last night,' she answered.

'Oh!' Marc exclaimed softly, and he slid his hand up her thigh under her black skirt until his fingers touched her curls. 'You played with this delightful little thing and satisfied yourself?'

'Twice,' she said, spreading her thighs as far as the slim-fitting skirt would permit, to let his fingers stroke her soft lips, 'and then I fell asleep. But when I woke up this morning I was still angry – with Victor and with you – and even with myself.'

Sne leaned over him and took his limp stalk in her gloved hand. His fingertips were between her petals of flesh, caressing gently. She dandled his limpness, trying to wake it up.

'No regrets?' Marc asked.

'It has been wonderful! I have never been so loved and cherished! I can't begin to tell you how very satisfied and happy I feel. Will you be at home tomorrow afternoon if I come to see you?'

'You may rely on it.'

For a little while they tried to excite each other, Marc with his hand up her tight skirt and she rubbing his stalk with her gloved hand until it almost became hard again. But it was obvious to both of them that they were played out for that day, and they kissed and parted.

During the next seven days Marc and Alice met almost daily and she tried hard to make up for all the time she had lost with Victor. Her experience of love-making had been severely restricted and she was eager to try out anything and everything which Marc suggested. His social life ceased to exist for that week – Alice was so demanding and he so anxious to show her all he knew, that he had no energy for anything else except to eat two hearty meals a day in a little restaurant near his apartment. For a week he was making love, eating or sleeping, but he consoled himself with the thought that when Alice's pent-up appetite was assuaged, their love-affair would settle down to a more comfortable routine.

In this he was optimistic, for events were to turn out otherwise. An invitation arrived from Victor for dinner on Saturday evening – a formal dinner, the invitation said. He guessed that Alice's hand was behind it, and he wondered what she was up to – it was no part of Marc's intention to become friendly with his cousin while he was making love to his wife. He arrived at the Darridan apartment to find himself one of a dinner-party of twelve, colleagues and friends of Victor's, and their wives, interested in talking of music and little else. The food and wines were superlatively good, but the conversation was painfully boring to Marc, seated between two middle-aged ladies who plied

280

him with questions about ballet, on the mistaken assumption that he was a keen amateur of the dance. Even with his good looks and natural charm it took him a long time to steer the conversation towards subjects less elevated and more congenial.

After dinner they went into the large and handsome salon. One of the guests persuaded Victor to play something for their entertainment – at first he affected diffidence, but when two or three of those who had enjoyed his lavish hospitality insisted, he took his seat at the grand piano that occupied one end of the salon. He played – whether well or ill, Marc was unable to say, though to his mind whatever it was, it was too long. There then followed a lengthy discussion of the merits of the piece which Victor had played, after which Aunt Berthe bid them all goodnight and retired to bed.

Marc flirted a little with the less unattractive of the ladies he had sat with at dinner, hinting that – if circumstances were different – it would give him enormous pleasure to do deliciously naughty little things to her. Madame Bouget had not had her legs apart for her husband – or any other man – for nearly a decade. At first she was dumbfounded, then a little annoyed that this young stranger should address her so impertinently – and then she was flattered that anyone would want to do delicious things to her sagging bosom and flabby belly and she blushed pink like a young girl and whispered her address to Marc.

It was after eleven when the guests made their preparations to depart, to Marc's relief. His only pleasure that evening, apart from teasing poor Madame Bouget, had been to look from time to time at Alice across the dinner-table, or across the salon, for she stayed well away from him out of discretion, and admire her breathtaking beauty. He diverted himself a little by speculating whether she was wearing knickers under her lavender evening frock, but there was never a moment when they were sufficiently apart from the others to ask her – or to feel her bottom through her thin frock and find out that way!

He approached Victor to thank him and wish him goodnight and was surprised when Victor asked him to stay for a few minutes to discuss something of importance. The request sent a tremor of apprehension through Marc, but he nodded and smiled.

When the other guests had gone Victor came back into the salon, where Marc was sitting and waiting.

'We can talk in confidence now,' said Victor portentously. 'I shall not detain you long.'

'What do you want to talk about?' Marc asked uneasily.

Alice came into the room and looked thoughtfully at the two men sitting facing each other. She went to the piano and busied herself collecting up the sheets of music, her back to her husband and Marc.

'Alice has told me everything,' said Victor. 'Needless to say, I was very surprised.'

Marc said nothing. He glanced at Alice, who was now posing gracefully and with extreme nonchalance, one hand on the shiny black piano top and the other touching the hair above her ear, as if to smooth it back.

'Admit it!' said Victor.

'I don't know what you mean,' Marc answered, trying to bluff it out.

'But you do!' said Victor, leaning forward in his chair to tap Marc on the knee. 'I would never have guessed it – you, of all people!'

'I can't imagine what Alice has told you – perhaps there is some misunderstanding . . .'

'There is no misunderstanding at all! She has told me of your love of music and your vast knowledge of it. I was astonished – my impression of you has always been that you were not much interested in serious cultural pursuits.'

'Alice is too kind,' said Marc, greatly relieved to hear himself accused of nothing more inconvenient than an interest in music. 'Compared with you I know nothing.'

'You are too modest. She mentioned that you met by chance while she was out shopping and had lunch together and talked about the performance of *Samson and Delilah* you attended with us.'

'Yes, we had lunch and talked about the opera,' Marc agreed.

It was true up to a point. He felt no need to mention to

Victor that he had unbuttoned Alice's blouse and felt her breasts while she babbled on about the opera – or that the lunch had been not in a restaurant but in his apartment, and Alice had been stark naked right through it.

'She told me what you thought of the performance,' Victor continued. 'Isn't that so, my dear?'

He turned his head to look at her as she stood behind him at the piano on the other side of the salon. Alice smiled prettily and nodded, her fingers entwined in the long pearl necklace she wore.

'My views are those of a mere novice,' said Marc, 'but the performance was excellent, I thought.' He was thinking of Alice spread out on his bed.

'Yes, an excellent performance,' Alice agreed.

'My dear Marc, your assessment was so much like mine that I was truly impressed,' said Victor. 'You even spotted the wrong note in the second act – you need a good ear for that!'

'Ah, the second act,' said Marc, 'it had its surprises.'

'You are a secret connoisseur!' said Victor.

Marc liked the phrase. 'A secret connoisseur,' he repeated. 'Yes, I think I may claim to be that.'

'Alice, my dear – a little glass of cognac for Marc while I try to obtain a favour from him,' said Victor, 'and one for me – to give me courage.'

'A favour? What can I possibly do for you?' Marc exclaimed.

'I too have a secret,' said Victor, smiling at him.

Alice brought the drinks. When her back was towards her husband she pouted her lips at Marc in a gesture of invitation. He let her see him stare briefly where her frock clung to her slender hips and he raised his eyebrows in a silent question. She understood and gave him an enigmatic smile.

'The truth is,' said Victor, 'I have been composing music for some years. I have at last completed the first piece with which I am sufficiently pleased to want to present to the public.'

'An opera?' Marc asked, wondering why there should be any secret about composing music.

'Nothing so ambitious! You think too highly of my poor talents, my dear Marc. It is a three-part rhapsody for the piano.'

'My congratulations – I'm sure it will be a great success.'

'Perhaps,' said Victor diffidently. 'First it must be heard.'

'Is there any problem about that? You are a wealthy man, Victor – I'm sure you can arrange a public performance of your rhapsody at any time.'

'Wealth is not enough. In fact, it is in a strange way an obstacle. If I were a professional musician – a teacher or a poor composer – my piece would be heard and judged on its merits. But there is a danger that it will be dismissed as the trifling of a rich dabbler.'

'I never knew that money could be an obstacle to anything,' said Marc, amazed by what he had heard.

'What I have in mind is this,' said Victor, emptying his glass in one long swallow. 'I shall try my piece on a small and very select audience of experts – friends from the Conservatory – you have met some of them this evening. I value their opinions highly. They were very kind when I played the Debussy to them after dinner.'

Marc wondered for a moment whether the kindness expressed by Victor's guests might in reality be an expression of gratitude for the superb dinner, rather than a professional opinion of his playing. But that seemed unduly cynical.

'I have no connections or influence in the world of music,' he said. 'What is the favour you want of me, Victor?'

'You have friends on a certain newspaper, I believe.'

At last the conversation began to make some sense to Marc. One of his friends was the son of the owner of a morning newspaper – not because Marc had any interest in the press, but because they had been friends at school and had grown up to enjoy the same sort of parties and women.

'How can that be of assistance to you, Victor?'

'The music critic of that newspaper is the most important in Paris – and therefore in the whole of France. He makes and breaks reputations with a few words. If he found merit in my work and said in the newspaper that it deserved a wider hearing, then the outcome would be guaranteed.'

Marc stared in thought over Victor's shoulder, to where Alice was sitting on the piano-stool. Behind her husband's back she was stroking her breasts delicately with both hands. And she was smiling at Marc.

'Where will your private performance be – here?' Marc asked.

'In this salon. There will be no more than twenty guests.'

'And through my connections you would like me to arrange to have this particular critic instructed to be present.'

'If it is not too much to ask,' said Victor, his tone humble.

'Suppose for a moment that this critic is too stupid to appreciate your music,' said Marc, watching Alice as she stroked the tips of her breasts through the thin silk of her frock, 'suppose he writes of it without understanding or sympathy? What then?'

'The public humiliation would crush me,' said Victor, his face turning white. 'There would be no alternative but to leave Paris at once and live in the country.'

'Oh!' Alice exclaimed, her hands dropping to her lap. 'That is too much! I don't think I would like to leave Paris.'

'There would be no choice, my dear. I would be a broken man and you would be my only companion.'

'You are forgetting your mother,' she reminded him.

'My dear mother, of course! She would be with us to sustain me through my agony.'

'Let us be more cheerful,' Marc said quickly. 'I guarantee that this critic person will be delighted by your music and write about it with unbounded enthusiasm. You will be famous, Victor.'

'Thank you – I hope that you are right.'

'Leave all that to me.'

Though he didn't think it worth mentioning to Victor, Marc thought it perfectly reasonable to assume that, if the critic could be instructed to attend a private performance, he could also be advised on what kind of review was wanted for publication. If it proved that the fellow had qualms about his integrity – a very strange concept when applied to a journalist – then an envelope containing bank-notes should ease his conscience.

He shook hands with Victor and said goodnight. Alice offered to see him to the door, the servants being by then in bed, or so she said. There followed a scene of comedy which Marc could never have imagined. Alice led him to the apartment door, opened it and said loudly, 'Au revoir, Marc' and closed the door again with both of them on the inside. With his hat in his hand, Marc followed her in silence back past the closed door to the salon and into another room, dark and empty. She put a finger to her lips to enjoin silence and closed the door and left him.

This is lunacy, Marc thought, hardly able to stop himself from roaring with laughter at the implications of his position. He moved away from the door with care and, in complete darkness, found a bed by hitting his shin against it painfully. He sat down to wait and after about ten minutes he heard voices outside. The door began to open and light came in from the passage. It was too late to hide under the bed and he could think of no excuse to explain his presence if Victor came in. For he was, Marc had no doubt, in Alice's bedroom. Suppose tonight, of all nights, Victor decided to exercise his conjugal rights!'

He need not have been anxious. The door was held ajar so that the bed was out of sight to those outside. Alice's hand came round the door to switch on the lights, making Marc blink. He heard her say, 'goodnight, Victor', and he heard her husband's answering murmur. Then she was in the room and the door was closed again. She pressed a finger to her lips once more to warn him of the necessity for silence and pointed to the wall behind him to indicate that Victor's room was on the other side of it. After that she ignored him as she prepared herself for bed – behaving as if he were not there at all.

Marc's heart speeded its beat as he watched Alice undress. She took off her earrings and necklace and put them in a box on her dressing-table – a large box with marquetry-work on the lid. She removed her frock and hung it in the wardrobe – and Marc saw that she had no underwear on at all. She sat on a padded chair to slip off her silk stockings, holding each up in turn to examine it for ladders.

She approached the bed, naked and very beautiful, and Marc got up from it and stood aside. It had been turned down by a maid and a lace-edged white night-dress laid out for her. She picked it up and for a moment or two Marc feared that she was going to slip it over her head and hide her body from his, but she tucked it under the pillows, got into bed and held her hand out towards him.

He was out of his clothes at once and beside her, kissing and caressing her in a frenzy of desire. Whether this was due to the casual manner in which she had undressed in front of him, or the bizarre circumstance that her husband was in the next room, who could say? All Marc knew was that he was on fire to plunge into her.

'Slow down, slow down!' Alice whispered, evidently afraid that he would have run his race and crossed the finishing line before she even left the start. In Marc's condition her words achieved nothing – his fingers had already pulled forcibly open the soft lips between her thighs and his hard stem was within centimetres of it. Alice reduced his frenzy by the simple expedient of nipping his throbbing part with her fingernails. He rolled away from her with a gasp of anguish and, while he was on his back, staring at her in pained surprise, she straddled his hips and impaled herself neatly on his spike.

'Be still now,' she murmured, leaning forward to bring her delightful little breasts within reach of his hands.

'That hurt!' he complained.

'But I'm making it better for you now,' she answered.

Marc lay still and let her ride him with all the skill she had learned during her visits to his apartment. The electric light was still on and he had a perfect view of her face, her eyes half-closed, with an expression of calm voluptuousness that reminded him of statues he had seen of Venus in museums. His slight hurt was forgotten and his passion blazed again under her ministrations – so much so

287

that it did not take long before she brought him to his critical moments. He heard Alice give a long moan of ecstasy just before her soft little belly drew his essence from him in quick spasms.

They lay quietly in each other's arms for a while and Marc began to wonder how he was to make his departure without waking the household. Was Victor a light sleeper, he wondered – was Aunt Berthe an insomniac? What of the servants, of whom there were several?

Alice had other ideas about his departure.

'This is my bed,' she said, close to his ear. 'It is for me to decide what I do in it.'

'Agreed.'

'If things were different. Victor would have the right to say what happens in my bed. But as he is not interested, the right is mine alone.'

'Of course.'

'So if I decide that I want to make love to you, I shall.'

'You did it superbly,' he told her.

'And in a little while I am going to do it to you again,' she informed him.

'Whenever you like!' His hand stroked her warm little bottom.

'Yes, for once it is as I like, here in my own home!'

The feel of her satin-skinned bottom reminded Marc that when she had taken her clothes off she had worn nothing under her lavender frock.

'You were bare-bottomed at dinner tonight, dear Alice – that must mean that you are in the mood for revenge on Victor.'

'What better place for my revenge than here in the bed he never visits?' she asked, and her hand trailed over his belly and touched his limp affair.

'There is a certain poetic justice in that,' said Marc.

She played with his equipment until it grew firm and bold enough for her purpose.

'It's marvellous, the way you recover so quickly,' she said. 'Lie on your back and prepare to be loved again!'

'You think that you will drain me dry in your revenge, dear little Alice – but you will not succeed! However often you ride me, I shall be ready for you again – it is you who will faint with ecstasy of love first.'

'As to that, time will tell,' she answered. 'My thirst for revenge is very strong, I warn you, and I shall probably grind you into the mattress and destroy you before I am satisfied!'

It was well after three in the morning when Marc left her. She guided him through the obstacles of the dark apartment to the door and stood there naked, like a pale statue of Venus in the gloom, while he kissed her and lightly touched the dark-curled little slot into which he had poured his heart and soul that night.

The streets were deserted at that hour and the chance of finding a taxi was remote unless he walked to the nearest railway station – the Gare de l'Est. He decided to make for Les Halles, which was closer, and refresh himself with a bowl of onion soup and a glass of cognac in one of the market-workers' cafés.

The truth of it was that the beautiful Alice had completely exhausted him, young and vigorous though he was. His boast of *as often as you like* had been taken quite literally by her and she had ridden him five times before her desire for revenge had been slaked that night. It had been very exciting indeed at the time – the fifth crisis was so intense that Marc had lost consciousness for a few moments and recovered to find himself still trying to jet his passion into Alice, though he had nothing left to give her. But after all that, he was now walking slowly along the Rue Poissonière with an aching back and legs that trembled beneath him.

He was very proud of his achievement that night. Alice was without doubt the most beautiful young woman he had ever seen – she had the face and the body of a goddess – to make love to her on so heroic a scale in the space of an hour or two was something of which he was sure any man in the world would have been proud. Granted, it was Alice herself who had done the work – which was just as well, for Marc doubted if he would have managed the fifth time otherwise. And if it had fatigued him, what of it? A long sleep would restore his energies for when he met her again.

There were other considerations for pride in this affair. He was Alice's first lover. Victor may have had the privilege of being the one to relieve her of her virginity, but that meant nothing, in the circumstances, for he had not aroused her to the pleasures of love. Spiritually, Alice was a virgin until she came to Marc's apartment the morning after the visit to the opera. *It was I who made her a woman*, Marc thought with satisfaction. *She is mine, not Victor's!*

As soon as the evening was arranged for Victor's debut as a composer of piano music, Marc kept his promise and spoke to his friend Jules, explaining what was required of the man who wrote on musical performances for his father's newspaper. Jules asked what was Marc's interest in the matter, and when he was told that it was a most delicate affair, he grinned and said that he understood perfectly.

When Marc arrived for the great event, there were already twenty people in the Darridans' salon. They were standing about, sipping champagne and talking of the musical treat to come – with the exception of one man who stood apart from the others. He was a lean-faced man with a sour expression and Marc guessed that he was the newspaper critic, present against his will.

After he had greeted Victor and kissed Alice's hand, Marc went back to the critic and drew him into the hall outside the salon for a private word.

'It is very good of you to accept my cousin's invitation, Monsieur Lebrun. We are all most grateful to you.'

Lebrun's lips moved in a grimace that resembled a snarl more than a polite smile.

'My cousin is an extremely modest man,' Marc continued. 'I have scribbled some details of his life and musical interests on a piece of paper for you, for it would embarrass him to talk about himself.'

From the inside pocket of his jacket he took an envelope and handed it to Lebrun.

'Wholly unnecessary,' the critic said unpleasantly.

The thickness of the envelope took him by surprise, however.

'What's this – your cousin's complete life-story?' he asked with a scowl.

He tore the envelope open and glanced inside. The instant that he caught sight of the wad of bank notes it contained, he thrust it quickly into his pocket.

'Your notes will be very useful when I write my review, Monsieur,' he said, and went back into the salon in pursuit of more champagne.

The servants were arranging rows of chairs facing the piano. When at last the audience was seated and the servants had withdrawn, Victor made a brief speech of welcome and thanked them for being present. He said a few words about the piece he had composed, and he was neither diffident nor effusive. His hearers clapped politely when he finished speaking, then he sat down at the grand piano, flexed his fingers a few times, took a deep breath and began to play.

Marc was standing just outside the open door of the salon. He considered that he had done his part and he had no particular wish to sit through the performance. He thought he might slip out and have a drink in a bar down the street while Victor was playing, and come back when it was all over. He could see Aunt Berthe in the front row, a hand cupped behind her ear to catch every note, a look of pride on her face at her son's achievement. Alice was in the back row, near the door, after supervising the seating and the departure of the servants. She was wearing the jet-black frock she had worn to the performance of *Samson and Delilah* at which Marc had touched her delicate flower for the first time and sent her into a climax of delight. Tonight she looked spectacularly beautiful and Marc experienced a familiar stirring in his trousers. Would she dare hide him in the apartment tonight for another night of love in her bed, he wondered – or would it be too risky: perhaps his debut as a composer would exhilarate Victor to the point where he wanted to sleep with his wife! All things considered, it looked like being a frustrating evening for Marc.

Alice glanced over her shoulder and saw him in the doorway, staring at her back. With the utmost caution, so that no one noticed her in their concentration on Victor's rhapsody, she got up from her chair and tiptoed out into the hall. She put a hand on Marc's arm to draw him out of

291

sight of the salon and then put her arms round his neck and kissed him warmly.

'Oh, Alice – I adore you!' he murmured. 'I was looking at you and remembering the last time we were together – two days is an eternity to be away from you.'

She kissed him again and he felt her hand tugging at his trouser-buttons.

'But this is insane!' he whispered as she pulled out his stiff stalk.

'I adore you too,' she told him, 'and I want you as much as you want me. Two days is far too long – last night in bed alone I had to pretend that my fingers were yours caressing me.'

Before Marc could raise any further objections to the imprudence of playing with his spindle in the hall, between the crowded salon on one side and the room where the servants were gathered on the other, Alice had her back against the wall and hoisted her frock up round her hips. If Marc had any objections, he forgot them instantly, and his hand slid between her thighs with all the familiarity of one travelling a path he knows well. Before he touched her he knew that she had no underwear beneath her frock. Her dark-curled notch opened to his fingers and he caressed her button while she stroked his stem – though only for a little while, before she pulled it towards the join of her thighs and Marc drove it into her.

'Yes, yes, yes,' she murmured fondly, and Marc grasped her bare bottom through the folds of her dress to steady her as he slid back and forth.

In the salon Victor had reached a fortissimo passage in his composition and the music boomed through the open door to the busy couple against the dividing wall outside. The chords seemed to echo in Marc's head, setting the rhythm for his movements, fast and assured. He gazed at Alice's beautiful face and was enchanted yet again – as he was every time – by the marvellous expression it assumed whenever he made love to her.

Then the music slowed and became dreamy and romantic – and without being aware of its effect on him, Marc slowed his pace. Alice was sighing gently in delight, the tip of her pink tongue visible between her red-rouged lips . Marc hands kneaded the warm cheeks of her bottom as he drove in and out of her with long slow thrusts.

'Oh, Marc,' she whispered, 'I have fallen in love with you!'

'And I love you, Alice,' he murmured back, his rhythm now a delicate diminuendo of calm delight.

'I shall leave Victor,' she said. 'I've had my revenge – I want love now.'

The piano burst out into the long triumphant final passage of the first part of the rhapsody, and simultaneously Marc's desire burst out in a fountain of ecstasy. Alice's tiny climactic cry was fortunately drowned by the final crashing chord from the piano.

'Do you truly love me, Marc?' she asked, her eyes still closed.

'With all my heart,' he answered, his legs still shaking beneath him.

It was with dismay that he acknowledged to Alice and to himself that he loved her, this being something he never intended or had foreseen. To play with her in bed in the afternoons and then be free to do what he wished in the evenings when she was back with her husband – that was what he had wanted. The unthinkable had happened and he had fallen in love with Alice!

'Do you love me enough to take me away from Victor?' she asked.

'I love you to distraction, Alice. I want you to leave this place now and come home with me and stay there forever.'

'I shall be ready in five minutes,' she said, disengaging herself from him.

She lowered her frock and hurried away towards her bedroom. Marc tucked his tail away and fastened his trousers, then moved back into the doorway of the salon and leaned idly against the door frame while Victor launched into the second part of his composition. The audience seemed rapt, staring at Victor fixedly as he played, except for Lebrun. He was sitting in the back row of chairs and he had his elbows on his knees and his face in his hands. Whether his posture indicated silent concentration or despair, it was impossible for Marc to determine.

Alice had become used to living in style, Marc pondered, and there was a danger that she would come to resent the less expansive way of life she would be sharing with him. It did not seem probable that Victor would make any financial arrangement for her after she had run away from him. Unless . . . a thought came into Marc's mind as he stared at Lebrun's back. There would be a complimentary review of Victor's music in the newspaper the next day – Lebrun had been instructed by his employer's son and cajoled by Marc's bundle of notes to write favourably. But to judge by Lebrun's posture – he was shaking his head from side to side, his hands pressed to his cheeks – Victor's music was not of the finest. Naturally, his assembled friends would assure him that it was wonderful, otherwise they would be asked to no more of Victor's superlative dinners.

Victor was going to be vulnerable to pressure of a certain sort, Marc realised. Suppose he was told that unless he behaved generously towards Alice the story would be spread about in the appropriate places that his musical success was based on deceit and bribery! A story like that in a rival newspaper would make his life impossible – he would scuttle off to the country, with only Aunt Berthe for a companion! All things considered, thought Marc, a little persuasion would induce Victor, who could well afford it, to make a regular monthly payment towards the upkeep of his estranged wife – and her lover.

It was more than five minutes before Alice returned, of course, though not *very* much more, and Victor was still banging the keyboard with diligence and concentration. She had changed into a less dramatic frock for her departure from the marital home, and wore a three-quarter length astrakhan coat over it. She was carrying a suitcase that presumably contained whatever clothes and jewellery she had decided to take with her. She gave the suitcase to Marc and they left the apartment quietly.

As they went down the stairs to the street, he told her that his happiness was so acute that he felt a little sorry for Victor.

'There is no need,' said Alice. 'He has what he wants – an audience for his music. And I have what I want. We are quits, he and I.'

'Why do you say that?'

'Because at the very moment of his musical triumph, he was betrayed.'

'Against the wall!' said Marc, grinning at her.

'It's a pity you didn't throw me on top of the piano and make love to me while he was playing,' said Alice, smiling sweetly. 'Victor wouldn't have noticed what you were doing to me, but at least we would have upset his mother!'

Remembrance of things past

She had chestnut-brown hair and a face that was broad at the cheekbones and curved gracefully to a pointed little chin. Her evening frock was of cream satin, cut in a wrap-over style with a bow at the right hip. She was full-breasted and very attractive – a woman in full bloom – and her age was thirty-six, exactly the same as Maurice Brissard's. He knew that for certain because, though it was twenty years since he last saw her, he had recognised her at second glance.

Naturally, it would have been far more romantic if he had recognised her as his lost childhood love at the first glance, but a man cannot always be thinking of these things, especially after so long. And if any further excuse was required, she was across the other side of Madame Hiver's salon and he had caught a mere glimpse of her, between little groups of chattering people with glasses in their hands. Even so, there was something familiar about her, something that sounded a chord in Maurice's memory. But he knew so many people that it was impossible to remember all their names. He talked to Yvonne Hiver for a few moments, his mind busy with the question of who the woman with chestnut-brown hair was. Then he turned to look across the salon again – and this time he knew! His sense of surprise was so great that he almost dropped his glass of champagne. Yvonne Hiver's eyes missed nothing – she gave him a knowing little smile.

'You are acquainted with Madame Lesquilles, Maurice?' she asked, though her tone made it clear that she was not asking a question at all.

'Lesquilles?' he said. 'I know no Madame Lesquilles.'

296

'And yet you are staring at her as if you were once her lover.' Yvonne gave a brittle little laugh. 'I know that look on a man's face, my dear. I should not be in the least offended if you looked at me like that.'

'Who knows what may happen!' said Maurice, to be polite, though he had no great ambition to become Yvonne Hiver's lover – that is to say her latest lover, for rumour had it that she changed lovers every few weeks. Certainly, almost every one of Maurice's men friends had been afforded the privilege of making full use of Yvonne's charms.

She put her bejewelled hand briefly on Maurice's arm and smiled at him in open invitation. At the same time she leaned towards him so her deeply décolleté frock gave him a brief glimpse of her bare breasts inside it – or at least, the major proportion of them.

'Then you don't know her?' she asked.

'She's Mireille Dulac – I knew her before she was married. Her husband worked for a company in Algeria, I was told.'

Yvonne gave a little moue of disappointment, but continued to speak cheerfully, her hopes of Maurice by no means abandoned.

'That's right,' she said. 'I believe he did quite well for himself out there. He transferred to Beirut after the War, when it became French, but they're back in Paris now.'

'Is Lesquilles here? I've never met him.'

'He goes out very little. His health is poor, that's why they've come back to France to live.'

'To judge by her frock and the diamonds round her neck the business opportunities in Beirut were rewarding,' said Maurice thoughtfully.

'That's all in the past now, my dear. They've taken an apartment in Neuilly and poor Mireille will have to manage on much less than she's been used to.'

'If you will excuse me, I shall pay my respects to her and see if she remembers me,' Maurice said, and seeing Yvonne's expression of discontent, he added, 'perhaps you will think me too bold, but I may find it impossible to prevent myself from telephoning you before long.'

'I like the sound of that,' she answered, smiling brilliantly at him. 'There are things I would love to discuss with you, dear Maurice, if we ever found ourselves together in a discreet place.'

'Until then,' he said, leaving her in a tremble of anticipation.

Mireille Lesquilles smiled broadly as Maurice approached her. 'I knew it was you the moment you entered the room,' she said.

Maurice kissed her hand, his heart beating a little faster than usual. 'Mireille! You are more beautiful now than you were as a girl!'

'Nonsense,' she said, though her smile indicated that his words pleased her. 'I was slender and delicate then, but not any more.'

'You had the beauty of a young girl then – and you have the beauty of a woman now,' he insisted. 'Is it true that you have returned to Paris to live?'

'The doctors told my husband that he would be dead inside a year unless he moved to a more temperate climate. He has problems with his liver.'

'So do many here,' said Maurice, 'those who drink too much.'

Mireille shrugged slightly and changed the subject. She wanted to know the details of Maurice's life – whom he had married, how many children he had, where he lived, and so on. While they talked happily together Maurice was staring at the fine and smooth skin of her bare arms, at the curve of her hips inside her frock, at her carefully made-up and expressive face – and at the prominent breasts under the thin satin that hid them.

After ten minutes Maurice's spectacularly beautiful wife joined them, thinking perhaps that he was taking just a little too much interest in a stranger. Maurice introduced them to each other and before long the two women were into the sort of conversation which excludes men, and Maurice drifted away. He became incautiously trapped in a corner by Yvonne, who asked him his opinion as to which gave a man the greater pleasure in bed – young girls with only their looks to commend them, or mature women of experience and sophistication.

Naturally, Maurice had taken care to discover precisely

where the Lesquilles home was located, so that he could telephone the next day and ask Mireille to have lunch with him. He took her to a little restaurant on the Left Bank, where the food was excellent and there was little chance that anyone he knew would be there to see him with Mireille. Maurice was a very discreet man and a loving husband – and he took care not to disturb his wife by allowing gossip about him to reach her ears. Besides that, Gaston Lesquilles was still an unknown quantity and it was prudent not to give him cause for concern.

They ate and drank very well, talked endlessly and were both in a mood of exhilaration when the table was cleared and a very fine old cognac appeared. Their original acquaintance had not been a long one – a mere month, when they were both nearly sixteen. In those days Maurice's father sent his wife and children to a house in the country near St Varent for the month of August each year, while he applied himself to whatever business a man applied himself to when his family were away. It was a large old house and Madame Brissard asked friends with children of about the same age as hers to stay with her. One summer it had been Madame Dulac with her daughter Mireille and her younger brother.

Over a glass of the cognac Maurice embarked upon his most treasured reminiscence, judging that Mireille was suitably prepared to hear it.

'Do you remember a day when you and I were alone in the orchard at St Varent, Mireille? We were sitting under a tree.'

'We were often in the orchard,' she answered, her cheeks a charming pink – perhaps from the emotions stirred up by memory, perhaps from the effects of the wine she had drunk with lunch and the cognac she was sipping.

'You know the day I mean! You let me kiss you.'

'Dear Maurice – you never stopped trying to kiss me!'

'I say *kiss*, but what really happened was that I pressed my mouth to yours,' Maurice continued, 'for I had no idea of how one really kisses a girl. But you were so pretty – and I was madly in love with you. In those days your hair was long – down to your shoulders – and parted in the middle.

299

The touch of our lips on the day I'm talking about sealed my destiny.'

'How important you make it sound! And we were neither of us sixteen at the time!' said Mireille, smiling at his foolishness.

'But it was important!' Maurice insisted. 'I remember it as if it were yesterday – when I kissed you under the tree your eyes were closed and your breath was warm against my lips.'

'You remember in such detail?' she asked, not really believing him.

'You let me open your blouse,' said Maurice. 'It was a grey blouse with a turn-down white collar. I pulled the top of your chemise down and saw your enchanting little breasts. I stared and stared, and you giggled and asked me if I wanted to touch them.'

'Ah, it was all my doing, was it!' Mireille exclaimed. 'That's not how I remember it – you thrust your hand into my clothes without any encouragement from me.'

'No, no!' Maurice protested with a little grin. 'I uncovered your breasts without an invitation, that is true – but after that it was your suggestion that I should play with them.'

'Memory can be very unreliable after twenty years – if it pleases you to believe your version, why not?' she answered. 'I suppose that in my heart I must have wanted you to play with them or I would have got up and run away from you.'

'Yes, you wanted me to – and you enjoyed it. You lay beside me under the tree with your eyes closed and you let me caress you for as long as I wanted to. My heart was beating so fast I thought I would die.'

'What children we were!' Mireille murmured. 'Your heart wouldn't beat like that today if you caressed me.'

'It would,' Maurice said at once, 'that I know for certain.'

'Dear Maurice – what nice things you say! But to continue with our little adventure in the orchard – do you remember what happened next?'

'Of course! While I was still playing with your pretty breasts you put your hand on my thigh. I shook like a leaf! And you felt upwards very slowly – it could only have been a second or two at most, but to me it was an eternity of blissful agony.'

'There was a bulge in your trousers,' said Mireille with a little laugh, 'a firmness – a stiffness! It was curiosity on my part, I suppose, that made me touch it.'

'Curiosity, desire – who can say what our motives were? But after you had found it and felt it through my trousers, you asked me to show you my *sparrow* – that was the word you used.'

'You're making this up!' Mireille exclaimed, reaching across the table to tap his hand in mock protest. 'I don't believe a word of it!'

'I'm telling the plain truth,' he replied. 'Deny it if you dare!'

'What a very immodest little girl I was,' said Mireille with a gurgle of laughter.

'I undid my trousers and got it out for you to see.'

'A sparrow sticking its head up out of its nest,' she said. 'How strange to remember all this – the days of our innocence!'

Maurice's voice was hushed as he spoke again. 'You took it in your hot little hand and I knew for certain that I loved you desperately, Mireille. I put my hand under your skirt and touched your knickers. I wanted you to take them off and let me look at you.'

'Days of innocence, did I say? You were not so innocent after all, to want to pull my knickers off. But I kept my legs together.'

'Almost,' he said, smiling at her across the table. 'I was able to slide my hand between your thighs and press against you, but you shook your head when I pleaded with you to let me go further.'

'I was a good girl, a virgin, and I had been taught that I must remain so until I married.'

'You were a virgin, yes – but a good girl? That is another matter. Your words have been imprinted on my memory ever since that day – you said, *Your sparrow wants to do something naughty, so I shall wring his neck.*'

Mireille burst into helpless laughter and Maurice joined in.

301

'Did I really say that? Oh, Maurice, what a memory you have!'

'We laugh now,' he said, still chuckling, 'but at the time we were very serious. I remember your expression as you leaned over me – your long hair was tumbling across your face – and there was an incredible moment when you gripped my fluttering sparrow and began to wring its neck.'

'At that moment I was not being a good girl,' Mireille said with a giggle, 'but you were a lucky boy – admit it!'

'I couldn't believe my luck – you, doing that to me! I didn't think that girls even knew about it. But my good fortune was short-lived, as you know. We heard your mother calling for you from the garden below the orchard. Perhaps she was not entirely convinced that you would remain a good girl – or even a virgin – if you were alone with me for too long. You were up on your feet at once and buttoning your blouse as you ran towards her through the trees.'

'My poor Maurice,' said Mireille, her red lips parting in a grin, 'how cruel to leave you in such a state of confusion. But what could I do?'

'And what could I do – in the state of excitement to which you had aroused me? I seized my sparrow and throttled him so fiercely that he coughed his life up on the grass immediately!'

Mireille laughed again and Maurice thought that he had rarely heard so pleasant a sound.

'I'm sure your mother suspected us,' he said. 'Perhaps your face was flushed when you reached her – perhaps not all your blouse buttons were fastened properly. She made sure that we were not left alone together after that. In another week she took you and your brother back to Paris, and we stayed on in the country. By the time we returned in September she'd taken you to Algeria.'

'Ours was a sad little love-story,' said Mireille, 'almost like Romeo and Juliet, don't you think? But unlike those two, we did not die for love. Here we are, twenty years later, amusing ourselves with memories of how it once was.'

'Memories of a broken heart,' said Maurice, reaching out to take her hand and squeeze it tenderly.

'Hearts break very easily when one is fifteen, nearly sixteen,' she said. 'How long did yours take to mend?'

'At least three months.'

'I never thought you were so fickle! It was at least half a year before I got over my longing for you.'

'But in a deeper sense, my heart was never mended at all,' said Maurice. 'I knew that when I met you again at Yvonne's party.'

Mireille looked at him pensively. 'When you asked me to lunch I knew that it was to talk about the old times,' she said, 'but I did not expect any of this. We knew each other for a short time, very long ago.'

'Enduring impressions can be made in moments, Mireille.'

'Evidently! Since we have talked so intimately, I expect you to be honest with me now. Are you trying to seduce me?'

'Naturally – I thought you understood that.'

His frankness neither dismayed nor offended her. She left her hand in his and stared at him in silent thought for some moments. Maurice knew that she was considering her position.

'Then you have succeeded,' she said at last, giving him a smile that was wholly enchanting. 'You have won my heart with your memories of those carefree and innocent days. I wish we could bring them back – but unlike you, my dear friend, I do not believe that it is even remotely possible. Too much has happened since then to both of us and we are no longer the wide-eyed children that we were, for whom a touch of hands was an adventure.'

'But?'

'But – I see that you have set your heart on trying to live again what nearly was and never was, and it would be cruel to deny you the chance.'

'Promise me that when I make love to you this time your mother will not call for you!' said Maurice, his eyes shining.

'I give you my word – she is too far away for me to hear

303

her, even if she does call my name.'

'And this time you will not refuse to take off your knickers?' Maurice asked, grinning at her and stroking the hand he held.

'I hope you will be gallant enough to take them off for me.'

'My heart will pound itself to pieces in my chest!' he sighed.

'And no doubt something else will pound away furiously,' she whispered across the table, 'though not in your chest.'

'You are still the naughty little good girl you were. I adore you for that. Did you manage to keep your virginity until you married?'

'Alas, no – in spite of all my mother's exhortations. Gaston was not the first to travel that path when we became engaged. A young army officer had been there before him.'

'How old were you when this soldier found out that you were not always a good girl?'

'Eighteen. Mother found out about him after six months or so and wanted me to marry him – but he was not the marrying kind. So about a year later she persuaded me to marry Gaston.'

'You listen too much to your mother – but I suppose that all young girls do.'

'Where will you take me?' Mireille asked, changing the subject. 'A hotel?'

'No, a discreet little place that I know. Come along, dear Mireille.'

'Now, you mean? This afternoon?'

'Of course! Do you think that I could live another hour without making love to you now that I have found you again?'

Without waiting for the bill, Maurice scattered money across the table, too much for what they had eaten and drunk, and pulled Mireille to her feet.

'Oh, Maurice – I believe I can see a long bulge in your trousers,' she whispered to him. 'What can it be – your keys?'

304

The proprietor came quickly across the restaurant as he saw them leaving without asking for the bill. His practised eye saw the amount Maurice had left on the table and he opened the door for them and bowed as they went out into the street.

Maurice took Mireille to the small apartment he maintained, unknown to his wife, family and friends, in the Rue Lafitte. He had for some years used this as a convenient and comfortable little retreat in which to entertain women friends in complete privacy. Not even the concierge knew his real name. If, when she cleaned for him, she came across any clue to his identity, she kept it to herself, not wanting to risk the possible loss of so open-handed a tenant.

'You must have been very sure of yourself,' said Mireille, as Maurice helped her off with her coat, 'to have this place ready, I mean.'

'I was very far from sure of anything,' he said, kissing the back of her neck, 'but when a man believes that there is a chance, however remote, that his most cherished dream may come true, he will go to any lengths to arrange that nothing shall get in the way of that incredible moment.'

'I suppose a friend of yours lives here?' she said, glancing round the small but elegantly furnished sitting-room.

'A good friend,' said Maurice, 'one I trust.'

He was pleased that Mireille had not suggested that this was his own secret apartment, to which he brought women for confidential conversations, for then he would have lied politely to her. Maurice disliked lies, except when they were necessary. He took her hand and led her to the bed-room.

When her green-striped frock came off he found that she was wearing satin and lace knickers in white and a brassière to match. The half-cups of the brassière supported her breasts but did nothing to conceal her prominent red-brown buds. Maurice thought it charming and drew her down to sit beside him on the bed so that he could kiss her buds while he undid the brassière. After he had removed it he saw that her breasts had lost the elasticity of extreme youth and hung a little heavy. Mireille saw the direction of his gaze and shrugged, setting her breasts wobbling.

'They're a lot bigger than when you saw them in the orchard,' she said. 'But what did you imagine? That was twenty years ago and I have three children.'

'They are magnificent!' said Maurice, caressing them full-handed. 'I remember them as pointed little delights, and now they have grown to be sumptuous.'

To reassure her that his little start when he removed her brassière had been surprise rather than disappointment, he kissed her buds and teased them with his tongue until they were firm and she was sighing. He laid her down on the bed and took off his clothes, dropping them on the floor. He was going to lie beside her and kiss her again, but she forestalled him by reaching up to take hold of his stiff pointer.

'Something else has grown larger since those days,' she said. 'You are to be congratulated, Maurice. I am certain that this has been fully indulged.'

'As to that,' he replied, arranging himself beside her so that he could play with her breasts, 'I can say with truth that it has given pleasure to a number of women.'

'Of whom I am to be the next?' she asked, tightening her grip on it.

'Dearest Mireille – you have not yet understood me,' he said, and his hands shook a little as he fondled her big soft breasts. 'Those days at St Varent have been in my mind ever since. We were little more than children, I know, but the fact is that I fell in love with you then and I have been in love with you ever since.'

'Flatterer!' she murmured, putting her hands over his to make him squeeze her breasts harder.

'It is the truth. I fell deeply in love with you, but our ways parted.'

'But surely you loved Marie-Thérèse when you married her?'

'I loved her – and I still do – but not with the wild and total commitment of youth.'

'You still make love to her?' Mireille asked, her hand stroking his hard stem.

It was not the sort of question usually asked by a woman of the world of the man lying naked beside her with his hand smoothing over her belly. Had it been another woman, Maurice would have been amazed and even offended. But with Mireille in his arms his normal composure had deserted him – he was sixteen again; eager, trusting and vulnerable. He could not be offended by anything said to him by the adored one beside him.

'Of course,' he replied.

'You're honest! And like all men, you have adventures?'

'But this is no adventure, I swear to you!'

'Then what is it?' she asked, breathing a little more rapidly as his fingers inserted themselves into her satin knickers.

'This is the fulfilment of a dream that I have cherished for twenty years.'

'This is your dream – to make love to me?'

'Yes,' he said with great earnestness, 'I love you – and I never thought that the day would come when you would be lying naked beside me.'

'Not altogether naked,' she said, smiling at him.

In his eagerness to explain his feelings to her, he had forgotten that he had started to remove her knickers. His fingers were hooked into them – he had pushed them down to the level of her furry mound and then stopped.

'My mother is too far away to interrupt you this time,' she went on. 'Do you want to take my knickers off, Maurice?'

In a moment he had her flimsy underwear off and was pressing his lips devoutly to the warm satin that had touched her body.

'Kiss *me*, my dear, not my underwear,' Mireille suggested.

'Whatever has been close to you is sacred to me!' he declared.

He dropped the lace and satin trifle as her legs parted and he kissed the chestnut curls between them – and then the warm and full lips under the curls.

'So, Maurice – this is the moment you have waited for,' she sighed. 'I hope that you are not disappointed – I am not sixteen now.'

'You are beautiful, beautiful,' Maurice murmured, opening her wide with his thumbs.

'Ah!' she sighed. 'I am yours to do with as you please – but do not be too hasty, even though you have waited for so long.'

Maurice was of the same mind – the realisation of his long-cherished dream was to be savoured to the full. He kissed every part of Mireille's comfortably fleshy body, not once but a dozen times, his fingers tracing every square millimetre of her skin, making her pant with desire.

'I want to feel you inside me, Maurice,' she murmured.

Over the years Maurice had slid his equipment into a great many of the tender little pockets with which women are blessed – but never with such quivering anticipation as he experienced at this moment. Mireille was wet, very wet, from his caresses and he uttered a little moan of delight as he slid into her

'Mireille – I adore you!' he murmured – not an original thing to say in the circumstances, but all that he was capable of just then.

He lay still on her, so as not to shorten the fantastic sensations he felt by precipitating a crisis, however much he wanted it.

'And I adore you,' she gasped, her legs up over his thighs to hold him as tightly as her arms round his neck. 'I think I always have!'

'Then you remember our days at St Varent as clearly as I do.'

'How could I ever forget them?'

'You unbuttoned your blouse and let me play with your pretty little breasts and I was in paradise – or so I thought then.'

'And now?' she asked faintly.

'This is paradise – to be inside you!'

'Yes, yes,' she sighed, 'I have never been so blissfully happy before!'

In all of this delightful exchange between the two of them as they lay joined on the bed there may perhaps be discerned a certain falsity and naivety. There is a popular saying that all cats are grey in the dark. The truth is that when human affections and sensibilities are deeply engaged, a man may very well derive more exquisite pleasure from a plump woman approaching middle age than he would from an eighteen-year-old dancer from the Folies Bergères. And a woman may well enjoy more in the embrace of a man she adores, whatever his age, than she would in the arms of a handsome young captain of Hussars. It is more often the mind which determines how much pleasure the body feels than the other way round.

Assuredly, neither Maurice nor Mireille were in the mood for philosophising about what they were experiencing. He lay lightly on her belly, supported on his elbows, so that he could see her face fully and kiss her mouth and then bend his neck to kiss her bounteous breasts, while sliding his engorged part in and out of her in a sedate rhythm. And she, clinging to him with intense eagerness, accepted his adoration in rapturous assent and moved her hips with slow grace to receive and return each stately thrust.

There was nothing frantic about Maurice's love-making that day, delayed though it had been by circumstances for twenty years. Together he and Mireille climbed at a steady pace up the long slope of enjoyment, in no haste to reach the peak they knew awaited them at the end of their journey. They sighed and kissed and gasped as they drew nearer to their ecstatic crisis, Mireille babbling without words and Maurice murmuring her name over and over again, his voice shaking from the force of his desire.

When the golden moment came, Maurice's eyes opened wide with incredulity as he gazed at her face, his loins jerking out of control and sending his homage rushing into her welcoming body. Mireille's mouth gaped open, but no sound issued from it, and she pulled his head down so that their mouths met in a long kiss. Her quaking belly thrust up against his and her heels drummed on the backs of his thighs.

'Maurice, Maurice!' she gasped into his open mouth as she shook.

It was some time before they were calm enough to speak again. Maurice lay on his back, Mireille's head on his shoulder, her fingers stroking his dark-haired chest.

'Well, my dear – your ambition has been realised,' she said, 'you have finally had what you desired all those years ago. Was it what you thought it would be?'

'It was better than I ever imagined,' he told her.

'How can you pretend that you have had anything out of the ordinary?' she asked. 'I am thirty-six years old and getting plump. My breasts are slack and my bottom is broad.'

'I won't have a word said against your breasts,' he answered, fondling them at once. 'To play with them is like getting a little drunk on the best wine. As for your bottom – I have not yet had time to examine it closely, but I shall do so before you rise from this bed.'

'Making love to me is one of life's greatest pleasures – is that what you're telling me?'

'I most certainly am. And I hope that you agree with me.'

'Oh, you did it marvellously well, Maurice! I don't think anyone has ever made love to me with so much devotion before.'

'It makes me very happy to hear you say that.'

'What follows then?' she asked.

'Why, in a little while I shall make love to you again, of course.'

'I meant what happens when we put our clothes on and leave this apartment?'

'I have not dared to think that far into the future,' said Maurice, 'but lovers seldom do.'

'Sixteen-year-old lovers, perhaps. But we are grown up and we are both married and have children. You are not so unworldly as not to have given some thought to tomorrow.'

'I have been so dazzled by the prospect of persuading you to let me make love to you that I have been in no condition to think rationally at all.'

'Perhaps,' she said, 'but there was never much doubt as to what was going to happen after we met at Yvonne's party, was there? It was a foregone conclusion that we would end up in bed together.'

'And I thought I had to persuade you!' he said with a chuckle. 'Oh, Mireille – how strong a hold the past has on both of us!'

'If there was any uncertainty, it was on your part,' she told him, 'and it was for another reason. You couldn't be sure that I'd be worth bothering with after you'd had me once – isn't that it?'

'Not for a moment!' said Maurice. 'The thing I was sure about was that if you let me love you, it would be as I'd always imagined – and I'd want to go on doing it again and again.'

'And is it so?'

'My god, it is!' he said softly, putting his hand between her warm thighs.

'I think I am beginning to believe you,' she whispered into his ear. 'Forgive me if I seemed cynical, Maurice, but I never expected to encounter such adoration in my life again.'

'Again? You've only encountered it once before,' he told her, 'and that was in the orchard at St Varent – with me.'

'That's true,' she murmured as his fingers traced the shape of the soft lips hidden by the chestnut curls between her legs. 'It has taken me this long to understand that. You are my one, true and only love, Maurice.'

They met again two days later in the apartment, late in the afternoon. Maurice was there half an hour early and smoked cigarettes impatiently while he waited. Mireille arrived wearing a three-quarter length coat in dark green, fastened right up to the throat, though it was a mild day. Maurice kissed both her hands, then took her in his arms and held her close while he kissed her mouth until she gasped for breath. When he let her go she laughed and took off her gloves and hat.

'You are as ardent as if you were sixteen again,' she said. 'Well, we must test this ardour.'

'Have no anxiety on that score,' said Maurice, misunderstanding her. 'I can still make love to you two or three times.'

'I'm sure you can. But that was not what was in my mind.'

311

'Then what?'

'Sit down and I will make everything clear to you.'

They were in the small sitting-room of the apartment. Maurice suggested that they should go to the bedroom, but Mireille shook her head and pointed to the leather sofa. Maurice sat down, hoping that he was not about to be lectured on family responsibilities and similar boring matters. He need not have worried about that – as soon as Mireille saw that he was sitting down she removed her coat and threw it across the nearest chair.

Maurice stared at her, his mouth open and his eyes shining. She was wearing a dove-grey silk blouse with a white turn-down collar.

'For the life of me I couldn't remember the colour of the skirt I was wearing that day in the orchard,' she said. 'I thought that black was the most likely colour.'

'It was a dark grey skirt,' said Maurice at once, 'a much darker shade than your blouse, but not quite black.'

She sat down beside him, put her hands on his shoulders and kissed him lightly on both cheeks.

'What were we talking about under the trees, Maurice?'

'I can't remember how we started – the events that followed wiped out the words – but I am sure that I told you that you were the prettiest girl I knew.'

'Was it true?'

'Completely. I must have said something in praise of your breasts, because it was then that you unbuttoned your blouse so that I could look at them.'

'That's your version, but it will do for now.' Then she smiled and went on in a hushed tone. 'Would you like to see my breasts, Maurice?'

He trembled as she slowly undid the buttons of her grey blouse – silk, not the cotton he recalled, but that was of no significance. She opened it wide for him and he stared at her plump breasts, lifted by the same sort of half-cup brassière she had worn two days before. This one had no lace edging, and her red-brown buds stood clear of the satin. Maurice sat staring in delight at the roundness and softness of what she had uncovered and a long sigh escaped him.

312

'Is that all you're going to do?' Mireille asked softly, 'Just look at them? Don't you want to feel them? You can if you want to.'

Maurice's heart raced as she enchanted him with this little replay of the scene in the orchard twenty years before. He freed her rolling breasts from the brassière and fondled them eagerly. Mireille leaned against him, supported by his arm round her waist, her eyes half-closed while he played with her until her buds were firm.

'I adore you, Mireille!' he gasped.

'So you should, now that I've let you feel me,' she said.

The words seemed to start an echo in his mind and he was lost in his dream of the past. Had she said that to him in the orchard – or was her memory faulty? He was sure that in another moment he would feel her hand on his thigh – and he was not disappointed. He sighed with pleasure when her fingers touched him and stroked upwards towards where his baton was quivering in his trousers.

'Maurice,' she whispered, 'there's a little bird trapped in here and trying to get out – I can feel it fluttering its wings. Is it a sparrow?'

'I think so,' he sighed.

'Show me your sparrow, Maurice.'

Those words again – across the gap of twenty years! He was sure that he had fallen in love with Mireille at the moment when she said that to him, and hearing her say it again confirmed his love, strengthened it – and made it blaze brightly, more brightly than ever before. He took his hand from her breasts and ripped his trousers open with a quick tug. Mireille's eyes were open now and she stared at the stiff part that poked jauntily out.

'It's bigger than I thought,' she said.

She clasped her hand round it and Maurice's whole body jerked at the pleasure of that simple touch. He put his own hand on her knee, then up her pleated skirt, sliding along her silk stocking, until his palm lay on the bare warm flesh above her garter.

'Your sparrow is fluttering so fast in my hand,' she murmured. 'It wants to escape – shall I let it go?'

'Hold on to it, Mireille – hold it tight!'

Her thighs were not very close together. Maurice's fingers touched the lace edge of her knickers and went into the loose leg to find her alcove.

'Oh!' she exclaimed, blinking two or three times. 'I didn't say you could touch me there, Maurice – nobody's allowed to touch me there.'

'But you have a warm little nest here,' he whispered. 'My sparrow wants to fly there.'

'Certainly not! Your sparrow would do something very naughty in my little nest if I let him. But I'll make sure he doesn't – I'll wring his neck first!'

Her fingers gripped the sparrow's neck and moved quickly. Maurice was so highly aroused by the little game they were playing together that his critical moment arrived almost immediately. He gave a long wail of delirious pleasure as the fluttering bird burst into liquid song, thereby proving that it was not a sparrow at all, but a nightingale, perhaps.

'Ah, ah, ah,' he warbled in time with the fluid notes pulsing from the jerking bird trapped between Mireille's fingers, until with a final trill, he slumped against the sofa-back.

'Your little bird has stopped fluttering,' Mireille announced.

'He sang his song for you,' Maurice sighed, his hand still held between her bare thighs under her skirt.

'And my mother did not interrupt!' she said with a chuckle.

'If anyone had interrupted, even your revered mother, I would have murdered them for committing sacrilege at such a moment. No judge in France, hearing my story of twenty years of heartache and loss, would have convicted me. It would have been a wholly justified crime of passion and I would be set free at once.'

'The memory that has haunted you for so long has now been thoroughly exorcised, my dear Maurice – you are a free man again.'

'On the contrary,' he said, 'until now it was only a memory that haunted me – now you have brought it to life!

314

'I shall never let you disappear from my life again, even if your mother does call out for you from behind the trees. I shall shout back at her and tell her that she can't have you because you are mine.'

'Dear Mama – she did not know what grief she caused that day! She did her best to look after me – she thought it ideal when I married Gaston, but it was not long before we both knew it was a mistake.'

'Of course it was a mistake! If she had stayed in Paris instead of dragging you and your brother to Algeria you and I would have been able to meet each other regularly. We should eventually have found the natural expression of our love and both our lives would have been different. Why did she go back there after your father died? She could have sold the property and land and lived in France.'

'She had a lover there,' said Mireille. 'He was married but she wanted to be with him whenever she could.'

'Was she happy – is she happy?'

'How can I say? I don't think she is.'

'Love-affairs ought to be happy,' said Maurice, 'otherwise there is no point in being in love.'

'And our love-affair – will that be happy?' Mireille asked, pressing her cheek to his.

'Yes, every day,' he promised.

'But it will not be possible for us to meet every day.'

'That may be, but on the days we are apart we shall remember the joys of being together and look forward with eagerness to being together again.'

'Here in your friend's apartment?' she said, raising an eyebrow.

'It is mine now,' Maurice replied. 'I have acquired it from him.'

'That was quick! When?'

'Immediately after we made love here – that very evening! The apartment is a shrine to our love – the bed is a holy place because of what we did on it. I could not tolerate the thought of anyone else using it!'

'So the apartment is yours? And no one else will come here?'

'Only you and I, Mireille.'

'Then this is to be the setting for our happiness,' she said, glancing round the sitting-room. 'There are some changes I would like to make, if you have no objections.'

'Whatever you wish.'

'And in the bedroom too,' she continued. 'After all, that will be the scene of our most delightful moments. Come and see what I have in mind.'

Maurice buttoned his trousers over his damp shirt and followed her.

'Your friend's taste can be improved on,' said Mireille.

She was standing in the doorway, looking with a critical eye round the bedroom. Maurice stood close behind her and put his arms round her. Her blouse was still unbuttoned and his hands clasped her big bare breasts.

'I doubt if you are in the right mood to pay attention to matters of interior decoration,' she said softly.

'I leave that to you,' he murmured. 'Order whatever pleases you and have the bills sent to me. The apartment is in the name of Lacroix – that was my friend's name – and I have left it unchanged, for the sake of discretion,'

'The room in which we make love must be elegant and intimate at the same time. You don't want me to spend my time in bed staring up at a plain white ceiling, do you?'

'You may cover the ceiling with brocade, if you wish. But I want you to spend your time in bed looking at me – when your eyes are open, that is.'

'And what happens when they are closed?'

'Then you will be in ecstasy.'

The warm tips of her breasts were firm to his caressing fingers and her soft bottom pressed back against his loins.

'That day in the orchard . . .' she began, and then hesitated, as if shy.

'What of it?'

'I refused to take my knickers off for you. But if you ask me now, you may get a different answer, Maurice.'

He steered her towards the bed, discarding his jacket on the way. They lay facing each other, as they had under the trees in the orchard, and Maurice pulled her blouse out of the waistband of her skirt and kissed her large round breasts with fervour.

'Where did you find it?' he asked.

'The blouse? If you only knew the trouble I had to find a grey blouse with a white collar! No one wears them any more, I was told. I went to six or seven shops before I found it.'

'You went to so much trouble for me?'

'There is no one in this world I would rather please than you, Maurice,' she said with great sincerity. 'Do not forget the memory of a summer day at St Varent is as much mine as it is yours. You have made me feel as if all the troubles of the past years have been wiped away forever and we are making a new start. For a man who can make me feel like that I will do anything! If you want me to dance naked for you on top of the Arc de Triomphe, say so and I will do it without hesitation.'

He kissed her tenderly for that and, a moment later, her hand touched his thigh.

'I've let you see my breasts, though I know I ought not to,' she whispered. 'Will you show me your sparrow?'

He smiled at the half-remembered words and tugged his trousers open again to let his stiff peg emerge. Mireille's hand closed round it and he spoke the words that changed the past for him.

'Mireille – pull your knickers down and let me look at yours.'

'Well . . .' she hesitated. 'You won't tell anyone?'

'I swear!'

'Promise you'll only look,' she said, keeping him in suspense, 'You mustn't touch me!'

'I promise,' he said at once.

He helped her pull her pleated black skirt up to her hips to bare her thighs. Her knickers were of pale green silk on which delicate flower-designs were embroidered. She slid them halfway down her thighs and showed him her chestnut-brown curls.

'That's so pretty!' he exclaimed.

'There, now you've seen it,' she said, continuing her young girl role.

'Wait – not so fast! I'm sure your curls go all the way between your legs.'

'What if they do?'

'Let me see, Mireille.'

'All right then,' she said with feigned reluctance. 'But no touching – you promised!'

Maurice eased the flimsy silk garment down her legs, took off her shoes and passed it over feet.

'Open your legs a little and let me look,' he pleaded.

Her thighs spread slowly apart to give him a glimpse of fleshy lips.

'Mama said I must never let a boy touch me between the legs,' she informed him.

'But I'm not touching you – I'm only looking.'

'That's true,' she said, her conscience apparently satisfied.

'So you're not doing anything your Mama said you mustn't,' said Maurice, to consolidate his gain before advancing further.

'I suppose so.'

'Did she say that you mustn't let anyone kiss you between the legs?'

'No,' she answered with a giggle. 'Who would want to do a thing like that?'

Maurice leaned over her, pushed her legs wider apart and licked his wet tongue along the warm folds of her entrance.

'Oh!' she exclaimed, as if alarmed.

'I'm only kissing you – I'm not touching you,' Maurice said hastily.

To the truth of that statement she was compelled to agree, for both his hands were under her crumpled-up skirt and stroking her belly, well away from the forbidden area between her legs, as she understood Mama's words.

'In that case it must be all right, as long as you don't touch me,' she murmured. 'Do it again, Maurice.'

His tongue flicked along her soft folds of flesh again – not once but a good many times – sending little throbs of pleasure through her.

'You won't try to do anything you shouldn't, will you?' Mireille asked faintly.

'No,' he said, 'but my sparrow wants to fly into your

little nest. Did your mother say anything about that?'

'No, she never mentioned sparrows – but what would he do there?'

'He'd sing a song for you – he's good at that.'

'He's a naughty sparrow – I ought to wring his neck.'

'He sings a marvellous song when he's happy – you'd enjoy it, Mireille.''

'Just this once then – but you mustn't tell anyone!'

Maurice lay gently on her and let his fluttering song-bird find its way into the warm nest it sought.

'That's not a sparrow!' Mireille exclaimed as it entered her fully. 'It's far too big! It must be a goose with a long neck!'

Maurice kissed her face as he thrust to and fro. Mireille sighed with pleasure and held him tight. Her blouse and skirt were rumped under her, half on, half off, and one of her stockings was laddered. Maurice was still fully dressed except for his jacket. His trousers were down round his knees and his shirt-collar was threatening to choke him as his emotions grew wilder. But of all this both he and she were blissfully unaware.

For Mireille, as for Maurice at this moment, their act of love was a dream come true, though her dream was not the same dream as his. After years of marriage to an unsatisfactory husband, she had found someone from her past who adored her to distraction. Better even than that, just when her husband's fortunes were going into irreversible decline, she had found a lover who was not only rich but would become richer – for that was the Brissard way. Maurice would give her not only the pleasures of love-making – he would insist that she had everything she wanted that money could buy.

Of course, it was a pity that she had no recollection of the day in the orchard at St Varent which had made so deep an impression on Maurice. Twenty years ago she had played a little with most of the boys she knew, as was natural. Maurice had been only one of half a dozen she had let feel her little breasts, and his was only one of the stiff little pegs she had held and stroked until they spat. Poor Maurice hadn't even had that from her! Nevertheless, by

319

listening to his reminiscences she had been able to learn enough to make it seem real to him again – and to persuade him that she shared his memories of the orchard. She fully intended to continue in this course, arousing and satisfying him as often as he wanted, to keep him devoted to her.

'Oh!' Maurice moaned as his bird sang its gasping song in her warm nest.

'Oh, yes!' Mireille exclaimed, delighted by the position in which she found herself.

FOLIES D'AMOUR

ANNE-MARIE VILLEFRANCHE AND HER FRIENDS

When I first began to translate into English the unpublished memoirs of Anne-Marie Villefranche it did not seem probable to me that these accounts of the intimate concerns of the people she knew would interest more than the few who take pleasure in scandalous gossip about the past. In this I under-estimated the appeal of tales of Paris in the 1920s, for there proved to be for that first volume, *Plaisir d'amour*, a large readership, not only in Britain but also elsewhere in Europe, in the United States – and even in far-off Japan.

This unexpected interest led to a request for more of her work and a further selection of her stories was published under the title of *Joie d'amour*. The demand for that book has resulted in a third collection, here presented as *Folies d'amour*.

The title of the present volume, as of the two former, was not chosen at random. As the reader will discover, the persons concerned in these stories involve themselves in extraordinary predicaments through their pursuit of illicit sexual pleasure.

To quote Anne-Marie's own words from *The fortune-teller*: 'The truth of the matter is that we each carry our destiny within us, for destiny is the outcome of character.' Seen from Anne-Marie's point of view, it may be said that events, whether fortunate or indecent, do not happen

1

by chance; they are the logical result of personality in action and, in that sense, they are deserved.

This can be seen plainly in the story of Marie-Claire Fénéon, whose devotion to narcissistic pleasures brings its own curious reward. Or again, in *The emancipated Madame Delaroque*, a man complicates his life by the pursuit of a fancied ideal which, when attained, proves comically different from his expectations.

Follies indeed! But it is the human capacity to be easily diverted from the path of social convention into the secret byways of pleasure that provides Anne-Marie with her material. She invites us to smile at the quirks of human nature, not at simple virtue.

How much of these memoirs is fact and how much should be attributed to Anne-Marie herself is not an easy question to resolve. As I reconstruct her method, she extracted from her friends as much of their adventures as they were willing to disclose. After that, her own knowledge of those concerned was used to fill in the gaps. Thus, in the narrative of Christope's disgraceful behaviour at Cannes, her confidant was obviously Christophe Larousse himself, who appears in the two previous volumes and seems to have been a favourite of hers. In the crystal room misadventure, Anne-Marie's source of information could only have been Marie-Claire Fénéon – presumably at a time much later than the events recorded, when she had perceived the truth about Giles and could take a more detached view of the whole episode.

Anne-Marie's own comments on the characters and motives of her friends are frequently wryly humorous. From them it is possible to form the view that she found the human comedy, particularly the pleasures and follies of love, endlessly amusing.

Jane Purcell
London 1984

2

MARCEL LEAVES HIS VISITING CARD

After the Bolshevik revolution in Russia and the establishment of a most monstrous tyranny by Lenin and his band of cut-throats, all who could fled the catastrophe that had overtaken their homeland. To be seen in public wearing a pair of clean shoes was a crime against the proletariat for which one could be shot against the nearest wall! In making their escape from this proletarian paradise Monsieur Diaghilev and the Ballets Russes brought to Paris a revolution of their own – the transformation of the classical dance into a colourful and vibrant spectacle.

The achievement, heralded throughout the whole of Europe, held little interest for Marcel Chalon, who did not find the ballet entertaining in any form, old or new. Yet he endured performances with good grace for the sake of his mother, who greatly enjoyed them. Since the tragic death of her husband a dozen years before, Madame Chalon had found no other male companion – indeed, she had not even sought one. Marcel, who still lived with her even though he was approaching thirty years of age, escorted his mother to the ballet whenever she wished.

One fine spring evening, events took an unusual course soon after the lights went down and the music started. As was her invariable custom, Madame Chalon insisted on occupying a seat next to the aisle – for what reason Marcel had never known and thought it impolite to ask. On the other side of him sat a pretty young woman and, beyond

3

her, an older woman whom he took to be her mother. Marcel surrendered to her the seat-arm between them – a courtesy she did not even acknowledge. Since his mother had already taken possession of the seat-arm on his other side, Marcel had nowhere at all to rest his elbows.

When the dancing began, Marcel amused himself by admiring the uncovered thighs of the female dancers on the stage. They were extremely beautiful, these thighs, shaped to perfection by years of hard practice – long, slender, gracefully muscled – how delightful it would be to have them gripping one's waist in the throes of passion!

But pleasant as it was at first to contemplate those thighs, it was inevitable that Marcel's interest diminished after a time, until eventually he was bored. The seats were not particularly comfortable and he had to make an effort not to disturb his mother's enjoyment of the spectacle by fidgeting. He fell back on his customary trick to keep himself amused – he recalled in as much detail as he could remember the most recent intimate encounter between himself and a beautiful woman – in this instance a certain Madame Bataille, two nights before. She was the wife of a friend of his and, needless to say, the friend knew nothing of his wife's excursions with Marcel. The memory of that encounter was a pleasant one and it served to arouse Marcel. The pressure of his trousers on his upright part diverted his attention from the stage and with a little luck would retain his interest until the intermission. Ah, dear friend, he silently addressed the source of his masculine pride between his legs, what charming adventures you have led me into!

He glanced down with affection into his lap, trying to discern in the darkened auditorium the long bulge he knew to be in the front of his trousers. He was embarrassed to see that, in sitting with his legs apart to accommodate his enjoyable stiffness, his left knee was touching the thigh of the young woman in the seat next to him.

4

How very rude she must think me – that was his first response, to be followed almost at once by a more pleasing thought – she had not moved her leg away! By way of experiment Marcel withdrew his own knee from contact with her, waited for a moment or two and then moved it back. She did not flinch away from the pressure – but nor did she return it. Could it be that she was so engrossed in the spectacle on the stage that she was unaware that a stranger's leg was pressing against her own?

Slowly, for he had no desire to attract the attention of his mother, Marcel half-turned his head to look at his unknown neighbour. She was hardly more than twenty years of age, he thought, dark-haired and wearing a short evening frock which, in the dimness of the auditorium, he took to be a shade of pale blue, with a narrow belt of the same colour. The frock was short enough to show her knees as she sat. It was also sleeveless, displaying slender arms with a gold bracelet on each wrist to match the gold chain round her neck. Most exciting of all to Marcel, needless to say, was that the frock was décolleté to a point between her breasts. Even if it had been possible to wear a chemise beneath so deep-cut a neck-line, Marcel knew instinctively that no woman with any pretention to style would have considered it for a moment. He gazed fondly at the gleaming skin of the upper curve of a breast as the young lady moved slightly and so caused her bosom to roll a little under the thin material of her frock. If he could but reach out and place his hand on that delicious rounded swelling nearest to him, he knew that he would be able to feel the warmth and softness of a tender little breast through the pale blue material.

Marcel's upstanding part bounded in his underwear at the very thought! It was urging him to carry out his wish and touch that tempting breast – to feel gently for the little bud through the frock – even if the action brought instant public disgrace upon him. The perfume she wore

5

was delightful – light and fragrant as befitted one so young – yet with a subtle promise. Marcel studied her profile as best he could out of the corner of his eye. Her hair was beautifully cut and left the lobes of her ears uncovered, and they were innocent of any jewellery. Her forehead was high and smooth, betokening intelligence. Her eyebrows were plucked to a fashionably thin line. Her little chin, under a brightly painted mouth, was firm and showed decisiveness of character, in Marcel's estimation. Altogether a most charming person to be seated next to – how was he to make her acquaintance, that was the question. In other circumstances he would have introduced himself and hoped for the best, but with his own Mama at his side and the girl's Mama at her side, so bold an enterprise was impossible.

His hands lay on his thighs, for without the benefit of arm-rests, the only other choices were to fold his arms across his chest or to clasp his hands in his lap. Marcel let his left hand brush against his neighbour's silk-clad knee, so lightly that it might be accidental and he would be able to apologise profusely for his clumsiness if she raised any objection. She made no move at all. He let his hand lie along his thigh, down near the knee, in such a way that the whole side of his palm was in light contact with her knee. He thought that he detected a tiny quiver of her leg at the touch, but she did not pull away from the contact. The delicate warmth of her flesh through the silk stocking made Marcel sigh with pleasure.

Up on the distant stage the dancers were flinging themselves about in a creative frenzy that went totally unremarked by Marcel. His attention was concentrated on the silken knee which his finger-tips were now caressing without pretence. A cautious half-glance at its owner's face showed him that she was still looking directly ahead at the stage, though even in the dim light he could perceive that her eye-lids were nearly closed and her red lips were a little open. Who could she be, he wondered,

6

this enchanting young woman who allowed him the exquisite pleasure of stroking her leg in a public place?

By now Marcel's hand had moved beyond its starting-point – had dipped slowly between her slightly parted knees and up under her frock a little, to caress the tender inside of her thigh. Again that delicious little tremor! This time he thought that she gave him a quick glance from the corner of her eye. Marcel was enraptured by having the boredom of sitting through a ballet performance dispelled in so unexpected and exciting a manner. If all the female dancers on the stage had, at that moment, stripped themselves and continued the ballet stark naked, he would have ignored them for the secret little delight of his hand lightly stroking his unknown neighbour's thigh.

When his fingers moved higher still and touched her garter, she reached out almost furtively to pull her frock down towards her knees again, for it was riding up toward her lap. But she accomplished this without impeding him in the slightest. At last he touched her bare thigh above her stocking-top and was rewarded with an unmistakable little tremor the length of her leg. The skin under his fingers was smooth as satin and warm to the touch – a combination of delights which so aroused Marcel that he felt a prickle of perspiration start in his arm-pits.

Ahead of him lay the incredible moment of discovery when, his fingers gliding slowly up that stretch of bare thigh, he would encounter her underwear – a hem of soft lace first, no doubt. After that – his mind reeled in sensual anticipation!

But it was not to be as he imagined. Her warm thighs closed on his hand, forbidding any further exploration of her secret charms! While he was trying to understand this sudden disappointment, she took hold of his wrist and pulled his hand away from her completely. A moment later the dancers froze into immobility, the music stopped and the audience applauded.

7

'Magnificent!' said Marcel's mother to him as she clapped her hands together, 'superb!'

'Superb,' Marcel agreed at once, though his compliment was intended for the young woman in the pale blue frock sitting next to him, 'the experience of a lifetime!'

Madame Chalon looked at her son as if he had lost his senses.

'I have never known you to be so enthusiastic before about the ballet,' she said, 'are you feeling all right?'

'The experience was enthralling – there is no other word to describe it, Mama.'

He said this loudly, to be overheard by his neighbour.

'Really?' Madame Chalon commented. 'You had better have something to drink, in this strange mood of yours. A small cognac, perhaps. Come along, Marcel.'

During the intermission Marcel thought furiously about how he was to make the acquaintance of the enchanting creature who had provided him with a most memorable interlude. He caught sight of her once or twice in the crowd, talking to the woman he was sure was her mother. But how? He could hardly walk up to her and pretend that he had met her before – not with that formidable mother standing at her side.

'Mama,' he said, 'that lady over there – the one in the black frock and the jet bead necklace – she looks familiar to me in some way. Is she not an acquaintance of yours? Perhaps I have seen her visiting you.'

Madame Chalon turned to look.

'The lady talking to the pretty young girl in blue, you mean?'

'Yes, that's the one.'

'No, I don't know her. She has a very unsympathetic look – I'm sure that I wouldn't want to know her.'

Marcel excused himself and, in the privacy of the men's toilet, scribbled a few words on the back of one of his visiting cards. It should not prove impossible to slip it into her hand unnoticed when the performance resumed.

The second part of the ballet was sheer delight for him. No sooner were the house lights lowered than his hand found its way discreetly under the pale blue frock. A most ingenious plan had presented itself to him during the return to his seat. In his palm, held flat by his thumb, was his visiting card! With infinite caution he slipped the thin card down the top of her stocking until it was held against her thigh by the pressure of her garter. That accomplished, his eager hand sought the smooth bare flesh between garter and underwear. What joy, what incredible joy surged through his heart at the touch! What wild thoughts whirled through his mind! More than anything in the world he wanted to be alone with this marvellous girl, to take her in his arms! He was on fire to kiss her trembling lips, to caress the sweet little breasts he half-discerned under her frock. Above all, he was full of an insane desire to press his lips to the warm and tender flesh of her thigh where his hand now rested!

As before, to his infinite sorrow, her legs clamped firmly together when he tried to reach her secret citadel, though not before his questing little finger touched the lace that hemmed her underwear. He was at the very threshold of success – his stiff part was quivering deliciously within the confines of his trousers. He risked a glance at her face in the dark, his eyes imploring her to relent and let him touch the summit of his desire. But she did not return his look – she stared fixedly at the stage, even though her pretty mouth was open in what Marcel believed to be faint sighs of pleasure.

All too soon she pushed his hand gently away. The orchestra reached a climactic finish and the audience applauded the end of the performance. With regret that his joy had ended, Marcel helped his mother into her fur wrap and took her arm to lead her out of the auditorium. The girl in pale blue gave him not one look as she and her mother made their preparations to depart. Yet seeing her full face and so close, Marcel was struck by the

9

exquisite refinement of her appearance and the air of slight haughtiness in the cast of her features. Yet she had permitted him, a stranger, such intimacies! Between her appearance and her actions there was so great a contradiction that Marcel was unable to understand it – yet he intended to do so.

He caught sight of her back in the foyer before she disappeared into the slow-moving crowd – just a glimpse of pale blue, a sable stole about her shoulders, going out of the main entrance. Impatient as he was to keep her in sight for as long as possible, Marcel could do nothing – his mother moved slowly, having a touch of arthritis in one hip, or so she claimed, so that it was impossible to hurry her along. Outside the theatre, there was no sign of the blue frock. Marcel shrugged in resignation and set about getting his mother into a taxi.

That night he dreamed about Mademoiselle Blue-frock, as was to be expected, for her charms had made a formidable impression on him. And besides, this was the third night since he had last enjoyed the company of Madame Bataille. In his dream Marcel was with the girl and together they were climbing the steps to the summit of the Eiffel Tower – an undertaking too daunting in waking life for Marcel ever to have considered. Yet here he was, clambering up the endless steps inside the cast-iron latticework of one of the legs of the giant edifice, the blue frock a step or two ahead of him. Under her frock the enchanting cheeks of her bottom moved up and down in turn as she climbed upwards.

'Can't you keep up with me, Marcel?' she asked over her shoulder.

'Let us not rush this ascent,' he answered.

'Are you tired already?'

'No, I can go on forever with you!'

'Put your hand between my legs, that will help you.'

He reached under her frock and felt his vertically-held hand clasped between the bare flesh of her thighs above her stockings. In this remarkable posture she seemed to draw him onwards and upwards, until the ground seemed a long way below when he looked down.

'How much further before we arrive at the summit?' he asked in wonder.

'There are one thousand six hundred and fifty-two steps to the top,' she answered sternly, as if surprised by his ignorance of so elementary a fact.

'But how many have we ascended so far?'

'Fifty-two,' she said, 'why didn't you count them?'

Marcel turned his hand sideways between her legs and clasped her tender mound, only the thin silk of her underwear between his palm and her soft fur.

'Let's stop and do it here,' he suggested.

At this moment he woke up. He lay thinking about his dream, trying to prolong for as long as he could the pleasant memory of his hand between her legs. But the remnants of the sleeping fantasy faded and left him with the reality of his male part at full stretch and no one in the bed with him.

The little ormolu clock at his bedside indicated that it was not much after three in the morning. Marcel pondered his predicament. He could dress and go out – fifteen minutes fast walk through the silent streets of sleeping Paris would bring him to the Bataille apartment, where Georgette would welcome him and offer a warm lodging for his homeless part – except that her husband had returned home the day before. It was too late to visit a private establishment Marcel held in esteem not far from the Opera – visitors were not admitted after two in the morning, so that the girls could sleep off the ravages of the evening and restore themselves for the following day's work.

Of course, there were still women offering all-night services in the streets around the Place Blanche and at the St Lazare railway station, which was even nearer. There were women available in the little cafes around

11

Les Halles market, looking for business from the market-porters just starting their day. But all that was repugnant to Marcel, the women to be encountered in such locations being ugly and coarse.

His hand was inside his pyjamas to fondle his stiff flesh. In his condition of high arousal a dozen or twenty strokes at most would be enough to bring about the emission which would relieve his emotions and allow him to go back to sleep. But to Marcel that course of action was an admission of defeat and unacceptable to his pride. A woman had caused this stiffness – a woman must provide the means to make it limp again. There was nothing for it but to risk a visit to Annette's room. He got out of bed in the dark, put on his long striped dressing-gown and opened his door with the utmost caution.

Annette was the younger of the two servants Marcel's mother employed. She was about thirty, plain but clean and well-fed. Marcel had availed himself of her willingly-rendered services on various occasions during the five years she had been with them – occasions when he had been in dire need of a woman's company, as now. But he had a fear that his mother might find out one of these times. That would be disastrous! Annette would be dismissed instantly, of course, and Marcel would be subjected to an angry lecture and his mother's contempt.

Nevertheless, dear Mama, he thought as he went silently towards the maid's room, sons have particular needs which mothers fail to understand sometimes. And not only sons – he wondered, not for the first time, if his mother had understood his father's particular needs, or whether his father had been driven to seek solace elsewhere.

Annette was fast asleep and snoring lightly when Marcel entered her room and closed the door carefully behind him. She had not drawn the curtains close and there was enough light through the window to guide him to her bedside. She was lying on her back, her hair tousled

12

over her forehead. He smoothed it back with a gentle hand, then stroked her cheek until her snoring stopped and her eyes opened. At once he pressed his hand delicately over her mouth to stop any exclamation of surprise which might disturb the household.

'Annette – it's me,' he whispered.

She stared at his face briefly and then nodded. He removed his hand.

'I awoke in a condition of loneliness,' he explained softly, 'will you comfort me a little, Annette?'

Her answer was to throw aside the bedcovers to make room for him. Marcel slipped off his beautiful dressing-gown and pyjama trousers and got into the narrow bed with her.

'I knew that you would understand,' he sighed, his hand feeling for her breasts.

Annette, as has been said, was well-fed – and well-fleshed as a result – broad of hip and solid of bottom. Her weighty breasts bore no comparison to the chic and pointed little breasts of women of fashion, naturally, but Marcel thought no worse of her for that. After all, she was a servant, a simple daughter of the people.

He helped her to pull her ankle-length cotton nightdress up round her neck so that he could roll her big slack breasts in his hands, and he noted that, as on previous occasions, their sheer size stimulated him in a strange way. She, meanwhile, had taken hold of his projecting member and was squeezing it clumsily but enthusiastically.

'I always say you've got a good one on you, M'sieu Marcel,' she whispered. 'You know I'm always ready to take care of it for you.'

What Annette's usual arrangements might be was not a subject to which Marcel had ever given more than passing consideration. With only one half-day free a week, it seemed improbable that she enjoyed much in the way of

13

the pleasures of love. Naturally, she welcomed Marcel's infrequent and furtive visits.

'You mustn't be too long about it,' she whispered, spreading her plump legs for him, 'and be careful about making the bed rattle. Old Louise next door is a light sleeper and you don't want her to know your business – she might tell your mother if she got suspicious.'

In spite of the limitations imposed upon him by her admonitions, Marcel positioned himself in great anticipation on Annette's broad and warm belly. A long push and he was well inserted where he wanted to be.

'God, what a ramrod,' she gasped, 'do it hard!'

Marcel plunged vigorously, closing his mind to the contrast between the elegant young woman whose thighs had so excited him and the hot and plain maidservant on whose body he lay.

'That feels good!' Annette exclaimed 'Harder!'

It did not take long before physical sensation overwhelmed Marcel and he fountained his climactic release into the maid's receptacle.

'That was quick,' she said as he withdrew from her and got out of her bed to dress himself.

'And most agreeable,' he said. 'Thank you, Annette.'

'Then if you are satisfied. . . goodnight, M'sieu Marcel.'

'On second thoughts,' he said, taking off his dressing-gown again, 'one should not stint oneself of the pleasures of life. If the meal is good, a second helping never comes amiss.'

He got back into bed with Annette, lying on his side, and told her to turn to lie with her back to him. In this position, like two spoons together, her big soft bottom pressed against his belly, he put his arms round her to fondle her breasts until his musket was reloaded – a process which never took him long. This time he adopted a more leisurely pace, ignoring Annette's gasps and sighs of pleasure while he imagined that it was Mademoiselle Blue-frock whose body he was enjoying. In this manner

14

the affair was concluded to the satisfaction of both participants.

'Thank you, M'sieu Marcel,' the maid said when he dressed for the second time, 'be careful going back to your room – there's a creaking floorboard that needs fixing just outside my door.'

Back in his own bed Marcel slept soundly, with no more dreams to disturb him, and woke up at nine o'clock feeling refreshed and full of hope for what the day might bring. Annette served his breakfast in bed – café au lait, two croissants still hot from the baker, with butter and apricot preserve. She winked broadly at him when she placed the tray across his lap and he gave her a handsome tip for her compliance.

That afternoon he took a taxi to the corner of the Place de la Bastille and strolled up the short and narrow rue de Birague into the Place des Vosges, timing himself to arrive there at five minutes before three o'clock. By common consent the Place des Vosges is one of the most beautiful squares in the whole of Paris and, on a fine spring afternoon, a perfect setting for a rendezvous. But would the young lady keep the assignation Marcel had scribbled on the card he had left under her garter?

He entered the little garden in the centre of the square and stood near the stone fountain to admire the elegant old mansions of red brick and pale stone that surrounded the square – buildings from the days of King Louis XIII. At the level of the street they were gracefully arcaded in stone, above that they rose two more stories to their steep roofs of grey slate broken by dormer windows. The sun was shining brightly and the little trees that fringed the garden were just showing their pink and white blossom – the scene could not have been improved upon! But would she come? Marcel made himself stroll slowly about the garden, trying to contain his rising agitation of spirit.

At ten minutes past three exactly he caught sight of her entering the garden on the other side from him. He uttered a great sigh of relief and strode quickly towards her. She was a very picture of elegance in a charcoal grey spring coat that fitted closely down to the waist and then flared out into a fuller skirt to her knees. It was trimmed with a little collar of grey fur, matched by cuffs of the same fur. Her little grey hat had a turned-back brim and in one white-gloved hand she held a square handbag of ultramarine blue. Marcel's heart bounded in time with his steps as he hurried towards her, a welcoming smile on his face – though her own expression remained tranquil.

They met close to the fountain. Marcel removed his hat and kissed her gloved hand. He stared with affection into her face, remembering each feature with pleasure. She was beautiful, no less, and her air of slight disdain enhanced her beauty enormously.

'I cannot tell you how enchanted I am to see you again,' he said, investing the commonplace words with a wealth of meaning.

'Your invitation was so unusual that it was difficult to refuse,' she replied, 'shall we walk together a little?'

Her words and her manner were cool, Marcel noted, but the mere fact that she had come to the assignation gave him hope.

Side by side they strolled at a leisurely pace around the Place des Vosges. Marcel was oblivious to the passers-by and the children playing under the stone arcades. He had his wish – he was with the marvellous young woman of his dream. But how ought he to proceed? On what terms were they? At the ballet she had allowed him certain intimacies, perhaps under the influence of the music and dance. But here and now – in the light of day? It might be that she regretted the generosity of her response to his advances the evening before and would repel him with indignation if he made reference to what had passed between them. Yet on the other hand – she had undoubtedly accepted the invitation on the back of the visiting card he had tucked down her stocking-top.

He decided that frankness was the least dangerous approach to the delicate situation.

'My name is Marcel Chalon, as you already know,' he began, 'I am unmarried and of independent means. I live at the address you have seen on my card, with my widowed mother, whom you saw last evening at the ballet.'

'You have told me nothing I did not know or could not guess,' she answered distantly. 'What then? Are there not certain improprieties on your part which require an explanation?'

'Without doubt,' said Marcel, 'and I must thank you with all my heart for giving me this opportunity of explaining my actions.'

'I am waiting.'

'My story is soon told. When I saw you sitting next to me yesterday evening I was so totally captivated by your beauty and elegance that I behaved with more boldness – one might even say rashness – than ever before in my life. I hope that you can understand and appreciate the formidable strength of the emotions which impelled me to do what I did.'

'I see,' she said, 'then it is not customary with you to put your hand up the clothes of women to whom you have not been introduced?'

Her directness took Marcel aback.

'No,' he answered, 'I was swept off my feet by the emotions you aroused in me.'

'What a pity,' she said, glancing at him thoughtfully.

'What do you mean?'

'I mean that I hoped to have found in you a man of spirit. The truth is that my life is dull, has always been dull and promises to always remain dull. I wish it to become adventurous and unpredictable. For a brief space I thought that you might be the person to make that happen, but I see now that I was mistaken. *Au revoir*, Monsieur.'

17

'Wait – don't go!' Marcel exclaimed urgently, putting his hand on her arm, 'I am exactly the person you are looking for. What I said before conveyed a false impression. Permit me to explain.'

'Then you do put your hand up the clothes of unknown women?'

Marcel smiled at her, beginning to appreciate her directness.

'Only give me the opportunity and I will transform your life, which you say is dull, into a veritable Arabian Nights adventure.'

She thought that over for a little while as they strolled along.

'Are you really capable of keeping that promise,' she said with a note of doubt in her voice, 'or does it mean no more than that you wish to take me to bed a few times for the sake of a quick thrill? That's not my idea of adventure.'

Marcel could hardly believe what he was hearing. Her appearance was so refined, her manner so well-bred – and yet her words implied a secret desire for incredible sensations. Perhaps this was the greatest moment of his life – perhaps he had accidentally encountered the one woman in the whole of Paris with whom he could realise his own desire to escape from the boredom of conventional society. He took her hand gently and raised it to his lips.

'You shall have no reason to complain,' he assured her, 'yesterday you experienced an unpredictable pleasure when I touched you. You cannot deny this, for I felt the delicate tremors when my fingers caressed your thigh. But that was no more than a modest overture. You shall enjoy remarkable sensations in improbable settings, I give you my word.'

'I am half-persuaded to give you an opportunity to prove that you mean what you say. But. . .' and she halted to turn and look him full in the face, 'disappoint me once and you will never see me again.'

'I understand. Now, tell me your name.'

'Marie-Madeleine. That's all you need to know.'

'No family name? No address? No telephone number?'

'If you attempt to discover any more about me I shall disappear forever.'

'Then Marie-Madeleine is enough for me,' Marcel said fervently.

'Good. Now, Monsieur, it is well after three o'clock and I must be home by six thirty to dress for dinner. Be so good as to begin the adventures you promised me.'

Marcel thought furiously. She had made it quite clear that to be taken to a hotel to be made love to was not her conception of an adventure. But that was what he had planned for! One false step now and he could lose this marvellous creature forever. What to do? Naturally, Marcel was not without extensive experience of women, married and unmarried. Most of his experiences had been fairly brief – affairs of a few weeks only – but twice in the last seven years he had formed deeper and longer-lasting liaisons with women, to the extent of maintaining them in an apartment which he visited several times a week – to the great disapproval of his mother every time he spent a night away from home – a disapproval no less ferocious because it was never spoken in words. The fact was that Madame Chalon fully expected her only son to marry, bring his bride to live in the family apartment and quickly produce grandchildren for her. Marcel had no inclination to fulfil these expectations.

'Well?' Marie-Madeleine demanded, 'are we to walk here all afternoon? Astonish me!'

'Certainly,' said Marcel, with more show of confidence than he felt at that moment, 'I intend to bath you in champagne.'

Her jet-black eyes opened wide and her mouth trembled. The disdainful expression was replaced by one of geniune astonishment. Marcel knew that he had struck the right note.

'In champagne!' she murmured.

'Before the War, in the days of the Belle Époque, so I have heard,' said Marcel; 'every great beauty of Paris was bathed in champagne by her special admirer. These famous devotees of Venus, whose glorious names are enshrined forever in history and legend – they bestowed their divine favours not on ordinary men of the sort one meets every day. No, they admitted to their intimate friendship the grandees of their day – Archdukes from Germany, Princes from Russia, Kings even, from Belgium and England.'

'Ah, yes,' Marie-Madeleine sighed, 'how magnificent!'

'Within the hour you shall be enrolled in this pantheon of great beauties worthy to receive this ultimate accolade. It will be my sacred privilege to perform for you, Marie-Madeleine, the most sumptuous rite of love.'

'Yes, yes,' she breathed, her eyes almost closed in delight, 'you are more marvellous than I could have imagined.'

The private hotel to which Marcel conducted her was not a hotel at all in the usual sense of the word. It was located in the rue Réaumur, completely anonymously, with a discreetly unmarked entrance door on the street that led directly to a flight of stairs to the first floor. It provided, for those who could afford the cost, elegantly furnished bedrooms and even more elegantly furnished suites of rooms, to lovers who desired to entertain their beloved for a few hours in luxury and in privacy. Naturally, establishments of this type are popular with men entertaining other men's wives – that most Parisian of pastimes!

From a small café only a short walk from the Place des Vosges Marcel telephoned ahead to ensure that a suite appropriate to his needs was immediately available. He also ordered a sufficient quantity of unchilled champagne for his purpose to be placed in the suite before his arrival.

As every man of distinction knows, it requires a minimum of eight dozen bottles to fill a bath of average size to a depth sufficient to impress a woman of quality. And remembering that the baths in the house to which he was taking Marie-Madeleine were of the large old-fashioned type, he ordered ten dozen bottles to be in readiness. To skimp on a few bottles at a moment like this might ruin beyond repair what promised to be a great adventure. The person to whom he spoke expressed not the least surprise at his request, as was to be expected in one who was accustomed to purveying special services to persons of adequate financial means. Marcel was a valued client, after all, and he was assured that the house would not charge him for any unopened bottles that might be left over.

The room in which Marie-Madeleine disrobed, with Marcel's expert assistance, had a certain fin-de-siècle charm which pleased her – long curtains of dark-red plush with tassels, a vast bed ornamented in white and gold with an oval plaque of porcelain let into its woodwork painted with a small and chubby Cupid about to let fly an arrow from a tiny bow. But for all the carefully-preserved pre-War finery, Marcel had eyes only for the beautiful young woman he had brought there – which was as it should be.

Her outer clothes removed, she stood gracefully, one hand at her cheek, so that Marcel could admire her slender figure in silk camiknickers of damson-red, an exquisitely flimsy garment which covered her from just above the point of her breasts to just below the join of her long thighs. Marcel sighed in delight at this vision of desire.

But then – an unimaginable shock caused him to gasp loudly! He caught sight for the first time of a ring on her finger – not a wedding-ring, for that would have meant nothing. But this!

'You are engaged?' he asked incredulously.

Marie-Madeleine raised her hand and frowned slightly at the offending ring. 'Does it matter to you?' she replied.

'No – but doesn't it matter to *you*?'

She shook her black-haired head gently.

'No, he's a boring man and I don't love him.'

'Then why are you engaged to be married to him, whoever he is?'

'I told you when we met – my life is dull. My parents are worthy, kind, dull people. They chose my fiancé for me and how could I refuse? He too is kind, worthy and dull – and most suitable, of course. Our marriage will be ideal in everyone's opinion except mine. We shall live in a large apartment, entertain a great deal, go to the most boring part of the country each summer and have two children. And that's it.'

'But this is frightful!' Marcel muttered.

'To you, perhaps. To me it is normal because that is the way I have been brought up. Now, Marcel. . .' and she used his name for the first time, 'you give every indication of becoming boring yourself. I am disappointed in you. I did not expect this conventional attitude. I shall dress and leave at once.'

'Don't go! It was only a moment of surprise and is now forgotten. Your first adventure is about to begin – let me kiss your knees.'

'That's better,' said Marie-Madeleine, smiling at him, 'no one has ever kissed my knees before.'

'Not even your fiancé?'

'I forbid you ever to mention him again.'

Marcel sank to the floor and kissed her pretty bare knees, his finger-tips lightly caressing the backs of her thighs. She gave every indication of enjoying what he was doing to her and by stages his hands moved up the loose legs of her silk *chemise-culotte* until he could squeeze and stroke the tender cheeks of her bottom. She let him continue this for some time before she gently pulled away and suggested that they might move into the bathroom together.

The bathroom was spacious and ornate, as befitted the establishment. Marcel opened a bottle and poured two glasses of champagne to drink with her a salute to the beginning of their adventures with each other. Marie-Madeleine sat on a chair, her bare knees gracefully crossed, sipping her wine and watching in total fascination as Marcel discarded his jacket and set to work popping corks and pouring fizzing champagne into the big and old-fashioned pink onyx bath. The delicate fumes of the wine filled the air, making Marie-Madeleine's eyes sparkle.

'But this is quite mad!' she exclaimed, laughing.

'Yes,' Marcel agreed, laughing with her as he stood, a bottle in each hand, champagne streaming into the bath.

He worked quickly, tearing open the packing cases, unwiring corks with a deft twist, until he had emptied the contents of eight dozen bottles and the floor was littered with corks, wires and empty bottles.

'Now,' he exclaimed, 'your bath is ready, my princess.'

Marie-Madeleine giggled and stood up, her arms stretched out towards him. Marcel kissed both hands and the insides of her wrists, then took her gently in his arms to kiss her adorable mouth. 'Oh Marcel, I think I am falling a little in love with you,' she breathed.

He slipped a hand between her warm thighs to undo the tiny mother of-pearl buttons of her camiknickers, then pulled the damson-red wisp of silk slowly up her body and over her head.

'You are truly beautiful,' he said, stepping back to look at her naked.

'Truly?' she asked, as if unsure – though no beautiful woman ever is.

'Utterly and breathtakingly beautiful,' he answered. 'Give me your hand.'

She put her hand in his and with great courtesy he helped her into the bath. She lay back in the pale gold champagne, a sight to dazzle the senses of any man.

The delicate pink tips of her breasts showed above the surface and the rest of her long svelte body and legs were visible through the wine. Marcel gazed in wonder at the good fortune which had made it possible for him to attract the interest of a woman as exquisitely beautiful as Marie-Madeleine. Those breasts of hers were works of fine art in their perfect proportion, as much a delight to the eye of the connoisseur as to his sense of touch – though Marcel fully intended to explore the truth of that with his hands in due course. For the moment he was content to regale his eyes! That elegantly curved little belly, with its circular navel, lay cradled between her slender hips in so artistic a manner that Marcel's heart missed a beat. To kiss it would be enchanting! And there, at the join of her long thighs, her neat triangle of fur was of thick curls that invited the fingers to comb through it!

'How the bubbles tickle!' Marie-Madeleine exclaimed with a little laugh, 'I love it.'

'Let them burst against that most sensitive part between your legs,' Marcel suggested 'open your thighs a little.'

A slight pinkness touched her face at the frankness of his suggestion, but only for a moment, then she moved her feet as widely apart as the bath allowed.

'Oh!' she cried a few seconds later. 'Oh! Marcel – the sensation is incredible !'

He watched her for a while as her eyes half-closed in her enjoyment of the tiny tickling of the champagne bubbles against the tender flesh between her thighs. Then, throwing off with reluctance the spell of her naked beauty, he tore open another case, popped two corks and let the frothing wine pour down over her breasts.

'Oh yes, yes!' she squealed, 'Oh, Marcel – how marvellous!'

She sat up and cupped her hands under her enticing

24

little breasts, holding them to receive the cascade of pale wine, her expression one of surprise and pleasure. Marcel opened two more bottles quickly and poured again from as high as he could hold the bottles, directing the two streams of champagne onto the pink buds of her breasts, where the wine foamed and sprayed out in a great torrent. The expression of her face had changed, he noted – the surprise had been replaced by that look of slight hauteur he loved so well. Her thinking had adjusted to the situation, he surmised – she now felt herself to be one of the great courtesans of the past receiving her rightful homage from an admirer. Her words confirmed his thought.

'Again!' she commanded, when the bottles were empty.

Again he cascaded foaming wine onto her pink buds, now engorged and firm. Her mouth slowly opened wide as if she were screaming, though no sound emerged. Her eyes stared at nothing, her long legs kicked abruptly, sending a deluge of champagne over the side of the bath onto the floor, then she sank back and lay trembling.

Marcel set down the bottles and reached for a large pink towel. In a few moments Marie-Madeleine's eyes opened and she looked at him with tenderness.

'Oh Marcel!' she murmured for the third time, her voice a little shaky this time.

She stood up and let him wrap her in the towel, which was big enough to cover her from shoulders to knees. Marcel picked her up and carried her into the bedroom, laid her on the broad bed and unwrapped her with a delicacy bordering on reverence. His clothes were off in seconds and he was beside her, kissing and caressing her. She sighed in great contentment as he kissed the tips of her breasts and tasted champagne.

'I believe that I am already a little in love with you,' she murmured.

'And I with you, Marie-Madeleine,' he replied, his lips moving over her belly, his hand between her thighs,

25

touching at last the warm treasure she had denied him at the ballet the evening before. He pressed his lips to the damp curls that tasted of champagne and to the soft folds of flesh the curls concealed.

They were both a little drunk from the fumes of so much wine. Marie-Madeleine's hands grasped him by the shoulders and pulled him towards her. At once he slid on top of her and, as her legs moved apart, brought his stiff projection to the voluptuous entrance to her enclosure.

The thought had been in his mind earlier, after what she had told him of the dullness of her life, that she might well be a virgin still. He pushed hard to overcome any such obstruction to pleasure, but the ease of his entry proved her to be otherwise. However boring a person her fiancé might be, at least he had displayed enough initiative to have relieved Marcel of any difficulty in that respect.

At this supreme moment Marcel tried to rein back his passion and to proceed at a canter rather than a gallop – to prolong the uniqueness of his first lovemaking with Marie-Madeleine. But her beautiful face so close to his expressed pure delight at what he was doing to her and the feel of her enchanting body under him was so stirring that, try as he might, nothing could restrain the sensations that were running away with him. His loins bucked wildly, Marie-Madeleine cried out in pleasure, and his passion erupted hotly within her.

In the weeks that followed their first encounter Marcel devised adventures to astonish her – he led her into erotic episodes unguessed at in her hitherto predictable life of prim conformity. Their meeting-place was always the Places des Vosges, the scene of their first rendezvous, and their arrangement was that he would wait for her by the little fountain at three in the afternoon. If she was not there by a quarter past the hour, then she would not come that day. Not knowing her family name or where she lived added to the uncertainty of when he would next see her and made the affair extraordinarily piquant for him. It was a veritable Arabian Nights story for him, a story in which he was the lover of a beautiful unknown – a mysterious princess who slipped away from the Caliph's harem at enormous danger to herself in order to be with the young man she loved! For Marie-Madeleine it was the same – she escaped for a few hours from the boring routine of life at home and with her fiancé into a world where the most improbable things happened to her.

One afternoon when a light spring rain was falling Marcel took her for a ride on the Metro, saying that he intended to show her something deliciously shameful. The words caught her imagination.

'But how can anything shameful be delicious?' she asked as they went down the steps from the street to the underground station.

'You will see,' he answered cryptically, purchasing two tickets.

At that time of the afternoon the trains were relatively little used and they were able to board an empty carriage. Instead of taking seats, Marcel led her to the end of the carriage and pressed her to the partition and, as the train jerked forward, slid his hand under her coat and skirt to rest for a moment between her thighs above her stockings! But only for a moment - then he had found his way into the loose leg of her knickers and was stroking the soft curls of her warm mound. Her face turned up to stare at him in amazement from under the brim of her little cloche hat.

Her red-painted mouth opened as if to protest, but showed instead the tip of her tongue as Marcel's fingers slowly parted the tender lips between her legs. It seemed to him that she gasped as his caressing fingers found her little bud of pleasure, but whatever sound she made was lost in the rattle of the train.

They had boarded the Metro at the Bastille station, heading westwards. By the Hôtel de Ville stop she was clinging tightly to him and he could feel her legs trembling against his own legs. Someone got into the carriage and sat down, but Marcel and Marie-Madeleine were too engrossed by then to pay any attention and he continued to caress her secret bud with great delicacy. Before they reached the next stop he felt her body convulse in passion and saw her eyes go blank in ecstasy. Still he kept his hand there, up her clothes, hiding what he was doing by his own body between her and whoever entered or left the carriage.

She was smiling up at him now, enchanted by the effrontery of his action in a public place.

'Deliciously shameful,' she whispered, just loud enough for him to hear as the train left the station.

Her smile broadened as his fingers began to move inside her again, wet now with the dew of her climactic emotions. This time she responded very quickly to his caress, rubbing herself rhythmically against his hand. The shuddering that announced that she had again reached the zenith of delight coincided with the train's arrival at the Étoile stop. Marcel stroked her quickly until she was still again, then removed his hand at last and kissed her cheek. They rode on to the Porte de Maillot and waited until the two or three other passengers had left the train before getting out themselves. On their way out of the station they passed an elderly couple. The woman glared at them and called out loudly that they should be ashamed of themselves, while her husband winked lewdly at Marcel.

Marie-Madeleine's cheeks were fiery red as they hurried away from the couple who had obviously shared the Metro carriage with them. As they entered the Bois de Boulogne she said:

'But suppose it had been someone who knows me!'

'Who, for instance?'

'My fiancé – what then?'

'But it wasn't, and you enjoyed the ride.'

'Marcel – you are impossible! And I adore you for it.'

'You adore me because I am unpredictable.'

'And without shame,' she added, 'I find that exciting.'

The spring shower had long stopped, the air in the Bois was fresh and sweet, Marcel led her off the road and under the trees, until he judged that they were out of sight of any but other lovers seeking privacy for their own pleasures. He stood Marie-Madeleine with her back against the trunk of a large tree and, without another word, opened the jacket of her spring costume – an elegant creation in peach-coloured silk of matching jacket and skirt. She was wearing a blouse of red and yellow stripes with a little collar that tied in a bow at the neckline. Marcel ran his hands over her breasts, then eased the blouse out of the waistband of her skirt, to find under it a chemise made wholly of fine lace. That too he pulled out of her skirt and up around her neck to bare her pretty breasts.

'But people like us don't do this sort of thing in the park,' she whispered as he fondled the marvellous little breasts he had uncovered.

'You and I do,' he replied, 'we are not like other people.'

'Marcel!' she murmured when he unbuttoned his trousers and brought out his hard part.

'Hold it in your hand,' he instructed her, 'until I find somewhere to put it.'

The touch of her white kid gloves on his sensitive protruberance was extraordinary, causing it to leap impatiently. Meanwhile, Marcel had lifted her skirt and pulled aside the loose leg of her flimsy underwear to reveal her black fur.

'There!' he said 'the ideal place for it. Put it in, Marie-Madeleine.'

Her lack of skill in effecting the conjuncture was ample proof that Marie-Madeleine's fiancé was a prosaic person who did no more than to arrange her on her back and penetrate her beautiful citadel of love with a brutal push. Nevertheless, in spite of her inexperience in handling a man's proud part, she persevered until matters were arranged to their mutual satisfaction. Marcel smiled at her in delight at the warm clasp of her flesh.

'Marie-Madeleine, I adore you,' he said, and meant it, 'hold up your clothes so that I can see your breasts.'

She leaned back against the bole of the tree, her gloved hands holding high the delectable creations of expensive couturier and lingerie-maker, so that he could have his wish. Marcel held her by the hips and slid his engorged part to and fro in an access of tranquil delight, intent on her changing expression as her composure disappeared under the impact of arousal.

'Marcel – I adore you too!' she exclaimed, as well she might at such a moment.

There ensued an interlude of sensual bliss, but all too soon Marcel reached the critical moment. His legs shook, he gripped Marie-Madeleine's hips strongly enough to bruise her delicate flesh, though she gave no sign of discomfort and surely felt none in her state of high excitement. He stared at her naked breasts bobbing up and down to the rhythm of his thrusting, then gasped out her name as he paid her his passionate respects.

To dress properly again afterwards she had to drop her peach-coloured skirt and smooth down chemise and blouse. Marcel went down on one knee on the still-wet grass and pressed a fond kiss to the warm lips between her thighs, breathing in the warm scent of her sensuality, before adjusting her knickers for her. When all was set to rights, they strolled back to the Place de la Porte Maillot arm in arm, where he put her into a taxi and waved goodbye as it sped away along the Avenue de la Grande Armée towards the Arc de Triomphe. She had said nothing to the taxi driver which offered a hint as to which part of Paris she lived in, only 'that way', accompanied by a nod of her head.

On one occasion she told Marcel that she was free the next evening and that she would like to be taken to the Opera. They met in the foyer and Marcel was pleased to see that she was wearing the pale blue evening frock in which he had first seen her – that marvellous evening when he had stroked her bare thigh. She looked charming, of course – and more than that, elegant. Her air of slight disdain when Marcel bowed to kiss her hand was enchanting!

Naturally, he had taken a box for the performance, a box for four, well-placed to give a perfect view of the stage. He was extremely attentive to Marie-Madeleine, moving the chairs a little to suit her, disposing of her fur wrap, obtaining a programme, using all his charm to keep her amused. He waved briefly to a man he recognised in a box across the other side of the auditorium, his vivacity conveying itself to Marie-Madeleine, so that she too smiled and talked more than usually. She had a habit of silence, he had observed at their previous meetings, the result no doubt of a dull home life.

As soon as the lights were lowered he put his hand on her knee, let it rest there for a moment or two, then moved it up under her frock until it rested on the bare flesh of her thigh above her garter – this with far more confidence than on that first occasion at the ballet. Her face turned towards him in the half-light and he saw that she was smiling, as if in reminiscence.

Needless to say, on this instance Marie-Madeleine did not press her legs together to restrain his hand from mounting a little higher, not even when his finger-tips reached her soft groin. She stared at the stage, so that it might be surmised that she was enjoying at the same time the intellectual pleasure of the performance and the sensual pleasure of the delicate touch between her thighs.

The presentation that evening was of *Manon Lescaut*, a favourite piece with Parisian audiences since its first production a little before the turn of the century. This

31

version of Prévost's romantic novel telling how the beautiful young Manon abandons everything to run away with her lover, leaves him for a richer one and then returns to the first to die in his arms in distant America – all this is so essentially French in spirit that its success was guaranteed from the first performance. It did not occur to Marcel, sitting in the darkened box, that Marie-Madeleine had asked him to take her to this particular opera because in her mind she perhaps identified herself with the heroine!

Be that as it may, Marcel's hand under her frock undid the tiny buttons of her silk camiknickers so that he could cup her furry mound and rub the curls lightly. He was, of course, an averagely selfish young man, intent on his own pleasure and he regarded others as means to that end. In due course his middle finger found its way between the succulent petals of her rose to touch the tiny stamen at its heart. She sighed and trembled, this well-bred young woman who was engaged to be married to a man of worth and substance – sighed not with outrage but with pleasure at the manner in which Marcel was handling her intimate parts. And he, his male stem achingly hard, took equally intense delight in flaunting public decency in this way. A sense of triumph suffused his being when Marie-Madeleine's hand clutched almost painfully hard the bulge inside his trousers and her whole body jerked as she attained the peak of her sensation. Not even the music of Puccini could compete for attention against that.

At the beginning of the second act Marcel led her silently to the rear of the box and seated himself on one of the chairs placed there. He turned her to face the stage, her back towards him and pulled the pale blue frock up over her bottom, then put his hand inside her opened underwear to fondle the elegant cheeks. She understood his intention at once and sank down onto his lap astride

32

his legs and impaled herself neatly on the fleshy spike he had freed from its place of decent concealment.

For a time Marcel was content to remain like that, enjoying the warm clasp of her body on his most sensitive part while he caressed her belly and breasts through the fine georgette of her frock. And Marie-Madeleine sat quiet, listening to the singers on the stage and savouring the feel of the hard intruder within her intimate enclosure. How ravishing such moments are, so tremulous with anticipation – though more usually experienced in private than in a box only just out of sight of two thousand people in evening dress! Eventually Marcel was impelled to take matters further – for once the fuse had been lit, to prevent the spark from reaching the gunpowder and causing an explosion is exceedingly difficult. Not that either of them had the least desire to pinch out the spark travelling the length of the fuse – far from it, the explosion was what they wanted. In his confined position and in circumstances requiring the greatest discretion, Marcel did not attempt to thrust himself into that exquisite aperture. By clenching and unclenching the muscles of his belly he was able to make his sturdy champion slide a centimetre or two inside her and this, continued for long enough, proved adequate in his emotional condition to precipitate the natural crisis.

To anyone other than Marcel and Marie-Madeleine these secret meetings of theirs would have seemed little more than the stages of a love affair. Perhaps not an ordinary love affair, in that Marie-Madeleine was engaged to be married to another man. There was also the fact that even after three months of demonstrating his passion for her, Marcel still did not know the identity of his beloved. That their love-making was often conducted in highly unsuitable places and at some risk of discovery - this also made their affair abnormal, not to say indiscreet. For persons of the status of Marcel and Marie-Madeleine there was no need for their amours to be discovered, and her beautiful bottom to be seen by the public, for example, under the colonnades of the Palais-Royal while Marcel stood close behind her and admired the view over her shoulder at the same time as he penetrated her under her raised skirt! Nor for her to play with his stiff part as they stood leaning over the parapet of the Pont des Arts, staring down into the Seine, into which the affectionate movement of her hand in due course made a libation of his vital essence. Behaviour of this sort might well have attracted the attention of the guardians of the law, with calamitous result for both. And worse than that, behaviour of this sort was, to say the least, in questionable taste. Yet to Marcel and Marie-Madeleine it seemed that they were living in a fairy-tale world of enchantment – a world of inviting doorways, arches and secret corners – where they would pause on their way to some high adventure devised by Marcel – adventures in improbable surroundings to put a keener edge on their appetite for each other.

Marie-Madeleine never spoke to him of her life with her family and from her silence he concluded that it continued to be boring and that he provided her with an escape route into delight.

For Marcel it was a marvellous time and also a difficult time. To plan the adventures they would share and then to live through them with Marie-Madeleine was exhilarating – more than that, it was intoxicating. But there were many afternoons when he waited for her in vain at their private rendezvous. She never afterwards explained why she had not been there, but joined enthusiastically in whatever he proposed. So the good days and the bad days alternated for Marcel, the days of utter sensual fulfilment and the days of bitter disappointment, when he paced for half an hour round the Place des Vosges and turned away at last, knowing that he would not see her that afternoon.

Naturally, his frustration at these times had to find release. He made his way to one of the better establishments to make use of the services of the prettiest young woman available. But it was never enough. The charms of a compliant professional were no adequate substitute for the delirious excitement which Marie-Madeleine aroused in him. These professional services relieved his immediate anguish, but only temporarily. After a disappointing afternoon of this type he would dream of Marie-Madeleine that night - usually half-dressed and in some impossible setting. In her flimsy silk underwear, for instance, at a table on the terrace of the Cafe de la Paix, or standing completely naked and embracing with both arms the tall obelisk in the Place Vendome. Or dancing with him, clad only in her stockings, in some back-street cafe concert - his feverish imagination devised a hundred ways of disturbing his sleep.

On these sleepless nights there was nothing for it but to make his way silently to the maid's room and bestow upon homely Annette the passion due to Marie-Madeleine. The frequency of his nocturnal visits increased as Marie-Madeleine, for reasons left unexplained, came to meet him less and less often. Eventually Marcel found himself in the most unsatisfactory position of making love to Marie-Madeleine no more than twice a week and getting into bed with Annette four or five times a week.

If Annette was surprised by the frequency of his visits to her bed she said nothing about it to him and always made him very welcome. For her, perhaps, these weeks were a period of regular gratification such as she had not previously enjoyed and she made the most of it, guessing that it would end as inexplicably as it had begun. Nowadays she awoke the moment Marcel set foot inside her small room and turned back the sheet for him while he was removing his dressing-gown and pyjamas. In the dark his questing hands found her cheap nightdress already up round her waist to give him instant access to her broad thighs and the fleshy mound between them.

Eventually, as his visits became almost a nightly occurrence, Annette ceased to trouble herself with night attire at all. Marcel would slip into her bed and find her totally naked, her big soft breasts ready for his hands. Sometimes he played with them and sucked her firm nipples for a long time, on other nights he squeezed them only briefly before rolling onto her wide belly to push inside her. Throughout all these encounters, whether his hands were full of the soft flesh of her breasts or his stiff projection was deep inside her hot inlet, in his imagination he was making love to Marie-Madeleine – slim-thighed and small-breasted Marie-Madeleine, the mysterious princess of his adventures!

He was waiting one afternoon in the little garden of the Place des Vosges, almost distraught with expectation. It was five days since he had last seen Marie-Madeleine – and on every one of those days he had been at the appointed place at three o'clock, aching to see her walking towards him – only to creep miserably away in savage disappointment when it was evident that she was not coming. For five nights he had transferred his desperate passion to Annette, belabouring her big body to the point of exhaustion. She made no complaint, of course, but last night, when he rolled her onto her side and pressed his belly against her big bottom to make his third entry within an hour – he thought that he had heard her sigh, perhaps in pleasure, but perhaps not. Whichever it was, by the time he relieved his despair into her very wet interior, she was asleep!

This is ridiculous, Marcel said to himself morosely as he paced round the little garden – I am madly in love with Marie-Madeleine and I am making love night after night to my mother's maid! This must stop at once! If Marie-Madeleine is not here today, I shall never come here again, never! It will be finished! I will not continue this absurd affair!

If she did arrive, what then? He thought about that and the conclusion he reached surprised him. If she came

36

today, he would ask her to marry him! He would refuse to listen to any objections about being engaged already. He loved her, he wanted her, he would have her! He would·drag her into the nearest taxi and insist – absolutely insist – that she took him to her home at once to be introduced to her parents. He would inform them in the clearest terms that he intended to marry their daughter at the earliest possible moment - certainly by the end of the week at the very latest, with or without their blessing. Then he would take Marie-Madeleine to the Ritz Hotel and bed her in their finest suite. He would make love to her all afternoon, have dinner served in the suite, take her back to bed and keep her there until midday tomorrow! After all, there were five days to be made up for.

They would be married by the end of the week and she would be with him day and night! They would travel to beautiful places in an endless round of pleasure – Venice, Florence, Rome, Athens, Constantinople – a year-long honeymoon of the adventure she craved. He would make love to her in gondolas, in palaces, beneath the Acropolis in the moonlight – inside the Great Pyramid, even! When they were alone together in their hotel, he would never let her be fully dressed. After long nights of love and a refreshing sleep in the cool hours of dawn they would breakfast together in their suite before huge open windows overlooking whatever the local sights happened to be – the Grand Canal, the Black Sea, the Adriatic – Marie-Madeleine's beautiful body tantalisingly half-revealed to him by an open peignoir of delicate silk – or perhaps she would be naked except for a brightly coloured silk bandanna draped loosely around her slender thighs. . .

He was so lost in his fantasy of married bliss that he started at a light tap on his arm. He half-turned – to find Marie-Madeleine standing beside him. An explosion of joy in his heart rendered him dumb for a moment. Of

37

course, she was exquisitely dressed in a summer frock of sunflower-yellow crepe satin cut with a cross-over bodice and a pleated skirt – and a matching little cloche hat! But Marcel had no eye for clothes just then – only for Marie-Madeleine herself.

'I adore you,' were his first words.

'And I adore you,' she said with a little smile.

'Before we move one step from this spot,' said Marcel, 'there is something of the utmost importance I must say to you.'

'Perhaps,' she replied, 'but first there is something I have to say to you, my dear. Walk with me down to the rue Saint Antoine – I told the taxi to wait for me there.'

'Excellent,' he said, for that fitted in well with his plan, and he took her arm as they strolled out of the square.

Her next words stopped him in his tracks.

'I have come to say goodbye, Marcel.'

'What? Goodbye? What do you mean?'

'This will be a shock to you, I know, but the fact is that I am to be married next week. Our adventures are over, my dear friend, and I must return to my dull and ordinary life.'

'But this is impossible! You cannot marry someone else!'

'Why not? You have always known that I was engaged. You must have realised what that implied – or did you think that my engagement would last for years?'

In his utter bewilderment he let her guide him gently forward along the narrow rue de Birague towards the main road.

'I forbid it!' he exclaimed. 'You must marry me – at once!'

'That is out of the question, Marcel. Everything is arranged.'

'You do not love this man – you told me so!'

'What of it? He will be a good husband.'

'I will be a better one!'

'No, you would be a better lover, Marcel, but not a better husband. I know you well enough to be sure of that. Be content, chéri – we have enjoyed some marvellous adventures together and now it is time to return to the real world.'

'Marry me and your entire life will be an adventure – I swear it!'

'Adventures must end sometime. I shall remember you with love and delight all my life, Marcel.'

To his horror he could see her taxi waiting at the end of the street, on the corner of the rue Saint Antoine.

'I cannot accept this parting,' he said firmly, 'I will not let you go.'

'Neither of us has a choice now.'

'Why do you say that?'

'There is something you do not know. I am pregnant, Marcel. Now you understand why it is necessary for me to be married quickly.'

The revelation took away Marcel's power of rational speech. He made gobbling noises as they continued down the street and reached the waiting taxi. Marie-Madeleine got in, closed the door and let down the window to speak to him.

'Goodbye, Marcel,' she said fondly.

'Tell me.' he stammered 'is the child mine?'

'Probably – but how can I be sure?' she answered calmly.

Marcel stood dumbfounded on the pavement, his mouth hanging open, as she spoke to the driver and the taxi pulled away. The encounter had totally deflated him. He made his way like a sleep-walker to the nearest bar and drank three glasses of cognac in quick succession.

'How can I be sure,' she had said. In other words, she had been allowing her stupid fiancé to make love to her all the time that she had been enjoying the most exotic and incredible adventures with Marcel! Yet why should that be a surprise, he asked himself bitterly – fiancés usually have certain privileges with the women they are to marry. Nevertheless, so cruel a reminder of that simple fact had dealt his feelings a vicious blow. He must put Marie-Madeleine out of his mind – even if she was pregnant by him. She had made her choice and if she was content to father Marcel's child on another man, so be it! But the perfidy of it – that was what hurt so deeply.

It was after six o'clock when he left the bar, about three-quarters drunk, and took a taxi home. The apartment seemed to be empty. He poured himself another glass of cognac and with that in his hand, made his way to the kitchen, staggering slightly. Annette was in the kitchen, scrubbing a saucepan at the sink.

'I thought I heard you come in, M'sieu Marcel,' she said, looking over her shoulder at his flushed face, 'will you be in for dinner this evening?'

'I don't want any dinner. Is my mother out?'

'Madame is visiting her sister and staying there to eat.'

'Yes, I think she mentioned that this morning,' he said vaguely.

'It's Louise's day off,' the maid added inconsequentially.

In his state of shock and fuddlement Marcel could concentrate only on the big bottom which filled out Annette's skirt. The sight, together with the amount of cognac he had drunk, aroused him.

'I've got a present for you, Annette,' he said, smiling foolishly.

'Really? What sort of present, M'sieu Marcel?'

He put his glass down on the kitchen table, unbuttoned his jacket and trousers and exposed his firm-standing part. Annette dropped the saucepan into the sink, wiped her hands on her apron and turned to face him.

'It's for you,' he said, advancing towards her, 'take it.'

She clasped it in her hand, still warm and slightly wet from washing up.

'It's like an iron bar!' she said with a little sigh.

By then Marcel had his hands on her breasts and was squeezing them through her frock.

'Are you sure you haven't had too much to drink?' she asked, her hand gliding up and down his proud champion, 'I've heard that it stops men from doing it.'

'It never stops me,' he answered, 'you'll see – turn round.'

He took her by the shoulders and moved her round to face the sink again, her back to him, then bent her over until her hands were in the soapy water, supporting herself.

'What are you doing?' she teased as he pulled her black skirt up over her backside and her plain knickers down her thighs.

He made no reply. There, below the twin melons of her bottom, in the fork of her solid thighs, lay the big split mound he had for so many nights made use of to relieve his unslaked passion for Marie-Madeleine. His thumbs dug into the soft flesh and dragged the brown-haired lips apart until he could stab his hard projection into her. His tipsy state caused him to drive so forcefully into the unprepared entrance that she gasped loudly in discomfort.

Once embedded, the frustration and anger of his dismissal by Marie-Madeleine that afternoon boiled over like an unwatched saucepan over a fire. Marcel rammed hard and fast, not even hearing Annette's cries for mercy, until at last the volcano within him erupted and gushed out his lava in frantic jets, until he was drained.

He pulled away from the maid, took a few short steps backwards, hardly knowing what he was doing, bumped against a wooden kitchen chair and collapsed into it. He stayed slumped there for a time, his eyes closed and his wet apparatus still protruding from his open trousers. Annette straightened up from the sink, dried her hands and turned to face him, while she adjusted her underwear and skirt.

'Do you feel better now, M'sieu Marcel?' she enquired.

He nodded briefly, all emotion spent in the brief and violent act.

His head was still spinning from the effects of the drink and the fierce purging of his emotions when she bent over him and he felt her wipe his softening projection dry and tuck it away.

'There is something I must talk to you about,' said Annette, fastening his trouser buttons for him.

'Yes?' he answered listlessly.

'The fact is, M'sieu Marcel, I am going to have a baby.'

The words were like a slap in the face. Marcel's eyes jerked open and his face turned pale as he sobered up fast.

'But that's impossible!' he blurted out.

'No, it's not,' she said firmly, 'it's a certainty.'

'But. . .'

'It's no use saying *but*. You've been doing it to me practically every night for three months – sometimes two or three times a night. What did you expect?'

'Oh my God!' he exclaimed, 'what will my mother say!'

'She'd be very angry, you can be sure of that. But there's no reason for her to find out, if we both behave sensibly.'

'What do you mean?' Marcel asked, grasping at the least hope, 'you are willing to get rid of it?'

Annette's face flushed dark red.

'How can you say such a wicked thing! That would be a terrible sin. What do you suppose Madame Chalon would say if she heard of that suggestion?'

'No, no!' Marcel gasped, distraught at the very idea. 'She must never hear of that, never! But what are we to do, then?'

'It's like this,' said the maid, seizing the advantage. 'I'm thirty-eight years old now and I've been a servant in one family or another ever since I was sixteen. I've had enough of it. What I want is a little house of my own in

42

the country and enough money to keep me and the child – it wouldn't be a lot.'

'I see. You think that I might provide that?'

'If you don't, M'sieu Marcel, I'm sure that Madame Chalon will – she's a very proper person and she wouldn't let a grandchild of hers beg in the streets.'

'Grandchild!' he echoed, dismayed by the word.

As indeed he might be! He knew his mother to be capable of insisting that the child be brought up in the family, right there in the apartment, whatever disposition was made for the maid. It was unthinkable – as also was the moral obloquy that his mother would heap upon Marcel's head. His life wouldn't be worth living!

'You are right, Annette,' he said, shuddering, 'I know where my duty lies. Tell my mother that you have been left a little house somewhere by a relation and give up your job here. Then go and find a place and I will buy it. You may rely on me.'

'Thank you. Excuse me for saying it, but it would ease my mind if you took me to a lawyer's office first and I got a signed piece of paper saying that I would have the little house and so much coming in every month to live on. That's reasonable, isn't it?'

Whether it was reasonable or not was not important – Marcel knew that he had no choice. He agreed to take her to see a discreet lawyer. While Annette, smiling now, made him a cup of strong coffee, he sat wondering if any man before had ever been presented with two unborn children on the same day. There seemed to him a sardonic cruelty in this accumulation of disasters that made him ask himself seriously whether Providence had arranged the world as well as it could be arranged. To leave one's visiting card carelessly was, he thought, an expensive business, emotionally and financially.

RAYMOND AT THE CIRCUS

There are those who will go to extraordinary lengths to acquire a reputation as a joker and usually it is those who have little else to commend them. One such was Georges Bonfils, a person whose predatory business practices might well have made him an outcast from decent society, except that his talent for devising the most elaborate farces somewhat softened the opinion of him which those who had dealings with him would otherwise have formed.

Knowing the man's reputation, Raymond was not astonished when he received from him a handsomely engraved invitation requesting the pleasure of his company at a performance of the Circus Émile. The formality of the wording on the card made him chuckle. Clearly it was one of Bonfils' jokes, something to astound and amuse those invited, something they would talk about for weeks afterwards. Undoubtedly the company would be small and carefully selected, that being Bonfils' style. As with all of these things, there would be a secret purpose – something to Bonfils' own advantage – but no one would mind that. Raymond wrote a formal note of acceptance and then asked around among his friends to discover who else had received an invitation. Quite a few had, the others looked at him enviously and said that their own invitations must surely be held up in the mail and would arrive shortly.

On the day specified, Raymond set out by car after lunch to arrive before three, the time on the card. It was no easy matter to locate the scene of the proposed entertainment. The Circus Émile waś not one of the large international circuses which toured the major towns and cities. Far from it, it was a small and down-at-heel venture which had pitched its threadbare tents on a piece of wasteland in a remote eastern suburb of Paris. That was only to be expected, Raymond reflected as he drove through dismal and depressing streets, for how otherwise could Bonfils have hired the facilities of the circus for whatever entertainment he proposed to stage?

When at last, in this unknown territory, he found the spot, Raymond saw that the main tent was small and shabby, the banner carrying its name was so weather-worn and battered that it was almost unreadable. The site was bounded on one side by a railway line along which a freight train rattled asthmatically, and the ground itself was strewn with rubbish that no one had troubled themselves to clear away. A bankrupt enterprise this, Raymond thought, a few families all related and banded together to make a poor living. It was doubtful whether Bonfils had paid them very much for the use of their facilities for an afternoon, yet however little it was, it was probably more than they would make in a week of their regular performances in so poor a neighbourhood.

The main entrance to the big tent was closed off by a flap of stained canvas, in front of which stood a muscular man with a big moustache. He was wearing a striped jersey and shapeless trousers and looked strong enough to cope single-handed with any sort of trouble which could conceivably arise. Not a person a sensible man would choose to quarrel with, Raymond said to himself as he parked his new Renault a few yards from the tent and walked across the littered ground. There were seven or eight big cars parked there already – evidently he was not the first to arrive.

The bruiser favoured him with a hard stare. Raymond responded by nodding pleasantly and handing him the engraved invitation card. The wording of it was formal in the extreme:

'Monsieur Georges Bonfils, a Commander of the Legion of Honour, requests the pleasure of the company of Monsieur Raymond Provost at a private performance of the Circus. . .' and so on. The man in the striped jersey – perhaps he was Émile himself – took it from him and glared at it briefly. The thought crossed Raymond's mind that it was improbable that striped-jersey was sufficiently literate to read what was printed on the card. Whether he was or not, he at least recognised it as the correct passport for the afternoon. He lifted the canvas flap and gestured Raymond through with a slight inclination of his head.

Inside it was stuffy. There were benches round the sides that would seat not more than a hundred and fifty spectators packed closely together. The sawdust-strewn ring in the centre was large enough for only the most modest of performances – a juggler or two, perhaps, a fire-eater, a dancing-bear with a ring through his nose, a knife-thrower with his board and unattractive wife as living target – the usual banalities. None of which would be presented today, of course, Bonfils must surely have made special arrangements for the entertainment of his guests.

The stuffiness in the tent was partly due to the lighting – hissing gas-flares from containers set in the corners. But the atmosphere was already convivial – about twenty well-dressed men were assembled on one side of the tent, chatting away, glasses in their hands. Two or three servants were busy with the refreshment – champagne bottles cooling in a row of dented zinc buckets and tubs filled with ice and water. The buckets at least looked as if they were circus property, the long-stemmed glasses the servants were handing round obviously were not.

Bonfils detached himself from the little crowd and came forward to shake Raymond's hand and welcome him. He was dressed very formally in a long and elegant morning-coat, cravat and black silk top hat. The monocle he affected was dangling on its thin gold chain against his white waistcoat. The whole attire, Raymond decided, was itself a part of the joke. Perhaps he should have dressed formally himself, but another glance at the other guests reassured him. They wore normal suits, though of mainly dark hues.

'How very pleased I am that you can be with us,' Bonfils exclaimed. 'You missed my last little circus entertainment, as I recall. It was so popular with everyone that I felt I had to arrange another. Come and have a drink. I think you know everyone here.'

'It was kind of you to invite me,' Raymond replied. 'Yes, I know many of your other guests.'

'Good, then there is no need for introductions.'

Raymond had already recognised a number of business associates, a few acquaintances from the Stock Exchange, a couple of important politicians, even a famous author he had once met at someone's reception – a man who had made a surprising amount of money from his boring sagas of tormented family life in the provinces. Glancing round the conservatively-dressed group of men, all wearing hats, Raymond smiled as he thought for a moment that the gathering could almost have been for a deceased colleague's funeral. The only jarring note was a vivid green tie worn by the writer, presumably as a sign of his creative ability.

Glass of champagne in hand, Raymond plunged into the throng, shaking hands, exchanging greetings, on easy terms with everyone there.

'Were you at Bonfils' last circus performance?' asked a friend, Xavier de Margeville, whom Raymond had known would be there. 'I can't remember.'

'I was away from Paris at the time and missed it. I've heard about it, of course.'

'It was the talk of Paris for a month afterwards. It inflated Georges' notoriety enormously.'

'But it didn't do him any harm, as I understand it,' said Raymond.

'Of course not! His invitations are so sought after that the most unlikely people do him favours in the hope of being added to the list, but he is very selective. Why, I was told just before you came in that Georges has disappointed a Minister of State today because he didn't regard him as useful enough. But that may be no more than one of Georges' own rumours to make himself more important. The gossip last year was that he had turned away a certain Eminence of the Church who wanted to be present, on the grounds that dignitaries of the Church knew so much about these things that he would find it boring.'

Raymond laughed and emptied his glass. At once a servant was at his side to refill it.

'On the other hand,' he said cheerfully, 'both tales might well be true, Xavier. Is today's performance to be a repetition of what I was told took place last autumn?'

'No, Georges has promised us something entirely different.'

The drinks flowed freely, the conversation became more animated and the gestures more expansive. Eventually the clanging of a handbell silenced the party. It was Bonfils, standing in the middle of the sawdust ring, his tall hat pushed to the back of his head.

'Gentlemen!' he bawled, 'your attention, please! You are about to witness the most amusing, the most daring, the most original circus performance ever to be presented in Paris – or anywhere else!'

'Since last year, you mean!' someone called out.

'No previous performance can possibly equal what you are to see today, you have my assurances,' Bonfils replied at once, greatly enjoying his role of ringmaster. 'This is the genuine, the unique, the once-in-a-lifetime performance, brought to you regardless of expense and trouble. Take your seats, if you please! The attendants will circulate among you with refreshments during the performance.'

With late arrivals the company now numbered about thirty. Everyone wanted to sit on the front row, of course, and the benches were rapidly filled round the edge of the sawdust ring.

Bonfils resumed his comical introduction when they were quiet again.

'Gentlemen, it is possible that in a gathering of important persons so distinguished in the fields of finance, commerce, politics – and the arts – there might possibly be one or two who have visited certain establishments in this city. Entirely for the purposes of study and observation, I need hardly say. In such establishments there is a remote possibility that you have been compelled to witness actions of a particular nature performed for the instruction of those present.'

'Shameful!' said someone who sounded very far from ashamed at this thought.

'Shameful indeed!' Bonfils continued. 'For I must inform you that these acts to which I refer are faked. They are fraudulent. They are deceptions! But today there will be no deception – you will be privileged to observe the real thing. Gentlemen, I give you, I proudly give you. . . Bonfils' *cirque erotique!*'

He paused and bowed to acknowledge the applause from his audience.

'Thank you, gentlemen – your appreciation is the only reward I seek. And now – for your entertainment, for your amazement, for your delectation, the Circus Bonfils – for one performance only – proudly presents. . .'

He clanged his handbell loudly, a threadbare curtain strung across one end of the tent was pulled aside by an unseen hand, while all eyes turned to catch the first glimpse of what was to be presented.

49

'Mademoiselle Marie!' Bonfils bawled.

Amid cries of emotion from the small audience a totally naked woman rode into the sawdust arena on an ordinary bicycle. She was in her twenties and reasonably pretty. Her breasts jumped up and down as she drove the pedals round energetically with her bare feet.

'Mademoiselle Jeanne!' Bonfils announced when the first rider was part way round the ring, and another equally naked young woman rode in, smiling and waving with one hand to the admiring little crowd on the benches.

'Mademoiselle Marianne!'

A third rider joined them, this one standing on the pedals and so giving a clear view of the patch of dark hair between her legs.

'Mademoiselle Sophie!'

There were four of them cycling round the small ring, smiling and acknowledging the applause, keeping their distance from each other. They were all about the same age and averagely attractive.

'Four of the most outstanding beauties of Paris for your delight!' Bonfils announced with gross exaggeration. 'Observe them as they ride, consider their merits. Estimate as best you can their strength and fortitude. And then, when the contest starts, pick your favourite and give her your whole-hearted support! Whichever of these lovelies you fancy – urge her on, encourage her! And in addition to your moral support, place a bet when the action becomes hot.'

'Surely they're not going to fight each other!' exclaimed Raymond, aghast.

'Of course not – that would be too brutal,' said de Margeville, 'something far more amusing. You'll see.'

'Are you ready, ladies?' Bonfils enquired loudly of the women circling him on their bicycles.

'Ready!' they chorused.

'Then prepare for the signal to begin. The prize to the

50

winner is a bottle of the finest champagne – and five thousand francs!'

All the women squealed pleasurably at that as they pedalled solemnly round in their circle.

'Go!' Bonfils called abruptly, clanging his bell again.

To Raymond's surprise they did not increase their speed at all – rather the opposite. Knowing that it was a contest between them, he had assumed that it was some sort of race. He turned to de Margeville, sitting next to him, to ask how the winner would be decided.

'Why, the winner will be the last one to remain on her bicycle.'

'An endurance test? Surely not – we'd be here all day and that would be excessively boring. Or are they allowed to knock each other off their bicycles?'

'No, they must not touch each other – that would bring disqualification. It is an endurance test of another kind. The saddles of those bicycles have been very well greased – see how the riders tend to slide a little on them with each thrust of their legs against the pedals.'

'What follows?' asked Raymond, still puzzled.

'My dear fellow – the intimate parts of our pretty bicyclists are being subjected to constant and rhythmic massage by the exertion of pedalling fast enough to stay upright. What do you suppose will be the result?'

'Heavens!' Raymond exclaimed in sudden understanding. 'You mean that the action of riding round will bring on the physical crisis more usually induced in a woman by her lover!'

'Exactly! Now you understand the amusement which Bonfils has arranged for us. As these women ride around under our close scrutiny, we shall observe the signs of their arousal. This one passing us now, for example – she is already pink of face. In a while you will see her little nipples become firm, her legs tremble! At the critical moment, each woman in turn will topple from the saddle, unable to continue to ride in her spasms of pleasure.'

51

'Until only one is left to claim Bonfils' prize! But what if there is cheating – if one of them should try to raise herself just off the saddle without being observed?'

'There is no chance of that going undetected. All four are watching each other closely to make sure no one wins the prize by cheating. And Bonfils is observing them – see how he stares at each as she passes in front of him! And finally, all of us here have the right to act as judges, to ensure that the rules are followed.'

'Champagne, Monsieur?' said a discreet voice at Raymond's elbow.

He turned to find one of Bonfils servants behind him with a bottle to refill his glass.

'Bonfils is the most salacious person I know,' said Raymond, sipping at the cold wine.

'Oh yes, but always in an original and interesting way,' de Margeville agreed, 'Look at this little beauty!'

It was Mademoiselle Marianne pedalling slowly past them. She was perhaps twenty-two or -three years old, somewhat broad-shouldered for her slender body. Her little breasts were set high, their buds a dark red that was almost crimson in intensity.

'See – she's well on the way,' Xavier de Margeville observed, 'and they've been round no more than three or four times. I shall not bet on her.'

'You intend to bet on this contest? I thought that Bonfils was joking when he said that.'

'It is part of the entertainment. Bonfils will accept all bets, however large, at the odds set by him. While there are four riders, the odds are three to one. Pick the winner and you may win a considerable sum.'

'One thousand francs on Mademoiselle Sophie!' a voice called from somewhere to Raymond's left.

He craned his neck to see who it was and recognised a well-known banker.

Bonfils, his handbell on the ground beside him, now held an open notebook and a thin gold pen. He scribbled the name of the banker, the amount and the name of the woman.

'Well done, dear friend!' he cried so that everyone would hear him. 'She seems a good choice to me – amateur that I am in such matters! One thousand francs is bet on Mademoiselle Sophie. Place your bets, gentlemen, while the odds are still three to one in your favour.'

'I understand,' said Raymond, 'the odds will shorten as we lose contestants.'

'Exactly. I do not think that Mademoiselle Sophie is my choice – look at the generous width of her bottom. In bed that would be a great advantage, but not here. She has that much weight bearing her down on the saddle and it must take its toll before long. No, I shall choose between Mademoiselle Jeanne and Mademoiselle Marianne. But which?'

'Where does Bonfils get the girls from?' Raymond enquired, 'They're too pretty and too clean to be part of the genuine circus.'

'I suppose he hires them from one of the better houses of pleasure.'

'You are wrong there,' said the man on Raymond's other side, 'I am well acquainted with the best houses in the ten years I have been a widower. These young women are unknown to me. Perhaps they are artists' models.'

'No one else is betting,' Raymond observed.

'They are studying form,' said de Margeville.

The most unusual spectacle of four young women riding round on bicycles and displaying their bodies had a certain piquancy, Raymond found. There were some interesting comparisons to make – the relative size and shape of breasts and bottoms – and their respective elasticity as they jiggled and bounced to their owners' movements. The relative length and meatiness or otherwise of all those thighs pumping up and down to turn the pedals! The colour and texture of the hair revealed by the action of those thighs. . .but above all, the interest lay in the expressions on the faces of the riders – that was truly fascinating.

All four had ridden into the arena smiling broadly to make the first lap – smiles that acknowledged the spontaneous applause and welcomed it. After all, these were women, whatever their profession, who experienced not the least embarrassment in displaying their naked bodies – on the contrary, they thrived on the admiration of men.

After a turn or two of the ring the smiles were still there on all four pretty faces – but they were becoming more like fixed grins as important and distracting sensations started to make themselves felt between the riders' legs. One by one even the grins disappeared as these sensations were intensified by the constant rubbing of the slippery saddles. Mademoiselle Marianne, for example, rode past with her mouth hanging open loosely and a faraway look in her eyes as she struggled against the crisis which threatened her.

'Heavens!' said de Margeville as he observed her, 'she won't last more than another time or two round the ring. This is the last opportunity of getting odds of three to one.'

He called out hurriedly to Bonfils in the middle of the arena.

'Five thousand on Mademoiselle Jeanne!'

Bonfils raised a finger in acknowledgment and scribbled in his notebook.

Raymond had also made up his mind by then.

'Ten thousand on Mademoiselle Sophie!'

Plump-bottomed Sophie, hearing her name, glanced over her shoulder and smiled vaguely in Raymond's direction. Her face was very flushed and Raymond wondered if he had made an expensive mistake. Xavier de Margeville certainly thought so.

'Not a hope,' he declared, 'not with that splendid bottom. Go for the thinnest, that's my advice.'

'And also mine,' the man on Raymond's other side

54

agreed and surprised him by betting fifty thousand francs on Mademoiselle Jeanne.

'Fifty thousand bet by Barras!' Bonfils announced loudly. 'That's more like it. He'll be able to pay his shareholders an extra dividend out of his winnings! Come along now, gentlemen – get your bets down while there's still time.'

At once several voices called out and kept Bonfils busy writing for a while, though no one approached or surpassed Barras' fifty thousand. In so far as Raymond could judge in the confusion of voices, most of the money was going on Mademoiselle Jeanne and Mademoiselle Marie and it was Mademoiselle Jeanne who was the favourite. He heard only one other wager placed on Mademoiselle Sophie, a circumstance which did not inspire him with confidence in her.

'Ah, look at Marianne!' de Margeville exclaimed, tapping Raymond on the knee, 'in a few more moments. . .'

Marianne on the far side of the sawdust ring was riding very slowly now, the front wheel of her bicycle wobbling. She was breathing quickly through her open mouth and her tiny breasts rose and fell with the heaving of her chest.

'She's cheating!' one of the other riders shouted shrilly, pointing at Marianne, 'she's off the saddle!'

Bonfils strode across to Mademoiselle Marianne and delivered a good-natured smack with his open hand on her bare bottom.

'Sit on the saddle properly,' he cried, 'no cheating allowed here!'

Marianne wobbled on, her course becoming more and more erratic. As she approached the bench where Raymond was sitting her head went slowly backwards until she was staring up at the shabby roof of the tent. She uttered a high-pitched squeal and toppled over sideways. There was a long gasp from the audience and many rose to their feet as Marianne rolled in the sawdust and lay on

55

her side, both hands pressed between her legs, her knees drawn up and jerking in the throes of her climactic moments.

'Mademoiselle Marianne withdraws from the contest,' Bonfils announced formally.

He raised his top hat in salute to the fallen competitor, then assisted her to her feet and gave her a friendly pat on the rump as she picked up her bicycle and wheeled it away.

All eyes were on the three women left in the ring as they circled slowly, each bright pink with emotion. The men who had not yet placed a bet were emboldened to do so now that the field had thinned out, though the odds were now at two to one only.

'Did anyone put money on Mademoiselle Marianne?' Raymond asked his friend.

'I think that Foucault over there had a few thousand francs on her. For the wrong reasons, alas. He knows nothing about betting, but he adores women with pointed little breasts like hers.'

'Who doesn't?' said Raymond, shrugging.

A groan of dismay arose from the benches as Mademoiselle Marie veered off course, her eyes closed and her belly shaking – to be followed by a shout of delight as she collided with a bench laden with spectators. The abrupt halting of her machine sent her sailing head-first over the handlebars into the laps of the onlookers – with such force that the bench tipped over backwards, depositing them all on the ground. Then a roar of laughter filled the tent as Marie writhed in ecstasy on top of two or three dark-clad businessmen who lay on the grass with their legs waving in the air.

When he could make himself heard, Bonfils announced that Mademoiselle Marie had withdrawn from the contest and that the odds had shortened to evens.

'That Sophie has more endurance than I gave her credit for,' said de Margeville, watching the two finalists pedalling slowly round, 'but mine will beat her – see how Sophie's thighs are trembling, while Jeanne's are steady and firm.'

In truth, Mademoiselle Sophie looked as if she was very close to the end of her ride. The flush of her face extended right down her neck and chest and her entire body gleamed with perspiration.

'Perhaps you are right, my dear fellow,' said Raymond doubtfully, 'but I retain my faith in her.'

'You will lose your money – and I shall win a hundred and fifty thousand francs from Bonfils!'

'You sound very confident,' Raymond responded, 'does your confidence extend to another ten thousand francs?'

'A side bet between you and me? But of course! Ten thousand from you to me when my woman wins – that will be very satisfactory.'

'Or vice-versa,' Raymond reminded him.

The vanquished Marie had not left the tent, Raymond noted. She was sitting on the bench between two of the men she had knocked over. Each had an arm round her naked waist and one of them – a banker named Weber who was nearer to his sixtieth birthday than his fiftieth – was whispering into her ear as he eyed her bare bosom. Mademoiselle Marie may have lost the prize money, Raymond concluded, but she will not return home empty-handed. Looking round the benches, he further observed that Mademoiselle Marianne, the first to be eliminated, had returned without her bicycle and was sitting bare-bottomed on the lap of the man who had wagered on her and lost.

With only two riders left in the arena, the contest must surely end very soon, for both of them appeared to be *in extremis*.

'One thousand francs on Mademoiselle Jeanne!' a voice called out, breaking the silent concentration of the spectators.

All heads turned to see who it was that had waited

until the final moments before committing himself at short odds. It was the famous author of novels for good Catholics.

'What a cautious fellow he must be!' said Raymond with a grin.

'There goes your girl!' de Margeville exclaimed in triumph, 'hand over the money!'

Mademoiselle Sophie was swaying dangerously from side to side on her slow-moving bicycle, her eyes closed to mere slits and a rapt expression on her red face. With bated breath the audience watched the last moments of the contest as the two women struggled to cling to the last shreds of self-control.

There was a long wail – and Mademoiselle Jeanne clapped a hand to the wet thatch between her legs! Her front wheel turned sideways and she slid to the sawdust and rolled onto her back, her legs kicking in the air as her climactic tension released itself. A long-drawn sigh from the audience acknowledged her defeat.

'Mademoiselle Jeanne withdraws from the contest!' Bonfils cried, 'The winner is Mademoiselle Sophie!'

'Well done, Mademoiselle Sophie!' Raymond called out to her, 'I have a bonus for you!'

He wasn't sure that she heard him because Bonfils' announcement was followed by prolonged applause for the victor. She managed another quarter lap, her swaying more pronounced, then dismounted quickly and sat in the sawdust, her knees drawn up and her arms round them, shaking violently.

Bonfils snapped his fingers and one of his servants hurried to him with a new bottle of champagne. When Mademoiselle Sophie's quivering had stopped, Bonfils tapped her on the shoulder and, as her head came up, he up-ended the bottle. She opened her mouth wide to catch the stream of champagne, swallowing as fast as she could, until she could drink no more. Bonfils poured the rest of the bottle over her bare breasts and belly to cool her off and she grinned.

During this interesting little interlude the spectators were clapping and cheering, all in exceptionally good humour at what they had witnessed in the arena, however the betting had gone. Bonfils had to ring his handbell for a long time to silence them and summon the four contestants to him. Weber seemed reluctant to free Mademoiselle Marie from his grasp.

'Let go of her!' Bonfils cried, laughing at him, 'you can have her back after the prize-giving, you naughty old banker!'

'I don't believe it,' Xavier de Margeville complained, handing Raymond ten thousand francs, 'I was absolutely certain that the one I bet on would last longest. In logic it could be no other way. Why did you bet on Sophie? She looked the least likely of them all.'

'Intuition,' said Raymond with a shrug, 'no more than that.'

Meanwhile the four naked young women arranged themselves before Bonfils in a row. Mademoiselle Sophie took a step forward and Bonfils congratulated her in the most grandiloquent manner on her triumph and presented the prize-money to her with a great flourish, a bow and a raising of his black top hat. For the others he had words of consolation. Not one of them looked disconsolate, from which Raymond deduced that they had established contacts that promised to more than compensate for what they had lost.

As soon as the women left the ring to dress themselves, Raymond went forward to claim his winnings from Bonfils, thinking that he was the only winner. He had forgotten that Desmoines had also wagered on Sophie, though a smaller amount. Bonfils counted out thirty thousand francs for Raymond and handed it to him with a grin.

'Congratulations – you are a shrewd judge of women, my dear fellow.'

'My congratulations to you,' said Raymond dryly, 'By my reckoning you must have made at least a quarter of a million francs.'

Bonfils winked at him.

'Ah, you must not overlook my expenses in arranging this little contest,' he answered, 'and you must agree that everyone has been greatly entertained. Just look – they're all trying to get their money back by drinking my champagne as if it were water. Take my advice – get a glass before it's all gone. I have the pleasant task of collecting all the money due to me before our friends begin to slip away, so you must excuse me.'

Raymond need not have feared that his offer of a bonus to Mademoiselle Sophie had gone unheard. He was standing among his friends, glass in hand, discussing the finer points of the contest they had witnessed – and she appeared at his elbow. She was wearing a plain black skirt and over it a long jumper that came down below her hips and had a zigzag pattern knitted into it.

'M'sieu,' she said, smiling at him.

Her bosom was fuller than was considered fashionable and her jumper emphasised it. But for the first time Raymond found himself looking at her face properly – it was round and pleasant, though her nose was perhaps a trifle broad. Her expression was one of good-nature, not the false friendliness of the professional.

'Ah, Mademoiselle Sophie! Permit me to congratulate you on a magnificent victory against very serious adversaries. I was inspired to bet on you and you did not disappoint my hopes. I feel that it is no more than justice to share my winnings with you – if you will do me the honour to accept this little gift.'

She smiled at him as he handed her five thousand francs of his winnings and – to his delight – she raised her black skirt and tucked the folded bank-notes into her garter.

Perhaps it was the wine he had drunk, perhaps it was the emotional impact of having seen four naked young women in the throes of passion – perhaps it was both – but Raymond at that moment found Mademoiselle Sophie very desirable.

'I have a car outside,' he murmured, 'it would give me great pleasure to offer you a ride back into the city.'

'You are very kind,' she said at once, 'perhaps you could drop me off where I live.'

The offer and the acceptance implied much more than a ride in his car, as they both understood completely. After another glass of Bonfils' rapidly diminishing stock of champagne they took their leave, while that enterprising person was still working his way through the crowd, note-book in hand and his pockets stuffed with bank-notes. Once in the car and on the way, formality vanished quickly. Raymond called her Sophie, told her his own name and drove with one hand, the other on her thigh above her garter – the one which did not hold her money. He was not acquainted with the district where she lived and they were driving back towards the city centre from a direction that was equally unfamiliar to him. After a longer drive than was probably necessary, he found the rue d'Alésia and followed it westwards until Sophie was able to direct him.

The building she indicated eventually was unprepossessing, but that was of no consequence. Her room was on the very top floor, as he had guessed it would be, and that too was of no consequence. Raymond was on fire from the long contact of his hand on Sophie's bare thigh under her skirt, his apparatus was fully extended and uncomfortable inside his clothes. Sophie too was quite ready – she was breathing even more quickly than the long climb up the stairs could be held responsible for.

The meagreness of her room and its poor furnishing made no impression whatsoever on Raymond, for no sooner were they inside than Sophie's hand was thrust urgently down the front of his trousers to give her a grip on the twin dependents below his upstanding part. At another time he might have found the grip a little too forcible for comfort, but in his heightened frame of mind her squeezing of those tender objects merely served to arouse him further.

'I'm dying for it!' she gasped. 'Do it to me!'

Raymond was exceptionally eager to oblige her. Bonfils' *cirque erotique* and the car ride afterwards had exacerbated his emotions to an impossible degree – and if that were not enough, the clasp of Sophie's hand brought his throbbing stiffness to almost the instant of explosion. He pushed her down onto the untidy bed, not at all gently, his hands clenched on her breasts through her jumper while she wriggled her bottom and pulled her skirt up to her waist – for her need and his were too demanding to waste time undressing. She groped between her parted thighs to rip open the buttons of her cami-knickers, while Raymond was treating his trouser buttons to the same violence.

He threw himself on her, catching one brief glimpse of the hair between her legs still plastered flat to her skin with the vaseline which had been spread liberally on the bicycle saddles. His distended member found her slippery channel of its own accord and slid inside. Sophie screamed in ecstatic release at once and thrashed about beneath him, her loins lifting to force him in further. For Raymond the sensation of that smooth penetration was too much – he made three short and rapid thrusts and fountained his release into her, amazed, delighted and dismayed – all at once – at the speed of his response.

'My God, I needed that,' said Sophie when he lay still on her at last. 'Now we can take our time and do it properly. How about getting undressed?'

Raymond slid from her embrace and together they removed their clothes.

'What a sight!' Sophie exclaimed, staring at her wispy

patch of hair, darkened and stuck flat, 'I must do something about that.'

She left him lying on the bed while she made preparations to wash herself.

The facilities afforded by her room were rudimentary – she took a large porcelain wash-basin from a rickety dressing table, set it on the floor and poured water into it from a jug. Raymond rolled onto his side to watch her at her toilet. She straddled the basin and crouched down to wash between her thighs.

'If this doesn't cool me down, nothing will,' she joked.

'God forbid,' said Raymond, 'it all happened so quickly that I feel that I have been cheated. But if that little plaything between your legs becomes chilled from the water, it will be a pleasure for me to warm it up again.'

'There's no fear of it going off the boil,' she assured him, 'when I get started, I can't stop – not even with all that riding round the circus for Monsieur Bonfils.'

She stood up and reached for a towel to dry herself.

'The speed with which it happened to us both is proof enough that the bicycle contest aroused you considerably,' said Raymond. 'It brought on a little crisis, for I saw you trembling and panting as you sat on the ground after you had won the prize.'

'Yes, I couldn't control myself that time,' said Sophie, 'though I managed to stay on the saddle through the others.'

She threw the towel aside carelessly and stood naked for him to see her, hands on her hips and a smile on her face. She was younger than Raymond had first thought, certainly not much more than twenty, but already her full breasts had lost some of their tautness and were a little slack. The slight loss in aesthetic appeal was more than compensated for, in Raymond's opinion, by the gain in sensual appeal, for a man could fondle them endlessly and find the experience rewarding – even hide his face between them – not to mention another part of his body!

63

But without doubt her most fascinating feature was the plump mound between her thighs. Under its covering of thin brown hair the lips were permanently separated by the overdeveloped inner lips pushing through.

'It is obvious why you are hot-natured,' Raymond commented affectionately 'In fact, I am surprised that you were able to endure the ride so long. What do you mean by *the others*? Are you saying that it happened to you while you were riding round the arena?'

'Five or six times,' she replied, getting back onto the bed with him, 'but as I had agreed to win it was necessary to continue.'

'Agreed to win? But what do you mean?'

Sophie grinned at him in a conspiratorial way as she stroked his belly.

'I'm giving away a secret when I shouldn't,' she said, 'but I like you, Raymond. The truth is that Monsieur Bonfils knows about my nature – how I have to go on when I've started. It's like waves on the sea – you must have seen it – the waves come rolling in, quite small ones, and then about every seventh wave is a much bigger one. At least, that's what I've been told. Well, that's how it is with me. I get aroused with a man and these little waves roll over me, one after the other, until the big one arrives.'

'That was when you were sitting in the sawdust?'

'No, of course not – that was a few minutes ago with you.'

Raymond was flattered that it should have been so.

'So there was an agreement between you and Bonfils to win the five thousand francs he offered as prize.'

Sophie winked at him, her hand sliding lower on his belly towards his most important asset.

'I trust you,' she said. 'The little agreement I had with Monsieur Bonfils was that I should receive ten thousand francs to enter and win.'

'But why?'

She shrugged impatiently at his slowness of comprehen-

64

sion and took hold of his awakening part to encourage its growth.

'Who did everyone bet on?' she asked. 'Monsieur Bonfils did very well for himself today, but I liked you straight off because you put your money on me. What made you do that – you weren't supposed to.'

Raymond chuckled at the thought of Bonfils' duplicity, now revealed to him. What a rogue the man was – yet with what entertaining cunning he brought off the coups which gave him his reputation!

'I liked the look of your bottom when you first rode past me on your bicycle,' he said, 'you have those round soft cheeks which indicate an amorous nature, not the tight little bottom of Mademoiselle Jeanne.'

'You think I've got a big bottom, do you?' Sophie asked, her hand sliding up and down his stiff part.

'A generous bottom, not a big one. Your centre of gravity is well down your body, which means that you are more at ease lying on your back than standing up – am I not right? And then those round soft breasts attracted my attention. One of the contestants had little pointed breasts set high on her chest – modish, of course, but disappointing when you have them in your hands. Yours, on first sight, were of a size and texture to please a man.'

He suited the action to the word by taking them in his hands and playing with them.

'Ah, I understand,' she said, 'you bet on me because you wanted to go to bed with me, not because you thought I could win the contest! I knew you were a sympathetic person as soon as I heard your voice calling out "Ten thousand francs on Mademoiselle Sophie"!'

'Now,' said Raymond, 'I wish to observe this interesting aspect of your nature you have described to me.'

His hand moved down her body to touch the soft and permanently pouting lips between her thighs.

'You won't collapse on me halfway through, will you?' she murmured, 'I can't stand it when that happens.'

'You may have every confidence in me,' said Raymond. 'My desire to see the little waves rolling in to the shore is so strong that I shall continue until the big wave breaks over us together.'

'Yes,' she said, 'get me started, Raymond chéri! I'll let you know when the big wave is on its way.'

THE SECRET OF MADAME DUPERRAY

Even in a society of beautiful and elegant women Madame Duperray was conspicuous. Everyone, including those who disliked her, agreed without the least hesitation that she was exceptionally beautiful and incredibly elegant. Her clothes were made for her by the most celebrated fashion designers in the whole of Paris and the effect was always stunning, whether it was a little velvet suit by Chanel for casual shopping, a short evening frock by Patou and a simple necklace of diamonds, or the full magnificence of a ball gown by Poiret – for Madame Duperray did not restrict her patronage to any one fashion house.

She was perfectly formed for the designers, being tall, slender, small-breasted, with exquisitely long legs. Her complexion was very fine and her hair a rich shade of dark brown that looked well with nearly every colour the couturiers decided was in fashion for that season. A further advantage was that she could afford anything they suggested, for she was rich – that is to say, her husband was rich and he allowed her a free hand.

A kind Providence had endowed Madame Duperray with gifts of intellect to match those of her form. She was intelligent, vivacious, well-informed, interested in everything from the classical theatre to American jazz. Invitations to her little luncheon parties – never more than twelve people – and to her sumptuous dinner parties were greatly esteemed as social occasions of particular importance. It was small wonder that her picture, with the charmingly humorous smile for which she was famous, should adorn the pages of the newspapers and magazines with great frequency.

No man who knew her had ever been heard to say a word of criticism of Madame Duperray. But there were women who disliked her, sad to say, and who made their opinions known to anyone who would listen. The worst that they could allege against her was that she changed her lovers more often than was decent for a woman in her position. No doubt there was an element of jealousy in this sort of gossip, for a regular lover can become as tedious as a husband to a woman of discernment.

If Monsieur Duperray was aware of this ill-natured tittle-tattle he seemed not to pay any attention to it. When he and his wife appeared together in public or entertained at home they were always on the best of terms – he most attentive to her and she to him. At fifty, or thereabouts, he was, of course, twenty years older than his wife but he had never been seen to exhibit any indication of the possessiveness of older men towards beautiful young wives. In short, the Duperrays gave every appearance of being paragons of domestic virtue.

Yet rumour persistently linked the name of Célestine Duperray with an extravagantly long list of young men, though without the smallest shred of evidence. Indeed, one well-known lady whose husband's name had been whispered as having been added to this legendary roll of honour had gone so far as to state that if Célestine Duperray were to charge at the going rate for her services, she would in a year or two be as rich as her husband! But that was mere spite, of course, and not taken seriously even by those who laughed at the joke.

Needless to say, men were absolutely charming towards Madame Duperray, and this was partly because it was impossible to be otherwise towards so great a beauty, and also perhaps in the hope that they might be invited to subscribe their name to the list of those who were supposed to have enjoyed her intimate favours. If any were honoured by so delicate an invitation, they kept very silent about it. In the whole of Paris it was impossible to find even one person who would admit to having been Célestine's lover. Very few women of any charm could rely on total discretion of that sort, men being such inveterate gossips. Even the lady who had started the impolite joke that Célestine could become rich by charging a few francs each time – even this lady was known by almost everyone except her husband to have been the very close friend of Charles Brissard for the past two years.

In these circumstances, the astounded delight of Nicolas Bruneau can be imagined when one evening Madame Duperray murmured secretly to him that she would call upon him the next day at three in the afternoon, if that was convenient! He could hardly believe his ears! He looked into her marvellous eyes and asked himself if he had suddenly gone mad, to imagine so fantastic a suggestion. Madame Duperray smiled her celebrated half-humorous smile and nodded and repeated:

'If that is convenient.'

Convenient! Dear God – whatever else he had planned for the next day was as nothing to the promise of a visit by Madame Duperray. To keep that rendezvous Nicolas was prepared to put off anything at all – even his mother's funeral, if she had had the poor judgment to have died just then – even the dignity of attending at the Élysée Palace to be invested a Chevalier of the Legion of Honour by the President of the Republic himself. Not that any such national recognition was due to him then, or ever likely to be. The truth of it was that Nicolas was already twenty-six, had achieved nothing much and had no great prospects before him, in spite of his family name. He was the second son of a good but impoverished old family which was once prominent but now, by reason of various calamities during the War, the nature of which is best forgotten, had receded into obscurity. Nicolas was a school-boy during his father's misfortunes and therefore not to be held in any way responsible, but his subsequent way of life was affected. His father gave him an annual allowance which kept him from starvation but was totally inadequate to permit him to live in the style he regarded as his natural right.

Happily, old times being soon forgotten, Nicolas's family name assured him of being received into the best circles and he supplemented his allowance by sporadic journalism for the newspapers and magazines which took an interest in the social activities of those eminent circles.

In this capacity he had met Madame Duperray more than once and had written suitably charming paragraphs about her, some of which had found their way into print under his name. After one of these pieces had been published, in which he mentioned her attendance at the races in the Bois de Boulogne, she had sent him a little note at the newspaper office, in her own elegant handwriting on delicately scented paper, saying how charmingly he wrote. He had acknowledged it gracefully, assuring her that it was impossible to write otherwise of so elegant a person, but that was the end of their correspondence.

The matter of her imputed lovers was one that had interested Nicolas since the first time he had seen her. Yet even his most diligent journalistic researches, including attempts to bribe servants all over Paris, had never led him to anyone who claimed this marvellous privilege. Nicolas had the inclination to dismiss the rumours as malicious gossip – and here now was an amazing indication of the most direct kind that there might be some truth in the stories after all!

The occasion at which the invitation – or at least, the suggestion – was murmured to him by Madame Duperray was at the Opera ball – a very grand function at which the richest, most fashionable, most glittering and most beautiful people were present. Nicolas was there, elegantly attired in evening tails, to collect enough names and details for a eulogistic column in the next day's newspaper. He knew almost everyone, of course, and circulated freely, exchanging greetings and compliments, even dancing with one or two of the younger women – those who were not overly enamoured of their partners. At a suitable moment he presented himself to Madame Duperray, while her husband was talking to someone else.

To say that she looked magnificent would be to understate matters. She wore a ball gown evidently created for this special evening by the most talented couturier in Paris – which means in the whole world. In its sophisticated simplicity it was stunning! A few metres of the finest tussore silk, no more than that, transformed into a sheath for her body, leaving her shoulders and arms bare – but the cut of it, that was sheer poetry translated into silk! The rich brown of her hair was accentuated by a strand of pearls woven into it by a hairdresser of genius. Nicolas wondered as he bowed over her white-gloved hand and kissed it how he would ever find words to describe the virtuosity of Madame Duperray's ball gown for his column in the newspaper.

Then she spoke, very softly, the words which so astounded him. His breath was quite taken away. He bowed again to signify his acceptance of so tremendous an honour and, before he was required to say anything, friends of hers came up to talk to her. Nicolas retired unobserved from the little group, his mind in a whirl, and made for the bar to fortify himself with cold champagne and gloat upon this incredible good fortune. Tomorrow at three! It was a date with destiny, no less!

In that he was correct, though not perhaps precisely the destiny he envisaged. But if it is destiny that orders our lives, then the next day's encounter with Madame Duperray was to change the entire course of Nicolas's life.

She had not enquired his address and that was in itself of interest. Months before, when he had acknowledged her note of tribute to his writing ability in the newspaper he had replied from his own address, not from the office. He was uncertain what to make of that. It could be that Madame Duperray had even then considered him to be a prospect for her alleged sequence of lovers – or it might mean no more than that she had a large address book into which she copied details of anyone ever likely to be useful in any way at all.

Nicolas's restricted financial means did not permit him to live in the style his family once had. He rented an apartment in one of the old buildings in the rue de Montmorency and, while it was small, he had taken pains to decorate and furnish it well. A number of the ladies he met during his journalistic work had visited him there – nearly all of them married – for an hour or two of diversion and Nicolas did not underestimate the importance of creating a good impression.

Madame Duperray arrived very punctually, a surprise in itself, and conducted herself towards him as if they had been friends all their lives. She allowed him to assist her out of her coat and roamed freely round his sitting-room, commenting in favourable terms on a picture here and a statuette there, as if they were works of art of value. She sat in one of his very modern black and gold armchairs – acquired for a mere song at a furniture auction – and chatted with easy familiarity about the people at the Opera ball. In effect, she conducted herself exactly as if this were an ordinary social call, with no suggestion of any more interesting motive.

This puzzled Nicolas at first. Perhaps she was nervous, he thought, although she certainly gave no sign of it. Eventually he came to realise that she was sizing him up before deciding whether to proceed any further. If the verdict went against him, she would ask for her coat and leave – and it would have been no more than an ordinary social call. Therefore it was up to Nicolas to take the initiative and persuade her subtly that she could, with advantage, trust to his savoire-faire and remove more than her coat and gloves!

Once his course was clear, Nicolas brought into play all his talents to charm and amuse. He made her laugh with little anecdotes about people she knew, incidents from his observation at social functions. He talked about people he knew well who were also known to her – he was a good talker, this Nicolas. When the moment was right, he began to talk about Madame Duperray herself – how exquisitely she dressed, what elegance of appearance she presented in public, how every man in Paris admired and adored her from afar – and so on and so on.

Célestine basked in his praise, her beautiful eyes shining with emotion. In due course Nicolas found himself, in the most natural way in the world, on his knees beside her chair, kissing her hands. Not long after that, sure of himself now, he kissed her silk-stockinged knees, very expertly and in a most flattering manner. Célestine stroked his hair and suggested that perhaps the time had come when he should show her the rest of his apartment.

By that she naturally meant the bed-room. Once in it, she held out her arms to Nicolas and he embraced her and kissed her with enthusiasm. If the truth were told it was rather more than enthusiasm – it was a sense of wonder he experienced. When he began to undress her he was like a man who has bought a lottery ticket for ten francs and learns that he has won a million! The dumb-struck winner stares at the prize being handed to him and cannot believe his luck. This, or something akin to it, was what Nicolas felt then – the beautiful and distinguished Célestine Duperray was in his bed-room, stripped to her stockings and flimsy silk knickers, her pretty little breasts offered to him to caress! He kissed them until their pink buds grew firm to his lips before completing her disrobing – and his own.

Seen naked, Célestine was incredibly beautiful, as he had guessed she would be. The skin of her expensively pampered body was like satin to the touch, its tones warm and delicate. Her breasts – each a delicious little handful! Her navel – a round and shallow dimple of enchanting shape, set in a belly so graceful that there could never be another to match it! The rich brown fur between her slender thighs was trimmed short to display to the best advantage the classical contour of her delightful mount of Venus. In short – though there was no reason in the world why any man should have wished to cut short the admiration of her charms when they were so generously offered to his view – her body displayed such a wealth of sensuous harmony to the eyes, the hands and the lips, that Nicolas, involved in aesthetic appreciation, almost forgot the purpose of Célestine's presence in his bed.

She reminded him, for even the most beautiful woman becomes faintly impatient if abstract adoration continues too long without any initiative to put her charms to their proper use. When Nicolas had sighed over her for as long as she considered sufficient, Célestine took hold of his rigid part and gave him to understand without words, that she could wait no longer for the pleasure of receiving it.

Her directness had the desired effect and when he was mounted Nicolas thought that he would burst with sheer joy! He was in possession of the splendours of that marvellous woman and the sensations were as magnificent as he could ever have imagined. He felt that he had at last entered into his true heritage. A person of his quality had a natural right to enjoy women like Célestine Duperray! It was only the misfortunes of his father that had until now cheated Nicolas of the prizes that were naturally his! Now that was all changed! The gorgeous Célestine had recognised his true worth and had responded in the only appropriate way! How perceptive she was, how refined her sensibilities!

Nicolas's excitement owed perhaps as much to gratified

pride as to physical desire – and it served him well. It called forth all the tender skills of which he was capable and extended the incredible moments of their intimate union into a long and delirious passage of ecstasy which left them both panting and trembling in explosively fulfilled desire.

'That was marvellous!' Célestine said, a smile of gratification on her face 'you really are very good at it, Nicolas.'

There does not live a man who is not flattered almost to imbecility when a beautiful woman praises his skill as a lover. Nicolas kissed her a hundred times at least – on the mouth, face, chin and neck – then changed his position and bestowed another hundred kisses or so on her elegant breasts.

It goes without saying that in the entire world there is no more superb sight than that of a woman lying naked on a bed, her eyes radiant with the love that she feels for the man beside her, her soft white skin delicately flushed from satisfied desire. This is the vision which painters have for centuries attempted to capture on canvas, though few have had any great measure of success. An exception, perhaps, is Edouard Manet's picture of Olympe, lying provocatively propped up on large pillows, a black ribbon round her neck to emphasise the pale sheen of her skin, her breasts thrust proudly forwards and one hand lying lightly across the join of her thighs, as if to preserve this final secret for her lover alone. As everyone knows, Olympe is in actuality a portrait of Victorine Meurent and the lover for whom she was preserving her most intimate secret was Manet himself.

It must not be supposed that Célestine was wholly passive during this extensive adoration of her attributes in the after-glow of emotion. One of her long-fingered hands caressed Nicolas' back and hip – before seeking to roam over more intimate parts of him, until her red-painted nails scratched lightly the sensitive skin of his inner thighs. By the time Nicolas's interminable kissing had descended to the neat little triangle of brown hair between Célestine's legs – the covering to the adorable private entrance through which he had penetrated to ecstasy not long before – his cavalier had recovered from the lassitude which follows active service and was fully alert again. Célestine was, after all, a woman of experience who knew how to obtain what she wanted. She held the head of his risen part delicately between forefinger and thumb, encouraging it to grow to the maximum.

When two people find themselves in these enchanting circumstances, there is only one course of action that can be followed. After another score or two of kisses to Célestine's open thighs and the warm satin skin of her groins, then some moments of exploring with the tip of his tongue the tender interior of the pouting lips between those groins, Nicolas once more positioned himself above Célestine and inserted into its rightful place the part of him which a benevolent Deity had expressly designed for this purpose.

Many men claim that the second amorous bout is superior to the first, their reasoning being that although the appetite is a little less keen, their natural part has been made more sensitive by its first use and therefore the sensations are greater. On the other hand, women rarely make comparisons of this kind, for the female experience is so different from the male experience in intimate concerns that physical comparisons miss the point completely.

Whatever the truth of it, the second turn was very greatly to the enjoyment of both Nicolas and Célestine, as their little sighs and exclamations testified to each other. Nicolas proceeded without haste, her face between his hands and his mouth touching hers in more kisses, until her legs rose from the bed to grip him tightly round the waist, her ankles crossed above his back. Then, the moment being right, he displayed his strength for her pleasure and before long brought them both to a climactic release.

'You're killing me with love!' Célestine sighed as they separated from each other, 'I adore you!'

These few words, spoken thousands of times a day by women in similar circumstances, no doubt, were enough to draw from Nicolas expressions of devotion, admiration, tenderness – he scarcely knew what he was saying.

They lay a little apart from each other to cool down, for they had become somewhat heated during the encounter, as was to be expected. Nicolas' hand lay between Célestine's thighs, just touching the little fur coat that adorned her. He had never been so happy in his life as at that moment – he had made love twice to this famous beauty and she adored him for it!

His happiness was compounded of sensual satisfaction, pride in his achievement and pleasant anticipation of being Célestine's lover for some considerable time to come – months perhaps – or even years!

Célestine rolled over to lie face down.

'How content I am,' she murmured, 'I must rest a little.'

Nicolas was too exhilarated to want to rest. He propped himself up on one elbow and stroked the cheeks of her bottom, exposed to him by the way she lay. They were superb, those cheeks – there was no other word for it – round, smooth as silk, warm and yielding to the touch.

'Ah,' she sighed, 'I see that I shall be given no rest – you are too virile for that.'

It was not until she praised him in this way that Nicolas decided that he must give her a third proof of his masculine vigour. In the normal course of events he found that twice in an afternoon was enough for him. He had the ability to go further, but to do so subjected him to a certain slight fatigue for the rest of the day. Of course, when a woman stayed all night in his apartment he expended himself fully, for then he was able to sleep late the next day.

No matter – now that the idea was fixed in his mind he intended to continue. A bottle of champagne before dinner would raise his spirits for the evening. But to continue meant that he must arouse Célestine, who had said that she was tired, since it would be discourteous to make use of her charming body for his own gratification unless she too enjoyed the proceeding. He knelt between her parted legs and fondled her bottom with both hands – a caress that usually interested a woman, he knew, to the point where she would be ready for the transfer of his hands to her breasts. After that, nature would take its course.

Célestine's bottom really was delicious. He stroked it and squeezed it until he heard her sigh with pleasure. Things were going well! He rotated those smooth cheeks in his palms and in doing so caught sight of the pink-brown little knot hidden between them – no uncommon sight for a lover and in the ordinary way of things wholly unremarkable. Yet on this occasion, to his surprise, he observed that her little fleshy knot was pulsating gently, clenching and unclenching!

A thought suggested itself to him. To test it he slipped a hand between her thighs and probed with a finger into the wet lips there until he touched and then tickled her secret bud. Ah yes – his theory held good! Célestine's external nodule pulsed in rhythm with his stimulation of her hidden bud! It was impossible not to draw the obvious conclusion from his observation – the normally unregarded part of Célestine between the cheeks of her bottom was for her a centre of acute pleasurable sensation. How pleasurable? he wondered – an experiment was called for. He touched the forefinger of his other hand to Célestine's sensuous nodule and caressed it lightly in time with his stimulation of her internal nodule. The effect of so simple a touch was remarkable. Célestine's legs jerked outwards to their widest stretch, her hands clawed at the bed sheet, dragging it up into two creased peaks and she gave voice to a long wail of ecstasy.

Nicolas was not an innocent, naturally, not one of those who knew no more than the simplest form of conjunction between man and woman. He had heard of the mode of pleasure now displayed for him by Célestine – and he had heard it spoken of as the Greek style of love. But that was the limit of his knowledge. He waited for Célestine's delicious throes to cease before he removed his fingers from her and she sighed, her flushed face pressed sideways into the pillow. Nicolas sighed too, the fact being that the paroxysm he had induced in her by his little experiment had aroused him again. So much so that there was no possibility of abandoning the exploration of this unfamiliar byway of love.

He lay over her back, his weight supported on his arms so that he could look down the length of his own body to steer the swollen head of his probe between the cheeks of her bottom and touch it to her sensitive little knot. How strange it seemed to him to be doing this – and yet, why not? There might be much to be learned and gained by so simple a course. Célestine moaned pleasurably and Nicolas could feel a tiny movement against the tip of his tenderest part, almost like a tiny mouth pressing kisses to the object of its desire. Célestine looked up at him over her shoulder, her dark brown eyes wide in wonder – and in loving admiration for the man who was able to give her these exquisite sensations. Even so, on her face was her familar half-smile with a hint of mockery in it! Then she too raised herself on one arm to try to see what was touching her eager nodule. Whether her contortion gave her a glimpse of Nicolas' straight part, poised at so intimate a spot, only she could say, but from their relative positions she knew that it was not his finger touching her but a stronger and more formidable limb.

She collapsed beneath him, sighing continuously, her body shuddering in the onset of passion. Nicolas pressed

79

forward slowly to complete her pleasure, hardly knowing what he was doing, his mind so dizzy with the strangeness of the moment. For an instant or two he made no progress, then that tiny aperture pouted and he gained a centimetre – then another, and it gaped wide to admit him freely. Almost in disbelief Nicolas felt himself sliding easily into her. He lowered himself onto her back, amazed at this extraordinary insertion.

Beneath him Célestine twitched in continuous spasms, moaning all the time in wordless delight. For Nicolas the experience was not merely new – there was an element of perversity in it which made it incredibly exciting. He lay still, not attempting to do anything at all – and no movement was necessary! Célestine's beautiful bottom was bouncing up and down under his belly and the greedy little mouth which held him was pulling at him. In moments it hurried him past the point of return and he too cried out as he delivered his offering into this improbable receptacle of hers. If she had moaned before, she screamed now as she received his jet and bucked so hard under him that he was almost thrown off her back and only kept his place by seizing her bare shoulders!

This time, he dimly understood, Célestine had reached some sort of culmination of desire and a tremendous release, infinitely greater then the climactic experiences he had effected by the use of his male part within her more usual ingress. What had been started as no more than a casual experiment had led him to make an astonishing discovery about her nature. He waited until her throes eased and she lay still beneath him.

'You were magnificent,' she murmured, 'I love you to distraction!'

Nicolas' emotions were more complicated than that.

'I've never before done it *à la Grecque*,' he confessed, wondering if she would think him foolish for saying so.

'And now that you have?'

'I hardly know what to think.'

80

'My dear, marvellous Nicolas,' she said in the most affectionate way, 'I cannot seriously believe that you are disturbed by so small a variation from the usual.'

'Not disturbed,' he hastened to assure her, his self-confidence returning now that he saw how casually she regarded the incident, 'no, not disturbed.'

'Then what?'

'A little surprised, perhaps – as I said, it was. the first time for me.'

'But not for me, you imply – and you are quite right.'

Nicolas removed himself from her elegant back and lay beside her.

'If I may ask,' he said, 'have you always preferred that manner of making love?'

'Not *always*. When I was a young girl I knew only the traditional way and I found that very pleasant. But I met a man who showed me a different way. His suggestion horrified me at first – it seemed unthinkable! But because I loved him I let him do whatever he wanted – for all I wanted was to please him! And to my astonishment, I must confess, I adored what he did to me from the very first time.'

'You are speaking of your husband, I assume.'

That made her chuckle. She turned to face him on the bed.

'No, not my husband. His tastes are completely traditional. But enough of that – tell me again that you love me, Nicolas!'

Again was pushing matters too far – he had told her several hundred times that she was adorable but he had not gone beyond that. However, the situation obviously demanded a declaration of that type and Nicolas obliged by saying that he loved her.

'Good, good!' she murmured, 'the truth is that I have fallen in love with you – head over heels! Oh, I am so happy! Kiss me, Nicolas!'

It was not much more than a week after his first encounter with Célestine that Nicolas found himself an involuntary participant in an unpleasant train of events which taught him that more was involved in being her lover then merely making love to her. He was strolling home very late one evening from the newspaper office when, in the rue Beaubourg, two men appeared from a dark doorway as he passed it and fell into step with him, one on either side. It was an unnerving experience at that time of night in a street devoid of other people – and it became even more unnerving when each of the men took him firmly by the arm. They were both large men, he noted, with facial expressions that did not indicate benevolence towards him. Nevertheless, he remained in possession of his wits.

'I have only a few hundred francs,' he told them, 'but you are welcome to them. I also have a watch, but that is not worth taking, I give you my word.'

That was a lie, as it happened – the watch was an extremely expensive one which had been given to him by Madame Duperray only two days before.

'Is your name Bruneau?' the man on his left demanded roughly

'It cannot be of any importance to you what my name is. I suggest you accept the little money I have and vanish before a guardian of the law makes an appearance.'

'I want to know,' said the ruffian in a threatening manner.

'But why?'

'To make sure we've got the right man. If you're not Bruneau I'll be so upset that you'll get a good kicking to make me feel better!'

'I am Nicolas Bruneau, I assure you!'

'Then you're coming with us – somebody wants to talk to you.'

'Really? Who might that be?'

There was no answer. They hurried him to the corner and into the back of a car waiting there. Now Nicolas was really frightened – this seemed more like a plot to murder him than to rob him. Perhaps it would have been better to deny his identity and endure the threatened beating! At least he would have survived that.

'Where are we going? I insist on being told,' he said with all the conviction he could muster, which was not much, but by way of reply he was told in the rudest possible way to keep his mouth shut.

He stared out of the window to check the route they were taking. The car turned east along the Boulevard St Denis and then, after a time, north again. The journey was not a long one and it terminated in a deserted street, where Nicolas was pushed out of the car and into a very ordinary looking apartment building.

They walked up to the first floor, one of the captors tapped discreetly on a door, received no answer and produced a key to unlock it. He led the way through an entrance hall into a large and well-furnished sitting-room, the other man prodding Nicolas in the back to move him along.

'Stay here,' the leading captor instructed, 'I'll tell the boss you're here.'

Nicolas waited – he could do no other, guarded by the other man, who in the light he could now see to be a burly young thug in dark clothes with a hat pulled down over his forehead. A particularly unpleasant type, thought Nicolas, somewhat reminiscent of the pimps one saw hanging round the Place Blanche while their women were servicing customers.

He decided to sit down, to give the impression of nonchalance, but at once the guardian thug scowled at him ferociously and made an insolent gesture that indicated that he should remain standing until he was invited to do otherwise.

In not more than five minutes the other ruffian reappeared at the door and stood aside to allow to enter – and Nicolas gasped as he recognised him – Monsieur

Raoul Duperray, husband of Célestine, landed proprietor, businessman extraordinary and a somewhat mysterious figure on the fringe of politics. This looked like being a most unpleasant encounter!

The last time Nicolas had seen Duperray was the night of the Opera ball, looking incredibly elegant in tails, the ribbon of the Legion of Honour on his lapel, his silvery hair most handsomely smoothed back from his forehead. But at this moment Monsieur Duperray's hair was in disarray and he wore only a crimson silk dressing gown and morocco leather slippers on his bare feet. Even so, for all his fifty years and the casual manner of his attire, Duperray looked like a formidable man to deal with.

'Ah, it's Monsieur Bruneau at last!' he said, staring hard at Nicolas, 'I'm pleased that you were able to come. Do sit down – would you like a drink?'

'Thank you, no,' said Nicolas, wondering whether he would survive a leap through a first-floor window to the pavement below if it became necessary to take fast evasive action. Then he remembered that there was another villain outside – the one who had driven the automobile. No, there was no escape that way.

Duperray told his two hirelings to wait outside and made himself comfortable in a striped armchair. To lessen his disadvantage, Nicolas also sat, but he kept his hat on as a gesture of independence.

'Another time of day would have been preferable for our discussion,' said Duperray, 'but it has taken those two idiots until now to find you. You are an elusive man – where do you get to all day long?'

'May I enquire the purpose of this abduction?' Nicolas retorted, his courage returning now that he saw that he was not to be murdered out of hand.

'I believe you know my wife,' Duperray said noncommitally.

'I have the honour of being acquainted with Madame Duperray,' Nicolas replied carefully, his tone neutral, 'as

I have the honour of being acquainted with many of the most prominent social figures, including the wife of the Minister of Justice.'

'I'm sure you do. It is about your acquaintance with my wife that I felt I must have a few words with you. Her happiness is very precious to me.'

'Naturally, Monsieur.'

'I shall speak frankly. You must understand that I am totally devoted to my dear wife. No doubt most men would claim as much, but in my case it happens to be literally true.'

The words had an ominous ring. Nicolas had never before been confronted by a jealous husband and felt himself to be at a loss – certainly when confronted by one with the wealth and influence of Duperray – a man who had shown that he could command thugs to bring people to him. And who, it could hardly be doubted, could issue instructions to break arms and legs, if need be, or even worse! Nicolas felt the situation to be extraordinarily delicate, to say the least.

'Your devotion does you credit, Monsieur Duperray,' he said very sincerely.

'Oh, but she deserves it! She is the most beautiful and fascinating woman in the world – she is worthy of nothing less than whole-hearted respect and admiration,' said Duperray.

'Very true,' Nicolas agreed.

'Our marriage has been enormously successful. We are the envy of everyone we know.'

'Of course.'

'But,' said Duperray, his face darkening and his mouth tightening, 'my wife has informed me that she is in love with you.'

Nicolas gulped. The moment he feared had arrived.

'She has informed you, Monsieur? Why should she do that?'

'Why not? We have no secrets from each other – we never have had secrets.'

'Then there is nothing I can say,' Nicolas murmured.

'There is a great deal you can say which I want to hear! First – is it your intention to try to persuade Célestine to leave me for you?' Duperray demanded.

'Heavens, no!' Nicolas exclaimed, 'nothing is further from my thoughts, Monsieur.'

'I am relieved to hear you say that. In my eyes the bond of marriage is sacred and I will not contemplate its dissolution in any circumstances. Do I make myself clear?'

'Very clear.'

'Think of the misery it would cause your parents, my dear Bruneau, if you were to be found floating in the Seine one early morning with your throat cut. They would be desolate!'

The desolation of his parents seemed irrelevant to Nicolas in comparison to his own misery in meeting so untimely an end.

'My dear parents must at all costs be protected from so profound an anguish,' he muttered.

'Spoken like a dutiful son! Parents' hearts are easily broken by the misfortunes of their children, and Paris can be a dangerous place for young men who are careless. Don't you agree?'

'Monsieur Duperray, have no fear on my account. I give you my solemn word that I shall never see Madame Duperray again. If you prefer, I will leave Paris this very night and take up residence elsewhere – Lyon, Marseilles, wherever you think most suitable.'

'What?' Duperray exclaimed, his face purple with rage. 'Are you insane? Didn't you hear what I said?'

'I don't understand,' Nicolas stammered 'what is it you want?'

'My wife loves you, though God alone knows why! She will be unhappy if she cannot see you regularly. Therefore you will put yourself at her disposal – do you understand me?'

'But you said. . .'

'You are not listening to me! Pay attention – I said that I will not permit my marriage to be destroyed. Have you got that?'

'Yes.'

'Célestine wants you, so she must have you. Do you understand that much?'

'But don't you mind?'

'Of course not – whatever gave you that idea?'

'You want me to be her lover – is that it, Monsieur?' Nicolas asked cautiously.

'At last! I began to think you were slow-witted. Yes, you are to be her lover until I tell you not to be.'

'This is a most irregular arrangement you are suggesting, Monsieur,' said Nicolas, feeling better now that Duperray's anger had subsided.

'Why should you care about that? You love her – she told me that too. Your compliance with your own instincts will make three people content. What more could you wish for?'

Nicolas at last removed his hat and held it on his knees – an unconscious sign of the decreasing tension, perhaps, or even a belated act of courtesy.

'You are looking puzzled,' said Duperray, his manner urbane once more 'let me explain. My marriage is perfect in every way but one – Célestine and I have different tastes in bed. But we are sensible people and we indulge our tastes separately – and with discretion.'

'That is very civilised, Monsieur. I congratulate you.'

'Then it's all agreed?'

'If that is what you really want.

'It is what I want and it is what Célestine wants. Therefore it is in your best interests to want the same. Otherwise the consequences would be too distressing to consider.'

'You may rely on me, Monsieur Duperray.'

'I knew that you'd see it my way if we talked things over rationally. One more thing, though – you earn a living in a trade notorious for spying through keyholes and bribing servants to obtain material so that you can print malicious lies about people of importance. I don't like that, not at any time, and especially not now that you have become a part of my own life. I suggest that you resign your job first thing in the morning.'

'I am happy to oblige you in every way I can, Monsieur Duperray, but you must realise that it is necessary for me to earn a living somehow and society journalism is the only way I have found.'

'Then you haven't looked very far.'

'I assure you I have. But I was never trained for any of the professions and I have no talent for business. My only asset is that I know everyone and can move about anywhere and be received on friendly terms.'

'Your father was lucky not to go to prison during the War,' said Duperray, 'I remember the scandal well. But that wasn't your fault. How much does it pay, this so-called journalism of yours?'

Nicolas told him, somewhat inflating the figure to preserve a shred of self-esteem.

'Is that all?' Duperray exclaimed 'why, those two employees of mine who escorted you here are paid that much and their only skill is in disposing of nuisances. You shall work for me.'

'I am grateful for the offer, but I must point out that I do not have the physique for their type of work.'

'I can see that. I suspect that you also lack the ruthlessness required to persuade a real nuisance to cease troubling me. What I have in mind is a continuation of your present work, but reporting to me alone, on the activities of certain people I shall designate from time to time – where they go, who they meet, who they sleep with, who gives them money, who they give money to – do you follow my meaning?'

'Spying?' Nicolas exclaimed in dismay.

'Certainly not – just what you do at present, but with fewer people to interest you and with more detail about them. The results will not be published. Or if they are, then it will not be under your name. Agreed?'

'What salary do your have in mind?'

'Twice what you earn now.'

'There will also be certain expenses, of course.'

'Of course – the people in whom I am interested do not dine in cheap cafés or ride around on the Metro. But I do not expect to be cheated on necessary expenses. That would disappoint me greatly, to find my confidence abused.'

'You may rely on me. I accept the offer.'

'That's very intelligent of you. Now that everything is cleared up between us, I need detain you no longer. My men will drive you home. Oh, by the way, forget about this address – it's a secret little bolt-hole of mine.'

'A most pleasant one,' said Nicolas, smiling for the first time since he had been pushed over the threshold of the apartment, 'I suppose you use it for entertaining. The décor is admirable.'

'You like it? Perhaps I'll give it to you if I find myself a better place. If you're good at your job, that is.'

'Which of my jobs, Monsieur? It seems to me that you have given me two jobs.'

Duperray laughed.

'Work hard at both and you will rise in my favour.'

'I shall be extremely diligent in both, Monsieur.'

'I think I'm beginning to see more in you than I thought. Perhaps Célestine has made a good choice this time. We shall see. If we've made a mistake, there are ways of putting it right.'

'I can assure you that I much prefer a warm bed to a cold river.'

'Spoken like a man of good sense! Having been associated with newspapers you will no doubt remember the sensation a couple of years ago when some young man whose name escapes me was fished out of the St Martin canal?'

'I regret that I do not recall the incident – so many unfortunates seek an end to their troubles that way.'

'Yes, the only reason that one sticks in my memory is that a post mortem examination revealed that he had been brutally deprived of the two objects necessary to sustain a love affair.'

'How hideous!' said Nicolas dismally.

'Well, as I told you, Paris can be a dangerous place for careless young men. But you need fear no such danger – you are my employee now and therefore under my protection.'

'Thank you, Monsieur.'

'Now, if you will excuse me, your mention of a warm bed reminded me of something I must attend to.'

Nicolas stood up politely.

'Of course, Monsieur Duperray. I had already guessed that you were entertaining a friend here tonight. I hope that you will accept my apologies for interrupting you at so delicate a moment.'

'Not your fault,' said Duperray graciously, 'it's those two idiots outside – all muscle and no brains. Still, they have their uses. And, to tell you the truth, a short break has not come amiss. At my age it is necessary to preserve one's strength to make it last out – I'm sure you understand me.'

'Then the interruption was well-timed. I wish you good night, Monsieur, and *bon appétit*!'

'Ah, if you only knew!'

Nicolas smiled in his most charming way, his curiosity whetted.

'I cannot even guess what marvellous delights a man of your eminence can command. To me the friendship of

Madame Duperray is the highest achievement I can imagine – and that is something you take for granted. I am lost in amazement at what you must regard as appropriate to your pleasure, Monsieur.'

Flattery, as Nicolas had learned well, will usually obtain a reward. Duperray warmed to him.

'Come with me and just peep round the door before you leave. You will see a sight to remember – and on your way home you can imagine my enjoyment. Perhaps that will inspire you to do your duty towards Célestine tomorrow – you are meeting her tomorrow, aren't you?'

Nicolas nodded, no longer in the least surprised that Duperray knew so much of his arrangements – either he had men watching his wife or, as he claimed, they kept no secrets from each other – an unusual state of affairs between married people. He followed Duperray along a passage to another door and Duperray turned the knob and pushed it open silently, just sufficiently for them to see into the room beyond.

It was a large bedroom, of course, furnished in the modern style with a broad and low bed. The covers were thrown back in disarray and there lay two girls entwined. They were both extremely pretty, Nicolas observed, and neither was older than sixteen – seventeen at the most – both of them slender and small-breasted. They were playing at *soixante-neuf*, one girl on her back with her legs spread impossibly wide, the other above her with her thighs clamped lovingly about her friend's head. The game was not a silent one – the room was filled with little cries, gasps, murmurs and even giggles! Nicolas thought it utterly charming – a scene of almost pastoral innocence. The spread thighs of the girl underneath were towards the door and as the uppermost girl raised her head for a moment, Nicolas had a view of the wet and pink little entrance she was holding open with her hands – an entrance which Duperray no doubt would make use of before the game was finished, in addition to the other little entrance not in view, but evidently receiving delicate attention, for the girl who had raised her head was sighing loudly.

'The little darlings!' Duperray whispered to Nicolas, 'they have become impatient without me. I have been away too long, discussing business matters with you. I must join them and take part in their little game. Goodnight, Monsieur Bruneau.'

Duperray's ruffians drove him home without a word – except when he got out of the car. The one who had spoken to him before took him by the arm in a grip that made him wince with pain and held him for a moment.

'The boss expects you to keep your mouth shut.'

'You may rely on it,' said Nicolas, trying to pull away, 'after all, I am in his employ now and I am a man of honour. I have given my word.'

The ruffian laughed most insultingly.

'You can be what you like as long as you keep your mouth shut,' he said, 'otherwise. . .'

By way of completing his threat he drew his forefinger across his throat.

When Madame Duperray arrived at Nicolas' apartment the next afternoon, the intervening events caused him to regard her in a somewhat different light. Of course, it was true that she had chosen him to be her lover because she recognised in him certain superior qualities – that had not changed. But he could no longer regard her as an ordinary married woman seeking affection and diversion away from her husband, as he had once assumed. In effect, she was the wife – and partner – of a man who had convincingly demonstrated his ability and willingness to arrange for the most unpleasant things to happen to anyone who annoyed him. During his visit earlier that day to the newspaper office to resign his position, Nicolas had looked back through the files to find the episode of the St Martin canal which Duperray had mentioned casually. And there it was – a young man of good family, taken from the murky water by the police and subsequently discovered to have been maimed, before drowning, in the manner Duperray had described. What he had been doing in so unlikely an area of Paris, what was the motive for the atrocity and who were the perpetrators – these things remained a mystery to the newspaper and to the authorities alike. Nicolas found the report very disturbing and it reinforced his belief that in dealing with Duperray one needed to be constantly on guard.

But for all that, as soon as Célestine was undressed and in his bed, all such considerations vanished from Nicolas' mind, for she was exceptionally beautiful and extremely well-disposed towards him. The feel of her breasts in his hands, the touch of her warm body pressed against him – this left no room in any man's mind for thoughts of caution or anything else except the enjoyment of the pleasures of love.

And such pleasures they were! Nicolas revelled in the beauties of her body and became intoxicated with sensation. In his heart he despised Duperray for taking half-grown girls as his playmates in preference to the sumptuous delight of making love to Célestine!

After the keenest of ecstasies and a gratifying tribute to Célestine's charms, vigorously deposited deep within her enchanting alcove, he lay beside her, holding her in his arms while he told her that he adored her. At that moment his feelings towards Duperray had been mellowed somewhat by the immense satisfaction of what he and Célestine had just experienced together. Although Duperray had forced an unexpected bargain upon him, Nicolas felt that perhaps after all he had the best of it. Not only had he acquired Célestine as a mistress – he was being paid to love her! A most remarkable position, for any young man!

Even when she rolled over onto her face and presented

to him her superb back and delicious bottom, his mood of exhilaration did not change. He stroked those round and satin-skinned cheeks and caressed with his finger-tip the little nodule between them. If that was what pleased her most, then so be it! Célestine gratified meant Duperray pleased – and Duperray pleased meant that Nicolas could advance in his service – away from the daily problem of making a living as a journalist into some position, perhaps slightly illegal, where he could live as befitted one of his background and abilities.

And besides, the first time he had done it to her that way, it had been an extremely interesting experience. So why not?

'Oh, Nicolas,' Célestine sighed 'yès, chéri!'

MARIE-CLAIRE AND HER CRYSTAL ROOM

In the large and elegant apartment of Maire-Claire Fénéon there was a room into which no one but she ever went. Her personal maid cleaned it, of course, when the room was not in use, but that did not count – and none of the other servants was allowed inside. The room was next to Marie-Claire's bedroom, where one would expect in the usual way of things to find a dressing-room. To some extent it was that, perhaps, but with a difference.

Marie-Claire had caused the walls of her secret room to be completely covered with mirror glass – even the inside of the doors and the long windows that opened onto the balcony overlooking the Avenue George V. And, naturally, the ceiling too. To be in this room was to be inside a glass cube, cut off from any contact with the world. The only item of furniture in it was a low and broad divan which stood in the centre of the floor – the floor at least was parquet, though without the usual carpets or rugs – and this divan was upholstered in pale yellow damask and piled with large cushions covered in apricot-coloured silk.

This was Marie-Claire's 'crystal room', though she never uttered its name aloud and spoke of it to no one, not even her closest friends, for to her it was a sacred place, an oratory, one might say, in which the prayers were not in words.

When the mirrored shutters to the balcony were closed

and the glass-covered door from the bedroom fast shut behind her, Marie-Claire was in a universe of her own making, where her whim was law. It was here that her private dreams became real, and her dreams were, to say, the least, stirring creations. For example, at such places of entertainment as the Casino de Paris and the Lido, where she had been taken by admirers assiduously paying court to so desirable an heiress as herself, she had been greatly impressed by the verve of the young women who passed across the stage or stood as a living backdrop for the main performers. To be one of them, what a delicious fantasy! To wear those skimpy and outrageous costumes and stand there for all to see! To show off one's body so freely – what bliss! The dream could be made to come true in Marie-Claire's crystal room, for behind one glass-panelled wall was a capacious wardrobe stocked with brightly-coloured creations bought from theatrical costumiers.

When she was in this mood, Marie-Claire would make up her face with exquisite care and then ransack the wardrobe to dress herself in the most outré style. A head-dress of tall white ostrich plumes, high-heeled silver shoes, fishnet stockings held halfway up her thighs by garters of ruched lace! Long white gloves stretching from her finger-tips to above her elbows! As for the rest, the expanse of gleaming skin between garters and head-dress, for that she wore no more than a tiny silver-coloured cache-sexe over the hair between her legs. Her breasts were bare, as she had seen the show-girls on the stage, and so apparelled she would strut gracefully to and fro across the room, humming a song, her arms outstretched, wholly beguiled by the effect in the mirrored walls. The glass on opposing walls threw her reflection back and forth in diminishing perspective, so that to Marie-Claire's delighted eyes it seemed that she was the leader of an endless chorus-line, each of the others following her slightest movement and gesture as she stepped and swayed. The sight was so magnificent that it almost took her breath away. Who else could produce, direct, choreograph and star in her own show whenever she chose?

On another day she would dress in skin-tight trousers of gold lamé that only just covered her hips and left her bare to a finger's breadth above the little patch of hair that guarded her secret place. From the sides, great lengths of the same material draped to her ankles and up again to be held over her forearms as she spread them wide in a ballet gesture. Two or three gold chains about her neck, looping down almost to her exposed breasts, on her head a close-fitting cap on which was mounted a single plume half a metre tall! Or more daring still when the mood took her, a huge Spanish mantilla of black lace, held at the back of her head by an ivory comb and draped elegantly round her in swirling folds. With that she wore nothing at all but black shoes – this being a spectacle she had once seen at the Folies Bergère – and when she swayed across the room, the gleam of her skin through the lace gave her a pleasure so intense that she became giddy after a while and was compelled to rest a little on the divan until she recovered. Even in that position she had the joy of seeing herself reflected full-length in the mirrored ceiling, pink and white through the lace. This vision of beauty she could contemplate in calm delight for a long time without becoming in the least bored.

On some visits to the crystal room her mood was different again and not inclined towards the stage. Then she would dress as if for going out visiting or shopping – a little cloche hat perhaps of peacock blue and a matching summer coat, fine silk stockings, shoes of black shiny patent leather – the effect was incredibly chic. She left the coat unfastened and as she moved about the room, choosing a pair of gloves to wear or checking the contents of her hand-bag, she caught tantalising glimpses of herself in the mirrors that made her utter tiny sighs of admiration

97

– for beneath the elegant coat she had put on nothing at all. A movement of her arm would cause the coat to part a little and let a pink-tipped breast peep briefly out. A half-turn would give a fleeting view of a lovely sleek thigh above a stocking-top. Marie-Claire was too much a connoisseur of herself to look fully in these moments – she behaved naturally, setting her hat at the best angle, twisting to check that her stockings were immaculate – teasing herself with sudden sly glimpses of some perfect part of herself. She could play this game of dressing to go out for at least an hour without tiring of it.

However prolonged or bizarre her games, they were in the end only preludes to her real intention – the adoration of her own naked body. Ah, the slow care and the controlled emotion as she approached this central act of worship! She stood before a mirrored wall, regarding herself full-face and at full-length, her gaze calm and steady as she removed one by one whatever garments she was wearing, until the glory of her beloved body was revealed to her eyes.

Time had no meaning while she observed in turn each part of herself from head to toe. Her hair, deep brown with just a hint of chestnut, so expertly cut to shape her head with soft waves and just show the lobes of her little ears! She ran her finger-tips over it very lightly to feel its soft texture without disarraying it in the slightest. How well its colour set off the flawless skin of her face and complemented her velvet-brown eyes under the high-arching and meticulously plucked eyebrows! But that face – classically beautiful, the cheek-bones slightly high and the nose firm and very straight! Her mouth was a poem in its expressiveness – the slightly pouting lips, painted a vibrant red, parting to show her small white teeth. It was a face to fall in love with at first sight, and many a man had done so, though none with the impassioned devotion of Marie-Claire herself.

Her neck was faultless, not short, not long – and not a

shadow or a trace of even the most microscopic of lines anywhere on it. The milky white luminescence of pearls or the bright cold fire of diamonds – both looked marvellously right against the skin of that neck. As for her shoulders – if an artist had carved a statue with shoulders like hers, Jean-Antoine Houdon at his best perhaps, or Antonio Canova at his most inspired – the work would have been instantly hailed a masterpiece.

In Marie-Claire's private opinion the much-admired sculpture by Canova of the Emperor Napoleon's sister Pauline had shoulders not as fine as her own. But then, presumably the artist was copying his model faithfully and if Pauline Bonaparte's shoulders were not as good as Marie-Claire's that was not Canova's fault.

At this point Marie-Claire crossed her arms over her breasts so that she could caress those gorgeous shoulders of hers. What good fortune that the fashion was for evening frocks that left the shoulders bare and so afforded her the opportunity to show off so dazzling a sight in restaurants and theatres around Paris! She took care not to look directly at her hands, for if there was any part of her less than perfect, she felt it was her hands. They were excellently well cared-for, of course – her maid manicured them and massaged them at least three times a week. The nails were coloured the same shade of bright red as her toe-nails – and yet, by the standards of beauty set by the rest of her, the hands failed a little. The fingers were just a little too short, the palms just a little too broad. Once it had vexed her, now she simply ignored this tiny flaw.

By turning herself a little to the side and looking over one shoulder Marie-Claire could see, in the mirror on the wall behind her, the elegance of her own back. It was long and narrow, curving in at her waist, then swelling out again to define her hips and the flawless globes of her bottom. She contemplated this dorsal aspect of herself with awed respect, as well she might, for she was certain that not even the ancient Greek statues of goddesses in

99

the Louvre Museum could be compared with it. If only she could arrange matters so that, at the time when the Museum was empty, she could convey herself and a long mirror into it – and then strip and compare her own back reflected in the mirror with the view of those over-rated statues!

When she had stroked her shoulders and viewed her elegant back to her great content, Marie-Claire uncrossed her slender arms and gazed in rapture at her breasts. The sight of them never failed to bring a small sigh of deepest approval to her lips. They were such miracles of symmetry in their delicate size and shape that she could find no words adequate to praise them. The gentle pink of their tiny buds – the effect against her satiny skin was completely captivating. No man who had ever been so greatly privileged as to see those breasts could prevent his hands from reaching out to touch them.

For Marie-Claire herself, it was equally impossible not to let her hands stray towards them as she stood before the mirror in profound appreciation of them. Her finger-tips slid very tenderly over the blush-pink tips, as lightly as a butterfly's kiss. Even so light a contact caused her to tremble with sheer pleasure. The little buds blushed an even more enticing shade – if that were possible – and stood up firmly.

How could anyone describe the beauty of Marie-Claire's belly? To say that it was smooth and most exquisitely curved, with a round navel set in it like a dimple – the words say nothing! Only the eye of a true connoisseur could appreciate the subtle beauty of that belly – and such a connoisseur would be inspired by his own admiration of it to trace its gentle curve with trembling finger-tips, as did Marie-Claire at this moment. At its base, where her impeccably rounded thighs joined, there was a small patch of deep brown hair, neatly trimmed into the shape of a heart! And what very superior hair it was – as silky as the hair on her head and with just the same hint of chestnut in it. Marie-Claire's fingers played in it, delighting in its adorable texture, until at last they touched the soft little lips it covered. She moved her feet apart so that she could see the reflection of the pink folds her fingers had opened like the petals of a superb rose. By now she was too giddy with pleasure to do more than stare at what she had revealed, as if hypnotised. She was in the same state – dare one say it? – as a female saint in mystical contemplation of the divine!

When the giddiness passed, or rather, when Marie-Claire became sufficiently accustomed to its hold on her to be able to walk without stumbling, she made her way with slow care to the divan in the centre of the crystal room and reposed herself upon it. She lay on her back on the apricot-coloured silk, her legs drawn up, her ankles crossed, thighs flat to the cushions and knees pointing in opposite directions. This was the position which gave her the best possible view in the mirror above her of the enchanting secret place between her legs. She stared with love and reverence, her heart beating a little faster. The spread of her thighs had parted the lips between them to give a view of the pink interior, a piquant contrast with the deep brown of the soft hair. The effect was ravishing!

At last, when her hands found their way to her thighs and then towards the shrine of love between them, it must not be supposed that she did anything so banal as to pleasure herself with her fingers. No doubt maid-servants relieved themselves with work-coarsened fingers in their lonely beds at night, perhaps even women of good family who were too plain to find themselves a man satisfied themselves in that manner. But that was by no means the same thing. That was mere self-gratification, of no more significance than blowing one's nose.

The difference was that Marie-Claire was engaged at this moment upon an act of worship, nothing less! The loving touch of her fingers on the tiny swollen bud within those pouting lips was a heartfelt tribute to her astonishing beauty.

Naturally, there could be nothing hurried or strained in such adoration – that would be completely out of place. Her fingers proceeded at a stately pace, Marie-Claire's eyes intent the whole time upon the reflection above her of her own naked body. Sighs of devotion escaped her as she observed the image of herself responding to her own veneration with little tremors of passion. Soon, very soon, she murmured over and over again *'Je t'aime. . .je t'aime. . .'* When the little tremors became long rhythmic shudders heralding the approach of the natural culmination of her act of homage to herself, Marie-Claire was not tempted to close her eyes and let herself be swept away by sensation. She stared fixedly at the glass ceiling, adoring every centimetre of the body she observed, until she saw her own back arch off the divan at the moment when her body accepted her true worship and bestowed its climactic benediction upon her.

In the profound peace which followed that benediction, she lay with her hands resting at her sides, still rapt in contemplation of her own enchanting beauty in the glass. At this time it seemed to her that she was in a state of grace – though no priest of the Church would have agreed with her on that! Sometimes she meditated for so long on her own loveliness that she dozed off into the sweetest of sleep. At other times, the memory of the blessing she had just received was so rapturous that her hands crept slowly back between her parted thighs to repeat her devotions.

It should not be supposed from this that Marie-Claire had no place in her life or thoughts for men and their love. On the contrary, she had a long-established intention to acquire some day a suitable husband. But *suitable* – that was where the problem lay.

A man must be of a certain status in society to merit even preliminary consideration as a candidate – that went without saying. After that, he must be extremely handsome, for Marie-Claire could not tolerate anything less than that in close proximity to her own beauty. Even her servants were chosen as much for their appearance as for their usefulness in the household.

Alas for Marie-Claire – so many of the best young Frenchmen had lost their lives in the War defending the sacred homeland that her area of choice had become sadly restricted. Admirers she had in abundance, being an heiress as well as beautiful. Of her admirers, the most eligible were permitted to become her lovers – the final test of their suitability! But it was then that her fastidiousness proved to be so insuperable a hurdle – so far not one of the candidates had measured up to the standards she set.

There was one of whom she had been very fond – but when he removed his clothes in her bedroom Marie-Claire could hardly suppress her gasp of horror. There was a thick pelt of black hair on his chest – and on his arms and legs! Even on his back! He resembled a bear, she thought in repulsion. Because of her affection for him, which ended at that moment, she allowed him to continue his love-making, but only in the dark. Throughout it her eyes were tightly closed and her teeth clenched, and although he was skilful enough to bring her to the moment of climax three times that night, she never invited him to her home again.

More often she found that the men who were acceptable in all other ways proved to be inadequate in the most important way of all – they failed to appreciate the immensity of the honour conferred upon them by being allowed to see and touch her magnificent body! Indeed, they were in general so crassly insensitive as to mistake her for an ordinarily beautiful woman whose charms existed merely to inflame their own sensual appetites! They did not adore her body as they should – they *used* it. They squashed her superb little breasts out of shape under their weight when they penetrated her, they beat

103

their bellies in the coarsest of manners against hers in their uncontrolled thrusting. At such times of disappointment and disillusion Marie-Claire recoiled in disgust. It was obvious to her that such men would not have been able to tell the difference if they had been mounted on her maid – or for that matter, on a street-woman. Marie-Claire's body was to them no more than a warm mattress with an accomodating hole!

By good fortune, soon after her thirtieth birthday, Marie-Claire became acquainted with a man only a year older than herself who seemed in every way to meet her exacting requirements. His name was Giles St Amand Mont-Royal and the circumstances in which they first met were much in his favour. In Marie-Claire's grand apartment there were displayed four portraits of her, as was perhaps to be expected, by different artists of whose style she approved. The earliest was a head and shoulders of her aged nineteen, in an evening frock which showed off those splendid shoulders of hers. The most recent was by a woman painter who called herself Monique Chabrol, to whose studio in Auteil Marie-Claire had been taken by her good friend Jeanne Verney. Monique and Jeanne were related by marriage, Marie-Claire learned – Jeanne's sister had been the wife of Alexandre St Amand Mont-Royal who, alas, had been killed in the War. Monique was his sister and Chabrol was her professional name as an artist.

Monique insisted on painting a full-length nude portrait of Marie-Claire. It depicted her lying on a chaise-longue, the merest corner of a Chantilly lace shawl just concealing that most precious part of her where her thighs joined. But for the fact that the finished picture would hang in her salon and be viewed by all visitors to her home, Marie-Claire would have dispensed with the shawl and displayed the rich brown of her heart-shaped little thatch. Throughout the sittings Monique Chabrol showed great and unexpected tenderness of approach to her subject and talked to Marie-Claire with as much affection as if they had been friends for years. At each session she took such care to arrange Marie-Claire's body and limbs in the pose she wanted that her lingering touch was almost a caress. From these indications Marie-Claire formed the conclusion that Monique was a lover of women and wondered what her own response would be if those sensitive fingers touched in an open invitation to love. But they never did and when the picture was completed Marie-Claire understood that Monique's appreciation of her beauty was aesthetic rather than sensual. For the picture was a great masterpiece, in Marie-Claire's judgment – it showed her not merely as beautiful but resplendent! The skin tones were sumptuous, the proportions breath-taking in their subtlety – and in the eyes there was a look of reverie such as Marie-Claire had when she was alone in her crystal room. If Monique had understood her so very exactly, it could only be because she herself in some measure shared Marie-Claire's own self-love.

Monique's younger brother, Giles St Amand Mont-Royal, had seen the portrait in only its half-finished state on a visit to her, but he had asked to be allowed to meet the sitter at once. Monique told him to be patient – her work was far too important to risk having the sittings disrupted in any way. After the painting was finished, she introduced him to Marie-Claire, who found him charming. He had the same glossy dark hair as his sister and the same widely-spaced eyes – though unlike hers, his were a marvellous shade of grey! His clothes were impeccable and the body inside them gave the impression of being robust and athletic. His compliments were well-expressed, somehow giving an appearance of being frank and courteous at the same time.

The first impressions being satisfactory, Marie-Claire accepted his invitation to dine with him. That too was a success, for he proved to be an amusing companion. From then on he arranged a variety of entertainments for her,

105

each pleasing in its different way. He took her riding in the Bois de Boulogne, making sure that they had the best mounts available. He was a magnificent horseman and Marie-Claire, looking utterly radiant in a new riding outfit, was secretly proud to be seen with him – an emotion which surprised her by its novelty! Giles' taste in theatre was for romantic comedy, which Marie-Claire also preferred to the tediousness of serious drama. He took her to only the best restaurants and was extremely exacting in his choice of food and wines – yet he ate and drank sparingly – and this won her approval, for nothing ruins a beautiful body more quickly than over-indulgence at the table.

By talking privately to Monique and to Jeanne Verney, Marie-Claire learned of some of Giles' previous liaisons – and what she heard was entirely to his credit. He had at some time in the past been the lover of the Vicomtesse de la Vergne, Monique related – a woman renowned and respected for her fastidious insistence on maintaining the manners and style of the pre-War era. More recently, according to Jeanne, he had been the intimate friend of Gabrielle de Michoux, the most refined person Marie-Claire had ever met. It was common knowledge among her woman friends that Gabrielle had her maid try out potential lovers for her in order to determine whether their style was adequate to please Gabrielle herself.

Thus reassured, Marie-Claire allowed Giles to become her lover – and he proved to be eminently acceptable. A surreptitious inspection of his body when he first undressed in her presence showed her that he was handsomely proportioned, broad of chest and narrow of waist. The hair on his chest was sparse and soft to the touch, not a bear's pelt to scrub against her delicate breasts. His male part was elegant, neither too large nor too small.

Above all else, it was Giles' manner of making love which won Marie-Claire's heart. He was strong and virile and very much in command of the situation – yet very considerate. When the caress of his hands and lips raised her to a near-pinnacle of delight, he did *not* roll onto her as if she were a living mattress. On their first occasion together he turned her gently onto her side, facing him, put pillows behind her to support her, then moved close and with great tenderness of touch slid his stiff worshipper into her sanctuary. In this way he could continue his reverent caress of her breasts while he paid homage to her – and more importantly, Marie-Claire could look down at her own marvellous body as it was worshipped. His passionate emission seemed to her like a prayer before an altar – a prayer which was answered instantly by her own graceful climax of ecstasy.

As their liaison developed, she learned that he had other postures of adoration. Sometimes he would sit her on the side of the bed in order to kneel between her parted legs and make his offering while contemplating the temple of love into which he had been admitted. Or again, he would lie on his back and seat her over his loins, her body fully open to his view – and to hers – while his trembling part was deep within her. Though satisfactory from the point of view of being able to see her own body in its gentle throes of passion, Marie-Claire did not much favour this position because it required her to make the movements that precipitated the delicious crisis – and her firm opinion was that Giles should do all that was neces- sary – for herself it was enough to be the inspiration for him. As soon as Giles understood this, he again showed how infinitely obliging he was by demonstrating other and more gratifying possibilities.

Their love affair was so perfect in every way that Marie- Claire eventually began to give careful consideration to the question of revealing to Giles her closely-guarded secret – the crystal room. By this time they had been lovers for three months and all her experience of him was entirely pleasing. In all that time there had not been sounded one false note, there had been not one awkward moment. She was starting to believe that in Giles she had found the love of a lifetime – a man completely in tune with herself, in bed and out of bed. He had not indicated in any way that he was thinking of a more permanent relationship than the one they were enjoying – but then, a man of his unquestioned virtues and qualities could choose almost any woman he wanted when he decided to settle down and take a wife – a thought which brought a tiny frown to her face.

On the other hand, he was so attentive and he assured her so very often of his devotion to her that Marie-Claire became convinced that in his heart a certain love for her must be dawning. A little more encouragement and he ought to be ready to ask her to marry him. Whether she would accept him or not was not finally clear to her, but the probability was that she would, to strengthen her hold on him, if no more than that.

Before that moment of decision was reached, she felt it to be essential to know what his reaction would be on being made aware of her secret. Even if they married, she had no intention of abandoning the pleasures of the crystal room – on the contrary, what she most desired was to have her admirer share those pleasures with her. She debated with herself for a long time – and who can blame her – no one had ever been into that room with her. To allow another person into it was like inviting him into her very soul. He might misunderstand, he might laugh, he might recoil in shock – any unfavourable response would destroy the marvellous liaison they already enjoyed.

Yet for all her misgivings, the day arrived when she made the decision and received Giles in her crystal room. He thought that her maid would usher him, as usual, into her salon, but they passed that door. Could it be her bedroom into which he was being shown? That would be most unusual and, to say the least, irregular. But that too they passed. The maid tapped at the door through which he had never stepped during his many visits to Marie-Claire's apartment. Giles entered and stared about him in blank astonishment as the door was closed behind him. He was in a room entirely lined with mirrors! His own reflection stared open-mouthed at him from the far wall.

Marie-Claire had spent half the day dressing for this momentous visit, trying on all sorts of costumes from her capacious wardrobe, discarding this and that, simple and bizarre. In the end she settled for simplicity – that is to say, for theatrical simplicity. On her head was a tall white toque which covered her hair completely and was draped around with strings of pearls. Around her neck was her diamond necklace, the stones glittering against her flawless skin. A long white skirt was held tightly around her waist by a broad belt of shiny black leather – a skirt with a train nearly a metre long and split up the front so that as she took a step forward to hold out her hand in greeting to Giles almost the whole length of one satin-skinned thigh was revealed. Between skirt and toque, apart from her diamonds, she wore nothing. She had found it impossible to bring herself to conceal her pretty breasts at this supreme moment in her life.

As for Giles, after that one instant of open-mouthed astonishment, he rose magnificently to the occasion. He went down on one knee as he took Marie-Claire's hand and kissed it, as if he were a courtier in the old days saluting a queen. He raised his eyes to her naked breasts and then to her face and told her that she was divine and that he loved her to distraction.

A smile of satisfaction and triumph revealed Marie-Claire's white little teeth. Giles had understood her! As soon as he had entered the crystal room and caught sight of her in her dramatic finery he had in an instant grasped her secret and he rejoiced in this new knowledge of her soul. She had chosen well – Giles was the man with whom she would spend her life in unending adoration of her beauty.

A bottle of champagne and two glasses stood ready by the divan. Marie-Claire herself poured the wine and handed a glass to her lover as he rose from his knee. They drank a toast to each other, then to their future together, then to their incomparable happiness – for both were entirely convinced that no two other people had ever tasted such profound delight together in the entire history of the world. It was a scene so charged with emotion that Giles' voice trembled and Marie-Claire almost wept tears of joy – except that to do so would have spoilt her careful make-up.

'Do you truly adore me, Giles?' she asked.

'I adore you as no woman has ever been adored – I swear it.'

'Then show me how you express your adoration.'

Giles set down his glass and removed her belt with reverence, sighing a little in pleasure as he uncovered her perfect dimple of a navel. He undid the fastening of her long white skirt and let it slide down her legs to the floor. He picked her up as if she were a sacred icon, kissed the pink tips of her breasts and laid her on the silk cushioned divan. In the mirrored ceiling Marie-Claire watched his dark-haired head moving lovingly over her breasts as he kissed them a hundred times and she felt the onset of that familiar dizziness of delight. Then his lips were on her soft belly and the hot tip of his tongue at its entrancing dimple. How he made the pleasure last! What delicacy, what finesse! Eventually, in the mirror above her, she watched him remove her pretty little silver-coloured cache-sexe and she felt his lips kiss the heart-shaped patch of deep-brown hair that clothed her mound of love.

He too must be naked – she permitted him to cease his attentions to her body for the short time it took him to strip. He lay beside her on the divan, murmuring words of love so fraught with emotion as to be almost incoherent. Marie-Claire's hand took hold of the hard stem of flesh standing from between his thighs. Not only was it pleasing to look at, it was a pleasure to hold it and feel its strength and resilience – and the throb of life in it. Yet her firm clasp was less for her own physical enjoyment as for the emotion of pride she experienced in laying claim to it for herself alone.

The many previous passages of love between Marie-Claire and Giles had been marvellously satisfactory but they were not to be compared with the sublimity of this grand occasion in her crystal room. In both her mind and his the importance of what was happening transcended mere love-making to become an act of pure worship. With all the imagination and savoir-faire expected of him, Giles devoted his attentions to her with incomparable though controlled enthusiasm.

At the supreme moment when she desired him to enter her so that she could watch her body while he served it, Giles demonstrated an understanding of her needs and an inventiveness which thrilled her almost to the climax of passion. With a strong sweep of his arms he lifted her from the divan and set her on her feet facing the nearest mirrored wall and only a few hands-breadths away from it. She gazed at her own beautiful naked body and was struck with love for Giles at this moment for affording her so marvellous a sight.

She felt his hands caress down her legs from hips to ankles, as he knelt behind her and showered kisses on the exquisite cheeks of her bottom. He eased her feet apart until he could move forward between them, sitting down on his haunches, until his knees touched the mirror. Marie-Claire's heart sang with joy as she realised his intention was to give her a full view of herself as he made love to her. She waited for his hands, on her hips again, urging her slowly downwards until she was kneeling over his folded legs, her back to him. His mouth pressed against her shoulders and the nape of her neck while she was still intent on her own glorious image, then slowly she looked lower in the glass to see the upright part which was poised to make its entrance.

One of Giles' hands moved lightly to her belly, the other was between her legs, parting the soft lips beneath the heart-shaped brown fur. The touch on her belly urged her downwards again until she felt the smooth head of his upright part within her portal. It was more than Marie-Claire could bear, so exquisite was this moment! Her eyes blinked as ecstasy coursed through her, but she forced them open to view the tremors of her body as it yielded to unbelievable pleasure.

Giles paused, supporting her by the hips, only the head of his quivering part within her. He too was surprised and delighted by her flattering response. He waited in patience until the climactic pleasure had completed itself and Marie-Claire whispered '*Je t'aime!*' Whether she meant that she loved him or loved herself was not a question that even occurred to him.

She was ready to renew that sublime experience in a very short time, stimulated as she was by the sight of her own body with the head of his stiff part lodged in it. She let herself sink fully onto Giles' lap and his patience was rewarded by the soft clasp of her body on his distended member. Over her shoulder he stared at the junction of their parts in the mirror, his eyes full of wonder. Without words – for the banality of speech would have been unthinkable in this meeting of souls – Giles took her wrists and spread her arms out sideways, then showed her how to lean forward until her palms were flat against the cool glass. This lifted her weight a little off his thighs and gave him the freedom of movement he wanted – a slow and rhythmic movement that sent tremors of pleasure through her belly.

For some moments he caressed her matchless breasts, but his hands returned to her hips, so that nothing of her reflection was obscured from his gaze – and hers. His grasp became a little firmer as his thrusts became longer

112

and more probing. Marie-Claire, looking away from her divine self in the mirror and at the reflection of his face, saw that his gaze was fixed upon her heart-shaped treasure into which he was plunged. The delicacy of those open pink lips almost sent her into another spasm of ecstasy – and below them she could see a centimetre or two of the hard stem that transfixed her.

Marie-Claire was in Paradise! Everything was supremely right – the shared adoration of her body – for at last she truly felt that she was sharing that incredible delight with another person. Oh, if these sublime sensations could last forever! But such intensity of emotion, however carefully nurtured, is necessarily of brief duration. Even so, the tremendous thought in Marie-Claire's mind, in so far as she was capable of holding a thought in her mind at that instant – was that this heavenly experience could be repeated again and again, day after day, with dear marvellous Giles.

Deep within her Marie-Claire felt with absolute certainty that what was about to happen to her would be the supreme moment of her life so far – a hitherto unconquered peak which ordinary women could not even see on the distant horizon. The certainty welled up with the divine sensations Giles was provoking in her. As she stared at the mirror image of the tender part of herself from which those incredible sensations emanated, her velvet-brown eyes were round with amazement. To be able to view the erect worshipper in her secret shrine, engaged upon his devotions at the very altar of love itself. . . the climactic ecstasy which swept through her then was totally unlike the gentle waves of gratification she had known all her life. This was a torrent, a tidal wave that engulfed in an instant her awareness of herself. Her eyes were shut tight, her mouth wide open in a piercing scream of unselfconscious delight!

The violence of her release brought on Giles' crisis at once. His strong part pulsed and leaped within Marie-

113

Claire's shaking body and he poured out his offering. His eyes remained open, and over her heaving shoulder his grey eyes stared fixedly in love and adoration at the reflection of his own handsome face.

CHRISTOPHE AT THE SEASIDE

The twin domes of the Carlton Hotel at Cannes are modelled, it is said, on the superb white breasts of a famous *cocotte* of the last century – one for whose charms men of the highest rank entered into expensive competition with each other. The thought of so graceful a tribute to a woman who had been the inspiration for much pleasure and anguish was pleasing to Christophe as he strolled in the hot sunshine of a beautiful morning, admiring the many delicious women to be seen along the Croisette. Nor was the admiration entirely on his part – he was an extremely good-looking young man and elegantly attired in a striped blazer, white trousers and a straw boater – the very epitome of casual style!

Naturally, before the War no one of any consequence would have been seen on the Côte d'Azur in the summer months. From the end of April the hotels closed down and the Casino was deserted. The season for visiting the southern coast was winter and it went without saying that during the summer months everyone went north to the fashionable resorts of Deauville and Le Touquet. However, all that changed a few years after the end of the War when rich Americans, much given to world travel to escape the cultural and culinary wilderness of their own country, discovered the Mediterranean coast of France. Even then, to go there in the heat of summer would have been regarded in Paris as no more than another eccentricity of an inexplicable nation, but for the whims

115

of women of style. Suddenly Chanel and Schiaparelli were designing the most ravishing and provocative beach clothes and showing them in their Paris boutiques. Every woman of taste wanted to wear these delicious and colourful little garments – it was almost like appearing naked in public to stroll about wearing these tiny shorts or these flimsily transparent beach pyjamas! In consequence, since it is women who rule the world from behind their husbands, within a year or two it was tremendously chic to holiday on the Côte d'Azur in the height of summer.

On his first visit to Cannes Christophe adored all that he saw. The women were so delicious in vivid tunics that displayed their bare brown legs to mid-thigh! And those in flimsy silk beach pyjamas with flaring trousers – marvellous! And in white linen trousers cut tight to display the curves of an elegant rump – exquisite!

Down by the edge of the sea itself, soaking in the sun, the most beautiful women imaginable revealed themselves in no more than skin-tight bathing costumes of thin woollen jersey in the brightest colours, cut to leave their backs bare to below the waist and their legs bare to within a few centimetres of the join of their thighs. What ravishing sights for a young man of Christophe's amorous disposition! He drank in the sight of these beautiful creatures walking barefoot in the sand, the tender buds of their breasts clearly visible through their clinging bathing costumes. The susceptibility of Christophe's nature guaranteed that his male part stood stiffly to attention in his white trousers for the whole length of his perambulation along the sea-shore.

Of course, the beautiful women who had so great an effect upon him were invariably surrounded by admirers, confident young men displaying expanses of sun-tanned skin and muscle. Or older men with receding hair and paunches, who had the appearance of being extremely rich – and to these the young beauties seemed even more attentive than to the young men. Christophe shrugged at the sight – that was the way of the world. His problem was that he was not rich.

Until quite recently he had believed himself to be on the right route to success in his uncle's business, especially when his elegant aunt had admitted him to her intimate friendship. How could such influence fail to guide him by acceptable stages to the very top of the business, with all the accompanying rewards? Alas, Jeanne Verney had ceased to visit Christophe's apartment when she became pregnant. That was the first cruel blow of fate – the second and equally devastating blow came when Verney's business interests were sold and Christophe's employment was terminated. Jeanne, gracious as always, had insisted that Christophe was given a sum of money by way of recompense for his disappointed hopes – a sum sufficient to maintain him for perhaps a year in reasonable style.

'What will you do now, Christophe?' she asked, 'stay in Paris or return to your mother in Lyon?'

'I shall go on a vacation while I think about my future,' he replied, no particular plan in his head.

'Excellent idea. Go to Cannes – I have friends there who will be pleased to see you.'

And there it was! Christophe travelled south on the Blue Train and engaged a room at the Carlton, it being early enough in the summer for that august establishment to be able to accomodate him for a few days. Needless to say, it was most imprudent of him to be staying in so expensive a hotel when the financial resources at his disposal were limited, but one lesson Christophe had learned from his time in Paris was that appearances mattered a great deal. What impression would he make on anyone of consequence if it became known that he was staying in a *pension* in a back-street? The idea was impossible.

On the Blue Train rushing south through the night Christophe had been unable to sleep. So it came about that, at the age of twenty-five, he took stock of himself for the first time in his life. As all the world knows, at three o'clock in the morning, a person alone finds himself face to face with the truth about himself, however displeasing it may be. Christophe knew that he would win no great prizes for his intellectual abilities, but what of it? Intellectuals were those who wrote boring books and lived in the discomfort of the Left Bank. He knew from his service in Verney's business enterprise that he would never become a giant of commerce by his own efforts, for he lacked the application it demanded. The learned professions were closed to him – that had been made obvious at school.

Yet Christophe had other virtues to offer. He was handsome, he wore clothes well, he had an endless fund of small-talk, he was attractive to women of all ages – and, at the top of the list of his qualities, he was an accomplished lover in bed, thanks to the devotion of his aunt Jeanne. He intended to use all these abilities to gain a position of acceptance in society. In short, his plan was to find and marry a rich woman, young and beautiful if possible, older than himself and plain if need be, so long as she was really rich and sufficiently in love with him to let him spend her money freely.

From Jeanne Christophe had an introduction to several friends of hers in Cannes, but he was in no hurry to pursue the matter. There was so much to see, so much to enjoy. Besides, he did not not wish to appear too eager to present himself to any of Jeanne's friends, as that might create a bad impression. Jeanne's friends were all people of importance, that went without saying. One of them even had a title, though there were no real titles in a Republic. To adorn one's name in this way, Christophe considered, indicated a certain nostalgia for the past and was the mark of a snob.

On his second day at the Carlton, he was taking breakfast on the terrace at about ten o'clock and reading the newspaper, when the course of his life changed in a dramatic manner. The lateness of the hour was due to the fact that he had been at the Casino the night before, observing the roulette players and taking stock of the general situation. Naturally, all the rich women there had escorts.

'M'sieu Larousse?' a respectful voice asked.

Christophe looked up from his newspaper to see, in considerable surprise, a tall man in dove-grey livery, a peaked hat tucked neatly under his arm, standing by his table.

'Who are you?'

'I am chauffeur to the Vicomtesse de la Vergne, M'sieu.'

That was the name of the titled lady which Jeanne had given Christophe.

'Madame la Vicomtesse presents her compliments,' the chauffeur said politely. 'She requests the pleasure of your company at lunch today.'

'That is most kind of her,' said Christophe. 'At what time?'

'I am to say, M'sieu, that as the Villa is at some distance from the town, Madame's car is at your disposal. I shall be outside the hotel to take you there whenever you are ready.'

'Very well. I shall finish my breakfast and accompany you shortly.'

'Thank you, M'sieu,' said the chauffeur, bowing as if Christophe had conferred an immense favour on him.

What thoughts passed through Christophe's mind as he folded his newspaper and poured another cup of coffee! Not that he wanted the coffee, but it gave him an excuse to remain at the table and think. A car with a uniformed chauffeur, no less! She began to be interesting, this so-called Vicomtesse. Yet how had she become aware that Christophe was in Cannes? Simple – Jeanne must have talked to her by telephone to tell her that he would be presenting himself in due course. He was confident that

119

Jeanne had recommended him highly to her friend, since she was still very affectionate towards him even though they had ceased to be lovers over a year ago.

Ah – but how had the Vicomtesse known to which hotel to send her messenger? Christophe hadn't known himself where he would be staying when he left Paris. He had got off the train and told a taxi driver to take him to the best hotel. Evidently the chauffeur had been told to enquire for a Monsieur Larousse at the two or three best hotels. Thank God, Christophe thought, that he had been inspired to make the expensive gesture and had not put up at some cheap *pension*!

Twenty minutes later, when he strolled out of the hotel with careful nonchalance, the sight of the car waiting for him almost made his mouth fall open in astonishment. It was a superb open tourer, the paintwork a gleaming maroon colour, the chrome polished to a degree that made it quite dazzling in the sun. The chauffeur stood at attention by his marvellous machine, his face impassive, and opened the rear door for Christophe – a door on which there appeared a small coat of arms! Christophe seated himself on the soft leather, tapped his straw boater firmly on his head at a jaunty angle and prepared to enjoy the ride.

The Villa was indeed at some distance from the town, as the chauffeur had told him. The route lay in the direction of Nice for some kilometres, then it wound upwards away from the sea. When their destination eventually came into sight it proved to be a large white house perched on a hillside, half-hidden from the road by a white-washed wall. Wrought-iron gates were swung open by a man whom, from his clothes, Christophe took to be a gardener. The long beautiful car entered and passed through a well-tended garden to halt outside the main entrance to the house.

The door opened as if his arrival had been anticipated to the second and a maid conducted him across a marble-floored entrance hall and a large salon stunningly decorated and furnished in the very latest style – all etched glass and sycamore – and out onto a broad paved terrace overlooking a swimming-pool. He stood still for a moment in the bright sunshine, his heart pounding for joy. Everything he had seen so far smelled of money, from the glass sculpture in the entrance hall to the ruinously expensive furnishings of the salon – and especially the people out by the swimming pool. He counted nine – five women and four men – four of them splashing about and laughing in the pool and the others sitting or lying in the sun on long reclining chairs of wood painted white and scarlet.

A young woman wearing the most elegant swimming costume Christophe had ever seen turned her head to stare calmly at him as he descended the broad stone steps from the terrace to the pool level. He guessed her age at twenty-one or two and thought that she might have Spanish or Italian blood, her hair was so dark and her skin so delicately olive-hued. She was so incredibly beautiful that Christophe fell in love with her instantly. He prayed silently to God to let this dazzling creature be the Vicomtesse de la Vergne and unmarried, so that he could marry her himself and live in conjugal bliss with her for the rest of his life. He would have crossed himself to reinforce his prayer, but that would have drawn her attention to him in a way that could not be regarded as stylish.

Naturally, she was not the Vicomtesse. The maid led Christophe to the opposite side of the pool, where a lady in pink reclined on a long chair. Her clothes were exquisite – beach pyjamas of chiffon so delicate that it was almost transparent – two strands of pearls about her neck and slave-bangles on the wrists of her bare sun-browned arms. But when she raised her head, under the broad brim of her sunhat Christophe encountered a fifty-year-old face, square-jawed and with a little too much make-up.

'You must be Christophe Larousse,' she said, extending

her hand to be kissed, 'I'm so pleased you could drop in for lunch.'

Christophe gave her his most charming smile as he removed his hat and bowed gracefully over her hand, a hand on which there were diamond rings on all four fingers.

'It was kind of you to invite me.'

'I've heard so much about you from Jeanne,' she said with a roguish smile, 'sit here beside me – Marie, bring cold drinks at once.'

She introduced him to the man and woman sitting close by her and while their names meant nothing to Christophe, their expensive casual clothes did. He set himself to make a good impression on his hostess and her friends. He succeeded so well that the shoulder strap of the woman's costume started slipping from her sun-tanned left shoulder in a manner that threatened to expose a breast! Each time she adjusted it she made sure that Christophe's attention was caught by the movement. The man, her husband, ignored her antics and continued to pay court to the Vicomtesse, who permitted a tiny frown to appear on her features the third or fourth time the strap slipped and suggested to Christophe that he might like to refresh himself after his journey by a swim. She dismissed his objection that he had brought nothing with him by waving vaguely towards a long and single-storey building to one side of the pool and telling him that he would find whatever he needed there.

He felt that it was best to do as she said, so as to retain her goodwill. Certainly she wanted him away from the pretty lady having problems with her shoulder strap! Perhaps she feared for his morals if he were exposed to so much temptation!

The single storey building had a veranda its whole length. Inside it was divided into half a dozen small rooms for changing, comfortably furnished and fully equipped with towels, bathing caps for the women and swimming costumes for both sexes. Christophe found a garment to fit him and undressed. Outside again, he stood for an instant on the edge of the pool and dived in, aiming for the life-size figure of a mermaid he could see on the tiles under the clear water.

One of the people now playing in the water was the black-haired girl with whom he had fallen in love. He surfaced beside her, slicked his hair back and smiled.

'My name is Christophe,' he introduced himself.

She returned his smile, then swam to the side and turned, one elbow on the edge to support herself while she looked at him.

'I am Nicolette Santana. You are very white-skinned still – have you just arrived?'

'Only yesterday. There is something I must tell you.'

'What?'

'I love you.'

'You don't know me,' she said, smiling at his impertinence.

'I have seen you – that is enough.'

'Do you usually fall in love so easily?'

'This is only the second time in my life.'

'And the first?'

'That is finished. Will you marry me, Nicolette?'

He said it light-heartedly, but with a touch of sincerity that no woman could miss. Her response was to laugh, but in her amusement Christophe thought he detected a hint of encouragement.

Seen at close quarters, Nicolette was so beautiful that Christophe's heart almost stopped beating. Her glossy hair, as blue-black as a raven's wing, was parted in the middle over an oval face of exquisite proportions, in which large eyes shone like polished jet-stones. Around her neck hung a simple strand of white coral beads – the same colour as her swimming costume, which was of the finest jersey wool and clung wetly to her perfect breasts, emphasising their full roundness.

All this Christophe noted avidly, as a man takes inventory of an apartment in which he intends to live for a long time. In his mind there was no doubt whatsoever – this marvellous girl was going to be his wife and he would never be unfaithful to her throughout his entire life. Unable to resist the impulse, he reached out under the water and ran his hand down her hip in a gesture that said everything that was in his heart. Before anyone could observe his action, before even Nicolette could respond, he said, 'Think about it,' and pushed off from the side of the pool with his feet, to swim at a furious speed across and' back. But by the time he had returned, she had climbed out of the water and was sunning herself. After a moment's thought, Christophe returned to the side of the Vicomtesse. The woman who had been troubled by her shoulder strap smiled prettily at him and studied quite openly the bulge under his wet swimsuit, but this time the Vicomtesse chose to ignore her.

'You have made the acquaintance of my niece,' she said brightly, 'a pretty girl – my sister's child.'

'Your niece?' said Christophe in surprise. 'Forgive me, but I see no family resemblance, Madame. You are fair-skinned, while she is dark.'

'Quite right! My sister married a Spanish nobleman. They were both lost on the *Lusitania*, coming back from America, murdered by the Boche!'

'Dreadful!'

'Fortunately the child was not with them on the voyage. I have made it my duty to give her a home and to educate her.'

'You are a very good-hearted person,' said Christophe. 'She is fortunate in having your protection and being brought up in France instead of Spain.'

'What a perceptive young man you are!' the Vicomtesse exclaimed. 'Her father's family wanted to take her after the tragedy, of course, but I refused to listen to any such plan. Of course, her name is not Nicolette – her father

124

insisted that she be called Isobel, but I soon changed that when she came to live with me.'

'You are no great admirer of the Spanish?' Christophe asked.

'Their cuisine is barbarous and their entertainments boring beyond words! Now, you'd better go and change – lunch will be in half an hour.'

In one of the changing rooms Christophe stripped off his borrowed swimsuit and threw it into a container placed there for that purpose. Before he had time to do any more the door opened – he had not bothered to turn the key in the lock – and there stood the Vicomtesse, from whom he had parted only a minute before. He reached for a towel from the neat stack to cover those parts of his body not normally displayed to mere acquaintances, but the Vicomtesse waved her hand in a gesture of indifference as she lowered herself into a chair.

'I have no regard for the idiocies of bourgeois modesty,' she announced. 'Tell me about my dear friend Jeanne – is she happy and well? And that frightful husband of hers – I have heard that he has become insane and has been locked away.'

'The report that has reached you is somewhat exaggerated, Madame,' said Christophe with an ironic smile, 'it is true that Monsieur Verney has suffered a breakdown of his health and requires constant care, but . . .'

'You must call me Régine,' the Vicomtesse interrupted. 'You are a very handsome young man, Christophe. How old are you?'

'Twenty-five,' he answered.

He made no attempt to conceal any part of himself as he rubbed himself dry with the towel – not a lengthy process, of course, for the hot sun had dried his skin by the side of the pool. But he thought it sensible to make a lengthy process of it. He stood facing the Vicomtesse while he raised each arm in turn to rub underneath, then sideways to her while he put a foot up on a white wooden stool and pretended to dry down his thigh and leg. In effect, he was posing for his hostess. He talked lightly of friends in Paris, bringing a smile to her lips, though whether that was the result of his words or the view of his body she was afforded – who could say?

Certainly she demonstrated her contempt for 'bourgeois morality' by studying him closely. Christophe had no misgivings on that account – he knew that he scored highly, being broad of shoulder and narrow of hip. His male appendage, to which the Vicomtesse seemed to be devoting considerable attention, was of pleasing proportions – he had been assured of that by several women of the world in whose experience he had every confidence. In the expert use of it he had been tutored by Jeanne Verney herself, though whether the Vicomtesse had been told that he did not know.

There came a time when he could hardly continue the pretence of drying himself further. His clothes were over the back of a chair close to where the Vicomtesse was sitting. He set aside the towel and reached for his shirt – and she also reached out, to cup his dependents in her palm.

'You have a good body, Christophe,' she said warmly. 'How long were you Jeanne's lover?'

'That is a question I cannot answer with propriety,' he said with a smile. 'You must ask her.'

'I did. She told me that you made her pregnant – a very inconsiderate thing to do.'

'A tragedy,' said Christophe, 'I lost her as a result.'

The Vicomtesse's other hand took possession of his fast-growing stem.

'Did you love her truly, Christophe?'

'I adored her,' he replied with complete honesty. 'My heart was broken when we ceased to be lovers.'

He was wondering if this strange and plain woman had it in mind to invite him to make love to her here in the changing room – and what his response would be if she

126

did. She had brought his accoutrement to full stand by her manipulation, but he felt no desire for her – only for the beautiful niece. Perhaps Madame la Vicomtesse read the expression in his eyes, for her broad face split in a grin.

'Not now,' she said, 'the others will be in to change in a moment. I may despise the common restrictions but I am a strong upholder of the social conventions.'

'And a strong upholder of something else at this moment, Régine.'

She laughed at that, ran her hand lightly up and down his stiff part a few times, then released it with a sigh.

'Dress yourself,' she said, 'we will talk again after lunch.'

She swept out of the little room in a flurry of pink chiffon. Christophe pulled his shirt over his head, hoping furiously that his tumescence would subside before he rejoined the other guests, but knowing from all past experience that it probably would not. As his head emerged through the neck of the shirt, he gasped in astonishment to see Nicolette, still in her tight white swimming costume, looking in through the door her aunt had left ajar – looking at the lower half of his body, still uncovered – looking at his stiff part sticking out like a baton!

Her eyes met his and she pouted at him.

'Nicolette!' he exclaimed, his appurtenance bounding at the sight of her.

He rushed to the door, not knowing what he would do – pull her inside the room and press her to him, tear off her costume . . . but when he put his head round the door she had disappeared into another of the changing rooms and coming along the corridor towards him was the lady who had experienced such difficulties with her shoulder strap. Christophe pulled his head back and closed the door quickly – and turned the key for safety!

Lunch was an enjoyable experience. Everyone was dressed elegantly, the food was delicious and the conversation lively. Afterwards everyone seemed to drift away, until Christophe found himself alone on the terrace. How could he find out which was Nicolette's room? The easiest way seemed to him to ask a servant and, as if on cue, out came the maid who had opened the door to him on his first arrival. But before he had time to make his enquiry, she informed him that Madame would like a few words with him. He shrugged and followed the maid.

The bedroom of the Vicomtesse, to which he was conducted, was large and modern in the most spectacular way. At one end the bed, fully two metres wide, stood in a niche lined with panelling of light beige wood, into which mother-of-pearl had been inlaid in a geometric pattern. At the other end of the room were arm chairs and a long sofa, all upholstered in beige silk. The lady herself, her ample body concealed in a feather-trimmed wrapper of floating chiffon the colour of newly-roasted coffee, sat on one of the chairs reading a letter, for which purpose she wore reading-glasses with tortoise-shell frames. On Christophe's entrance she put aside letter and reading-glasses and smiled at him fondly.

The room impressed Christophe as deeply as the other parts of the Villa he had seen. He knew himself to be in the presence of formidable wealth – wealth used with good taste, for not only did she surround herself with expensive and beautiful objects, but also with fascinating people, to judge from the conversation over lunch. In Christophe's opinion, his hostess was worthy of respect, perhaps even admiration.

She waved him to a chair with a bejewelled hand.

'I like an hour's rest at this time of the day,' she informed him, 'but today I do not feel like sleeping. I need to be amused – I hope you don't mind talking to me, though I'm sure you'd rather be out by the pool with the other young people.'

Christophe assured her that he was well content to be

received by her in so informal a setting. The use of the word 'informal' caused her to glance at the bed.

'To you I must seem a foolish old woman,' she said, 'but I find young people utterly irresistible – the good-looking ones, that is to say. I find it impossible to deny them whatever they want.'

She had said 'young people', Christophe noted, not just young *men*. Perhaps her tastes embraced both sexes. He raised his eyes from the heavy diamond rings on her hand to gaze with as much good grace as he could muster into her pudgy face.

'I am at your service, Régine,' he said, taking the plunge boldly.

'Of course you are,' she replied, 'every handsome young man I've ever met with no money of his own has been willing to oblige me. I have come to expect it.'

'You are very candid,' said Christophe, not at all pleased by the direction of the conversation.

'I can afford to be.'

She stood for a moment to slip off her coffee-coloured peignoir and sat down again, completely naked except for her high-heeled shoes.

'Look at *me*, not at my diamonds,' she commanded, 'what do you see?'

Christophe looked carefully. The Vicomtesse's neck was short and thick, her breasts were heavy, her belly plump almost to the point of being fat. Her thighs were certainly thick and the thin hair between them was so fresh a brown that it was surely dyed.

'I see a woman,' he answered her question.

'I cannot dispute that,' she said, 'but you see a woman who has lived a little too well for a little too long, to the detriment of the beautiful body of her youth. Does the sight repel you, my dear young friend? You are surely used to the sight of pretty young women with firm breasts and flat bellies.'

'I am not repelled.'

'They all say that,' she remarked. 'And for obvious reasons they are not looking at *these*,' – she put her hands under her big and sagging breasts to lift them up – 'they are looking at the rings on my hands instead. When they kiss my nipples, in their minds they are kissing my diamonds.'

Christophe was experiencing a distinct feeling of uneasiness at the outspoken manner of the Vicomtesse. Her philosophy was her own affair and he had no desire to listen to it. Besides, it was unjust – he had asked for nothing, not even the invitation to lunch. She had sent her car for him. Why should he be subjected to this display of middle-aged cynicism?

'When they put their hand between my legs, these charming and obliging young men,' she continued, 'they are in reality stroking one of my fur coats – the sable, perhaps, or the Russian fox – I have a wardrobe full of such coats.'

'Really, Madame!' Christophe exclaimed in a sudden flash of irritation.

'Worst of all,' she went on, as if unaware of his presence, 'when they finally bring themselves to push their stiff little things in *here*,' and she parted her thighs widely so that Christophe saw the thick and pouting lips within the tinted brown hair, 'they are only making love to my bank account. Do you believe that a bank account feels ecstasy when a young man squirts his little spoonful into it?'

Christophe felt that it was intolerable to be insulted in this way. He saw two courses of action that would put an end to it. The most obvious was to walk out and leave the woman to her melancholy victory. The other was to play her at her own game and beat her at it. He got up swiftly and took two steps towards her, seized her flabby breasts and tugged sharply, so that she winced.

'You seem well acquainted with the ways of gigolos, Madame,' he sneered. 'If you had been a little less self-indulgent in the past, perhaps you would have less cause for self-pity now.'

'How dare you speak to me like that!' she exclaimed.

'I speak as I wish,' he replied sharply, tugging at her breasts again, her further expostulations cut off by a little shriek.

'You said that you wished to be amused,' he reminded her, 'then you insult me as if I were a male prostitute you had summoned to give you a quick thrill to occupy a dull afternoon. Your behaviour towards me has been disgraceful and I shall see to it that everyone hears about it.'

'No!' she said quickly, 'I am sorry – it was wrong of me, perhaps. But you let me touch you in the changing room. You let me think that you would not deny me.'

'Courtesy prevented me from taking exception to your uninvited familiarity,' he said, putting anger into his tone. 'But this! You summon me here and bare your body to me as a prelude to a tirade of abuse! It is too much!'

'Forgive me, I implore you,' the Vicomtesse gasped, her face red.

'Your actions have been unforgivable,' he declared and squeezed her breasts so hard that she whimpered. 'Was it your intention to order me to make love to you and then throw me a few francs afterwards? If you were a man I would beat you senseless and leave you sprawled here on the floor.'

Something in his words brought a quick glint into her eyes.

'If I were a man I should not be here naked with your hands on my breasts,' she pointed out.

That was obvious enough, but it left Christophe without words for a moment. Before he could recover, the Vicomtesse slid her jewelled hand up his thighs and began to unbutton his trousers.

'You looked at me and said that you saw a woman,' she said huskily, 'perhaps you spoke truthfully – perhaps

131

you looked at me and saw a woman and not a pile of gold coins. I must know!'

She pulled his male part out into the light of day and, astonished, Christophe became aware at that moment that it was stiff. In spite of the disagreeable nature of their conversation, the sight of her naked body had brought about the usual effect, even though her body had held no particular interest for him – or so he thought. The truth was, though he had never admitted it to himself, that he was so susceptible to women that any pair of breasts, no matter how drooping, could bring him to a state of readiness. That was not to say he threw himself with abandon at every women who gave him to understand that she would not discourage his advances. Certainly he had no intention of allowing the Vicomtesse to lure him into an intimate encounter – she had injured his masculine pride by her words.

'This is too much!' he exclaimed in irritation as she rolled his upright staff between her palms.

He released her breasts to grasp her wrists and pull her hands away. But the Vicomtesse did not wish to surrender her possession of this cherished part so quickly! In the struggle that ensued, she was dragged to the very edge of her chair, then off it altogether, so that she fell sideways to the floor. Even then she retained her double-handed grip and Christophe, to save himself from anguish or damage, was forced to fall to his knees beside her. Still she held on in her ridiculous frenzy of possession, but he was the stronger and at last he prised her hands loose. The Vicomtesse rolled over face down, perhaps to conceal her expression of angry frustration, the tantrum of a spoiled child from whom a favourite toy has been taken. She lay sprawled on the rug and, she being naked but for her shoes, Christophe saw her bottom for the first time.

It infuriated him, that bottom! The rest of her body, which she had displayed uninvited to him during her tirade, was pudgy and unattractive – it spoke all too

132

plainly of years of over-indulgence at the table and lack of exercise. But her bottom! It had escaped the ravages of time and could have been that of a twenty-year-old girl. The cheeks were gracefully rounded, the skin smooth and unblemished! And the colour – a delicate ivory! The golden tan of her legs terminated just below those beautiful cheeks, the tan of her back above them, and this piebald effect seemed to accentuate at the same time the luscious tenderness of her rump and to make it seem somehow more naked than the rest of her.

Christophe found it intolerable that this harpy who expected him to perform on command should be blessed with a bottom that would be the envy of most women half her age. At that moment he hated her and wanted to punish her presumption. Without a thought, directed only by the furious emotion that filled his heart, he straddled her back, facing her feet, and held her pinned face-down to the floor with his weight while he slapped with both hands at the pretty cheeks that had annoyed him so much.

'Stop that! You're hurting me!' the Vicomtesse shrieked, wriggling beneath him to try to escape.

Christophe was deaf to her pleas. He took a fierce revenge for the humiliation to which she had subjected him – and also perhaps for the injustice, as he perceived it, that this middle-aged woman should be so extremely rich and a handsome young man like himself should be without the means to sustain the style to which he felt himself to be entitled. His disappointments in Paris, the uncertainty of his future – he purged all these emotions from his heart by smacking the Vicomtesse's rump until his hands were stinging. By then the ivory cheeks were bright red and the Vicomtesse was sobbing miserably.

After relieving his emotions Christophe felt remarkably light-hearted. His male appendage hang passive and limp outside his trousers as if he had just made love to the Vicomtesse! The change in his mood was so great that he was even well-disposed towards the Vicomtesse herself, she having been the means by which he had attained his happy state of emotional balance.

Her bottom looked painfully red. He touched it lightly and she winced. Something should be done about it, Christophe thought benignly, or she will take her meals standing up for the next day or two. With this in mind, he adjusted his trousers and searched around the room for some means of alleviating her distress. On the dressing-table he discovered a large jar of cold cream – most delicately scented when he removed the lid and sniffed at the contents. With this he returned to the victim of his wrath – still quietly sobbing – and seated himself cross-legged on the rug beside her.

'This will take away the pain,' he said.

He scooped generous quantities of the expensive cream from the jar, one for each cheek, and smoothed it gently into her skin, using both palms. She uttered a little squeal at the first touch, then fell silent as he continued and the emollient cream cooled her fiery bottom.

'Is that better, Madame?' he enquired.

'Yes, it helps. Please continue,' she answered faintly.

He smeared on another double scoop and resumed his light massage. It seemed to him so peaceful, sitting there on the floor, rubbing cold cream into the Vicomtesse's bottom – peaceful and pleasant. Certainly it was a very sensible way to pass an afternoon – much better than baking oneself alive out in the sun by the swimming pool. Nicolette was out there, perhaps, but there was little opportunity of talking to her in private with so many guests at the Villa. Now if it had been *her* bottom he was massaging . . . the thought caused him to sigh gently. With an image of Nicolette in his mind, he stroked the Vicomtesse's rump dreamily, not even noticing when her legs eased themselves apart on the rug, not even aware that his hands were caressing slowly into the divide

134

between the cheeks he had assailed so brutally only five minutes before.

His palms were gliding over warm and supple skin, but his finger-tips were touching short curls, yet still he paid no attention. More cream – the jar was almost empty now – right down between those superb cheeks this time. How pleasant an object was a woman's bottom, he thought as if in a reverie, how delicious to handle! With what genius the good Lord had fashioned the female body in all its parts!

His fingers were in the curls, smoothing cold cream into the soft lips of flesh between Madame's legs. A few moments later Christophe realised with a start that he had the finger-tips of both hands inside those lips! The slipperiness he felt was no longer cold cream but the dew of her arousal! He gasped at the thought, almost stopped, then told himself that to abandon a woman in this condition, after bringing her to it, was out of the question. To leave any woman, Vicomtesse or not, at this point would be the act of a person without manners or style.

Now that he was fully aware of what he was doing, Christophe began to employ the skills he had learned from Jeanne Verney when she and he had been lovers. The most vivid memories of his adult life were of the long afternoons in his little apartment in the rue Vavin, when Jeanne lay naked on his bed and he caressed her elegant breasts and belly, finding out how far she could be aroused before she pulled him on top of her to finish her off. Together they had played this game endlessly and sometimes they had both misjudged the level of her excitement and she had reached a gasping and trembling climax before he could penetrate her wet fleece.

He had been with many women since his affaire with Jeanne had come to an end, but on nights when he slept alone those golden afternoons sometimes returned in his dreams and he awoke erect and disconsolate. It seemed strange to him now that one of Jeanne's friends, the plain

135

and middle-aged Vicomtesse, was enjoying the benefit of those adventures into sensuality.

Of the Vicomtesse's present enjoyment there could be no possible doubt. Her diamond-laden fingers were scrabbling in the rug and she was moaning in delight to his expert touch between her legs. Earlier on, when she had been seated on the chair, she had deliberately parted her thighs to display to him the thick and pouting lips within her brown curls. It had been no more than a glimpse, he staring in surprise at her expression of cynicism, but his close attention to those parts now as she lay face-down on the floor, made it obvious to him that the entrance between the Vicomtesse's thighs was more than usually generous in dimension. Whether that was by nature or by diligent use over many years, who could say? But what in most women of his acquaintance was a shrine of love was, in her case, a veritable cathedral! It would be an extraordinary man who could fill that, he considered, for the eight fingers of his two hands fitted into it without undue difficulty. That being so, he was able to use them all to excite in her such shudders of passion that her feet drummed on the floor until her high-heeled shoes fell off!

Christophe may not have been particularly intelligent, but he was not a fool – no young man in his position could afford to be that. The lady he was pleasuring in so curious a manner was very rich – of that he had seen ample evidence. The private parts to which he was attending might well be the key to his own future happiness and prosperity. With so formidable a possibility to motivate him, Christophe employed all his skill to make the occasion one she would remember with gratitude.

Over a period of perhaps a quarter of an hour his artful fingers brought her a dozen times to the very brink of climactic release, then hesitated delicately, so that she never quite reached the zenith her entire body was straining to achieve. Her moans had long ceased – all that she was capable of was a harsh and heavy breathing

136

through her wide open mouth. Her broad back was shiny with perspiration and she had broken one finger-nail by clawing at the rug.

At last Christophe judged that it was enough. His fingers fluttered wetly within her gaping portal as he applied the final stimulation to her distended bud. The result was dramatic in the extreme – every muscle in her body contracted. Her shoulder blades stood out from her back, the sinews stood out on her neck, her legs stiffened as if they were made of iron and her feet pointed straight downwards. She gave voice to a long wailing shriek as the spasms of ecstasy gripped her and shook her. She was bouncing up and down on her belly and thrashing about with her arms as if she were swimming in her own pool.

'Stupendous!' Christophe said aloud in awe at the effect he had produced.

She lay exhausted for some time after that, as was to be expected. Christophe sat quietly on the floor, his hands resting on his knees, waiting for her to recover.

'Christophe,' she whispered eventually, 'I adore you.'

Of course, it would have been courteous, to put it no higher, to respond with the same words, but that was further than Christophe was prepared to go. His silence passed unnoticed and the Vicomtesse continued, her voice regaining a little strength.

'I did not understand what a very special person you are, my dear,' she said, 'I took you for just another good-looking young man trying to make his fortune with his penis. You were right to beat me – I said dreadful things to you. Forgive me, I implore you.'

'We understand each other at last,' he answered mildly, 'I am glad of it.'

What a stupid woman, he was thinking – all I did was to smack her backside until she wept and then give her a slow feel! And for that she falls in love with me! Thanks be to the divine Providence that set this woman's brains between her legs instead of in her head!

Without getting up from the rug, the Vicomtesse shuffled herself round until her head was towards Christophe. She reached up to lay her hands over his hands.

'Say that I am forgiven,' she pleaded, 'say my name!'

'Régine – we are good friends now, I hope. Let there be no talk of forgiveness. To understand all is to forgive all.'

'Say it again!' she breathed, her eyes on his face in abject devotion.

'Régine.'

She shuffled a little closer until her head was between his knees. Her hands left his and touched his trouser buttons timidly, a look of entreaty in her brown eyes.

'Only if I have your permission,' she murmured, 'but it means so much to me now, my dear Christophe, so very much!'

He made no objection this time as she undid his buttons slowly and extracted his male part. It was full-grown again, naturally – no man can handle a woman as he had handled her without becoming aroused himself. Arousal demands relief, and for this reason he let her have her way, not because he had any desire to become her lover.

Régine fondled him with great respect.

'He is very sturdy,' she said in a hushed voice, 'yet so regal! Yes, he is a king – a king of love!'

To his amazement she slipped one of her diamond rings off a finger and crowned his upright part with it.

'See!' she exclaimed, 'a crown for His Majesty!'

Christophe was tempted to burst into laughter at her ludicrous behaviour but he succeeded in controlling himself. Only half an hour ago his male part had been a mere object of utility to Régine, to be employed for her own pleasure and paid for at whatever rate she decided. Now it had become a royal sceptre, to be adorned with diamonds. That was real progress! Before he could think of any suitable response – not that there was any need of one, for Régine hardly ever listened to what other people

138

were saying – she bowed her head as if in homage and the tip of her tongue swept the diamond ring from its place of honour. Her lips touched His Majesty's crimson head in a respectful kiss. Not content with so simple an act of obeisance, her painted lips opened and at once His Majesty was deep inside her mouth!

Christophe uttered a little sigh of pleasure as her hot and wet tongue applied itself to his most sensitive part. He closed his eyes and instead of the top of Régine's head he conjured up in his mind's eye a vision of Nicolette as he had seen her at the swimming pool. The buds of her beautiful breasts were prominent through her white bathing costume and she was smiling at him in love and desire. He reached out to touch her and his fingers encountered bare flesh – that of Régine's shoulder, of course, but he dismissed that thought from his mind and imagined that it was Nicolette's graceful shoulder under his hand.

His ruse was so successful – and Régine's ministrations so ardent – that it seemed only moments before enormous sensations overwhelmed him and he discharged his passion into her hot mouth. His finger-nails dug into her shoulder fiercely as ecstasy shook him, but she made no complaint.

When it was over she looked up into his face almost shyly.

'Thank you, Christophe, thank you,' she said, 'did I please you a little?'

He nodded, surprised by her humble tone.

'I'm so glad,' she said, 'I've only done that for a man once before in my life, when I was very young, but it seemed the right thing to do to show you my affection for you. I know that you cannot love me or feel for me a tenth of what I feel for you, but I am sure that we can be very close friends.'

The diamond ring with which she had crowned his pride

lay on the rug between them. Régine picked it up, but did not replace it on her finger.

'His Majesty does not wish to wear his crown any more,' she said playfully. 'See – his head is drooping! Take the ring, Christophe, as a memento of this day.'

'No!' he said sharply, 'I am not to be bought with trinkets. You forget yourself, Madame!'

In truth, he was playing for higher stakes than a ring, valuable or not. If he allowed Régine to believe that she could purchase his favours, as she had doubtlessly purchased young men's favours many times before, then he would be nothing more than an employee.

Her pudgy face creased as if she were about to weep again.

'Christophe – please!' she stammered. 'It was not meant as an insult, I assure you! Just a small present between good friends, that's all.'

'Then I will take your suggestion in the spirit in which it was intended,' he replied, maintaining an aloof manner, 'but I will not take the ring. Put it back on your finger.'

'Yes, Christophe,' she said hastily. 'Please don't call me Madame – it makes you sound so distant and I can't bear that. I want to be close to you, my dear.'

'Régine, you have much to learn about me if we are to be good friends.'

'Yes, Christophe,' she said, smiling at hearing him say her name.

After dinner that evening Régine decided that all her guests should accompany her to the Casino. This journey was not in the open touring car – at least not for Madame herself, Christophe and two others – but in a tall and luxurious limousine, complete with a flexible tube through which Régine could convey her instructions, should there be any, to the chauffeur in front behind his glass panel.

The gaming room was full when they arrived, the men very distinguished in gleaming white shirt-fronts and black tail coats, the ladies – ah, the elegance of their evening frocks and the bright glitter of their jewels! Somewhat to Christophe's dismay hemlines had begun to lengthen a year or so earlier, in response to heaven alone knew what, and by this summer they were at ankle-length. He thought it sad that beautiful women should deprive admirers the sight of their graceful legs in sheer silk stockings – but who could argue against the dictates of fashion? Putting that consideration aside, he felt himself very much at home in this society, proud of his handsome face and good figure. Régine was magnificent in a close-cut frock of the Napoleonic style, bare-armed, the waist-line high up under her bosom, so that the exquisite work of Schiaparelli concealed a certain ungainliness, and the jewels around her neck, wrists and fingers diverted attention from too close consideration of any shortcoming in her physical appearance.

While Régine busied herself at one of the roulette tables, exchanging greetings with everyone – for she knew everyone and they knew her – Christophe tried to attach himself to Nicolette but was thwarted in his attempt by the young man who had elected himself her escort for the evening. He therefore decided to observe everything around him with care – the gambling, the people, the style and, above all else, the women who were gambling. One needed to know the proper way to do things – how to bet, how to win with restrained enthusiasm, how to lose with good grace.

There was a moment when the lively chatter in the salon was hushed, the chanting of the croupiers' *Rien ne va plus*' was stilled and only the tiny clicks of a ball round a roulette wheel broke the silence as all eyes turned towards the entrance. Christophe turned to see what had caused so great an effect – surely some person of immense importance! There, advancing into the gaming room was a man in his middle years, well-dressed and confident, but in no way distinguished in Christophe's eyes – except

141

that on each arm he had a small and beautiful woman –
and the two women were identical! Christophe stared
openly at the vivacious twins, whose large dark eyes shone
in their exquisite faces under nearly black hair worn in a
fringe over broad foreheads. The diamonds they both
wore were fabulous in size and in quantity, making Régine
appear almost unadorned by comparison.

The lull in conversation and activity lasted while the
newcomers paraded in grand style the length of the salon
to the end table, then all turned back to their own absorb-
ing pursuits, the croupiers took up their polite admonitions and the wheels spun again.

'But who are they!' Christophe asked Régine as she
slid a large plaque onto the red.

'Who?' she retorted, as if she had not noticed the trio.

'The people who just came in.'

'Oh, those! Don't you know? They call themselves the
Dolly sisters – they are entertainers. They used to appear
in the Paris music-halls. They are foreigners, of course –
Hungarian, I understand – probably gypsies, if the truth
were known.'

'I have heard of them, but I have never seen them on
stage.'

'You never will now, not while they have a rich friend
to take care of them.'

'The gentleman with them, you mean. Who is he?'

'An American, of course, what else? His name is
Gordon Selfridge and he is said to own a large shop in
London.'

'How extraordinary!' said Christophe, lost in
admiration.

Régine made it very clear that she did not share that
generous emotion.

'He rarely brings them here,' she said coldly, 'they stay
in Monte Carlo – it's very raffish there, you know. But
perhaps he wanted a change of wheel tonight to change
his luck.'

To Christophe it appeared that, with the delicious twins at his side, Monsieur Selfridge had no need to trouble himself with the banalities of luck.

'They are both his little friends, do you suppose, the Mesdemoiselles Dolly?' he asked, eager to pursue his enquiries even though he was aware that Régine disapproved of the subject. On what grounds he was uncertain, for she had professed herself to be contemptuous of what she called 'bourgeois morality' and by her actions earlier that day had proved it.

'It is said that Rosy, whichever one that is, is his particular friend,' Régine answered, 'the other one is named Jenny. But it is my own view that the two of them are interchangeable.'

Great God! Christophe thought in awe, interpreting her words according to his own disposition – to have two beautiful women in one's bed at the same time!

The splendour of so lavish a feast of warm mouths, soft breasts and silky thighs dazzled his senses and caused to tremble within his evening trousers that part of him to which Régine had paid homage a few hours ago. His interest in roulette, such as it was, and his interest in the people in the salon, evaporated like a thin morning mist when the sun rises. He had eyes for nothing but the two gorgeous women at the distant table. It was not long before Régine noticed his mood. In the hour that they had been in the Casino she had won a few thousand francs and lost them again – not that she was there to gamble, only to be seen in society.

'You are bored with all this,' she said, with a gesture that embraced the salon, 'And so am I. There are other ways to amuse ourselves. Come – we'll leave the others here and send the car back for them.'

In the back of the beautiful limousine Régine sat upright and serene, a strand of diamonds woven into her hair, a costly fur wrap about her bare shoulders, a three-strand diamond necklace around her neck – all this of immense interest to Christophe, far more than the interest he took in her person. Between the passenger compartment of the vehicle and the chauffeur up front there was a thick glass panel, over which a blind of oyster coloured silk had been lowered. Outside it was dark, though not deserted, inside the limousine Christophe felt that he and Madame la Vicomtesse were isolated in a small and luxurious world of their own. If only it had been Nicolette with whom he was making this journey from the town to the Villa!

'You may amuse me,' said Régine, turning to look fully at him, 'but with care – I do not wish to arrive bedraggled, to be an object of derision to the servants.'

Christophe nodded acknowledgment and knelt on the thickly carpeted floor of the limousine to turn up her skirt over her knees. Her legs, clad in the most delicate silk stockings he had ever seen, were not at all bad, he decided on close inspection. Her ankles and calves were well-shaped, in fact, and it was only above the knees that there was rather too much flesh for elegance. But her thighs were warm to his hands, he noted as he turned the Schiaparelli creation further back – and warm thighs are a great encouragement to a man.

Régine raised her broad bottom from the seat so that he could turn her frock right up to her waist. Her stockings were held up by suspenders attached to a corselet, designed to compress her over-abundant belly. Christophe expected therefore to encounter lace-trimmed knickers, but to his surprise she wore no such garment that evening and, when her thighs moved apart on the seat, there was the tuft of bright brown hair he had viewed that afternoon. He stroked it cautiously, not at all sure whether it was her own hair tinted or a tiny wig made to fit over her mound.

'You may continue,' Régine said softly.

He seated himself beside her to let his fingers glide over the object of his attentions. For a time he teased the pouting lips, then reached underneath to gain admission. She was already moist within and as his fingers parted the inner lips and touched her swollen bud, she sighed pleasurably. He stimulated her quickly, intent on pleasing her but wanting it to be over as soon as possible. Régine responded swiftly, her belly and loins rolling rhythmically to press against his fingers – for by this time he had all four of them embedded inside her.

'Oh!' she exclaimed, 'something incredibly nice is about to happen!'

Christophe put the palm of his other hand flat on her bare belly to squeeze in time with his rubbing movements. In another moment or two Régine began to squirm, her legs as wide apart as they would go. Christophe, staring at her face, saw her eyes bulge suddenly, her mouth gape open – and then she was panting hoarsely in her ecstatic release.

When she was finished, he let her rest for a while, his hand lying lightly on her exposed thigh. To impress her he flicked the white silk handerchief from his breast pocket and murmuring 'If you will permit me . . . ' he wiped her gently dry and then rearranged her frock.

They arrived at the villa shortly afterwards. The imperturbable chauffeur opened the limousine door and handed Régine out. An attentive maid opened the house door for her to enter. Régine took all this for granted, Christophe noted, giving not the slightest acknowledgment of any service performed for her – not even the intimate service he had rendered on the journey home.

'Does Madame require anything?' the maid enquired.

'Bring a bottle of champagne to my room,' said Régine, 'with two glasses. And tell Henri to return to the Casino and wait for the others.'

Christophe felt that it was time to assert himself before he slipped back into the role of employee on scarcely a higher level than that of maid or chauffeur.

'Bring the champagne to the pool,' he instructed the maid. 'We wish to enjoy the moonlight.'

The maid stared at him, aghast at his presumption in countermanding Madame's instructions. Régine herself gave him a startled look, then nodded her consent.

'You may be right, Christophe,' she said when the maid had left them, 'perhaps I am too much in the habit of telling others what to do. But in the years I have been alone I have been compelled to make every decision for myself. That is not good for a woman.'

They sat on the patio, overlooking the pool, while the maid served wonderfully chilled champagne. It was a warm and cloudless night, a three-quarters full moon in the sky to light the scene – a night ideal for lovers, if they had been lovers. Christophe took up something Régine had said a little before.

'How long have you been alone?' he asked sympathetically.

Alone was not the word he would have used to describe her way of life, with a niece and a house full of guests, but it had been her own word.

'For nearly fifteen years.'

'Your husband, the Vicomte, was he killed in the War?'

'I wish he had been, the callous brute!' she answered angrily. 'But no – he left me. He lives abroad.'

Evidently Christophe had started his hostess along a route which would lead only to unpleasantness. To change the mood, on a sudden whim, he stood up and began to take off his clothes – tail-coat, white bow-tie, patent leather shoes. Régine looked at him in amazement.

'What are you doing?'

'I am going to swim in the moonlight – and you are going to do the same.'

'But I have no swimming costume here!'

'Nor have I,' he said, stepping out of his underpants to stand naked.

146

'How handsome you are, Christophe – come closer and let me touch you.'

'We are going to swim,' he said firmly.

'You expect me to undress here?'

'Why not? This is your house.'

He reached out his hand and she took it. Once on her feet she continued to protest as he undid the bodice of her frock and pulled it off her, revealing a corset in black moiré encasing her body from her breasts to the join of her thighs.

'But this is mad!' she exclaimed as he unfastened her suspenders.

'What of it?'

He rolled her stockings down her legs and undid the corset. She was as naked as he, except that she still had diamonds in her hair, around her neck and on her fingers. Christophe studied her for a moment, his head on one side. Deprived of support, her ample breasts hung heavily and her belly bulged more than could be considered attractive. All the same, the diamonds made a good showing. And if a man liked big breasts . . . Christophe took them in his hands, as if to assess their weight. Régine gave him a pleading look.

'Christophe, do not despise me,' she whispered.

'Why should I despise you?'

'Because I am no longer young and beautiful.'

'You're not so bad.'

He urged her to the edge of the pool with little pats of encouragement on her bare bottom.

'We can be seen from every window in the house,' she sighed.

By way of reply, Christophe put an arm around her waist and jumped, pulling her with him into the clear water. They hit the surface with a mighty splash and went under in a tangle of limbs. When his feet struck the tiled bottom of the pool Christophe released her and pushed upwards, shook the water from his hair and swam slowly

147

round in a circle until Régine broke the surface, spluttering and laughing at the same time.

'You are insane,' she told him, 'but I love you for it.'

As frisky as a young girl, she splashed water at him with her hands and he splashed back at her. They played this game for a long time, laughing at each other, until the water began to feel cool and Christophe decided that action was necessary.

'Time to swim now,' he said, 'five times up and down the pool.'

'It is too much – I shall drown!'

'I won't let you – and the exercise will make you feel good.'

He led the way at a leisurely pace and Régine struggled along beside him, puffing and panting after the first length of the pool. After the fourth she refused to go any further and clung exhausted to the edge. She was a strange sight, drops of water rolling down her breasts and her necklace gleaming in the moonlight. Her once carefully arranged hair was plastered close to her head and the strand of diamonds hung loosely round her ears.

'Let me help you out of the water,' said Christophe, 'and I will get towels from the changing room to rub you warm and dry.'

It was easier said than done. Régine was fatigued by the exertion of swimming so far and it required all of Christophe's strength to hoist her wet bulk up out of the water. But at last they stood on the side of the pool, he half-supporting her with an arm about her waist, she with one arm clinging round his shoulders to ease her trembling legs.

It was at this most vulnerable moment that an unexpected burst of laughter and some impertinent clapping intruded itself upon them! Their heads turned and, horror, there on the patio stood Régine's guests, elegant in evening attire and greatly amused by the spectacle before them.

'My God!' Régine wailed.

Her heavy body swung round quickly to present her back to the unwelcome spectators and so preserve from their curious eyes the sight of her oversize female attributes in their nakedness. Alas, the tiles were wet and smooth. In her haste to protect her modesty she lost her footing and went headlong into the water, taking Christophe with her, her legs thrashing high above her head as she fell, exposing all that she had wished to conceal.

The shock of the immersion, added to that of discovery in so compromising a situation, dazed Régine. She rose to the surface from the depths like a sounding whale, then sank again with no effort to save herself. Christophe, alarmed, flipped over and dived after her, found her on the bottom and got her by the back of the neck. He got her as quickly as he could to the surface and towed her to the side, her breasts and belly standing clear of the water like the superstructure of a sinking ship.

The men in the party rushed forward to assist, still choking back their laughter at these unfortunate circumstances. Régine was hauled limply out of the pool and arranged face-down, where she lay coughing up water. As Christophe got his hands on the edge to pull himself out of the water, one of the helpers accidently trod on his hand and, with a howl of pain, he sank back into the depths. When next he surfaced he saw that Régine had been turned over and that one of the rescuers had gallantly spread Christophe's discarded tail-coat over her wet bulk – for the sake of decency, of course. In the general solicitude for Régine, Christophe was entirely forgotten. He watched them pick her up and carry her into the house, then at last he felt it was safe to clamber out of the pool. He sat for a time with his arms around his knees, getting his breath back and feeling most uneasy about what had occurred.

'You will catch cold if you stay like that,' a voice said casually.

He looked up to see Nicolette standing near him.

'Everyone really is mad here,' he said slowly, 'it must be the perpetual sunshine which boils your brains.'

He got to his feet, ignoring her glance at his male part, shrunk to a diminutive size by the coolness of the water. Without bothering to dry himself he put on his shirt and shoes.

His hand still hurt but there seemed to be no bones broken.

'Shouldn't you be helping to look after your aunt?' he asked coldly.

'She's in bed and her maid is attending to her. She'll come to no harm – she's too tough for that.'

'With that I heartily agree,' said Christophe moodily. 'Goodnight, Mademoiselle.'

'Wait a minute – I want to talk to you.'

'But I want a hot bath and a glass of cognac.'

'Tell me one thing.'

'What?'

'Are you a gigolo?'

'I find that question insulting,' and he turned away from her and made for the house.

Nicolette trotted beside him.

'There's no need to be angry,' she said, 'most of Régine's young men are, you know. What makes you different?'

'The fact that I shall leave this madhouse forever the moment I am dressed and ready.'

'Then why were you invited to stay here?'

She pursued him with her questions through the house and right into the bathroom.

'It can be of no concern to you,' said Christophe, 'but an aunt of mine in Paris informed Régine that I was staying in Cannes at the Carlton. I knew nothing of this, or of your aunt, until a chauffeur arrived with an invitation to lunch.'

He turned on the taps and watched the hot water gushing into the bath. His wet shirt was clinging coldly to his skin and he was shivering.

'Now, if you will excuse me, it is my intention to get into the bath.'

She pouted at him and left. He was lying in the hot and scented water, his eyes closed peacefully, when Nicolette returned with a bottle of cognac and two glasses. She poured a generous measure for him, much less for herself, and perched on the edge of the huge bath to sip her drink. Christophe tasted the cognac and felt its warmth glowing inside him. Why Nicolette should be interested in his relations with her aunt he did not know, nor why she should be here in the bathroom with him, but he put it down to the general eccentricity which seemed to pervade the entire villa.

'That's interesting,' she said.

'What is?'

'When you got out of the swimming pool it was tiny, but now that you're in a hot bath it's grown considerably.'

Not believing what he had heard, Christophe stared up at Nicolette's beautiful oval face and in her large shining eyes he saw a lively curiosity. She was not Régine's niece for nothing, he decided.

'I ask myself whether, if you were naked in this bath and I were sitting there looking at you, you would accept my compliments or tell me to leave at once?' he said lightly.

'Who can say?' she replied. 'It would depend on my mood, I imagine.'

'And at the moment your mood is to observe a part of me which is not usually displayed to young ladies, except in special circumstances.'

'I believe that it's getting bigger still,' she remarked.

'While you sit there it will continue to do so.'

'I can't think why – after all, I am fully dressed.'

'But you are here with me, and that is enough to make it grow bigger.'

'Very much bigger, or just bigger?' she enquired.

'You must judge that for yourself,' Christophe sighed, watching the head of his rapidly stiffening part emerge above the surface of the bath water.

'Nicolette – what would Madame la Vicomtesse say if she knew that you were observing me in this way?' he asked.

'I don't know – or care. Are you afraid of her?'

'Why should I be?' he countered. 'In any case, I'm leaving early in the morning.'

'You said you were going tonight. Why the delay?'

'Because I am at last with the only member of this crazy household for whom I care.'

'Of course – when we first met. you declared that you loved me. That was in the pool – you appear to have many adventures there.'

'I told you the truth,' he said, absolutely sincere now. 'The moment I saw you my heart pounded as if it would burst. I knew at once that this was the love of a lifetime – a tremendous and enduring passion – even though I did not know who you were.'

'Very flattering, but I am not at all sure that I need another lover at present,' she said.

'I am not offering myself as *another* lover, Nicolette, but as one who loves you to distraction – there is a world of difference.'

'A bathroom is an unusual place for declarations of eternal love. But then, I never did believe in standing on ceremony. Apart from this great love of yours, Christophe, what else do you have to recommend yourself to me?'

So much sophistication at so young an age – Christophe blinked at the implications and was grateful for the schooling in affairs of the heart which he had received in Paris.

'Only what you can see,' he answered, 'I must tell you openly that I have very little money and no particular prospects.'

'What I can see is not without a certain attraction. It has grown *very* much bigger. Does hot water always have that effect on you?'

'It is not the water, as you well know – it is your nearness that has this effect, and always will.'

'Always is a long time – you should not exaggerate.'

'And love is a rare commodity, Nicolette.'

'So I believe, and God knows that my dear aunt spends enough money trying to buy it.'

Christophe held her gaze, looking into her eyes and willing her with all his heart to recognise the expression of his devotion in his own eyes. After a while she looked away almost demurely.

'I'm going to my room,' she said shortly, 'when you are ready, join me there and we will continue this conversation in more suitable surroundings.'

She was hardly through the door before Christophe was out of the bath and rubbing himself dry briskly. The farce in the swimming pool with Régine was no longer a humiliation, for it had caused Nicolette to take notice of him at last. Then he remembered that he could not present himself to Nicolette wearing a soaking wet evening shirt and creased black trousers – he would have to go to his own room first for something else.

But in the event he need not have troubled himself. When he went into her room she had undressed and was lying on her bed, propped up with big square satin pillows and wearing only a night dress made entirely of Chantilly lace, so short that the hem was only halfway down her thighs.

The next morning, before breakfast, Christophe and Nicolette ran away together. That is to say, before Régine or any of her guests were stirring, they loaded six pieces of luggage into the open tourer – one containing

Christophe's entire wardrobe and five containing a selection of Nicolette's clothes – and had the chauffeur drive them into Cannes to the railway station. There are, after all, ways of doing these things. On the long journey to Paris Christophe, besotted with love though he was, learned with relief that Nicolette was an heiress in her own right and not dependent on the Vicomtesse.

THE LITTLE ANGEL

The gullibility of human nature is such that almost everything that can be eaten or drunk without risk of death – and even some substances with that risk – has been used as an aphrodisiac to intensify desire. In the ancient days, as is well known and recorded, the nobility availed themselves of the testicles of stags and bulls for this purpose, no doubt sliced and lightly grilled in breadcrumbs.

In more recent times celery and asparagus have been considered efficacious, for no better reason than that they have the same general shape as the masculine part in a condition of excitement! Little need be said of the expensive potions and powders that can be obtained from dubious pharmacists, for while some of these are only tinctured sugar to deceive the purchaser, some are known to be truly inflammatory and to carry the danger of death in proportion to their power to arouse. It is less than thirty years since the President of the Republic, Félix Faure, died naked in the arms of his young mistress – of a surfeit of special pills he had taken to stimulate his desires. It was with the greatest difficulty that a public scandal was averted on that sad occasion.

And yet there is an aphrodisiac which never fails to have its effect, which carries no dangerous toxicity, and which costs nothing – the imagination. No one can have failed to observe how a man's imagination can be so stimulated that he mistakes an ordinarily pretty woman for a goddess of beauty, whose favours he must seek at

155

whatever inconvenience to himself. This was the case of André Giroud, who fell in love with a woman before he had seen her, entirely because of what he was told about her. The words he heard wrought such vivid images in his mind that his imagination became instantly obsessed.

It happened while he was dining in a restaurant one evening with a business acquaintance, Adolphe Lacoste, a man much older than himself and with a more extensive knowledge of the private arrangements of persons of importance in the circle of finance and business in Paris. The conversation ranged widely until Lacoste began to speak of the days before the War, when he had first come to Paris to establish himself. He had, he related to André, cultivated the acquaintance of a certain Monsieur Moncourbier, a personage whose financial dealings extended into many areas.

'Moncourbier was a great gourmet,' Lacoste said. 'He employed servants of talent, particularly his chef de cuisine. The first time he invited me to lunch at his private residence, the food was superb, the wines were a connoisseur's delight, the service was impeccable. He was about fifty years old and had no wife. His household was managed by a woman named Cabuchon. She was a small and tireless woman, somewhere between thirty and forty, I estimated, rather plain, one must say. She dressed somewhat above her station, to my way of thinking, though one would not describe her as elegant. A woman of the shopkeeper class who had been translated above her proper place in life.'

'She was Moncourbier's mistress, I suppose, plain or not,' said André.

'I thought for a time that was her station and naturally I was not impressed by Moncourbier's taste in choosing her. But the unfolding of events that afternoon led me to conclude that she was no more than his housekeeper.'

'Another woman was introduced?'

'Not exactly. Picture the scene – after that regal meal

Moncourbier and I were sitting at our ease in his impressive salon while the servants cleared the dining-room. Madame Cabuchon was with us and served us coffee – a blend fit for an Emperor. We were comfortably replete and in the very best of humours. To tell the truth, Moncourbier was more than replete – he was jovial from the effects of the wines we had enjoyed with lunch and the magnificent cognac we sipped with the coffee.'

'He became expansive?' André suggested. 'He confided some private affair to you?'

'He did more than that. He instructed Madame Cabuchon to bring his "little angel" to him. And while she was out of the room, he told me that the housekeeper's daughter was the light of his life. Naturally I assumed that she was his own child by the housekeeper, but he made it clear that she was not, as you will see. To my question of whether she was a pretty child he replied that she was astonishingly beautiful and that he adored her purity and innocence – and much more in that strain. I've forgotten his words after so many years but I remember that he was most eloquent – to the point where I felt embarrassed.'

'He was a gourmet, you said?'

'In everything. And as you would expect, he was grossly fat. I can still visualise him sitting there that afternoon, at ease in his own house, slightly drunk and full of geniality towards the whole world at that moment. His several chins shook as he talked to me and his vast paunch bulged out so much that he had to sit with his legs widely apart to accommodate it. It had been many years since he had last seen his own feet. He had spilled cigar ash down the front of his jacket and made no attempt to brush it off. He had very little hair left, except over his ears, and his bald pate was pink and flushed from the food and wine.'

'You paint a vivid picture,' André commented, 'though not an appealing one.'

'Moncourbier was not an appealing man, merely a very clever one.'

'And the housekeeper's daughter?'

'Ah, yes,' said Lacoste, 'that was a different matter – one in which Moncourbier displayed his gourmet's talent. Madame Cabuchon returned after some time with her daughter, whose name was Lucette, I was informed. I could hardly believe my eyes, I assure you! I saw a young girl of thirteen or fourteen at most, marvellously pretty, slender of form and with long and very light blonde hair.'

André shrugged dismissively and said:

'There are men with a taste for very young girls. I find it pathetic.'

'If it were as banal as that I would not weary you with the story.'

'Then I hope you will pardon my interruption and continue,' said André.

'With pleasure. Lucette entered the salon bare-foot. She was wearing a sleeveless garment cut like a tunic, round at the neck, tied at the waist with a length of golden cord, and ending about halfway down her thighs. The most surprising thing about this curious garment was that while it covered her young body, it did nothing to conceal it at all. It was made, you understand, of some gauze-like transparent tissue. And there was a further surprise – on her shoulders she had small golden wings.'

'Wings? I don't believe it.'

Lacoste nodded and smiled, pleased by the effect he had created on his listener.

'I give you my word. She had small wings made of gauze stretched on thin wire frames, attached to her back by some device or other.'

'She really was dressed up as a "little angel", you mean?'

'Exactly so, except for the indecency of her tunic. My astonishment must have shown on my face because Moncourbier chuckled and shook and spilled more cigar ash down his chest and then asked me if I had ever seen so beautiful a creature.'

158

'She was pretty, you said.'

'Exquisite, my dear André, in face and in body. Through her transparent garment I could clearly see her small growing breasts and their pointed pink tips. And, though I tried not to look, I observed between her thighs a most enchanting little mound, very lightly covered in blonde floss. When she went to Moncourbier and kissed him on his pink bald head, she presented her rear to me – and it was as adorable as her front view. Below the silly little wings she had a long and sinuous back like a kitten, and a bottom! How can I describe it – the cheeks of her bottom were like two very round and rosy apples.'

'Adolphe!' exclaimed André. 'You speak with such warmth that I begin to believe that you were physically attracted to this child.'

'That was the very question I was asking myself as I sat there, glass in hand, watching Moncourbier fuss over his living toy – for that's what she was, of course. Like you, I have always regarded old men who want little girls as perverse and unpleasant creatures, probably impotent. Yet even so I felt the attractions of that particular child, though with a sense of shame.'

'Was she at all self-conscious in your presence, the girl?'

'Not in the least. She smiled at me prettily when Moncourbier told her that I was a friend of his.'

'A remarkable scene,' said André. 'How did you escape from it?'

'There was no escape for me just then. I was lunching with Moncourbier in private to interest him in a business deal of the greatest delicacy – a matter of enormous importance to me at that time. To avoid giving him offence I was prepared to endure anything.'

'What happened, then?'

'You will find it hard to believe, but I give you my word that it is true. After a while Madame Cabuchon seated herself at the piano and struck a chord. Lucette went to stand in the centre of the salon, some distance from us, in a spot where the afternoon sun shone through the windows to create a long beam of gold across the floor. The effect was highly theatrical, for her tiny wings glittered and her tunic became even more transparent, if that were possible. Then – to her mother's accompaniment – she sang to us!'

'Well or badly?' André asked, the scene vivid in his mind's eye.

'Quite well. She had a pleasing little voice and evidently had been given singing lessons.'

'I hardly dare ask what it was that she sang.'

'You are right to be apprehensive,' said Lacoste, grinning at him. 'She sang the Ave Maria to that syrupy tune by Gounod!'

André laughed at the thought.

'My dear friend,' he said at last, 'the way you describe that scene makes it sound absolutely ridiculous. How did you prevent yourself from bursting into laughter?'

'It *was* ridiculous,' Lacoste agreed, 'a half-naked child warbling away in Moncourbier's salon. Yet the effect on Moncourbier was bizarre! I swear to you that tears rolled down his fat cheeks! Perhaps he was secretly gloating over the sight of her adolescent breasts, perhaps he was moved by the religious sentiment of the words she sang – perhaps both – I could not tell. But to him the experience was evidently sublime.'

'The girl had been trained by her mother to take advantage of Moncourbier's little weaknesses, of course,' said André.

'But of course! And she had trained the child very well. By the end of the recital old Moncourbier was sobbing into a handkerchief the size of a table-cloth. I hid my embarrassment because of my urgent need to get him to back my particular business venture, but there was worse embarrassment to come. After he had dried his cheeks, Lucette went to him and sat upon his knee and kissed his forehead. He called her his little angel a score of times.

He raised his eyes to the ceiling and implored God and the Holy Virgin and all the saints in heaven to protect this dear child – he went on like that for a long time.'

'And the mother?'

'Madame Cabuchon sat primly at the piano, a badly concealed smirk on her face.'

'He was a sentimentalist of some sort, this Moncourbier,' said André.

'Of some sort, yes. But during this lengthy monologue he addressed to Heaven I noticed that his pudgy hands were stroking Lucette's thighs under her short tunic. The question that came into my mind was, that if he did this openly with a stranger present, what familiarities did he permit himself at other times? Lucette was not at all troubled by his caresses – it was obvious to me that she was no stranger to them.'

'The mother's training must have been extensive.'

'All this time,' said Lacoste, 'old mother Cabuchon sat pretending to notice nothing. It was extraordinary. Moncourbier got redder and redder in the face, the child giggled as he stroked her, his arm up her tunic to the elbow. He lowered his head as far as his thick neck allowed and pressed his cheek to her tiny breasts under the thin material. It was only then that Madame Cabuchon rose from the piano and announced that it was time for Lucette to leave so that Monsieur Moncourbier could discuss business with his guest.'

'And that was that?'

'Moncourbier surrendered the child to her mother with reluctance, but he neither argued nor complained at the abrupt termination of his pleasure. Yet there was one thing which stayed in my memory after that day. La Cabuchon held the girl by the hand to lead her out of the room – and instructed her to say "*Au revoir*" to me before she went. Lucette turned her pretty face towards me, said the words and winked!'

André laughed again, but incredulously this time.

'That is imagination,' he told Lacoste, 'perhaps the child blinked.'

Lacoste shook his head, smiling.

'There was no mistake,' he said, 'Lucette winked at me deliberately. It was a tiny conspiratorial gesture that said more than words could. She was letting me know that she and I both knew that Moncourbier was a silly old fool.'

'Then she was a most precocious child, this little Lucette.'

'More than you can imagine – there was also an invitation in that wink.'

'An invitation? No, that's too much – I don't believe you.'

'You were not there to see it, André – but I was. The invitation from that remarkable child was to take her away from Moncourbier and become her playmate, if I had a mind to. And, of course, if I had the means to maintain her and her Mama in the style to which Moncourbier had accustomed them.'

'All that in one wink? Surely not!'

Lacoste shrugged.

'Believe what you like,' he said, not in the least put out. 'There was no intention on my part of accepting the child's invitation, of course.'

'That I believe. How did your business dealings with Moncourbier go?'

'Very successfully. Moncourbier was a clever man in financial matters, however foolish he may have been in other ways. The deal went through and we both made a very good profit out of it. For me that was a turning-point in my life. Until that time I had been successful in Orleans, where I was born, but this venture in association with Moncourbier was my debut in Parisian business circles. The War started the next year and the opportunities for a businessman to make money were unlimited – so long as one was not required for military service.'

'So I have been told,' said André. 'My services were

required and I still have a small piece of Boche shrapnel in my right thigh as a souvenir.'

'Alas,' said Lacoste, 'it was found that I had a disorder of the liver which prevented me from serving France in the trenches.'

'A sad circumstance,' André commented dryly. 'And your friend Moncourbier – doubtless he also found it impossible not to make a fortune during the War years?'

'To my astonishment, he did find it impossible. He made some calamitous investments. By 1916 he was in very deep water and borrowing from everyone he knew. He crashed the year after that – he was bankrupt for an enormous sum. There was even talk of prosecuting him – it seems that some of the means he had employed to try to prevent the crash were uncomfortably close to outright fraud. But in the end he managed to talk his way out of so dreadful a fate and disappeared from the sight of his reproachful creditors.'

'Is he still alive?'

'Certainly. The old rogue saved something from the disaster. He had a secret fund concealed somewhere out of reach. Since he was forced to quit Paris he has lived quietly in Biarritz. He has a small apartment there and a sufficient income to live modestly, or so I am informed.'

'But his great days are over, it would seem.'

Lacoste nodded and smiled sadly.

'Yes, a lesson to all of us to be prudent in business affairs,' he said.

'And Lucette, the little angel, now grown into a woman – did you ever hear of her again?'

'Our paths crossed again after the War, in the strangest circumstances. It seems that old mother Cabuchon also saved something from the wreck. Where she took her daughter to complete her education I do not know. But soon after the end of the War Lucette reappeared in Paris, an enchanting young beauty of about twenty, and soon made her mark in circles where her looks and other talents were of more importance than her virtue. She became the protégé of a Russian Prince for a year or two. He was not one of those Russian nobles who had fled penniless from the Bolsheviks to become a taxi-driver or restaurant doorman in Paris. By no means! He had transferred a good part of the family fortune here long before the War. Lucette was very well off with him.'

'And after him?' André enquired.

'There was someone else, you may be sure.'

'Is she still in Paris now?'

'Why yes, I am surprised that you have not made her acquaintance. Who her present protector is, I am unable to say. Presumably the man she is dining with over there.'

André turned to look across the restaurant at the table Lacoste indicated. He saw a woman of twenty-seven or -eight, her straw-blonde hair cut short and close to her head, framing a delicate profile. Her evening frock was of marvellous elegance – a tight-fitting bodice of white crêpe-de-Chine that left her slender arms bare and was very deeply decolléte. Around the long column of her neck she wore four strands of matched pearls – and similar bracelets on both wrists.

'I believe that the jewellery she is wearing was a present from the Prince,' said Lacoste.

What thoughts were stirred in André by the sight of this woman – she who was once in her childhood the 'little angel' of a rich man's fantasy. She had grown into a woman of great distinction. This Moncourbier, her first protector, he who had paraded her almost naked to please himself, what more had he done? André speculated feverishly. He had fondled her thighs in the presence of Lacoste without shame. After Lacoste had taken his leave, no doubt the old Turk had removed the child's tunic to feast his eyes on her body and run his hands over her tiny breasts. Had he gone even further – no, that would have been impossible if he were as fat as Lacoste described him. But he would have devised other little games . . . André was still staring in fascination at Lucette Cabuchon across the restaurant. Those childish thighs which had pleased Moncourbier were now long and sleek under the skirt of her expensive frock. The tiny breasts had rounded out into shapes of elegant beauty.

Lucette realised that she was being stared at, turned her head and looked straight at André. Her face was heart-shaped, her nose long and straight – but the most expressive feature of her beautiful face was her mouth, wide, generous and good-humoured. She returned André's look without embarrassment, until he realised with a start that he was behaving most impolitely in staring at her. He turned back to Lacoste, to find him grinning.

'I know the man she is with,' said André, to cover his confusion, 'his name is Malplaquet and he is a bullion dealer. Strange – I never thought of him as an adventurous man. Quite the contrary, he has always seemed to me to be dull and cautious. Yet there he sits with that marvellous woman, his face beaming with pleasure, as well it might!'

'My dear André – I believe that you are interested in Lucette!'

'Your little story has fascinated me, I admit. I feel that I must make her acquaintance. Let us finish our meal before they do and on our way out we will pause at Malplaquet's table and I will introduce you to him.'

'And in turn be introduced to Lucette,' said Lacoste.

'Naturally. It would give me pleasure to kiss her hand.'

'Her hand . . . of course,' said Lacoste, his knowing smile suggesting that other parts of Mademoiselle Cabuchon's exquisite person were well worth kissing.

'You said that your path and hers crossed again some years ago,' André prompted him, 'that suggests that she had remembered you, which is not easy to believe. It was a good many years after your disreputable friend had let you see her as a half-naked child.'

'Half-naked is so ambiguous a term,' said Lacoste, 'it

165

seems to suggest that she was naked from the waist up and clothed below, so exposing her tiny breasts – or that she was clothed above the waist and naked below, revealing her girlish charms. In fact, I was privileged to observe all her young treasures through that indecently transparent tunic. She had a tiny oval mole to the left of her dimple of a navel – no doubt she still has, if one were permitted to see her undressed.'

'Enchanting thought!' said André. 'If it is not too indelicate a question, on what terms did you renew your acquaintance with her when she was grown up?'

'It was entirely a business arrangement. I told you that she was under the protection of a Prince for a year or two at the end of the War. Like all Russians he was half-mad, of course. He had moods of black depression at times and then he would drink enormous quantities of cognac and take occasional shots with a revolver at the statues round his house – even at the pictures on the walls. And at his servants, if they were rash enough to intrude on his melancholy. He wounded a footman or two, but he was able to pay them off with large sums of money and so escape the attentions of the police. In short, he was like King Saul in the Old Testament. Lucette was the one who could soothe his black imaginings and restore him to himself.'

'She is brave, as well as beautiful,' said André.

'I think she was very fond of him. At other times the Prince became exuberant beyond reason. He gave vast parties and was absurdly generous. In one such interlude he gave Lucette a handful of deeds as a little present for pleasing him in some way or other. When he died, she consulted me as to whether to retain the property he had given her or to sell it.'

'I find it impossible to believe that she had remembered you, Adolphe.'

'You're quite right. It was her mother who had remembered my name from the days of my successful venture

with Moncourbier. After all, it was the old man's last big·
coup and Madame Cabuchon gave me the credit for it.'

'Was it a valuable property she had been given?'

'Not particularly so. It was a small, neglected and
unprofitable vineyard somewhere in the vicinity of St.
Etienne. I know nothing about such things so in turn I
consulted your esteemed uncle, Aristide Brissard, whom
I knew. I understood that he was always interested in the
purchase and sale of land, among other things.'

'What did he advise?'

'He said that, unprofitable or not, land of that sort
was the best of longterm investments. He suggested that
Lucette should keep it and spend money on putting it to
rights. Or if she decided against that, then he offered to
buy it from her at whatever price she regarded as fair.'

'Did he?'

'Oh yes, little Lucette wanted cash just then, not the
problems of vinegrowing. She sold it to him – and paid
me a commission for arranging the sale! By now I imagine
that your uncle has set his vineyard to rights and is making
a reasonable profit on it.'

'I'm sure of it,' said André, 'everything Uncle Aristide
touches produces a profit, believe me! And yet no one,
not even those inside the family, ever quite knows the
extent of his interests. If Mademoiselle Cabuchon was
short of money, I assume that the Prince died
unexpectedly.'

'The manner of his death was as bizarre as his life. He
was roaming the house in one of his black moods, revolver
in hand. Lucette had been sent for hurriedly – I think she
was visiting her mother at the time. The Prince, at the
top of his grand staircase, took a shot at a bust of Napoleon the Third, or some such worthy. The bullet glanced
off the bust, then off the marble balustrade and hit the
Prince in the leg. He fell head over heels down the staircase and broke his neck. The servants heard the noise of
his fall and guessed that he had hurt himself, but they

were too afraid for their lives to go near him – after all, they knew he had his revolver and could not be sure that he was unconscious. Alas, he was dead. He lay there at the foot of his own stairs until Lucette arrived much later and she had the courage to go to him. But he had been dead for several hours by then and there was nothing to do but send for a priest.'

'A terrible shock for a young woman,' said André thoughtfully.

'Yes, she was fond of him, as I believe I told you. She stayed with his body until the servants had carried him back upstairs and laid him out on his bed. She knelt and prayed for his soul at the foot of the bed while the priest carried out his sad office. Then, there being no more to be done, she packed her jewels and clothes and sent for a taxi to take her away from there. And if she packed a little more than was rightfully hers – a small objet d'art or two – who shall blame her? She had to face the expense of setting up her own home and maintaining herself in good style until such time as another rich man felt constrained to take care of her living costs.'

'From what you have told me about her,' said André, 'I feel that she is a most remarkable woman. If you have finished, let's call for the bill and go across to Malplaquet's table. I must meet her.'

So he was introduced to her. The next day he telephoned her. Two days later she accepted his invitation to dinner – the brief process was totally uncomplicated because of André's determination to recognise no obstacles or refusals. The truth was that in his mind she had become the most desirable woman in Paris. Reason should have informed him that, like all beautiful women, Lucette was possessed of a head, two arms, two breasts, two legs – and certain other enchanting bodily attributes of the female. But the voice of reason goes unheard when a man's imagination is aroused. If a friend had been disposed to discuss with André the nature and quality of

Lucette's charms, then he – with no direct experience of them – would undoubtedly have been prepared to argue that she had breasts more shapely than those of any other woman, that her legs were more elegant, her skin smoother, her personality more engaging, her conversation more amusing – and this from no more than a minute's formal conversation when he was introduced to her in a restaurant! Lacoste's vivid account of some episodes in her early life had fixed in André's mind the idea that Lucette was a semi-divine creature of love, trained from childhood in the arts of delighting men, immensely skilled in the ways of pleasure and passion.

They dined together, they talked, they danced and drank champagne. It was well after two in the morning when André escorted her back to her apartment in the rue de Monceau, near the park. She unlocked the door herself and went in without a word. André following close behind. It was not until they had traversed the apartment and were in her bedroom that she turned and stared briefly at him, as if in surprise.

'Oh, you're here,' she said with a half-mocking smile.

'But of course,' he answered, sure that he was on the verge of experiencing a night of considerable pleasure with her – or at least as much of the night as was left.

'How hot and uncomfortable I am!' she sighed.

It was a very warm summer night, to be sure, still and airless, even with the long windows wide open. Lucette's elegant frock covered only those areas of her body which decency and good style required, but there was a light sheen of perspiration on her pretty neck and her bare back. André, in full evening attire, was feeling the heat himself – his shirt was stuck clammily to his back and he was wet under the arms.

'I must take a cool bath,' Lucette declared, 'I couldn't stand being touched in this state. It would be inconsiderate to wake my maid at this hour, so you must assist me.'

'With the greatest of pleasure,' André murmured fervently.

Lucette kicked off her high-heeled shoes, loosened something at her waist, shrugged off the shoulder-straps of her cyclamen-red frock and let it slide down her body to the floor. She stood revealed in ivory lace knickers and her stockings – apart from her four-stranded pearl choker, of course. André contemplated her perfectly rounded little breasts, his urgent part rising to attention in his trousers as he tried to imagine the bliss of kissing the delicate pink buds displayed before him.

'Do you think you can take my stockings off without ruining them?' she asked.

He went down on one knee and touched his fingers to her embroidered garters, trying to discern the shape of her mound through the thin material that hid it from sight. Slowly he eased one garter down from where it held her stocking-top halfway up her creamy-skinned thighs, slid it over her knee and all the way down her superb leg and over her small foot. He repeated the performance with the other one, and then rolled her stockings down, finding them as fine as cobweb to his touch.

Before he could reach for the only garment she now wore – the last lace covering of her feminine modesty – she stepped away from him and moved across the room. After a moment of stunned immobility, he leaped to his feet and went after her, desperate not to let her escape him for a second now that he had touched her thighs, though only with his finger-tips and that briefly. She was in her bathroom, bending over to control the taps to produce the cool temperature of water she wanted. It was a very pretty bathroom, the walls a pale gold colour, hung with small pictures and silhouette portraits, but at the moment André had eyes for nothing except the delicious cheeks of her bottom, the ivory material stretched over them as she learned forward.

She took a crystal bottle from a side-table and poured

170

some of its expensive contents into the water. At once the water frothed up and a delicate scent permeated the air.

'Sit there and talk to me,' Lucette said to him over her bare shoulder.

He seated himself on an armchair of wickerwork lacquered gold and attempted to converse as best he could, though his attention was transfixed by Lucette's long and narrow back and the curves of her bottom. He broke off what he was saying and caught his breath as she hooked her thumbs in the sides of her ivory knickers and pushed them down her legs, her back still towards him. He stared at the satin-smooth skin of those marvellous little globes, his heart beating faster. He almost caught a glimpse of blonde fur between her thighs as she stepped into the bath – or did he? Perhaps it was only a trick of his fevered imagination.

Lucette lay in the water, only her head above the scented foam. She rested the back of her blonde head on the edge of the bath, where a Greek key pattern in pale blue traced the outline of the rim. It was only then that André noticed that she still had her choker on – the strands of pearls set off the column of the neck perfectly as it rose from the water.

'Oh, that's good,' she said in satisfaction, 'I was hot enough to burst!' ·

'That would be a catastrophe of the first order,' he said, smiling at her.

'Well, if not burst, then at least melt away,' she said.

'That too would be a calamity. You are so adorable that not one gramme of you must be lost.'

She smiled at him as if he had said something witty.

'You look very hot yourself, André. Why don't you take your clothes off and get in here with me? There's plenty of room.'

What man could have hesitated over such an invitation? In moments André's black evening clothes were off and

171

strewn across the wicker chair, followed by socks, underwear – everything, and he stepped into the cool water to sit down facing Lucette. She raised her knees and sat up a little to give him more space. The change of position caused her breasts to bob up just above the surface, their pink tips touched with the scented foam of the bath essence.

'Is that better,' she asked.

'Much,' he answered in relief.

'You looked like a boiled lobster in those clothes.'

'I was beginning to feel like one. Though truth compels me to confess that it was not entirely the effect of a warm night. There was another and more important reason, as you must be aware.'

'Truly? What was that?'

'You are laughing at me. You understand very well, dear Lucette, that the sight of you naked in your bath is more than enough to raise any man's temperature.'

He was sitting with his legs outside hers, his feet just touching her hips on either side.

'Thank heaven we cooled you down in time,' she said.

Even as she spoke, she reached forward through the delicately opaque water – he felt her hand touch the inside of his open thighs and take hold of his upright stem of flesh.

'The water hasn't cooled this fellow at all,' she commented with a smile.

'How could it, when you are so close to me?' he murmured.

Lucette's bath essence produced an emollient effect on the water, and no doubt was intended to produce the same effect on her skin. André experienced a sensation of pleasant slipperiness as her hand moved slowly up and down his tautness.

'Oh heavens, it's getting hotter!' she exclaimed. 'How is that possible?'

172

'Like a volcano, it is building up its forces for an eruption,' he told her.

Lucette rose to her knees and moved forward to straddle his thighs. Under the water he felt her hands positioning him before she lowered herself carefully, her small navel with the oval mole alongside it disappearing back under the surface as she sank down. The mole was as Lacoste had described it, was the silly thought in André's mind at this marvellous moment. He sighed as the cool touch of water was replaced by the warm clasp of soft flesh. His hands moved with gentle appetite up her wet body to cup her little breasts.

'Have you shared a bath with many women?' she asked casually.

She was moving gracefully up and down his embedded pride.

'You are the first,' he admitted, his pleasure immense at what was happening to him.

'Really?' Lucette said. 'Does that mean that you prefer in hot weather to make love under a shower? I've never much cared for that myself – the standing position is not a comfortable one.'

'Yet in a sudden emergency . . .' he sighed, 'even a standing position is acceptable.'

'In circumstances that make it the only possibility, everything is permissible,' she agreed softly. 'Are there many emergencies of that sort in your daily life, my poor André?'

'Not in the ordinary way . . . but there have been occasions . . .'

'How very interesting – tell me of the most recent one,' she teased him as she maintained her slow up and down ride on his imprisoned part.

'Tonight – while we were dancing,' he responded at once, 'you must have been aware of a certain pressure against you as I held you to me.'

'Oh that!' she said lightly, 'that was quite normal. Every

173

man I dance with gives me similar proof of his emotions towards me – anything less would be ungallant and insulting. No, my dear, you used the word *emergency*. That refers to a far more serious event. Tell me of your last real emergency.'

'It was at a ball given by the Marquise de Casa Maury back in the spring . . . perhaps you were also a guest?'

'What caused your desperation at the ball?'

'A woman to whom I was introduced and with whom I danced. I had consumed a great deal of champagne . . . and as we moved to the music I glanced down her frock and saw her breasts quite plainly – at once I was on fire – I can't explain why even now . . . yet I knew that unless . . . '

His words trailed off as the sensations of pleasure through his body intensified.

'Go on – what did you do?'

But before André could find suitable words to describe the events that befell him at the Marquise's ball, an emergency of a more expected kind silenced him – a crisis induced by the slow massage of his stiffness by that marvellous inlet of Lucette's beautiful body which a generous Providence had designed for this very purpose. A series of miniature tidal waves rolled the length of the scented bath water as his body convulsed in long spasms and paid her the compliment due to her talents as a lover.

In the weeks that followed his first encounter with her in her bath, André came to understand and appreciate how remarkable Lucette's talents were. The usual course of intimate events between men and women can be described in a few words – it is to kiss, to remove the clothes, to caress each other, to join bodies together in whichever of the well-known positions seems best to them – and so to induce in each other those sublime sensations that accompany the discharge of passion. With Lucette it was never on any occasion either so familiar or so

174

uncomplicated. There was in her nature, André discovered, a deep-seated desire for play-acting, which made of each act of love a drama pitched in a different mood – tender, comic, sardonic – or whatever her mood dictated.

There was a time in her childhood, he reminded himself, when she had played at being old Moncourbier's 'little angel' while his hand felt between her legs. Now that she was a grown woman she still enjoyed acting out roles, though they had become much more sophisticated since those far-off days. She had another attribute, which he only slowly understood – from seemingly casual conversation she gathered tiny indications and analysed them until she came to know a man's unspoken fantasies. To his astonishment, he would find himself playing them out with her at some later meeting! Astonishment was by no means the only emotion aroused by her on such occasions, of course – there was also intense pleasure and surging desire.

Take, for example, an afternoon not long after André had become established as her lover. She greeted him in her salon looking marvellously chic, her golden hair smooth to her head, her long arms bare – and much else besides, for she was wearing a single garment of crimson silk, much like lounging pyjamas. It was all in one piece – of necessity, for the upper part covered only her pretty breasts, leaving her sides – and her back – uncovered. Even that does not quite do the creation justice, for as André suddenly perceived, the back was cut so low that the beginning of the enchanting crease between the cheeks of her bottom was just visible. The trouser section fitted very closely round her long thighs, then flared out from the knees to give very wide bottoms that hid her feet and showed only the high heels of her white shoes.

'I want to dance,' she said, before he could utter a word, and whirled away from his arms to the gramophone, wound it up and put on a record.

175

André was instantly ready to indugle her whims, for experience had shown him that the result was always pleasurable. He moved aside a chair or two, took her in his arms and led her, dipping and striding, in the steps of a popular tango across the room. At first his hand rested lightly on the smooth skin of her bare back, up between her shoulder-blades. Inevitably, as the dance continued and he warmed to it – and to her – the hand slid downwards, at first to her waist and, eventually, lower still until his little finger rested comfortably in the crease where her bottom began. Lucette's eyes sparkled at the touch and the half-mocking smile that was so characteristic of her appeared on her face.

When the music ran out, André rewound the gramophone while Lucette turned over the record. He took her in his arms, ready to move off, his hand now thrust down the low-cut back of her lounging pyjamas to rest fully on her satin-skinned bottom – for as he had suspected, she wore no underwear that afternoon.

'Ah, you intend to be impolite, Monsieur Giroud,' she said in mock disapproval. 'You believe that because I asked you to dance with me you can give yourself liberty to handle me at will! Two can play at that game, Monsieur.'

Before he had time to comprehend her intent, she had unbuttoned the jacket of his beautiful blue suit – and the buttons of his trousers! Her adroit fingers flicked his male part out into full exposure, she put one hand on his shoulder, the other on his outstretched hand – and they were dancing again. As they performed the intricate steps, André was acutely aware of the sensation of his exposed part flopping about in this indecent freedom. But not for long – the very sensations he experienced quickly stimulated him to the point where what had been limp before now became firm and upright. After that, each time that Lucette brushed past him, the silk of her garment touching his aroused part, little spasms of pleasure ran through him, until his face was pink with emotion.

They were close to the gramophone when the music stopped.

'Did you enjoy that dance?' she asked him.

'Very much. I think that we should sit the next one out, chérie.'

'Not yet – I want to dance again. Turn the handle while I choose another record.'

This time she selected a slower piece of music, one that made it possible for her to press her body closely against him. The slide of silk over his bared stem provoked such delicious tremors of emotion in André that he hardly heard the music at all. His hand was right down the back of her pyjamas to grasp and squeeze those soft round cheeks.

'Lucette . . . ' he murmured dizzily, 'come, let us sit down . . . '

'I love this tune – don't you?' she asked, her face with its half-mocking, half-sensual smile turned up towards his, 'I often ask the band to play it for me when I'm out dancing. Of course, here at the Marquise's ball one cannot make requests of the band – that would be presumptious and ill-mannered. But I am so glad they are playing it.'

The night of the Marquise's ball! Memories floated up into André's mind, half-dazed as it was by the passion stirring in him. The urgency of his desire that night after dancing twice with Françoise . . . his rapid and fevered search to find some empty and convenient corner anywhere to conceal her and himself while he relieved that tremendous desire she had aroused.

He dropped Lucette's hand and put his arm round her waist. The hand fondling her rump gripped hard and pressed her belly against his throbbing passion. He gave a long sigh and fountained his tribute up the front of her crimson pyjamas. Lucette held him by the waist with both hands, rubbing her silk-clad body against him until he had finished.

'Yes, I see that you do like that tune,' she said, as calmly as if nothing had occurred, though her eyes were laughing at him.

'I find it very exciting,' André responded, trying to match her mood.

'Of that you have provided adequate proof,' she said, breaking away from him. As she stepped back he saw the evidence of his passion in a darkening stain on her pyjamas.

'I must take this off at once and put it to soak before any irreparable damage is done,' she observed.

'I shall replace it,' he offered at once.

'Yes, but in the meantime, dear impetuous André, I can hardly let my maid see me in this condition. Perhaps you will accompany me to my bedroom to assist me in removing this compromised pyjama suit.'

'But of course,' he said, smiling at her.

It occurred to him that his male part, now beginning to loll after its exertions, was still openly displayed. He lowered his hands to put the matter right and Lucette laughed at him.

'No need to hide it away,' she said, 'I'm sure that we shall find a further use for it when you have helped me out of my clothes.'

Naturally they found a use for it, that day and many days to follow. It would not be too much to say that Lucette had a touch of near-genius in finding uses for that interesting part of André's anatomy, making his private visits to her occasions of surprise and delight. In public her behaviour was always correct, whether they were at the races or dining out or attending someone's reception together or at the theatre. At such times she was a lively and amusing companion, but with no hint of her ability to devise unusual and secret pleasures, unless in the half-mocking smile that crept over her pretty face from time to time.

As was to be expected, the once amicable relations between André and Jacques Malplaquet turned sour. Malplaquet had once been privileged to enjoy Lucette's little games and now that he had been displaced in her affections by André he took it badly. He went so far as to ignore André's greeting when their paths crossed, turning his face deliberately away from him, even at social functions. André shrugged and paid no attention – after all, that was life. He felt that Malplaquet might have conceded defeat a little more graciously, but he never voiced this opinion to anyone, not even mutual friends. Since Malplaquet adopted that offended attitude, there was nothing to be done. There was a rumour that came to André's ears that his dispossessed rival had lost a lot of money on an ill-considered business venture and he was sorry for the man – but he felt it best not to approach him to offer condolences, for that surely would have been taken amiss. The rumour also said that Lacoste, of all people, had made money in the same deal, which seemed most unlikely to André, who knew that Lacoste had never dabbled in that branch of business. But it was only a vague rumour, one of many circulating among a certain circle of businessmen and André gave it no more than a passing thought. His life held far more pleasant mysteries to think about – such as what would be Lucette's next whim.

Lucette expressed herself as much impressed by André's abilities as a lover, by the style of his clothes, the trappings of his style of life – by almost everything about him. Her open admiration greatly increased the satisfaction which André derived from his liaison with her. She was even impressed by the fact that he was a member of the Brissard family, through his mother.

'I have met Monsieur Aristide Brissard,' she told him with some pride, 'he advised me over a small matter of business a few years ago. He is a most distinguished man – I could almost have fallen in love with him. And you are his nephew – anyone could guess that – you have the same air of distinction as he.'

'To be precise, I am only half Brissard,' said André modestly, 'my father is also distinguished. The name of Giroud is highly esteemed in certain circles.'

'But of course,' said Lucette.

She was sitting on his lap at this moment, a circumstance which imparted a strange touch to their conversation. They had been to hear Lucienne Boyer sing that evening and were delighted, as was all Paris, by her tender love songs and the gracefulness of her slender figure and, pale oval face. Afterwards they had enjoyed a late supper and a bottle or two of excellent chilled Sancerre, before returning to Lucette's apartment for the main event of the evening.

Lucette was looking more than usually elegant that night. Her blonde hair was cut very short and smooth to her head, parted on one side – the effect was boyish, except for the delicately feminine profile and the thin arched eyebrows. Her frock was simplicity itself – the simplicity which only the most expensive of master couturiers can achieve. It was of ivory silk, sleeveless and cut deep between her impertinent breasts and cut even lower down her back – close fitting down to the waist, then a fuller skirt to her knees, showing off her slender and immaculately shaped legs.

André was sitting on the sofa in her salon, while she poured him a glass of cool champagne and brought it to him. The sofa was from the illustrious past, André had thought the first time he saw it, to judge by the shape of its feet and legs and the excellence of the carving on them. But it had been stripped of whatever upholstery its makers had given it and recovered in gold damask to match the style of Lucette's salon. He expected that she would seat herself beside him, but after she had handed him the glass, she asked him to put his feet up.

Most obligingly, André swung up his legs and half-sat, half reclined, the length of the sofa. He raised an eyebrow in surprise and delight as she leaned over him to undo the buttons on his white evening waistcoat – and then the buttons of his black trousers.

'Ah!' he exclaimed in pleasure as she pulled up his shirt-front and released his most cherished part from its place of concealment. From the moment they had entered her apartment it had begun to stir itself in anticipation of what was to follow. The touch of her hand completed the process and it was at full stretch in an instant.

She straightened her back and stood looking down at what she had laid bare. Then with her smile of secret amusement she took hold of her skirt and slowly, centimetre by centimetre, raised it. André was fascinated as the rising hem revealed her garters of pale pink trimmed with tiny white rosebuds, her stocking-tops, then the satin skin of her thighs. Still the hem rose – exquisitely slowly – to the level where he expected to see the lace-trimmed edge of her underwear. But there was only the smooth pale columns of her thighs and his heart was thumping in his breast.

The upward movement stopped and André raised his eyes to her face. She was staring at him with an expression of amusement on her face, her scarlet-painted lips open to display her small white teeth.

'*Voyeur*!' she teased him.

'Yes,' he said, agreeing with her wholeheartedly. 'How beautiful you are, Lucette!'

'You think I've got good legs, do you?'

'Your legs are enchanting – and so is the rest of you.'

'Words are easy enough,' she said, smiling again, 'but the way that great thing of yours is jumping about gives me confidence that you mean what you are saying.'

181

'Assuredly,' André replied. 'He is nodding his head in agreement with me.'

Her skirt rose another centimetre and André sighed loudly as he spied at last the join of her thighs and the beginning of her blonde floss. It rose higher – and all was revealed to him – her plump little mound and its silky fur coat.

'But you are not wearing any underwear!' he babbled foolishly.

She held the front of her frock up around her waist, so that he half-glimpsed her navel and the little oval mole to the side of it.

'It was too hot this evening,' she answered casually, straddling his lap as he reclined on the sofa.

'You mean that all evening . . . ' André gasped as her hand took hold of his upright part firmly to guide it into the direction she intended, ' . . . you were wearing nothing but that flimsy frock?'

'Ah, now if you'd known!' she said with a smile.

'If only I had known!' he murmured as she sank slowly across him to push his firmness into her soft recess.

'You'd have had your hand up my clothes all evening, I suppose,' said Lucette. 'Next time we dine out together you can amuse yourself by speculating whether I've got any underwear under my frock or whether I'm bare-bottomed. That will keep you in a state of confusion for hours.'

She arranged her ivory-white skirt over her thighs so that he could see nothing of what was happening. But the sensations were more than adequate to keep him informed of her intentions – she was rocking slowly and gently back and forth, a movement almost imperceptible to the eye (particularly the eye made dim with emotion) but the effect on his imprisoned flesh was most gratifying.

'It would be polite to drink a toast to me,' she informed him, her hand gesturing towards the glass of champagne he still held.

'Forgive me,' he said, trembling with pleasure, 'you are so adorable and so beautiful that I was struck dumb for a moment. I raise my glass in salute to you, dear Lucette.'

As best he could in the circumstances, he lifted the glass and gulped down the champagne. Her rocking had become a little faster and firmer as she spoke and little spasms of exquisite feeling were rippling through his belly and groins.

Had another person entered the room just then – Lucette's maid, for example – nothing unseemly was to be seen. The juxtaposition of the two on the sofa was most unusual, of course. But apart from that, André was still elegant in his formal evening attire, his white bow tie neatly in place above his stiff shirt-front, his tail-coat on, his black patent leather shoes sticking out of the ends of his trousers. Lucette, astride him, had arranged her full white skirt almost primly, so that not even her knees were uncovered. Yet underneath that silk skirt – ah, what voluptuous sensations were being experienced by the closely joined parts! It was at this moment that Lucette introduced the topic of André's connection with the Brissard family. The conversation was incongruous in the extreme, yet André attempted to play the role required of him in Lucette's game.

'It is a great honour to be so intimately connected with a member of so important a family,' she said dreamily, rocking away.

'As for me, it is a privilege to be on such close terms with so beautiful and elegant a person as you,' André gabbled, hardly knowing what he was saying.

'Ever since I met your Uncle I have wanted to know more about your family,' Lucette murmured, her delicate movements becoming almost jerky.

'You shall! Whatever you want!' he gasped.

'Oh, André – I believe that something delightful is going to happen to me!'

'And to me!'

A moment later she was writhing on his lap as she reached the apex of her passion, her curled fingers digging into his belly through her skirt. André bucked hard as his own critical moments arrived, flooding her with his torrential release.

For a woman like Lucette, a man will do anything she requires – for skills like hers are rare and highly prized. It is not to be wondered at that many a woman who has reached the pinnacle of wordly success as the mistress of a rich and important man is – if her friends spoke the truth – plain of face and undistinguished of figure. Yet in spite of these natural disadvantages she becomes the owner of grand houses, a chateau perhaps, jewels, wardrobes full of the finest clothes, expensive motor-cars – even power, for many will approach her with a fine present in the hope that she will put a word in their favour into the ear of the man she has enchanted by her abilities in the bedroom. So it has always been – the portraits of the mistresses of Kings from our glorious history show them to be only averagely good-looking, even though it is certain that the Court painter flattered them to a considerable extent in his work.

Imagination – that is the unfailing aphrodisiac – and Lucette had it in full measure. One memorable afternoon when André called upon her, she announced that she proposed to give him a body massage. In the ordinary way, a masseur treats the client's body with the hands. Lucette's version was far more interesting than that. She massaged André's body with her own.

'Imagine that you have travelled to the Far East,' she instructed him, 'I am small and have golden skin, black hair and slanting eyes – yes? I am about to demonstrate to you one of the cultural specialities of my country.'

That she was blonde, tall and had alabaster skin was no barrier to André's imagination when it was aroused.

He bowed to her, half-seriously and half-comically, and requested her to be so kind as to proceed.

Her bed had been stripped of sheets and covered with an impermeable sheet of thin black rubber. André undressed completely and lay on it while she covered his body and limbs with sweet-smelling oil. He watched her with great interest as she sat naked beside him and oiled her own body too.

'Face down,' she said.

He turned over, his face cradled on his slippery arms and felt the weight of her slender body on his back. She lay on him and slid herself up and down his spine, her hands hooked over his shoulders to give herself a grip. André shuddered with pleasure as he felt her soft breasts squashed against his skin, rubbing up and down gently – and her warm belly sliding over him. As she moved downwards he experienced the exquisite sensation of the soft hair between her legs rubbing over the cheeks of his bottom.

'Honourable white master like Oriental massage?' she enquired in a mock-Chinese accent.

'Oh, yes!' he sighed, trying to savour all the sensations at once.

By the time she had been on his back for five minutes, André was in a high state of arousal. She pretended to be astonished when he turned over to her command and revealed his male projection at full stretch.

'Honourable white master think bad thoughts,' she said in the sing-song accent, 'maybe massage too much for white foreigners. This person stop now.'

'No, don't stop!' André pleaded.

She sat astride his belly and slithered up and down, massaging him from chest to thighs with that most tender part between her legs. Her eyes were sparkling.

'Slave girl begin to think bad thoughts now,' she said, 'must change massage before this person brings shame on herself.'

She indicated that he should part his legs so that she could lie on the rubber between them and massage him with her small slippery breasts, starting at his navel and working slowly downwards until his upright part was quivering between those pliant delights.

André was near the end of his tether. He grasped at her shoulders to pull her up his body and turn her onto her back so that he could assume the superior position and plunge into her. But she was so slippery from the oil that he could not take hold of her – each time he attempted it she slid easily out of his hands.

'Now honourable visitor understand purpose of oil,' she giggled, 'only way poor girl can be saved from ravishment by every customer.'

André was in heaven – experiencing that sweet frustration and certain of eventual success. His chest heaved to his rapid breathing, his distended part slithered across Lucette's belly as he strove to roll her underneath him, she laughing and resisting to prolong for a few more moments the thrilling struggle.

Yet it was at this supreme moment that their game was interrupted by an insistent tapping on the bedroom door!

'Go away!' Lucette cried out furiously.

'Madame,' her maid's voice insisted, 'it is a matter of the utmost urgency!'

'What is it? Is the building on fire?'

'No, Madame – you must come to the telephone. There is an emergency.'

To André's horror Lucette freed herself from him and skipped off the bed. She leaned over to kiss his mouth, her hand giving his straining appendage a playful tug.

'Be patient for only a moment,' she murmured, 'while I put an end to this nonsense.'

He watched her walk swiftly across the room to the door, still naked, her marvellous body gleaming with oil. She turned for an instant to smile lasciviously at him and was gone. Poor André lay on the impermeable sheet, hands under his head, staring at his disappointed but still uprearing limb. So near, he thought, another second or two and she would have surrendered! And you, dear friend, would have slid yourself into that soft little slit of hers! Not all the telephones in the world could then have prevented you from discharging your duty. But this! To be almost at the moment of supreme pleasure – and then abandoned! It is atrocious! As soon as she returns and you have relieved me of this monstrous burden of desire, I shall demand an explanation from Lucette, believe me. Nothing like this shall ever happen again – I give you my word.

To a man in André's condition seconds are like hours. He twisted about on the bed in his discomfort, grinding his teeth and clenching his fists. There was no clock in the room, his own watch was with his clothes and he had no way of knowing how much time had elapsed since the dreadful moment when Lucette slipped out of his hands. He groaned and rolled over face down – then gasped as the slide of his sensitive member along the oily rubber sheet almost precipitated the crisis for which his body was yearning. Hurriedly he turned over onto his side to avoid the catastrophe, at the very moment when the door was flung open with a crash and Lucette rushed in, her eyes blazing with anger.

'Pig!' she screamed at him. 'Traitor! Deceiver! I never want to see you again!'

André stared at her in amazement, wondering if perhaps some bad news conveyed to her by telephone had rendered her insane. But what?

'What are you saying, Lucette?'

'You have betrayed me!'

'Not so! I have not been with another woman since the day I met you.'

'I'm not talking about that! You know very well what I mean!'

She was a magnificent sight, naked and enraged, as she

paced up and down at the foot of the bed, her breasts and belly gleaming with oil.

'I really don't understand what you are saying. How have I betrayed you?'

'The Verney business – you deliberately lied to me to make a fool of me!'

'What Verney business?' André asked, puzzled by her words.

Then his memory stirred and he recalled telling her casually, a week or two before, something his cousin Maurice Brissard had confided to him.

'But anything I said about that is a private family matter,' he said, becoming angry himself at the ludicrous situation he was in.

'Because of your lies I have lost a lot of money,' Lucette said with great bitterness. 'And a good friend of mine has lost millions. I suppose you find that amusing? Get out of here!'

She strode to where his clothes lay across a chair, bundled them up and flung them through the open bedroom door, pointing after them with a shaking finger.

'Get out!' she screamed.

André was seething with rage as he got up and stalked out of the room, hearing the door slam behind him and a key turn in the lock. It did not improve his temper to see Lucette's maid peeping at him from around another door, her hand going to her mouth to cover a grin as she spied his glistening member waving about in front of him. He took his clothes into the bathroom to dress away from the maid's sniggering and realised that he needed to bath to rid himself of the massage oil that covered him from neck to knees. Nevertheless, he had no intention of remaining a moment longer than necessary in Lucette's apartment.

He took a big fluffy towel to wipe himself as dry as possible before dressing, muttering incoherently under his breath as he scrubbed at his shoulders and chest. His anger was not directed against Lucette, as might have been thought, but against his cousin Maurice. André had fitted the puzzle together in his mind – Maurice had intentionally given him information which he had passed on heedlessly to Lucette – and for some reason André did not yet understand, the information had been false. It was Lucette, that marvellous lover, who had incurred a financial loss as a result! And at what a moment this treachery on the part of Maurice had been discovered! Maurice must be made to suffer!

Muttering in this fashion to himself, André rubbed his belly briskly to soak up the oil, then his stiff part – utterly without regard for the condition it was in! At once a spasm of ecstasy flashed through him like a lightning-bolt. He jerked the towel away, contracted the muscles of his belly tightly to arrest the process that he knew was beginning – but it was too late! There was a roaring in his ears and his heart pounded – his fleshy staff bounded and André doubled over helplessly as it spat its essence into the bath-tub in long jets. Yet even in this moment of humiliation, in his mind's eye he saw a vision of Lucette as she had been in the bedroom, naked and magnificent, pointing at him in her fury, her pretty breasts heaving with the vehemence of her denunciation of him.

When, after a visit to his own home for a bath and change of clothes, André confronted his cousin, his mood was one of implacable hatred. He spoke loudly and with malign intensity, accusing Maurice of double-dealing, perjury, deception, fraud – whatever came into his mind. His mood grew even blacker when Maurice burst into laughter.

'My dear André – do sit down,' said Maurice, regaining control of himself, 'there are things I must explain to you.'

'I want no explanations from you – I want justice!' André told him.

'Very well, you shall have justice then. What do you regard as justice?'

'An apology to me for the disgraceful way you have used my good nature for your own questionable purposes. And for Mademoiselle Cabuchon, full restitution of whatever she has lost in this affair.'

'Ah,' said Maurice, 'but would that be justice? Before we decide, let me tell you of one or two details in Mademoiselle Cabuchon's background of which you are obviously unaware. I am sure that you remember your history lessons at school, in particular, the manner in which Catherine de Medici ruled when she was Queen Mother of France during the infancy of her children.'

'We may dispense with the history and fables and legends,' said André, 'get to the point.'

'But it is the point. Queen Catherine hit upon an excellent device for keeping herself informed of the activities of her political opponents. She recruited and supervised the training of what came to be known as her "flying squad" – now do you remember?'

'No I do not,' said André angrily, 'What the devil have I to do with political espionage and intrigue?'

'Nothing, I hope, but the principle is the same. The "flying squad" was composed of pretty young women selected from the families of impoverished small gentry. If my memory serves me well, the ages of these volunteers ranged from fifteen to about twenty-five. They were infiltrated into the houses of persons known to be enemies of the Queen Mother and her policies, by the simple device of becoming the cherished mistresses of her opponents. They remained loyal to Catherine and reported to her the pillow-talk of the men she most distrusted. Now do you understand?'

'You are suggesting that Mademoiselle Cabuchon is playing a similar part for some other person? I find that offensive in the extreme!'

190

'I am not suggesting, André. I am telling you as a matter of established fact that she does precisely that.'

'Who is the monstrous person involved? I shall kill him!'

'Ask yourself – who brought you and Mademoiselle together?'

'Lacoste!'

'You have your answer.'

'I do not believe you – this is all a fabrication,' said André, the fight going out of him so that at last he sank into a chair.

'Consider then, who was it who had the honour of being Mademoiselle's most intimate friend before you, André?'

'That is no concern of yours.'

'My question was rhetorical,' said Maurice pleasantly, 'there is no necessity to answer it. It was Jacques Malplaquet, there is no secret about that. Poor Malplaquet suffered a sharp loss in a business arrangement with Lacoste very shortly after Mademoiselle Cabuchon transferred her favours to you. And while I do not wish to distress you by labouring the point, before him there was another who encountered the same unexpected business reversal. I will not name him.'

'Have I been duped?' André asked in dismay.

'There is something else you perhaps ought to know, unpleasant though you may find it. Those favours you esteem so highly – and why not? She is a very beautiful woman – have in the past year or two been offered very discreetly to me and to my brother Charles. Of course, knowing of her allegiance to Lacoste, we declined politely.'

'But this is a nightmare!' André exclaimed faintly.

'When you began to ask questions and display an interest in business,' Maurice went on, 'this was so far out of character that I become interested in your motives. It was easy enough to ascertain that you had become

Mademoiselle Cabuchon's close friend. The connection was clear – Lacoste intended to obtain private information through you which he could use to our disadvantage and to his own gain.'

'So you told me a false story,' said André thoughtfully.

'Not entirely – that would have been seen by Lacoste for what it was. It is well known that my sister Jeanne's husband is not able for reasons of health to look after his business. Since he became indisposed I have been taking care of it in the interests of my sister and her children. I have neither the time nor the inclination to continue like that forever and so it was decided between Jeanne and me, and agreed by her husband, that the business should be sold and the proceeds invested to provide a proper income. All that was required was a buyer at the right price.'

'And that was Lacoste,' said André, suddenly smiling, 'you are clever, Maurice, that I do not deny.'

'He bought it at a very high price because he had a strange idea that Verney's company was about to be awarded an enormous contract from the Army. Where such a thought came from, I find it hard to imagine.'

'You sly devil! You hinted to me that you personally had bribed a high government official to get the contract – you even named him to me!' said André, laughing at last.

'You must have misunderstood whatever I said to you,' Maurice answered suavely but very firmly, 'I have never bribed a government official in my life – the idea is unthinkable.'

'But of course. Tell me then, what has Lacoste really bought?'

'A business which is in difficulty.'

'And the Verneys have secured their position, thanks to your little intrigue! You are most ingenious – I forgive you everything.'

'Most unfortunately Mademoiselle Cabuchon has lost

the commission which Lacoste pays on the deals he arranges on information supplied by her.'

'She is a whore!' exclaimed André viciously, 'She deserves it.'

'That is a cruel word to describe so enchanting a person.'

'Enchanting, yes – but false. I shall go to her apartment and spit in her face!'

'You must do no such ill-mannered thing, André. Go to her apartment and make love to her – that will be far more satisfactory for both of you. I have been told that she has remarkable talents in the bedroom.'

'She threw me out! Can you believe it – *she* threw *me* naked out of her bedroom!'

'A lovers' quarrel – a moment of pique – easily remedied.'

'Do you think so?' André asked, hope rising in his heart.

'Certainly. You may be sure that after this episode which has cost him so very much money Lacoste will want nothing more to do with Mademoiselle Cabuchon. She is alone in the world – except for an aged mother she supports in some distant suburb. When she has reconsidered her position I am sure that she will welcome you back.'

André got up to shake his cousin's hand warmly.

'Maurice, how can I ever thank you?' he said, his voice charged with emotion.

THE FORTUNE-TELLER

It is because women are the most rational of creatures, contrary to what men believe about them, that they pay attention to fortune-tellers. The superficial logic which enslaves male thinking compels them to brush aside the arts of divination by cards, palms, mirrors and other means as nothing more than superstition. But women know that events and situations have a certain knack of repeating themselves and from that there follows the ineluctable conclusion that each person's life forms a particular pattern. If the individual pattern can be discerned in good time, then it can be used to advantage.

Naturally, it is only some bizarre and heretical Protestant sects which suppose that the course of one's life is predetermined from the moment of birth, a belief running contrary to religion, commonsense and experience. The truth of the matter is that we each carry our destiny within us, for destiny is the outcome of character. For this reason alone a skilled and gifted fortune-teller, who can see through the veils behind which we conceal our true selves, can assess character and predict the probable course of an individual's life.

It was therefore to a fortune-teller that Yvonne Daladier had recourse in a time of indecision. At the age of twenty-five she believed that she had endured more than a fair share of disappointment. She was, as all her friends agreed, a beautiful young woman. She dressed well, when she could afford to do so. She was lively and intelligent

194

– and she was a charming lover. Yet with so many qualities to recommend her, she had neither a husband nor a permanent lover.

The reason for her unfortunate condition, Yvonne had come to realise, was that she invariably chose unsuitable men. They fell in love with her, they set her up in well-furnished apartments and bought fashionable clothes for her, they entertained her in the very best places and they made love to her in a satisfactory manner. Not one of the five who had so far been accorded these privileges had ever proposed marriage to her, though that was understandable in the case of the two who already had wives and families. But apart from that, these lovers eventually went off elsewhere, leaving her to pay a rent she could not afford. Altogether, it was infuriating!

Her latest protector was Paul-Henri Courval, a handsome man only a few years older than Yvonne herself. He had plenty of money, that went without saying. He was not very clever and not at all witty, but that was of no importance. In some ways it was a distinct advantage, in that after a month or so of the enjoyment of Yvonne's very considerable charms, he declared himself to be madly in love with her. Yvonne found that most satisfactory, not merely because it made Paul-Henri especially generous towards her but because it held the promise of a longer relationship between them and made it possible for her to nudge him imperceptibly towards the idea of marriage.

At the same time, she felt it would be sensible to seek advice from one who could read the secrets of the human heart. If Paul-Henri was going to prove unsuitable eventually, then the sooner she knew the truth, the better. On the other hand, if she had made a sensible choice this time, then she could go ahead with the steps necessary to bring him to a proposal of marriage and thereby guarantee her own future comfort and happiness.

One night, as they lay naked together on her bed after a tempestuous act of love which left Yvonne feeling somewhat exhausted, she stroked his chest gently while she introduced the topic that had been in her mind all day. Paul-Henri, resting comfortably on his back after his amorous exertions, was in a very good humour – as well he might be – and disposed to listen to her. Even so, he was surprised.

'A fortune-teller!' he exclaimed. 'But why?'

'She's very good,' Yvonne assured him, her finger-tips gliding over his flat nipples in a way calculated to soothe him.

'When did you see her?'

'This morning. A friend recommended her to me. It was very strange – she told me things which she couldn't possibly have known about.'

'But evidently she did know – she probably got a few facts about you from your friend – they're clever at wheedling information out of unsuspecting customers.'

'Not even my friend knew some of the things.'

'Friends often know, or guess, more than you think. They are all charlatans, these fortune-tellers – they make a living out of gullibility.'

'That may be true of most of them, but this one is different. She upset me.'

'But that's dreadful!' said Paul-Henri, taking her into his arms to comfort her, 'what did she say?'

'I can't tell you that – I gave my word. But if she is right, then our love will not last long.'

'What nonsense! I adore you, chérie, and you know that. This person is a fraud who should be brought to the attention of the police.'

'Perhaps – but promise me one thing first.'

'Anything,' he said expansively, his hands fondling the smooth cheeks of her bottom, 'you have only to ask.'

'Go and see her yourself tomorrow. If you tell me afterwards that she is wrong, then I will believe you and that will be the end of my worries.'

Paul-Henri hadn't expected that, but he rose to the occasion.

'To please you, dear Yvonne, I will go and see this lying fraud and tell her that to her face.'

As is well known, promises made in bed often lead to unfortunate results. Be that as it may, on the next day at eleven in the morning Paul-Henri made his way by taxi to the Butte Montmartre to confront the fortune-teller who had given anxiety to the woman he loved. The address he sought was not to be found in the Montmartre known to foreign tourists – the Montmartre of entertainment and music and small restaurants – but in a narrow back-street of shabby houses that seemed not to have been painted or cleaned since they were built in the previous century. On the ground floor of the number he had been given he discovered a small bar with a dirty floor and a zinc-topped counter at which stood two or three scruffy men he judged to be of the petty criminal class.

The bar-tender, collarless, unshaven and with only one eye, sold him a small glass of abominable cognac and told him that Mademoiselle Marie lived on the top floor. Paul-Henri was amazed that the fastidious Yvonne should have visited so squalid a place and he regarded it as one more proof of the irrationality of women. If Fate is to speak to us, he thought, it will not be in a filthy den like this.

The men at the bar were whispering together and occasionally glancing at him. His expensive clothes marked him as a target for larceny, he realised, and he already knew what he would do if attacked. He would fling the wretched spirit in his glass into the eyes of the leading assailant, instantly blinding him for life, kick the second one very hard between the legs to incapacitate him permanently, then snatch the cognac bottle from the bar where One-Eye had placed it in the hope that he would order a second drink and smash it over the head of the third man, breaking his skull at the very least and possibly killing him outright. The bar-tender by then would be cowering behind his unwiped bar and would offer no resistance as Paul-Henri left the thieves' rat-hole and strolled down the narrow street to find a representative of the law – if any were to be found in this district.

Nothing of the sort occurred, of course, and he had no opportunity to demonstrate his courage. He left his unfinished drink on the bar and climbed the creaking stairs to the top floor. There was no landing – the stairs ended abruptly at a wooden door from which the green paint of fifty years ago was peeling. He knocked and went in.

The room in which he found himself was made smaller by a shabby grey curtain stretched from wall to wall to divide it in two. The only illumination was that of a sky-light in the sloping roof, the floor was bare and unswept – all this Paul-Henri saw in a glance of distaste that wrinkled his nose. But then he saw the fortune-teller.

She sat, this Mademoiselle Marie, with her back to the curtain, at a small square table on which she was laying out playing cards in parallel rows. She looked up as the door closed behind him and he stood still. He had expected to meet an old woman, though he could not have explained why. Mademoiselle Marie was not yet thirty – hardly older than Yvonne, he thought.

She had a flowered scarf tied round her head and, from under it, her long black hair hung down to well below her shoulders. Paul-Henri had never seen such long hair on a woman in all his life and it held him spell-bound for a moment. It was hopelessly unstylish, but it was magnificent, he thought. Marie's face was broad, with high cheek-bones, a strong nose and a broad mouth. But it was her eyes that compelled attention. They were set wide apart, they were black, they shone – and they were unblinking.

'Sit down, M'sieu,' she said, breaking the silence.

On the near side of the table stood a rickety chair that

looked to have been bought in the Flea Market for a few centimes. Paul-Henri sat and looked at Marie across the table, suddenly aware of her perfume. It was a heavy and sensual fragrance that hinted at . . . but he closed his mind to thoughts of that kind and concentrated on the reason for his visit.

'You wish to consult me?' she prompted him.

'Yes . . . that is to say, no . . . the fact is, Mademoiselle, a very dear friend of mine came to see you yesterday and was disturbed by some nonsense or other you told her. I must make my position clear – I refuse to allow her to be upset like this. What did you say to her?'

Marie was wearing a short-sleeved frock of shiny black satin that buttoned down the bodice. That is to say, more precisely, it could be buttoned down the bodice for, as Paul-Henri saw, the buttons were open from the scalloped neckline to between her breasts. More than that, as she moved her arm to lay another card from the pack face-down on one of the rows on the table, her breasts rolled under the frock to give a view extensive enough to inform Paul-Henri that they were large and bare beneath the thin black material. He found the sight very distracting and almost missed what she said.

'Several clients consulted me yesterday. Which one of them was your dear, dear friend, M'sieu?'

'Mademoiselle Daladier,' Paul-Henri replied, offended by the impertinent way in which she had phrased the question.

'Ah, the pretty one – yes, I might have guessed that a distinguished man like you would be interested in her.'

'If you please,' said Paul-Henri curtly, 'I do not wish to have my personal affairs discussed. I am here to clear up what may have been a misunderstanding.'

He took out his note-case, thinking that the sight of money would inspire the fortune-teller to a prediction of good fortune, long life and happiness which he could carry back triumphantly to Yvonne. But Marie shook her head slowly from side to side.

'Put your money away, M'sieu. My clients pay me after I have told them what I see, not before.'

'As you wish. What did you see for Mademoiselle Daladier?'

'That is confidential between her and me. But I'll tell you this much – she came to consult me about you.'

'About me? That's ridiculous!'

'Perhaps. I could tell her nothing about you because I'd never seen you. But now you're here – let me see your palms, M'sieu.'

'I didn't come here to have my hands read.'

'Maybe not – but it will give you something to tell your friend to ease her mind.'

'Oh, very well then,' Paul-Henri agreed impatiently.

He put his forearms on the table with his palms upwards. Marie studied them carefully, comparing the lines on his left hand with those on his right hand, tracing them with her finger-tip. It took a long time, during which she said nothing to him.

Her touch had an unexpected effect on Paul-Henri. In spite of the extreme inappropriateness of the circumstances, his male part grew stiff and long and he found himself trying to see more of Marie's breasts as she leaned over the table to look at his hands.

But this is terrible, he said to himself. Last night I loved myself to a standstill with my beautiful Yvonne – and here I am getting excited over an overweight gypsy! It's that damned perfume of hers – I must get out of here at once before I am tempted to do something stupid.

Marie settled the matter by laying her own hands flat on his. Her palms were warm and dry and it was as if an electric current passed through Paul-Henri – from his palms, up his arms, down through his spine and up his erect part! He gasped at the sensation, certain that he would discharge into his underwear unless the contact with Marie was broken at once. But her eyes held him – her unblinking stare kept him in his seat, trembling on the brink of an involuntary climax of passion.

'Your hands tell me that you are as honest as any, as selfish as most, open-handed to those you love, deaf to the rest – in short, an average normal man, though with more money than most have.'

'Is that all?' he managed to say through the hot emotions that both delighted and appalled him as he trembled under her touch.

Not being a complete fool, he was by then wondering how much Marie would ask to take her clothes off and let him relieve the monstrous desire she had aroused. After all, his experience was that all women of her sort – gypsies, vagabonds, cafe singers, circus folk and the rest – they were readily available to the man who had money in his pocket and was not afraid to spend it. Marie looked into his flushed face and nodded, as if reading his thoughts – no great feat, and one requiring no particular powers of clairvoyance, for one look at him in that condition would have told any woman what was in his mind.

'Come with me,' she said, releasing his hands.

When she stood up from the table Paul-Henri saw that her shiny black frock was held in tightly at her waist by a broad belt of black leather with a big silver buckle, so emphasising the outward swell of her bosom and hips. With one hand she pulled aside the dingy curtain behind her, making the wooden rings on which it hung rattle together, and with the other hand she gestured him through. With a sigh of relief, he got up and walked past her, so close that his arm brushed lightly against her breasts. She made no move to avoid the contact.

There was no window in the back of the room and, when the curtain was drawn back into place again, it was half-dark in there. The space divided off for Marie's private apartment was tiny and most of the space in it was occupied by a low divan pushed up close to the wall.

There was only one touch of colour in this unprepossessing cubicle – a marvellously embroidered Spanish shawl in crimson and black spread over the divan.

Marie stood with her back to the curtain, seeming hardly to breathe, an enigmatic expression on her face as she waited for Paul-Henri's reaction. He was momentarily at a loss and awaited a sign from her.

'Not what you expected?' she asked casually.

He shrugged, not wanting to give offence.

'You must remember, M'sieu, that I am not a whore. I don't take men to a comfortable bedroom to sell my body. I tell fortunes.'

All the same, Paul-Henri thought, here we are in her sleeping-quarters and money will assuredly pass between us before I depart – so what does that make her?

'You seem a little confused,' Marie said. 'You've never met anyone like me before, have you?'

She took a step towards him as she spoke and again he was aware of the musky perfume she wore. It seemed to affect the nerves and make him breathe a little faster. Her hand reached up to touch his cheek.

'Put yourself in my hands,' she said, 'do not be afraid – unless you are afraid of the truth.'

'Whatever the truth may be,' he said, as jauntily as possible, 'I am sure that I can face it with equanimity.'

'Good, good,' she said, almost absent-mindedly.

Her hand left his cheek to trail down his chest and belly until she could trace the outline of his hardness through his trousers.

'Yes, that's as it should be,' she said, as if to herself, 'otherwise I can achieve nothing.'

'Nor I,' Paul-Henri said with a nervous smile.

Her fingers were busy with his trouser buttons, but she frowned at his little joke.

'This is not a process to be laughed at,' she reproached him.

'Forgive me – I have never had my fortune told before. At least, not like this.'

'No, but *this* has been in a woman's hand before.'

She had the emblem of his virility out of his trousers and was gripping it firmly, her touch increasing its rigidity. Paul-Henri sighed with pleasure.

'You must answer all my questions if I am to be of service to you, M'sieu.'

'I took your question to be rhetorical, Mademoiselle. But yes, as you say, that part of me has been in a woman's hand before – and in more delectable parts of her body.'

'Just answer my questions – I don't need to know your life history. You have been with more than one woman, naturally. Your pretty friend was not the first to play with this, was she?'

'No, nor the second – I am nearly thirty years old – what do you expect?'

'I didn't ask you that,' and she tugged sharply at his swollen projection.

'My apologies, Mademoiselle.'

'That's better. Do you know where a man's heart is to be found?'

'Why, in his chest, I suppose.'

'Wrong – it is lower down. This is your heart I am holding in my hand – this length of stiff flesh you think of by another name. This is what guides your affections and passions.'

Paul-Henri was beginning to tremble at the knees as a result of her attentions to what he must now learn to think of as his *heart*.

'And where are a man's brains to be found,' she asked, 'do you know that?'

'You must tell me,' he murmured.

One of her hands unclasped itself from his *heart*, burrowed inside his open trousers and took hold of his dependents.

203

'Here,' she said, 'your brains are in these. Does that surprise you?'

'Your words astonish me,' Paul-Henri sighed.

In his mind was the thought that in a few more moments it would be Marie's turn to be surprised when her vigorous manipulation caused him to pour out his excitement onto her black frock.

'Do not mock me or it will be the worse for you,' she warned him, the hand clasping his *brains* tightening to the point where it was almost painful. 'These are what control your actions, and what is in your head merely complies – that is the truth of the matter.'

He gasped as her hands left him suddenly. He swayed as he stood, his male part sticking stiffly out of his trousers. Marie unfastened the silver buckle at her waist and let the belt fall to the floor. In another moment her frock was up and over her head. Without it she was completely naked, Paul-Henri noted with delight – but he was treated to the briefest of glimpses of her full breasts before she stepped past him towards the divan. He had a moment or two to admire the firm round cheeks of her bottom as she flicked the gorgeous Spanish shawl out of the way and then she seated herself on the divan, facing him again, her knees apart and her bare feet solidly on the dusty floor.

Paul-Henri was very nearly at the apex of excitement from her fondling and the sight of her naked body fired him to action. He stepped forward to fling himself on her, carry her over onto her back and drive straight in to assuage the incredible desire she had aroused. But it was not to be so – Marie moved as quickly as a cat, one strong leg bending upwards between them so that the sole of her foot stopped him, planted against his quivering projection and holding it flat to his belly.

'You're not here to do that,' she informed him sharply, 'you are here to have your fortune told.'

204

'For God's sake!' he gasped, 'I'm desperate! I can't stop now – I'll give you whatever you want!'

'I told you that I am not a whore for sale,' she reminded him. 'Do you think that you can rape me?'

He stared at her sturdy arms and legs, at the muscles of her thighs and her confident expression. Perhaps he could and perhaps not – either way it would be a long and noisy struggle that would surely bring the criminals up from the bar below to her aid.

'I implore you!' he said.

'That's better. Down on your knees!'

She removed her foot and Paul-Henri sank to his knees between her parted legs.

How desirable she was, he thought feverishly, her skin a rich olive-brown colour – ah, with a gasp of surprise he noticed for the first time that she had a little five-pointed star tattooed in blue on the upper curve of one breast.

'What does that mean?' he asked, trying to touch it, but she pushed his hand away.

'That's none of your business. Put your hands on my hips – and otherwise don't move at all, understand?'

Paul-Henri nodded and did as she said. Her fleshy hips were warm and yielding under his hands and he groaned in frustration. To achieve his goal meant that he would have to go along with her ludicrous mystification and to pretend that he fully believed her claim not to be for sale – but he hoped with every fibre of his being that she would not spin out this farce too long before allowing him to proceed to the natural culmination of his passion. Her perfume was heavy in his nostrils – it seemed to emanate from every part of her body, as if she soaked herself in it from head to foot. He could scent it in her long black hair hanging down over her shoulders, on her meaty breasts – it even rose from her thighs and groin! He looked down at the mat of coarse black hair which covered the lower part of her belly – and while he was staring, she raised her legs and wrapped them tightly round his waist.

'Keep your hands on my hips,' she warned him.

She took a firm grasp of his engorged part once more and for a delicious moment he believed that she intended to insert its swollen head into the plump lips between her legs, now exposed to him by the position of her thighs around his middle. But his hope was dashed – she laid his projection the length of those warm lips and, with the flat of her hand, pressed it against her crinkly fur. Inadequate though this arrangement was, Paul-Henri still found a fierce excitement in the contact between their most intimate parts.

'Look into my eyes,' Marie instructed him.

He forced himself to look away from his baulked pride, so very close to where he wanted it to be, yet trapped under her hand. His gaze travelled slowly up her broad belly, up to her breasts and paused at the tattoo mark, then up to her unsmiling face at last. The eyes he looked into gleamed with an emotion he found it impossible to identify.

'Tell me your name,' she said.

'You know it already.'

'Tell me your full name!'

'Paul-Henri Courval.'

'Good, keep looking into my eyes.'

He had no choice – her compelling stare held him immobile.'

'What do you see?' she asked.

'In your eyes? A certain darkness – but it has depth . . . there is a sense of an impending revelation . . . I can't describe it.'

'Look through my eyes into my soul. In a moment the clouds will part and you will understand.'

Paul-Henri was held almost as if in a trance by her bright and unblinking stare. His state of arousal had dulled his critical faculties and, even while he trembled with pleasurable sensation, he was unaware that the hand that pressed his erection to her mat of hair was moving insidiously. His only thought was that his whole body was hot and shaking and that some overwhelming event was about to take place.

'What do you see?' Marie repeated.

'I see . . . I see . . . '

Before he could determine what it was that he believed he could see in her eyes, his body convulsed in a paroxysm of gratification and his tormented passion gushed out beneath her hand.

'No!' he exclaimed in consternation, 'No!'

' . . . four, five, six, seven . . . ' he heard her counting aloud as the spasms shook him.

Then he was still, an angry discontent in his heart at the way in which this so-called fortune-teller had led him to expect much and then tricked him. He tried to pull away from her, his intention to leave at once with an appropriately rude remark or two about fraudulent practices. But she held him fast between her strong legs, her hand still clamping his disappointed part to her.

'Wait,' she said, 'I have it now.'

'Whatever it is that you have,' Paul-Henri said curtly, 'it is not where I expected you to have it. Release me – or is it part of your scheme to provoke me into forcing you to let me go?'

'Don't you want to hear your fortune? You find my methods unusual, perhaps, but they are effective.'

'I wish this entire transaction to end now.'

'As you wish,' and she removed her legs from his waist.

He was on his feet at once, buttoning his trousers. Marie remained seated on the divan, the evidence of his passion visible on the thick black hair which adorned her belly.

'Your fee?' Paul-Henri demanded.

'You owe me nothing, M'sieu, since I haven't told you anything.'

He had not the least intention of letting this creature extend her victory over him by a display of generosity. He delved into his pocket for all his loose change and flung the handful of coins onto the floor between her bare feet. She smiled in mockery at his gesture and, as he left abruptly, she called after him:

'You'll be back – we'll talk about payment then.'

Paul-Henri was in an extremely bad temper as he strode through the narrow streets until he found himself in a part of Montmartre he recognised. He went into the first decent bar he could find and drunk a glass of good cognac – not the rot-gut he had been offered before – while he set his chaotic thoughts in order.

What could have been the fortune-teller's purpose in leading him into so wretched a substitute for an act of love? That was the question he found impossible to answer to his satisfaction. She had not done it for gain, evidently, for she had refused to take money from him. She had not done it to tell his fortune through some bizarre form of bodily contact, as she had hinted, for that was too absurd an idea to contemplate at all. Unless she was in some way deranged, perhaps . . . ? But that seemed unlikely. She had given every indication of intelligence and purpose. Did she suffer from some type of perversion that gave her pleasure from handling men in that particular way? That seemed the most probable hypothesis, even though he had not observed any signs of pleasure in her demeanour during the episode or afterwards. The whole affair was an enigma for a doctor or a priest to resolve!

When Paul-Henri left the bar and strolled on, he was more puzzled than angry. He came eventually to the Place du Tertre, where the usual crowd of hopeful but penniless artists were exhibiting their paintings under the trees in the middle of the square. At first glance the pictures appeared to be about equally divided between views of old Montmartre, views of the white-domed church of

Sacré-Coeur and views of naked women in various poses. Painters, Paul-Henri reflected, seemed to be much devoted to naked women as a subject for their work. One or two of them were passably painted, many were not. He almost grunted with surprise at the sight of one that depicted a big-breasted woman sitting on the side of a bed in almost exactly the position the fortune-teller was in when he left her room. But closer examination showed it to be a portrait of a different woman, with light-brown hair arranged in a fringe over her forehead and a somewhat stupid expression. And without the strange blue star tattoo on her breast, needless to say!

When he had seen as much of the exhibition as he found interesting, Paul-Henri decided that he was hungry. He lunched well in one of the little restaurants for which Montmartre is known – an excellent piece of filet de boeuf and a bottle of good red burgundy. He was unable to dismiss from his mind the fortune-teller's parting words to him: 'You'll be back.' She had said it with such confidence! To a man she had just tricked in the most despicable manner!

There is, as everyone knows, no better or more certain way to banish a man's annoyance and to reconcile him to the world than good food and good wine. As his spirits were raised, Paul-Henri found himself dwelling upon the memory of Mademoiselle Marie's very obvious physical advantages – all of which had been presented to his view, if to no other part of him. The clasp of her legs about his waist was, in retrospect, very enjoyable. It would without question be an exceptionally gratifying experience to feel those legs round his waist again while he lay on her broad belly and flattened her breasts under him in the pleasant exertion of discharging his passion into her secret recess!

More than that, not only would it be gratifying, but he owed it to himself to even the score between them.

For all Marie's talk of not selling her body, Paul-Henri was still convinced that it was only a matter of how much money she was offered. He would return to her rat-hole of a room and place on the table before her more money than she had ever seen before at one time in her life – and then she would agree to do anything he wanted. After all, she had made it clear that she expected him to return. She had gone so far as to say that they would then discuss her fee. Paul-Henri's mind was made up – he called for his bill and was soon on his way back to where she lived.

Through the street-level window he saw that the same two or three idlers were in the bar – well, what else could one expect from that type of person? He climbed the dusty stairs to the top floor and, without knocking, entered Marie's room. The reason for not knocking was one of pride. To knock is to seek permission to enter – and Paul-Henri was not here as a supplicant but as a man come to purchase a certain service.

The fortune-teller was not there. Her cards were spread carelessly on the table as if she had completed a reading and then swept her hand across the rows to break up the pattern. A faint trace of her perfume lingered in the air and made his nostrils dilate as he sought to savour this evanescent memory.

It was decidedly strange, of course, that a man of his subtle tastes and refined pleasures should find anything to interest him in a woman he regarded as coarse. He found it difficult to explain to himself why he was on fire for her and in what lay the appeal of her earthy sensuality. But the simple truth is that men, however delicate their tastes become, remain part animal in their nature, most especially in all matters relating to the appendage between their thighs – to which they ascribe a ridiculously inflated importance. Let a man be without the company of the woman he loves for a day or two and even a washer-woman, so long as she is not grotesque of appearance, has the power to stiffen his male part. And if he has been without the intimate friendship of a woman for a week or more, then even a washerwoman of grotesque appearance will serve his turn. Any harbour in a storm, as seafarers say! Marie, though not beautiful by any stretch of the imagination, was not ugly.

How long Paul-Henri stood by the table in the dimly-lit room, his homburg hat on his head, his lemon yellow gloved hands clasped in front of him, he could never afterwards determine. His reverie was disturbed by a sound from behind the grey curtain which divided the room – the sound of a long sigh.

It was unmistakable that sigh – the sound of a woman with her lover! Marie was at home, after all! And more than that, she was lying on the divan behind the curtain in the throes of pleasure! The realisation aroused Paul-Henri immediately – his face flushed red and in three sudden jerks his male part stood erect. He also experienced an overwhelming curiosity as to what sort of man Marie allowed these intimacies. One of her own type, he thought, probably one of the ruffians he had earlier seen drinking rum in the bar below. But not necessarily – it might be someone like himself, a man of intelligence and status.

He put his hat on the table and took a few silent steps to the wall, where the curtain met it. With the greatest caution, so that the wooden rings should not rattle and give him away, he moved the curtain just enough to see into the alcove.

Marie's broad back was towards him as she lay on the divan, propped on one elbow, her head scarf removed and her mane of black hair hanging loosely down almost like a wimple. She had one knee up to part her thighs lasciviously and her companion, who was hidden from Paul-Henri, was evidently caressing her between those strong thighs, for at that moment Marie sighed again – a long exhalation that expressed the keenest pleasure.

Paul-Henri had only to wait, he knew, and before long Marie would be on her back with her partner on top of her – and he would see what sort of lover she preferred.

211

That he was intruding unpardonably into the private concerns of another person never entered his mind – he was too aroused for niceties of conscience to mean anything to him just then. Perhaps too, though of this one cannot be certain, he did not regard Marie the fortune-teller as a person worthy enough in relation to himself to be accorded the ordinary courtesies of social behaviour. And when one cannot be sure, one must be charitable – and attribute his spying to his condition of acute excitement.

Still sighing pleasurably, Marie's big body moved languorously and her head descended towards her lover. It was then that Paul-Henri received the second surprise since he had entered, uninvited, her room. The other person on the divan with Marie was also a woman!

He stared in total amazement, hardly able to accept what he saw. But it was true – Marie's new position revealed to him the thighs and belly of her companion – soft, rounded thighs between which lay a small patch of curly brown hair, and not the slightest indication of a hard stem like that which quivered inside his own trousers. Even as he watched, Marie's hand covered the patch and her fingers parted the lips they found there and probed within. She had bowed her head, he realised, to kiss the tips of her lover's breasts, which were still concealed from him.

After the initial shock of seeing two women engaged in pleasuring each other Paul-Henri experienced a state of arousal that made him shiver so violently that he found it necessary to lean against the wall to support himself on his trembling legs. His erect part was fluttering in his underwear – a sensation painful, delicious and intolerable at the same time. He was unable to stop himself from ripping open his trousers to let his monstrously swollen stem jut out.

'That's good, that's good!' Marie moaned to her friend, 'faster now!'

With the back of his glove Paul-Henri wiped from his forehead the drops of perspiration which were threatening to trickle down into his staring eyes. The movement of his arm made the curtain rings click together a little, but fortunately for him the two women on the divan were far too engrossed in each other and their own emotions to take note of so small a sound. Marie's friend was gasping without pause as the hand between her thighs continued its impetuous ministrations. Soon, very soon now . . . Paul-Henri would observe both women attain the climax of their passion! The thought was overwhelming!

It was almost too overwhelming! His hand was clutching the hard-standing part he had released from his trousers, squeezing it tightly. Two or three fast flicks would be enough to spray the dusty grey curtain with a climactic release of his own! But no, he insisted to his raging desire – wait! Very soon now there will be a choice of two warm receptacles for this throbbing part!

Marie's friend screamed briefly and her bottom lifted off the divan as her critical moments arrived. And immediately afterwards Marie's body jerked furiously for a moment or two – Paul-Henri's eyes were bulging almost out of his head! The engorged stem in his hand was shaking so furiously that he knew what was about to happen to him!

The fortune-teller's ecstasy was brief. While her friend was still gasping and kicking her heels against the mattress, Marie was off the divan and, with a sweep of her arm, flung back the curtains to reveal Paul-Henri! Unlike the first two surprises of the last quarter of an hour, this third great shock was extremely disagreeable. Paul-Henri leaned against the wall, open-mouthed, petrified with the horror of the situation and unable to move a muscle.

Marie was within arm's reach of him, her big round breasts heaving from her recent exertions on the divan, a drop or two of perspiration running down her belly towards the expanse of black fur that concealed her secret treasure.

'M'sieu Courval,' she said, a smile on her broad face, 'I knew you'd be back.'

It was the most ghastly moment of Paul-Henri's life and he could do no more than babble incoherently.

'You've arrived at a good time,' said Marie, 'in fact, you couldn't have chosen a better time.'

'But . . . but . . . '

'And you're all prepared for it,' she added, looking down at his bared and distended part, still firmly grasped in his yellow-gloved hand.

'But . . . but . . . '

'Come and join us,' she said with a grin.

She brushed his arm aside and took him by his projection as if it were a handle and pulled him towards the divan. The warmth of her body accentuated her perfume and Paul-Henri was dizzy from its effect. Perhaps it was that, perhaps it was the grasp of her hand on his male part – but it was too much! What he had feared a moment or two ago now happened – his legs felt like rubber, his loins twitched convulsively and he fountained his pent-up desire onto the divan!

The fourth shock of the afternoon was a coup-de-grace! As he tottered on unsteady legs, spattering the mattress, there before him he saw, still trembling in the aftermath of passion – Yvonne!

THE EMANCIPATED MADAME DELAROQUE

The very first time that Laurence saw her he was absolutely sure that she had just been making love. She was coming down the stairs from a second floor apartment in the Boulevard Beaumarchais and he was going up. Her clothes were distinctly elegant – a neat little summer suit in pale green silk, with an exquisitely pleated skirt. Under a pull-down hat in a matching shade her face was beautifully serene, yet to Laurence's perceptive eye there was about her an air of satisfied desire that left no room for doubt as to what she had been doing.

He stood aside politely to let her pass and raised his hat to her. She was no more than twenty-five years old and extremely attractive. She acknowledged his courtesy with a nod but did not return his smile – perhaps she read in his eyes his instinctive awareness of her recent pleasures. The subtlety of her expensive perfume was not lost on Laurence as she passed close to him and he thought he could even detect a hint of the exciting natural fragrance of a woman who has just been loved, but that might have been his imagination. Her white gloves were very fine, he noted, with criss-cross stitching on the backs in a contrasting colour.

In short, he desired her greatly from the moment he saw her. If she had returned his smile he would have tried to engage her in conversation then and there, with a view to persuading her to meet him at some later date. But she did no more than nod graciously and went on down the stairs.

It was almost six in the evening and Laurence was on his way to call upon a friend to invite him out to dinner and an evening of whatever entertainment presented itself as suitable to two young and unmarried men. There was also a little matter of business of the most interesting sort to be discussed between them. The friend, Jean-Claude Sorbier, greeted him warmly and settled him down with a drink while they debated which of the scores of restaurants they knew and liked should be their starting-point for the evening. Eventually Laurence could contain his curiosity no longer.

'On the way up the stairs I passed a most enchanting lady,' he said, 'does she have an apartment in this building?'

'I don't really know any of my neighbours,' Jean-Claude replied, 'I'm out so much, you know.'

'You couldn't possibly live in the same building as this one and not know about it,' Laurence protested. 'About twenty-five, wearing a light green suit – quite magnificent in every way. You must have seen her.'

'I don't think anyone like that lives here,' Jean-Claude said vaguely.

'But you've been here for years – you must have passed all your neighbours on the stairs at some time!'

Jean-Claude shrugged and Laurence guessed the truth at last.

'You devil!' he said with a grin. 'She was here to visit you – I might have known it! You lucky dog – she is superb! Who is she?'

'Well, since you've found me out, her name is Marcelle Delaroque. But please don't breath a word to anyone – her husband is a jealous man from what I hear and I don't want to cause any problems for her.'

'Naturally,' said Laurence, 'but Delaroque – the name seems familiar, though I can't place it. Who is he?'

'No one of importance – he's one of our representatives at the League of Nations. But surely you've heard of Marcelle Delaroque?'

'Of course – she's the woman who campaigns for education for women! The newspapers always have articles by her. I started to read one of them once but I couldn't get through it. But she's a perfect beauty – and I'd imagined that the writer of those articles must be a plain old maid. She can't be Delaroque's first wife – he's at least sixty.'

'His third.'

Laurence tried to question Jean-Claude further about his charming friend, but achieved nothing. Discretion was of the utmost importance, Jean-Claude insisted, and they returned to the question of where they should have dinner.

The little matter of business which Laurence raised over dinner was an opportunity which had come his way of acquiring for a reasonable sum of money the lease of a cottage in the country, not much more than an hour's drive out of Paris. In the nature of things, the ladies who became intimate friends of gallant young men like Laurence and Jean-Claude were frequently married and therefore the greatest of discretion was necessary to preserve the social decencies. This occasioned short and sometimes hurried encounters, when the pleasures of love really required more time and security from interruption by inconsiderate visitors or observation by servants.

From time to time it was possible for married ladies to explain to their husbands why they would be away for a night or two, staying with their sisters outside Paris, or some other convenient relative – and it was especially easy to explain such absences to husbands who had urgent preoccupations of their own with other married women, and easiest of all if a husband was conducting an intimate friendship with an unmarried woman he was also supporting. To provide for assignations arising from considerations like these, there were a number of small but very comfortable hotels within an hour or two of the city. They were well-frequented, particularly at week-ends.

The problem was that one might meet inconvenient acquaintances in these places, engaged in the same activities. More than one story was told of married couples each accompanied by someone else, meeting by chance in a small country hotel – with disastrous results! Whether these stories had any basis in fact or were merely idle gossip to amuse was neither here nor there – the possibility, however remote, of an unwanted encounter was enough to give rise to a certain nervousness.

To have a small house of one's own in the country – that was a proposition of real merit. The cost was fairly high, of course, since the owners of suitable properties were no fools and knew the value of what they had to offer. But shared between two good friends who trusted each other, the cost was reasonable and the advantages obvious. In a cottage of one's own there would be space and privacy to play love-games which were not practical in a hotel room. Jean-Claude congratulated Laurence on finding such a place and said that an opportunity like that must not be missed. They would take the cottage at once and divide the costs equally.

After that the evening continued merrily, with a visit to the Moulin Rouge to see the last show, then visits to numerous low dance halls with accordion music and singers in sequins who claimed to be Spanish, until they found their way towards dawn to a café near Les Halles, to round off the night with thick onion soup and a little glass of marc.

So the arrangements were completed, the cottage leased and plans made for the inaugural visit. At that time Laurence was on grounds of close amity with Marie-Véronique Blois, the charming cousin of another of his friends, Charles Brissard, through whom he had met her. To say that Marie-Véronique was charming was true, up to a point. She was pretty, she dressed well, she enjoyed the pleasures of love – all the qualities a man looks for in a woman with whom he intends to maintain an intimate relationship. But sadly, Marie-Véronique had proved to be an uninteresting conversationalist. She had a tendency, which Laurence found boring, to talk about domestic matters – and this to a lover!

In the tender throes of love-making Marie-Véronique always remained silent, even at the supreme moment itself. At first Laurence had attributed this rare character-istic to the profundity of her passion, but on longer acquaintance with her he began to ask himself if it might perhaps be because she was silently planning tomorrow's meals for her family. At all events, it seemed to him that their close friendship was not destined to last for very long. Nevertheless, for the present – that is, until someone else appeared in his life – he was content to leave things as they were and to enjoy what Marie-Véronique had to offer.

It was therefore Marie-Véronique that he drove into the country to assist in putting the newly acquired cottage to its proposed use. She had no great difficulty in absenting herself from her family for a day or two – one of her complaints against her husband was that he no longer loved her and was away too much. It was no secret to Laurence and most of the people he knew that Marie-Véronique's husband had for the past two or three years been conducting a tempestuous love-affair with a Polish opera singer, but Marie-Véronique herself never made any reference to that. Either she did not know or she chose not to believe it.

Naturally, Jean-Claude invited Marcelle Delaroque. According to what he told Laurence, she had declined outright when she heard that others would be present. But Jean-Claude had eventually succeeded in overcoming her objections by assuring her that his life-long friend Laurence was completely trustworthy. As for Marie-

Véronique, she was clearly in no position to reveal to anyone who she might have met at a place she should not herself have been in.

Both the women were delighted by the cottage itself when they saw it. It had evidently been built originally as a superior type of farm-house and much improved by its present owner. Running water had been installed, and even a bath-room, but the rustic touch had been preserved in the heavy wooden furniture and white-washed walls. The kitchen floor was stone-flagged and had a big open range for cooking – and this room also served as a dining-room. Upstairs there were two bed-rooms, each furnished with an old-fashioned high bed, sturdily built of wood and ideal for amorous cavortings.

There was no telephone or electricity, of course, which added to the rural charm. An excellent dinner, prepared by the ladies themselves, with plenty of good wine, was enjoyed in the soft glow of an oil-lamp suspended from the kitchen ceiling. The entire scenario was romantic in the extreme and even Marie-Véronique was able to forget her domestic preoccupations. Indeed, stimulated by Marcelle Delaroque, who was a witty and lively talker, Marie-Véronique positively blossomed. All in all, it was a most enjoyable evening.

Well before midnight the two couples retired to their bedrooms for the most important part of their expedition into the country. Laurence undressed Marie-Véronique in the golden candle-light which was the only illumination upstairs, kissing her breasts as he uncovered them. Once in bed, her unaccustomed vivacity continued and their love-making had a greater degree of exhilaration than ever before. She sighed and gasped as he embraced her – something she had never ventured previously, and when he mounted her, her legs clasped him boldly! Oh, the marvels that are wrought by good country air, lively companionship and enough excellent wine! Laurence rode her proudly and was rewarded at the critical moment by hearing her gasp his name lovingly as he delivered his passionate offering into the shrine of love.

He lay trembling on her warm body, holding her close and delighted by what had happened. He had judged her too harshly, he thought; he had been unkind and over-critical. In truth, she was a marvellous woman to have as a mistress.

Through the wall that separated them from the room into which Jean-Claude and Marcelle had retired, he heard a woman's voice exclaim '*Ah! Ah! Ah!*' – the exclamation rising in crescendo to a long wail of ecstasy. It was Marcelle in a devastating climax of love, there could be no doubt of that.

'She's very noisy,' Marie-Véronique whispered beneath him.

Laurence's pleasure in his own love-making was destroyed like a toy balloon pricked by a pin. He had thought Marie-Véronique exceptionally responsive that night – yet here thrust upon his attention was a contrast which made him realise how timid her responses really were. What he wanted was a woman like Marcelle – one who plunged so completely into love-making that all else was forgotten in her orgasmic release. In short, he wanted Marcelle in bed with him, not Marie-Véronique.

How strangely self-defeating are the whims of men! The plain fact of the matter was that Laurence was in bed with a most amiable young woman who had just given him the supreme satisfaction of love. Even now her warm breasts were cushioning his chest and her tender prize still clasped his shrinking male pride. A reasonable man would have been well content – yet Laurence was fretting silently because he wanted a different woman beneath him. The emotions of affection and gratitude which he should by rights be experiencing towards Marie-Véronique were not in his heart. By this example it may be seen that men are, for the most part, idiots.

He moved to lie beside Marie-Véronique and hold her

in his arms – for the sake of appearances rather than for the proper reasons – while he contemplated his situation. Now that he considered the matter, he had wanted Marcelle ever since the moment he saw her coming down the stairs from Jean-Claude's apartment.

'Do you want to do it again?' Marie-Véronique asked in a whisper.

She had never asked that before – it had been understood without words that their pleasures would be repeated. Perhaps she felt with feminine intuition that all was not well – that he had turned away from her in his heart.

'Are you tired, chérie?' he asked, as graciously as he was able.

'Yes – it must be the fresh air. Would you mind very much if I went to sleep now? We have all day tomorrow.'

'Of course – go to sleep in my arms.'

No more was said and in only a few minutes her regular breathing told him that she was asleep. Laurence lay awake for a very long time, thoroughly miserable because of the cry of delight he had heard through the wall. His misery deepened when, in due course, that cry was repeated, this time with even more abandon than before. Laurence's male equipment stirred and stood erect at the sound, but he had no heart to make love to Marie-Véronique again – and besides, she was sound asleep. What was he going to do? he asked himself. To free himself from his affair with Marie-Véronique was easy enough – but how to win Marcelle away from Jean-Claude? Evidently she was devoted to him, or she would not be here. No doubt she could be persuaded to transfer her affections – Laurence never under-estimated his own abilities to please women of the world – but Jean-Claude would then be mortally offended by what he would surely regard as treachery by his oldest friend.

In a dilemma of this kind, friendship loses every time. Laurence resolved to win Marcelle for himself and, if

Jean-Claude never spoke to him again, so much the worse for him. The priorities were self-evident!

The excitement he was experiencing made him picture her – with what pangs of gnawing jealousy – in Jean-Claude's bed and the events that had led up to that cry of ecstasy. Naked, stretched out on her back, Jean-Claude's hand busy between her thighs and his mouth at her breasts! Or Marcelle sprawled in abandon across Jean-Claude, her fingers playing with his upright part! Oh, it was too much – it was intolerable to lie here in the dark while all that he desired most in the world was separated from him by the thickness of a wall!

Marie-Véronique had turned away from him in her sleep and was breathing peacefully – while he lay in a fever of frustrated desire, his erect part pushing up the sheet like a tent-pole. He had never known such torment in his life before. But there was worse to come – a repetition of Marcelle's long cry of delight, this time prolonged beyond the point of credibility.

For Laurence in his state of acute arousal it was too much. His trembling hand seized his hard projection and rubbed frantically. The echo of Marcelle's wailing cry still sounded inside his head and in seconds his frustrated part jerked mightily and poured its wasted passion in a stream onto his bare belly. After that, though he was not contented, he was at least fatigued by the strength of the despairing emotions he had experienced and eventually he drifted off to sleep.

The unfamiliar sound of birds singing in the trees about the cottage to greet a new day awoke him some hours later. He had no idea what time it was and through the bedroom window the sky looked pale – presumably it was very early indeed. Marie-Véronique slept on, lying on her back with one slender arm above her head on the pillow. Her pretty face was calm and she looked no more than twenty, innocent and vulnerable. Laurence's conscience began to trouble him when he recalled his unworthy emotions of the night before. After all, this dear woman had taken a deliberate risk with her domestic happiness to be with him. She had responded warmly to his love-making, putting herself utterly at his disposal – and how had he repaid her trust and affection? Laurence was ashamed of himself, most of all when he remembered his furious act of self-gratification while she slept at his side.

He drew the covers down gently so as not to disturb her and contemplated her captivating little breasts. In truth, Marie-Véronique was a very desirable woman and he had behaved towards her with unforgivable ingratitude. He touched the tip of his tongue lightly to the rosebud that adorned one of her breasts and inhaled the delicate perfume of her skin. He had been much to blame, he freely confessed that to himself. Between his legs there stirred the part that demonstrated his masculinity and, by the time he turned his attention to her other delicious breast, he was at full stretch.

Marie-Véronique sighed in her sleep, dreaming of love, no doubt, as a result of the enjoyable sensations which Laurence's gentle ministrations were giving her. He pushed the covers down further to admire her smooth belly and then he stroked it very lightly. She is beautiful, he thought – a verdict which was confirmed enthusiastically by his quivering male part.

She was lying with her legs slightly apart. Laurence's finger-tips brushed through the dark brown fleece between them and came to rest on her secret lips. So warm, so tender! Laurence sighed in appreciation, his heart overflowing now with profound affection for Marie-Véronique, whom only the night before he had spurned. She sighed too as the growing sensations of delight urged her towards wakefulness. Laurence's questing finger inserted itself with delicate skill between the soft lips he had been caressing and – ah, yes, the dew of arousal was already manifesting itself within her luxurious little alcove! He touched her hidden bud as lightly as a butterfly settling itself with fragile beating wings on a summer flower. She sighed again, almost awake now, and her elegant legs moved slowly apart in a most touching gesture of surrender. Laurence's finger caressed a little more firmly until, with a gasp of pleasure, she became fully awake, her deep brown eyes opening to gaze at him in rapture.

'Oh, Laurence!' she whispered in delight.

Her arm went about his neck, pulling him towards her. He rolled lightly onto her and, as her knees bent upwards, the head of his ready projection found of its own accord the entrance to her warm grotto of Venus and an easy push lodged him within. Laurence's heart was full of the tenderest emotions towards her – he made love to her with deeply affectionate passion, intent on her pleasure as much as his own. In circumstances such as these, when mutual esteem and desire are equally matched, the outcome is guaranteed to be enormously satisfactory to both partners. The pace quickened, became urgent – and at the moment when Laurence paid his respects to her in a passionate flood, Marie-Véronique arched her back in delight and gasped out that she adored him.

After many murmured declarations of mutual love, they at last lay in each other's arms and, because it was still ridiculously early in the morning, Marie-Véronique soon fell asleep again, an expression of utter content on her face. Laurence also tried to sleep, but his gratification at his renewed affection for Marie-Véronique did not permit him to do so. He lay awake, happy and pleased with himself, at peace with the world. In due course a growing awareness of the need to visit the bathroom to ease the pressure of the wine he had drunk the night before compelled him to get out of bed. He moved cautiously, not wishing to disturb his darling Marie-Véronique and, still naked, went to the bedroom door and lifted the old-fashioned iron latch without a sound.

The door to the bathroom was opposite and to the

right. At the very moment that Laurence pulled open his bedroom door – at the instant he stood there with one bare foot over the threshold – the bathroom door opened and Marcelle came out. She too was naked, evidently not thinking it worthwhile to put on a peignoir for the short journey from bed to bathroom. Laurence stood frozen in mid-step, staring at her, his new-found content gone in an instant. That she was beautiful was obvious to everyone – but Laurence had not realised how entrancingly beautiful she was until this moment when he saw her naked. His heart stood still and he forgot to breathe.

She was of middle height, neither too tall nor too short, and gracefully slender of form. Her hair had been dishevelled by the loving exertions of the night and, as yet uncombed and unbrushed, floated about her head in a silky haze of light brown, with strands of an even lighter hue, almost blonde, in it. Her eyes were wide-set and large – their tint a fascinating grey-green. Her mouth was wide and generous, her little chin had the delicate squareness of a woman who knew her own mind.

All this, of course, Laurence had seen before and admired greatly – her ready smile as she talked over dinner, the way her eyes shone when she became animated in discussion. What held his attention during this unexpected encounter at dawn was what he had not seen before – her exquisite naked body. He stared and stared and could not believe what he was privileged to see.

Beauty, it is said, is in the eye of the beholder. Perhaps it was so with Laurence. Marcelle's breasts were stylishly small and perfectly round, decorated with pink buds – and this description can be applied to many thousands of young women. Her waist was narrow, her hips broadened out in curves of restrained voluptuousness. An anatomist would have regarded her as a good specimen of adult womanhood, but to Laurence she was the most alluring person he had ever seen in his entire life. Her belly, for example, was a masterpiece whose subtle shape was accentuated by a round and shallow navel – a subject for a poet rather than an anatomist!

Descriptions in words are banal and futile to a man in so emotional a condition as Laurence was at that moment. *Impression* is all, not detail – and the impression he received was one of richness of visual and tactile beauty. Still there was more – a fleshy and luxurious mound adorned with neatly clipped and curly hair – dark brown – much darker than the hair of her head! This luscious treasure was set between thighs and legs the sight of which would have made the most talented of sculptors shed tears of despair at the thought of attempting to reproduce their perfection of line.

The passage of time was suspended for Laurence. He had lived through a lifetime, and seen Marcelle and received so powerful an impression of her beauty that, given pencil and paper, he could have drawn her from memory with the utmost accuracy – all in the space of perhaps a second and a half. For Marcelle glimpsed him from the corner of her eye and turned her head to look fully at him, without the least sign of embarrassment at being caught naked and unaware. How she interpreted the expression on his face at that moment, who can say? Her grey-green eyes flickered downwards briefly to take note of his male equipment, hanging limply after its recent attentions to Marie-Véronique, then she looked up to his face again and smiled in a way that was both friendly and casual. There was also a hint of amusement in that smile – and a touch of conspiracy – as if to say: *I know what you've been doing, and I've been doing the same*.

She turned away and went to her bedroom, leaving Laurence with a last glimpse of her long and slender back and the firm little cheeks of her bottom.

He let out his pent-up breath in a long sigh and a great truth forced itself upon him – he was in love with Marcelle Delaroque.

If anyone had been curious enough to ask him *why*?

he could not have answered the question. Even if some rational part of his own mind had induced him to make a comparison between Marcelle and Marie-Véronique, he would have been unable to exercise the detachment necessary to consider the differences and the likenesses. Certainly he could never have been brought to see that the likenesses were greater than the differences. Yet the facts were that Marcelle and Marie-Véronique were of much the same age, give a year or so, of about the same height, of the same social class. They were both attractive and amiable, they were both marvellously well designed by Providence for the uses and delights of love. In comparison to all that, a reasonable man would have found the differences trifling. Marie-Véronique's hair was a darker shade of brown than Marcelle's, that was true, and her breasts were a little fuller – an advantage in the eyes of many men. The most important point of difference was also in her favour – she loved Laurence, and Marcelle did not.

When all that is said, when the rational mind has enumerated all the excellent reasons why Laurence should cling to Marie-Véronique and pay no more attention to Marcelle than courtesy required, the truth was that Laurence did not love the charming woman to whom, only a quarter of an hour before, he had made love most tenderly. He stood like a naked statue in the doorway of his bedroom staring down an empty passage, struck dumb by the amazing discovery that he was hopelessly in love with a woman whose ecstasies in the arms of Jean-Claude had disturbed his sleep.

A further thought made his blood run cold – he would hear those sounds of ecstasy again in the night to come! Last night was bad enough, but now that he was fully aware of his feelings towards Marcelle, it was impossible! Separated from him by only a thin wall, that superb body would be bared for the kisses of Jean-Claude! And horrible to contemplate – it would be Jean-Claude gasping out his passion as he burrowed into Marcelle's plump little mound! Ah no, that was intolerable!

Laurence decided then and there to return to Paris immediately after breakfast, to spare himself so much agony. He must think of an excuse – some remembered appointment – anything to remove himself urgently from the country cottage which had been acquired as a place of pleasure and had so quickly become a place of torment for him.

To be fair to him, he was not a bad sort of fellow, this Laurence. He was handsome, well-liked and, in the normal course of events, he behaved with consideration for others. He had been the intimate friend of innumerable pretty women, some married, some not, and he treated them all well. Needless to say, he had never before been in love. At the age of almost thirty he was utterly unprepared for the formidable impact of that emotion!

In the weeks that followed the visit to the country Laurence found that it was excessively difficult to speak to Marcelle, either in person or by telephone. For he was obsessed by his passion and thought of little else but the pursuit of it. Alas, Marcelle proved to be extraordinarily busy, it seemed, and almost never at home, except when she and her husband were entertaining guests. Her presence was required in Geneva when her husband was at meetings of the League of Nations, and that seemed to account for half her time. As for the rest, her interest in promoting the cause of education for women took her to speaking engagements in cities all over France. When she was in Paris without her husband, her servants never seemed to know where she was – which indicated to Laurence that she was with Jean-Claude.

Weeks passed in this infuriating way. From time to time Laurence called upon Jean-Claude and, after some general talk, asked casually about Marcelle. The answers he received were never very satisfactory.

229

'She was here yesterday afternoon. She left for Geneva this morning.'

Or even worse:

'Marcelle? We were down at the cottage for a couple of nights and came back yesterday. She's off to Marseilles to address some worthy group of people on her favourite subject.'

And even more frustrating:

'Marcelle – oh, she becomes more beautiful every day! How is Marie-Véronique – have you taken her to the country recently?'

Truth to tell, Laurence had invited Marie-Véronique once more to the country cottage after the first fateful visit and she had accepted. After all, because a man is dying of love for a woman he cannot possess, his natural instincts do not disappear! In the absence of Marcelle, the visit had been, one might say, a success. Laurence enjoyed Marie-Véronique's compliance in bed and she appeared to be well content. Yet, even as he enjoyed himself, Laurence could not prevent the thought flitting through his mind that this, in some manner, was not the real thing, only a second-best. And on getting up in the morning, he found himself staring at the bathroom door, where once he had seen Marcelle in her naked beauty, foolishly hoping that the door would open and she appear to him – and knowing full well that she was a long way away and certainly not thinking of him.

The problem was to arrange to meet Marcelle when she was not with her husband and not with Jean-Claude. Laurence gave the matter some prolonged thought and made a plan. He telephoned to the office of the newspaper in which Marcelle's articles on education were most often published and acquired the information that she was to make a speech to an audience in Bordeaux in three days time. A few more telephone calls to the best hotels in that city produced the further information as to where a reservation had been made for Madame Delaroque.

Laurence reserved a suite for himself in the same hotel and congratulated himself upon his sagacity. Marcelle would be alone in a hotel, far from her home and friends. She would be surprised and pleased to meet someone she knew, apparently by chance. They would talk, Laurence would remind her subtly of the circumstances in which they had accidentally viewed each other naked. The rest would follow naturally.

On the due day, he took the train to Bordeaux, dined alone in the hotel and then sat with a glass of cognac where he could watch the entrance and be seen by her when she returned from her meeting. Time passed very slowly, because of his eagerness to see her. He ordered another cognac and rehearsed in his mind the explanation he had concocted for his presence in Bordeaux.

It was after ten o'clock when at last Marcelle came into the hotel – accompanied by two other women, all of them talking at the same time. Laurence stood up, an expression of false surprise on his face.

'Madame Delaroque – how very pleasant to meet you again! And how unexpected!'

'Monsieur Callot – what are you doing here?' she said, smiling at him.

There was a babble of introductions and Laurence kissed hands – his story about being in Bordeaux on a business matter completely lost in the fuss. At last he succeeded in getting the ladies seated and drinking champagne while he listened to Marcelle's account of her speech and the enthusiasm of her two companions. One of the ladies was a school-teacher, he gathered, the other a librarian. They were both devoted to Marcelle – they admired her courage, her intellect, her clothes, everything about her! She was what they would both have wanted to have been if they had had the inestimable privilege of being born in Paris – and of having her looks and position, of course!

Laurence judged that things were going well and he

ordered more champagne. The two disciples would decide that it was time for them to go home before long – for surely no one stayed up until midnight in Bordeaux! He would be alone with Marcelle! The moment would arrive when he persuaded her to accompany him to his suite! Or perhaps she would prefer to invite him to her room, who could say? Not long after that she would be in his arms! He would assist her out of her clothes and cover that beautiful body with hot kisses! After that – ah, the imagination could not reach far enough to encompass the felicities of what would happen then! But he would hear that orgasmic cry of hers and know that it was his doing – and, he promised himself as the champagne bubbled through him, he would hear that cry of hers at least three times before he let her sleep! At least three!

Quite suddenly, the plan changed entirely. Marcelle stood up and said 'Goodnight' to them all and offered her hand to Laurence.

'I must leave you,' she said. 'It is late and I am catching an early train to Geneva tomorrow.'

Then she was gone! Laurence sat down again, thunderstruck. This wasn't his plan at all! The two friends were supposed to leave – but here he was, left with them – both of them chatting away and drinking his champagne – the third bottle!

After a while his normal good nature reasserted itself and he accepted the fact that the situation was ridiculous. But the hours of anticipation of the pleasures of love could not be dismissed easily. He looked at the two women he had been left with and gave them his most charming smile.

They were a contrasting pair. Mademoiselle Bergerac was well over thirty – nearer forty, perhaps – a plump woman in a dark blue summer suit that had obviously been bought in a department store. She was a teacher, he had been told, a vocation which Laurence did not esteem highly, but above her round and pink cheeks there was a certain sparkle in her brown eyes that suggested she might know more interesting things than those she taught to children in the class-room. Her friend, Mademoiselle Clavel, was younger – about thirty, perhaps – and, by comparison, thin. She wore rimless spectacles and gave an impression of seriousness when she spoke – even when she laughed. For all that, her skirt had crept above her knees as she sat, revealing a hint of green garter.

In ordinary circumstances Laurence would not have given these ladies a second glance, of course. But situated as he was, alone in a strange city, bereft of the object of his desire, his blood up – why not? He did not expect to meet them ever again. There was nothing to lose.

'Ladies,' he said, 'it would be a pity to end our conversation. May I make a suggestion?'

'Of course, Monsieur Callot,' said Mademoiselle Bergerac, eyeing him cautiously.

'We could continue our most interesting discussion in my suite, over another glass of champagne.'

Mademoiselle Clavel and Mademoiselle Bergerac looked at each other in silence for a moment or two. It was plump Mademoiselle Bergerac who spoke eventually.

'You are very kind, Monsieur, but this is not Paris, you must understand. Things are very different here. It is out of the question for a woman to accept an invitation to a hotel room – unless she is of a certain type, if you follow me. Since you are a stranger here, we take no offence at your suggestion, since it was surely made in good faith and friendship and with no intention of being insulting.'

'My most profound apologies,' said Laurence in his most gracious manner, 'I assure you that I have the greatest of respect for you.'

'Because you are a friend of Madame Delaroque,' Mademoiselle Bergerac continued, 'that alters the circumstances. We both have the highest regard for her.'

So do I,' Laurence assured her, 'I admire her greatly.'

'It is because of these special circumstances that we feel

able to accept your invitation,' Mademoiselle Bergerac concluded.

In the expectation of entertaining Marcelle, Laurence had reserved for himself a fine suite in the hotel. Mademoiselle Bergerac was impressed when she saw it, and said so at length. So was Mademoiselle Clavel, though she said less. The conversation continued, becoming even more vivacious after another glass or two of champagne. At some point the formal titles of Monsieur and Mademoiselle were abandoned in favour of Laurence, Brigitte and Marianne. Not long after that Brigitte, the plump one, declared that she was hot and removed the jacket of her summer suit to reveal a white satin blouse well filled out in front. Thus encouraged, Marianne took off the short jacket she wore over her striped frock. She seemed to have very little bosom but, as Laurence could not help but notice, her skirt kept riding up as she twisted about in her chair until a gleam of bare flesh appeared above her stocking-top.

Laurence asked permission to shed his jacket, agreeing that it was a warm night – a marvellous night – a night made for love, dare he say? At once the conversation turned to love and the ladies explained to him at some length how exceptionally difficult it was in their home-town for a woman possessed of education and taste to meet, in the right circumstances, a man worthy enough to be entrusted with their tender emotions. Laurence commiserated with them, his sincerity so apparent that, without anyone appearing to move, all three found themselves on the sofa together, Laurence in the middle, with an arm round each of them.

Naturally, they were all a little drunk by now and in very good spirits. So much so that when Laurence's arms slid a little down their shoulders and his hands eased their way under their arms until each hand rested on a breast, neither Brigitte nor Marianne was in the least shocked. On the contrary, they seemed to regard this development

234

as perfectly natural. Laurence sat in great comfort, a big soft breast in his left hand and a small flat one in his right. He too found it quite natural and not in the least outrageous when Brigitte's hand found its way inside his shirt to stroke his chest and Marianne's warm palm rested on his thigh, about midway between knee and the source of his pride. On the contrary, his extensible part was puffed up with pride at that time.

Marianne seemed content to leave her hand where it was and make no further advance but Brigitte's fingers had begun to tease Laurence's nipples slowly. Yet it was Marianne, her spectacles glinting, who insisted in all seriousness that between good friends there should be no secrets. As soon as Laurence agreed with her proposition of frankness, Marianne stood up and pulled her frock over her head to show herself in plain pink camiknickers. These too she removed to let Laurence view plainly her thin body and childish breasts – but her belly was enticing, he thought, very smooth and flat – and her lean thighs had a sinewy look about them that was interesting. She sat down again within his arm and pressed herself closely to him, her palm moving a little higher up his thigh as he caressed one of her tiny rosebuds with the ball of his thumb.

'There!' she whispered, 'I have no secrets from you, Laurence.'

'I admire your strength of character,' he said. 'You have demonstrated with total clarity that you are a person of principle – you mean what you say. Do you not agree, Brigitte?'

'But of course,' Brigitte exclaimed. 'Her courage is to be admired also. She believes that men do not think her truly feminine because her breasts are so small. But she displays them to you and that requires real courage.'

'I am honoured,' said Laurence, 'I praise your courage as well as your principles, Marianne, and I assure you that I have no doubts whatsoever of your femininity. Nor do I think that your breasts are too small – I think they are enchanting.'

To prove his assertion he continued to play with the one he could reach until the little rosebud was standing up firmly.

'Fine words,' said Brigitte on his other side, 'but words are cheap enough. What of your secrets, Laurence, are they to remain concealed from us?'

'As a man of honour I can do no less than follow the example set by Marianne,' he answered cheerfully.

He rose to his feet and stripped himself recklessly, hurling clothes and shoes to the furthest corners of the room. When he sat down again between the two women both stared at his bare muscular thighs and the strong stem which rose from between them. A hand crept up each thigh – one with short and plump fingers and one narrow hand with long thin fingers – until they met and both took hold of the part of him created to give pleasure to women. It felt strange, and very exciting, to be handled by two women at the same time.

'Now, Brigitte,' he murmured, 'you are the only one still hiding secrets from your friends. This raises serious doubts as to your sincerity and friendship – don't you agree, Marianne?'

'She is always like that,' Marianne declared, 'quick to speak but slow to act. Come on, Brigitte, what are you waiting for? Off with your clothes and let's see those big fat breasts of yours, even if they do dangle more than they should.'

Stung by the gibe, Brigitte unbuttoned her blouse, then stood up to drop her skirt. She was wearing a full-length chemise, embroidered over the bosom and plain at the hem. She hoisted it over her head and, as she bent over to remove her matching knickers, Laurence stared in fascination at the immense round cheeks of her bottom.

'Ah!' said Marianne, 'the sight of your backside made

him jerk in my hand. Look out for yourself, Brigitte, he might be one of those who prefer the back door!'

'Have no fear,' said Laurence, amused by the suggestion, 'my tastes in these matters are orthodox. I have always found the front entrance adequate for my purpose.'

'As to that,' said Marianne, 'We shall see.'

Brigitte was still on her feet and had turned to present to him her frontal aspect. The big bouncy breasts she had boasted in her youth had indeed become somewhat slack with time, but they were still most presentable. Laurence reached out to squeeze one of them appreciatively.

'My dears,' he said, 'the moment has surely come, now that we have exchanged secrets, to move ourselves into a more appropriate part of the suite so that we can investigate these secrets more thoroughly in a comfortable position.'

'The horizontal position,' Marianne suggested.

'Exactly.'

Laurence, wearing nothing at all, led the women – wearing only their stockings and garters – to the bedroom, each of his arms round a bare waist. He was wondering how the decision could be made as to which of them would first receive his tribute without the other one becoming offended. It was an engrossing and amusing train of thought.

His concern proved unnecessary. The instant that the three of them were on the bed, Marianne's spectacles removed at last, matters arranged themselves. The only light was that of the moon through the open windows – a most suitable setting for what was enacted there! As they rolled about together on the broad bed they ceased in some strange manner to be three distinct and separate persons. There was warm flesh, wet mouths and caressing hands – and that was all! There were hands between Laurence's legs, hands stroking his chest and belly, hands manipulating his upright part, mouths pressed to his mouth, mouths pressed to his body and thighs. His own hands grasped and fondled breasts, bottoms, soft-haired little mounds!

Together they writhed, sighed and gasped – now Laurence was on his back with a warm belly across his, a breast squeezed down over his mouth as he worried at its firm bud with his lips. Then he was face-down on a yielding body, his head between open thighs, darting his tongue into smooth groins, while above him a warm and wet mound was being rubbed against his back and fingernails were digging pleasurably into the cheeks of his bottom. The woman beneath him rolled and he was on his side, his face pressed into a hot belly, a pair of thighs clamped round his waist and his fingers deep within a wet little aperture.

These frenetic exercises and the sensations they induced brought Laurence very nearly to the point of climactic release. His whole body was trembling, as if in delirium, and he tried to grasp a pair of hips – any pair – to force one of the women onto her back and get between her legs urgently. But even as he tried, four hands seized him, one under the chin, one by his hair, one by the ankle and one by his fluttering stem. He was rolled onto his back, a leg was thrown over his chest and, an instant later, one of the women was sitting astride his chest. He raised his head to nip playfully at the bottom pinning him down and even as he did so, he became aware of certain voluptuous sensations elsewhere that informed him that the other woman had taken her seat astride his loins and that his engorged pride had been expertly guided into a tunnel of warm flesh.

Laurence sighed and shook, his hands over the thighs so near his face to get at the tender lips between them – only to discover that other hands were there before him! He rubbed urgently at the busy hands, half-wondering whose they were, until the jolting of the woman astride his belly, who had taken his hard-standing part into her tender care – this jolting produced the desired explosion and he cried out '*Ah, ah, ah!*' as his spasms fountained his passion upwards into its destined receptacle. The woman seated across his chest wailed in exquisite pleasure as the fingers rubbing between her legs brought her to a climax of sensation – the jolting over his loins increased in speed, halted abruptly for the length of an in-drawn breath, then resumed furiously for a few more strokes, accompanied by a long sobbing wail of ecstasy.

Soon after that the two women sagged slowly sideways, pulling Laurence onto his side. There were adjustments of limbs, then all three lay quietly for a while, Laurence with his head on a smooth thigh and a head pillowed on his belly.

'My dears,' he said eventually, 'that was astonishing.'

'I suppose that in Paris you have little amusements like that every day,' said a voice in the near-darkness, 'it wasn't too boring for you, was it?'

He recognised the voice as Marianne's.

'It was magnificent,' he sighed, his hand moving gently over a big soft breast which must be Brigitte's.

'It is good of you to say so,' said the owner of the breast he was fondling, 'but we realise that here in the provinces we cannot hope to equal the pleasures taken for granted by a man of the world like you. I mean, after Madame Delaroque Marianne and I must seem extremely ordinary to you.'

'You do yourself an injustice,' Laurence protested.

He wished with all his heart that she had not reminded him that the divine Marcelle was in another bed in the hotel. To some extent it spoiled the pleasure he had just enjoyed by making his companions seem to him, as Brigitte herself had said, extremely ordinary. He sighed, and it was not with pleasure.

But there was a hand caressing his limp part affectionately and, as it began to respond, the memory of Marcelle faded from Laurence's thoughts. After all, it is impossible

239

for a man to be remembering and sighing over the love of his life at every moment of the day and night – especially when he is in bed with two other women totally unrestrained in their enjoyment of the delights of love. With the hand that was not fondling Brigitte's breasts he reached out to touch Marianne's belly in the dark and let his fingers move to the secret place between her slim thighs. How deliciously wet it was there! In this way – muted and gentle – there commenced the second movement of the symphony. Naturally it became livelier and more energetic as it proceeded, the tempo quickened and a delightful *agitato* made itself apparent.

At the height of it, Laurence found himself sitting upright on his heels, a woman across his thighs and his baton enclosed within the soft container intended for it. It was the plump Brigitte who was affording him this accomodation – he knew that by the feel of her breasts squashed against his chest – and from that fact he guessed that it had been Marianne who had received his first offering. Not that she was content to be left out of things – she was kneeling behind Brigitte and rubbing her little breasts against her friend's broad back! Nor was that the limit of her participation – as Laurence's hands moved everywhere over feverishly hot flesh, he found that one of Brigitte's arms was behind her, in a position, as far as he could judge, to put her hand between Marianne's splayed thighs!

Brigitte responded very quickly to the thrilling stimulus of Laurence's hard appurtenance within her. She moaned and shook violently in her ecstasy, the pulsating grip of her inner muscles causing him to attain the culmination of desire much earlier than he had expected. But the pleasure was none the less for that – he forced his hands between their bodies and squeezed her breasts tightly throughout his critical moments, enravished by sensation. Marianne was a little slower – presumably impaled on Brigitte's fingers – but she too at last uttered the sobbing

240

cry that denoted her arrival at the supreme peak of.
pleasure.

'*Mesdemoiselles* – you are a delight!' said Laurence. 'I
don't know when I last enjoyed myself so much! But if
one may ask – do you always seek your amusements
together in this way?'

'Of course not!' Brigitte exclaimed, unseating herself
from his thighs. 'What must you think of us! This is the
first time we've ever been together with a man!'

'Then I am very greatly honoured. I beg you not to be
offended by questions meant only in a spirit of friendly
curiosity about two persons for whom I have the very
highest regard. What made you decide this evening to, so
to speak, share your diversions?'

'We both liked the look of you,' said Marianne,
entering the conversation at last, 'neither of us could bear
to let the other have you to herself when you invited us
to your suite, so here we both are.'

'That is very flattering! I hope most sincerely that you
are not disappointed by the outcome of your decision.'

'I think you're marvellous,' said Marianne, reaching
over to stroke his thigh tenderly, 'don't you, Brigitte?'

'Superb!' Brigitte sighed.

In the traditional manner, the symphony of love had
four movements and, after an appropriate pause for the
players to recover from their exertions, the third movement got under way. And then the fourth, by which time
it was late into the night and the moon was down and the
room in almost total darkness. When the final chords
were sounded at last, all three were fatigued and content.
Laurence drifted off to sleep, pleased with his night's
work.

He was awakened some time later by a persistent
shaking of the mattress beneath him. His eyes opened
lazily to see, in the half-light which heralds dawn, plump
Brigitte sprawled on her back and Marianne crouching
over her. Laurence's eyes opened wider and with a sudden

241

shock of excitement he understood what he was seeing. One of Marianne's hands was between Brigitte's parted thighs, moving rhythmically, while her mouth was at Brigitte's breasts. The shaking that had woken him was caused by Brigitte's legs trembling hard against the mattress as delightful sensations coursed through her. Laurence propped himself up on one elbow to observe more closely – Marianne glanced up from the breasts to which she was ministering and her eyes met his for a moment. Or more exactly, his eyes met hers, for without her spectacles she stared myopically at him for an instant, then bowed her head to resume her labour of love, her nimble fingers moving swiftly between Brigitte's thighs.

Brigitte cried out in orgasmic delight, her legs thrashing at the mattress. Before her convulsions were finished, before her legs were still, Marianne turned as quickly as a cat and spread herself the length of Brigitte's trembling body, her slender legs between her friend's plump legs. She pressed her soft-haired little mound tightly against the one beneath her and rode it furiously, as if she were a man! Brigitte lay still at last, her ecstasy over, letting her friend have her way with her until in a final fury of thrusting Marianne achieved her aim and moaned loudly in release, her open mouth over Brigitte's mouth.

The observation of this strange proceeding aroused Laurence mightily. His male extension was at full stretch long before Marianne reached her moments of culmination. Hardly had her throes of delight faded to a delicious nervous twitching as she lay on Brigitte than Laurence took her by her narrow hips and pulled her off her friend and towards him, until she lay on her side with her back to him. It was the work of a moment to lift her topmost leg and burrow his stiffness between the soft lips still pouting from her climactic pleasure of not five seconds ago. Marianne cried out in surprise as she felt herself invaded in this manner, then jerked her little bottom against his belly to make him begin.

He held her by her waist and thrust easily, enchanted by this unexpected turn of events. Brigitte rolled over to face Marianne and squeezed her fat breasts against her friend's flat little breasts. Her arm was over Marianne, to grasp Laurence by the hip and pull him closer, so that he felt that he was making love to both women at the same time.

It was in Laurence's mind that this charming little interlude would be of considerable duration, given his supreme exertions of an hour or two earlier and for this reason he set himself a gentle pace that could be sustained to a satisfactory conclusion. In this he was mistaken. He had been extremely aroused by the sight of Marianne lying on Brigitte's plump belly and utilising it in so masculine a fashion that he found himself soon plunging hard and fast into Marianne's very moist convenience. As for Marianne herself, her most tender parts were evidently very sensitive from the pleasure they had just received and she returned his thrusts most firmly – and the instant that Laurence sighed and delivered his offering within her, she too cried out and hugged Brigitte to her.

He fell asleep again at once, still joined intimately to Marianne, an arm over her waist and his hand resting between Brigitte's warm thighs. When he awoke it was broad daylight and he was alone – his companions of the night had departed without disturbing his rest. He lay in the incredibly rumpled bed, content with the world, recalling with the greatest of pleasure the escapades of the night. When he looked at his watch it was after ten o'clock and he was very hungry.

He found a scribbled note in the sitting-room of his suite when he sat down to the breakfast a waiter brought him. The note thanked him for a most enjoyable occasion and gave an address at which he was requested to call when he was next in Bordeaux. It was unsigned and Laurence smiled and put it into his wallet as a souvenir of a memorable encounter.

243

On the train back to Paris his thoughts turned to Marcelle Delaroque. She, after all, was the cause of his long journey – and his plan to get her alone had proved to be totally futile. Naturally, his tremendous passion for her had not been diminished in the slightest degree by his adventure with her acquaintances. He loved her madly and desired her to distraction! There was only one thing for it, he decided – no more subterfuges! He would go to her and explain frankly his emotions towards her, in the hope that she would be moved to take pity on him.

In the event, to find Marcelle at home and alone for the simple purpose of declaring his passion proved to be exceedingly difficult to achieve. It was always the same when he called at her apartment or telephoned: *Madame is away. Madame is out.* But Laurence persevered and, after seemingly endless attempts, he succeeded, about ten days after his return from Bordeaux, in speaking to her on the telephone.

He told her that there was a matter of the utmost importance and discretion that he must discuss with her immediately! Marcelle seemed not disposed to take this completely seriously – certainly not as seriously as he would have wished – and made half a dozen excuses to put him off. But Laurence was not to be put off any longer, having reached this point. To settle things, he said that he would call at her apartment in a quarter of an hour – and put the telephone down before she had time to say no.

There was no time to change his clothes, visit his barber – no time for anything at all except to find a taxi and bribe the driver to get through the traffic at high speed. Even then, it took rather longer than the quarter of an hour he had specified.

A maid opened the door to him – no doubt the one who had been dashing his hopes for so long by her constant reiteration of *Madame is not at home*. Laurence told her his name and she ushered him into Marcelle's salon. How his heart was beating at this moment – he was alone with Marcelle at last!

She was sitting in a large arm-chair and was dressed most elegantly in a close-fitting frock of moire silk in a delicate shade of moss-rose, a belt of the same material very low round her hips, with a round silver buckle in front.

Laurence sped across the room to bow over her hand and kiss it.

'You can only stay for a moment,' she said, 'I'm going out. There is something you want to say to me – can it be that urgent?'

'You cannot imagine how urgent,' said Laurence, at a loss how to begin in these unauspicious circumstances.

'Then tell me and I shall know.'

'Marcelle – since the first moment I saw you there has been growing in my heart a certain emotion, though it may be that you are unaware of this.'

'Of what should I be aware?'

There was nothing to be done but blurt it out and hope for the best – and this he did.

'I am in love with you, Marcelle.'

'Are you?' she said calmly, 'you've given no signs of it. Have you been drinking? You look a little flushed.'

'No, I assure you that I am sober. The agitation you see comes from the very powerful emotions I am experiencing.'

'And you have been in love with me since the first time you saw me – not just since lunch-time, is that what I am to believe?'

'Exactly that! At first I did not understand my own feelings. But then it struck me like a blow. Since then I have not been able to get you out of my mind.'

'When did this blow strike you?'

'That early morning when I saw you coming out of the bathroom of the cottage.'

'By chance you saw me with nothing on,' Marcelle said.

'Do you fall in love with every woman you see like that – Marie-Véronique, for example?'

'No, I do not love her!'

'I am sorry to hear it – she is devoted to you, from what I observed.'

'These things can't be regulated. I have an affection for her, but that is another matter entirely.'

'Well, you have told me your urgent news,' said Marcelle, 'I must go now or I shall be late.'

'Please – don't go yet!'

'I must. There are people waiting for me.'

'You cannot leave before I have an answer!' he said in great distress of mind.

'You haven't asked a question, so how can I answer it? What is it that you want?'

'You.'

Marcelle looked slightly puzzled.

'Are you suggesting that I should break off my friendship with Jean-Claude and . . . ' she left the sentence unfinished and shrugged.

'Yes, yes, yes! Forget Jean-Claude and think only of me.'

'But I thought that you and he were old friends.'

'We are, but nothing matters to me except to obtain your love – nothing!'

'Such vehemence! But as you said a moment ago, these things can't be regulated.'

'You don't love him, I know that.'

'You sound very sure,' she answered, smiling a little.

'I am.'

'All this talk of love is beginning to become faintly tiresome. I really must go now.'

'One word before you do – unless I make love to you very soon I shall either go mad or die – that's the state I'm in.'

'Is *that* all you want!' Marcelle exclaimed. 'Heavens, why didn't you say so before instead of sitting there talking about love? Well, it will have to be quick – I have an appointment in ten minutes.'

Before Laurence had fully grasped the implications of her words Marcelle was on her feet and raising the hem of her frock. He saw the embroidered garters which held up her fine silk stockings – then, a sight to make him gasp aloud in delight – her bare thighs above her stocking-tops. He stared in disbelief at the lace edge of her knickers and he broke. out into perspiration as she slipped the knickers down her legs and to her ankles!

How could it be possible that a hunger that had gnawed away at him for so long should be so easily appeased? Yet there she was, hopping from left foot to right foot as she removed that intimate garment completely and dropped it casually onto the chair where she had been sitting.

'You are not to crease my frock,' she said, 'I haven't time to change and make up again.'

Laurence nodded, dumb with amazement.

'Open your trousers,' she said, a touch of impatience in her tone.

He fumbled with his buttons awkwardly. This was not at all how he imagined the scene would be played between them. He had envisaged a lengthy – but interesting – dialogue in which he advanced his cause and she was at first modest, then more responsive – and finally welcoming, won over by his respectful fervour. Then kisses, dozens of them, on her mouth and face! That would be followed by. the leisurely and completely intriguing process of undressing her to fondle her breasts – and so on! That was the usual procedure, as Laurence understood it, from his past experience. It was a shock to see Marcelle standing before him, her underwear discarded at almost his first word.

Impatient with his fumbling, she reached down into his lap, flicked open his trouser buttons and pulled out his stiff part.

'At least that's ready for action!' she said with a chuckle.

She raised her skirt with one hand – up to her navel – uncovering the neat tuft of brown hair between her legs. Her other hand was at her mouth – she licked her fingers and passed them between the lips hidden in her tuft, to moisten the entrance for him. A moment later she was astride his lap and he felt himself guided into place by her hand, then jammed inside her as she sat down forcefully across his thighs.

'There we are!' she said cheerfully. 'Now you've got what you wanted. Why didn't you tell me before? Today is very inconvenient.'

'Oh Marcelle!' he gasped, not knowing what to reply.

She rode up and down sharply on his embedded spike of flesh, very adept at the task.

'Does that feel good?' she asked. 'No, you mustn't touch my breasts – you'll ruin my frock. Sit still and let things take their course.'

However unprepared spiritually Laurence was for the event which was taking place with him as a participant, his body responded to the stimulus in a natural way. Marcelle's brisk up and down motion produced sensations of the keenest pleasure that made his emotions surge. Something else too surged and he uttered a final gasp of surprise as Marcelle drained him of his passion.

'There now!' she said, her movements ceasing at once, 'now I've made you happy! And you've made me late for my appointment – I must fly! Call for me at about twelve tomorrow and you can take me to lunch – and then we can go to your apartment for the whole afternoon – I shall be free until dinner.'

Before Laurence could say a word, she was off him and out of the room, snatching up her pretty silk underwear from the chair as she went.

Romance of Lust
Anonymous

The Romance of Lust is that rare combination of graphic sensuality, literary success, and historical importance that is loved by critics and readers alike.—*The Times*

"Truly remarkable. All the pleasure of fine historical fiction combined with the most intimate descriptions of explicit lovemaking."
—*Herald Tribune*

"This justly famous novel has been a secret bestseller for a hundred years."

The Altar of Venus
Anonymous

Our author, a gentleman of wealth and privilege, is introduced to desire's delights at a tender age, and then and there commits himself to a life-long sensual expedition. As he enters manhood, he progresses from schoolgirls' charms to older women's enticements, especially those of acquaintances' mothers and wives. Later, he moves beyond common London brothels to sophisticated entertainments available only in Paris. Truly, he has become a lord among libertines.

Caning Able
Stan Kent

Caning Able is a modern-day version of the melodramatic tales of Victorian erotica. Full of dastardly villains, regimented discipline, corporal punishment and forbidden sexual liaisons, the novel features the brilliant and beautiful Jasmine, a seemingly helpless heroine who reigns triumphant despite dire peril. By mixing libidinous prose with a changing business world, Caning Able gives treasured plots a welcome twist: women who are definitely not the weaker sex.

The Blue Moon Erotic Reader III

Once again, Blue Moon presents its unique collection of stories of passion, desire, and experimentation

A testimonial to the publication of quality erotica, The Blue Moon Erotic Reader III presents more than twenty-five romantic and exciting excerpts from selections spanning a variety of periods and themes. This is a historical compilation that combines generous extracts from the finest forbidden books with the most extravagant samplings that the modern erotic imagination has created. The result is a collection that is evocative and entertaining, perhaps even enlightening. It encompasses memorable scenes of youthful initiations into the mysteries of sex, notorious confessions, and scandalous adventures of the powerful, wealthy, and notable. The Blue Moon Erotic Reader III is a stirring complement to the senses. Good taste, and passion, and an exalted desire are all here, making for a union of sex and sensibility that is available only once in a Blue Moon.

Beauty in the Birch
Anonymous

Beauty in the Birch is a remarkable description of exotic Victorian sexual episodes. Reportedly first published in Paris in 1905, the letters reveal the exploits of the handsome thirty-year-old rake Charles, who finds employment in a country mansion for wayward girls, and the impetuous and mischievous Lizzie, who, as the daughter of Britannia's plenipotentiary in an Arabian territory, makes herself privy to all the pleasures and punishments of the royal harem.